Passion

Jude Morgan

review

First published in Great Britain in 2004
by Review

First published in paperback in Great Britain in 2005
by Review

An imprint of Headline Book Publishing

4

ISBN 978-0-7553-0403-5

Typeset in Bembo by
Letterpart Limited, Reigate, Surrey

Printed and bound in Great Britain by
Clays Ltd, St Ives plc

Headline's policy is to use papers that are natural, renewable and
recyclable products and made from wood grown in sustainable forests.
The logging and manufacturing processes are expected to conform
to the environmental regulations of the country of origin.

HEADLINE BOOK PUBLISHING
A division of Hodder Headline
338 Euston Road
LONDON NW1 3BH

www.reviewbooks.co.uk
www.hodderheadline.com

For Adam Wilson - welcome

Special thanks to:

Virginia Murray
Keith Smith
Judith Stronach

Prologue

Falling

No one is watching the woman on her way towards death.

She is seen, unconsciously witnessed. A tall handsome woman in a white muslin gown and red handkerchief shawl walking alone in the October rain.

Not strolling. A boy driving a cow passes her on the Chelsea road. And he feels for a moment, like a gust, her strenuousness and purpose as she plunges past him.

She has come out of London, that rampart of smoke on the horizon, and she has walked all the way, and her skirts are crusted with mud. A housemaid in cloak and clip-clapping pattens, returning from an errand to her master's villa at the riverside, notices that: stares: sees the high eager colour in the woman's cheeks, her straggles of auburn hair. Forgets, by the time she reaches the kitchen fire.

Low flat plashy meadows, and no more colour than an engraving. From time to time the woman looks up at the sky and studies its complexion. Downriver a pumping-house chimney smokes, a windmill makes an unmoving cross.

At Battersea Bridge, for the first time, her stride slows. She appears irresolute: halts: looks up and down the river. Decides.

The boatman spits absently, considering the strange request of this strange woman who has come at him out of the grey twilight.

'All very well,' he says, scratching his neck, and 'I don't say I don't trust you. Only . . .' The boat is for hire, yes, but he rows it:

1

that is his trade. 'I can't allow . . .' But there has been no work at the little timber wharf all day, and the woman has money. She rattles the coins in her large white cupped hand like dice, impatiently.

Soon she is in the boat and rowing, with the same strength and determination, upriver and away from wharves and warehouses. Willows loom under clotted clouds, and light retreats as the rain comes down harder, fluttering on the water. Now she is evading human eyes altogether: no one to see as she brings the boat in to the bank, down below Putney Bridge.

She steps out, not minding sodden skirts, liking them so, and stands for a minute with her arms up against the timber struts of the bridge, examining the water with sharp sips of breath. A faint moan, then she stoops and scrabbles for stones, fills her pockets. Her step is still vigorous when she goes up to the bridge.

But – a setback – there is a toll-gate: she must ring the bell for the keeper, and pay him a halfpenny to get to her death. No matter for the cost, but she would rather he did not see her. He claws the halfpenny from her, snivels under his dripping hat-brim, darts back to his booth. Not interested. Good.

Good, and now there is only the right spot to be sought.

A packhorse crosses the bridge, and then a travelling-coach with the glasses up and lamps lit. No one observes the woman pressing herself into the shelter of one of the bridge-bays. The coach-lamps smear away into the glistening darkness, the rattle and crunch give way to the unquenchable hiss of rain. And now a swift upward movement.

The woman climbs up on the wooden railing of the bridge, and in the moment before she leaps, standing upright on the top bar, her figure is all there is of definition in the liquefying night.

Her name is Mary, and she is a mother though no wife, and in the last moment, as she looks down at the river, like a rippling floor twenty feet below her, she feels less fear than familiarity. Misery is home ground, and she has only ever made excursions into the far country of happiness. Her infant daughter is awaiting her return – she puts out chubby arms in Mary's mind – but Mary blinks that away. Mary is intent upon dying.

She jumps. Her heavy clothes cling to her as she plunges straight down through the rainy air.

Catch her.

She may as well, her father was saying as he tenderly tilted the bottle, she may as well go: it is the best she can hope for, after all: she is never going to make a good marriage.

He spoke with authority, for once. Failure was something he knew all about.

Her mother wept vague, selfish tears. Mary's sisters were away at school, and without Mary she would have to manage him by herself. When he uncorked the demons of the second bottle, there would be no Mary to get between them. But Mary was tired of that: it was not as if her mother would ever admit the truth.

'When I was a girl, Mama,' she told her, during the packing of her trunk, 'I would often sleep on the landing outside your bedchamber, on the worst nights, so that—'

'Oh, my dear, whatever for?' her mother trilled. 'Curious child!' She lifted the striped sleeve of a gown from the trunk with disdainful fingers and sighed. 'You don't seem to *like* pretty things.'

So goodbye to home, but no home, only the latest in a succession of houses. Whenever her father could not bear himself any longer, he moved them on. A good solid-sounding name, Wollstonecraft: and he bought a farm in the Welsh hills, as if he would fix and root it there. The roots did not take. He drifted back to London. Perhaps his sons would change things. From sons would come establishment. He had them, thank heaven, as well as daughters, who were for marrying. Mary being unable to grasp this simple fact, he adopted a thorough uninterest in her. Her studies he merely laughed at, except once when he came in from shooting, sat down to pie and ale, and found her books in his way. He flung open the window and sent them flying. His daughter ran out after them, a retriever.

No respectable young woman left her family except to get married, or to take employment if absolutely driven to it by poverty. Why? The way things were. Mary found it did not do to ask these questions. Still she asked them: they rose violently to her lips, they were ungovernable. She walked out into the world interrogating it, fierce, dowdy, plain-looking because she chose to be. Why should a woman beautify herself – for men? Why were men not rational beings, who could esteem a woman on rational terms? And if they were taught to be like that, why couldn't they be taught differently?

Out in the world there were only a few things she could do. Be a paid companion: be a governess: teach. Mary did them all. She supported herself. Supporting her in turn was a springy mesh of hope. Even when she fell and plunged, as she often did when melancholy undercut pride, she was caught up by hope and returned to life. Something better was awaiting, though she was not sure of its shape.

Not man-shaped: that was certain. Men were her father, and her all-conquering, all-inheriting brother, and the boor her sister had married who was drunk at his own wedding and mauled his wife in her childbed. Where Mary knew love was in female friendship. She dreamed of a mutual tender attachment of equals, perhaps in a cottage, although it was also vaguely like a library. Even her dreams did not fit.

Her mother fell ill, and Mary was called home to the daughter's duty, at the slow deathbed. Mrs Wollstonecraft did not seem to understand what was happening to her. Pain and peevishness gave way, as she thinned, to stark flat surprise: surely this had only been the first act – not the whole play. Surely? The question was still on her bony face when her eyes finally dimmed. Mary screamed, and the curate who had come to talk comfort nodded, smiling: ah, so there was sensibility in this unnatural virago after all.

But the scream was fear and realization. Her mother had never done or thought or felt anything very much, so death was no break: merely more, or less, of the same. Everlasting ladyism. Mary took it in. She took in the lesson of her next employers, aristocrats, young, powdered, idle, marooned in their thousands of Irish acres: the master of the house dwelled on Mary's breasts with bored rake's eyes, his wife passionately kissed the grazed paw of her favourite dog while not listening to her daughter recite. And when the daughter became too attached to Mary, and her mother dismissed Mary because of it, that bitter lesson was taken in too. What had been done to women did not necessarily make them allies. The footman shrugged off the hand of the beggar: the mudlarks that she watched when she came back jobless and penniless to London, rooting in the filth of low tide beneath London Bridge, fought like dogs over their pickings.

She took it all in, and tried to vent it with her pen. She must write or burn. Paternoster Row, St Paul's Churchyard, Ave Maria Lane: the names reeked of the unenlightened past, all the oppressive lumber she would throw off the bent back of human-kind, but here she found her place, here where the booksellers and stationers and publishers had founded a little republic of print. Authors exhibited their candlelight complexions in these shady quiet streets – the quietest in London, with posts set up across the thoroughfare to discourage wheeled traffic, so that the noise of the city was like a near seashore. Mary wrote, and was paid and printed. Stories, reviews, translations: she gobbled up the work that made her short-sighted, ink-stained, and independent.

A *bluestocking*. Her father's sneer was easy to imagine, she did not need or want to see it. He was ensconced in Wales now, with a second wife, a simple, devoted countrywoman: a good wife to him, apparently.

'What the world commonly calls a good wife,' Mary said, 'is indistinguishable from an outright slave.'

It was at her publisher's house that she began to say these things. He was her publisher, employer, landlord, and friend:

every afternoon he gathered his authors about his dining-table – painters, scholars, politicians too – and they traded in heady talk. Radical talk. Up in the air went the conventions, the old worn ideas: bang went their intensely rational arguments and shattered them. Mary had never known a space that a governess could occupy and say such things in. Here was thought: here was no powder and damned finicking lace.

And here, alas, was love. Bad love. (That other, arrested Mary, endlessly falling towards black water, knows that with her it has always been so, ever thus – a plunge from reason into darkness.) Love nearly spoiled that good place: she made a hysterical fool of herself over a man, clung and begged.

She survived it, thank God – or thank that vaguer deity that she was learning to honour in those days. And then those days became suddenly glorious: first her place, and now her time.

No longer a misfit, she heard Revolution yell across the Channel like a child to a mother.

'Eighty-nine: the world completely changed. To Mary, it finally turned the right way up.

'Liberty.' Say the word: feel its delicate effect in the mouth, its consonants a lick, a kiss and a chuckle. Sensual; and there were some of her set who went around pronouncing the magnificent word wantonly, as fresh news came daily of the tumble and rush of events in Paris. They would renege, as the novelty wore off: take fright at the scale of the remaking. Not Mary. A citizeness to her soul, she did not see the Revolutionary cause as something you could take up or put down at will. This was mankind's turning-point and we were all in it. Thank that dwindling Godhead (almost departed now from Mary's once-devout soul, where she had set up a shrine to Reason, spanking new as a Brighton villa) that she had been born in this time, the greatest time in all history. She embraced it – and it embraced her. Mary, the eternal governess, the scribbling bluestocking, had a part to play as Revolution rose and, sun-like, flooded the world's horizon.

Who is Mary, the wretched woman some seconds and yards from drowning herself like an unwanted pup?

Not so long ago she had been the most famous woman in Europe.

(And Mary, falling, sees in a tiny instant the fallacy, that the times were made for her, that the world was made for her, for it is in truth a thing all separate and alien, and when in a few minutes she is dead it will go smoothly on without her. And in this last agonizing truth and terror the oracle of Reason is dumb.)

The Rights of Man. The book that started it was by Tom Paine – Norfolk Quaker originally, then fighter for American freedom, then taunting scourge of John Bull and his flunkeyish notions of Church and King. In Paine's face – an eagle turned fleshy – you could see something of all these: Mary saw it often at the dinners in St Paul's Churchyard, until his incendiary little volume had sold so many copies that the government arrested him for it. By then she had written at sleepless speed her own paean to the new age. It did not satisfy her. Impatient of words, she took one word and made it stand out, and invoked a new revolution.

Man.

'*A Vindication of the Rights of Woman*,' the young lady was saying, in the bookshop, doing petulant things with her gauze mantle. 'That's what I mean – it sounds so – I do not think I will like it.'

'Probably you will not like it. It's a very silly violent book, in part – quite wild.' That was an older woman, aunt or mamma, with a rich, amused voice. 'It is also entirely true, and I think we are all a little afraid of it. Buy it, my dear. My copy is all fallen to pieces from lending.' Mary, in the back of the shop, listened frozen and thrilled: the authoress.

No word from her father, of course, lurking soused in his Welsh farmstead, waited on by a mind-sucked yes-woman. No spectral cry of recognition from her mother's futile grave. But other voices, many, responded to Mary's shout of protest: women and men, at home and abroad. The letters tottered in heaps.

'I confess I still do not understand what you imagine that

women *want*,' said a liberal clergyman, snuff-dose poised in his pinched fingers as if he were cracking a flea.

'That *want* suggests a complaining child, who must be pacified with a jelly or tart. But it is the notion of women being treated specially, in whatever way, that is the root of the mischief. We wish simply to be rational human creatures, whose wants are neither indulged nor denied.'

'Oh dear me – but where does this leave chivalry – gallantry?'

'It leaves it, I hope, sir, in the dead past where it belongs.'

The clergyman (crushed) was – she remembers – young and pale and not unsuited, not unhandsome, in his clerical black. He would look at her when she was not talking – as men did then, she found, not with pleasure but with interest. Past thirty, she wondered about this beauty that she seemed to have strayed into like some unexpected byway. Was it real?

'Your fame,' said her visitor, uneasily inspecting the rush-bottomed chair before he sat down. 'I could not consider a visit to London complete without waiting upon the esteemed Miss – Wollstonecraft.' French and mellifluous, he made his way with difficulty through that thorny thicket of consonants.

'I am indeed honoured, sir. *Your* fame – and the great, the very great interest taken in the events in Paris by everyone here who is a friend to liberty, to the progress of humankind . . .'

Charles Maurice Talleyrand-Périgord, late Bishop of Autun, special envoy of Revolutionary France, sat with pained, courteous elegance in her shabby parlour. Wine? A thousand thanks, a little wine, to be sure. He did not look very sure when she gave him sweet canary in a teacup. But he stayed. She was overwhelmed. Admiring from afar, she had dedicated her book to him. Now he was here, politely attending to her arguments that France must lead the way in educating women to be the rational, sensible, useful equals of men in society.

'To be sure,' he agreed, and, 'It must be our first consideration, when the constitution is settled. Alas! I do not find so very many friends to liberty in England. Those in authority have given me a cold welcome. This distresses me. In France, war clouds gather.' But with his delicate upward gesture he made them seem somehow fluffy and pink. 'My great fear – I will be frank – is that England joins in war against us. In that I see disaster.'

'The more we follow reason, the less will we be inclined to the barbaric nonsense of war. France must be our example. And if by my pen I can advance that cause . . .' Modesty stopped her abruptly, modesty discovered like a fading bruise on the arm – where had that come from? And for a moment it was not Talleyrand, glossy and cultivated, who sat before her but her father, lolling in boots and buckskins and yawning his scorn at her—

'Prating of her book-learning! It's not natural. You have not raised her aright, ma'am,' he threw out at her mother, who cringed in agreement. 'Don't talk this stuff before company, Mary. Really it is not natural.'

'. . . Natural man is virtuous.' Mary argued it out with the same pale clergyman, who had been to see a public execution at Newgate, and deplored the callous antics of the crowd. 'It is the arrangements of society that have distorted and corrupted him.'

'And her?'

'Aye, aye – only a vulgar mind can be occupied with these quibbles.' She never knew when she was being rude. 'What was the poor man being hanged?'

'He was a forger – and not poor, for he had got a deal of money by it.'

'You reinforce my point. What is forgery but talent and ingenuity misapplied? In crime there is only energy wrongly directed. One day these things will be understood.'

He shook his head. 'You make no allowance for the passions.'

Didn't she? Her misguided passion, her bad love, had made her writhe and weep. He was an artist, clever, ugly, self-admiring: wrong, wrong. Writing alone at her bureau, her dusty study scoured with summer-dry light, Mary watched a bluebottle endlessly hammering itself against the window-glass, and saw there love as she knew it, a painful beating against nothingness.

France: it was in her thoughts, in her heart, and many of her friends were going to see for themselves. Mary packed her well-travelled trunk. Goodbye to the old unhappy kingdom: greetings to the smiling republic of virtue. On the beach at Dover the sailor helping her into the rowing-boat took the opportunity to grope her buttocks; he grinned in her frowning face. A thin, dandified elderly man saw.

'You travel alone,' he said, part explanation, part enquiry, as they were rowed out to the packet-ship. 'You have heard, madam, that they are slaughtering people over there?'

'It is partly to discover the truth behind these rumours that I go. If they are true – which I doubt – then it is much to be regretted.'

'But still you go.'

'I still contend for the principles the French have adopted: not their violent practice.'

'You suppose the two can be separated,' he said, with the same half-question.

'Why do you go, sir?' she said, annoyed.

'I have property interests in Rouen,' he said, yawning, 'and it is all one to me. I am not a friend of humanity – don't like it much.'

She turned away from him, shook the sluggish sand of Dover off her petticoat-hem, and put her face into the ebullient Channel wind. (Later she remembered him. Now, in the plunging dying now, she remembers him.)

'I am still a spinster on the wing,' she wrote to a friend.

Paris was all cold winter light. She watched it harden on the whitewashed wall of her bedchamber-lodging at the echoing top of the merchant's house in the Marais. Outside, the dawn cry of the water-seller, mournful in the high narrow gully of a street, shattered her with homesickness.

'Madame,' said the maid, when she left the house, tapping her own head and winking, 'hat, hat.' The tricolour cockade: it was best to wear one in your hat – bullish *sansculottes* might accost you in the street otherwise, question your sympathies. *She*, of all people.

Paris was not London. At first she could not get over this simple fact. No ramble of scrubby suburbs: it was country then city. No veil of coal-smoke. Mary was disdainful of appearances, and it was a shock to find herself unable, for a long time, to see past them. Coffee-houses, billiard-halls, *rôtisseurs*, wine-shops, teeming and heaving. Then, gaps and vacancies, an effect of pulled teeth: statues gone from plinths, the mansions of the nobility in the Faubourg St Honoré standing bare. A terrible snarl and rattle of ironshod wheels on the terrible potholed streets – wagons, *diligences*, *fiacres*: all shabby and lumbering, all dragged by bony creatures too small for them, horses only by resemblance. In the rue du Temple, she watched egg-dancers. They set out their painted eggs like stepping-stones not to be stepped on, then blindfolded they leapt and pranced, over and around and betwixt and between. Why did one watch? In admiration: or in the suspense of wanting them to fail, to hear the crack and crunch.

Further down the rue du Temple, within the old city wall, the Temple itself drew the reluctant eye, like a coffin in a room. In the medieval tower the imprisoned King waited, with his family, for the Revolution to decide what to do with him.

'You heard about the Queen's friend, the Princesse de Lamballe? After they cut off her head?' An acquaintance from London, who took her to White's Hotel where the English visitors gathered. He smiled thinly, the *blasé* expatriate. 'They put it on a pike and waved it outside the tower window where the Queen could see it. Say hello to your friend, they said. Such excesses. Of course, Antoinette is not a blameless woman, not by any means.'

In the arcades of the Palais-Royal the *demi-mondaines* paraded in filmy muslins. It was a cold winter: Mary could see the gooseflesh on their arms. Other women she saw actually wearing

11

the striped trousers of the *sansculottes*: they shouldered through the crowded street like workmen, shouting about the price of bread. Things seen, heard. One January day in particular, divided between silence and sound, like black squares on white: the grind and crash of the city gates shutting: marching feet: drums; and then the white silence stretching out until, at last, the black roar from the place de la Révolution, where they were cutting off the King's head.

The Father of his People. Mary kept to her room, staring at the fog dripping from the eaves. Things seen, slowly made sense of.

'The voice of the people is the voice of God.' They discussed that at White's, the little circle of English sympathizers, observing, scribbling. Mary had her subject: women: would the Revolution begin the new world for women she had been searching for?

'No.' That was Madame Roland, the interior minister's wife. Her salon was the Revolutionary schoolroom and Mary was an eager scholar. Frustration, too, at this pretty dark self-possessed woman who became her friend but not her ally. 'We must find other ways, other channels to fulfil our destiny as women. It may be as wife, as mother, as helpmeet. Nature does not allow us to stand alone.' But from Manon Roland's dinner-table, it was said, plots and policies were spun out: her husband ran the ministry but she ran him. She calmly confided to Mary that she found him physically repulsive. Tangled in Madame Roland's charm, Mary still felt that none of this was quite right.

'If the voice of the people is the voice of God,' Mary said, 'then the reverse must be true as the two halves of an equation must be interchangeable. Therefore the voice of God is the voice of the people, which makes him our construction or invention.'

'Atheism?' Madame Roland smiled. 'Does it frighten you?'

No . . . Except when she saw certain things. An old tisane-seller in the rue St Antoine, bent double from the keg on his back borne all his blank crippling years, swaying along like some grotesque great snail or turtle and on his caved-in face a meaningless, appalling grin. A graffito on a wall outside the Temple showing the Queen impaled on a spike and on her face the same grin, but this time of leering pleasure. Then Mary reached for faith like a blind woman groping for a stair-rail that suddenly wasn't there: felt herself falling . . .

As she falls now, a tumbler in dark air, about to hit dark water . . .

As she fell in Paris, while Revolution became Terror: fell headlong deep in love.

Imlay.

His name: two simple syllables that came, for Mary, to encompass the world. Including heaven and hell.

'I disliked you very much when I first saw you,' she told him, as she lay in the lumpy inn-room bed watching him dress.

'Well, I must say that's uncommon,' he said, grinning, pulling shirt over narrow sinewy torso, over the scar where a bear's claws had raked him. 'But, then, you are an uncommon woman.'

'Is this uncommon?' she asked, partly from anxiety, partly from a sheer seeking of information, when she eagerly took him to her for a second time. 'What I feel . . .?'

He was reassuring. He was experienced with women – not as a rake, but as a sincere lover. An intimate partnership of equals, that was his ideal: not the stifling conventions of marriage. 'Two prize turkeys strung up together.' Gilbert Imlay was an American, late captain in the army of the young republic, and when he spoke of prize turkeys and flung out his rangy arms, laughing, he seemed to bring a bracing gust of air from the great forests of the wild where he had tracked and explored.

'That's what he *says*,' she overheard someone muttering at White's. France and England were at war now, and the expatriate circle at White's dining-table was dwindling. Those who remained were growing sour and suspicious even as they huddled together. 'Why did he come away from America, then? The great hunter?'

13

'What he *hunts*,' someone said, 'is—' The rest was spluttering laughter.

Business. That was what had brought Imlay to Europe. He had a share in a ship. Also he had written a book, published in London. Also he was a sympathizer with the Revolution. Why was this not satisfactory: why must people be pinned down to a category? thought Mary, helpless with love.

Bliss must have a bower. Hers was a little house he found for her outside the city at Neuilly, amid smoky green clouds, woods on all sides. From there Paris faded to a rumour of tramping feet and clanging tocsins. The Revolution was a serpent eating its own tail. The prisons were filling with the denounced and proscribed. Manon Roland was among them. When she was alone in the house, Mary had nightmares. But mostly she was not alone: Imlay came to her from Paris, lean and humorous and ardent, with news, delicacies, kisses.

A mistress in a cottage. Well, let people see it in that light. She knew it was different. (And yet she shuddered in terror when she missed her menses and began to be sick: and to the dungeons of her nightmares was added the figure of her lover turning his back and walking away with that loose-limbed shrug.)

'Why, I was never more happy, my dear. Who could not be? A child is a joyous thing. I love children.' He laughed at her expression. 'Why so surprised? I almost like children better than adults. Fresh and natural: what could be better?' He held her hand tenderly, kissing the fingertips, looking searchingly at her. 'Do you fear loss of reputation? We're agreed – I think – on our opinion of those nonsensical old conventions. And you know I consider you the wife of my heart. Oh, yes.'

In Paris, where Mary returned for her pregnancy, a nonsensical old convention was finally got rid of when Queen Marie Antoinette was executed on the *machine* of Dr Guillotin – once mistrusted, now much used. Mary hugged the swelling life within her, amid the multiplication of death. The republic dosed its ills with a vigorous application of *terreur*. Faces she knew from

Madame Roland's *salon* stared out from the tumbrils, under cropped hair. Madame Roland's turn came. She died, Mary heard, bravely. Madame Roland had said that the Revolution must be cemented with blood. She was a literary person, and literary people sometimes say such things. They are perhaps not quite to be trusted with words. Mary wrote, kept her lodging, tried to keep her faith. Imlay was gone to the coast, to Le Havre, on ship business. Foreigners were proscribed, and there were few of her old circle about. She was safe because Imlay was American and he called her his wife. Only *called* her so, the few muttered.

'Marriage vows,' she told them, 'would clog my soul.'

But still she had nightmares, and sometimes the kicking of her baby seemed like the frenzy of a prisoner battering at his walls.

Walking out alone, she crossed the place de la Révolution. There was the guillotine on its platform: a modest apparatus, like an oversized cider-press; one saw the surprise on the faces of provincials who expected the *machine* to tower dramatically into the sky. The work had been done earlier, but there were still soldiers about, and a group of *sansculottes* seated about the pedestal of a vanished statue, enjoying a *fête révolutionnaire* – bread, a few bits of fruit and vegetables set out on handkerchiefs. A man bit right into a whole onion as she passed, with a hideous crunching that seemed to scour her ear. She had never been so close to the guillotine: a sort of fascination drew her nearer. Then she cried aloud.

The ground under her feet was sticky. No stranger to the mud of Paris streets, she did not for a moment realize that it was congealed blood that had sucked the heel of her shoe downward.

'Oh, God – oh, dear God – we do wrong here.' She began to shout. 'Does no one see it? Is everyone blind . . .?'

'No, Madame,' hissed a voice in her ear, 'no, not blind, just preferring to live rather than die.' A fat pursy man in striped trousers and cockaded hat, he firmly took her arm and propelled her away. 'You have two lives to protect, I see. So, consider, Madame, consider the prudence of *silence…*' He hissed it as he relinquished her.

Feeling faint, she sat down on a mounting-block, until urged away by a soldier. He seemed to find her distasteful: alone, pregnant, stormy-looking – this would not do. The republic was pure and virtuous and domestic.

Mary ground her shoe as she went away, and a childhood memory struck her. The farm in Yorkshire: the visit of the pig-killer. Her father, who would blaze away at game-birds as if they had done him a wrong, absented himself from the terrible squeals. Mary's little brother, left to her charge, toddled off to investigate the strange outhouse ruckus, and she had to pursue. She caught him at the open outhouse door, amid ghastly spurtings.

Three Marys: the girl, slipping and almost falling in the pig's blood: the woman, retreating in angry disgust from the place de la Révolution: and Mary now, hitting the water below Putney Bridge heavily and flat. Stunned, as if she has landed on paving-stones, she sinks.

In Le Havre, where she had followed him – where he had not invited her, though he welcomed her as if he had, after the first fleeting frown – where the waterside prostitutes winked at her as if they knew something about her, where fat-armed red-bonneted fishwives embraced her and told her to have many more for the republic – in Le Havre she gave easy birth to her daughter.

'Look at her,' he said, his long fingers gently caressing the baby's hair as she sucked at Mary's breast. 'Strong as a little she-bear. She'll soon be writing *The Rights of Woman*, Part Two.'

'Where are you going?'

'Oh, the Customs House again. Some infernal confusion about the bills of lading. I wish the Revolution had made our dear French more efficient.' He cocked an eyebrow at her. 'Why, you're not about to go into a passion again, my love? Don't – it sours the milk, for one thing – I swear little Fanny wrinkled her nose at it yesterday.' He kissed the top of her head.

'It is because I love you,' she said, but he was already out of the room.

She went to the window. Their lodging was in a merchant's house, overlooking the quayside. Below, Imlay's tall figure strode away. The cobbles were greasy with refuse, but he did not look as if he would ever slip.

'Your father,' she told her nuzzling baby. So here they were: love for a man, and domesticity, and motherhood – things she had pitilessly dissected as specimens. But in the living flesh . . .? She didn't know. There was something in front of her, perhaps happiness: Mary hesitated, like someone in a fairy-tale being offered a tempting dish that might be poisoned. Was that it? Again she didn't know. She disapproved of fairy-tales. They were not rational.

Incredible, the cold, the pain, as if her lungs are packed with ice. Water sings in her ears: her eyes sting, blinded. Still she lives, suffers. The iron-smelling river pulls her down only to thrust her up. Gasping, Mary tries to push down her ballooning skirts. Perhaps this is death – not a ceasing, just the agony of life infinitely prolonged.

Probably he began to be unfaithful the winter after the baby's birth, when Mary returned with her to Paris, and he sailed off on business. It wasn't important to pinpoint dates, though she wasted energy trying to do so, at first, simply because she thought that way she might find out what had gone wrong.

'Fidelity is a somewhat artificial virtue,' he said. 'Isn't it? Isn't it putting fetters on the heart? The feelings—'

'What about *my* feelings? Do you not see how wretched I am?'

'Well, yes, I do. And perhaps that is a sure sign that – well, we do not appear to make each other happy any more, and so—'

'Don't say it. No – please don't. I will master myself better. It's only that I – I haven't been sleeping, and I start thinking and thinking . . .'

'My dear, you're a self-tormentor,' he said lightly. 'I don't think, you know, that I ever fostered any illusions about myself.'

That was in London. Business had taken him there, supposedly; and detained him so long that at last she followed him. It was a stormy crossing: little Fanny screamed and was miserably sick: they were rowed ashore at Brighton in a shower of needle-like hail. So Mary's mother country greeted her return. Imlay was not there to meet her.

Imlay had a woman, perhaps more than one, in London. Knowing this, Mary kept loving him. The love had brought her in the end to this dark water, here, now. Humiliation: perhaps only the very proud can know its full bitterness. And Mary who is very proud, strong-willed, independent – an Amazon, they have called her – knows it. She is a deep scholar of humiliation now, can parse its grammar and solve its equations at sight, she has outstripped everyone in it. Thrashing, drowning, Mary's mind is still rich with humiliation lore: the time she tried to kill herself with laudanum: the voyage she made to Denmark, for him, to sort out his business affairs there, while he stayed in London: the return, when he was all evasive charm, and it was his servant who finally told Mary that he was involved with a young actress.

'Pretty little thing. Smart as a button. He says they're going to keep house together. Well, you know him – he don't give a fig!'

Mary knows it all. Pretty little thing. Down, down. Numbness, seizing every limb, slowing the heart: only her ever-restless mind still busy. My dear, you're a self-tormentor. You don't seem to *like* pretty things. Down, hearing the last thing, the creak and clunk of oars, seeing the last thing, a hand reaching for her.

'Where——?'

'You're in the Duke's Head. Gently now – a sip, try a sip.'

In whose head? So all the creeds were wrong: when you died, you became a thought in someone else's head. Mary burst out laughing, then vomited up the brandy they had given her and wept.

'Blow that smoke t'other way, Tom – can't you see how green she is?'

It was a tavern taproom, with spit-stained flagstones and tarry beams. She was on a settle by the fire. Her clothes were steaming, and so was a kettle on the hob, and there were tobacco-pipes smoking: she shaped faces dimly through the fug. An old woman in a starched cap took away the brandy-glass and proffered her a cloth. Men in mufflers, fustian jackets, one with an old-fashioned scratch wig, gazed on her with frank curiosity.

'Why did you do it, mistress?'

'Leave the poor creature be, Tom,' the old woman snapped to the man who had spoken. 'Rest back, dear – don't speak.'

Shivering violently, Mary retched drily, wiped her mouth. 'Why did I do it? Because – because, I think, I am nothing.'

The man grunted. 'Aye, I've felt so sometimes. Never so far as that, though.'

'Tom and Andrew here, they fetched you out,' the old woman said.

'Just laying the boat up, we were. It was lucky. A few minutes more . . .'

A doctor came, a blue-nosed sawbones, who examined her untenderly. His eyes went to her belly, looking for the old story. Not this one, she thought: but then again, perhaps it was after all.

In France, the fall of Robespierre has brought an end to the Terror, and the new government has settled down to some good old-fashioned corruption, while its vigorous armies are shaking down windfalls from the trembling tree of Europe, and the exploits of a young commander named Bonaparte are the thrill of the public prints. In England, in London, in the dusty byways of St Paul's Churchyard, Mary having failed to die must learn how to live.

It was Imlay who at last sent a carriage to fetch her from the riverside tavern back to town. For a little while it seemed – but no. The half-drowning has done this for her at least. He will, if she cleaves still to him, go on forever looking at her in that wry bewildered way; no more.

She is very bleak. It was, she tells her friends, a rational act. Meanwhile, her little girl, Fanny, clings and trembles as if she feels the cold water closing over them.

Traitor.

It is a word much in the air. The days are gone when sympathy for the Revolution could be safely expressed. The government stamps on such seditious talk: sends spies to radical tea-parties. *Philosopher* is another suspect word, liable to get you your house burnt down by a mob yelling for Church and King. As for female philosophers, they are the worst of all, combining everything that's beastly and unnatural. Mary sees the spirit of John Bull at his most jowly, heavy-booted and piggy-eyed stomping across the land: he strongly resembles her father.

So she is bleaker still. She has tried to live, and tried to die, according to her beliefs. Building the world from the head up, as in France. Instead the fall of the angled blade, the fall into dark water. She can see no way up, out.

Brushing her hair in front of the mirror one morning, she says to herself, unexpectedly, 'I am lonely.' And with that it is as if a new Mary emerges from the chrysalis of the past, shaking her sad wings.

Friends gather round, performing little unheroic acts, nudging her towards life. 'Come to the theatre with me – I have two tickets, I don't want to go alone.' She is seen again at dinner-tables, if seldom heard. Admirers are directed to the celebrated author of the *Vindication*. 'I have come three hundred and fifty miles, ma'am, to shake this hand.'

Mary's French maid excitedly notes the day she goes out alone, calling, neatly dressed: 'Madame is off walking like a man again!'

Soon she is strong enough to debate, to argue. Being less sure of everything now, she is more convincing. Among her hearers, one takes shape, for her, for us: from the figured frieze of radical literary London – see spectacles, dowdy powdered hair, bluestocking bosoms unhindered by stays, striped coats *à la*

Robespierre – steps forward one particular figure. What does he represent, this round-shouldered scholar, fortyish, thin-haired, with the mild eyes and the long, unfortunate nose?

'Love,' writes Mary, 'is a want of my heart.' The bleak mood often visits her still – or, rather, it does not visit so much as brutally burst in like a ravisher. That is Mary: there are no suburbs to her personality: before you know it you are at her heart.

The man is named William Godwin. He moves in her circles, has seen her about before: has had the startling experience of being gently corrected by her, indeed, when he was holding forth about something. That doesn't happen often. In their circles, this man is revered much as Tom Paine was. Behind the domed forehead radical ideas revolve: in cool prose he slaughters every sacred cow from monarchy to marriage. He is a bachelor with holes in his stockings, living by his pen, devoted to humanity in the abstract. The woman who corrected him was an annoying blur on the edge of his myopia.

Now there is a change. Someone tells him the story of Mary's life. He carries it home like a brimming vessel.

She calls on him at his lodgings in Somers Town, where black beetles scuttle and a shabby dancing-master practises on a kit-fiddle next door hour after squeaking hour. She looks quite at home. Romantically, he begins to feel that his myopia has been more than physical. When she has gone, he finds himself trembling. Never a dextrous man, he drops his plate while preparing his solitary bread and cheese supper: lucky poverty – the plate is mere pewter, and goes rolling and rippling and wobbling around the floorboards for a remarkably long time, so that he finds himself watching its erratic course in fascination, wondering where it will end up.

How he ended up here, the apostle of anarchism, is quite as curious. He was a country boy. He grew up in the East Anglian fens, where the horizon ruled its severe, logical line between earth and sky, where the rivers ran straight, where the square box of the meeting-house stood up against the flatness, awaiting him.

For young William was to be a minister like his father. They trained him for the pulpit: his fastidious mind led him, by neat stepping-stones of reason, to atheism. Now, writer, philosopher, scourge, he would see all pulpits brought down, along with all institutions – but not violently. There is no fiery element in him. Back in the fens, he saw what the slow, unstoppable rising of the waters could do.

'So, you have made the pilgrimage,' says a friend to Mary, archly. 'Did you get a blessing?'

Young men, intent on world-changing, bring their panting ideals to Somers Town, sit at Godwin's feet. But Mary does not worship, not Godwin, even as she begins to see more of him; and to look forward to it; and to think of him as soon as she wakes up in the morning; and to spend deep evenings *tête-à-tête* that only end with wild mutual glances of disbelief at the clock. She remembers what it was like to worship, and where it ultimately took her.

'Do you mean you are falling in love rationally?' says the same arch friend.

Answers Mary, 'Why not?'

'I disliked you very much when I first saw you,' Mary tells him, in the warm free space made by their first kiss.

And then memory seizes her, horribly.

She has said that before.

But this is not Imlay. 'Did you?' Godwin says, in his pondering way. 'Yes, we began badly, I think. We didn't know each other then, of course. It just goes to show, as I have always argued–' a smile lights his wintry face '–that the extension of knowledge must always lead to the enlargement of happiness.' And they laugh.

'Those two? Good God, it will never work,' says the arch friend – a little jealously.

'Well, she is certainly in good looks,' says another.

Mary, coming up from the depths, returning to the sparkling surface of life, reveals beauty. At thirty-seven she has more bloom and glow than at twenty. The raw angry glare is gone. There is roundness and amplitude.

Ah. At last, a little too much of that.

Well, they are rationalists: it is because they share the same strong ideas that they have begun sharing the same bed; therefore, let us rationally discuss what is best to be done.

It does not quite work out like that. The winds of emotion get up: they are both a little battered and bruised by the end.

'Of course there is a stigma,' he says, 'and the child must become aware of it; but as soon as the child is of an age to understand, we can instruct it that this stigma has no foundation in reason, and is only the consequence of the unenlightened state of society.'

'Talking of stigma,' she says, tight-lipped, 'there is the stigma upon *me*. Fanny was born out of wedlock, though I passed as Mrs Imlay. This one – this one will mark me down as a whore, William – that is certain – sure as a juggler's box, as my father used to say – oh, and how *he* would smirk . . .'

Watching her in bafflement, Godwin says, 'But you don't believe in that false morality. Your beliefs—'

'I know my beliefs, thank you – and this is not a time to be talking of them!'

'These fears . . .' He shakes his head. It seems a lapse into gallantry, but what he says is simply honest: 'I never supposed you could fear anything!'

Her coppery head is down. What she does not say: *I fear that you will abandon me too.*

Godwin paces his narrow parlour. All around are books, unhelpful heaps of them. There is a volume of her own writing on the table, and on the floor one by him: idly she picks his up and places it on top of hers: there – perhaps a pamphlet will be born. She laughs and puts her face in her hands.

'My dear.' His arms are around her. 'My love.'

'Well,' Godwin says, nervous but smiling, as they stand in a wedge of spring sunlight outside St Pancras Church, 'this is, you know, entirely contrary to my principles.'

'Mine also,' says Mary. 'Come, let us go in and be married.'

This unborn child is quiet. Unlike Fanny, who sometimes comes and puts an ear to Mary's belly and listens dubiously, he does not kick the womb with violent assertion. (They are sure the baby will be a boy, and already refer to him as William.) Instead there are only gentle interrogative nudgings, which Mary imagines as little questions, courteously put, about the world outside. In the afternoons, when she consents to take a little rest – for Mary wishes to work, walk, and live full right up to the birth – she sits in the bedroom window with a view of hayfields to the north, and conducts a colloquy within herself, through blood and heartbeat to the stranger inside.

Where is your father? He's working – just over there – Evesham Buildings. He has rooms there. Well, yes, he lives here with us also, but he keeps a separate establishment during the day. Yes, it is uncommon, but it suits us. It is not reasonable for two independent creatures, even if they love each other, to be forever in each other's pockets. Not that I mind when he is here: not at all. This place? Well, I hope you will like it. It's called the Polygon – that means many-sided. Quite new-built, and very well planned, though by no means fashionable – I hope you will never care for that. We are on the edge of London here, and there are meadows nearby, and good air, and those things are much more important.

Yes, hot today. A strange summer it has been – burning heat, then sudden downpours, and the most terrific and sublime thunderstorms I ever knew. I fancy those hayfields were quite worthless this year – which is a great pity – these are such dear times, because of the war. I must confess to thrilling at a storm, though – you must have felt it yourself – the great stirring, and the electricity in the air. Your father, I think, does not feel so. To him it is just a meteorological phenomenon, which of course it is. Still . . .

Oh, no, he has a very feeling heart, your father. Fanny loves him. Handsome? Perhaps not, though he has a noble profile, I think, and a most musical voice – you've surely heard him reading aloud in the evenings, after the cloth is taken away and the lamp lit – my favourite times . . . I tell him that a husband is a much more useful and pleasant domestic article than I ever supposed. Well, you see, it is our little joke, for we have both of us written much against the institution of marriage, and now we go and get married ourselves. Some are happy for us: some do sneer. That, my dear, is something you must accustom yourself to in this world, if you are to live any kind of independent, feeling, worthwhile life, and not just go on like an automaton of convention. The fact is, it's better to be born from married parents, for nonsensical reasons. And I am weary of being scandalous. I want to go forward and be happy. It sounds easy, doesn't it? And yet it is the thorniest thing . . . By your time, I hope, it will be easier.

I hope and believe. These times are rather cruel and bitter, my dear, that should have been so good and bright. We thought the world was being made anew. Instead the old world is being clamped down over us like a cage. There are men in government now who would defame your father to the depths of disgrace – and me also. They spy upon their own people. Honest men who meet to talk over their country's affairs are thrown in prison for it. And as for women, we are bid to hold our tongues when we have scarcely gained the use of them.

But this cannot go on. Once the path of improvement opens, humankind *must* walk it at last. This I believe.

And do you know what? You have a star attending your birth! Yes, a romantic notion, is it not? But quite true. There is a new comet seen in the sky. And do you know who discovered it?

Madame Herschel – the Astronomer Royal's sister. A woman.
    Yes, that does make me very happy.

The Polygon, Somers Town, London, Sunday, the third of
September 1797. Late summer still, in the pink cobwebbed sky:
summer in the flowering gardens enclosed by the ring of tall
houses. Not fashionable, true, and in thirty years' time it will be
very down-at-heel. But on this Sunday a pleasant place, with a
pleasant little world circling around it, a world of artisans and
their families, French refugees living on very little but still curled
and powdered, market-gardeners who carefully brush the brick-
kiln dust from their growing greens, miniature-painters, authors.
The man in the stiff blue coat with gilt buttons, exchanging
greetings with a chair-maker sitting at his open window beside
his whistling caged bird, is a City clerk; on his arm, his wife in a
wrapover gown and coquelicot shawl, plump and cheerful. They
are returning from a walk out to one of the many favoured
Sunday spots between here and Hampstead, the tea-gardens and
bowling-greens and skittle-grounds, the dairies where you can
drink milk fresh from the cow and go on to watch an Italian
puppet-show in the innyard, the flat fields where Cockney
sportsmen bang merrily and hopelessly away with their guns and
come home strutting. Sundayfied peace, and a sleepy glow on the
wooded heights of Highgate and Hampstead: a swaddling atmosphere, just right for the household at number twenty-nine where
a new baby, five days old, breathes the temperate air and squints at
the mellow light.

Not a new William after all, but a new Mary. The midwife
who delivered the baby girl, after a long and difficult labour,
chuckled when she saw Godwin's expression of surprise, and said
how curious it was that parents got these notions in their heads,
when they had no means of telling.

But the adjustment was quickly made. 'Beautiful,' Godwin
murmured, peering short-sightedly at the suckling mite, 'indeed.'
    'Such pain you gave me, my dear – Lord, you half killed me!'

Mary tenderly addressed her baby. 'But now you are so good, and so sweet, and I am quite recompensed.'

A difficult labour – and afterwards, more travail. The afterbirth did not come, an alarming development. Godwin raced in the middle of the night to the Westminster Hospital, fetched the best doctor that could be had. The best that the best doctor could do was try to remove the afterbirth by hand – buttered, groping, agony-inflicting hand.

'I am confident,' he told Godwin at last, coming downstairs in the bleary morning, his face grey, 'confident, yes, that no more of the placenta is retained.'

'No more?'

'It unluckily disintegrated. Hence the prolonged – prolonged work. However. I am confident. Have you breakfasted?'

Mary lay drowsing: her skin looked like paper. The midwife muttered apologetically about the bloodied sheets.

'You did not cry out,' Godwin said. 'I was listening – and yet it must have been—'

'It was the worst pain I have ever known,' Mary said. 'But it was borne – and is over. Thank heaven. No, my dear, I shall not make you a widower yet.'

So she slept, and strengthened, and began to feed the baby – the little Mary, thriving. Fanny, a little girl of baneful timidity, peeped in the cradle at her half-sister as if at a monster's great paw half concealed. The stairs resounded with the brisk feet of visitors. Mother and father discussed the future, theories of education, Rousseau, names: agreed there could only be one. She urged him to go across to his study and work: she intended doing the same herself, very soon.

And now it is Sunday, and Godwin comes back to the Polygon from a long walk, passing the strollers, the City clerk, the whistling caged bird, and at his door is met by the maid – the French girl who came with Mary from Paris, and has seen her mistress at the heights and in the depths – and who just looks at him, dumb, round-mouthed, stricken.

27

★ ★ ★

'Her shivering,' says Godwin, shivering, 'that – that is no ordinary ague.'

'Well, of course it is a moot question,' says the doctor, 'whether there is ever any such thing as an ordinary ague.'

Godwin stares. Not a humorous man, even in his lightest moments, here at the darkest he finds himself on the brink of a joke: nearly saying: *I am the dry pedant in this house, thank you.* Instead he mutters, 'I invited some people to dine. They had better not come.'

He eats alone, not in the dining room on the first floor but in the little parlour below. Later he goes upstairs, pauses, steps into the dining room. The bedroom is directly above. The ceiling is juddering and hammering as if a great engine were working up there. That is his wife shivering.

'My dear, this is a sad change. You must have a lot more rest, I think. Shall I move that pillow up?'

'No – keep hold of my hand – there. That terrible shaking is gone – feel it? Somehow I overcame it. A struggle.' She smiles weakly. 'It's all a struggle, isn't it?'

'To be sure.' He holds her hot hand, and tries not to avert his face at the smell of her breath. 'The baby—'

'Where is she?'

'The doctors think it best she goes to nurse. They fear your milk is – not good for her at present.'

'Puppies?' Godwin says, distractedly. 'Puppies?'

'Or kittens, at a pinch – but there is the matter of sharp claws. Puppies, preferably, for comfort,' the doctor says. 'To drain off the milk, sir, which may have a poisonous effect if retained. Also it may offer stimulation to the whole womanly system. If there is still placental matter, the womb must be encouraged to expel it. Alternatively, a further manual operation. I know a surgeon who would make the attempt.'

'Puppies. I don't know – there must be some, I suppose, in the vicinity – but I am hardly acquainted with our neighbours. The maid – the maid will know.'

Puppies, squirming at Mary's swollen breasts. 'I have appeared many things to you, my dear,' she says to him, through clenched smiling teeth, 'but never absurd before – I hope.'

'Absurd? Heroic, I think. Something of Romulus and Remus, in reverse.'

Later the surgeon comes, looks, shakes his head.

'She is too low. She is . . .'

Sinking, sinking.

The sixth day. Unthinkable that she can live through such days. The trouble is, she wants to.

He has been at her bedside for hours, comes down groggy and half blind from fatigue. He sees the maid hovering. 'No – nothing for me, thank you. She said – a most curious thing – she said she was in heaven. I am not sure what she could mean – whether she meant perhaps that her symptoms were feeling a little easier.'

The maid thinks: How pompous he is. She misses the little girl, Fanny, who has been sent to stay with friends: she does not think she will like it here without the mistress. She has an admirer down the street, a Frenchman. I'll marry him, she thinks. No babies, though. It's too hard for women in this world.

'My dear – do you hear me aright? There is something I wish to say – about the children.'

A bare whisper. 'I know what you are thinking of.'

And then neither of them can say any more. Such silence. Outside, the slow footsteps of the lamplighter sound like the tread of a giant, hunting.

Another Sunday; but such is the difference a week can make, now the sky is a cold, reserved blue, and there is a pinch of autumn in the air.

In the kitchen of number twenty-nine, the maid is crying into a towel. A man comes out of the house, balding, round-shouldered, with a scholar's complexion, and walks across to Evesham Buildings: walks heavily, as if he were mentally wading. Goes into his rooms there, sits down in his study, opens his journal. Mends a pen, dips it. Writes, under today's date, the words *20 minutes before 8*, and then scores a heavy black line, as straight as if he used a ruler.

He feels that there is somewhere he should go. But he cannot think of anywhere. The meeting-house on the fen is a long way away, if it was ever there.

Later, to a friend attempting consolation: 'The dead do not live.'

A week later, there is a new commotion on the stairs of the house in the Polygon. The other day it was a carrying-down. Now it is a carrying-up: Godwin is moving all his things into the house, will live and work and bring up the children here.

The baby, Mary, is held aloft by the maid, who looks for resemblance in the tiny crab-apple face.

'You have a lot to live up to.' She sighs. And for a moment she fancies a flash of understanding in the baby's drunken eyes, as if she knows that very well.

Part One

Let us recollect our sensations as children. What a distinct and intense apprehension had we of the world and of ourselves . . . We less habitually distinguished all that we saw and felt, from ourselves! They seemed, as it were, to constitute one mass.

Shelley, 'On Life'

Sorrow is knowledge.

Byron, *Manfred*

Thou art a dreaming thing,
A fever of thyself.

Keats, *The Fall of Hyperion*

1

Girlhoods: Augusta

Like it? Yes, Augusta was sure she would like it at the Marquise's school. Augusta never thought of giving any other reply. First, because she never disliked anything very much: second, because it was Grandmother placing her there, Grandmother who was the kindest and dearest of her connections. That was the word that best expressed the loose links of family and friends connecting Augusta to the world. Imprecise, perhaps – but that never troubled Augusta.

'What is this you have written here?' demanded the Marquise, who condescended to teach French herself, when she was well enough. She suffered from bilious headaches. From brandy, the music-mistress would whisper, with a vivid mime of tossing back a glass; and sometimes indeed the Marquise would talk in maudlin tones of the property she had had in France before the Revolution drove her out, and then set her teeth and make chopping gestures. 'What is this? "*Le chaise*", or "*la chaise*"? It looks as if it could be either.'

'Yes,' Augusta said agreeably. It seemed a very good solution.

Grandmother hoped she would not be too shy. Again, that was the nearest word. Augusta could be so quiet, still and self-contained, you forgot she was there. But it wasn't fear. She was content to let people be what they were – which was much grander, fuller, more significant figures than her – while she comfortably observed.

'Grand' was precisely the word to describe her grandmother.

As a little girl Augusta had supposed that was why she was called Grandmother; and when she discovered that other people had grandmothers, who weren't necessarily grand, she was faintly disappointed. Only faintly: her mind remained pleased with the concept, and at some level felt it was still true. Augusta's mind was like that. It was the mental equivalent of being double-jointed.

Grandmother was Lady Holdernesse, still handsome at past seventy and upright as a dragoon. Years ago the late Earl of Holdernesse had been a favourite of the Court, even for a time governor to the turbulent young Prince of Wales; and about Lady Holdernesse there clung still an antique Hanoverian atmosphere of snuff and powder, paduasoy and ruffles. Where the Marquise, who took all the fashion papers, wore the new style of high-waisted gown, loose and flowing, Lady Holdernesse remained rigidly encased in stays. Regularly she received friendly little notes in mangled French from Queen Charlotte herself – that dreadful old dowd, as the other girls at the school called her.

'They say the Queen knits all evening,' said vivacious Miss Edwards, 'and no one is allowed to sit in her presence, or sneeze or cough or make a noise, and then she goes to bed at ten. And she is so frugal that no one gets a drop or a crumb the whole time, and sometimes the equerries faint dead away, only they do it *quietly*.'

'Curious how the Prince has turned out so very different,' said languorous Miss Lane, flat on her back. 'Such dissipation!' They all loved that word: they loved to say it hissingly, luxuriate in the images it evoked – although these were really rather vague. Bottles, sofas, cards, bed-curtains, with perhaps a bailiff at the door. In the schoolroom they efficiently put the cut-out map of Europe together, but sinfulness was a country of repute only, its borders indefinite, its extent unknown.

'Not curious at all,' said Miss Edwards, with heavy wisdom. 'His upbringing was so stern and severe, it was no wonder he would fly out and rebel. Anyone could have seen that.'

'And your grandmother is actually a Lady of the Bedchamber!'

Miss Lane said, yawning at Augusta. 'I aver, how monstrous dull for her!'

Still, the connection was impressive: it gave her some lustre in the other girls' eyes. The difficulty was explaining it. Was her grandmother, then, her only family? Not really, though her parents were both dead. It was a long story and rather sad . . .

Augusta's story: it had become for her almost like something she had read in a book. Much of it concerned people she had never seen, or could not remember seeing. Her mother, spoiled and beautiful only daughter of Lady Holdernesse, had been the centre of a great scandal. Respectably married to the Marquess of Carmarthen, she had thrown up everything for a passionate affair with a dashing officer in the Coldstream Guards. They were not discreet: they were flagrant. The Marquess, being a Marquess, was able to get a sorrowful divorce. She, with her reputation in tatters, promptly married her dashing captain. He promptly spent all her money. The carefree ways that had been so engaging in a bachelor were less attractive once she was married to them. From this unlucky alliance came one child – Augusta. Her mother was never well after the birth, and died on Augusta's first birthday.

'Do you have not the faintest memory of her?' asked Miss Morton, who was strong on sensibility. 'Some say that even the tiniest infant can receive these impressions, and revive them in later life.'

'Do they?' said Augusta, always respectful of what others said. 'Well, it may be so. But not for me. I cannot remember anything of her.'

Nor much of the years that followed. According to the story, Grandmother took charge of her, bitterly blaming her father for her mother's death. Meanwhile the dashing captain resumed his old ways. Soon he was hock-deep in debt and resorting to the marriage-market of Bath to mend his fortunes. There he snared his second bride, a Scots heiress with the refinement and allure of an oatmeal pudding, and eagerly began working his way through her twenty thousand pounds.

And now there came a patch of memory, like a coloured picture pasted into the story. Her father and his new wife came to claim Augusta from her grandmother.

She was not yet five; but the later Augusta retained a clear image of an interview at Holdernesse House, with Grandmother sitting straight-backed and chin up; and seated at what seemed a great distance, as if they were going to urge their chairs into a trot and joust at each other, the fat black-haired lady whom her father had married. Somewhere between were Augusta and her father. He was crouching down, and smiling, and holding out his arms invitingly: a handsome man with laughing eyes, fair hair tied in a queue, a froth of cravat. And Augusta looked from one to the other, searching their faces, not knowing what to do. She had a sense that she ought to please someone, somehow, but could not think how to go about it.

'If you must,' her grandmother was saying. There was more, but these were the words, several times repeated, that stayed with Augusta. 'If you must.' Grandmother sounded cold and unhappy, not like herself. She had been born a Dutchwoman, and there was always a gentle accent, a shading in her voice that to Augusta was the essential sound of kindness. Grandmother was very devout. Augusta's mind, by one of its ready transitions, always conceived the voice of angels, even of God, speaking with that accent.

The fat lady was saying, 'She will do very well with us,' and patting her ample belly. And at this point the memory dissolved in incoherence and alarm. The fat lady, Augusta's stepmother, went on: 'There is a little brother or sister for her here – what d'ye think of that, missie?' And Augusta burst into tears and ran to her grandmother's skirts, hiding her face. There was some sort of fear or misapprehension in her that the fat lady was going to produce, conjurer-like, a little baby there and then. It was all too much. All too much partly because of fascination. She wanted to see the brother or sister, as well as dreading it. She wanted everything to be as it was before. She howled.

And curiously, though she was taken away by her father and stepmother, she remembered very little of that. There was a glimpse of the parting with Grandmother, who was shaking. Not with tears, not with cold: it was contempt that sent that quiver through her proud stiff-corseted bosom. She despised Augusta's father and his fleshy Aberdeen bride. She could not disguise it. In the carriage, after, her stepmother shook a hamlike fist.

'Such airs! Such airs as the old body gives herself!' And then, looking down at Augusta, who was quietly weeping: 'Lord, I hope you'll not keep *that* up.'

But she didn't, not Augusta – she had an innate sense of the value of being no trouble. Certainly her memories of the brief period that followed, living with her father and stepmother, were such that she seemed hardly to be in them at all. She was a sketchy figure on the edge of the canvas, where the gorgeously coloured figures of stepmother and father contested the centre of the composition.

Why did they want her? She was not sure, then or now. If there was some notion of their being a happy family together, it soon evaporated in the heat of quarrels, money troubles, wine, separations. And Augusta never could quite grasp that notion – what family was, who belonged to it, who did not. It was perhaps from this time that she developed the roomy idea of her 'connections'. But she did nourish a little secret hope for long after – that her father had taken her simply for love of her.

Darkness blotted out the story then. Apparently they all went to France, to escape the captain's creditors; and there, apparently, Augusta fell ill, and her stepmother nursed her before bringing her back to England, alone. Out of all this Augusta could summon only fragments: a pitching boat, her father brushing something unpleasant from the sleeve of his gold-laced coat, her own scream at the sight of a surgeon's leech in a glass jar. It was not a long passage in the story. Settling into London lodgings to await the birth of her own child, with the debt-stricken captain still in France, her stepmother decided Augusta was one trouble

too many. Grandmother's maid came from Holdernesse House to
fetch her back. Grandmother was very glad to reclaim her, but
she could not trust herself to look Augusta's stepmother in the
face.

'You will never suffer like that again, my child,' Grandmother
said, clutching Augusta's small hands in her long dry bony ones:
here memory became full and clear and rounded again. 'I shall see
to it. I promise it. I had no power to refuse him, do you see?
Because he is your father. He has his rights.' The dry hands
tightened convulsively. 'Well, we shall see. If he tries to claim
them again . . .'

Grandmother looked grim; the gaunt sinews stood out in her
stately neck. Perhaps because of that, because even then she
sought pleasantness at any price, Augusta said: 'I didn't mind,
Grandmother. He is very good really.'

'God help you, my dear,' Grandmother said, shaking her head,
'and God bless you, but he is not.' The grim gaunt look softened,
though, to Augusta's intense relief. 'Natural, I suppose. You have a
warm heart, Augusta. I hope it will not hurt you.'

'Oh, I shouldn't think so.'

So she was not to see the baby brother or sister after all.
'Half-brother,' Grandmother said, when news came that her
stepmother had been safely delivered of a boy. 'He is to be
George.'

'George.' Augusta tried the name over. There was something
irresistible about it. She had a baby brother named George; these
simple facts seemed to solve much that was problematical and
unsatisfying about her young life. 'My brother George.'

'Half-brother. But you need not trouble your head about him,
I think, my dear. They say she intends taking him back to
Scotland. She will need to beg from her family, of course.'

So it proved. Her stepmother decamped with her baby brother
to Aberdeen, a place that Augusta used to think of as practically
polar in remoteness, beyond ice-strewn seas. Her father was there
also for a while – sponging, they said – before taking his debts off

to France again. By then Augusta was in a new place herself.

'Is this Derbyshire?' she asked them, when they first took her into the house. And later, when they took her out to the paddock to see the pony and the donkey there, 'Is this still Derbyshire?'

The lady laughed, and hugged her. Augusta had been quite serious – Grandmother had told her she was going to live in Derbyshire, and when at the end of the long journey Grandmother's travelling-coach pulled up in front of a rambling grey ivy-mantled building near a church, Augusta thought this was it – but laugh, hug and lady were all very agreeable. This was a happy part of the story.

The lady was Mrs Alderson: the genial man with the bloodhound eyes was her husband, the rector of this rural parish and her grandmother's chaplain. They had kind hearts, three small children, and plenty of room. For eight untroubled years Augusta lived with the Aldersons. They breathed good limestone air, ate tender spring lamb and crisp apples and drank creamy milk that was never watered down or frothed up with snails: they played cup-and-ball and spillikins and charades: they had prayers with the accent on mercy not punishment. Augusta shed her sickliness, throve, and knew a family life at last.

Except, of course, that this was not her family. More confusion – until she decided not to trouble about it. She would let affection lead her. She could never turn down love. Perhaps for others it was like an annuity that could always be relied upon, but for Augusta it was a special gift to be received gratefully.

At the rectory in deepest Derbyshire she was a long way from her father, and the more responsible of her connections saw to it that she stayed that way. The captain was not told where she was, lest he steal her away – or, more likely, threaten to, so they would have to pay him not to. Understanding this, Augusta's flexible mind still embraced a wish that she could see him, somehow, while keeping this peaceful life as well. It was an impossibility, but Augusta lived quite comfortably with impossibilities.

This one was not to be. When she was eight, her father died of drink and debility, penniless and alone, in the French town of Valenciennes. Mad Jack, as he was known, was only thirty-six – but, then, he had surely lived twice as fast as most people. Now that he was only a memory, a sketch of dazzle and dash, he could be harmlessly allowed into Augusta's mental circle of those she loved. Also ushered into that inner and inward circle was the little half-brother she had never seen, who had inherited their father's debts and, it was said, his good looks. Alas, they were spoiled, because the little boy in far-off Aberdeen was, Grandmother reported, terribly lame – club-footed, in fact.

Augusta knew what that was. There was a youth who looked after the mules for the nearby coal-mine, and he could be seen from the rectory windows sometimes leading the poor creatures to grass. 'Poor creature,' was said of him too: his lameness was spectacular, he lurched and swung and teetered; village children followed, mimicking cruelly and with deadly accuracy. Yet the imagined brother in the circle of Augusta's mind, shadowy as he was, certainly did not move like that; he was all grace.

So: Augusta's story brought up to date – the long, tranquil passage among healthful hills ended, warm, loving goodbyes to the Aldersons, and a new chapter opening at the Marquise's boarding-school in Barnes. Just outside London, here: this whole tract of Thames-side, through Fulham to Chelsea, had been liberally planted with Young Ladies' Academies. Any day you might see crocodiles of girls going on walks, goggling at other crocodiles across the way – 'Did you *see* her? Did you *see* the sabot sleeves? Did you ever see such a fright in your *life*?' – looking in, if indulged, at milliner's and circulating-library, exercising pencil and sensibility at riverside beauty-spots. Down to peaceful Putney Bridge was one such walk: and here you could still hear the local gossip of last autumn, when a woman tried to drown herself by jumping off the bridge, and was rescued in the nick of time by watermen.

Poor creature, thought Augusta. She could not imagine such

potent unhappiness: it even seemed a human achievement beyond her capability, like genius or Herculean strength.

Not quite London, but London very near at hand, and that was apt for Augusta, for she was sent to the school to be groomed and polished and prepared for that little, huge world just downriver, where Grandmother lived. Society. The landmarks of that world stood out to the minds of the Marquise's young charges like vivid peaks. There, if you were lucky, you had your coming-out at Almack's, paraded Rotten Row in the fashions of a Bond Street *modiste*, went late to routs and crushes in the mansions of the squares out west, or to Vauxhall Gardens, or to the theatre in the fascinatingly sinful purlieus of Covent Garden. And there were men.

Oh, there were men everywhere, of course, like the drawing-master who breathed noisily through his nose and jumped as if electrified when his hand accidentally brushed yours – but this was different. In that waiting world, men were superb, terrifying, and other. They lolled in the bow-windows of their clubs, White's and Brooks's and Boodle's, and stared out at St James's Street that was all theirs, for no respectable woman could walk there. Yet they were also after you, in that world. That was why you entered it: to join a sort of mutual hunt through the groves of the Season. Somewhere there was the man who would make you his prize.

The girls talked of him as they lounged on summer evenings in the stifling bedrooms on the top floor of the Marquise's house. In the dry heat there was a prickle and crackle of muslin gowns and restlessly combed hair. At the sound of hoofs and wheels in the street they always left a silence, as if it just might be Destiny bowling towards them.

'I'm so bored,' said Miss Lane the ever-languid, her face in the counterpane.

'Have you noticed,' said Miss Edwards, 'how old Garside puts her hand on her cunny when she talks about Rousseau?'

They let out a fizzing laugh, scandalized, also contemptuous.

Miss Garside was a teacher, and thus old, dowdy, hopeless: they would never be like her.

'Rousseau was a great spirit,' said sentimental Miss Morton. 'The one place in the world I wish to visit above all others is Rousseau's grave.'

'I aver, you have the most curious notions,' sighed Miss Lane. 'I aver' was all the rage with them at the moment: these favourite phrases, like 'beyond anything great' and 'monstrous mortifying', came and went mysteriously. 'Who could care to go and see a grave? It would quite put me in the dismals.'

'Don't let the Marquise find your volume of Rousseau,' said Miss Edwards. 'She says he caused the Revolution.'

'It was people like the Marquise who caused the Revolution,' Miss Lane said, with sleepy tartness. 'What would you *do* at the grave?'

'Lay a laurel wreath. Weep.'

'Lord. Though I suppose anything is better than this boredom.' She sat up and looked over at Augusta. 'Aren't you bored? You never look it.'

'Oh, sometimes,' Augusta said, though in truth she wasn't. Seat her comfortably, and she could happily contemplate the landscape of her own skirt, shoe, sofa.

'Not you.' Miss Lane levered herself up, regarded Augusta with tousled head on one side. 'I can see you in a dozen years – a mother—'

'Oh, Lord!' breathed Augusta.

'Yes, and a good one, a doting one. The sort I wish *I* had, instead of the old strumpet.' Miss Lane's mother was a fashionable widow, reputed to be having an affair with her young lawyer. Once a month she wrote her daughter a short letter – half the page blank. 'My dear child', they always began: Miss Lane said it was because her mother couldn't remember her name. 'Yes, a happy wife and mother, and you'll be very genteel and settled, but the young people will adore you because you're not severe, and bring you their love-troubles.'

This was amazing. Augusta could never picture anything in this way, unless she had already seen it or had it described to her.

Miss Morton said, 'What about me?'

'Oh – I think – I can see eastern costume,' Miss Lane said, satisfactorily. Miss Morton had a favourite uncle in India, and would often talk knowledgeably about 'the fabled East', and claim an exotic soul.

'And me?' said Miss Edwards.

'I don't know, I'm tired,' Miss Lane groaned, collapsing again, 'and so bored,' and she stared up at the sun-filled window as if her stare might crack and burst it out.

'Shall I read from *The Monk*?' Miss Morton suggested. 'Shall I read the part where they get Cunegunda and bind her and gag her, and Agnes dresses as the ghost of the Bleeding Nun? It is so wonderfully horrid.'

'Not so horrid the tenth time round.' Miss Lane sighed.

And then Augusta spoke up – not with self-assertion, for that was not like her, but simply because she felt their dullness and wanted to cheer them. They loved the thrill of the Gothic, and she could bring it closer.

'You know, my brother has an abbey, or will have. A real Gothic abbey.'

They clamoured. Even Miss Lane was alert. How, how, tell.

'Well, my brother is heir to the Barony of Rochdale, through our father. *He* was only nephew to the fifth Baron, but now the main line has all died out because the heir was killed at the siege of Calvi, very bravely. And so when the old lord dies, which cannot be long, my little brother will become the sixth lord – all quite unexpected. And he will get the ancestral house in Nottinghamshire, which is a genuine old abbey, called Newstead. No, I have never seen it, but I have heard all about it. Nor my brother neither. Yes – half-brother – though I don't feel that makes any difference. Oh, I don't know how old – only that it is monstrous old, and it does have a Haunted Room, that I can swear to.'

It was a sensation. Miss Morton declared herself about to burst with envy. And this from Augusta – who was so quiet and unassuming, who was the despair of the drawing-master because she would painstakingly draw every leaf upon a tree instead of suggesting them with a few strokes. It was—

'Romantic!' cried Miss Morton. 'The most romantic thing I ever heard!'

'But when your brother inherits, will you be able to see the abbey then?' Miss Edwards demanded. 'Will you go and stay? Or even live there with him?'

'I don't know,' Augusta said. 'I haven't thought about it.'

But in her understated way she had. The inner circle of her mind now contained a locale as well as people – a Gothic abbey, turreted, convincing, bathed in perpetual moonlight.

And was it, somehow, her place? She couldn't tell: Augusta had no conception of her future as something she could control. Fate must direct. Yet she trusted. She felt that life did not unfold or unroll in any consequential manner – it proceeded by a chain of small miracles. So one never knew.

Miss Edwards, her round cheeks rich with blushes, wanted to know: 'How old is your brother?'

'He is five years younger than me – so he is nine.'

'And so six years younger than me,' Miss Edwards said, thinking. 'Well, it is not such a great difference. I could still marry him.'

'Lord, as if he should want you!' chuckled Miss Lane, lazily slapping out.

'Well, he might. He might marry any one of us,' Miss Edwards insisted: then, her eye falling on Augusta, 'Well, not you, of course.'

And that set them all off on one of their laughing fits, which came like sudden showers from a clear sky, and could go on and on until they wept and hiccoughed and had to drag out the chamber-pot hastily, and would subside only to begin again with a single glance and shriek. This time it was so noisy that the

Marquise herself came to the door, brandy-nosed and tetchy, to demand if they were young ladies or hyenas.

'And you,' she said, wagging a departing finger at Augusta, 'I am surprised at *you*, Miss Byron.'

2

Girlhoods: Caroline

If you're going to be born towards the end of the eighteenth century of the Christian era, probably the most favourable location is England, taking into account such things as infant-mortality rates, life expectancy, freedom from natural disasters and military incursions, and comparative material wealth. And the section of English society that it is most favourable to be born into is, of course, the upper section. Even the best that medical science can offer is no great matter at this date, but such as it is, the upper class can command it: likewise food, clothes, room, distance from epidemic breeding-places, warmth, safety and security.

Try to be born into the aristocracy, then. Not the lower reaches, where there are quite a few out-at-elbows lordlings squatting dismally amid their mortgaged and weed-choked acres. (There is one such to be found at Newstead Abbey, in Nottinghamshire, just at this moment: the Wicked Lord Byron, as they used to call the fifth Baron, though now the old man is more strange than wicked, living off hard cheese in brooding retirement and holding discourse only with the clicking horde of crickets that infest the filthy kitchen. He is trying to train them.) Nor is it a good idea to aim higher, and be actually born into the royal family, not riven as they are by the bitter loathing between King George III and his son the Prince of Wales – or Whales, as the satirists will soon begin to call the dandified scapegrace when fat claims him as hungrily as he would claim the throne.

No, better by far, best of all, be born into one of the highest aristocratic families – rich as kings, only a little less powerful, and unhindered by responsibility. And surely the most eligible of all is the great Whig clan that includes the Duke of Devonshire, owner of no less than six country houses, and his spectacular young wife Georgiana, who has accumulated sixty thousand pounds' worth of gambling debts since her marriage and, most piquantly, is not quite sure *how*. So, how about Georgiana's sister, likewise a beauty but not so intensely subject to public scrutiny, and well married to a man who will be Earl of Bessborough and has no obvious vices? There will be a country place, of course, but try to be born in town, at the family's London mansion, where medical attention can be more swiftly summoned, and the rooms more easily heated, as the date appointed for the birth is November (summer with its muggy fevers being the worst season). And as the mother in this case already has two boys and fancies a change, try to be born a girl.

There. Every chance is now maximized. It is hardly possible in 1785 to enter the world more auspiciously. Draw your first breath, Caroline Ponsonby.

'Now there is a child,' says the physician who has attended the birth to the *accoucheur* at the door of the Cavendish Square house, 'who will never want for anything.'

And the fairies popularly supposed to gather around the cradle – do they hear those words, and smile ironically? Fairies, if anyone, surely know about the deceptiveness of appearances.

The growing Caroline seems, at any rate, fairy-influenced. She is light and slender, her hair a wild red-gold cloud of curls, her face pure pixie with its pert nose and huge brown eyes. They call her 'little sprite', Ariel. Her elder brothers toss her, bird-boned and squealing and delighted, from one to the other, like a toy.

'John, Frederick, stop it. You'll make her sick.'

'Caro likes it, Mama! She likes it beyond anything.'

'She'll be over-excited. Now you know where that leads.'

Quite early on, Caroline knows that this means her temper.

At first she thinks of it as a thing that has come to live with them, a troublesome outsider. When her temper has done naughty things, she looks in the mirror to try and see it, like a demon at her shoulder. But she sees only her own face, flushed and contorted.

It is a great pity, everyone agrees. She is generally so quick, clever, happy, and loving. This above all. Perhaps that's the problem.

'She must learn to moderate her feelings,' says the doctor, called in to examine her after she has exhausted herself with a screaming fit. 'What is this about a kitten?'

'It was lame. We had it drowned,' her father says reasonably.

Loving, yes: early on she knows what it is to be shaken by love. 'These passionate attachments,' people say, dismissively, and Caroline wants to cry out that *attachment* is just right, for she is already as sensitive to words as everything else, and when she loves it is like a bonding and tearing, like when she roamed down to the kitchen of Aunt Georgiana's house and picked up a plate from the stove and realized, with fascination momentarily postponing the agony, that it was so hot her fingers had stuck to it like wax.

That is what it feels like when she dreams her favourite spaniel has run away, and she has to scurry down in her night-rail sobbing and put her arms round him in his basket, where they find her in the morning with her thin bare feet blue with cold.

So, perhaps the fairies did more at the cradle: perhaps she is a true changeling.

'I don't think she can have got it from my side,' says her father – likely enough, thinks the doctor: the man is such a thundering bore.

'We don't need to talk in those terms,' says the doctor. 'Miss Ponsonby is overly vivacious. But her mental powers are uncommonly quick. There is no suggestion—'

'She cannot have got it from my side either,' puts in Caroline's mother. 'There is assuredly no instability there.'

Well, no, thinks the doctor. But then again.

Caroline's maternal grandmother, Lady Spencer, is eccentric. She dresses in a mannish riding-habit, keeps pet snakes, dines on grey porridge while she pores over books of metaphysics. Into the world she sent two beautiful daughters. The eldest is that fabulous Georgiana who married the Duke of Devonshire and has imperilled even his unthinkable wealth with her extravagance: meanwhile he is sleeping with her best friend. The younger, Caroline's mother, has gambled away a few fortunes likewise, but her main recreation seems to have been collecting admirers. Everyone from the Prince of Wales down, the doctor has heard; and they don't stop at admiration.

'Well,' the doctor says, shrugging, 'for the excitability at night, there is always laudanum.'

Caroline makes up stories. They pop into her head unbidden. Sometimes they have fairies in them, and witches and goblins: sometimes stranger things. 'A sugar loaf as big as a house, and on the top there lived a mouse, with whiskers on his chin, and he made such a din when he fell in the well and broke his nose and tore his hose so he ate his toes . . .'

'It doesn't make sense, Caro,' complains Frederick. 'Tell the one about the soldier. This one's silly. How can he eat his toes?'

'With a knife and fork.'

'It doesn't make sense.'

But Caroline is used to that. Many things in her world do not make sense. She has seen Papa shouting at Mama, and his fingers fiercely gripping her arm just as they grip the reins of a half-broken horse. In a world that made sense, that would be as bad as her temper. But it's not, apparently; and she is not even to mention that she saw it. Indeed, it did not happen at all. Which makes no sense.

Caroline loves to dress up: to appear, suddenly, transformed and dramatic.

'What are you today?' her nurse says.

'I am an Egyptian queen, of course.'

'Like Cleopatra?'

'*Like* Cleopatra. But someone else.'

'Someone who wears a gold-fringed curtain.'

'It's a royal robe.'

'And where did the royal robe come from?'

'Well, it came down from a window.'

'On its own? Or did the Egyptian queen help it?'

'Oh, it doesn't matter, you know.' Nothing like that does. She has a hazy idea that her family owns the world. It gives her a peculiar fearlessness. Not for her the childhood dread of getting lost. She has only to go up to any door, knock, and be admitted.

So when the whole family, Bessboroughs and Devonshires, travel abroad, and she, as quite a little girl, rides through the new-made France, seeing the burnt shells of convents, passing under Revolutionary arches of flowers crowned with the red caps of liberty, she is not afraid or upset or homesick. The Alps appear to her an excellent idea, Italy only a little less so: her fair skin soon burns under the hot southern sun. But she is not fussy about appearances, otherwise she might ask her father to have it turned down a little.

At Naples she scrambles about the slopes of Vesuvius, violently throws her lava samples at a muleteer she sees beating his animal, gallops with a pet fox about the sweet-smelling garden of the villa, chatters in macaronic fragments of French and Italian.

And tries to look after her mother. Mama's health was poor before coming abroad. She had a paralytic seizure from which she is only lately recovered. But now Mama has a new malady. 'What is it, Mama? What's wrong? Oh, tell me, tell me else I'll die!'

She has not seen her mother for some time: the adults have been engaged in a round of sightseeing expeditions, sailing-parties, receptions at the Neopolitan court. Now her mother is in Caroline's room at the top of the house, where Caroline is made to rest in the warm afternoon, and she is crying.

'Oh, Mama, stop, or I shall die!' With anyone else, this might be a piece of childish exaggeration, but with Caroline at such moments there is a stark conviction: she can almost feel the life slipping from her.

Through brimming eyes Lady Bessborough looks about her for a chair: the room is not familiar to her. 'It's nothing, my dear,' she says, half laughing. 'It's love.'

Later Caroline hears her nurse talking to her mother's maid. 'Oh, he's a pretty fellow all right – very pretty – and so he should be, considering he's ten years younger than her.'

'More, I've heard. Ugh, pardon, I'm bilious from this damn saucy mucky food. More than ten, I've heard. I don't reckon he's even of age. What does she think she's about?'

'Oh, well, she's always had more of an itch than his lordship can scratch. From what I've heard—'

Caroline owns a little silver-mounted riding-crop, given to her by her uncle the Duke, and without knowing how, she has it in her hands and is thrashing her nurse's jerking rump with it. 'Beast, filthy beast, dirty old crow, old worm—'

'Miss, you'll stop that at once – stop it – your pa shall hear of it.' And having grappled the riding-crop away from her at last, the nurse gives a great sigh and, over Caroline's head, says, 'You see? See how *this* one's turning out.'

Her father is more remote than ever at this time. He seems always to be riding, has diminished to a smell of leather and sweat, a creak of boots, a grim profile.

One day she catches him. 'Papa, listen. You must help – Mama is so poorly. She's got love.' She sees him flinch, but she does not understand it yet, though she will soon, sooner than she should. 'She's always weeping, and coming and going—'

'Oh, Caroline,' he snaps, 'don't prattle so,' and he looks around in perplexity, as if she were some troublesome small animal and he were trying to locate the cage she has escaped from.

Aunt Georgiana walks with her in the garden and is, as ever, vaguely comforting. Just her presence: tall, plump, pretty, milky-skinned, embraceable, to little elfin Caroline she really *is* Devonshire, a whole rich landscape of pleasantness.

'Your mama is quite well, Caro,' she says. 'Don't trouble yourself about it. I declare you've taught those dogs tricks already – however do you do it?'

The two dogs frisking about the garden are gifts from a Neapolitan countess, and Caroline has made the adults laugh by remarking how curious it is that they understand commands in English. She can always do that – make them laugh. It's almost too easy. Sometimes it seems most of the adults around her have shut off the part of their minds that thinks of funny things.

'She says she can't sleep.'

'Well, that's not like her,' Georgiana says, with a faint touch of sisterly malice. 'But as long as *you* sleep, my dear, that's the main thing.'

Caroline never really likes going to sleep: she resists that surrender, that nothingness. But lately it is worse. She sits up thinking of her mother and staring out at the sky above the bay, where between them, spreading night and the smoke of Vesuvius horribly claim the sky. This garden too, loud with bees, obscene with roses, now disturbs her. Here the other day she found a wonderful butterfly, iridescent and big as her hand, and caught it in a downturned glass jar. She only meant it to be in there while she looked and admired. When something called her into the house, she only meant to be a moment. It was the next morning before she remembered, shrieking aloud, running. The butterfly was dead, faded, like a leaf. Caroline pinched and punched her own arms, seeking punishment, though she knew that would be up to God in the end.

'I hate love!' she bursts out. 'It just makes people cry, I hate it.'

'It might seem that way, Caro,' Aunt Georgiana says. 'But – well, never mind. You'll see when you're older.'

Caroline, hardly listening, points a trembling finger at the dogs. 'Oh! I never taught them that. What are they doing?'

'Oh, Lord.' Aunt Georgiana steers her away. 'Never mind, don't pay them any heed, my dear.'

'Scappa's hurting Roma – look.'

'No, no.' She is trying to suppress – Caroline can see it – a faint smile.

That is another thing about adults. When they do laugh, it's at things that aren't funny.

But compensations: she has never before been so close to Mama. Often Mama will come in with a candle when Caroline is already in bed, sit down by her with a wonderful whisper of silk from her evening-gown, and talk to her as if she were another adult.

'I am a great fool, am I not, Caro?'

'No, Mama. Never!'

'It's what people are saying. It's what they are all saying.' Since her illness, perhaps, there has been this slow, lisping quality about Mama's speech – though Aunt Georgiana has something of it too. Like a fire, it is luxuriant, and lulls you.

'Oh, who cares what people think?' says Caroline stoutly. 'Not me.'

'I shall have to go away, I think. I can't bear to be here. He – he torments me.'

'No, don't go. Please, Mama.'

'Little Squirrel. You know you do very well without me.'

'I don't.' And then, just as when she was learning to ride and instinctively understood how to distribute her weight, Caroline's mind makes a deft adjustment. 'If you go, he'll think it's because of him. And then that makes him the winner.'

Mama turns, her eyes shining in the candlelight. 'The things you do think of!' she says after a moment.

In truth, Lady Bessborough's affair with her Adonis, young Granville Leveson-Gower, only mildly tickles the English colony at Naples. Gathered around the baroque court of the Two Sicilies – with its dwarfs and clockwork toys and ripe whiff of

53

corruption, and its illiterate king, Ferdinand the Big-Nosed, superstitious as an old peasant-woman, addicted to the hunt, gobbling dishes of macaroni in the royal box at the opera – they are not very shockable. There was lately the scandal of the British minister, dry old Sir William Hamilton, presenting a buxom new bride half his age and no better than she should be; but they are getting used to Lady Hamilton's ways now. Then there is the diversion of a Royal Navy squadron coming into the bay, with a mission to the allied court. Young Captain Nelson, dining ashore, is quizzed: Where are the troops to go? Is it true that French royalists have taken Toulon? Does he not think this war will very soon fizzle out? And some draw their own conclusions from his cautious replies, and begin to think of home. Young Captain Nelson departs, and the chances of war will take him to Corsica, and to the siege of Calvi, where he will lose his right eye to splinters from cannon-shot; and where an even more fateful cannonball will snuff out the life of one William Byron, making a little lame boy living obscurely in Scotland heir to a barony.

But as for Lady Bessborough and her pretty lover – well, as someone says, it gives her something to do.

Learning: Caroline is not doing enough of it, according to Grandmama Spencer, who is teaching herself German and conjugates verbs as she stomps about the Royal Gardens. Mama talks vaguely of hearing Caroline's daily lesson, and Grandmama Spencer herself sometimes sits her down to arithmetic; but the child needs, she says, a proper governess.

Caroline is learning, though, all the time. She has picked up enough French to write a letter home in it: Italian too: she scribbles verses, rhyming for ever, and in her sketchbook draws tiny devastating caricatures. She even has an ear for dialect, for language beyond the pale.

'*Cazzo.*' She has heard their guide say it. It means what you tread in, regularly, in the unswept streets. When she is taken to a firework display in the Royal Gardens, and everyone is cooing exclamations, Caroline cries out in the same tone: 'Ah, *cazzo!*' And her mischief is rewarded by a beaming smile from a bewigged expatriate gentlewoman sitting close by, who remarks: 'How charming – the way the little ones pick up the language!'

Learning, by unconventional means. Aunt Georgiana has already gone home to England – why? To be with her husband the Duke and her children, whom she loves so dearly. But why, then, did she go away from them? Hush. And why did she have a big belly when we first came away to France, and then it got small again? Hush, hush. Eager linguist, she begins to interpret *hush*, a word conveying a multiplicity of meanings, but all of them bringing to her mind the two dogs in the garden, hunched, grotesquely urgent.

Learning: they are going home at last, and break their journey at Rome, after a passage perilous through bandit country – pistol-shots echoing round the narrow defiles, the guide sweating and moaning *cazzo, cazzo*, and unburied corpses at the roadside – one with a Vesuvius of flies erupting from its burst belly – and only Caroline unafraid. (The merely *real* does not frighten her.) In the inn-room her mother sets out her writing-desk (portable – their moving emporium of luggage is watched like a carnival parade by hungry faces) and after writing for a few minutes stares into space.

Caroline comes up, looks over her arm, and reads the name at the top of the letter.

'Oh!' she says in disappointment, for it is the name of the young man at Naples, familiar to Caroline from those anguished talks at night by the moonlit bay. 'Oh, you are writing to him. I thought that was done. I thought that was why we were going home—'

'What?' Her mother comes to herself, as if from far distances, and her dreamy heavy-eyed face turns stern. 'Yes, yes, to be sure. But we do not – we do not *speak* of these things, my dear. I had thought you would understand that by now. Come – let us have no more of it.'

Caroline, wordless for once, thinks of those soft Neapolitan nights with her mother sitting on her bed, telling her fears and secrets to her daughter-confessor.

A brief sharp kiss, a turn of the shoulder. 'Now go, go, let me write in peace, my dear.'

'Oh . . . What shall I do, then, Mama?'

'Whatever you like, Caro,' Lady Bessborough says, busily writing.

'And what are you today, Caroline?'

'A boy. My name is – Charles.'

'I see. That is why you have your brother's clothes on, I suppose. And that – good God, that's a knife! Put it down at once. Where—'

'It's only a butter-knife. Boys are allowed to have knives.'

'Caroline, put it down at once. See the marks you have made on that table.'

'I can't hear you, I'm Charles, you'll have to call me by my name.'

Sigh. 'It's high time you stopped all this pretending.'

'Why?'

'Because you are growing up . . . And now what are you laughing at?'

Lady Bessborough says: 'I cannot control her. She is simply beyond me. She has been worse since we came back to England, much worse.' It is three o'clock in the afternoon. Lady Bessborough has been up for an hour. No letter from her lover today. When is he coming to London? Soon perhaps she can begin dressing for dinner, slowly: then there will be dinner: then the evening, and the gaming-tables will make the time go. 'She is not like the boys. I miss them so.' They are at Harrow: no letter from them today either.

'Well, she is a girl,' Lord Bessborough grunts.

'I was a girl once,' Lady Bessborough says, drifting over to the fireplace to confront herself in the pier-glass. She sounds unconvinced.

'Try her with your mother a while. She responds well to your mother.' Lord Bessborough fidgets with his riding-crop, wearing his perpetual look of a man impatient to get away. 'That's my notion.'

'I see. And what about me?' Lady Bessborough addresses him in the glass.

'I didn't suppose we were talking of you, my dear,' he answers, already going.

Lady Bessborough, after long contemplation, looks at the clock on the mantel, and observes with mild despair that it is only two minutes past three.

Grandmama Spencer, happy to take Caroline in hand, finds her a governess and oversees an improving regime. She spends long weeks in the country, away from the temptation to show off: when her temper gets the better of her, only echoing silence greets her frenzied yelling. There is progress. The doctor says there is nothing wrong with her beyond excitability: she feels too much.

'How can I feel less?' she asks Grandmama Spencer – not teasing: a serious question.

'It's a matter of what you reveal. A matter of restraint. I saw you with the dogs this morning, Caro – actually licking their faces.'

'They were licking mine. It's their way of showing love, so I wanted to show them back. Besides, they'd just been bathed. I bathed them. And they wriggled so much they bathed me so it all comes in a circle.'

Grandmama Spencer smiles reluctantly. 'You know I would always have you think for yourself, my dear. The mind *must* have freedom. But the heart does not always profit from it.'

'I think I should have been a boy – a soldier. That's what I should have been.'

'A soldier? Why so?'

'Oh, I could go marching off, and not be a nuisance.'

She remains irrepressible. Words seize her fancy, intensely: she cannot understand how people take them for granted. 'Mercurial': that was one she delighted in, just at first sight, and when she discovers its meaning she runs about feeling mercurial, imagining wings at her heels, darting, changing. Lay an image in her mind, and she nourishes it to cuckoo size. When Grandmama Spencer shows her the family tree, Caroline cannot help picturing a great gnarled tree with all of them dangling from the branches. 'There never was such a tree!' she tells her Devonshire cousins. 'All the fruits are different. With this hair I must be what else but a chestnut, and then Grandmama Spencer is, I am afraid to say, a crab-apple, and then you . . .'

The cousins laugh explosively. She is their master of ceremonies and their court jester – sometimes also the maker of trouble and the bringer-down of vengeance: the price for entertainment. What with sleeping, and being poorly, and having a lover, Lady Bessborough has not much time to look after Caroline, and much of her bringing-up is spent at Devonshire House with her Aunt Georgiana's children. Little G, the eldest, has her mother's beguiling pleasantness: Caroline thinks of her like a draught of warm milk. Hary-o is a fierce, downright little dumpling of a girl – a refreshing drink of unsweetened lemonade. The youngest, Hart, son and heir, is troubled with deafness and shyness, and seems to look up to Caroline with an anguished attention – just, alas, plain water. There are others in the nursery, apparently of the family, though Caroline soon learns not to try placing them exactly on the family tree. That is one of the things we do not talk about.

Devonshire House stands huge and assertive in St James's – at the centre of the world, indeed – overlooking Green Park with Buckingham House across the way. Within, Caroline and her cousins torment the governess and tumble in wild, juvenile cataracts from one floor to the next. There are no regular mealtimes: a descent on the vast basement kitchen will usually produce something eatable. They sit on the stairs gobbling from silver plates. A benign neglect is easy to achieve in Devonshire House, which is so big that a thousand people can parade through the public rooms. Once Caroline spends the whole day wearing a frizzed powdered wig, filched from a bedroom, and no one notices.

Sometimes her uncle the Duke will droop into the schoolroom and bestow his papery kisses – not often: it is Aunt Georgiana who rules this fabulous roost. (Caroline is used to this – men dull and shadowy behind vivid womenfolk. She supposes it is a natural attribute of the species of manhood, just as moths are always brownish and dusty.) Georgiana has suffered lately. No longer the statuesque charmer painted by Gainsborough in a great cartwheel hat of her own design that sent the ladies of the *ton* rushing to their milliners for a copy, the Duchess of Devonshire bears the marks of marital griefs, the shock at the execution of her friend Marie Antoinette of France, and the bungling efforts of medical science to operate on an eye condition that has left her face lopsided and given her family the memory of the most horrifying screams anyone ever heard. Still, she is a great figure – a politician, if women could be politicians – and Devonshire House the resort of other great figures: rulers – or would-be rulers. For this is the pole-star of the Whig world, and the Whigs are out.

'What is a Tory, you say?' Caroline's father makes one of his rare jokes. 'Oh, it's what we all are nowadays.'

It is the Revolution in France that has holed the Whigs below the water-line. Some have continued to hail it: others have drawn away in alarm. Divided, they watch as young Mr Pitt wraps himself in the toga of loyalty to Church and King and looks set to rule more or less for ever. Peeping through the banisters before being chased to bed by a harassed nurse, Caroline and the other gilded urchins often witness the Whig leaders arriving for suppers, card-parties, receptions. Mr Fox one knows straight away – the bushy black eyebrows and swarthy jaw are just as in the print-shop caricatures, where he is always being wicked and unpatriotic. And Mr Sheridan, once the writer of plays, lifted from stage to statesman, with his drinker's ruined raspberry face: once, too, the lover of Caroline's mama, and still, it is whispered, panting for her. And now and then, Prinny himself – the Prince of Wales, with his sauntering, fleshy, dainty walk, acre of white waistcoat, sausage curls: the one great friend and hope of the Whigs, if only his father would die, or go mad again so that Prinny is made Regent.

The Whigs are out, but the sufferings of political exile are borne stoically enough. Boredom can always be relieved by gambling, that most artificial of excitements, like a galvanic charge applied to a lifeless limb. Both Georgiana and Caroline's mothers continue to lose thousands at faro and macao. Grandmama Spencer is grey-faced when she speaks of it.

'But, Grandmama, didn't you used to game? I've heard Papa say that when Grandpapa was alive you and he would be at cards and dice all night. And when you ran out of money you'd throw your rings on the table—'

A blasting, withering look silences Caroline.

'I conquered that vice,' Grandmama Spencer says at last, with her ramrod back to her, 'through prayer – effort – discipline. It's what we must all do. You too, Caroline. Your vices – the wildness and thoughtlessness – you must destroy them or they will destroy you.'

'Oh, I know,' Caroline says tremulously: for she does know: her versatile imagination is capable of anything, including black ends and catastrophes.

'I say this out of love for you.'

'Oh, I know that too.' And she does. Tears spring to her eyes: emotions always flare in her like this, like oil spattered on to flame. She longs acutely for an embrace. But Grandmama Spencer, riding-habited, snake-handling, prayerful, does not deal in embraces.

Nor do the whole family, in fact – except embraces of the

sexual kind. Caroline now knows about, if she does not understand, this strange force of passion that lurks beneath the surface
of adult life, impelling them in unforeseen directions, like the
schoolroom magnet under the table rolling the iron filings about.
It is the key to most mysteries. Yet still she does not make the
connection, at first, when mystery afflicts her own body. She is
staying with Grandmama Spencer at her country house near St
Albans when she wakes to find herself bleeding.

Caroline, looking down at the sheet, thinks quite calmly: Here
it is then: punishment. She does not doubt that she merits it, only
the manner of it is surprising. Will this lead to death, then, and
how soon? Only later, practising on the pianoforte, does she
break down, because she adores music, and when she bleeds to
death she will have to leave it behind.

Grandmama Spencer, severely practical, elicits the truth, briskly
tells her what it means and shows her how to deal with it. Caroline
gabbles with delighted relief. 'So Mama has it, and Aunt Georgiana,
and Nurse and Mrs Trimmer and everyone! And yet they never
seem to say! How odd – or perhaps I've just not noticed—'

'We do not talk about it, Caroline.'

'But if everyone has it—'

'It is not a fit subject for conversation.' She sighed. 'I thought
you would understand.'

Understanding. There are two sorts of understanding, it seems.
There is the understanding of music and mathematics and Italian,
and that proceeds smoothly enough, like a walk on a good gravel
path. And there is the other sort of understanding, which is
shifting sands and stormy currents, and has glimpses of beauty and
terror, and does not translate into words very easily. As, when
Caroline washes and washes her face, scrubbing at her cheeks
until they shine like red, painful apples. Grandmama Spencer
cannot understand that, and Caroline cannot explain.

The same shadowy sort of understanding hovers about her
mama's temporary retirement from the world, after a fall downstairs. Has she hurt herself very badly? No – but she must rest, she

must have seclusion for a couple of months at least. Caroline, staying with Grandmama Spencer, can hardly say when it is that she grasps what is going on, putting together bits of servants' gossip, the tone of her father's letters. But she knows at last that Mama is producing a little brother or sister, though not one she will meet: this is a token of Mama's enduring affair with the beautiful, cruel young man she first met at Naples. It is not spoken of. It is understood.

Even Caroline, with her uncontrollable tongue, does not speak of it. But this is a time of turning points for her. Solemn in a white gown she is confirmed at Westminster Abbey. At first, as she walks down the nave with her cousin Little G, her mind is busy with all its old monkey chatter. *Enter stage right one red-haired loon – the Westmonster of Westminster – come on, commune, come one come all, the bishop wears lawn sleeves and I wear forlorn sleeves, skinny limbs like spillikins, all goosefleshed and all flesh is grass, like* pâté de foie gras, *and grass makes a lawn, and so we get Greensleeves.* But when it comes to the laying-on of hands, the nonsense stops and she trembles under the eye of heaven. Caroline has no doubts about God. It is the material world she cannot quite believe in.

Another turning point: she has a fever and the doctors, as they often do, order her long hair cut off to apply blisters. Recovered, she views the cropped coppery cluster in the mirror with a curious feeling – like recognition. After a long voyage, the landfall of identity is in sight at last.

And at a Devonshire House dinner, she finds herself seated next to the eldest son of Lord Melbourne and hardly able to eat for looking at him – his thick-set shoulders, strong jaw, coal-dark brows and eyes. He is a grown man, of course, and beside him she is a child. But he, steadily munching, steadily listening, steadily blinking the dark-lantern eyes, does not treat her like one: not William Lamb.

3
Girlhoods: Mary

In the beginning there was her father. He knew all and saw all and he was never wrong. He was her creator, and she was his only creature.

Not strictly true: there was her sister Fanny. But though Fanny was the elder, she was meek and timid and viewed him with uncomprehending awe – like an idol. But for Mary the deity wore a human face, which made him all the more wonderful. Her reverence was suffused with love.

He was alone. That, too, was grandly fitting. It was part of his tremendousness. For Mary there was Fanny to sit beside at lessons and to whisper to when the nursery candle was put out: the maid had a young man down the street she laughed and joked with: even the poorest and shabbiest of the French *émigrés* who shuffled about their neighbourhood would gather at the Abbé's hospice to pray and sing together, sad hands patting thin shoulders. But Mary's father worked alone and slept alone, and when business took him away he got on the coach alone and came back alone – stepping carefully in his short-sighted, stooped way down on to the innyard cobbles and then courteously handing out a lady passenger before turning with a flash of spectacles to look for Mary, who breathlessly waited with her hand gripping her nurse's so hard that Nurse complained she had quite stopped the blood.

He had not always been alone. There was another, complementary principle in this cosmos, beautiful and tender as he was grave and austere. Its image hung in the study, above his desk:

Mary had gazed long at it and when she closed her eyes at night could summon it in perfect reproduction. The portrait of the woman in a white wrapover gown and black cap, soft auburn hair waving about her strong, glowing, gentle face: her mother.

Her mother was dead, and very early on her father had explained to Mary what that meant – the sad but natural end to which everyone came after their stay on earth. Their memories were kept alive by their friends, while their bodies were put away. Mary's mother had been put away in St Pancras churchyard, and Mary had often been there and seen the gravestone. As she could not remember ever being unable to read, she could not recall ever being shocked that the name on the gravestone was her own.

For she was named after that great personage – which made her feel, even more, the centre of a universe freighted with importance. Most dizzying of all, her mother had died in giving birth to her.

Her father had explained it, in his lucid and methodical way. But even before then Mary had perceived difference about herself. Other children had mothers who continued in life alongside them. But the woman in the portrait had had to relinquish life in the ordeal of getting Mary into the world. Heroically she had placed her child on this ledge of safety before being dragged down into the abyss. This was stirring, terrible: it made life ferociously meaningful. From a little girl, Mary could never understand it when people yawned, whistled, twitched in vacancy: they must be half dead.

Although he was alone, her father had many visitors. Mary soon realized that they came to the house in the Polygon rather as others – slaves of superstition and unreason, as her father named them – crowded into the church. The visitors came to shake his hand, to hear him talk, to submit questions to his judgement. 'I come, honoured sir,' said one shining-eyed young man, 'to sit at your feet.'

But he did not do so: they both sat on chairs in the study, and talked about monarchy and republics. What the young man had said, as her father patiently explained, was a figure of speech. It was the same when another of his visitors commiserated with him on being violently attacked last week.

'Who attacked you, Papa? Where – what did they do?' Mary cried, imagining stoically hidden injuries, cracked bones.

'The attack,' her father said, with his small, rationed smile, 'was not a physical one, my dear. It was someone writing in a newspaper, saying I am a bad man because of the things I believe. These calumnies,' he went on, turning back to his companion, 'are only to be expected. When they fear the ideas, they will hasten to malign the character of their originator.' And with a devout upward glance at the portrait: 'The late Mrs Godwin knew that all too well.'

Often the visitors stood in admiration before that picture. And once Mary heard her father say to one of them: 'A good likeness? Oh, yes, indeed. That is exactly how she appeared – before death stole her from me.' And she knew, again, that that was a figure of speech. But knowledge could not prevent the nightmares, in which death came like a looming giant to steal her father away too.

Sometimes the visitors would look at Mary also, in the same way as they looked at her father and her mother's portrait, and though it was strange at first she got used to it. She was special, exceptional, because of who she was. There was pride in this – and responsibility. She must try all the harder when, for example, she was sluggish over the spelling-book or sums. Her father did not indulge her, nor did she expect it. 'If I tell you it is right when it is wrong,' he said, 'then I tell a lie. I think you would not wish me to tell a lie, any more than I would wish you to tell a lie. We must be truthful. Do you see?' She saw.

Sometimes her father would ask the visitors for money. And somehow this was an aspect of his glory too, like the newspapers attacking him and calling him bad: he was a deity who knew poverty and enmity. Thinking of that, Mary sometimes wanted to weep – but did not. Once when she got into a passion he told

65

her, with his soft severity, that tears were idle and wasteful. So, unlike poor tremulous Fanny, Mary as a child very seldom cried. She supposed that tears must be saved up for a time when they would really be needed.

'Such a pretty mite!' said one of the Godwin aunts, lowly as he was lofty, with a shake of mobcapped head. 'I do hope she'll not grow up vain of it.'

'Looks are nature's dispensation,' he said, 'and as such we can have no reason to be proud of them or otherwise. That is what Mary will be taught.'

'If you say so,' huffed the aunt, who privately thought the house was like a tomb and the children sad little spectres.

People admired Mary's fine honey-gold hair, her delicate straight features. Fanny sighed over them. 'You're much prettier than me,' she observed, uncomplainingly. 'Or – than I, rather. That's right, isn't it?' she added, with a nervous glance over her shoulder, but their father was not nearby.

Young Mr Coleridge was one of the visitors Mary would look out for: there was a fascination about his looks, perhaps because they seemed the opposite of her father's in some defining way. Her father angular, dry, bony, pale, all hollows and sockets: Mr Coleridge made of circles, his round dark-curled head like her own drawings, a red ring of lips and full cheeks. Indeed he looked like a child – the essence of childhood as her father was of the adult. He even talked like one – not in his matter, which was often beyond her, but in the fact that he was hardly ever silent. It was curious that he had a child of his own, a son.

'You might marry him when you are grown, Mary,' Mr Coleridge said – not with condescension, just with speculative wonder at how things might turn out.

Mary thought. 'I'm going to stay with my papa,' she said.

Mr Coleridge seemed to understand that, like a lot of things. When he asked her if she said her prayers at night, he whispered it with a smile: for her father did not believe in prayers. Quite rightly: such things were for lesser beings like her.

'Always keep them up, my dear,' Mr Coleridge said, winking his round eyes, 'even if only in here,' and he tapped his chest.

So she would. But not without trouble. Belief: her first shameful secret kept from her father.

When the calamity came, Mary was four years old. Long after, she heard someone claim that the human mind keeps very few memories before the age of five. But she could remember everything before the fall: the leathery smell of books in her father's study, the old man who weeded the Polygon gardens wearing a horsehair wig that looked like a great mushroom, the worn-down milestone by the path to St Pancras churchyard where she would always sit for a moment because it was just her size, the map-like shape of the damp stain on the ceiling above her bed. The engine of memory was so powerful that sometimes it seemed it might even take her all the way back to birth itself, to that violent expulsion into light, the new terrible burden of life.

'You have a new neighbour, I see,' said one of the visitors. 'Have you met her?'

'I have met her,' Mary's father said, with something more than his usual precision, fussing over the simple syllables. 'I have, yes, met her. Her name is Mrs Clairmont.'

'A widow?'

'Hm? To be sure. Yes, a widow. Quite an agreeable woman,' her father said, as if he were thinking of something else.

But he wasn't.

'I used to believe,' her father said, wiping his brow, 'that the single state was best for a man with work to do. It was your dear mother who taught me otherwise. And now I have met Mrs Clairmont, who though she is not like your mother has many equally amiable qualities. And as we like each other, we have decided to be together, as man and wife. That is to marry, and live together, in the same house – this house.' He folded and refolded his handkerchief. 'It is a good – it is a reasonable arrangement in all ways: for though I am greatly fond of you, as you must know, and there is no alteration in that fondness, I am ever aware that our lives – your lives – would be considerably improved by the presence of a figure who, while not a mother, may fulfil something of a maternal role.' Having folded the handkerchief into a neat square, he shook it out and mopped his brow again. 'So, my dear, I think you understand?'

Mary stared at him.

'Come. It is plain enough. Is there something you wish to ask me about it?'

Mary stared: lanced him with her silence. With an irritable snap of the handkerchief, he turned to Fanny. 'Well, now – you understand, don't you, Fanny?'

'Oh! yes, Papa.' Docility was all Fanny had: at last it had come into its own. Her face shone as he patted her hand.

'Very well. And your powers of understanding, Mary, are quite as strong as Fanny's, that I know.' He sighed: his tone grew plaintive. 'I hope you will not be stubborn about this. If you have a care for me, you will not: for it is not an easy thing I am doing. It is hard, and painful.'

Then why, thought Mary, after she had continued to stare him right out of the room, then why do it?

Like the swift descent of a decapitating blade, like cannon-shot whining through the air to its target, like violent revolution the Clairmonts erupted into Mary's life, cutting off irrevocably all that had gone before.

'Of Swiss extraction,' her father urbanely told his friends, 'with French connections.' ('Mongrel,' said one, out of his hearing.)

Mrs Clairmont was forever out of doors. The houses of the Polygon had little first-floor balconies: let her father step out on to his, and out would pop Mrs Clairmont at number twenty-seven to hail him. If he took a turn in the garden, there she was likewise, hallooing over the fence. She called him 'Immortal Philosopher' and 'Great Being'. Mary had seen her tramping about the garden on the chance of seeing her distinguished neighbour, in the worst of weathers: rain, gales, it did not affect Mrs Clairmont. She had a strenuous thumping stride, like a postilion in high boots. Entering a room, she heedlessly sent delicate things flying. Her vast bottom usurped the view like the balloon Mary had seen ascend and soar over London from Vauxhall Gardens.

'I should think you are mighty quick at your lessons, aren't you? That's your father in you, of course. Lord, I hope you know what a prodigy your pa is!' Mrs Clairmont, having thrust her flat bespectacled face into Mary's, withdrew it with a titter. 'Not that you could know the half of it. Dear me, no.' And her father, hovering nearby, smirked.

She wore green spectacles in imitation of Robespierre. (Devoutly, Mary hoped that she would come to the same end.) Certainly the spectacles seemed to do nothing for her vision: always she put her face close to yours to address you. There was no escape and you could scarcely even breathe for the warm must that came up like an exhalation from her impending chasm of powdered cleavage.

Sometimes the same smell would be discernible on her father's clothes. Mary had never quite liked it when he unbent to one of his rare embraces, for this was godhead stooping: now she eluded them altogether.

'It is, isn't it, a pity,' Mrs Clairmont said, 'that she is not more forthcoming? This reserve.' That 'isn't it' was so like her: she was forever demanding assent. 'She'll learn otherwise from my two, perhaps. Now *there* is frankness and openness for you.'

Are, thought Mary: the right word is 'are'. But her father did not correct Mrs Clairmont. He just smirked on.

They all went together to the theatre: Mary with her father and Fanny, and Mrs Clairmont with those wonders of frankness and openness, her two children.

High holiday: the expense of a hackney to take them across the city, over the river to the drab streets of Southwark. Squeezed in, Mary had no choice but to face the monster's children, seated either side of their mother like little waterspouts flanking the main gargoyle.

Like her they had flat, piggy-nosed faces. Worse was their eyes, black staring blobs that made her think of pastry men in the windows of cookshops. The boy, Charles, was very much a boy and occupied with kicking his fat worsted-stockinged legs and reinvestigating unspeakable things in his pockets. But from the first the girl – Jane – fixed her attention on Mary. It was as if never in her life had she seen anything like Mary, nor ever would again: as if the whole world were one kind of thing and Mary utterly another: and only amazement prevented her trumpeting the difference to the stars.

They had a box at Astley's, the Equestrian Amphitheatre on Westminster Bridge Road, home of spectacular musical panto-mimes with real galloping horses, smelling of sawdust and candle-wax and orange-peel, favourite of family parties. The children, like a family, were ranged at the front of the box. The noisome Jane, beside Mary, began prodding and whispering before there was anything to see. 'Look': the musicians tuning up in the orchestra pit. 'Look': her own reflection in the gilded pier-glass. When the play began, Mary managed to forget her for a time. In spite of herself, she got wrapped up in the story. Then she noticed Jane was watching her more than the performance, and that when she gasped, Jane gasped, and when she laughed, Jane laughed. So, she decided to show nothing at all.

Mary kept it up. (It came easily to her.) Out of the corner of her eye she observed Jane's staring currant-eyed bafflement. Her victory came when the scenes in the circus-ring began, with the clowns and the horse-riders. Mary did not much care for this part, but Jane was transfixed. She forgot to watch Mary. She bobbed up and down with the equestrienne, she shrieked at the clowns' pratfalls, and when the hero's horse rolled in the sawdust, pretending to die from the villain's pretend gunshot, she sobbed and wailed. Behind her, Mrs Clairmont chuckled and told her to hush. Still Jane howled, at last turning her streaked square-mouthed face to Mary's as if in desperate appeal: did *she* not feel it?

'The horse isn't really dead,' Mary said. 'Look. He's got up. It's make-believe.'

Jane gazed and gasped and gulped: it was true: she scrubbed her cheeks and laughed and cheered, and took hold of Mary's hand and squeezed it tightly. And though Mary got her hand away as quickly as she could, it was not soon enough to banish doubts that her victory was really a species of defeat.

When they returned home the summer night was welling up like molten iron over the dark brim of the city. By hackney again, over the Thames with its spawn of mist and cat's-cradle of rigging, through the dusty labyrinth of streets; and all the way Jane talked, faster than the turn of the wheels. When she ran out of words she sang, or buzzed or gurgled. The black eyes looked no more capable than a gingerbread man's of closing, ever. Mary regarded her with a deep, dull distaste.

'Well, well,' her father said, at the Polygon before they parted, beaming round, 'I am delighted – delighted that we are all good friends.'

This seemed to Mary so plainly untrue that she wondered what her father, so scrupulously truthful, could mean by it. And then, looking up at him, she had a horrible momentary vision of his face as something quite different: instead of its usual sombre benevolence, it rearranged itself into a sly mask, a mask of a man perpetually striking a bargain. Then it was gone. She was so relieved that once indoors she flung herself, unprecedentedly, into his nerveless arms.

He was surprised – pleased also. He took it as acquiescence. It was not.

One cold morning her father brushed his best coat, redistributed his thin hair across his scalp, and set out to a distant church to be married to Mrs Clairmont: thus plainly, simply, rationally began his new life of conjugal felicity, uniting the two families under one roof in domestic congeniality.

Perhaps he believed it. Fanny, at least, gave him no reason to think otherwise. The noisy flood of Clairmonts quenched her utterly. Not Mary: she burned.

'Lord, I never saw such quaint arrangements in all my life! Only look at this trivet – did you ever see the like? And this meat-jack – just look. Oh, and the curtain about the washstand – you would hardly believe . . .' That was the Clairmont woman on first joining the household. She kept disappearing to fetch and display these things as she talked, though her voice didn't fade, she just raised it to compensate for distance. With a meaningless chuckle, perspiration frosting her lip, she flourished them to nobody in particular. It was stupid, Mary thought: for she and Fanny and her father could not be expected to share in her amusement at their domestic arrangements, and Charles and Jane were too little to know any better. So what was she doing it for? What was the point of it?

Often Mary itched to say these things. Weeks, months, years did not diminish the desire. 'Oh,' the woman said, when a neighbour complained of his chimney smoking, 'that is quite the same with us. Worse – we can hardly breathe sometimes.' This was not true, and it was not something said untruthfully to make someone feel better, as when she herself told struggling Fanny she found a lesson hard too: so why say it? One of her father's visitors wore mourning for, as he explained, a brother lost at sea. The Clairmont took over. 'Aye, there are sad things about, aren't there? Look at my poor friend Abby, over at Islington – her husband's cousin has gone into a shocking consumption – says she never saw a man decline so fast, not that he was ever entirely strong, but a great change. That is a shocking sad thing to think of, is it not?' And the bewildered visitor agreed with her instead of asking, as Mary wanted to, why on earth he should care about this distant stranger more than his own brother.

She thought and did not speak, but the monster her step-mother (so she must call her) seemed to feel the hostile glare of her mind.

'I declare there is something quite uncomfortable about the child sometimes,' she remarked, as if wishing to be heard by a deaf person on the other side of a stout door. 'Fanny is always amenable, but this one . . . Well, she may learn ease from my little ones, perhaps.'

One blessed day the whole Clairmont brood went out with her father, and Mary with a cold was allowed to stay at home. (Some demurral from the stepmother, a believer in bracing treatments, long walks in country air.) Mary crept into her father's study, and for some time sat listening. At last she spoke to the portrait above the desk, like a window on to a better world.

'I love you, Mama,' she said. 'You are so quiet.'

'Can you draw? Can you draw a tree? I can draw a tree – I can draw a big tree – the biggest that ever was. There. See?'

Mary looked dispassionately at Jane's tongue-poking labours. 'How can you tell it's a big tree? It could be any sort of tree.'

'Because I *say*.' There followed a familiar pattern of angry defiance, then dubious looks, then tears. Jane could cry hugely at a moment's notice. Her sleeves were never dry. Sometimes the pattern ended with something hurled or smashed and a stomping exit: sometimes, and more frequently as time passed, with appeal. 'Show me, then. How? Make it big.'

Mary drew, at the base of the tree, the tiniest human figures she could manage.

'Oh,' Jane said, in a post-crying gasp, wiping her nose with an absent arm. 'You can draw.'

Through the months and years this childish competition went on – Mary never imagined it could do so – like the Trojan War, unending, epic.

'Can you dance?'

There Mary yielded ground: that was of no interest to her.

Jane's satisfaction vaulted: oh, *she* could dance. Her mother, seeing that here her child had the advantage, arranged music lessons. Jane trilled and pirouetted, to her mother's raptures.

'I shall be on the stage,' Jane crowed, 'and you shall come and see me, Mary, and, *oh* how you will clap.'

'I do like to see these cheerful spirits in a girl,' her mother cooed. 'There is – isn't there? – something so warm and natural.'

And deliberately subtracting the smile from her face she met Mary's cool straight gaze. She couldn't keep it up, though: it was like when you stared at a cat or dog; the woman was always the first to look away.

Nor was this her stepmother's only defeat. The Clairmont jeopardized her own campaign with her violent temper. Her little angel could swiftly become a little devil, to be tugged and screamed at and finally slapped – hard, dainty, accurate strokes across the legs that had Jane squirming and howling. (Try that with me, Mary silently begged: do try that with me. But her stepmother kept within her limits.) Afterwards Jane would weep in a way that in any other child would have seemed inconsolable. Mary knew it would pass at the sound of a ballad-seller's bell or the sight of a crawling ladybird. But it was always Mary she sought out.

'Mama whipped me.'

'I know.'

'I hate her. She's a fat bitch.'

'Hush, you shouldn't say such things.'

'Other people do. I've heard them.' Sometimes a long crying fit would bring Jane to a peculiar bleak clarity, as if she had shed stupidity along with the salt. 'They wonder why your pa ever married her. I bet you think she's a fat bitch too.'

'Hush, you mustn't . . .' Mary felt strange: part guilty, part excited. It was rather like when they went to church – her stepmother's innovation, overruling her father's atheism for the sake of appearances – and she would consciously open her eyes during the prayers, and look around at everybody bent-headed and blind, and feel that something ought to happen to her but it didn't.

'One day,' Jane said hoarsely, 'I'll show her. When I'm big, she'll see. She'll wish she'd treated me better.'

'What do you mean?' In spite of everything, this was new and startling to Mary: the idea that parents would one day be less than they are now.

'I'll make *her* cry.'

'How?'

'Don't know.'

'You'll forget by then,' Mary said sceptically. Jane was always forgetting things: unlike Mary.

'I won't.' Jane suddenly stood on her head. 'Can you do this?'

When she was first told by her father that the woman was going to have a baby, Mary felt sick. Then, thinking of her own mother and how she had died, she allowed herself to entertain a terrible hope – just briefly: then guilt crashed in like migraine. She entreated forgiveness, and it seemed natural to do so, with anguished whisperings, before her mother's portrait.

Her stepmother came across her: gave a great sniff.

'I am rather afraid, my dear,' the woman said later to her father, 'that Mary is morbid in her temperament. And this forever going off to her mother's grave – I don't, of course, disapprove filial tenderness; but you would be the first to deplore unhealthy excess in any sentiment, that I do know. And then there is Jane who is so impressionable. To think of her being dragged along to gloomy graveyards . . .'

Ah, but there was the rub. No one dragged her. Jane wanted to do whatever Mary was doing, even though the tombstones gave her the horrors and she squealed about seeing a skeleton in the bushes. Mary began to realize a most odd rarefied pleasure: power over someone you despise.

Sometimes she would even mimic her stepmother and make Jane treacherously snigger. The way the woman would sail into the room when her father had a visitor and her father and the visitor were laughing at a joke, and the woman would laugh showily as she came in *even though she hadn't heard the joke.*

After the first revulsion, she soon got over her stepmother being pregnant. In a way the Clairmont – fat, volatile, sentimental, attention-demanding – was only being more intensely herself: in a way she had always been pregnant. When she produced, with typical ease, a plump Clairmontish boy, Mary's father was delighted: at last he had his William. Mary regarded the latest intruder with immovable disinterest. Another crier.

Mr Coleridge came – or a version of him. Mary stared. The round face had become a sallow pudding of flesh; the round eyes shallow, fishy.

'Mary. You are prettier than ever. And I hear cleverer than ever.' He shook her hand: his felt like dough. 'You must stop when you get to be cleverer than me, for no one is allowed to be that, you know.'

'You haven't been to see us for ages,' she said, reproachful: his absence seemed part of the downfall, an aspect of the Clairmonts.

'Not because I didn't want to. I went abroad for my health.'

'I'm afraid,' she said gravely, looking at him, 'that you didn't find it.'

'Mary!' Her stepmother, with hen-like flappings, bore down on her. 'Such things you say. Really, these children had better, hadn't they, be up in the nursery?'

It was never like that. Her father had always encouraged her to keep company with adults: she had spoken to Mr Coleridge as another adult might.

But her stepmother took possession of Mr Coleridge. Soon she was inviting him to dinner: they had only cold pork and pease but, 'What need ceremony, with such old friends!' she said, with a girlish laugh.

She was not old friends with Mr Coleridge at all. It was another of her rewritings of family history. Through dinner she asked him about his travels, cutting off his answers and telling him all about the places he had been to and she hadn't.

'You will read to us, later, I hope,' Mary's father said. 'Mrs Godwin has never heard you give the *Mariner*.'

'Oh, I would love that beyond anything!' cried her step-mother, not listening: the prospect might as well have been a jig on the table.

Mary knew that Mr Coleridge was a poet: knew he did something with words that was very different from what her father, great throbbing brain that he was, did at his desk in his slow methodical way: something sorcerous. It drew Mary as the confectioner's shop window drew Jane and Charles, who would breathe a sensual duet of greed against the misting glass. So she had a plan when the time came for banishment to the nursery. Before the adults moved from dining-table to parlour she crept down and hid under the sofa.

Alone was the plan – but, of course, Jane came too.

'What are you going to do? Let me – I'm coming.'

'There isn't room for us both.'

'Well, then I'll tell,' Jane said, with great reasonableness.

There was room, just. It was uncomfortable: when the adults' feet walked in, Jane nearly erupted in giggles. But when Mr Coleridge began to recite, in his rich, woody, faintly snuffly voice, Mary forgot everything. She forgot where she was – except insofar as she was, truly, where she belonged.

' "There was a ship." ' There was: Mary was on it. She saw the ringed horizon and heard the flap of the sails and felt the icy air of polar seas freezing her wide-open eyelashes. She felt the bloody feathery weight of the albatross round her neck. ' "Water, water, everywhere, Nor any drop to drink." ' She felt the terror of that: simple: stark: somehow pure, like beauty, like the love that filled her when she looked at her mother's picture, like the love that used to fill her when her father smiled on her. ' "Her skin was white as leprosy, The nightmare LIFE-IN-DEATH was she." ' And she felt the terror of that too – but in her mind. She understood that it was worse, worse than death. She even understood that Mr Coleridge, with his vague, benign, sick look, knew all about it, too much about it.

Then – it was dusty under there – Jane sneezed. The next moment the Clairmont was dragging them out, scolding, yelling. Like most foolish people, she dreaded being made to look a fool. Mr Coleridge was staring. She shook Jane like a doll, viciously, while her other hand gripped Mary's shoulder, holding her in place.

'Go on then,' Mary cried, 'beat me – you beat me, and see what Papa thinks of you *then*.'

She was almost disappointed when the woman did not.

Later, lying tearless in the nursery, staring at the ceiling damp-stains with their archipelagos and fretted islands, she listened to Jane's ceaseless boohooing and to the voices of her father and stepmother quarrelling downstairs. Soon came the expected slam of the door. 'I shall *not* come back! Don't think it – don't you think it!' Mary had no clock, but she reckoned an hour before she heard the woman's return. All the time she lay perfectly still, while Jane sniffled herself into a doze. Now it was her stepmother's turn to weep, loudly and talkatively, with dramatic roulades and melismas. Mary thought, drily: 'Water, water everywhere.'

But when she slept she had nightmares. She was drowning in bubbly blue water, rising only to sink again, and there was a hand extended that she did not want to take.

'Can you fly?' Jane whispered one morning in the nursery, when they were under strict instructions to be quiet over their books: Fanny was poorly. 'I can fly.'

Mary just gave her a look.

'Do you think I can't? I can, you know. Do you mean I'm a liar? Do you?' She began to pinch Mary's leg under the table. She kept pinching, unmercifully, harder and harder, wanting Mary to cry out under the governess's eye. Mary bit her lips and held her silence. At last, when the governess went out of the room, when her leg felt a mass of bruises, she turned and put her lips to Jane's ear and screamed into it: '*Liar!*'

There was no doubt of who was behind the move from the Polygon. Having married her father, the Clairmont now set about changing him. He was to be a man of business.

Skinner Street, Holborn: nearby amenities included Smithfield market, with the sounds and smells of the slaughterhouses making it impossible to open a window in summer, and Snow Hill like a slimy river of dung, and Newgate gaol where crowds gathered to watch men hang and die. For this they left the fresh air of Somers Town, the gracious French *émigrés* and the market-gardens, and the grave of Mary's mother in quiet St Pancras. It was a shock: not a surprise.

The house stood on the corner, tall, narrow, candle-shaped, with ground-floor bow-windows where the books would be displayed. This was to be the making of Mary's perpetually distressed father: writing, publishing and selling children's books from these premises, with her stepmother running the shop. Mary's stepbrother Charles was gone away to Charterhouse, and the infant William, always indulged, stamped about the house with his fat, cross, spoiled look. For the girls, there was a ready-made prospect – Mary knew it: downstairs the counter and the ledger-book and the bow-windows where she might watch the cattle driven steaming to their death or strain for a glimpse of the coaches bucketing away from the Saracen's Head for the north country. Meanwhile her stepmother's brazen voice rang up and down the house, which echoed it like a well.

Clairmontland. It was Mary's first indication that a person could change the world.

'Mary,' her father notified her, 'I wish you would show yourself less sullen, and more obliging to Mrs Godwin.'

He had called her into his library above the shop. Here, with

79

the portrait of her mother rehung, and the smell of books and the light shining from her father's domed forehead and his low musical voice, she found the past not quite obliterated. Her heart throbbed. 'Yes, Papa,' she said. 'Whatever you say.'

'Now, now: you know that isn't how I like things. I would not have you obedient to whatever I say. If I were to say something foolish or unreasonable, I hope you would not agree to it. But this request I think is a wholly reasonable one. It would make life here much more harmonious. It would be a proof of that eminent sense I know you to possess, to a much greater degree than most girls of your years. And it would please me.'

'Then I will try – truly I will try, Papa, and I'll do as you wish,' she said, ardently: her god was on his throne again and she longed to make sacrifices.

'Mrs Godwin has the greatest care for you, Mary, though you are not her own child. I would like to see you appreciate that.'

'I will, Papa. You'll be pleased with me, I promise.'

'You will do it only to please me? That is not what I ask.'

'But it still comes to the same . . .' She gave it up: how could she chop logic with William Godwin?

'If you were unhappy, my dear,' her father went on, taking up a knife and beginning to mend his pen, 'I should hope you would be able to talk to me about it.'

Mary stared at his hands, recalling a trip to a country tea-garden where her stepmother, thinking no one saw, had taken his hand and placed it deep in her muslined lap. The pen-nib was all crooked, and worse the more he scraped at it: gods were not made for such things.

'Papa,' she said suddenly, 'shall I show you my French grammar exercises?'

He frowned. 'Surely that is Fanny who—'

'But I've done them too. See.' She ran to fetch her workbook: stood quivering at his elbow, nearly touching him as he went over them. She had spent hours over them, outpacing Fanny, using a secreted candle-stub to carry on after dark.

Her father said, 'There are several incorrect tenses.' He held out the book, turning away. 'I have marked them.'

The schoolroom was at the top of the house. Eastward, St Paul's was moored in smutty sooty air. Northward, if you craned out, you could still make out the lost landmarks of her old home, the better world.

She had been sickly – headaches, eczema – and there was talk of her going away to school, in a better air, by the sea perhaps. Good. She wished it were now: wished that like fibbing Jane she could fly: step on to the windowsill and launch herself away from this overbrimming house, this well of noise and temper, this competing crowd caged in brick. She dreamed, watching a crow, well feasted from Smithfield gore, cross the sky like a piece of smoke quickened, dreams of an undivided love – hers alone, never shared, unencumbered, to come.

4

Girlhoods: Fanny

The crow flies north, towards those green heights beyond the smoke – our direction, now.

But instead of going as the crow flies, go this way: away from the booksellers' quarter with its narrow houses squeezed in like slender volumes packed on a shelf: through the shadow of Newgate, London's own Bastille, massive, crowned with iron spikes, and by St Bartholomew's Hospital, old Bart's – not much less alarming to the mind, place of bonesaws and leather straps – and by London Wall into the real City of merchants and counting-houses (place of high stools and brass rails and a whiff of nutmeg from East India fortunes) and into Moorfields and into the yard of one of London's great coaching inns, the Swan and Hoop. Not to linger: just mark the scale – a hundred feet of gabled, latticed, inviting frontage, broad arch, broader yard, steaming stables, clattering kitchens – and, before taking coach, the touch of confusion, the less than smooth running that suggests new management. That old ostler with the gaitered bow-legs and mulberry cheeks will confirm it. Yes: things have been a mite arsy-versy last year or so. Mr Keats had the running of the place, nice and smooth, and then he died sudden – thrown from his horse – shocking thing, and he not above thirty. Left a widow with children, and what's the first thing *she* must do but marry again when he's hardly cold in his grave. No knowing what she saw in number two – he couldn't manage the place, nor manage her, for she left him; and so he gave it up to a new man, and now they're only just getting straight again. Where Mrs Keats is now, he couldn't say: a great shame: a great fall. But now, look at *this* for a turn-out . . .

This is a coach, shuddering over cobbles and then roaring over flagstones, swinging and struggling via the City Road north (going our way), by Somers Town and St Pancras where Mary's mother and Mary's memories lie buried, and then climbing past Camden Town, where London falls away, where smoke from each chimney becomes a separate event. Depart now from the highway: rural roads conduct us to pleasant obscurity. Away from places where people are very rich or very poor, or very scandalous, or very intellectual.

But not to remoteness: this is Hampstead, which is to London like a pretty dower-house in the grounds of a frowning mansion. From the healthful heights of the Heath, you can see the city spread out like a great fungus in the Thames's damp hollow: while near at hand, spruce cottages and villas perch on the slopes, amid holly-trees and dog-roses. Now, down the hill, and strike the field-path to the hamlet of West End. Gorse, garden-plots, beehives: in the stubble, women in stays and short-sleeved shifts, gleaning, and one or two children playing around them. Not those, though: a little further, to the sturdy brick farmhouse in its miniature avenue of beeches. There – in front of the house, the little girl in the white gown and black sash, with sugar-brown hair, and eyes of a remarkable blue – laughing eyes – even as she turns and squints at you in the sun, holding a kitten, weightless and prickly, under her chin, and wondering.

Why the attention? Why, indeed? Frances Brawne, Fanny Brawne, careless, skips away in the sun, in the absolute luxury of inexpectation.

There is so little to say and so much to say. What can leave less impress upon the world than a happy childhood? Nothing graven in stone: only delicate jottings.

Discovery that if you lie awake and look at the night-light, you can, by half closing your eyes to differing degrees, make the darting rays seem to dance towards your eyes. Discovery: you can amuse yourself. Little Fanny Brawne is never bored.

First they are walking across the Heath, the three of them – Fanny, mother, father. She is in the middle, a hand given to each, and from time to time they lift her – delicious anticipation, *not* to be spoiled by a signal – and she floats along for a few steps. Later they are four, and it is Samuel, her little brother, who is in the middle and laughing at the sudden levitations. Discovery: there is an equivalent pleasure in watching him, in slipping out of her own skin and entering into his enjoyment.

Samuel suffers night terrors. Fanny, hearing him crying out in the adjoining bedroom, ballet-walks the creaking floorboards to his bedside and croons consolation.

'It will get light soon, Samuel. It always does.'

'Does it?' His curly hair, silhouetted, is wild with sweat.

'Well, I'm quite old, you know' – eight – she can look back with amusement at the pitiable innocence of six and the gaucheness of seven – 'and it's never stayed dark in all the time I can remember.'

'But the gumbler.' Samuel points to the linen-cupboard in the corner of the room. 'The gumbler keeps coming out.'

She can never fathom what the gumbler is or where he got the word. But she decides on a way to deal with it.

'Now then, gumbler.' She marches to the cupboard, opens it slightly, peering into the darker darkness. 'Gumbler? Listen to me. I won't have you scaring Samuel. It's very naughty. I'm older, you know, I can tell gumblers off, I'm quite big enough. So you stop it at once.'

She closes the cupboard firmly. Samuel breathes wondering satisfaction. Only when she gets back to her own bed does the thought occur to her: what if, when she had addressed the open cupboard, a gumbler hand had shot out and grabbed her?

And then the idea makes her laugh so hard she has to half choke herself with the corner of the counterpane. Discovery: laughter can defeat anything.

★ ★ ★

She loves the business of making. When the tailor comes about a new suit of clothes for her father, with rolls of material and pattern-books under his arm, she hovers about in an agony of fascination, longing to put pins in her mouth like that, to measure and assess and make the first bold cuts in the cloth.

'I should like to be a dressmaker when I'm grown,' she informs her mother.

'My dear Frances, if I were a superstitious woman I'd be rather alarmed – in case saying the thing should make it come true. Heaven forbid!'

'Why? Is it a bad thing to be a dressmaker?'

'It is a very good thing,' her mother says, after a careful moment, 'for those who are in trade in that way, and make an honest living by it. But you cannot do that and be genteel. It is a different thing.'

'Oh. Are we genteel?'

'Dear, dear,' her mother says, with her round, comfortable, slightly absent laugh, 'what a question.'

And obviously one that, from time to time, vexes Mr and Mrs Brawne, causing them to have one of their rare disagreements. ('Chiding' is the word they use – 'My dear, you need not chide me for that' – always with a sort of half-smile, as if it has some secret meaning for them, and prevents them ever quarrelling seriously. Fanny watches, fascinated.) Now, when the tailor sends in his bill, there is a little chiding over when it is to be paid.

'You would not have me dress as if I were taking corn to market, I think, my dear?'

'Now you take me up wrong, Mr Brawne: you know you do.'

'Then I beg your pardon. Only you did seem to have your *ricketty* face on just then.'

'Time was, you adored my *ricketty* face, Mr Brawne.'

'I adore all your faces, my dear: that don't change.' He lightly kisses the back of her neck. 'I adore it all.' Again, fascinating: they would come through the disagreement to something even Fanny could tell was warm, burning.

'Ricketty' is another of their private words, easy enough to interpret. Ricketts was her mother's maiden name. There are a Grandfather Ricketts at Walworth and an Uncle John Ricketts at Stoke Newington: rather stern and splendid and occasional figures, like doctors treating the family health. Behind them, one feels the presence of an august ancestry of Ricketts, who had been governors in the West Indies and garnered honours and riches. Marriage to a Brawne is a downward step. Only a small step – but the narrower these distinctions, the more they matter.

Yet Fanny cannot conceive of anyone more genteel-looking than her father. He has fine, youthful features and wears neatly barbered sidepieces that Fanny, sitting on his knee, likes to grasp and pull so that the skin stretches out like india-rubber. He winces, but smilingly. (Later that look of patient pain will become a fixture and by then she will not dream of the mock tuggings. Not yet.)

No, not yet: for ten years time, unstinting, offers every benefit, with no sign that the store can run out.

Gentility means you do not make anything – or if you do you are discreet about it. Thus Mrs Brawne declares herself strictly not at home on the day allotted to dipping rushes. Armouring herself with an apron she retreats to the kitchen where the great pan of hot fat and the pile of bulrushes stand ready on the deal table, maid at attention waiting to be supervised. There is a sort of ceremonious pride in Mrs Brawne's humiliation as she dips the first rush in the fat and lays it to cool: like a pontiff stooping to perform the Maundy foot-washing. In the parlour, in company, they burn only good expensive wax candles, but the malodorous rushlights must suffice for the kitchen and the bedrooms.

And if company calls when Mrs Brawne is doing the darning, she spirits it away and, with conjurer's dexterity, substitutes her embroidery-hoop. Fanny is amused by these swift droppings and raisings of the veil of gentility – though not with malice. Laughter only seasons her love. And still the business of making draws her. At the druggist's shop in Heath Street she leans her nose on the counter and watches the careful spooning of the four ha'porths – laudanum, paregoric, aniseed and peppermint – snuffing up the smell, liking and disliking it. The druggist is grimly jocular.

'A purge for you today, Miss Frances? A good strong dose of jalap and aloes?'

'No, thank you!' She knows what this is like. Illness: there are some people, invalids, who fuss over it and indulge it: Fanny hates it, intends to have nothing to do with it.

Making: the blind broom-tyer sits at the open door of his cottage on the Heath, face turned up to catch the sun while his hands, like someone else's, stroke and sort and straighten the gathered heather that will form the besom-head. Fanny could watch all day, but Samuel tugs: can't they go home? Those milky-filmed eyes scare him. He is forever preyed upon, from two sides, by fears and sympathies. Later, crossing the Heath, she sees a soldier in the distance take a tumble from his horse, and quickly she covers Samuel's eyes with her shawl. Why? Nurse wants to know (an obliging girl from the village who takes them on walks – but in the genteel version, their nurse).

'Well, if Samuel had seen him, he would have cried for him, and wanted him – and how on earth would we get a soldier home?'

Red coats are as familiar a sight to her as the water-lilies on the Hampstead ponds. Soldiers exercise on the Heath, descend like demigods on the assembly rooms or on carpet-dances in private houses where young ladies palpitate and mothers smile anxiously. Soldiers get spontaneous cheers at this time, when the bonfires stand ready on the heights to flare their warning if Bonaparte comes.

Bonaparte: the menace, the terror, the name on everyone's lips. Fanny has an old parasol as a plaything, and when the whalebone strut snaps in two, releasing a faint fishy odour, she thinks, *Bone-apart*: laughs: and from that moment is free of fear. Not so Samuel, whom the nurse unwisely disciplines by threatening him with the vengeance of that monster Boney: new nightmares.

Mr Brawne painstakingly reassures. 'People call Bonaparte a monster, but in truth he is just a man, Samuel, that's all – a mischief-making man. Part of his mischief is making war on us in England, or so he thinks. But to get here, he would have to cross the sea, where our great ships would shoot at him; and even if he got past them, our soldiers would be waiting for him when he landed – and *they* would soon deal with him. Lord, just let him try!'

Later Fanny overhears her mother remark to her father: 'Well, my dear, you said that quite as if you believed it.'

So does everyone. They sing patriotic songs: 'Britons Strike Home' is on top of every pianoforte. But when Fanny hears 'United and Hearty, Have at Bonapartee!' she has to run away and laugh herself almost sick. That's the glory of funny things: you can keep them in your mind, as if in a box, and take them out to cheer you in a dull moment. And the trouble with them too. Sometimes they occur to you when they shouldn't, when you're meant to be serious, when you're in Sunday clothes going to church or, worse, actually in church. One hot Sabbath, in the middle of a dusty sermon, the old-fashioned vicar takes off his old-fashioned wig and places it on the wig-stand beside the pulpit; and as Fanny looks at the carved bewigged blank the thought comes to her, as if someone else has put it there: *Yes, give him a turn, he can't do any worse*. And she is so afraid she is going to shriek out that she has to pinch her own flesh hard and make a pain.

If that doesn't work you must think of sad things. Oh, they are there: like the little baby brother she hardly saw, who died and was gone in the middle of a blustery night, but whom she can summon as a physical memory of tiny fingers ringing her own, and their softness that was also somehow roughness, and was warm and damp and startlingly intimate. And even worse, perhaps, the neighbour's little boy who drowned in one of the ponds. One day he was bowling a hoop along Haverstock Hill: the next found face down and waxen, his hair floating.

The exact spot becomes, immediately, naturally, a place of ghoulish pilgrimage. 'Just think,' says Nurse. 'Just here!'

Fanny looks, but the water is only water: neutral. Quite different, though, is the solitary hawthorn a little further along the path.

Nurse and Samuel go on while Fanny stands arrested.

This hawthorn is an old, old, ugly thing: swart and powerful: twisted into a mad, strenuous, suggestive shape like a hellish man trying to strangle himself. Fanny gasps. I am here all the time, the thorn-bush says, with a grimace of spikes: when you laugh, when the sun comes out and warms and brightens, I am still here. I am the dark god, the everlasting enemy – and I will make demands on you.

She knows. Suffering, pain, the bad side, she knows they are inescapably there. But her faith is that they are partial. There is something called credit, which her father and mother often talk about (with a little chiding sometimes). Credit means you owe something, and will have to give up something else if you don't pay for it in the end. And so with the bad side, Fanny believes. Evil is a creditor. It may send in a bill now and then, even take something from you. But it cannot rule.

So she believes. The ugly hawthorn, though, tests her faith. You don't know, it says, leering, what I am capable of.

Fanny runs. Runs back to her good small world, where every sight presents, like a calling-card, its benign meaning.

The baker bearing aloft his two great square baskets, and that smell and creak of wicker inseparable from bread so that when she sits on the wicker footstool in her mother's bedroom she thinks of crumbs and butter.

The postman in his red coat and blue lapels, his bell and canvas bag slung at his side as he raps his special rap and always, fascinatingly, looking away as he does so, into a far distance, as if being a postman were the merest unconsidered distraction on the edge of his real life.

In winter, skating on the ponds, and chairs on the ice – dining-chairs, that is the real fun for Fanny, the absurdity, like the way portly old gentlemen and dry curates always seem to be very good at it, sailing by with black-stockinged leg gravely extended.

The butcher, a dainty man, always in his white hand the whisk to shoo the flies away from the meat and which he plies delicately as a lady with a fan; and then he will purse and chirrup at the bullfinch he keeps in a cage that can whistle 'God Save the King'.

Outings: a trip to Sadler's Wells, gorgeous theatricals in the open air with lamplight on the lake and between the trees, the strong-man bending iron bars with a careless look and the tightrope-dancer, legs shockingly exposed in white tights (great rippling hams in truth and the tightrope bowing surely lower than it should) and the fiddlers and tootlers making Fanny bubble in her seat, and most piquant of all – confirming her belief in a world admirably contrived – a little shelf running along the backs of the benches on which you place your pasties and bottle of wine.

Outings: Wimbledon Common, and a grand review of troops before the Prince; barouches full of picnickers looking down on the massed redcoat ranks, and then a deafening crackle of running fire all along the line that makes the horses bolt and babies cry while the fat Prince, a swimming blob of pantomime uniform in the glass O of a borrowed telescope, manfully maintains the salute.

Interiors: the soft white-capped heads of ladies, Mama and friends bent over tea (glint of the precious caddy-key at her waist, best Hyson at sixteen shillings a pound now and a little chiding over it sometimes and whether company would really know if it were mixed with blackberry leaves) and meanwhile Fanny at the cheek-burning hearth serving Samuel a mock feast with the little sand-glasses from the writing-desk as goblets and slices from a sealing-wax joint.

A dare: stay awake till the gong-farmer's cart comes round and then when he is right outside emptying the cess throw open the window and breathe deep, deep into your lungs. (She does it, and is not sick, at least not till after Samuel is admiringly asleep.)

All this, and the good smells like orange wine in the still-room and on autumn nights the drift of chops and onions roasted at the old brick-kilns by the seasonal labourers come down to harvest the market-gardens, and the good feels like cambric and poplin and sarcenet and tabby and lutestring (for Fanny their names and their textures almost, wonderfully, one and the same) and the good sounds like the bray of the mail-coach horn and sometimes, in the woods at twilight, the song of a nightingale, clear and separate, as if mounted in a silver frame of silence.

The changes come all at once. Fanny likes the first one: the birth of little Margaret. Entrusted with the pewter feeding-bottle, smiling indulgently at the screeches, Fanny feels herself proudly stationed half-way up the stairs to adulthood. As she does, more disturbingly, when her father walks alone in the garden after a great quarrel (beyond chiding this time) and Fanny, watching his slow, high-shouldered circuit, goes out to him.

'Ah, my dear.' He puts his hand on her shoulder. 'We have had a difficult time of it, haven't we, since poor Grandfather Ricketts died?'

She doesn't know what to say to this. The passing of Grandfather Ricketts seemed merely of a piece with his general awful impressiveness, rather as if he had built a new coach-house. And while there has been crêpe, she has noticed no grieving.

'Fanny, if you hear people gossip about his money, and where it has gone, you must pay them no heed.'

'Why, where has it gone? Has someone stolen it?' She is excited – can't help it: she thrills to hear of burglaries, murders, footpads leaping from hedges.

'No, no.' He clucks his tongue, but Mr Brawne's fine-drawn

face wears the look as ever of a man who has exhausted his strength doing something strenuously noble. 'The money goes, quite rightly, to your mother. In a trust. And after her, to you and the other children. What people may talk about is that none of it goes to *me*.'

'Oh. Oh, but Mama will let you have some, you know. And if ever I get some, I will too – you can have it all—'

'My dear Fanny.' He is laughing hard and silently, his hand hard also on her shoulder. 'Never mind. I wish, in a way, you didn't have to learn about the world.'

Fanny listens respectfully, withholding agreement: she wants to learn.

'Listen. When you are a woman, and come to marry,' he says, ignoring her embarrassed squirm, 'make sure he is someone you need never apologize for. Make sure he is above all someone *suitable*.' He hisses it like a curse, and a roosting bird flurries off in alarm.

Another change is a move, to a rented villa in the hamlet of Kentish Town, off the Highgate road. She doesn't understand. People come here from the city to shoot, which her father never does: or, as invalids, for the air. You see them wheeled around in Bath-chairs or sitting out on garden-seats under rugs. There is a word much used here that foxes her too, at first. The word is consumption.

She thought she knew it. Sometimes her mother, sighing over the account-book, laments the servants' consumption of cheese and bacon: thus, it must mean eating. And so, in a dreadful way, it is in Kentish Town, where the silent pale people in the garden-seats narrow and dwindle as they stare across green meadow and deer-park. Only their eyes seem to stay the same – and so, at the end, are huge, unbearable, when the consumption has eaten the rest away.

'It is a malady of the lungs,' primly states the mistress of the little day-school she attends, 'and is often observed to run in families.'

Still Fanny does not quite realize that her own father is being consumed – even though she observes the sharpening cheek-bones and is woken by his houndlike coughs – until she is skipping along behind her mother and father and Samuel one day, and Samuel, with a hand in each of theirs, crows to be lifted, to float, and Fanny sees that her father no longer has the strength to raise his little boy an inch from the grass.

More crêpe: bombazine: velvet: jet. No relish in these for Fanny, and she hates black and will for ever.

'We are provided,' her mother is saying tearfully to the visiting curate, gingerly cradling her glass of port-wine as if she cannot think what to do with it, 'yes, to a degree, I thank you, sir, we are provided by the foresight of my late father – though it is only such a provision as may secure us from absolute want – and can hardly quiet the fears of a widow left with three children and quite unaccustomed to dealing with the world.' With despairing decision, she swallows the port-wine all down; flushes tremendously.

'Ah,' says the curate wisely. 'The world, ma'am, is a snare.' His eyes wander to the view of fields at the window: hare-coursing is his true love, the Church a marriage of convenience. 'A snare.'

Samuel continually weeps, confronting the simple outrage: 'Where is Papa?' But Fanny notices, cumulatively, other absences. The applelike shine on the end of the windsor arm-chair where he would sit, his thin hand rubbing meditatively, begins to fade to dullness. The books he was reading – always two at a time, as if mistrusting that one might mislead him – are put away, their marker spills used to light the candles. The sound of male footsteps on the path outside empties of meaning, becomes an inexpectancy. Mr Brawne, the light-boned, well-mannered, unremarkable five foot six of him, makes a great subtraction from the world.

The maid is occupied long in his bedchamber after, scrubbing. Dying he coughed a fountain. No one has told Fanny this but, childlike, her ears get to it. Likewise the debts.

'I'm sure I don't know what is to become of us,' repeats Mrs Brawne, pretty in cap and weepers. 'I'm sure I do not know.' She sounds more decisive than plaintive.

Fanny goes to school, and in quiet Brompton with its neat railings and neat poplars she negotiates French and German verbs with the same deftness as the intricate steps of the quadrille. Her teachers are impressed: already there is something sharply defined about little Miss Brawne when other girls are still unformed, shedding childhood in awkward clumps. There is no trouble with fees. Uncle John Ricketts (jingling watch-chain and fobs, creaking boots, kindly frown, Fanny's aquiline nose) observes his duty to his widowed sister. Does not presume to advise: but caution, my dear, prudence, discretion, reason, *cannot* be too early impressed upon the young.

On an outing by the coach to Hampstead – 'A place,' Mrs Brawne loyally proclaims, 'I shall always associate with felicity' – Fanny seeks out the pond where the boy drowned, and the hawthorn – the ugly twisted shape expressive of the world's wrong.

She stands before it, prodded by the spring wind. Very well, she addresses it. You have done what you can. Breaking, hurting, spoiling. Made me cry, to your satisfaction. But now what? You've drawn so much from the bank they surely won't let you spend any more. You're in debt to me now. I don't fear you. What else can you do?

She turns her back on it, and with untied bonnet-strings and hitched skirts trots away to her mother and brother and sister, a charming family group arranged against purple heath, and it is only the wind that she hears shiver through the deformed branches like a muttering laugh.

Part Two

Great is their love who love in sin and fear.

Byron, *Heaven and Earth*

True love in this differs from gold and clay,
That to divide is not to take away.

Shelley, *Epipsychidion*

Even bees, the little almsmen of spring-bowers,
Know there is richest juice in poison-flowers.

Keats, *Isabella; or, The Pot of Basil*

1

Testing the Waters

His Majesty King George III of Great Britain and Ireland seized Augusta's hand and grasped it as if it were some small but lively cage-bird.

'Well, now. Well, now. Miss Byron promises fair. Eh? You are to be congratulated, madam—' to her grandmother. 'I never saw a young woman turned out so elegant. Such a niceness in deportment. Such a – and so on. But then that's you, my dear Lady Holdernesse – what better example could she have had? What?' Retaining Augusta's hand, the King turned his protuberant eyes back to her with a faint surprised, quizzing look, as if he had forgotten who she was. 'What? But she hardly says a word. Quite the tittlemouse! Not that that won't stand you in good stead, Miss Byron, in this world of ours, for upon my soul men don't care for a talking woman. Not they! Men like to be talking themselves, ain't that so, my dear madam?'

'So it is,' answered the Queen, sending her husband a little sharp reminding gesture: he let go of Augusta's hand. 'But now tell me, my friend, are you truly recovered? I vow I turned quite faint when of the operation I heard. And I am not a fainting woman.'

'There was pain,' Grandmother said, with a shrug. 'I offered it to God. God sustained me.'

'I prayed,' the Queen said. 'And you, Miss Byron, I am sure you also your prayers offered.'

'Yes, Your Majesty,' lied Augusta.

97

The thing was, she had never really doubted that Grandmother would be all right. When first she heard that Grandmother had a cancer of the breast and that the surgeons were going to cut off the breast, Augusta went on a long walk, thinking. She thought of Grandmother's goodness and courage, and at the end she found she had come to a conclusion. All would be well: all *must* be well: and to pray would be, somehow, to deny the faith, to betray a doubt. When Grandmother survived, Augusta was joyful and thankful, but not surprised. (Augusta was kept away from Holdernesse House on the day of the operation. Grandmother spoke not a word of it after, and when one of the servants experimentally mentioned screams and sobs, Augusta firmly hushed her.)

But, of course, this could not be explained to the old gabbling gobbling King or dumpy Queen Charlotte, guttural and Germanic, whose little eyes seemed only to be counting the flowers in the carpet-pattern but missed nothing. They were as pious as dear Grandmother – Lady Holiness, as some nicknamed her – and, besides, Augusta's natural reserve was intensified in such company. Nothing if not correct, Augusta knew that you did not speak to Their Majesties unless spoken to, you started no conversational subjects, you followed their lead. Even in such exceptional circumstances as this – for here they were in the drawing room of Grandmother's house in Hertford Street, and the King and Queen were actually the *callers*. They had begun this habit since Grandmother's illness had made her housebound: such was the Queen's affection for her old friend.

Well, that was entirely natural, Augusta thought. Still, she was profoundly impressed, and a little alarmed, whenever the royal carriage drew up. Since leaving the Marquise's academy she had kept up a correspondence with several of her schoolfellows, and was always perplexed as to how to mention the royal intimacy without sounding boastful. Also her friends wanted to know things that were, if understandable, difficult to reconcile with respect – such as just how ugly *was* the Queen, and did the King ever talk in that way – you know – in that shocking way he did when he went mad?

Well, he certainly talked. Augusta's own habit of silence had met its opposite. The King's conversation was like a page in which even the margins had been filled with scribbles.

'And so you are finished and complete, now, Miss Byron, and have your French and your fine sewing and what-naught? Accomplishments, you know, a young lady cannot have too many of them – of course she *may*, and then make herself tedious and a bluestocking, but I see nothing of that in you, my dear. But you must be fond of music – I am sure you are – I am never wrong on these matters – the woman who knows music will never be at a loss for solace and diversion, and the man neither – heaven knows I have always loved it and it has loved *me* – by that I mean it has never failed me. Even at the worst. You know Handel, of course – he is incomparable – is he not? What? Is there anything to compare – *Judas Maccabeus* but then yes, *Saul*, to be sure even finer – we shall play some over, my dear, some time when your grandmama's nerves are equal to it. And your husband, you know – he will love to hear it. Ha! I have shocked you, because you have no husband – but I mean the one you *shall* have, and pretty soon.'

'Time enough for that,' said Queen Charlotte. 'She is not so grown, sir, as you suppose.'

'Never too early to think of it.' The King paced cumbrously, his great jaw working. 'Now there's young Major What's-his-name – fine fellow – I have his name, it won't come, no matter – just back from India. A little burnt, but I dare say you don't mind that, hey, Miss Byron, a little weathered in the complexion? Though how he bore the heat I don't know – I asked him – and he said – for I cannot bear, cannot endure for a moment too great a heat, it kills me – and India, now – was there ever anything so curious? I confess I cannot conceive what it is like – what? Can you, Miss Byron?'

And then Augusta surprised herself. 'Well,' she said, 'at school I knew a girl who had an uncle out in India, Your Majesty, and she was full of stories about it. Once she said he had shot a tiger from the back of an elephant – only then she thought it might have been the other way around; which did make me wonder whether the stories were more exciting than genuine.'

The old King, after a goggling pause, laughed, stamping and shouting. Even the Queen's pickle-mouth expressed a smile. Augusta blushed. She had never attempted to sparkle before. Her success embarrassed her.

'No, no,' the King said at last, 'not him – not Major Thing – I *know* his name,' he reproached himself with a fierce punch on his own thigh. 'Never mind, he won't do, he is too – we must set ourselves to thinking of someone – someone just right. Nay, don't colour up, Miss Byron, matrimony is the finest thing – marital felicity, *I* know it, the very finest thing – I am a great friend to marriage. You are the same, Lady Holdernesse, what?'

'Not every history is so happy,' said the Queen, metallically, exchanging a look with grim, gaunt Grandmother; and for a moment the air prickled with ghosts, Augusta's ruined mother, Mad Jack Byron grinning from the bankrupt grave.

'I have my other granddaughter to see settled just now,' Lady Holdernesse said. 'Then it will be time enough to think of Augusta.'

'Other granddaughter?' said the King.

'From my daughter's first marriage,' Lady Holdernesse said – with a wince: but then her face was swollen, with a toothache she claimed.

'Ah!' the King said, drawing it out so long he seemed about to sing. Then, 'It's my belief that *people*,' he said, with such emphasis he might have been referring to something outlandish and obscure – porcupines or snuff-grinders, 'should only marry *once*.'

'Once,' said the Queen to the carpet, 'is enough.'

Other granddaughter: again the complexities of Augusta's connections. But this set of people she was getting to know, since leaving school and returning to Grandmother's house, and to like, and to think of simply as her mama-kin. They were the grown children of her mother's first, respectable marriage to the Marquess of Carmarthen. They were very wealthy and well set-up – the eldest was Duke of Leeds no less – but they were kind to their solitary stepsister, invited her to their various houses, and were relieved that she showed no traits of Mad Jack Byron. While Augusta, taking in the grandeur, the marble, the plate, the sheer solidity of her mama-kin's world, could only wonder at that lost wild father of hers, for whom her mother had willingly thrown all this away. One could hardly conceive of a mere person making such a change: he must have been a hurricane, a heatwave, an explosion.

'But you are so shy!' they would say pleasantly, at dinners and routs, and they did not realize, when Augusta smiled and agreed that she was rather, that this showed she was not. If she were she would have choked, snuffled, or stomped away denying it. Augusta was something different. She just did not know what, yet.

Grandmother's toothache did not go away. Her still handsome face swelled and swelled. Her eyes grew slitted. She could hardly eat, though the Queen sent titbits from the royal farms, and called and pressed her to try them.

'Please don't protect me,' Augusta said one day to the doctor, ambushing him as he was leaving her grandmother's bedchamber. 'It is not the toothache, is it?'

He hesitated only a moment, shrugged. 'It is the cancer again. It has spread to the jaw, the tongue. She is eighty. There is nothing to be done.'

Augusta took that in. 'She is in a great deal of pain, I think.'

The doctor sniffed, as if he felt his professional competence impugned, or thought he ought to: then nodded. 'A lesser woman would sink under it.'

'I see. Thank you.'

Augusta did her weeping in her own room. She knew there

could be no reprieve this time. But when Grandmother died, a Bible under her translucent hand, Augusta had found her ground of consolation: no more of that pain. Hence a better though a sad thing. She was grieved that life should be so hard, but she did not see it as cruel.

After the funeral, looking about at her room, she did sigh for the impermanence of her footing in the world. 'Her' room so briefly, like all her rooms: Holdernesse House was to be sold, although Grandmother's will was to provide her with a modest inheritance. But where she was to go next did not seem such a great matter. Grandmother, in her last lucid time, had consulted all her connections: there would be somewhere for her.

She didn't want much, Augusta. But she did want something. She felt it like a headache either just gone or about to come as she wandered the house, disregarded, among lawyer's clerks and surveyors with ledgers.

And then a letter came for her, from Brighton. She did not recognize the hectic script, but as she read she heard the long-ago voice quite clearly, the chesty Scots voice she thought she had quite forgotten. The fat lady with the raisin eyes, her short-time stepmother, her papa-kin, Catherine Byron, wrote to condole with her on the death of Lady Holdernesse (mutual loathing sharply mentioned) and to assure Augusta of her friendship, and that of her half-brother, who in spite of their never having met was always speaking of Augusta, Mrs Byron wrote, in the most affectionate terms.

I knew it, thought Augusta, with vague, vast pleasure: I am in his circle as he is in mine. The young lord of Newstead Abbey, and me wandering here among the dust-sheets: who could be less connected? And so, who could be more? She had a taste for paradox.

Mrs Byron concluded, loftily, that her son was presently at Harrow School, and that she saw no reason now to keep him and Augusta apart.

Twiddling the cornelian ring Grandmother had left her,

Augusta thought: I do need someone to be close to. Then she looked at the thought in amazement. Often her own thoughts were like this — surprise packages for her.

I'm sorry, Grandmother. I know you hated her — hated my father too: probably you had good reason. But you could sit still through a two-hour sermon in a cold church, and I can't. And I'm not good at hating either. Too — I suppose — strenuous.

The only disappointment in the letter was that Mrs Byron spoke of Augusta and her brother meeting, but made no arrangement. Never mind: that would work out, somehow. Augusta had a taste for fate too.

'I shall be glad,' the Duke of Devonshire sighed, when the year 1800 was about to come in with a small fortune's worth of blazing candles and popping corks at Devonshire House, 'when the eighteenth century is over,' as if speaking of a dull visit to a district with no hunting; and patted his dog's head. And when in 1802 the peace was declared, after nine years of war between England and France, the Duke sighed, 'I dare say we can go over to Paris again now,' as if a good shop had reopened after a fire; and patted his dog's head.

The Peace of Amiens: the two punch-drunk prizefighters unable to carry on any longer: 'a genuine reconciliation between the two first nations of the world', according to 'Doctor' Addington, the new Prime Minister: the peace, quipped the wits, that passeth all understanding. Too much conceded to Bonaparte, securer now in power as First Consul than any king, and lording it over Europe: wouldn't last: bad times ahead. But for now, a feeling of relief and freedom. The tight little island had begun to seem like a prison. The fashionable world packed its trunks and headed for the Channel. Of course Boney and his upstart crew were devils, but who could resist a little tour of hell, just to see what it was like?

The Duke did not go, in the end, because of his gout. But everyone else did — 'everyone', in this case, being roughly the whole section of English society that in France would have been guillotined.

Caroline: she is here, with her parents, tottering ashore at watchtower-girded Calais, putting up at crowded Dessain's, sick, excited, seventeen.

In truth, no regrets that her uncle the Duke is not coming. He is very kind (in fact has lately rescued her parents from gambling-induced bankruptcy) but, alas, dull work as company. Also, and alas, he is so very like his son and heir, Hart, cousin and playmate of Caroline's childhood and now at Harrow where he daily grows in resemblance to his father (a doleful, milky sort of face, like a pup whose eyes have only just opened) and is, reliably, in love with Caroline.

Why, she can't think: for Caroline, outgoing, outspoken as she is, has no very high opinion of herself. Indeed she thinks in many ways she is a very bad person. But she knows she is simply no good for dogged, quiet Hart, nor he for her. (He is no sparkler at Harrow, as he cheerfully admits: compared to dazzlers like that young lame Byron, a mere ninnyhammer: but he tries.)

Caroline is better, though, than the frenetic girl who was examined by perplexed doctors. It is as if she has concluded her own inner peace treaty, withdrawn the troops and decommissioned the ships. Partly the diplomatic settlement at home has helped. Her father has got used to her mother's lover: at least there is just the one. And Caroline herself is in love. This new France of Bonaparte is certainly interesting, if silly: 'First Consul!' she cries. 'How very toga-ish!' But more interesting is the development in her heart. She sees the whole pageant through this shimmering glass. Her one wish, all the time, is to tell her love about it. So she does, inside. Propriety forbids correspondence, but no one can prevent Caroline composing her mental letter to him.

Now: my dear William. So I may call you, as this letter is inscribed nowhere, unless on the whirls of my brain – I believe the brain, from what I saw once in a medical engraving, is composed of whirls or whorls and it would seem to me very likely, I am sure my brain feels exactly like that sometimes. Of course you know before I left everyone was talking of this flirtation between us. That's all it is to them – a little supplementary gossip of the season. To me it is so much more. To you too, I think, I hope, I believe, after the way you spoke at Little G's ball. And when we walked on the terrace at Brocket. When you taught me about Theocritus and, you know, people can be very obtuse, can't they, even those one loves – for Hary-O said to me after What were you two talking of so hugger-mugger and I answered Theocritus and she said Oh to be sure and went into the most monstrous bray of laughter. When it was quite true. As if lovers can only talk of love. I love it when we talk of history and books and politics. I love your verses. I love your ambitions. I love, yes, your mind but you are also the handsomest man I ever saw, make no mistake about that. I have the greatest fancy for those mighty dark brows and eyes of yours.

Which I should not say. And I gather should not even think. These conventions. I think they are, as the new slang has it, a bore. By which I don't mean morals, though: I am a very moral person. Sometimes I behave badly, yet that doesn't alter it.

Of course it will be better, in terms of convention, when I am out. Next year, probably – I dare say Cousin Hary-O and I will be presented at Court at the same time. Mama already has me practising the curtsy. And *then* – if you still feel – but I won't say any more now – I won't tempt Fate.

And now shall I tell you about France? Well, I *think* it is France. So many voices one hears are English. Raised and strident, I fear, too often. Complaining about the prices, the service, this and that. One looks at them afresh. The men especially, the fashionable ones. They are so very sleek, some of them, in their tight coats and polished hessians, and they seem to need nothing else in the world but what they already have or can easily get, and you feel that if they made love to you they would

105

only be doing it to themselves, really, with you as the admiring audience to the performance.

Of course I should not think of such things. But I am not innocent. That is, I know. But only as I know Latin – that thing in books – which is different from being a Roman.

In truth I am rather afraid of the whole matter.

You by the way are not like those sleek men, my dear William. I see you not feline but canine even ursine. My Bear-Lamb. Oh but on the subject of Romans yes Bonaparte's whole style is very toga-ish, not that an actual toga would suit him his legs being altogether too short, for yes indeed I have seen him in the abbreviated flesh and I shall tell you all.

From Calais we proceeded in our own carriage by I must confess a very decent gravel road – Artois peaceful, peasants in the fields looking as if they hadn't altered since the days of Louis XIV, old flea-trap inns with the horrible *table d'hôte* and the earth-closets of Hades and everyone spitting happily on the floor, little villages, hardly any commerce, a feeling of stopped clocks – and so no, Bonaparte has not turned France into one great barrack. We did see some soldiers at Amiens, cavalrymen in great plumed shakoes – I couldn't decide whether they looked splendid or vulgar. Oh, and we saw churches that had been half demolished in the Revolution being repaired – that's Bonaparte – he has given the French back their religion. I think he is probably very clever.

Then through Picardy. Here, the John Bullish will be delighted to know, I did see women wearing wooden shoes just like in the prints. Then at last Paris – oh it is shabby and run-down you think – then spanking new boulevards and gingerbread mansions rear up to confound you – and so it continues. I cannot make up my mind. The newspapers are mere parrots for Bonaparte's policy – he has looted Italy's art treasures and heaped them in the Louvre like any robber with his cave of plunder – and in Paris yes soldiers soldiers, they even keep order in the opera-house – and yet—

Here all is very much *alive* – and if I were French I think I could forgive Boney much for that alone. It is how I felt when you first *dwelled* upon me with those eyes, William – it is how I think I could never bear *not* to feel. Oh, it is absurd in parts – the toga-ish aspects – the martial columns and statues, and the cult of republican virtue rubbing along with the prostitutes in the Palais Royal and the ordnance contractors smirking over their paunches. And a great fuss is made of the First Consul sharing the one plain bedchamber in the consular apartments with his wife, which I think is rather humbug.

And yet *she* – Madame Bonaparte – is quite an entrancing creature. We saw her at an evening party, with her daughter. Both beauties, and the mother not at all shamed by the comparison – only her teeth are bad and she keeps them covered. It gives her a secret look. And gazing at her I could not help wondering – what is it like? To be her, I mean – to know what she knows – to have burned such a trail through the dry old world.

I wonder.

Well, there have been parties galore, receptions, levées, dinners, suppers, dancing till four in the morning breaking up only for cards – I have never seen a candle put out, they burn through until daylight cancels them – it is as if the whole of Paris society has taken a vow not to sleep, at least while the English are here. One evening we dined at Les Trois Frères Provençaux – not an inn but a *restaurant* – now there for once is a very creditable invention of the Grand Nation – and there were some English travellers there a-mourning and a-moping. For where if you please said they was the old gracious France they knew – now it is all new money and tawdry vulgarity. And the fashions are positively *indecent*, they said. Huffing puffing.

It is true that the whole toga-ish business has made the ladies look very *undressed*. The gowns are meant to be classical – Greekesses or Romanesses off a frieze or a dug-up vase you know. So the stuffs are of the finest, slightest, thinnest – transparent indeed – with flesh-coloured stockings and sandals and bare arms and very – very – little underneath. Still, this is only the body that God gave us, is it not? Which cannot be wrong. Though I am learning not to say these things as people do not seem to think as I do.

You are different of course – my William.

But – you don't want to hear about ladies' frocks, of course not – what of Bonaparte himself? – the conqueror and saviour, the *cynosure* of Europe (I have always longed to use that word, look at it, it is so *unlikely*). I shall give you him then as I saw him.

There were Mama and Papa and I in a balcony overlooking the place du Carrousel – below picture Bonaparte riding a grey horse (the dead King's own, they say, the poor decapitated Capet's own nag) to take the salute of his guards. Uniforms, brilliant and showy – general and mistaken impression that one cannot have too *much* gold braid. Boney's own Egyptian Mamelukes attending him – imagine Indian jugglers turned fierce – and his generals following, each dazzling with about a hundred medals apiece – there cannot have been *so* many victories so I fancy such honours as the Grand Order of Getting Up In The Morning. But as for the man himself – dressed quite plain – the uniform of the Chasseur Guards, blue coat, cocked hat unlaced, no fripperies. And lo! He is not a swarthy dwarf with a crook nose as we have been led to believe. I was quite close enough to see that. Indeed I met eyes with the Corsican ogre for a moment. I think.

He is smallish: rather pale and fine-drawn than otherwise, in that like a poet more than a soldier: with a look of alertness and deep resolution. You may tell I found the fellow, unadorned, not unimpressive. As for what the French think of him – well, make of this what you will: I thought the crowd cheered him to the echo – while Mama said to me afterwards did I not observe how silently and sullenly they received him.

Of course whatever else he is, he is a shocking villain: but which of us is not? Well you I think my dearest William. There – you are to be my redeemer no less – I hope that does not alarm you. Only I do feel that if I had someone – like you – clever, handsome, splendid – to be *all in all* to – as in the Middle Ages religion used to be from birth to death – then I think I could be so much better.

Papa has brought several new bronzes: Mama some Angoulême china. So they are each happy in their own way. Which is how they live. Oh William it will not be like that for us – now if I were truly writing this I would hesitate whether to put a question mark there. It would seem lack of faith, and I have such faith in the might of love.

Now I have been meaning to speak about *your* mother – and what she thinks of me. That is not something I usually give a jot about – my trouble perhaps! But this is a different case. I fear she does not approve of me – though perhaps that is simply her manner – which is somewhat tart and sharp – forgive me. I dare say like the taste of capers or limes it is something one acquires a relish for. Lord knows I am no plain-roast-and-boiled myself – how one might describe the flavour of *me* I can't guess. Conceive me a dish of cherries chicken chives and chutney baked in a gypsy's fire and served on a fool's-gold platter with a garnish of minced manna – now this is an odd dish but could you call it a *dull* one?

But no more in this strain. I think your mother would not like it. And of course this is not a letter she could ever get her hands on – written on my brain – yet I fear if anyone could do it – get their fingers right into your brain I mean – it would be her. Forgive me.

My dear William, I take up my invisible pen for the last time, as we are on our way home, and soon I hope I shall see you in the flesh. For now I have much leisure to write you, as we are stuck fast at Calais waiting for a wind, or rather an absence of wind as a gale is ripping the sea up and the packet will not sail.

Well: you will recall my account of Bonaparte. Now will you believe that on our last night in Paris I had the most shocking dream about him. Yes I will confess it, there was Bonaparte parting the curtains and actually climbing into my bed – this though he is not at all the species of man I should so entertain – but such is the strangeness of our dream-life. And out of that strangeness I spoke quite plain and prim to him thus: 'No, no. You are a very bad man.' And he answered me (in English if you please), 'Yes I am, madam. But is it not better to do bad things than to do nothing?'

In the dream I had no answer.

What do you think, William?

You I know mean to do great things. I hope I shall be at your side. I hope—

Well here is an illustration. This at Calais is only the last in a series of wretched delays we have had since leaving Paris. First a wheel broke on the carriage. Papa sent Mama and me ahead by post while he had it mended – and we had to wait for hours at the most Stygian inn. One could really fancy it the resort of bandits like in *The Monk* – and indeed Mama was all a-tremble fearing we would be murdered any minute and the clothes stripped off our backs. Well at last along comes Papa – and we go on and then before Montreuil there is another wheel gone – and before the coast a third – was there ever such luck? And all the time Papa cursing and Mama lamenting – and yet here is the terrible thing. They were all the time quite *separate* in their distresses. No pretending even to cheer or support the other. And one knew – I knew – that what they found most intolerable about the delay was having to spend more time in each other's company. Not hatred: worse: boredom, distaste, weariness, indifference.

The bandits I did not fear for a moment. But this I fear.

We have just had news that the packet will sail with the morning tide. So hey-ho for England! There is a man at the *table d'hôte* who is something to do with the Foreign Office, and he says there will be war with France again soon. I regret but am not surprised. It does not feel settled here. It feels like storms.

So, William, I sign myself your Caroline. Hoping for the day when I may truly do so.

★ ★ ★

'Peripatetic,' said the young gentleman helpfully, when Augusta was hesitating how to describe her life.

'Oh, no,' she said, 'very happy.' She had misheard. *Very pathetic*, she thought he had said.

Peripatetic, he explained, meaning moving from place to place. Oh, yes, she agreed, that was how she lived at present.

Augusta revolved around her relations. Her mama-kin welcomed her to their various town and country houses, and she enjoyed long stays with her papa-kin in the imposing shape of the Earl of Carlisle at Castle Howard. She loved it there and was fond of the domineering old Earl whose caged-eagle expression softened whenever he saw her: the family resemblance, he said, plucked at his heart. Just where he stood on the family tree was not quite so easy to say. She believed he was her second cousin. Certainly he was official guardian to her half-brother – though in answer to Augusta's eager question, he said he had met the boy only once, and then smiled thinly – and seemed to be the venerable elder of their scattered tribe. Sometimes, so vast was the house and so many the guests, he would forget she was there. 'My dear Augusta, when did you get back?'

'I have not been away, sir.'

'You don't say so? Well, well, all the better. There is a young fellow I wanted to introduce to you. Been at sea. Some remarkable tales . . .' That might have been the one who said *peripatetic* – she wasn't sure. She might well indeed have been related to him: she wasn't sure of that either. He was quite agreeable and forgettable, like most of the young men she met.

They tended to think the same of her. Augusta was now tall, well fleshed, with dreaming eyes like shaded lamps, and an untroubled mouth. Her columnar white neck and sloping shoulders looked well in the new bare fashions. She danced elegantly and had not many opinions. She had a small income from the seven thousand pounds' legacy left her by her grandmother. She was not quite a poor relation: she was certainly no catch. Some might have noted the irony that Augusta Byron, who could find a temporary home at the grandest mansion in the kingdom, had no real home of her own.

She preferred to think, with her natural optimism, that she had many homes. Reading much, she found in novels characters forever agonizing over divided affections. This she rejected. Why couldn't one divide them? It might even be better: you stood more chance of retaining some of them, on the principle of eggs in baskets. But she kept quiet.

'Ah, my dear. A surprise – you still here.'

'Here' was the library of the Earl's London house, in Grosvenor Place, whither they had migrated after Christmas, and where he found Augusta a lone sentry behind the parapets of books.

'Yes, sir. It's tomorrow I leave – you recall you were good enough to order the carriage ready for me.'

'To be sure. Portman Square, wasn't it?'

'Yes, sir – that is, Portland Place. The Harcourts. They were very good friends of my grandmother's, and have been kind enough to treat me almost as one of the family.'

'I remember,' the Earl said vaguely. He had lately developed a tremor in his right hand, and he fought it with the other for an angry moment. 'What's that you have there? Poems of Pope, eh? You may know that I have versified a little in my time. Oh, nothing to come up to that great fellow. Though no less a judge than Dr Johnson saw fit to praise my tragedy.' Testily he waved her to silence, as if she had brought it up. 'That is past. I prefer now to be a diner at the banquet of the arts rather than a toiler in the kitchens.' His own metaphor cheered him: he mouthed silently as if committing it to memory. 'Well, I hope you will have a pleasant stay with the – with those people, my dear. You must come to us again soon. Do they entertain? Wait, of course they do. He is quite high at Court. I know them. Oh, you will do famously there, they are forever entertaining.'

'They do like to have young people about them. Indeed I have

hopes, sir, that I may meet my brother there at last, as he has been
there—'

'Who? Oh, him. He will be down from Harrow, I dare say. I
suppose I should step over there and get a report of him some
time. I don't mind that. It's his mother. She – well, have you any
recollection of her, my dear? You were kept away, I think. Lucky
for you.'

Augusta only nodded. Since receiving the letter from
Catherine Byron, she had heard things. Her stepmother was
eager to learn, apparently, what Grandmother had left her. This
was disappointing. But the figure of her half-brother was only
thrown into more luminous relief. He was untouched. He had
written her his own letter, full of schoolboyish gravity. Her
half-brother was to Augusta a most delightful idea.

'Well, I'm glad you enjoy Pope,' the Earl said, turning away
and attacking his rebellious hand again. 'There are no such
geniuses now.'

Long afterwards Augusta would think back to her first meeting
with him – with Byron – and investigate it for significance.

And, of course, with hindsight – but that was precisely it,
Augusta's mind objected mildly. How else could you see any
experience except mounted and glazed in the frame of hindsight?
When things were actually happening to you, they were just a
swirl and a flicker: every morning on waking you simply fell into
life as into a deep pool. And that was hard to recapture, without a
great deal of effort, and Augusta cordially disliked effort.

Still, what she got was something like this: the scene is the big
drawing room of her friends the Harcourts' house in Portland
Place. Time, Easter: and the cold splashy sunlight of that season
painting stripes on the morning-gowns of seated women and
starring the coat-buttons of men who are strutting and lounging
awkwardly or consequentially but always with bulk, so that the
room seems abnormally filled up, even for one of the sociable
Harcourts' receptions. Noisy too: talk of the renewal of the war,

the perfidy of Bonaparte, the Prince of Wales's debts, the fashion for black gauze: one young woman with a peculiar pointless repeated yelp of a laugh, like a stab to the ear. Scents of beeswax from the rosewood pianoforte – lustrously polished and reflecting the sausagelike breeches of a dull stout young man (face a blank) monopolizing Augusta – and pomade and attar of roses and the spicy ghost of General Harcourt's devilled breakfast.

Feelings: Augusta a little excited, knowing he is coming today – Byron (and that naked name is not hindsight, it is thus she thinks of her half-brother from the first meeting) – for they have written via the family lawyer, with whom he is staying for the Easter holidays, and it is all arranged. But as there always are, other feelings, the background hum of the emotions: irritation with the laughing girl, lingering puzzlement over a lost stocking, first faint grinding suggestion of her menses on their way.

Then he is there – in the doorway, looking about him.

Augusta stands up abruptly.

How does she know? Because for a moment there is the sheer shock you get when confronted with a mirror you don't expect to be there. Those eyes scanning the room are *her* eyes.

Of course, no one can really judge their own appearance; still, after a few seconds Augusta realizes that the physical correspondences between her and her brother are limited. White skin, more tendency to flesh than bone, the bowed shape of the lips, perhaps: chiefly, those large, clear blue eyes. Even then, what she recognizes with that terrific jolt of identity is less a look than a feeling – what it is like to be behind those eyes. To view the world with a profound bafflement – amused, interested, but still wondering why it is there.

Augusta realizes that she has always felt like someone entering a roomful of people in which all the seats are taken and no one gets up; and if she can just keep carrying it off, being unassuming and unobtrusive, no one will notice her standing about. She sees that in those eyes too, for all the swaggering set of the boy's shoulders and the careless pout.

She raises her hand. The eyes meet hers. A shy smile touches them. Then he begins to make his way towards her and she remembers – how could she forget? – that he is lame.

Very lame. Later she grew so used to it she stopped noticing it. But here, in the bright rippling pool of the now, it hits her like a slap. Her brother's limp gives him an up-and-down teetering gait. His eyes measure the crowded room between them like an obstacle course. Gowns trail and tea-tables glint.

'Oh!' says her boring monopolist, as Augusta leaves him. 'You know, I haven't finished talking.'

'Yes, I know,' she says politely back, and threads her way through to her brother, extending her hand.

The youth takes it, briefly. She is conscious of being nearly twenty, of having safely traversed ground he has yet to make up. He is fifteen, well grown, with a very little heaviness that reminds Augusta of his mother and that he seems on the brink, like a brisk wet dog, of shaking off altogether. He is in between many things: boyhood and manhood, shyness and confidence, obscurity and society, naturalness and artifice, innocence and knowledge, puppy-fat and leanness. At the axis of all these, he can touch them all and hence the confusion about him, the unfinished, shifting look: near at hand, too, is an exceptional physical beauty of which the dark curls and crisp cameolike profile offer a vivid first sketch.

'You're Miss Byron.' Even his voice is undecided, between gruffness and lisp.

'And you're Lord Byron.'

They exchange their first mutual smile at absurdity.

'Was there ever such a curious meeting?' he says quickly. 'And yet, you know, I feel I have known you for a long time. Which is curious also.' With a little lurch he gets over to a chair and stands, with obvious relief, clutching the back of it.

'That's precisely how I feel. You must call me Augusta, by the by.'

'Must I?' He gives her a tricksy half-smile. 'You seem very sure

115

that we are going to like each other. Augusta.'

'I am very sure. And I am hardly ever sure of *anything* in life, so you see this is quite exceptional.'

He laughs. 'I like nonsense – and you do too, don't you? I could tell from your letters.'

'I like it better than sense.'

Suddenly his smile fades to a stricken baleful look: he seems to make a mental hop backward to before they first spoke and, glaring away, says, 'I hate meeting people for the first time. Don't you?'

'I do indeed.'

'Yet you *seem* mighty calm.'

After a moment she says, honestly, 'I know. I can't account for it. It's just the way I am. Somehow my feelings don't show on the surface. Even my tears, you know, are very small – the merest droplets.'

Byron laughs, a youth's laugh, buoyant and a little coarse. 'You do have a talent for nonsense.'

In fact Augusta meant it quite seriously. But she smiles and agrees, glad to have restored him. 'There,' she says, 'that seat will be free in a moment, at last – see the couple getting up? They are engaged – and yet they will persist in making much of one another, just as if they were not. Was there ever anything more tiresome?'

With interest, Augusta sees that she has impressed him. Her tone: she has picked it up unconsciously from the circles she moves in. She remembers the years when he was the boy in Aberdeen, distant obscurity. She breathes deep: feels this meeting has done her good already.

'And so how do you get on at Harrow?'

Seated by her, he is more relaxed, and his eyes cease their suspicious flicking over her shoulder.

'Thank you – *now* I get on very well. Not that I am ready to fancy it heaven, but at least I no longer equate it with the other place.'

'Oh, was it so very disagreeable? Still, it must be a great wrench to go and live away from home so young.'

'Well, if it were only *that* . . .' He seems to measure her for a moment. 'The fact is, when you cram boys together by the hundred, the result isn't always pleasant, or edifying.'

'I suppose not,' she says vaguely: she can think only of the Marquise's little school with its tense boredom and lukewarm gossip.

'And then I had a high old quarrel with one of the masters, who threatened to expel me. As if I cared for *that*. Well, I shall have the beating of him at last.'

'How will you do that?' Augusta says wonderingly: challenge to authority seems to her a sheer physical impossibility.

'Why,' he says, with a beautiful transfiguring smile – she cannot decide whether it is like the taking off or putting on of a mask, 'I shall make him love me, of course. How else?'

'You are a singular creature!' she says, sitting back, gazing.

'Ah, but that's just what I'm not. That's why I called you Miss Byron – most deliberately, for the pleasure of saying it. I am not the only one, thank God!'

'It is a nice feeling, isn't it? Of course, there is your mother besides.'

'She is Mrs Byron by virtue of having married our father – but that's as far as it goes,' he says, his face mottling. 'No, I'm saying nothing she would not endorse herself, whole-heartedly. My mother's chief amusement is to abuse our father's character, and when she is most incensed against me to compare me with him, and complain that I am a true Byron, and say she cannot conceive a greater insult than that. Pretty in her, ain't it?'

'Dear, dear. And yet she married him, you know, and no one made her.'

'To be sure! – and though he seems to have been something of a scamp, I cannot learn any worse of him than his inability to live with my mother. And that seems to me only evidence of the soundest good sense. I know *I* cannot do it.'

117

'Well, I remember very little of Mrs Byron, and know little more. But that is not kind in her to make you unhappy – and over our father too. I confess I have always had a tenderness for his memory, and never liked to hear it defamed. But perhaps – if she has a hasty temper, she merely says these things—'

'When you mentioned going away from home just now,' he says, shaking his head, 'I only had a blank feeling. When I must, I lodge with my mother, at Bath or in town or wherever – it's all the same – I never have had a home.' He chuckles gloomily. 'How very pathetic!'

'Peripatetic,' she says automatically.

'What?'

'Oh – someone was asking about how I lived, and they said it was peripatetic, and I misheard it as "very pathetic", and said no, quite happy thank you . . .' He is already laughing: she joins in: for a while they are helpless. 'I hear quite well, you know. It's only that my mind doesn't listen, somehow . . .'

Sobering, he says, 'You have no home either.'

'I dare say.' And indeed it is for the first time she has dared to say it, even to herself. 'Oh, but what about Newstead? Can't you call that home?'

'Newstead is let. When I come of age, I shall live there. Part of the time, at any rate. I mean to go out into the world, not rusticate like some poor booby squire. And you,' he flushes, consciously seigneurial, not quite able to laugh at himself for it, 'you, I hope, will always find a home there if you want – that is, I hope you know that.'

'Thank you. You are very kind.'

'Kind, no – you are my nearest tie, you know – my truest and nearest tie.' He is hoarse and solemn: then it is wiped away, and the mischief is back. 'It's a curious way to meet a sister, but maybe the best after all, for we have missed seeing each other daily as brats, when I would have pulled your hair, and you would have tattled tales of me, and we would have laid the grounds for a good old solid conventional brotherly-sisterly dislike for the rest of our conventional lives.'

'Oh, for shame – surely it need not be like that.'

'I fear so – look to your Bible – the very first conventional family, Papa Adam and Mama Eve all under the one happy roof, or tent at least – and *that* ended in bloody murder.'

'Now I must play the elder sister, and reprove you. This is irreligious.'

Byron is delighted. 'Oh, you are devout? Then I am sorry for it – I mean if I offend. But as to the Bible, I don't speak out of puling ignorance. When I was a boy in Scotland I had it well dinned into me by my dear nurse, who was always preparing me for the fire to come by beating me blue – a little hell on account, you might say. Naughty I may be, but no one can catch me on the Bible for I know it back to front.'

'Hm. Well, you know they say the Devil can cite scripture for his own purposes.'

'He would not be much of a Devil if he could not,' says Byron gleefully.

He is cleverer than me, thinks Augusta randomly, without surprise, and: How alike our hands are. And then she wonders about the right foot that he keeps carefully tucked away under the sofa. 'You needn't fear, I shan't belabour you with religion,' she says. 'Mine is a comfort to me – but I was taught a different kind, I think.'

'What, no thumping reminders of your sins?'

'I know I'm not perfect. But I don't think about the fact all the time.'

'Ha – you should try living with my mother,' he says, with a gnawing smile. 'Then you could not fail to be eternally conscious of your *imperfection*.'

'Dear, dear,' she says again, helplessly. 'This is a thousand pities!'

'Oh, not half so many. Look – our hostess is coming over: we'd better compose ourselves.' He laughs at her. 'I only said compose yourself, sister — not look as if you've done something terribly bad.'

'Is that how I look?' she asks, interested.

'No. Not really. You look as if you have never done anything terribly bad.'

'Well, I don't think I have, in truth. Nor ever wanted to.'

He quizzes her with slitted eyes. 'Haven't you?'

'No. And don't tell me you want to, else I shall have to reprove you again.'

'Oh, but there's such attraction in the notion. If only to get your jab in first. I mean, the world will never hesitate to do something terribly bad to *you* — now, will it?'

'Tut, nonsense,' says Augusta, thinking: A youth's cynicism, forced and callow.

And yet she has a momentary image of Grandmother, her face swollen to the size of two faces with cancer; and she can almost believe he sees it too, and other things inside her, quickly, like a brief riffling of pages.

Then their hostess is upon them, and all the vivid detail fades as if a shutter has been closed. In the presence of a third person, her brother becomes just a pale shy boy stiffly presenting his compliments and biting his thumbnail in between. If anything in Augusta has changed, she is not aware of it. But the self is a deep well, the windlass is rusty, and Augusta disinclined to effort. She leans back comfortable as a cat, idly wondering what boys can get up to at school that is so unpleasant.

The pattern: Augusta continued to circulate round the home of her connections like a redirected letter, and when London residence and school holidays coincided she met up with young Lord Byron, very gladly and cordially.

'You are very obliging,' he said, challengingly, on one of these occasions, when their talk had been interrupted by some half-sister's cousin's stepbrother's fiancée, entreating her to join a drive out to Twickenham tomorrow.

'Well, she wants a chaperone,' Augusta said, with a shrug, 'so I'm quite happy to go.'

'You mean you don't *mind* going. That's a different thing.'

'Is it?'

'My dear sister,' he said, with one of his characteristic rushes of affection, seizing her hand, 'you are the very best creature that ever was – you are – and I would maintain it against an army.'

'Thank you, brother,' she said placidly. 'I do hope, however, that no army ever invades us with the aim of settling that point. I should feel dreadfully responsible.' They laughed. They were always laughing together: it made people look and frown.

Sometimes, though, her half-brother was in black and resentful mood. The caster of all these shadows, it seemed, was his mother.

'She can be very amiable,' he said, 'and is capable, besides, of being the most sensible woman in England. The mystery then, you'll agree, is why she should choose instead to be the most intolerable, and the most stupid, for such a great part of the time that it is torment to be with her. A sample, if you like, of my mother's elegant conversation, taken from this very morning. "What do you do there?" – in a voice like a costive crow. What I was doing there was prying at the paw of the neighbour's cat, which is always coming in – it had a thorn or such, I could tell from the way it held it, and so I found and managed to pull it out – but to say *this* to my mother is to invite apocalypse. "Cat – what's that to you – a better thing if you had a care for my megrim. But not you – see my reward for cherishing you when you were such a wretched little brat I'd have been commended for drowning you like an unwanted pup?" She is fit as an ox, by the by, and the megrim doesn't prevent her embarking on an energetic description of our father's faults, and how many I have inherited. And then later, in company, she tipples wine and bawls that I am the sweetest son that ever was and she would cut her throat for me. And when people laugh she laughs too and doesn't see that the joke is at her expense.'

121

Once, haunted by these domestic pictures, she went to their kinsman the Earl of Carlisle.

'He and Mrs Byron disagree, do they?' the old man said, hovering over his curio cabinets. 'I've heard something of it. Nor does it surprise me. Where that lady is concerned, I'm afraid I . . .' He half shrugged, half shivered, as if shaking something loathsome off his back. 'But there's nothing I can do, my dear. My duty is to oversee my ward's education, and so forth, but really I can't involve myself with the family. Besides, he will be grown soon enough, and then . . .' He pursed his lips. 'Well, then we shall see.'

'He is surely a young man of great promise,' Augusta said.

'Is he? Well, of course, my dear, you have a sister's partiality. Quite commendable. Now, did you ever see the Titian I bought for one guinea?'

She was coming to see that the young lord of Newstead, who had cut such a figure in the world of her imagination, was in the wider world no such matter. In the impeccable drawing rooms of her mama-kin, her crested cousinry, his name created no stir.

'Who? What is it? A barony? Oh. Wait, wasn't there some old scandal? They used to call his grandfather the Wicked Lord, or something.'

'His great-uncle,' Augusta said.

'Oh. Always a pity, I think, when titles don't descend direct. Never know who you're going to get. Oh, but no, I'm sure he'll do very well.'

That they were not at all distinguished was a revelation that to Augusta, with her intensely modest sense of self, caused no pain. She felt it only for her brother. There was not just the physical insecurity of that lame leg: he was, she saw, socially unsure of himself. And nothing betrayed this more than his blustery moods, when he was all lofty arrogance.

'Southwell!' He groaned. 'That's where she's taking a house. That's where she intends to bury me alive during the holidays.'

'Where is that?'

'Well you might ask, sister. It is the smallest and nothingest of all small nothingy provincial towns. Even the name sounds like something made up in a second-rate novel. Clorinda's grandfather retired to his native hamlet of Southwell, where at length he expired, lulled by the sweet sounds of rural tranquillity, and bored out of existence . . . Oh, it's in Nottinghamshire. Near enough to Newstead, at least: I can go over and stay with the steward sometimes. But think of being trapped in some dismal borough – old maids playing penny whist in fancy-work parlours – smirking curates reading Shakespeare aloud, badly, and no one knowing any better – apple-cheeked dunderheads telling you how many birds they bagged – was there ever such a hell devised? I know she is intent on revenging herself on me for Father's derelictions, but this is carrying it a little far.'

'My poor brother! I shall miss you.'

'I shall miss you, Gus – I shall miss everyone connected with light and life and having a trace of wit. But if I *can* get to town, I *shall*; and I promise to refrain from putting a bullet in my brain, on condition that you send me a great budget of a letter by every post, to Harrow and to this other pest-hole. Do you promise?'

'Of course,' she said. 'What else have I to do?'

After an awkward laugh, he said: 'Fight off the suitors.'

Augusta was intrigued to find herself blushing. 'Oh, no,' she said. 'Letters it shall be.'

Byron lunged at her hand. 'Thank God I've got you!'

She was pleased. 'Well,' she said, smiling, 'so there is one heavenly dispensation with which you are *not* inclined to quarrel.'

She did write – more often than he did – and he was often in her thoughts; but by the autumn the landscape of her life had changed so much that it was hard to keep in sight any of the old landmarks. The always-unexpected thing happened. Augusta fell in love.

Enter George Leigh.

You'll hear him first, as Augusta did, for he is noisy, a genial laugher, a jingler of change – and then his clothes are an orchestra in themselves. When he is in uniform, they are a military band: for George Leigh is Colonel of the 10th Light Dragoons, the Prince of Wales's Own – *the* regiment for fashion – and is rattlingly covered in braid and buttons, sashes and crossbelts and tassels and spurs. Out of uniform, there is the *più piano* creak and crackle of leather and starch, for George Leigh is also a dandy, like his friend and ex-officer of the 10th, Beau Brummell. (The famous Beau, in his rise to power as the despot of elegance, has left behind some decidedly middling family connections, including the obscure Brawnes of Hampstead.) As for Colonel George Leigh's family – well, inevitably, unsurprisingly, he is yet another of Augusta's cousins.

Not that they knew each other before. George's father, General Leigh, separated early from his wife and from the rest of the family, and has carefully kept his distance. It is quite by chance, at the Earl of Carlisle's townhouse, that Augusta and George are brought together. Though, of course, the very introduction is significant.

'My cousin!' George cries. 'Well, this is a delightful discovery.'

And Augusta's ever-lowered eyes slowly travel up the tall, tall, slender figure, the hessians and pantaloons, the coat like a mould into which the narrow waist and broad chest have been poured, the high cravat like a white chimney-pot, to the fair, smiling, full-lipped face with its magnificently chiselled Roman nose and light hair in the new Windswept style.

'Miss Byron.' He snaps into a bow, part military, part rapscallion. White teeth glint: the slightly bloodshot grey eyes crinkle. 'I am your humble servant.' He retains her hand impudently in his. 'Or shall I say slave?'

Well, really, what is Augusta to do?

Other girls, she knew, kept journals in which they poured out their hearts. Augusta had never been of that sort. She felt she would simply not know what to write. Even the great event of her life so far, the falling in love with Colonel George Leigh, gave her no impulse to record. It just whirled her onward. Sometimes in her dreamy way, watching autumn leaves swirl in the wind, Augusta had fancied the leaves were enjoying themselves. That was her, being whisked through Hyde Park in George Leigh's curricle behind a pair of matched greys.

'How high up we are! I never imagined.' The high-perch carriage felt no stouter or heavier than bamboo, and the wheels seemed hardly to touch the ground.

'You're not frightened, are you?' George said, with a grin.

'No,' she said truthfully.

'She's high, but she ain't tittupy,' said George; then, negligently gathering the reins in his left hand, he covered hers with his right. 'And I'll look after you, you know.'

'Oh, I know.' She liked the feel of his hand: she was fascinated by the way his face wrinkled when he smiled yet still looked fresh and young. He was just past thirty, and had lived. He brought exuberance and confidence. He brought a world. And to Augusta, who never felt there was quite enough about her to justify her existence, this was very welcome.

The world he brought was fashionable, horsy, raffish, male: Brightonish not Bathish. He was equerry to the Prince of Wales. At reviews and race-meetings he sat at the Prince's right hand. He judged, bought, sold, and trained horses for the Prince, told him of good bets, and backed his fancies with huge wagers of his own.

'Oh, there isn't much the Prince *wouldn't* trust me with, I think,' he told Augusta. 'But, then, I've known him since I was a little sprat. I think of His Highness as a firm friend and a deuced good fellow – can't help it.'

Augusta, through her grandmother, had always been inclined to take the side of the old King and Queen against the scapegrace Prince who was always breaking their hearts. From George Leigh she learnt another side.

'Why, the Prince does have a feeling heart, you may be sure of

125

that. The fact is, the King was so devilish cold and harsh upon him when he was a lad, that it poisoned things between 'em. As for the Prince being eager to take the throne, I dare say he is – but that's only because he fears for the country, if the old King should turn mad again. Oh, the Prince is the best of fellows, believe me. After all,' he said, winking solemnly at her, 'he thinks well of *me*. Now that must be to his credit – mustn't it?'

She tapped his great bony knee. 'You conceited creature.'

He laughed at that – his huge, deep-chested, satisfying laugh. She never had to burst herself with wit for George: he was easily amused.

When he first kissed her there were several surprises: the roughness of the male face, the way he seemed to become all at once tremulous and shy and subservient, the tumultuousness of her own response. For a moment she wanted to behave with tremendous indecency.

He brought a world, and for much of the time he stayed in it. He haunted Tattersall's and the clubs of St James's, went off to Newmarket or Brighton, joined house-parties and shoots. Catty acquaintances suggested there might be other ladies. Augusta knew, or trusted, better. George was simply meant for her. When he was troubled or unhappy, he sought her out. He revealed his weakness, and to do that was to give a kind of gift, Augusta thought.

'Yes – yes, I am little hipped, I fear. Fact is, I lost a deal of money on the stupidest wager and now the old 'un's taken me up sharp on it. Said I was a fool. And – made me feel like one.'

'I don't think you a fool,' she said. She could never judge anyone so harshly, for immediately she would think how it must feel: she entered into the feelings of others rather more easily than her own.

'Don't you?' He blinked in perplexity. They were at an evening party at the Earl of Carlisle's house, and the Earl himself was close by, engaged with friends in a learned dispute on the Pindaric ode. Blinking again, George said, 'I can't think of clever things to say, you know, like that. Never could.'

'No more can I,' she said, and under the deft cover of her skirts pressed his foot.

'You are a famous girl!' George said, with a gust of warmth.

'Oh dear.' She knew that 'famous' was one of his favourite slang words of approval – he spoke of famous punch or a famous gun – but just for a moment she took it literally, and shuddered. She would hate to be famous, she thought. Augusta wanted to fit into the world like a tile in a mosaic.

'I say – look here, I haven't said anything wrong, have I?' he said anxiously. Little-boy eyes: protectiveness stirred in her. 'Only – I do admire you so extremely. And I thought that you—'

'You thought quite rightly,' she said, pressing his foot again.

The Earl of Carlisle said: 'I have no jurisdiction over you, my dear. I speak only as your kinsman and friend. And as you lack a parent's care . . .'

'I am very grateful for your solicitude, sir.'

'Well, I'm afraid you won't be. As I'm bound to say that I don't consider this connection with Colonel Leigh a propitious one.'

Love loosened Augusta's normally obedient tongue. 'I don't see why, sir. Colonel Leigh is well placed with the Prince.'

'That's as may be. The fact is, he lives high. He games. Oh, yes, so did I when I was young. But living in that sort of style must be supported, do you see? And you have, what, a few hundred a year?'

'Yes. Which surely proves,' she said with a smile, 'that Colonel Leigh is not interested in me for my money.'

'But this is precisely it. His father will surely urge him to look for a fortune when he marries. My dear, it's not that you aren't eligible. You are well connected. And if either you or he had a fortune—' He broke off, frowning, to fight the tremor in his hand. 'This wretched palsy. Makes me look a dodderer – which I am *not* . . .'

'No one could suppose it, sir. And again I am grateful for your concern. But Colonel Leigh and I have a – a strong mutual attachment, which stands above all other considerations.'

The Earl stared at her, mirroring her own surprise. Under the fluid layers of her nature, love had uncovered this unsuspected bedrock: stubbornness.

'Well, I've spoken to the old 'un,' George said gloomily, on one of their drives. 'And he's just as stiff-necked as before.'

George's father, the General, was an upright old martinet with little puffs of white hair coming out of his ears, as if his dyspepsia were actually burning him up from inside. He had always been quite correct and polite to Augusta – and why not? She was not a person he ever intended being closely connected to.

'You explained to him, didn't you, that we would have enough to live on, without calling upon his purse?'

'Oh! to be sure – well enough,' George said vaguely. 'The fact is, there's your name as well – and your pa's reputation. He sees you as a poor bet altogether. Wants me to marry some golden dolly.' He pouted or, as Augusta saw it, set his jaw. 'Damn it, it's like him to balk, just because you're *my* choice. Always the same. Never trusted me with anything. Well, we'll see, old 'un, we'll see.'

'What shall we do?'

'Never fear, my sweet. He won't have the beating of me: I'll win him round at last. Needs time, that's all.' He flicked the whip, lovingly. 'Of course, some might say I should just go on without his consent – but I simply can't be that kind of cold fish, my darling. And I don't imagine you'd want me to be.'

'Oh, no,' said Augusta. Even with her new firmness, she could not entertain defiance. Other people still came first.

'So it may mean waiting, I'm afraid.'

'Then I'll wait,' she said.

Marriage: Caroline, too, swims against the tide.

'It isn't that we don't like him, Caro,' her mother says, at a family conference. She looks helplessly at Caroline's father. That 'we' is so unaccustomed, there has been so little pretence of 'we' for so long, that everyone feels its absurdity. 'It's just that we thought – it has always been thought that you might marry Hart. He is so very fond of you. Isn't he?' Again Lady Bessborough turns flounderingly to her husband, lacking even a ready name to call him.

Hart – Caroline's cousin, the Devonshire heir, the boy who used to tumble with her about the echoing corridors of Aunt Georgiana's house – is desolate at the thought of Caroline becoming engaged to William Lamb. Hart, now an awkward youth with spaniel eyes and a melancholy, undeniable nose (*proboscis*, thinks Caroline, and reproaches herself, she must not think it but when he bends his mild doomed gaze on her she cannot help it *proboscis proboscis*), hopes it will not happen. There are some grounds for his hope. There are objections.

William's family: no one could call them poor or insignificant, but certainly to the Devonshire House set their lack of pedigree is noticeable. William's father is Lord Melbourne – the very *first* Lord Melbourne, and an Irish peerage at that. Still, there is money, and Lady Melbourne has been a notable hostess, and has made Melbourne House in Whitehall one of the half-dozen places to be in society. So, not an insuperable objection.

Then there is William's position as a younger son: he is training for the bar, will have to make his own way; this is unpromising. But now fate lends a hand. William's elder brother dies of a galloping consumption. Now William stands heir to the Melbourne title and estates. The family expectations shift to him: a parliamentary seat is sought. He is a coming man.

There remains the objection that there is something about the Melbournes generally, something grasping and scrambling and pitiless. But this is hard to put into words; and against it stands Caroline's obvious and overwhelming love for him. A love match: well, well: stranger things have happened.

'He is certainly very handsome,' murmurs Caroline's mother, wistfully.

'It's you I love,' William says to Caroline, in his forceful way. They are at her family's villa in Roehampton, and have stolen a walk together in the sodden gardens. 'It's you I want. Not your family. That doesn't matter. Likewise with you, I hope.'

'Yes. Yes. And if only it could be that way.'

He gives a great sniff, which in its heartiness, its gusto, is typically William. When he shoots, his gun sounds louder than everyone else's. His very hair, Samson-like, seems to grow with extraordinary strength, straight up from the root, black and thick as wire.

'One of the things I first loved about you,' he says, 'was your courage. I saw you breaking in that colt that none of the grooms could manage—'

'I had no idea. Where were you?'

'Never mind. I was watching. I have long been watching you.'

'How perfect! But have you really lurked in bushes – and disguised yourself as trees—'

'You won't distract me from my point, Caroline. You seemed fearless. It was wonderful. It still is. So, don't be afraid of the world. Square up to it, knock it down. It's easy.'

She hears him respectfully. Indeed, everything does seem easy for William Lamb. Give him a book, and in half an hour he will have the gist of it. Looking up to him, Caroline quells the occasional thought that there is more to a book than the gist of it, more to a matter than the heart of it. She adores, and adoration must not be qualified.

'When I'm with you, it's easy,' she says. 'When I'm away from you, I doubt – I weaken. Sometimes I feel just like that—' pointing to a worm, wriggling stranded on the brick path.

William picks up the worm with the end of his cane and deposits it in the soil of the flower-bed. 'Easy,' he says.

Caroline stands still, her eyes filling with tears. 'I love you,' she says. 'Oh, dear God.'

'You're addressing me I hope, not the deity,' William says, nervous, glowing, reaching out for her – with a glance first at the house.

A woman should not make avowals of love before the man has formally addressed her parents. Just the kind of fuss Caroline hates: anyway, everyone must know about it. When William makes his proposal, in a beautiful letter, she feels martyred with the suspense of waiting for her parents' approval. Her mother comes back late from a family meeting at Devonshire House. Well, she says, the decision is Caroline's. Caroline half strangles her with embraces. The next day she and her mother meet William in their box at Drury Lane. He sees at once, and in his delight hugs and kisses Lady Bessborough, who looks wistful again.

At Devonshire House, alas, Hart sobs at the news. 'I always thought you would marry me. I know I'm young. But if you could just have waited – as soon as I was old enough—'

'My dear Hart,' Caroline says wretchedly, trying not to look at his running nose, 'you are very dear to me as you have always been. But between us, you know, there has never – I have never supposed—' Hart howls. In the end Aunt Georgiana sends for the doctor: he does have these turns. Caroline pities, and sympathizes. She remembers her own troubles. Gone now, thank heaven.

Hart will get over it. Caroline's sky is blue: there is only one cloud in it.

Cloud – shadow – some sort of shape. It says much for the effect Caroline's future mother-in-law has on her that her usually fertile imagination struggles to re-create her.

'The Gorgon'. Mentally she tries that out for a while, but it's inadequate. You might apply it to an old woman who is formidable but commonplace enough beneath the temper. Lady Melbourne is not like that. 'The Harpy'. That has a hint of desperate spinsterish resentment; and no, Lady Melbourne is not like that either. Nor Fury, nor Dragon, nor Hell-kite. They all have too much conventional mother-in-law hyperbole about them. You might even, conceivably, use them with a sort of fondness. Lady Melbourne cannot be approached with *fondness* any more than the night or the certainty of death.

When Lady Melbourne learnt who her son's bride was to be, she remarked that she hoped the girl would turn out better than her mother. She did not say it in Caroline's hearing – that was not her way – but she made sure it got back to her.

'Your William appears so absolutely in love,' a friend said to her, 'and she with him. Surely a good beginning, at least.'

Lady Melbourne only smiled a remote smile. She did not believe in happy marriages.

She had been a beauty: now, in her fifties, the beauty was still visible in the way of the spent moon that sometimes lingers in a winter morning's sky. She was buxom and had admirably pale skin that she habitually set off with white muslin and a jet choker. Her nose was William's, high-ridged and hawkish. Other family resemblances were more complex, as it was generally agreed that only the dead eldest had been her husband's child, and that various lovers had fathered the rest on Lady Melbourne's ample form. The blood of the Prince himself was supposedly mixed in there somewhere. But Lady Melbourne kept her secrets.

She did not go out much in society now, preferring to have it come to her at Melbourne House. As she was clever, influential, piquant, society came: and it congratulated her on her son's match. Which was, after all, a good one, fastening them to the Devonshire House set, highest of the high. Lady Melbourne acknowledged society's congratulations and smiled her tight-lipped smile, looking as if she knew a thousand discreditable things she did not care to divulge. Which she probably did. That was why society, some of it, was frightened of her, and had a name for her: the Spider.

Spider, malign spinner of webs, entangling and entrapping. Caroline, in her search for a name, chose to ignore that one.

Perhaps because she liked to be original: perhaps also it was too horrible. She loathed spiders. And against all the evidence, perhaps she wanted to believe there was a kind woman inside the conventional monster. In fact she was determined at least to try and like her mother-in-law. It seemed worth the attempt, as she and William were going to be living with her at Melbourne House.

So Caroline shut out thoughts of pale, bloated bodies and scuttling legs and flies dying in stickiness. She shut out her own insight, which saw in Lady Melbourne a woman past the age of sexual conquest who still wanted to conquer. As in vanquish, defeat, destroy.

Though there had been letters – more from her than him – Augusta had not seen Byron for a year. When they met at Grosvenor Place, it seemed more like ten. He was taller, thinner, more defined, the rosiness of the boy replaced by a pale, nocturnal complexion. So much might have been expected. But this piercing look that came into his eyes like a blown coal, only to turn ashy the next moment – and a moment after that, a look as if you had been sharing a great joke, with in the next instant a different fire like sulky gunpowder – all this in the seconds between two shuddering yawns, as if he had scaled a thin-aired mountain to get to this drawing room . . . Beside him Augusta felt that she must somehow be living too slowly, her heartbeats spaced and ponderous like a whale's.

'Hell is pictured wrong,' he told her. 'Flames and lakes and wailing and demons a-prodding you with sharp implements – this is horrible but also *interesting* – you would goggle as you roasted. For a true hell there must be horrible *nothingness* – and there you have Southwell, in a nutshell. A nutshell hell. Hades with ladies. The next artist who is commissioned to illustrate Dante, let him attend a Southwell carpet-dance, and there he may draw from life such terrors as will make his engravers faint away at copying 'em. I am miserable there.' But he laughed.

'And now you leave Harrow. Things happen so fast.'

'Harrow I could hardly bear to leave, if there were only Southwell and *she* to go to. Thank God for Cambridge.'

'Well, for your sake I thank God for it, as your mother makes you so unhappy. But I hear very shocking things about young gentlemen at the universities, and I hope I shall not hear them about *you*.'

'Oh, if you mean the ordinary shocking things, you won't: I've no taste for the ordinary. But here – when am I to congratulate you, and my future brother-in-law? You must have a notion, even if things are still sticky with the old General. You can trust your own brother with the secret. When's the day – and how many carriages – and will there be lobster-salad at the breakfast? Oh, Lord,' he said, reading her expression. 'You mean it's no further forrard?'

'Colonel Leigh's father is still not reconciled to the match,' Augusta said quietly.

'Reconciled to the match! There's language to freeze a pond. Reconciled to the – well, why doesn't Colonel Leigh strip him down, or let him go hang?'

'George is doing everything he can. But he does not want us to begin married life under such a cloud as disapproval from his father – and, if it comes to that, neither do I.'

Her brother's eyebrows went up satirically – but then he read her again: read the tender loyalty that asked not to be touched.

'Heyo,' he said, veering, 'love troubles – how the two words go together. Was there ever anything so pestilential? And yet of so very little account, once you boil it down.' Now he swaggered, and five years fell off his age. Amused, Augusta shaded her smile down to sympathetic agreement. 'For my part I don't know why we mortals let ourselves be tormented by it. You may surmise I've had a few pains in that regard myself of late. Believe me, Gus, they fade fast – like one of those little bruises you find on your arm, and wonder how you came by it.'

'Do they?' Memories of last night, when George had been so

sighing, so downcast. You don't have to wait, he'd said: it's not fair on you, after all: you could choose to be free and no one would blame you. Augusta had said no with all her mild might, baffled: she could not understand what was so grand about freedom. 'Well, I shall take your word for it. But these troubles – was Southwell their scene? And as you tell me the town is inhabited only by old maids and parsons, pray which of the two was it that raised the pleasing passion in your breast?'

Their old healing laughter. Augusta had missed it: love, especially thwarted love, was so clenched and intense.

'And shall you stay at Southwell before you go up to Cambridge?'

He shrugged. 'No help for it. If there were anywhere else . . . There was Newstead. But that's no go.'

'What happened? The last I heard you were staying there with your tenant – something Grey, was it? Quite a young man, and it all sounded very pleasant—'

'So it was,' Byron said sharply, 'was, was. Grimmest word in the language. Aye, I liked being there very much. We shot and quaffed and it was Bachelor-hall. He was a very good friend to me. And then my mother wanted him to be a very good friend to *her*.'

'Oh – oh, but you cannot mean—'

'My dearest Goose,' he said, flinging himself back in his seat, 'it is a thing I cannot talk of to anyone – even you – though if there were anyone . . . All I'll say is this: she will always take from me whatever she can. My friend Grey was fool enough not to see it. I don't propose competing with *her* for anybody's affection. Thankfully she won't try to steal *you* from me, as she thinks as badly of you as me,' he said brutally.

'Yes. I have had one or two rather unkind letters from her. About my engagement. It doesn't reflect well on the family, apparently.'

'It's because you're a Byron. If I could think she was simply mad it would be better. Then I might be able to feel pity as well

135

as shame.' Yes, he had changed: so dark and mordant. 'What I must accept is that my mother is no mother. What she should be to me, I only have in you, Gus.'

She touched his arm. He jumped as violently as if he had thought himself alone.

'I'm glad,' she said.

'Are you?' His mood slid skittishly. 'Even though I have as good as called you maternal – which is to paint you an old woman of forty? To double a woman's age and get away without a stinging slap – there's impunity defined . . . Poor Gus, what you do look, as well as elegant and splendid and as many nice things as you like, is weary. I'm willing to believe part of that is the bore of entertaining me but not all, no – it's this engagement, ain't it? Really, can't the two of you skip off to Gretna and be damned to everything else?'

'I'm not weary,' Augusta said. 'I'm patient. When you come to fall in love – I mean truly and properly – then above all, you'll find, you believe in that person. It's like – well, I know you are monstrously irreligious, but all I can say is it's like faith.'

'I see.' His smile was sweet, not quite mocking. 'And the other person has that same faith in you?'

'Oh, yes.'

'Ah – that's the part I can't see happening. Not with me. I think all these things are going to be different with me.'

'Do you? Oh dear.' To Augusta, the idea of diverging from the common fate was uncomfortable: something like going off the coach-road and plunging into the darkness of foggy fields.

'Faith. Patience.' Byron tugged at his springy black curls. 'They sound like the two spinstery daughters of a Baptist minister.'

'You may mock me all you like, my dear brother,' she said calmly.

'I know. And that's why I never would. I must go.' Getting up, Byron seemed to throw himself pettishly out of his seat as if annoyed with you, but Augusta understood it by now: he was disguising the limp. 'Write me, won't you, Goose? The longest letters imaginable.' With bent head and hidden eyes he seized her hand. 'You are the best person I know, or ever will.'

On the evening of 3 June 1805, in the drawing room of her family home in Cavendish Square, Lady Caroline Ponsonby was very nearly not married to William Lamb.

Three nights previously, she was standing in her bedroom, naked, looking at herself sideways in her dressing-table mirror. At twenty she was still slight and angular. Candlelight drew the line of her collarbone, traced a thin piping on her straight limbs. Folding her arms across her small breasts, Caroline tightened her stomach and buttocks, met her own mournful speculative eyes. There. Now she might be a young girl, or a boy.

'I wish I was,' she said experimentally into the silence. 'I wish I was anything but a woman.'

It was natural, her mother told her when they walked together in the square: these doubts and fears. Every woman had them.

'Did you, Mama?'

'Oh, come now.' Her mother fluttered: even now she shrank from such directness as from a physical assault. 'Women in general. Just before they marry, they have these thoughts. It is such a great change in life. But after all, you do love William, don't you?'

'I adore him.' Caroline groaned.

'Ah. Of course, your grandmama would say it's better to love than adore.'

'I know. I can't think like that.'

'Well.' Lady Bessborough put up her parasol. 'Think how fine you'll look in your wedding gown. I never saw anything as pretty as those long lace sleeves. And how handsome William will look beside you. Dear, dear. You lucky thing.'

Gazing into the mirror, Caroline wondered: Why do we alone, out of all the creatures, have to have clothes? Why must we undertake the laborious business of assembling various bits of cloth and ingeniously covering our bodies with them? Perhaps it might be better if we all went naked like the savages who, after all, don't *think* of themselves as naked, because all do the same and have never known any different . . . Suddenly she took her hands away from her breasts and began to caper in a wild dance. She laughed at herself, giddily. Then she stopped with a gasp. Out of nowhere, she had imagined William's face in the corner of the room, watching her. She slunk to cover herself.

Earth and air: that was what they said about the match between William Lamb and Caroline. As if they were opposites in everything as they were physically – he so solid, she so light. Not so. Caroline had got to know him well, his lights and shades, and there was much in common. (So, it was not William: among the doubts and agonies of those few days, she was firm on that: whatever was wrong, it was not William.) He had, for instance, a roaring temper like her own, though it took a lot to rouse it. She saw him lose it once with one of his brothers – loud, hard, assuming young men, like William filed sharp, with a taste for horseplay. Tiring of the taste one evening, William turned on his brother like a furious devil. Later, when Caroline's ears still rang disbelievingly, he spoke of it with restored placidity.

'A roasting? – yes, I suppose I did give him a roasting – well, no – only a moderate broiling really. He won't even remember it. Why? Are you surprised?'

'Yes. No. I don't know. I'm vastly *intrigued* – I never thought—'

'Oh, you must have,' he said, with his clever coaxing smile. 'Are we not passionately attached? And didn't your inward voice tell you, now there is the person who is like me – even to his worst side? I have seen you angry, Caro, and what I felt was recognition. That seizure of the spirit, in which you would scorch and burn and lay waste the whole world if only you had a Titan's power – and what a fortunate thing it is that you haven't.'

'Now I am surprised. Strange man! – you have felt it too!'

He laughed gently, very urbane. 'And I know how quickly it passes. Leaving one feeling rather foolish.'

'Yes,' she said: but in truth, no. When the old fury did come upon her – which, thank heaven, was infrequently now – she could never find such a short path back to rationality. She would wander in the wild wake of the storm for an age. But she said yes because she wanted to learn. William would teach her. William was like her but without the wickedness. Oh, she was indeed very lucky.

The day before the wedding there was a reception for the couple at Devonshire House. The presents stood in extravagant heaps, as if making up for something: sugar with the medicine. Caroline stared at her family all around her: her mother and father giving her their amiably puzzled look, as if they could not think how they got her but were quite pleased that they had: kind Aunt Georgiana, her beauty a stately ruin, and her husband the Duke actually absent-mindedly looking the other way, like one of his own dogs made to wave a paw: her Devonshire cousins, including Hart bravely (*proboscis no proboscis*) bearing it.

And here also were William's family. Sheer nonsense, this feeling that they should not be there, that they were intruders. Above all, this feeling that Mama and Papa and Aunt Georgiana and Hart and everyone were being replaced by them: Caroline being handed over. It was something to do, perhaps, with the way Lady Melbourne, Her Spidership, her almost mother-in-law, seemed to loom over the proceedings like some monumental idol, hewn, incarnate.

'I hope you like it, my dear,' Lady Melbourne said, when Caroline opened her gift – a circlet of diamonds and amethysts. 'If you don't, you must say so. We mustn't begin by being untruthful with one another.' She had a smooth, rich voice like cream pouring off a spoon.

'It's beautiful.'

'As befits the bride.' She said this with a sort of game sprightliness: the great lady thanking the gardener's boy for the tattered bunch of violets. *I know how to behave, my dear, though of course one doesn't mean any of it.*

139

'Thank you. I shall wear it tomorrow.'

'Ah, tomorrow! I dare say you can hardly wait.' *To get your hands on my son.*

'It is a beautiful gift,' Caroline said, 'and there is one more thing I would like.'

'Yes?'

'Your blessing.'

Just for a moment Lady Melbourne was silenced. Then, 'My dear, how could you ever suppose you did not have it? Curious child! I think I shall like you.'

A smart recovery. Still, Caroline thought, she had not given it.

She couldn't help it: she let herself down. Again she told herself it wasn't William, it was the things around him and to do with him – the fact that there was such a strong facial resemblance between him and Lady Melbourne, the way his family gathered so hulkingly in the Cavendish Square drawing room for the wedding, that feeling of being handed over, traded. Not William. He was the one who got her through the service, inclining his great warm shoulder against her, encouraging her with his compelling eyes. But afterwards, when it was time to leave with him, she broke down. Perhaps she should not have been married from her parents' house: it made everything horribly symbolic.

The carriage stood before the door. Onlookers lounging in the warm evening came to gape. Caroline turned to say goodbye to her mother and father, and began to howl. She wrapped herself round her astonished father, begging to stay.

'My dear Caro – your place is with William now.' Her father patted her gingerly, as if she might break.

'Well, then, let him stay here – with us – only I can't go away from you, from home, it isn't right—' She didn't know what she was saying or why. Something felt unfinished.

'It's only nerves,' her mother said. 'That's all. Now, Caro, please. People are looking.'

'I will not go – I will not.' She wept and screamed. Then

William stepped up calmly, took her in his arms, and carried her easily to the carriage.

'I'm sorry,' she said dully, when they had been driving for some minutes. She raised her eyes: she had been unable to look at him, since they left Cavendish Square. 'William—'

'Don't be, my love,' he said. 'It's quite natural. I understand entirely.'

He always did understand: nothing ever baffled his cleverness. Sometimes indeed he seemed bored by his own capacity for understanding, as if it made life too easy. However, he did not look bored now.

Later, at Brocket Hall, the Melbourne country place in Hertfordshire, he lit a second candle from the first, looked smiling down at her, tousled hair in his eyes. 'Caroline Lamb. How do you do?'

She pulled the bedsheet up to her chin. 'I do very well, sir. Considering.'

'Considering what?'

'Considering you have made an old married woman of me. How dreadful – I must take up penny whist and good works and wear a lace cap—'

'If you do I shall be unfaithful,' he said, laughing. 'But serious, how *do* you do?'

'Quite well – quite moderately well,' she said, inching the bedsheet further up. 'It's rather odd, isn't it?'

Again he rumbled with laughter. 'That's the first time I've heard it described in quite that way.'

'Is it? Well, yes, I suppose – of course, it wouldn't be new to you. You already know about it. But isn't it odd, again, that men can have these experiences, while we women must wait till the wedding night?'

'Not odd at all,' he said, stretching. 'Men are freer. Biology sees to that. And I *know* a good deal more than this, my love. Oh, your great eyes! You are a married woman now, Caro, you're allowed to learn these things.'

'I suppose I am. But it is rather shocking to think – well, surprising to think, you know – what is going on all the time behind curtains and doors.'

'You would indeed be surprised.'

'Would I? And – is it right? I mean – a little while ago, when you stopped and did that – that other thing. Is that right?'

'Did it feel right?'

'I don't know. Yes – oh, you provoking man! You answer like a politician.'

'Well, that's promising. My love, I truly think you are innocent, aren't you? However did you manage it?'

She sat up. 'What do you mean?'

'I mean,' he said yawning, 'in this wicked world of ours. I like it. It's another thing about you that's enchanting.'

'Then you are not disappointed in me?'

'Good God, no. Now where are you going?'

'Well – I am going to stool, sir, if you must know.'

'Nonsense, the passage is dark, you'll get lost. Here – use the convenient vessel. Only the best china at Brocket.'

She hesitated. 'I'm not sure I care for you to see—'

'Caro,' he said chuckling, 'you are delicious. Consider, my love, the time for modesty is past.' He winked at her.

'You are quite a fiend. Well, give me that. I shall go behind that screen at any rate.' Retiring, she tried to be quiet about it. 'Earth and air . . . I don't know. I think there is a good deal of fire in you, William Lamb.'

'And there is a good deal of water in you, by the sound of it.'

'Oh!' Coming out, she saw his grin as he lay on his front, one hand propping up his handsome head. She leapt on to the bed and slapped at his buttocks. 'Incorrigible creature!'

'Piss-pot.'

'I shall slap you again, sir!'

'Very well.' And something about the candlelight made his grin so very much more wolf than lamb that she had to bury her head in his shoulder so as not to see it.

Voices around Augusta.

–Oh, yes, Miss Byron: patience on a monument, they call her.

–That, or monumentally stupid.

–I do believe her engagement has lasted longer than either of her father's marriages.

–Are they waiting for the old General to die, do you suppose?

–It'll be a long wait. He's tough as a packman's saddle.

–She'll be married in white – it will match her hair.

–She bears up wonderfully, you know, under the strain.

–And so does Colonel Leigh. They say, from the way he carries on, you would hardly know he was engaged at all.

–Miss Byron, how do you do? You are so quiet – one would hardly know – how do you do?

He had given her a pearl ring, engraved with the words *To Augusta M. Byron, from George*. Sometimes she would take it off and reread the words. Then she would put the ring back on again. Always.

Yes, she was sad. Sad that the old General could not think well of her: sad that George's character was not such that he could assert himself against his father. But this, mind, was a different thing from wishing George other than he was, or wanting to change him. Augusta would never have presumed. After all, he loved her just as she was, and she surely had nothing special about her.

Now she had another sadness, one that made her cleave all the more loyally to George: she seemed to have lost her brother.

How the rift had come about was difficult to say, which made Augusta feel that it must be her own fault. Byron had gone up to Cambridge, and begun living in the usual fashion of a young lord off the leash. His letters hinted at bacchanals by the Cam: rumour amplified them. Even for a young lord he was living it high, and there were tales of novel extravagances – keeping a bear in his rooms, bringing his own fencing-master up to Cambridge. Augusta was first amused, then faintly troubled. The Byron title, she knew, did not bring much money with it. She also knew – with a different kind of knowledge, deep in her blood – that her brother would insist on keeping up with, in surpassing his contemporaries, no matter how much richer than him.

So when he wrote her with news of his debts, she was not surprised. What did take her aback was the way the letter went on. After swearing her to secrecy, Byron told her of his scheme to raise funds from a money-lender. All he needed was someone to co-sign the note with him and act as his security. She was the only person he could ask.

She was frightened. Direful tales were told of what happened when you got into the hands of money-lenders – that was always the phrase: Augusta's literal mind could not help picturing thumbscrews and molestations. Not knowing how to say no, she wrote back offering to lend him the money instead. She was relieved when he proudly refused: then alarmed as it became clear he thought she meant to go along with the first scheme after all. For the first time in her life Augusta, lover of bed and connoisseur of dreams, found herself unable to sleep at night. She was staying at Castle Howard with the Earl of Carlisle – her brother's guardian, and the one person to whom he had enjoined her above all not to mention the matter. The Earl noticed the smudges under her eyes: what was wrong?

Like sickness she poured it out. The Earl told her she was quite right to have nothing to do with it, and said he would arrange a meeting with her brother at the family lawyer's. That night Augusta slept at last.

And her brother felt she had betrayed him.

He did not say so. It was the injured silence that fell. No letters: her own, increasingly plaintive, went unanswered. She heard later that he had raised the loan at last with another guarantor. She was sorry for it. He would ruin himself, she thought: that was why she had refused. Yet as his silence continued, and she caught the hum of reproach in it, Augusta began to doubt her own motives. Perhaps she had been acting selfishly after all. And then to break a confidence . . .

After Cambridge, she heard, he was planning to go abroad. She had liked having a brother. It was all very sad – also bitter, a taste to which her palate was not accustomed. She did not despair; but sometimes when the despondent fit came over George, and he sat holding his coiffure and crooning the wrongs he had done her tying her to his wretched fate, she had to hush him sharply. Because if there was no hope here – then where?

Salvation came in an unexpected shape: the Prince of Wales.

Whose shape is certainly unexpected if you do not know him. The Prince, Prinny, who wants to be Regent and presently, finally, will be, is at this time a man in his disappointed forties, prisoned in burgeoning flesh, jaded from disastrous amours, loathed by his kingly father and by a large proportion of his future subjects. Caricaturists and satirists whimper, hardly knowing where to begin: the bloated tippling dandy, raising the fantasy minarets of Brighton Pavilion, designing operatic uniforms, longing for Dad to go mad. He has always been there, in the background that he now steps out of to change Augusta's life. As a girl Caroline watched him through the banisters at Devonshire House, favouring Whig gatherings with his famous inimitably elegant bow; and in his slimmer past he was one of the flies caught in Lady Melbourne's web. These worlds, Augusta's and Caroline's, have faintly touched before now: Caroline's Devonshire cousins have stayed at house-parties alongside Augusta, know her by sight, think of her as an odd, quiet, quizzical creature. Now the stuffed-cushion figure of the Prince, stepping in to help his old friend George Leigh, brings them together again – but still only briefly, tangentially. The true link being forged between their fates is soft and malleable, yet to be tempered: the beautiful wounding young man who while still at Cambridge is publishing his first poetry, and whose name will soon become more than a name, will be a battle-cry, an erotic moan, an explosion.

Names matter; but sometimes they must be ignored. When the Prince offers George Leigh and his fiancée a house, only the name can be objected to – Six Mile Bottom. (In the future, when that chain is forged, Caroline will be unable to think of that name without going into transports.) For now, the important thing is that an obstacle has been removed. If they go ahead and marry, they will have somewhere to live. A word from the Prince in the General's ear also smooths the way: the old curmudgeon, while not approving, stops making difficulties.

This is generous of the Prince, who has his generous side. For all the girth and guzzling and absurdity, he is an unhappy man who wants, like everyone, to be liked and to feel that he matters. In his case, he wants to command: he wants to be England's riposte to Napoleon, sword in hand at the head of his very well-dressed troops: to be a hero; and his father will not have it.

But he is a hero to Augusta when he makes the gift of the house, and enables her at last to marry the man she loves. Six Mile Bottom is a modest lodge outside Newmarket, with stables and paddocks to gladden a horseman's heart, and, of course, the very temple of the turf close by: even the cows in the meadows look ready to break into a canter. The house itself is about the size of one of Castle Howard's outbuildings. Augusta, no horsewoman, doesn't mind. At last, at the age of twenty-four, she has a home.

And here she anticipates a retired life of quiet contentment, raising children, sending out no ripples into the wider world. She does not expect to have any truck with genius, fame, passion: neither does Caroline Lamb, settling into a choppy married life of sharp quarrels and prompt reconciliations: neither does Mary Godwin, growing up in Grub Street among tension and debt: neither does Fanny Brawne, yawning her way through French verbs in the obscure suburbs of gentility.

But it is coming.

2

On the Heights

When Mary first went to live away from home, it was not her father but her stepmother – the Clairmont – who wondered if she would bear it.

'Poor mite! She looks so little. I really don't know that she should go.' The Clairmont did a lot of handkerchief-wringing and patting of her bosom. For show, of course: this was at the coach-office, where people looked on in admiration of her sensibility.

But Mary suspected the presence of a little fear too. She would be away from the Clairmont's influence and power: she would grow and change. She might, in short, become even more of a thorn in the puddingy flesh of her stepmother, who often sighed to Godwin about the rebellious and unnatural spirit that lurked in that girl.

Mary knew that she could be formidable. It was not that she was volatile, like her stepsister Jane with her tempests of quickly dried tears. Mary's emotional temperature, even through the hectic season of adolescence, was habitually cool. But she could go to white heat in seconds if goaded to it. Also she had a powerfully retentive memory not only for facts but feelings. She did not brood on slights, but she never forgot them.

'I look, Mary, for improvement,' her father said to her in farewell. 'You know why this is. Not in any spirit of carping criticism: you promise well, you are quick and keen, you have many parts. And as the daughter of so estimable a mother, and as a rational creature, you must surely wish to do justice to these qualities, and not see them impaired and stifled by defects of temper.' He shook her hand. Her heart howled, while she boarded the coach in silence. (You've got thin lips, blossoming Jane had said in scorn lately: tight lips, really, Mary thought, that was where the thinness came from. Tight.)

The first time away was not a success: an undistinguished school – it was the cheapest – in fashionable Ramsgate. From the grimed windows Mary watched elegant young ladies parading arm-in-arm on their way to and from expensive seminaries. Behind her the unwanted daughters of country attorneys kicked each other under the table and struggled with lessons she had mastered in infancy. There was nothing on either side of the smeared glass that she wanted. She made no friends. The skin condition that the seaside air was meant to ameliorate still burned and itched.

'Dear God, you'd think, wouldn't you, that such fine air as Ramsgate would set anyone up?' her stepmother lamented, when Mary after six months was brought back to Skinner Street. The Clairmont viewed ill-health as a sort of tiresomeness. Her Charles and Jane, she went on unwisely, were always well.

'It's like you're always saying,' Mary snapped. 'Where there's no sense there's no feeling.'

In his study, among the blessedly unproblematic books, her father sighed and polished his spectacles. He needed new ones, but his finances were as precarious as ever: the shop seemed to swallow money instead of making it. In his naked eyes Mary glimpsed again that foxy bargaining look: also since coming home she had noticed something conscious and pompous about the way he carried himself, as if balancing the precious weight of his reputation on his head. Yet this did not alter her feelings about him, not at the root: even when hating him she would have died to please him.

'I am sad, chiefly, that you are still prey to these foibles. It is a grievous misdirection of energy. Your mother used to remark that the skill and ingenuity applied by the housebreaker would be of great benefit to society if properly channelled.'

'I have broken into no houses, Papa.'

'Yet you show the same destructive spirit. Nay, worse, for want, ill-education and the inequality of laws usually drive the criminal. You suffer from none of these.'

'Unhappiness,' Mary blurted. 'That's what makes people bad. Isn't it? So you have always taught me.'

He inclined his head cautiously. 'The human creature is naturally virtuous. Social and environmental influences may impair his happiness and turn him towards vice. This I think I have conclusively proved in my work. However—'

'Well, I have proved it in my life, then,' she said impetuously. 'If my conduct is not good, then there must be causes—'

'Ah.' He held up a finger: in his rarefied way he was enjoying this. 'But are the causes rational? They are not. The causes, Mary, consist in your continued resentment and antagonism towards your stepmother. And as she is good, kind, and concerned for your welfare, this is not rational in you.'

Q.E.D. His smile suffocated her. She made a bow – not an apology – and fled. He could always out-argue her. It was because he never let his passions interfere with his reasoning. Deep inside she felt that reasoning which ignored passion was no reasoning at all, but she could find no way to say so.

'She is such a cold little creature!' the Clairmont sniffed later, in Mary's hearing. And Mary thought: How stupid she is. It was the coldest winter she could remember, with a fair on the frozen Thames, and at Skinner Street with its meagre fires there were ferns of ice on every window-pane. Even the stupidest person, Mary thought, knew what happened when you touched the ice. Ice burned.

'Papa has had another letter from that young man,' Jane said. 'He showed me. His is the most wonderful story—'

'You shouldn't call him Papa,' Mary said.

'Why not?'

'Because he isn't your real father.'

'Pom-ti-pom. He's just as fond of me as he is of you, so it makes no difference.'

Mary glared at her. There was a thaw, so she and Jane and Fanny had been allowed to take a morning walk over to Holborn Hill, but the ground was still treacherous with slush. While Mary went carefully, Jane strode out, curly head up, looking as if she could never fall.

'Why do you say these things?' Mary said.

Jane snorted. 'They're only words.'

'There's no such thing as *only* words . . . Wait, those are my gloves you're wearing.'

'No, they're not.'

Mary appealed to Fanny: always the arbiter of truth. 'Fanny? You know those gloves?'

'Yes, Mary. They are yours.'

'Oh, well,' shrugged Jane, who never minded in the least being caught out in a lie, 'it doesn't matter. Mine are worn out, and yours aren't. And Papa always says that those who have should give freely to those who don't. We are rational creatures, and rational creatures cannot wish to see their fellows in want, and so—'

'I know what my papa says, thank you.'

'He is kind and loves us all,' Fanny put in quietly, 'and I think that's all that matters.'

Both Mary and Jane listened to her with a kind of weary respect. At seventeen she was the eldest: she was plain and dutiful and caused no trouble. Also they knew that with her the whole subject was ticklish. She was the product of an earlier liaison of Mary's mother, an outsider with no true parent at Skinner Street. It was understood but not talked about. It was a great pity. And if only she were not so dull . . .

'What does this young man want from Papa, I wonder?' Mary said, putting her shawl to her nose: the thaw had revived the thick blood smell of the Smithfield slaughterhouses. 'Ugh. I wish we need not kill animals to eat.'

'Well, they kill each other, after all. No, he doesn't want anything – he's quite plain about that. Quite the reverse. He's Papa's *admirer.*' She seized Mary's arm, giggling in her ear. 'And that's why Papa's making such a fuss, because nobody thought he had any of *those* left nowadays.'

'Hush, you shouldn't . . .' murmured Mary: but a part of her wanted to laugh too, just as another part ached at the picture of her father scribbling and struggling in obscurity, even his notoriety now a forgotten shadow.

'He wants to help Papa,' Fanny said, 'on Papa's own principles. It is very noble.'

'Fanny's already in love with him,' Jane jeered, 'but you're out of luck, Fanny – he's married. It was monstrous romantic. This girl's father kept the Mount Street Coffee-house – and was most horridly tyrannical to her, and this young man saw it, and fell in love, and whisked her away and so they eloped. *He* is of very good family – heir to a baronetcy in Sussex – but his father is a shocking tyrant too. Always trying to keep down his spirit. Which has been quite irrepressible – he was expelled from Eton – and then from Oxford because of atheism – and his father actually said he wished he could have sent him to the war in Spain so that he would be killed and so put out of the way – is it not monstrous?'

'It rather sounds as if you are the one who is in love with him,' Mary remarked drily.

'Pom-ti-pom. I bet you will run to read his next letter. What other excitement is there in our wretched lives?' Jane said, with a sudden plunge into vicious gloom, aiming a kick at a dirty ball of snow.

Fanny, her heavy cheeks glowing, said tentatively, 'It is a pity about the atheism.'

'Oh, Fanny, he is a philosopher like Papa, he would not suit your prim notions at all,' Jane said.

'Do I have prim notions?'

'Woman as a domestic beast, with no independence of mind or action,' suggested Mary.

'Well,' Fanny said, in her muted way, 'if a woman wishes simply to live a domestic life, I can't see what's wrong with it.'

Mary and Jane, who so seldom agreed, were united in their scorn for that.

'When I'm a great actress,' Jane said magnanimously, 'you can come and live with me, Fanny, and see how an independent woman gets on in the world. Oh – let's look in Forster's window – there might be some new bonnets.'

'There aren't,' Mary said. 'Let's go home. It's too cold.'

'I'm not cold. I'm never cold,' Jane said. She was thirteen, well grown and rounded, graceful where she had been hoydenish, and for parts of each day indistinguishable from a woman. Then the endlessly competitive tongue-poking little girl would slip out like a bottle-imp. 'I'm stronger than you.'

'To be sure,' Mary said. 'Curious then that you need the gloves.'

Jane grimaced, stuck. Then she chuckled. 'I know why you want to go home. You want to read Mr Shelley's letter for yourself.'

Corporation Hall, Fetter Lane, off Fleet Street: the weather still bitter, the streetlamps mere pinpricks in the grey fleece of fog and coal-smoke: the audience gathering in the ill-lit lecture room, bronchial and impatient: the speaker stepping up to the lectern nervous, wiping and wiping his palms, his round dark eyes made rounder and darker by the opium-induced expansion of his pupils.

He is Mr Coleridge, old friend of Mary's father, who has been eagerly publicizing this series of lectures for him, and who has now brought Mary along to hear the last of them. The subjects are Shakespeare and Milton; and Mr Coleridge, whose vast brain has grown labyrinthine with German metaphysics and opium, is not a man to make such weighty subjects any lighter. Even Mary's father, dome-skulled and sympathetic, can be seen wincing as he tries to keep hold of the speaker's evanescent thread.

Still, the hall is well filled, for such things are fashionable. Scientific gentlemen exhibit vacuum-pumps and electrical piles to large audiences who go on to discuss them at West End routs and crushes. It is, in the new slang, quite the thing. For Mary, whose needle-sharp mind is as capable as any there of pinning down the speaker's meaning, personal memories haunt the vaporous air: Mr Coleridge young and energetic as a March wind, catechizing her in the old house at Somers Town before Clairmonts were thought of: Mr Coleridge heavier, troubled, reciting his *Ancient Mariner* while Mary and Jane hid under the sofa. She has heard her father tell a friend that while Coleridge's genius has survived his dissipations, his fire has gone out: he is a conservative now, a Church-and-King man. Mary keeps thinking of this. She is a prey to surges of anger and dismay. She wishes for consistency in a world full of betrayals (and where her own body is following the trend, startling her with strange pains and embarrassing transformations). In a consistent world, Mr Coleridge would not have turned sad and timid. Bonaparte would not have crowned himself Emperor. Her father would not have married the Clairmont. Everyone would be true to their beliefs. Ice-like, Mary burns.

It is possible that her intensity, combined with her slenderness and fairness and the spectacular amber of her hair, catches at least for a moment the eye of the young man muffled up in a great black cloak a few rows away, or that he, pallid likewise, tranced by thought, briefly senses it like an emanation, as even the closed eyes of a sleeper will register a light suddenly lit. With these people, nothing is unlikely. But at any rate the moment passes, the orbits brush and separate again, and at the end of the lecture Mary walks home with her father to hot posset and an early bed, and George Gordon, Lord Byron, takes a hackney to Covent Garden to drink till the morning.

★ ★ ★

Oh. There you are. Yes, it's me. Caroline.

You'd know at once, of course. I haven't changed a bit. How's this for a figure, in a married woman who's borne three children? Enviable, is it not? Not, perhaps. I'm too thin. Sometimes I wear six pairs of stockings to give my legs some shape. I've overheard *them* – William's family – referring to me as the Skeleton. Delightful in them, is it not? Perhaps I insufficiently disguise my own feelings about *them*. A parcel of brutes. How William escaped being like them I don't know. Or nearly escaped, at least. I am full of qualifications tonight.

What am I doing sitting on the stairs? Oh, we have had one of our quarrels, and William has gone off. I don't know – to cool his head somewhere. I want to show him, when he comes back, that I've been – you know. Regretting.

Hush. We must talk quietly. Just up there is the bedchamber of Lord and Lady Melbourne. My mother-in-law, the one they call the Spider, yes. Unfair, I think. I keep trying to be fair. You imagine she's horrid to me? Not at all. Only – sometimes she looks at me if I were some exotic and hideous plant that had been given her, and that she had fully expected to die in our climate. But it hasn't yet, and she can only look on in well-bred wonderment, and when the housekeeper says shall I not throw the nasty thing out ma'am, she says no, there is still some amusement in its very ghastliness.

Oh, Lord Melbourne? Well, he is a stubby, squat man with a crab-apple face and temper. He doesn't think much of me. But then no one thinks much of him. Not next to his wife. She makes him invisible. So – that is where they sleep. Just down the passage from our own bedchamber. One can hear his snores. I dread to think what they can hear.

Yes, I suppose it is strange, but that's how we live here at Melbourne House, and one gets used to it. William and I do have our own suite of rooms, on the first floor. Thus to get to them, you have to pass *hers*. There she always is: the sleepless sentry of my moral siege.

I'm over-dramatizing again, as William would say. Lately we were talking to a man who goes to every public hanging at Newgate. It is his choicest amusement. I ventured to suggest a likeness to Lady Melbourne, spectating upon our lives. William was not cross with me. Just sighed, frowned in a bemused way: Caro, Caro. Or sometimes: Tut tut, Car. So my name reduces: will I be nothing but C at last? Or perhaps that will go too – and there will be nothing to my name at all – and so nothing to me? That would be a way of disposing of a person, wouldn't it? Look over there, there's – no name – nobody – nothing. How funny.

I'm sorry. I got carried away for a moment.

Time was, William would smile in admiration and say, Caro, Caro – oh, still bemused – but fascinated. It is a great thing to fascinate. It is a terrible thing to cease to do so.

I am unfair to Lady Melbourne. In truth I quite admire her and wish I could learn by her example. She is so very self-possessed. And I scarcely possess myself at all it seems to me – as if my self was mortgaged long ago – to whom I know not – the higher spirits, I would hope – but it may be, alas, the Devil. I pray not. But it would explain a good deal.

Self-possession – oh she has it to the tips of her fingers. She can sit still for hours on end, like her own marble image with only the eyes ever working, seeing, estimating. It is as if she has no nerve-ends. Perhaps I got hers for I seem to have more than my share. I am, you know, you remember, a connoisseur of words. Here is one I came across: *ganglion*. It is a bundle of nerves. It is a word I cannot get out of my head lately. It has such suggestiveness of tangling and gangling and I think of signing myself in a letter Lady Caroline Ganglion. And just seeing.

Probably no one would be surprised. Certainly not William. I do not think it is in my power to surprise him now – of course he is very clever and sophisticated anyhow and so it would be hard but still I think I used to. Now I sometimes feel that he is looking at me rather in the way of his mother – as a curious spectacle about which his feelings are neutral.

Oh, only sometimes.

Quarrel often? I dare say – not so much as we used to – still more than many a couple after six years of marriage – which so often opens the epoch of indifference or era of don't-care. We are often passionate – in both senses of the word – if less so than at first – that, I suppose, is natural. But yes, thank heaven there is still fire. Which is life. Is it not?

Well, you may be right. But, oh, such regular set-tos – such champion-of-all-England bare-handed bouts – such powder kegs set alight as marked our early matrimonial days! For William, you know, though he burns slow burns fierce – and as for me, well, you know about me – and so there would be such storms, and I would walk out, or he would – I remember once hurling down his ring at my parents' house and how, a thing that could never happen again if you tried, it actually bounced from the floor back to my hand. But such reunions – there is nothing sweeter than the love that follows a quarrel. Sometimes a quarrel may be worth making, for the sake of that sweetness.

This is cultivating extremes, you say – well, your look says it – but what then? Is it better to cultivate mediocrity and tedium and dreary conventional nothingness? Do you say that that is better? Do you?

I beg your pardon. I am a little tired – but fidgety – cannot sleep.

It's cold here. Curious: though we burn such quantities of coal, all our houses are like this – Mama's, and Devonshire House, and Brocket – all bleak and chill and draughty-shrill once you go beyond the few rooms that are used. That says something, perhaps: perhaps not. The frightening thing for me is that everything seems to brim with meaning. Yet if everything is meaningful then everything is meaningless. Is that not so?

Forgive me. You were asking about our children. Well, there is only one living. Yes, sad. He is dear, dear. The others—

Well, I blame Lord Nelson. I do! – not that he could help it he being a corpse at the time. It was his funeral, when they brought him home after Trafalgar – January of the year six. Vast lamentations – even if one did not approve all his actions public and private there was no doubt that here was a hero, a man who had scrambled on to the shoulders of the world – and so we got a room high up by Temple Bar to watch the funeral procession go by – Mama and my Aunt Georgiana and I, mightily pregnant. It was very awful and impressive. I wondered what all those horses must be thinking, all caparisoned in black, and whether they understood. It was bitter cold and the room was damp and the procession went on for ever. And I verily believe that I took a chill that day that lowered me, and so when I was brought to bed three weeks later, the little baby was born dead. Not really Nelson's fault. No one's fault. But I think my dear Aunt Georgiana was never well following that, and she died not long after. The Duke remarried, you know. Married his mistress. Not a popular move. And I could only feel that my family seemed to be crumbling away. While William's remain, and increase. Like sturdy weeds – only that is not fair—

Not William, no, not William. He will be a great man, you know. Everyone says it. I remember when he was chosen to make the speech in reply to the Address from the Throne in Parliament – and I so wanted to hear him – so I did what any ingenious person would do. I borrowed my brother's clothes and got myself smuggled into the Commons as a young secretary. I make a tolerably handsome young man when dressed up – and it is so very piquant – going where you would not be allowed to go, and hearing what would normally be spared your ears. Most revealing. Of course, my mother-in-law did not approve. She did not say much – but she has this way of drawing down her eyelids like blinds – as if she would shut out the very sight of you—

William said he would not scold, but I must realize why this species of behaviour was improper. I did not – at least, I was impudent and said why was it improper when sometimes in the bedchamber I will dress a certain way – and he will do things – even here in the dark I blush to tell you so I will just say he likes to do things in a schoolmastery sort of way. You understand? Ah! You see, I never suspected these habits existed until I was married. And for long I thought them wrong – until William disabused me – teaching me that morality is entirely relative to the world we live in – not absolute as I had always supposed it. Well – when I mentioned this – he sighed and adopted what I think of as his Honourable Member tone – saying that it was *appearance* that was all. What people do in private does not *appear*.

Of course he is much cleverer than me – and I am always willing to learn from him. When he found it hard to read my writing, I engaged a writing-master so as to improve it. To improve is the great aim of my life.

Oh, and my son – to love and cherish him. He is a fine boy – the true Lamb stoutness – and when he was born I confess he cost me some tears – he so big and I so slight. But now he is five and I could not wish a finer boy.

It is true he is not quite like others. The doctors do not know quite what to say – for he is certainly hearty – yet there is something difficult about his mind – a shadow over it. I have heard people say he is simple. I think of it as a beautiful simplicity. But I know William is disappointed. Such a clever man as he is – he surely wished for a son to raise and teach and follow in his footsteps. And that I fear poor Augustus can never do.

Sometimes I see William making a great fuss of his dogs, petting them and calling them his clever fellows, while Augustus sits by, disregarded. Yes, it's sad. Augustus doesn't seem to mind, however. He asks for very little.

I think – sometimes – he is my punishment. And then I think that that is nonsense for I would not change him, not a jot, and love him entirely.

I had another little girl. She died within twelve hours – dear, this is a melancholy, maudlin report is it not? – and not what you expect of me, I'm sure. Never fear – from dawn to dusk I am quite as wild and absurd as you could wish – and I shall soon have done with my woes, which are, after all, the common lot of women the world over. I will only say it is a great pity – that William, with all his talents, could not bring me the one small thing I desired – comfort – and yet he grieved and suffered in his own way I am sure – a man's way, silent and separate.

I know, I know the passion of those first days does not last. One must settle down to matrimonial harmony – played as a quiet *adagio* and no more *allegro* – this I know. And yet – sometimes I fear I am different from everyone else, that I have a different climate as it were – they are all temperate regions and I am a tropic, racked with storms and downpours and burning suns. Of course there is only *one* sun. Language is a slippery matter. Now on that subject – there is the most wonderful new book out – a verse narrative of quite a new kind that has fairly set me raving – remind me to show it to you. No, I am not discontented. Perhaps I appear so. William said to me not long ago, when I was impatient for his attention, that we *cannot always be honeymooning*.

Of course not. And yet how ghastly. That bowing before necessity. Why can we at least not shake a fist at it? I think I screamed something of the sort at him. But he got bored and shrugged and went away.

It was not long after this that I made a fool of myself over a man. Yes – I shall conceal nothing from you – why should I? You are a piece of posterity, and must be in possession of all the facts. But in truth there is not much to tell. I did not, in the end, commit adultery. Yes, I prefer that Biblical phrase. It brings in the seriousness. If it were to happen – it would not be lightly. I know I am an odd frisk of a woman – but you know I never do anything lightly – without readiness for its full consequences – no no. Well, he was a soldier, very brave and gallant. My dearest brother Frederick is with the army too – in the Peninsula – and I am quite pierced through with pride in him and anxiety for him – and curiously I think it was partly that which made me look favourably on my suitor in his splendid uniform. He thought much of me. William, I conceived, did not think much of me, for he was always occupied with parliamentary business. And so there were sighings and meetings and a few kisses – oh, you can imagine it. William found out. I suppose I wanted him to. He seemed chiefly irritated that, if I were going to do this, I was so indiscreet about it. Appearance again. But it was my heart that put a stop to it. My heart revolted at my own actions – tore down the Bastille of my nonsensical sentiments – sent my absurd dreams to the guillotine – and returned rejoicing to William. For I only want one love: one true love.

He was pleased, I think. We got on rather better after, for a time. My mother-in-law watched us from beneath those blinds. Seeing us happy together, she made some remark about living in an age of miracles. She seems always *waiting* for something from me: some promised revelation.

Then William and I had a sad falling-out, on the night of our sixth wedding anniversary. I am quite vexed with myself to think of it. There was a ball, and William was for home at midnight, for he soon gets bored – and I would not go with him and said you go, I shall stay – for there was waltzing, the new dance – you know it? But of course you do. Well, I adore it and would not leave off – even though it was our wedding anniversary – so off he went in a black mood and I stayed till near five in the morning. And when I came home I hated myself and knew that I had not been happy, not really, all that time. I think there has been a general coolness between us since then.

And coolness I detest – so I am glad in a way that we have had this flare-up tonight. At least the heart speaks and is not muzzled. I do wonder where he has gone. Formerly, I may as well say, he has vented his spirit after our quarrels by going to other women. Oh, not affairs. Biddable, buyable creatures. I could smell them on him. But he only shrugged and brushed it aside in his most worldly way. There were things, he said, that I had shown myself loath to do, and as he did not believe in a wife being forced to such points, he sought relief elsewhere. It meant nothing. I, being somewhat constrained carnally, would not understand these matters, he said. Well. I did not like to be thought so. Therefore I took some pains to be more obliging – and was, I believe, a quick learner in this as everything. It is curious that we venerate innocence – and yet it is a quality that no one wants to possess.

But I don't think that's where he has gone tonight. His club perhaps. Or simply a long walk. It is a dark night – but I don't fear for him – he would best any footpad.

Oh, that book. It is downstairs – and I had better not stir to get it, for that will mean making a light, and Lady Melbourne may see it and come out demanding explanations. But you may get a copy yourself, for there will be more printing, I am sure, for it is such a grand success. *Childe Harold's Pilgrimage* is its title. I drank it down like nectar. I have written to the author praising it. He is, they say, a young man of mark – and I can well believe it – and yet one never knows. I have a strong fancy to find out.

How cold it is. I wonder if I shall ever feel warm again.

It happened at Christmas, which until then had been Fanny Brawne's favourite season. It was her special rite, it had everything that she loved, conviviality and sociability, warm rooms full of music and games and cheerful people. It fitted her conception of religion – the log-fire, not the hell-fire: a bright promise not a dark threat. She had heard that debtors could not be arrested on Sundays ('debtors', a word to be whispered with a certain anxious disdain in her mother's circles where gentility was a cobbled shoe that pinched tight) and in Fanny's mind Christmas had much the same feeling of blessed exemption. Life relented of its demands at Christmas, tradesmen did not present bills, squabbles were suspended, worries over Samuel's schooling or Margaret's habit of eating mud were put aside.

And then when she was twelve, and home from school for Christmas with her head full of the steps for the quadrille and the desirability of feathers in the headdress, the strange regrettable thing happened. Christmas did not keep it at bay. Afterwards she wondered whether she would ever feel the same about her beloved feast. She did: but not about other things.

She first saw the man when she sat up one evening waiting for her mother to come home from a party at a neighbour's. From the parlour window of the little Kentish Town house she watched for her mother's return, her embroidery-hoop in her lap, her mind visiting at its leisure a thousand locations between the constellated stars that shone above the roofs. She was glad her mother was accepting such invitations again: it was two years since Mr Brawne had died, and she belonged at a party, with her pretty, glowing, guileless look and her readiness to be entertained.

The carriage that stopped at the gate was not a post-chaise: it must belong to the gentleman who handed her mother out and with a rather conscious stiff, high-stepping look, like a man in a play, escorted her to the door. He was a soberly dressed, long-faced man of forty with a lined, strained brow like a headache made visible. He retained her mother's hand a moment before he bowed and left her.

'Oh! no, not a new acquaintance by any means,' her mother said, with a fluttered, absent look. She kept patting her chest as she did when pickles had made her bilious.

Fanny would have thought nothing of it. But the gentleman sent his carriage round to take them to church on Sunday: then on Christmas Eve her mother went to another party and came back so late that Fanny had fallen asleep in the parlour.

'My dear, the candles are quite down. You'll get a stiff neck sitting there. Come, kiss me and off to bed.'

There was the sweetness of wine on her mother's breath. Normally, even at Christmas, she would take only tea.

'Did that gentleman bring you home again, Mama?'

Mrs Brawne hesitated, then shook her head as if annoyed with herself for doing so. 'Yes. Yes, he did, which was most obliging of him. The ground is frozen hard again. We're lucky your kind Uncle John sent us all those coals. We must be sure and send some down to old Mrs Ebury at West Hill – she suffers so with her joints—'

'Who is that gentleman, Mama?'

'My dear, you are quite the inquisitor tonight. He is a friend – an old friend.' Her mother's eyes were like polished coins in the dimness. 'If you must know, he is someone I knew a long time ago – before your father. He was, if you like, my first sweetheart.'

'Oh! Oh, Mama, fancy!'

'Yes. Fancy.' Mrs Brawne, an inveterate folder and smoother, suddenly took off her mantle and gaily tossed it down on the sofa. 'I was quite a young girl – and he was my first admirer. He even wrote me verses. They were not very good verses—' she chuckled in a low, throaty, unaccustomed way '—and we were laughing tonight, recalling them – but still, a verse is a verse. He was, you know, very much smitten with me at the time: it was the talk of the neighbourhood.'

Fanny picked up the mantle and folded it edge to edge, carefully. 'Fancy,' she said.

'Well, it was not to be. We parted friends, and then I met your father. Still – he was very much in earnest, this man. He once said that he was dying of love for me.' Mrs Brawne drifted over to the window. 'And, you know, he has never married.'

Fanny, watching her mother's back, nearly said, 'Fancy', again. But instead she picked up the last guttering candle and said, 'Let's go to bed, Mama.'

'Yes . . . Yes, I am tired,' Mrs Brawne said, and sprang up the stairs.

On St Stephen's Day Fanny overheard Nurse talking to the maid about 'the missus's new beau'. By then she had done some thinking. She had got over the strangeness and was willing to find it, as her mother plainly did, charming that she should run into her old sweetheart so many years later. She even went to her mother and asked her to tell the tale; and was rewarded with an account of her mother's youth, too irresistible with its piled, powdered hair and face-patches and whalebone and rib-crushing bodices. What people wore in the past was a fascination to Fanny. She painstakingly drew historical costumes in her notebooks and set herself to imagining what they must have been like to wear: she was sure this was not trivial: how you were dressed determined much of what you felt and thought. (And this too, she thought, will one day be utterly remote and peculiar – this absolutely normal costume of high-waisted muslin gown with sash and low slippers – and Uncle John Ricketts's plain blue coat and starched neckcloth and creaky squeaky boots . . .)

And creaking, squeaking, Uncle John Ricketts came to them after Christmas and sat a long time in the parlour clearing his throat and glancing at the Dutch clock as if he expected it to tell him something other than the time.

Timidly Mrs Brawne said: 'Will you take more tea, John?'

'No – I thank you – no,' he said sharply, as if she had suggested something indecent. Then he shifted to a position even more awkward and uncomfortable than his habitual one, and went on, 'My dear Frances, I hope you will be frank with me. I hear reports that you are considering marrying again.'

'My dear brother,' Mrs Brawne said, with a fair degree of composure, 'then you hear what is not true.'

'Ah. I don't, of course, listen to gossip. Nor – nor could it be truly any of my concern if you were – if this gossip had substance. In theory at least.' There was a shaving-nick right in the middle of Uncle John's chin. Fanny could not help staring: fought down the laughter. It was so wonderfully central. And Uncle John was so serious. 'In theory. In practice, of course, I am always concerned for you. My nearest kin – I would add the dearest.'

'Thank you, John. It is my greatest happiness to know that I am secure in your regard. As for this gossip, I know well how it has got about—'

'I don't listen to it, of course.'

'To be sure. The gentleman in question is an old acquaintance – from my youth. And if we like to sit and talk over old times, in the way of people past the prime of life, I do not think there is anything surprising in that.'

'Indeed. Indeed. You are amused, Fanny?'

'No, sir. I was just thinking of your kind gift, and what I shall spend it on.'

'Well, be sure and spend it wisely. Wisdom. Yes. That, my dear Frances, is my theme.' He congratulated himself on the transition with a pat on his great bony knee. 'If – I only say *if* – there were to be any such step taken, I hope it would be with due wisdom. Prudence. Consideration of what was, perhaps, not considered before. You know I was very fond of your late husband: he had many qualities. Still, he was not . . .' Uncle John looked expressively around the little parlour, then seemed all at once to lose heart. 'I have said enough, perhaps. Fanny, it occurs to me that rather than spend, you might save your gift.'

After he was gone Fanny put her arms round her mother's slim waist and said: 'I'm so proud of you, Mama.'

'Are you, my dear? I can't think why.'

'You didn't let Uncle John bully you.'

Mrs Brawne smiled away, folding Fanny's hands into her own. 'Didn't I?'

When the gentleman with the lined forehead called, Fanny made sure to shoo Samuel away from the parlour so that he and her mother could be private. This was being adult: Fanny liked it: it was tact, civility, discretion, words she enjoyed – they even thrilled her in the way that knights and crags and tempests were supposed to.

'Who's that man?'

'A friend of Mama's.'

'Mama's funny lately.'

'No, she isn't. Go fetch the cup-and-ball, and we'll see if you can beat me this time.' He couldn't: Fanny could catch the ball a hundred times without missing. But she missed deliberately in the end to let him win. That made him over-excited, and later at dinner he was so noisy and boisterous that Mrs Brawne, who had

165

been staring fixedly at the soup-tureen, said with a sudden snap that it was hard, very hard, for a lone woman to manage such children day after day.

'I think you have one of your megrims, Mama,' Fanny said.

'I think I have. I shall go to bed early. We are all out of sorts lately. I shall be glad when Christmas is over.'

Fanny went to bed early too, slept at once, and woke to find herself, astonishingly, on her feet, in the doorway of her mother's room, and weeping.

'Oh, my dear,' Mrs Brawne said sitting up in bed, 'you're sleepwalking.'

Launching herself at her mother, Fanny cried, 'I don't want you to – I don't want you to, Mama, please . . .'

'Dear, dear. What, my love? Was it a nightmare?'

'I don't want you to marry that man,' Fanny moaned, clutching at her. 'I'm sorry – I don't know why – only I want it to be just us – or else Papa, but he's gone and I wish he never had – I'm sorry.'

'Hush, hush. Whatever – well, I won't say what put this into your head. Because of course you are not stupid, my dear. But you needn't fear. There is – has been – an offer. An eligible offer in many respects. I have declined. I don't wish to marry again. My heart is entirely given to your father's memory. And no material considerations can outweigh that.' Mrs Brawne spoke as if she had had the words long in her mind. 'I'm sorry you've been grieving over this, Fanny. I didn't know. I should have, perhaps. Dear, how cold you are: get in beside me a minute.'

Fanny huddled against her mother's soft, scented warmth. She closed her eyes. Soon, she knew, there must be a farewell to this: the adulthood she desired did not admit of it. But soon, soon, not now.

Then, a thought.

'Was the gentleman sad?'

She felt her mother's breath held, pent for a paining moment. 'He – he was very polite as ever. Certainly he was disappointed.

He said – referring to those verses long ago – that I would be the death of him at last.' She dabbed a tight kiss on the crown of Fanny's head. 'In jest, of course.'

The gentleman did not call any more. The parties ended. Fanny returned to school in Brompton, glad that things were back to normal – or hoping they were. A new mistress, turbaned and eccentric, introduced Fanny to Shakespeare. The tragedies oppressed her, but she fell deeply and delightedly into the comedies. For hours she warmed her mind at the glow of *Twelfth Night*: the poplars of Brompton became the Forest of Arden.

'Men have died from time to time, and worms have eaten them, but not for love.'

When she first came across that line, Fanny felt a thrill of recognition. Here was someone who said what she thought, or did not know she had thought until it was set so beautifully before her. And, of course, there was consolation. She knew the gentleman had not died. He had gone back to his place in Berkshire and from there had sent a respectful present of game. Still, it had nagged at her: the thought of a man dying for love of her mother. It was an image of awful, unthinkable burden. But here was a poet who took her aside and said smilingly, 'You see?'

And later she found herself feeling aggrieved at the gentleman for talking so freely about death. She thought of the loss of her father, of the boy floating in the Hampstead pond, of the hideous careless thorn. There was death's true nature: not the trifling disappointments of love affairs. So. Fanny was glad to have settled these things so early in her life. She moved on to *Much Ado About Nothing*, adored it, and longed to be Beatrice cutting a man to pieces with wit.

'They say he is very beautiful and very mysterious,' she heard one of the older girls saying, one day when she was beginning *The Taming of the Shrew*, 'and there is no telling what he has done – only that it is marked on his face.'

'Who?' Fanny put in.

'Childe Harold. Well, not him – the man who wrote the

poem. Lord Byron. You must have heard of him.'

'No. Is that the book? May I see?'

'Be very careful with it – Papa only bought it me with much grumbling – it's so expensive. Oh, but worth it. The spell – the fire – the power – I have never felt such agitating sensations within me.'

'Lord, is it a poem or a dish of devilled kidneys?' Fanny said, opening the octavo volume.

'You know, Fanny, there is such a thing as being too clever.'

No, Fanny thought, beginning to read with quickening interest, no, there is not.

'Who? Oh. Your brother, I suppose.'

Colonel George Leigh – but no longer, strictly, entitled to call himself Colonel at all – glanced dully across the breakfast table at Augusta's letter, then returned to dipping his pink lips in weak tea. His eyelids were puffed, slug-like: there was a deep groove between his brows. Augusta felt sorry for him. Drink still revenged itself on him as painfully as if he were an unfledged youth instead of a bottle-hardened man of forty. The trouble was, she thought, he did not know where to stop: and his cronies egged him on. And then she couldn't blame him for indulging just now, when things were so difficult.

'Yes,' Augusta said. 'My brother. Will you eat something, George?'

'Can't stomach it, old girl. Extraordinary thing – fellow at Cheveley was talking of your brother – Drummond, young Drummie we call him – bought that nice little bay mare last year – remember?'

'I'm not sure.' Georgie's friends: Drummies and Harrys and Jemmies, they all blended into one composite figure in her mind, hessian-booted, starched, whisker-toying, loud-laughing, expert in fetlocks and faro. (And vacant. Thus, in parentheses, Augusta puts any disloyal thoughts: consigns them to brackets of the mind.)

'You must remember. Anyhow he was talking of your brother – absolutely all the rage in town just now apparently – every hostess must have him – quite the lion. And Drummie himself was curious to see the fellow, that's the extraordinary part.'

'Why so?'

'Oh, well, I thought it was only your tea-table ladies, your blues and chatterers, who'd be dangling after him. Oh, nothing against the fellow. But, after all, he's only been abroad and come back and written verses. Oh – oh, really!' George burst out in disgust, as their second child, Augusta Charlotte, reminded them of her presence at the table by being sick down her front.

'She was poorly again last night.' Augusta wiped, dabbed, soothed. 'I thought of sending for the doctor – but I fancy she's only colicky. George, wait.'

'Sorry, old girl. Not with my stomach as it is. Really, we should have a nursery for them to eat in . . .'

She caught up with him in the hall, shrugging on his riding-coat. She took the letter with her. 'George – I was going to tell you about my brother's letter. He does seem – as you say – to be much in society just now—'

'Good for him,' George said stonily. 'Now I want to go into Newmarket to see a fellow.'

'He has met the Prince.'

His back to her, George froze. 'Jolly for him. Well, must get on.'

'George, please. What Byron says – how very agreeable the Prince was – it's set me thinking again that surely the time has come to—'

'To what, old girl?' George said turning. 'Creep and crawl? No, no. That ain't Georgy's style, you know, and never will be, God willing.' His hand on the door-handle he went on briskly: 'I may step over to Cheveley later – don't wait supper.'

'Oh, George, I didn't marry you never to be with you!' That doesn't make sense, she thought, inwardly calm even in distress, and: How odd my voice sounds. A marital protest from Augusta was such a rarity that it was almost as if a stranger had spoken.

George certainly seemed to think so. 'Eh? Old girl, what's this, what's this? You're ill, I think. Lie down – I should lie down.'

'I'm not ill. I'm just concerned for you, George. You – I know you keep yourself busy with things—'

'Busy, I should say so. There's that new cob in stable only half broke yet. Though I think the farrier should look him over – I suspect a touch of sweet-itch, don't you think?'

'I've never understood the diseases of horses, you know,' she said, stroking his lapels.

Reassured, his brow clearing, he chuckled. 'No, you haven't, have you? Funny thing. Well, well, so he's met the Prince, has he? Just on account of scribbling?'

'The Prince greatly admires *Childe Harold*, it seems.'

'Devil of a thing. Mind, the Prince always did like putting his nose in a book. Couldn't understand it myself – here was a man who had the finest stable in Europe, wasting his time with silly novels and verses. Don't know what his stable's like now, mind.' George thrust out his lower lip. 'Wish you hadn't made me think of that, old girl. Put me in the dumps again.'

'Well, that's why. Because I want to see you happier – see you well placed again.'

'Well placed – I should think I was – sharing the Prince's own barouche at the races, if you please. I think any man would call that well placed,' George said bitterly. 'And any man would consider himself pretty hard done by to lose it as I did. But whose fault was that, eh?'

(Yours, George. Only in parenthesis.) 'I know. It was horribly unfair. But, you know, time has passed, and Byron says the Prince is in very affable case, and now that he has all the powers of Regency confirmed, it's surely time to—'

'He should have been Regent long ago,' George said. (Pompously.)

'And now that he is, it's surely worth approaching him – submitting yourself to his mercy—'

'Oho! Which is as much as to say, I admit doing wrong. And I didn't, old girl. There's the sticking-point, you see.'

'Oh – wrong, and right . . . These things are only what you care to make them,' Augusta said, in her vague way: though she meant it. 'George, I'm sure the Prince would look favourably on you, if you made the overture. But it must come from you. He is the Prince Regent after all, and you the subject. That's the way it's done.'

George looked at her as if she had asked him to scale a mountain. 'Lord,' he said, 'you really are beating me about the ears with this, old girl. No wonder my poor old head aches.' He flung open the door. (He was good at things like that. Uncorking bottles, letting down carriage steps, walking with a swinging genial stride. Eating.) 'As for the Prince, if he wants me he can summon me.'

Before Augusta could call after him, the nursemaid appeared. 'Mrs Leigh, littlest wants his feed. Hark at him scream.'

Littlest was their six-week-old son, George. Augusta picked him up. He fastened his enraged little head at her breast as if he would suck her soul out. George.

'Married – but not so you'd notice.' That had been the common joke about Augusta and George Leigh, from very early on. She hadn't minded. George loved horse-racing and cards and shooting-parties. She had known that when she married him. She did not suppose that he would cease loving them, or wishing to spend much of his time with them, once they were married: she didn't think that was natural. Couples who tried to be all in all to one another were, she believed, heading for trouble. And one of the things she had first loved about George was his immense capacity for being happy – on horseback, with a glass of good brandy, dressing gorgeously in new-pressed regimentals, making love to her, winning a wager. They did pretty well, she thought, even if she wished he did not go away quite so much: and if those good things of life were chiefly bought on credit, well, she was not exacting. Everything – it

171

remained her creed – would be all right.

And it remained her creed even when everything began to go wrong.

First George's regiment was sent abroad, to the war in the Peninsula. In the rustic seclusion of Six Mile Bottom Augusta gardened and baked and nursed little Georgiana, their firstborn, and woke gasping from nightmares in which George was shot and she felt the bullet actually pounding into her own body and jolting her from the mattress. But George came back in one piece – all that Augusta wanted. She covered his sunburnt gaunt face with kisses.

'Steady, old girl. I haven't had clean linen in a fortnight.'

'You're a hero,' she said – though that did not greatly interest her: Augusta was not comfortable with heroism.

Unfortunately George had won his spurs in the retreat from Corunna – and, courage and endurance notwithstanding, a retreat was a retreat. Hearing the sniffs and sneers of his countrymen, George set his jaw in an expression that Augusta was to come to know and regret: a misunderstood look, wounded and stubborn. That look accompanied him throughout the next year, in which his own disgrace was slowly paraded before the public eye like a file of shabby deserters.

Absent-mindedness: that was what lay behind the first part of it, Augusta was sure. She knew all about absent-mindedness: she was always discovering half-drunk cups of cold tea that she could not remember pouring. George, as the Prince's trusted buyer and seller of horses, had simply forgotten that the money he had received for a sale was not his. He had not meant to keep it. He was not good at accounts, tended to keep track of his transactions in his head. He had not stolen from the Prince. Of that Augusta was certain. Or as near certain as made no difference.

'They are all against me, old girl. I am most basely insulted. As a gentleman it was the only thing I could do. You see that, don't you?'

In righteous indignation he had resigned as the Prince's

equerry. The Prince, he declared, had used him shabbily. Augusta made loyal noises, aware that the Prince had not made any move to dismiss George, aware that the Prince kept this roof over their heads. But at least George still had his colonelcy.

Then, with recrimination in the air, there was an enquiry into the regimental accounts of the 10th Hussars. Fraud, profiteering, peculation: they were as much a part of the army as pipe-clay and canvas. So George grumbled over his brandy, as the enquiry ferreted deeper: and then hotly told Augusta that that did not mean, of course it did not mean, that he was guilty of them: only that . . . Well, if she was determined to be against him too, then he might as well put a bullet in his brain and have done . . .

Augusta suffered. For a while her only thoughts of George were the bracketed ones, traitorous, unthinkable. A chasm opened between them. He spent much time in London and Brighton, chivying fellow officers, protesting his innocence, drinking. Then Augusta happened to hear a new curate preach in their parish on the woman taken in adultery. Casting the first stone. That story had always lain at the heart of her beliefs. She reproached herself, though not bitterly: even on herself Augusta could not be hard. He was in London again, and came home in the midst of a downpour. Soaked and shivering he sat down to stare miserably into the parlour fire. Augusta brought him a hot toddy, stood and watched him swallow it, then put her arms round him.

He gasped: then buried his face in her neck. 'Oh! Old girl,' he sobbed. 'I'm so unhappy – so damned unhappy.'

She kissed his wet blond head. He smelt like some small helpless pet let in from the rain. 'Never fear, George,' she said. 'We're back now. We're back.'

Soon she was his partisan. George was, she wrote to her friends, being made a scapegoat. Whatever had been going on with the regimental accounts, there were many others involved, and it was all very complex; but only George was to suffer. This was surely not fair. So she banished altogether those bracketed thoughts. It was easier because of her remoteness at Six Mile Bottom. Miles from anywhere, with no town, no society, seldom even a newspaper unless George brought an old one over from the Green Man Inn across the muddy road, she felt very cut off, virtuously so, from the great world. She had not been to London since the birth of Augusta Charlotte and came to think of it as a place of toils and wiles and glittering deception. What chance did straightforward country-dwellers like themselves stand, when that sophisticated world turned against them? (Of course George spent much of his time away from Six Mile Bottom, moving around that very world – but there, she was done with such thoughts.)

Augusta did not mind the isolation. Domesticity suited her. Her eye appreciated the bulbous shine on silver, the neat rhythm of stacked crockery, the haze of poured flour, in the way a painter would respond to colour. She was a devoted mother – and she hoped a good one; though she could never be strict with her children, and sometimes would recline in a daydream while they scrambled half dressed over the ample terrain of her body. Augusta submerged herself in these things while George's career staggered to its inglorious close.

'Never,' he said, when it was whispered to him that he must resign his commission or face a court-martial. 'Never. You understand, don't you, old girl?' And later, when he resigned, 'Had to. A court-martial would finish us. You understand, don't you, old girl?'

'Of course, George. There was nothing else you could do. Never mind: at least I shall have you more to myself now.'

It did not happen quite like that. For a while George lurked at home. He played sad-eyed games with Georgiana, ceased to tease his coiffure, did much sorrowful resting of his head on Augusta's bosom. But though he no longer had any position or prospects, there were still horses, there was still the turf and gambling and shooting and house-parties and smoking-rooms: the kingdom of Georgeland still stood. 'A race-meet would be just the thing to cheer me up, I fancy,' he said, the first time he went back to Newmarket. Then it was Doncaster. Soon he was his old self again – never there. *Married – but not so you'd notice.*

Augusta was very sick throughout her third pregnancy. But part of that might have been the unpaid bills, which she studied and collected and sifted for relative urgency until she felt faint with it. 'I think my luck will turn soon,' George would say, with a shrug, or, 'Once that colt's broken in I'll get a good price. Trust me, old girl.'

She did, of course. (But she didn't. Thus the unspeakable thoughts crept back.)

While George could get away to the racecourse or the hunting-field, Augusta's only avenue of escape was in her mind. It was a long, straight avenue, rising in the distance to a tremendous eminence soaked in sunlight. It was her brother.

Through the bars of her matrimonial maternal birdcage, Augusta peeped at Byron, in curiosity, in affection, in wonder. They had not met: through those five dampening, tarnishing years since her marriage her brother had again been an absent presence, felt through letters, mutual acquaintance, gossip – and imagination. The breach between them had been simply repaired: Byron wrote to her as if nothing had happened. As this was precisely Augusta's way of dealing with unpleasant things, they were very soon on the warmest of terms again. He was her spectacle. George studied the form of racehorses, his stable-master followed Napoleon's latest campaigns with hand-inked maps, and some women took all the fashion-papers and kept abreast of every new hemline and bonnet-trimming. Augusta had Byron. She pieced him together in the same way. When after Cambridge he went abroad on his travels, his letters grew infrequent, but she worked out his itinerary, and tried to re-create it in her mind. Portugal: Spain: Malta: Albania: Greece: Turkey. For most of it she had only the dimmest ideas – burning skies, harbours, sashes and sabres: but she conjured such mental land-scapes as she could while she suckled and changed clouts and combed reluctant round heads. Just as when she was a girl, her brother was myth, reality, and consolation.

Though not quite as when she was a girl. Then the future was an empty stage, on which he might perhaps be one of the bright actors. Now— ('now' needs brackets: now there is no future except a perpetual more of the same.)

And then he had returned to England, a well-travelled, notable and – she heard – particularly handsome young man, far from the unfinished youth she remembered. He had Newstead Abbey: he had, perhaps, genius, from his ventures into poetry: he surely had a fine future. But shortly after his return something happened that seemed to confirm a notion that her brother had spoken of before, and that Augusta had always dismissed – the notion that there was something doomed about the Byrons. On landing in England he had taken lodgings in London, intending to go up soon to Newstead, where his mother was living. As far as he knew, Catherine Byron was well, or as well as a woman overly fond of both drink and attention could ever be. He postponed the reunion: probably he was not anxious to see the mother with whom he had had such spectacular quarrels.

But he loved her: Augusta could tell from his broken-up response to her death. There was a swift, acute illness, and he set out for Newstead as soon as he heard, and arrived too late. His mother had died the day before. His mourning letters did not say the words 'if only', but they were stamped all over them.

And now, today, a happier letter from Byron slipped through the bars of the birdcage, and Augusta glanced over it again as she suckled her tiny greedy Georgeling. Her brother was indeed, as Drummie or whoever he was had said, the idol of society, the catch of the London season, the rage, the *dernier cri*. Hostesses angled for his presence. People walked out of parties because he was not there. Even statesmen took notice: he had given his first speech in the House of Lords in support of the workmen who were smashing up the new machines in the north. Daring and even shocking to Augusta, whose opinions were old-fashioned:

but still very Byron. And everywhere people talked of the grand poem he had brought back from his travels. He had sent Augusta a first copy of *Childe Harold's Pilgrimage*, and it stood in a solitary place of honour on her bureau. Now and then George would pick it up and turn it over in his hands with a bemused look, as if expecting it to do something – open up like a clasp-knife or play a tune. As well as some of the verses, Augusta knew the inscription on the title-page by heart.

> To Augusta, my dearest sister, and my best friend, who has ever loved me better than I deserved, this volume is presented by her father's son, and most affectionate brother, B.

And now he had been introduced to the Prince Regent: the man who, Augusta gathered, still bore some goodwill to George Leigh – if only George would apply to him. Just that.

'Well,' she said aloud, 'he has his pride. And that is a very fine thing.'

For once, for a mercy, little George went down quietly after his feed. Easing her sore breasts, Augusta crossed the draughty passage to the kitchen. Seeing to the ordering of dinner was a complex matter. Very probably George would not be joining her, but if he did come in, he expected there to be enough for him and was cross if not; but if she were to dine alone, she must make sure it was not a wasteful amount and that what went uneaten could be reused. But plainly – George was a roast-and-boiled man, and had hooted disdain at attempted *ragouts* and *fricassées*.

The groom was at the outside door. He wanted to know when the Colonel would be back.

'That I don't know, Tom,' Augusta said. (He's not a colonel any more. We all pretend.)

'Ah. Only there's another load of hay mouldy. Fit for nothing. Second time this month. I do believe that feed-man's out to cheat us.'

'I'll tell the Colonel when I see him, Tom.' (Yes, in Georgeland even the feed-merchant is a persecutor.)

Augusta inspected the larder. She found herself staring at a cold saddle of greasy mutton. She wondered if the sheep had had a happy life. She stood there so long that the cook-maid came up and asked curiously, 'Anything you need, ma'am?'

'No,' Augusta said, 'nothing.' (God, God, I need something.)

3

Rondo Romantique

Mary's second time away. No shabby-genteel Ramsgate this time: she was going to Scotland.

'Such a long way away!' Jane cooed. 'I shouldn't care to be sent so far. It's almost as if they don't ever want you to come back.'

'If you are still here, I don't want to,' Mary said. These stepsisterly needlings were reflexive, ritual as church responses: they did not preclude a certain fondness. Besides, both knew that Mary's trip was quite enviable. For the past few years Walter Scott's ballads had been the favourite reading of every fireside. England was level and tame: it was the land of the mountain and the flood that stirred young hearts. Mary was going where young Lochinvar swept you on to his galloping steed.

Or rather, Dundee. 'A solid, prosperous town,' Godwin said, with watery amusement, 'not, perhaps, amenable to those picturesque fancies.' But there was to be the bracing air and exercise that her sickliness needed. The town, and the family she would be staying with, were of strong Radical sympathies, sober, learned. It was to be the making of her – at least, in the image that Godwin approved.

The Clairmont did not come down to the quay to see Mary off. She had one of the tactical headaches she invoked whenever it seemed that someone else was going to claim the attention. This way, Godwin would be worrying about her even as he was saying goodbye to his daughter. Perceiving these things had become so easy for Mary that she had almost ceased to heed

179

them: they were like simple arithmetic learnt long ago.

The ship lay below St Katherine's Stairs and was called the *Osnaburgh*. It had a fishy smell and the deck was pasted with sailors' spittle like so many oysters. 'She,' Godwin said, nervously watching Mary's boxes being carried below. 'A boat or ship is always referred to as feminine. Can you think of any other examples of this peculiar nomenclature?'

'A country or nation,' Mary said, feeling sick, 'considered in diplomatic or military terms.'

'Good. I recall that in my birthplace in the fens, windmills were also given a feminine appellation by their keepers. Ah, there's a motherly-looking lady coming aboard: we can ask her to keep her eye on you, Mary. Coachmen also I believe refer to their vehicles as she. A curious question why: perhaps all these things have a certain unpredictability about them. And so the vulgar prejudice about the changefulness of women's characters attaches. Your mother would have had something pertinent to say on the subject, I'm sure.'

Jane, having run all over the ship and even hung perilously, monkey-like, over the taff-rail, now came pink-cheeked and solemn-eyed to take Mary's hand and then – astonishing Mary – to wail, 'It's not right – Papa, don't do it – you can't make Mary go off alone, she's only fifteen, you can't, it's too horrible—'

'Hush,' said Fanny, the Clairmont's absence lending her a faint shade of authority, 'people are looking.'

'I don't care about that. I don't want Mary to *go*.'

'Well, I shall still be here,' Fanny said.

'But you're dull. And she isn't.'

Fanny, well used to being hit glancing blows by flying insults, just looked perplexed. 'Yet you are always quarrelling.'

'A natural affection,' Godwin said, half anxious, half sententious, 'quite normal, for those brought up as sisters – including the little disagreements. Jane, you must consider that Mary goes, only to return to us some time quite soon. As for going alone, it has always been my belief, as it was her mother's, that women should be afforded independent action, even as young as Mary. Besides — besides, you know it is not within our means for me to purchase a passage to Dundee also, as well as a passage back. But let us ask Mary. Are you unhappy to go, Mary?'

Mary pulled her hand gently from Jane's sweaty clutch. Her hands were always as cool as Jane's were warm. 'No, Papa. I am content to go, if it is what you want.'

Her father nodded, opened his mouth. She stopped him, going on: 'Only,' she said, fighting down a wave of nausea, 'only if it is what you want — and not her. My stepmother,' she added grudgingly. 'If this is her notion, to send me away, then I don't want to go. Though I shall still go, of course.'

Godwin sighed and shook his head. 'Do you have your money tucked away safe?'

'Yes, Papa. In my stays.' He was becoming good at evasion, she thought.

'Very well. I shall go and speak to that lady, and then we had better leave the ship: it looks as if they are making sail. Say your goodbyes, my dears.'

Fanny drily presented a kiss and mumbled something about prayers. Jane stared at her with her intent berryish black eyes for a long time, as if to imprint the significance of what she was about to do, and then kissed Mary with a hot sudden looming, brushing the side of Mary's mouth.

'We'll write,' she said, 'we'll write and write — everything. All the news about Mr Shelley. Now he's back from Ireland perhaps we shall see him at last at Skinner Street and — Lord! To think I might meet him first, without you!' Jane grimaced, momentarily torn between triumph and tenderness. 'Mind, I think they're sending me back to that school at Walham Green. I hate it. Well, I don't really. Lord, you're so calm! How can you be so calm?'

'I'm not,' Mary said. 'I'm terrified. They say it takes six days to get there. I feel sick, I can't sail for six days.'

'I could: it doesn't bother me. Oh, I shall be so vexed if Mr Shelley comes and I'm not there!'

'Perhaps he won't.' Mary was slightly bored with Mr Shelley, the young Godwin-worshipper whose letters to her father were still hallowed like psalms at Skinner Street. Jane and Fanny were always making such a fuss about him. 'He has other things to do.'

'Oh, he will. Papa will see to that.' Jane's face became a gleeful mask of knowingness. '*Because* of Mr Shelley's money.' She rubbed her hands together cackling.

'You make Papa sound as if – you know Mr Shelley has offered to help him. That's different.'

'It's always different with Papa. If I pick my nose it's because I'm dirty. If he does it it's because he's natural and unaffected. Will you be sleeping in a hammock?'

'No. You're crying.'

'Of course I'm crying, it's sad. Don't you ever cry?'

'Sometimes. Thank you, by the way.'

'What for?'

'For not wanting me to go.'

'Well, that's worn off a bit. I do love you, sort of. Look out, here comes your papa.'

Mary looked her surprise. 'You called him my papa.'

'Yes. Well, he is, isn't he? Truly. I bet he'll be crying tonight. Though he won't show it, like you.'

Last farewells: her father and Jane and Fanny back to the dockside, where they waved handkerchiefs while the sails bellied and the captain bawled commands. The matronly lady, yawning onions, told Mary she would look out for her, then went away. Her father's bald dome was lost in diminishing detail: London faded. Mary was sick three times before Gravesend. The matronly lady was nowhere to be seen. Slumped against the rail, Mary fell into an exhausted doze and woke to find that her money had been stolen. The captain shrugged when she told him. Never had she been so absolutely alone.

Curiously enough, it felt perfectly normal.

Listen: that rhythm. That *rhythm*. The WALTZ.

And it comes from the lands of the Germans, with metaphysicians and hock, and with folk-tales of forests and ballads of bogles. In London the Frenchified fashions give place to the Rhine in these days of Napoleon's ultimate sway, when Europe's his vassal and everyone's scared of his long (dwarfish) shadow (the view of *The Times* this, and right-thinking Britons, though not necessarily everyone whom you may meet in the salons and levées, and Byron for one is a kind of admirer of Boney the darer, the symbol of energy, will, and assertion). It thrills through the ballrooms this year like a current, electric, galvanic – the same that the new pioneers of the science have passed through the corpses of frogs and, now, felons, unhooked from the gallows and used in experiments, seeming to show through their twitching and jerking that life might be made this way – shocking, immoral, compelling thought, just as this German dance merits those adjectives. Everyone knows it, and those who won't do it will talk of it – say it corrupts, and that no one in their day would dream of such mauling, in public, in daylight.

For *waltzing* (the name of this flagrant new caper) is different, entirely, from all of the dances society favoured in previous times. It entails a new posture: the man *holds* the woman. His arms are right round her, their faces together; the whole thing suggestive, the outraged say hotly, of – what they won't mention. The scandal is swelled by the bareness of fashion, for women wear little now – gauzy, transparent, their gowns are like shifts, and the gleam of their shoulders and crests of their breasts may be dizzily viewed in the swirl of the dance-floor. Which moralists moan is the lobby of Sodom. To waltz is to fornicate upright to music. No wonder it's popular.

Come: to the party. The year, 1812, and the season – the Season: the time between Christmas and June. And the place, here in Whitehall, the locus of power, the hub of the kingdom: the house, see its pillars, its portico. All very classical. Hints at serenity. (Just don't expect it – not in *this* mansion.) The Melbournes reside here – my lord and my lady – the crab and the

183

spider – though they don't concern us, or not just at present. The waltz-party – hear it? – is held at the top there – look up the rotunda (we're in now) – and there, on the first floor, the Lambs' own apartments. And that's where the lilting of triple time rhythms proceeds to entice us. It's morning (which means roughly noon, in these circles) and numerous people are noisily cramming the sunlit reception rooms. One, with the floor cleared, is sacred to waltzing; and here is the music, the tingle and jangle of Broadwood piano, the whisking of feet and the rustle of gowns, and the murmur of watchers. It can't be denied that the thing is compelling. Compared with the line-up to which they're accustomed – the squares and the sets, like a genteel parade-ground – the waltz is anarchic: no pattern of partners, no end or beginning, it whirls in a circle like energy visible. Strangest of all is its privacy. Couples who waltz are alone while in public. It makes the spectator a voyeur of sorts.

And the liveliest waltzer? The one who seems born for this airy amusement? No other than Caroline. Hers is the curly head, cropped like a pageboy's, that always revolves on the Melbourne House whirligig. Light as a thistle (as sharp too, as spiky) she floats in the arms of a series of smilers, who gaze in her eyes and guffaw at her flow of fantastical nonsense, and fancy their chances – and yet there is something about her that hinders their ardour. A flare of intensity, more than they bargain for: some of them, yes, are a little afraid of her.

Not of her husband, urbane and detached, who is glad that his turbulent wife has a pastime. Apparently, anyway: William has never been easy to read.

'Well, I'll say this for Caro – she does *entertain*,' a guest says acerbically.

Caroline's ways are flamboyant – she's known for it. Hers are the filmiest muslins; she damps them, reputedly, making them cling and reveal even more. In the crush of a drawing room, balked of an exit, Caro will leap over sofas and tables. At dinner she'll offer a vivid account of a book she has read about cannibals, canvassing views from her neighbours on which of the bodily parts they would favour, supposing they *had* to (consensus of thigh, which she finds rather telling). Once she decides to omit the word *the* from whatever she says, and for days she maintains it with brilliant resourcefulness (just as devotedly, someone pronounces, as if it were something that mattered). And always about her, this feeling of peril. Whatever will Caro do next, is the sigh of her mother; and *anything* seems the correctest reply.

But today there's a tension about her, a watchfulness: eyes in the back of her head, you might say. And the reason is making his way up the staircase, and not without trouble, because of his limp. From the moment he enters the suite there's a ripple, a shiver of notice. It spreads, like a breeze through a field, to the ballroom, and Caroline knows that her moment has come.

And so Byron's accepted her kind invitation – the phrase every hostess is longing to hear. For the craze of the season is snaring this poet, this brooding young aristo, bearing his aura of beauty and strangeness. To drawing rooms stale with a fug of old gossip a gust of the new, the exotic, the daring is brought by the man who is watching the waltzing (excluded from dancing, of course, by the lameness). He's travelled to places where fabulous indolent sultans and viziers loll in their harems, and bandits descend from authentic sierras, and everything's olives and myrtle and pashas and minarets. Thrilling – but mostly because it is *he* who has seen them. And he is a mystery – partly revealed, like a glimpse through a keyhole, or portion of nudity. Known are the facts: he is young, and a genius, lately returned from his travels, and owning an abbey near Nottingham, Radical, fierce in the Lords on behalf of the labourers. Plain the appearances: no one mistakes him, the pallor, the underlook (so they describe it, his female admirers, the beam of his eyes from the shadow of glowering brow) and the mouth like a wound, with its bitterness, humour and petulance. Dubious, though, are the stories surrounding him: orgies at Newstead, and something about him suggestive of *darkness,* as if he has done an unspeakable thing and it preys on him.

No one has been, in fact, such a sensation as Byron is, now, in the salons of London society. Caro is only the latest to hook the celebrity: that's how it seems, to the waltzers and watchers. And one of the latter – the lady in lilac, who sits in her chair as if seated in judgement – is watching intently.

A bosomy, pretty, yet icy young lady, her hands neatly folded, her lips like a drawstring, so scornfully tight. As her hostess detaches herself from the dancing, and shimmers, as limber and fleet as a fish in the shallows, her way through the crowd to the newest arrival, the lady in lilac observes, with dispassion. Her name: Annabella. For now, a spectator, who seems to see nothing in Byron (a curiously tentative smile on his lips as he bows to his hostess) but one further instance of Caro's extravagance – liveried pageboys, and ice with the wine, and a poet. But she is another who cannot be easily read (by herself, least of all, perhaps). Time has her card. We shall meet her again. Annabella: your moment will come.

But the music is fading – in Caroline's ears, it is fading, as Byron presents to her, seeming amused at himself (yet he trembles), a rose and carnation the colour of blood. And: 'Your ladyship likes, I am told,' he says, 'all that is newest and rare – for a moment.'

A moment . . .

Liberty, equality, fraternity.

Throughout these years, the famous trio of epithets has hovered over history, public and personal, just as they were painted in large red letters above the doors of Parisian houses at the height of Revolutionary ardour. Mary's mother saw them often, when she was living in Paris in the days when the guillotine was never dry. Later Caroline saw them, occasionally, faded or half scrubbed out, when she joined the English visitors flocking to Citizen General Bonaparte's primped and pacified capital. In their name, or something like it, the armies of Bonaparte have conquered most of Europe, even while the General has made them ring hollow by crowning himself the Emperor Napoleon; and the consequent war with England still grinds on in Spain, where Colonel George Leigh had his brief blooding. Here there are still a few hardy souls who cleave to those three incendiary principles: embattled solitaries like Godwin, and his enthusiastic correspondent, that young Mr Shelley who is drawing into view. But the prevailing mood is against them – bitterly so. Last result of the trio: they have driven England into the arms of a fierce and repressive reaction. To the passionate young its touch feels deathly.

And when Caroline Lamb crouches, bird-boned, goose-fleshed and nightgowned, at her desk on the draughty second floor of Melbourne House, and scribbles her journal in her long-tailed looping script, she is not inscribing upon history like revolutionaries and conquerors. She is performing a private act (very private – even William must not see). And yet perhaps Caroline of all people, with her quivering nerves, her many-windowed mind, can sense prophecy and presentiment as she dips her pen and invokes another trinity to describe the man she is falling in love with.

Mad, bad, and dangerous to know.

Lady Melbourne, privately taking tea with friends, shrugged off the question. 'I have never had the faintest notion what my daughter-in-law supposes she is doing,' she said, 'and nor have I now.'

'So it is true, then?' put in a sharp-faced lady, friend of a friend, who seemed to be aiming to outdo Lady Melbourne's style of bitch-grandeur, even down to the black choker round her neck. Good luck.

'To be sure, Lord Byron is forever calling, and it is Caroline he comes to see. This can hardly be news, even to those who are not entirely up with the *ton*.' Lady Melbourne beckoned a prompt footman with a twitch: refill the teapot. Bloomy reflections from the silver did unflattering things to her skin.

'Is that why there's a rope rail going up the stairs?' the first friend said. 'I hear he has a lame leg. Some say he's actually cloven-footed.'

'There is a lot of nonsense talked about him,' the sharp-faced lady said, peering into her tea as if she suspected it was poisoned. Not entirely fanciful, when Lady Melbourne was your hostess. 'I hear he is quite graceful, and of uncommon looks. But perhaps you can tell us, Lady Melbourne. Have you seen him?'

'To be sure. There's not much I don't see. Every caller must pass my apartments. He is a pretty sort of man.'

'But he has not introduced himself here? You have not met him?' Unwisely pressing.

'No: in this regard at least, my dear, I am as ignorant as you.' Someone spluttered into their cup.

Sharp-face made a game stab. 'Well, of course he is young – not above three-and-twenty, they say – and you know what that's like: he probably thinks of you merely as an old woman.'

Later, alone, Lady Melbourne brushed her hair before her mirror. The friend of a friend would not be invited again; and with a twitch on one of her many threads, Lady Melbourne would set going a vibration of gossip that would finish the woman's reputation in a fortnight. Still, a small matter.

With bleak eyes she studied her equinoctial beauty in the glass. Though she would have died rather than admit it, she feared the winter had come.

Still, she had great control over herself. It was three hours since the sharp-faced woman had said what she had said, and only now did Lady Melbourne allow the flush to creep up her face, a stinging surge of shame, mortification, longing, and rage.

Before this, Caroline thought, looking down at the young turmoil of his black curls, before this everything in my life was just that – *before*: awaited, in the offing, not yet begun. Hard to explain.

'What's another word for "before"?' she asked him.

'Previously,' Byron said yawning. 'Anterior, prior.'

'No. Those aren't right.' Caroline shifted, caressing him with her bare foot.

'After, then.'

'You provoking man. That is the opposite.'

'No. The same. Just depends upon where you stand. Instance – you washed your hands before breakfast this morning, didn't you?'

'Certainly.'

'But when you did that, you were also washing them *after* breakfast – that is, yesterday's breakfast. You do not deny that today is after yesterday?'

'Wait. I'm thinking. This only holds true for repeated actions, surely. Whereas if I only ever ate *one* breakfast in my life—'

'Which might indeed be true – look how slender you are.'

'That bit is not slender. Where was I? Yes, if I only had one in my life, then there would be a time before it and a time after it and they would not be the same. Surely?'

'Well, time is only the little slice that we mortals know of eternity. And eternity, by its nature having no beginning and no end, must be circular, which means that no time can be before or after another. Damn it!' He chuckled hoarsely. 'A fine theme to be fretting ourselves with on a sweet spring morn.'

'Which is also a grey winter's night, if all times are the same times. But, my darling – think what a mighty theme for poetry, if it could be done – eternity, immortality—'

'Pooh, too cloudy altogether. Leave that sort of misty matter to old Turdsworth. And as for immortality, I don't believe in it. No gainsaying eternity. But neither you nor I will be there, or here, or anywhere, to record it creeping by. Thank heaven.'

'The heaven you don't believe in. Shocking infidel.'

'You do, don't you?'

'Wildly. And no doubt you will mock me for it.'

'No,' he said, turning and sitting up. 'I wouldn't. Because it's sincere. It's cant I can't abide. Pretending.'

'I knew that as soon as I read you,' she said, threading her fingers through his. ' " 'Here,' said I, 'is an enemy of the hypocrites. A scourge of the Pharisees.' " No one thinks as you and I do, you know.'

'I'm not even sure I think as I do,' he said, with a slight, separate smile. 'Who mocks you for your religion? Someone does.'

'Oh . . . William's family. I say nothing against them – only that they are very different. I keep thinking of that miserable expression "down to earth".'

'I see.' He was amused. 'And with you, I keep thinking of a skylark. A human skylark, flying higher and disdaining the earth altogether. But then even they must come down to earth sometimes – don't they? – I confess I know no nature lore. I am adrift in a hedgerow – a castaway in a cow-pasture – but I have a fancy skylarks descend, at least to make a nest.'

'Yes,' she said, with a sudden plunge of spirits, 'they have to make a nest.'

He saw it. 'By the by, can one believe something wildly?' he said, with a playful pinch.

'Tormentor,' she cried delightedly, swooping up at once, 'of course one can, if I say so. Haven't I told you of my empire over the sublunary earth? Haven't I told you that if you step out of St James's and find yourself being rained on, that raincloud was sent by me?'

'To be sure, I had forgot your omnipotence. Presumably I have you to thank for that bilious attack I suffered yester-eve,' he said, as they lolled back together.

'Yes – I despatched it to teach you a lesson – in case you had forgot me for a second.' His indolent closeness delighted her: at first he would not do this. After the act of love, he had been quick to dress, draw away. She had no doubt of his experience, but wondered about its quality. Perhaps all his bedmates before had sought only the immediate passion and release – to Caroline the very least of it. Perhaps she was differently made, wanting more, wanting deeper, finer. Perhaps they were, simply, meant for each other.

'Ah, then I have that much liberty from your thrall? A second—'

'No,' she said, pouncingly, and even while she smiled in jest her heart did not, it was deadly earnest. 'That's too much – only for a fraction – a sliver or shaving of a second may you not think of me.'

'That thin, eh? Like the ham at Vauxhall Gardens. And you are under an equal obligation, I trust, to think of me?'

'You needn't fear for that. Your name is in my mind as often as a clock ticks.'

'Lucky it ain't Farquharson then,' he said, his lips lazily smiling, his eyes more alert, thorough.

Caroline looked away. 'I believe everything wildly,' she said, 'by the by.'

'Yes. It's a beguiling new thought to me – quite a fluffy yellow new-hatched idea. Belief has always seemed to me calm somehow – steady – well upholstered.'

'Is that because you lack it? Surely not. Oh, there is such force in you, such passion—'

'I know – I know the seeming,' he said, flinging himself back with one white sculpted arm above his head. He had a beautiful, dreadful look just then of dying of some titanic sting. 'Oh, I feel it in me. And then I think it is all like a set of fellows in an orchestra pit – tuning up their fiddles and tightening their drumskins – all ready to play their hearts out – but not one of them has a page of music to read, and no one is there to conduct them, and the whole thing is quite without a point.' Abruptly, gazing up, he laughed as if he had read a joke written on the ceiling. 'Which is probably what every young pup says when the world don't satisfy him. How exquisitely long your neck is.'

191

'Thank you. I shall hang very well then, shan't I? I mean if you desert me, and I am obliged to come after you and thrust a knife into your heart.'

'You are rather confident you will find it. I'm not sure it's there at all.' Byron had closed his eyes, his high smooth chest rising and falling in smooth rhythm: now he opened one grey eye to her. 'Marrying is a fool's game, I think. Isn't it?'

Caroline said, surprised at herself: 'No.' She thought his one-eyed face seemed to fall, as if on the edge of a scowl. 'No. Well, it depends.'

'Come here.'

She did so, shivering a little, guilty, needy. 'I thought we were still talking of immortality, sir.'

'Not I. It's a thing I cannot conceive.'

More seriously, even as she surrendered to his hands, she said: 'Well, this moment. This – us. Isn't this immortal?' She had a kind of half-aroused seizure of panic, gripping his hair. 'Isn't it? Else why exist so?'

'Oh, stick at time. Time's enough to think of. Look – like I said – before and after, all the same. I kissed your cunny before we made love, but also after. Which is also before the next time. And yes, my tremendous Caro, this is not immortality. But won't it do?'

Before and after. Even though she worshipped Byron and venerated his mind above all, Caroline still believed in the notion of before and after, simply because her life proved it.

It's like this: a theatre. To Caroline, her life before Byron is a theatre on a winter's morning. Dark, dusty, chill, echoing, smelling of must and faded orange-peel and old spent candles. You can move about in it, sit down on the cold hard benches, look up at the lustreless chandeliers: you can step down into the orchestra pit among the bentwood chairs and the stacked music-stands, you can even climb on to the bare stage and hear your feet resound on its dull boards and gaze out at the house, the gilded boxes occupied by shadows. But there's no one here and nothing happening and no reason – terrifyingly, if you stop wandering about and really think – for it to be here at all.

That's before.

And now there is Byron – and the lights blaze, the benches and boxes are crowded with colourfully dressed, animated, chattering figures, music strikes up with a purposeful crash and flourish, and the wave of warm hubbub recedes as the rich red curtain draws puckering away to begin the fabulous drama.

A comedy or a tragedy? She doesn't know, or care.

Scenes from the drama.

The backdrop is the fashionable West End of London in 1812. Small sunlit world: you can easily walk, as Byron often does, from his rooms in St James's Street to Melbourne House in Whitehall. Along the way there are the clubs, Brooks's and White's and Boodle's, where gamesters throw fortunes down the wells of green baize. Having everything, they court nothing, just to excite themselves. The dandy in full plumage parades these broad streets with their strew of horse dung and straw: often the celebrated Brummell himself, in moulded coat and champagne-polished boots. Over there, Carlton House, the Regent's louche lair: yonder the parks, haunt of bloods on blood horses, elegant equestriennes, carriage-drivers in barouches and landaus and curricles and phaetons. All backdrops are illusory, but this perhaps more than most. The carriages are fantasies, high and delicate, always seeming on the edge of overturning: the ladies they carry are gauzy-clad, tissuey, about to blow away. For all the solidity of the Piccadilly mansions, much of the money here is a fiction. Brummell struts above an abyss of debt; Corinthian bucks run up railinged steps to brass-handled doors with creditors at their clipping heels. In some ways it is the slenderest of façades, thin as the pasteboard that makes the playing-cards shuffled at faro-tables and the gilt-edged calling cards that forge the alliances and declare the wars of society: turn it one way and it all but disappears.

Scene: Caroline's first meeting with Byron. She refuses an introduction and walks away from him. It is at Lady Westmorland's. Young women are clustered round him like, Caroline thinks, farmyard geese round an intruding hound. Not thus: not for her. His eyes are on her, like a clinging thread at nape and ear, as she goes.

Scene: second meeting. She is calling at Holland House after a ride through Hyde Park when Byron is announced. Sweaty and dishevelled, she leaps from the sofa, begs the use of a dressing room, and runs to wash and tidy herself. Returning, she could curse the mutual acquaintance who says: 'You are fortunate indeed, Lord Byron. Here has Lady Caroline been sitting happily with *us* in all her muck – but when she heard you were coming, she ran off to beautify herself.' Now, she thinks, he will suppose me just one of the gaggle. Another goose. Which I am.

'Your ladyship refused an introduction before,' Byron says, with a fencing look. 'Might I ask why?'

Goose, yes, thinks Caroline, my goose is cooked, my fate is sealed, the die is cast, and every other expression suggestive of momentous overthrow. 'I feared for your life, Lord Byron.' Men are handsome: William is handsome: this man is beautiful.

'For my life, how so?'

I don't know why I am mirthful. Perhaps because this is so serious. Cupid's arrow has been so prettified, pettified: but it is not so, it is not a brooch-pin, it thrusts and stabs and, oh, hurts. 'Because you appeared to me quite surfeited with introductions – and I know from my history how fatal a surfeit can be – the old kings were always perishing of it, all those confusing Edwards and Richards dying of a surfeit of lampreys or oysters. So in a manner I have saved your life.'

He smiles and detains her hand: he has a look that makes you the only people in the room, sharers of ineffably amusing secrets. 'My preserver. You know that in parts of the East it is the custom that one who has saved another's life must stay at his side for the rest of their lives?' A thrilling voice, the faint hint of Scots burr like the nap of a flock material against the skin. Thus things begin: publicly, in the presence of others: with an audience.

Scene: the two of them in his carriage, after a reception: the blinds down, a guttering lamp, rain tapping at the glasses as if to be admitted, or in warning. Byron begins kissing her palms and wrists.

He sits back.

'I think you must kiss me now,' he says lightly.

'Upon the hands, sir? Are you turned Pope or—'

'On the mouth.'

She lowers her eyes. 'I daren't.'

'Oh!' he breathes, and in the dimness his smiling teeth, very white, flash a sardonic crescent. 'Then I have found it at last. The thing that no one supposed existed – the north-west passage and the philosopher's stone and the unicorn rolled into one – the thing that Lady Caroline Lamb *dared not do*.' He reached out across the carriage to place his open hand soft against her cheek. 'And yet it is such a small thing.'

'But it isn't,' she says. And kisses him.

Scene: Caroline has made love with Byron for the first time, in his bed. There is a human skull by the pillow, a brace of pistols – primed and loaded, she knows – at hand; lying in lassitude she examines them with interest. 'How marvellous the human mind is that can contrive such things,' she murmurs, cocking a pistol.

'And yet it is only a bag of mush, like a blood pudding, contained in a space like this,' Byron says, fondly touching the skull.

When she first saw these things in his bedchamber, alongside his cane and fencing-foil, she stared and cried: 'So the tales are true – that at Newstead you quaff wine from a cup made from a human skull!'

'Aye, so – they make handsome vessels, polished up and mounted. Why is *quaffing* so much less moral than drinking, I wonder?' Conversationally he added, 'Caro, do you think me mad?'

'A little. Only in the way that one should be, in this world, to feel anything.' In truth the pistols alarmed her at first: but when she was perched atop him, naked, she reached a wild pitched moment that made her grab the pistols and brandish them, gasping and laughing. She would have fired them if his hands had not, at last, gently overpowered and dissuaded her.

Scene: Caroline's own, small, neat, rather modest bedchamber at Melbourne House. (More revealing of the true Caroline, perhaps, than her public antics.) With her, Byron: but no pyrotechnical sensualities. As often, they have been reading together. He has read hugely and omnivorously and is opening up new worlds to her, and this is a large part of her excitement. Beautiful eyes are very well, but what chains and enchants her is genius. And now, as often, her son Augustus has been brought down from the nursery, at the forgettable top of the house where the servants sleep in little cells, and is contentedly sitting on Byron's lap. He is five years old, with all the sturdy bigness of the Lambs, but none of their cleverness: no cleverness at all.

'He is not – not adroit, perhaps,' Caroline says, kissing his fat cheek. 'But he is, steadily, a very good, very dear boy. Aren't you?'

The big little boy swivels his heavy head, smiling as if peeping round a corner.

'Well,' says Byron, jiggling his charge up and down so that Augustus mewls with delight, 'who wants to be adroit, after all? You know what it means, my friend. It's French, it's *droit*, it means "right", and right is straight and proper and correct and pompous and priggish and dull. Who wants to be those? Not I. Nor can I be, my lambkin. Because I have never been right. I was born all wrong and have always been all wrong.'

'Wrong,' Augustus says, looking with drugged wonder in Byron's face.

'Quite so, my friend. Or do you mean to correct me? It's true, I swear. The other night a link-boy in Piccadilly called me by name. The friend who was with me said, "Ah, look how your fame has spread." But it wasn't that. The lad knew me by my deformity. As everyone does.'

Caroline says: 'You shouldn't talk so.'

'Of course – because it makes others uncomfortable. Isn't that why this poor fellow is forever banished upstairs?'

'I would not have it so. But William – I think William is not comfortable with him.' And sometimes, she thinks, it is almost as if William hates him. Is it because he sees himself there – himself without the intelligence, coarse and unleavened, creature of reflex and appetite? Disloyal thoughts: they always set off a breeze of denial in her. 'Not that he does not love his son, dearly and absolutely. He is the best of men: he is too good for me.'

Byron assesses her over the boy's tufted head. 'Why do you talk about him so much to me? Doesn't it make you feel worse?'

'I wasn't aware I did,' Caroline says, turning away and going to the window-seat.

'Or is it to make me jealous? Which is rather odd. Usually the unstated aim is to make the husband jealous.'

'Don't,' she cries, 'don't say *usually* like that. It makes it seem small and foul . . . Are you jealous?'

'When you talk of your love for him, yes. Not rational in me, I know. But then one doesn't walk into a woman's arms rationally.'

'I think you are more rational than me. You didn't want us to leave Holland House together the other night. You said it would be too obvious.'

He laughs. 'And you would prefer me to carry you out in my arms? So that everyone should mark it, and your husband be shamed and your mother-in-law scandalized, and we should be forced to leave off altogether?'

'Together,' Augustus says.

'Very good, my friend. Together – like this.' Byron gently presses the boy's hands palm to palm. 'That's what we want to be, Caro – isn't it? And to be so, we must sometimes be apart.'

'I'm sorry. I'm foolish. I am, I know I am, I'm always being foolish and the only thing to stop me is to – *stop* me. Be firm and fierce with me and then I take heed.'

'Lord. I don't mean to begin chastising, if that's what you mean.'

'Well, it is natural. For men and women to enjoy correction – discipline. So I have heard.'

'Have you? Do you mean William . . . ? Good God.'

'Apart,' says Augustus, spreading his hands.

'Excellent, bravo.' Byron returns his attention, seemingly with relief, to the boy. 'I think you have ample sense, you know, my friend. You simply don't go about shouting and bragging, which is the way to commendation in this world.'

Caroline finds her eyes filling with tears. This often happens now, sudden and random as a sneeze. She stares out at rippling St James's Park. 'I saw a balloon ascent here once. I was half dead with envy of the people in the basket. It looked so beautiful. But the trouble is, I would never want to come down.'

'Perhaps that's how it is with this little fellow. He's up in his own balloon, and doesn't want to come down – and who can blame him?'

Surreptitiously Caroline wipes her eyes: she knows Byron hates tears. 'Sometimes I dream he is an angel. A real flying angel floating above my head. But I'm always afraid he will float quite away . . . Is it true that in the East the simple-minded are revered, because they are nearer God?'

'Well, there are many Easts, but certainly I never saw the barbarities of Bedlam on my travels. Your good Muslim considers charity to the unfortunate his prime duty – unlike your Englishman who puts it somewhere below changing his linen. I met many a Turk who was as good a Christian as most Christians, as 'twere.'

'But they oppress the Greeks most cruelly, do they not?'

'So they do – almost as cruelly as if they were Irish.' His smile is wolfish. 'The two have a deal in common. Only the Greeks are much prettier.'

Caroline throws a cushion at him. 'I don't want to hear about your Greek ladies, thank you.'

'I wasn't just talking about the ladies.'

'Hush. You cannot mean what I think you mean. It is too . . .'

'Shocking? Surely not. I love you because you don't find things shocking. Nor pretend to.'

She gazes at him. Sometimes she suffers this feeling that he is not really here at all, that she has projected him by some enormous effort of imagination, and that if she reaches out a hand it will go through him, ghost-like. With a groan she falls on her knees.

'The shocking thing,' she says, 'is how much I love you.'

Byron never flushes: he seems instead to turn even paler, so that his eyes stand out like ice-coloured gems.

'Call it amazing,' he says huskily, 'astounding, astonishing, awesome, admirable, damn them must they all be As – but not shocking, Caro.'

'If you knew what was inside me,' she says, touching her breast, 'you would be shocked.'

The icy gems seem to crackle. 'So would you.'

Scene: a pageboy in scarlet hussar jacket and fawn pantaloons springs lightly up the stairs to Byron's lodging. The knowing may recognize the livery as that worn by the household of Lady Caroline Lamb, who likes to design these things herself. But they would have to be very knowing indeed to recognize that slight youthful figure as none other than Caroline herself.

She has walked here from Melbourne House, walked with an ease and freedom she can never enjoy in woman's garb. She has looked boldly in people's faces, tingled with the thrill of their *not knowing*. Now she wonders what Byron will make of it. Occasionally, when her wildness sweeps over her, she senses him taking a mental step back: it reminds her of the anarchic childhood days at Devonshire House, when she dared her cousin Hart to jump down the first flight of stairs with her, stood tensed at the top with his damp hand in hers, and then at the moment of launching felt the hand tighten in a mute tug of refusal.

Byron's valet, Fletcher, lets her in. (She is a little breathless: she has given up waltzing for Byron, and misses the exercise.) She puts a finger to her lips at Fletcher's stare, and goes through to the bedchamber where, as she suspected, Byron is only just stirring, dressing-gowned and bleary over hock-and-soda after a punishing night. But the sight of her wakes him up: definitely.

The bed is still warm when she lies down on it.

'No,' he says, a catch in his throat, when she begins to unbutton the scarlet jacket. 'No. Leave it on.'

Scene: Caroline returning to Melbourne House after a morning shopping. The door to the downstairs state room stands open, and as she walks by Lady Melbourne's voice rings like a peremptory bell. 'Caroline. Step in, my dear: here is your husband returned. You'll wish to greet him, of course.'

William has been away for a couple of days on political business: he often is. Less usual is this tête-à-tête with his mother, which he tends to avoid: she badgers him so, he says. Caroline presents her cheek to be kissed. The touch of William's lips makes her feel happy and wretched all at once: she longs to change the world and make it better and tells herself she would die on the spot if she could do it.

'And so they are going to hang the man who shot Mr Perceval,' she says, sitting down. 'A wicked crime, of course, but is the poor man not out of his wits? How could he suppose the Prime Minister responsible for his troubles? Lord Byron is going to see him hanged. He says he cannot help himself. Have you seen Augustus?'

'I'll go up later,' William says. 'The man must pay, if only to satisfy society. Caroline, if there is an election this summer, would you wish me to stand?'

'Of course. Because you belong in public life – it's your destiny.' Caroline believes this: she is no hypocrite. As she loves William less, she admires him more. 'Though I fear, now that the Prince has made his peace with the Tories, your party will still be out of office. But no matter, you must be there, you must—'

'I have doubts,' William says harshly. 'There is the expense of being returned to Parliament. There are – difficulties.'

'I must say,' remarks Lady Melbourne, apparently addressing the teapot on the side-table, 'this loyalty is as charming as it is surprising. I had not thought to hear it from one who seems more concerned to link the name of Lamb with folly and absurdity.'

'I know well that I am foolish and absurd,' Caroline says, submissively, 'but I hope I only hurt myself with them.'

'I doubt I will stand,' William says, folding his arms with his characteristic look of giving up on the world as on a tiresome card game. 'Perhaps I'll write my memoirs.'

'Of course you will stand,' snaps Lady Melbourne; and then, apparently to the milk-jug: 'These follies, of course, are how you *present* yourself to the eyes of the world, and as such are necessary to you. For they secure attention – and that, Caroline, is what you must have, is it not?'

'Oh, I think I know precisely how much and how little attention to pay to Car – don't I, my love?' William says genially. 'I don't believe in making a great fuss about something that doesn't deserve a great fuss. This is the art of balance.'

'It is the art that will make you a great statesman, William,' Caroline says.

'Except I'm not standing.' He laughs.

'It is an art that can be taken to excess,' puts in Lady Melbourne sharply, not liking this outbreak of old marital rapport. 'This trifling cast of mind dismays me exceedingly. Why, when I was your age—'

'Oh, but we are not discussing ancient history, Mama,' says William. It is a style of remark common among the bruising Lambs, but Lady Melbourne meets it frostily, and frowns – at Caroline.

'Ma'am, I shall try to be good,' Caroline says, finding her voice leaking out as a whisper and – why *does* it happen? – her eyes smarting with tears again.

'Hm?' Lady Melbourne, reaching for the teapot, looks at her as if she has said she would try to learn Portuguese. 'Oh, who cares about that? I'm talking about life, my dear.' Lady Melbourne's 'dear' is a marvel – it is everything that is not meant by *dear*: it is deft and short as an assassin's stiletto.

'Appearances,' Caroline says faintly.

'Why does Lord Byron want to see this hanging?' William enquires, languidly. 'Does he think to make a poem of it?'

'I think he is fascinated by men who have done something bad – something terrible,' Caroline says. 'And what it does to their souls.'

'It is, I must admit, a piquant speculation,' William says, with a nod.

I am discussing my lover with my husband, Caroline thinks. The world is mad. But then I have always known that, haven't I?

Pouring tea, Lady Melbourne says: 'You do not think appearances important, Caroline—'

'No, I do not.'

Lady Melbourne regards her with a fresh, inhaling, high-chinned look. 'I did not mean it,' she says, 'as a question.' And then the shutters come down.

Scene: Byron low-spirited, in Caroline's apartments at Melbourne House: honeyed sun pouring in, Byron just come from 'Gentleman' Jackson's boxing rooms at Bond Street, a favourite haunt where he spars and fences and whence he usually comes vivacious, parrying and stabbing at dust-motes with his cane; but listless today. He is, and can no longer pretend he is not, hopelessly in debt. Newstead Abbey will have to be sold.

Ominous thought. At the best of times there seems little enough to fasten him to England, this restless exotic with his Asiatic mementoes, his loathing of the ordinary, his edgy look of perpetual departure. In any room, Byron always makes sure he can see the door.

Caroline says: 'I have jewels. I could sell them.'

'Sweet of you,' he murmurs absently, shaking his head, prowling. He comes to a halt at the window and lounges, saturnine profile against the crimson curtain, an intaglio of melancholy. She has seen him fall into this attitude at parties and receptions, when he is bored. She knows that sometimes there is calculation in it: it is a pose or, more strictly, a mask. But sometimes it is real, very real. She is suddenly visited by a horrible vision of a mask melting on to a face, becoming one with it. 'Sell . . . Why on earth should you do that?'

Because . . . She is silent. He has to ask.

Annabella Milbanke, handsome, clever, and rich, with a comfortable home and happy disposition, seemed to unite some of the best blessings of existence; and had lived nearly twenty-one years in the world with very little to distress or vex her.

She was the daughter of Sir Ralph Milbanke, a baronet whose estates lay in the far northern county of Durham, and his lady the former Miss Noel, a scion of the distinguished family of Lords Wentworth. Fifteen years had elapsed between their marriage, and the birth of their only child; a circumstance that rendered Annabella doubly precious in the eyes of parents who had all but despaired of producing an heir, and who were consequently inclined to treat her as a species of miracle irrespective of her character and attainments. These soon revealed themselves to be, however, of a superior order. From a little child, Annabella furnished proofs of a precocious intelligence, which her parents were very ready to foster. Sir Ralph was a genial and inoffensive man, whose principal ambition was for a parliamentary seat; and a just assessment of his talents must have concluded that any higher eminence was entirely beyond him. Accordingly he stood in awe of his daughter's brilliance, to which he was prepared to defer when she was scarcely taller than his cane; while Lady Milbanke, whose mind was more developed than her husband's, was eager to encourage an intellectual growth, which in her own case had been somewhat suppressed by the circumstances of her marriage.

The powers of reason and understanding thus cultivated in Annabella, showed themselves most markedly in a predilection for mathematics. – Her tutors pronounced her a prodigy; and soon she had so far outstripped them as to make her arithmetical studies necessarily a private amusement, undertaken alone with a book of Euclid and the best hot-pressed paper. Her other precocity was in the matter of religion. Prayers, for the infant Annabella, were never a mere matter of custom; and as she grew older she manifested a stern devotion, and attachment to religious principle, perhaps more narrow than generous in their fervour, and more impressive than comfortable. However, it was not in the nature of Sir Ralph and Lady Milbanke to see fault in their remarkable offspring. Nor was there at Seaham, Sir Ralph's seat on the remote coast, a large circle of society with whom Annabella might have learnt the lessons of comparison. The village was a bare hamlet, in which the Milbankes were not merely first in consequence, but solitary in that state; and the district was a scanty one, scarcely able to muster sufficient couples for a creditable county ball. It was hardly to be wondered at that Annabella entered upon womanhood with very decided opinions, particularly upon the failings of others; a subject on which she was the more ready to pronounce, as she had never detected any in herself.

Little inclined as she was for the frivolities of society, Annabella was nevertheless expected to make a figure in it. She was the heiress not only of her parents, but of her uncle Lord Wentworth. The expenses that had been required to lever Sir Ralph at last into Parliament had left the family in need of some temporary economies; but ultimately, Annabella would be wealthy. Nor were her personal charms insignificant. The world is readier to bestow the title of a *beauty* upon a woman who is well dressed, well bred and well connected, than on the same woman lacking these attributes, who might indeed be pronounced no better than tolerable. – So Annabella's looks did very well; and with the aid of London fashions, and the air of poise consequent on her favoured upbringing, she contrived to impress everyone as a fine young woman, without any peril of dazzling the men into folly, or the women into envy. She was of no more than the middle height; her figure was good, if too full for complete elegance: her hair of the true auburn, and curling without the aid of tongs or papers: her face more round than oval, with a glowing complexion: her eyes unusually large and brilliant, and for once justifying that poetic epithet of orbs, which went some way to offsetting a mouth a little ungenerous and indrawn. She had a soft but clear voice, which struck the ear all the more musically for not being overused; for she was oftener content to be an observer than a participator in conversation, especially if it was of a light or trivial kind. In all there was about her a quality of quiet self-containment that could not fail to elicit admiration, even where it did not inspire affection. It was expected that she would marry well; and in pursuance of that object, she was introduced in her twentieth year to the London Season.

The first essay was a success, in that Annabella added polish and address to her habitual self-command, gained a useful circle of acquaintance, and was the object of serious attention from several eligible gentlemen. — But Annabella's taste was fastidious: far from finding her head turned, her fond parents observed it more firmly fixed on her shoulders than ever. She was not about to make any rash decisions, applying as she did to the conundrum of matrimony the same analytical mind that she brought to bear on geometrical figures.

With such evident steadiness of character, Annabella did not appear likely to her parents to suffer from their absence during her second Season. Economy had required that Sir Ralph give up his house in town; and accordingly, he and Lady Milbanke elected to remain at Seaham, while Annabella spent the Season in the care of relatives in London. Chief among these was her aunt, Lady Melbourne. The social prominence of this lady ensured that Annabella would lack no profitable introductions. Less to be commended, in Annabella's strict view, was her aunt's character; which, while secured from *present* or *future* scandal by her invincibly sixty years, was far from stainless in retrospect. Lady Melbourne was certainly a worldly woman, indifferent to virtue, invulnerable to religion, and concerned above all for the advancement of her family in power and consequence. But she made Annabella very welcome, taking her under her wing, and throwing Melbourne House open to her at all times; and Annabella so far returned her aunt's regard, as to think of her only as critically as she did everyone else.

Her acquaintance with her aunt's notorious daughter-in-law was less happy. Lady Caroline Lamb took up her connection from the country with typical enthusiasm: made much of Annabella, extended to her a hundred invitations, and would have drawn her into her circle of intimates. But Lady Melbourne, observing this, felt it her duty to warn Annabella of the pernicious influence of which her daughter-in-law was capable; allowing Caroline to be of good heart, she nevertheless could not commend her temper, her judgement, or her morals. To these admonitions, Annabella very soon added the fruits of observation, which confirmed Lady Caroline in the character regretfully given her by her mother-in-law. The great fool she made of herself over the young poet, Lord Byron, sufficed to lower Lady Caroline permanently in Annabella's estimation. But Byron himself was at least partially exempt from her disapprobating conclusion. – Annabella found him, as she calmly reported to her parents, rather interesting.

This was in spite of her determination to have nothing to do with the *lionizing* to which the young lord was subject that Season. The spectacle of young women jostling to be the object of his scornful notice was one that afforded her a good deal of amusement; but she did not allow her inward laughter to seduce her from a very firm reprehension. – There was neither dignity nor sense in these demonstrations. Of Lord Byron's genius she had no doubt – it was a well-read mind that Annabella brought to the perusal of his poetry: but she could as little approve the violent passions expressed there, as she could applaud the celebrity they had caused. When she first set eyes on him, at a morning waltz-party of Lady Caroline's, she was divided between admiration of his beauty, deprecation of his manner, and a pitying apprehension that the injudicious attention being paid him must be the means of further corrupting a nature compromised by indulgence, and debilitated by vice.

It was her settled intention not to be a worshipper at this polluted shrine. But moving in the Melbourne House set, it was inevitable that their acquaintance should ripen at least to civility. – It went further. In conversation with Lord Byron, she found a very different man from the jaded and sensual Childe Harold of popular imagination. There was a gentleness, on which the harsh cynicism was, she thought, the merest veneer. Plainly he had seen and known much, and more, perhaps, than a man of his or any age should have, for the peace of his soul; but this in itself might be the instrument of his regeneration. It had made him – like Annabella – a shrewd observer of mankind's follies and vices. Like her, he saw from a height; and if the eminence was not, as in her case, the lofty perch of piety, there was nothing to prevent its becoming so, one day, under the right influence.

Alas! how deplorably different were the influences Annabella *did* see operating upon Lord Byron, during the succeeding months. – Lady Caroline Lamb threw herself at him most shamelessly. It was plain to Annabella that Byron's true instincts disinclined him to such society: his refusal to join in the waltz, which to Annabella appeared a disgraceful exhibition, confirmed him in her eyes as a man of right principles. But Lady Caroline exerted herself so thoroughly to capture him that the result could hardly be in doubt. Annabella found herself watching the progress of an illicit connection that both parties seemed resolved upon enacting in the most public manner possible. The latest indiscretion or, better, quarrel of Lord Byron and Lady Caroline Lamb was soon the favourite subject of every drawing-room conversation – it was more amusing than the latest play – more exciting than the news from the war.

Fortunately for her peace, Annabella's regret at witnessing the entanglement of a noble nature in the toils of an adventuress, and its consequent surrender to its own baser instincts, was tempered by her resolute possession of her feelings. She was not about to be betrayed into susceptibility by a too active sympathy, nor by the consciousness that when Lord Byron was talking to her, he was a better man. – Her heart, she could confidently assert, was safe. Knowing she was in no danger of being fascinated, she was able to converse rationally with Lord Byron, in a manner that seemed to refresh him, who was so accustomed to ladies being too *impressed* for fluency, or even intelligibility. She had lately attempted some verses of her own; and in the same sensible spirit, gave them to Lady Caroline, with a request that she pass them to Lord Byron, so that she might have his candid comments on their worth. – He was highly complimentary; but to her continent satisfaction at this was added the disagreeable observation of Lady Caroline's jealousy. Her cousin-in-law reported to her that Lord Byron would willingly see more of her poems; but, with a vulgar forwardness that not even her well-attested eccentricity could excuse, went on to suggest that any hopes Annabella might be entertaining in Lord Byron's direction were rendered vain by a prior claim on Lady Caroline's part, the immoral nature of which she did not scruple to assert. – Indecency Arabella was fortified against: absurdity she could tolerate; but the two together were beyond endurance. Her valiant efforts to find her cousin-in-law anything but tiresome, she now gladly abandoned. Any unease that this wild accusation might have started was quickly overcome by Annabella's contemplation of her own motives, which she could pronounce to be as pure as ever. – As for her opinion of Lord Byron himself, which this distasteful intelligence might have forced her to revise, it was confirmed in its initial warmth by a new development.

'Byron is coming to his senses about Caro Lamb.' – Some such overheard piece of gossip was her first intimation. As it was Annabella's fixed principle never to listen to tattle, the impression these words made on her forced her to the rueful conclusion that her disinterest, when it came to Lord Byron's affairs, was less than complete. But on further reflection, she acquitted herself of all but a desire to see a man of genius live up to his promise, which such an intrigue must be preventing. Other proofs were not long in coming, of Lord Byron's deploring the connection, and at last perceiving in Lady Caroline the baneful influence that had long been plain to Annabella's undazzled eyes. His attempts at a dignified detachment from the lady's more public excesses won her silent applause: the embarrassments he was put to, by her hysterical responses, elicited her silent pity. – She felt for him; and when a visit by Lady Caroline's family to the country removed her agitating presence from town for a while, Annabella seemed to herself to share his very sighs of relief.

It appeared to her highly probable that a man in his situation, and possessing those undoubted qualities that acrimony could not hide, nor dissipation impair, must seek sooner or later to leave behind the sins of his youth, and embark upon a new and restorative course. Lady Melbourne dropt one or two hints in that direction, the full import of which her niece did not chuse to construe; though she must admit it as a truth universally acknowledged, that a single man *not* in possession of a good fortune must be in want of a wife.

4

The Fire of Love, The Love of Fire

Oh: there you are.

So you have followed me all this way. A beautiful old church, don't you think? Once an abbey. My paternal grandmother is buried here. She had the same name as me. That is always curious, is it not? Even when your name is relatively common as Caroline is. It feels as if a part of you is stolen, somehow.

No, I never knew her. I have been hearkening for her ghost, but nothing sounds. No matter. I like to sit here, in the silence.

What do I want to hear from her? Well: what one always wants from elders. Sense, wisdom, advice. To be sure, that is unfair. Next month I shall be twenty-seven – which as a girl I remember thinking as the farther reaches – the *ne plus ultra* – the Antipodes of experience and discretion. And yet look at me now.

Thin, you say? I must say you are niggardly with the compliments – and you know I have always been thin – but true, true, I know I am grown quite spectral of late. And when I look in my mirror I see eyes – nothing but eyes – and am hard put to it to find a face around them. But I am a little *better* than I was – you find this hard to credit but you should have seen me when I first came here. The air, the peace, the change is doing me good after all. The distance from London – from *him* – is a different matter: that is killing me by inches.

But then so was being near him.

Listen: that lowing cow. Sounds travel so far here – the emptiness, I suppose – and that soft air. She only wants milking I should think – and some people find the lowing of cows so blissful and comfortable a music – but I always hear it as a terrible cry of anguish – I don't know why.

Well, and how do you like Ireland? You have seen my father's place, Bessborough House, up the hill? Yes, very handsome, quite new. Whenever we come, he says he had forgot how pleasant it is, and wonders why he doesn't come oftener. If you are fond of fishing, you will find wonderful trout here. Fine views. And society, if you want it, at Waterford. Yes, we are pretty well placed – more so than my poor dear cousin Hart, who has been at *his* Irish place over at Lismore Castle – improving it for it was quite a ruin – but alas it is still horribly damp. When we visited I fetched a frog from the grounds and ceremoniously invited him into the drawing room – where I said he would feel quite at home.

So, you see, my old spirits are not quite cast down and crushed – in spite of everything.

Everything? Byron. Everything.

That's why I, we, are here. I have been hustled across the Irish Sea as from a contagion or plague – though I don't know whether I am the plague myself – or he—

Let me say first that I am not your common adulterous woman. (Indeed I suspect none are.) William is with me here – and though we have had our storms – yet that *understanding* of his splendid mind has never failed. Nor my affection. But a continuance of *intense* love beyond the first year or two of marriage is, all must agree, a rarity. And if I had strayed out of mere idleness and cupidity – a stupidity of cupidity, say – shown myself a mere Bonaparte of the boudoir greedy for conquests – then I might have incurred William's disgust as I *have not*. For what came upon me was an infliction, a visitation – truly a passion.

Now the last sufferings of Our Lord are named also the Passion in theology – and I beg you don't think me guilty of any light impiety when I mention this. If you could see into my heart you would know that is the last thing I would be guilty of – though certainly I might be and perhaps am guilty of everything else. No, I mention it because it points to passion's true nature. And ours, as human creatures. And this one thing I have learnt: we do not, cannot, know ourselves.

As this thought is terrifying beyond endurance, I try not to think of it.

No, I do very well, thank you – I must walk about a little. I am restless. My failing, I know. It was one of the things that drew me to Byron. He cannot rest content for a single second. Before that I had supposed myself unique in this – everyone else I saw seemed to me like a *tree* – that is, fixed to some spot in the earth – while I alone drifted free – drifted, floated, tumbled.

So we turned and twined in the air together. I thought.

You know, he said to me once: 'You are the only woman who has never bored me.'

I had better go back soon. They will be worried about me: Mama, Papa, William. I have been a great trouble to them lately.

Well, I will tell you what happened, in brief. First I must ask you if you tipple. Oh, pray don't be offended – I mean do you know how a tippler is? How they cannot take *one* drink or *two* – they may as well have none as that. They must go on and on, until there is – not satisfaction, for if they were the sort of people who *could* be satisfied, then they would not be tipplers – but oblivion, I suppose. Mr Pitt, even when he was Prime Minister, was one such. I remember Mr Fox telling us about his unthinkable wine bills. Well, I – no, you have me quite wrong, I do not mean I am addicted to the bottle.

I mean that Byron was, is, my tipple.

I mean I could not, cannot, ever have enough of him.

Sometimes in London, at night – when I was not with him – I would look out of my bedchamber window across the city, the lights all like pearls sewn on a dark shawl, and I would almost – I felt I could very nearly, by sheer pressure of my mind, pinpoint where he was in all that crowded expanse. That I could locate him, as my dog can sniff out a titbit hidden under a blanket.

He also said to me, later, that this affair of ours was a mere mad fancy such as we had both had a hundred times before, and would have a hundred times again. And I could not find the words to tell him how wrong he was.

He will come to know it. Of that I am still certain.

Well, what have you heard about the whole thing? Then I can tell you which parts are true and which are mere gossip. Mind, I would add that if there is anything that strikes you as particularly unlikely, that is probably true. That was the way we were. Is the way we are.

Yes: sometimes it fell out that I was not invited to certain balls or parties. Probably because of my habit of making a spectacle of myself − or of showing my feelings, which apparently comes to the same thing. And yes, if Byron was invited, I would go to the house and wait outside so that I could see him when he left. This I cannot conceive a crime. If harmful to anyone then only to myself − my waiting about in all weathers. But it was mostly mild. Once or twice a soaking − but my constitution is curiously proof against such things − perhaps because I am so *very* thin that really *very* little rain can fall on me − unless I run around in it − do you suppose that's it? Well: no harm as I say, and I came to know several coachmen pretty well, from waiting about, and have shared a nip from their flasks, and learnt all sorts of new words.

You have heard talk also of *scenes* I dare say − and if it be a *scene* to show your mortification when the man you love consumedly is deliberately paying attention to another woman before dinner − then a *scene* let it be − for my part I can see no alternative in such a situation but a brute insensibility—

I beg your pardon. I was not aware I was shouting.

Yes, we quarrelled more and more. He said I was suffocating him. I said this was because he had begun to hold me at arm's length − and that having sacrificed my reputation to him I could not endure doubts, I must have assurance that I was loved yet and not abandoned. He said that when we met I had no reputation to lose. I struck out at him and then fell at his feet. These are unhappy recollections. There are better ones – he would write me with the gentlest letter regretting the thorny pass we had come to – wondering what other course there was for us – the clean end to the affair or the slow grubby decline of mutual esteem. And then I knew there must be another – in love there are no impossibilities as I often told him—

Yes – yes, I dare say that is true, I did send him four or five letters a day, sometimes. But do you suppose I was *counting*?

Well, no one can hear.

It is true that I would get into his rooms sometimes by putting on a man's or a boy's disguise. What you must understand – and I cannot be entirely candid here – is that we had had a sort of game, once, to do with this. So it would not have been so very surprising or shocking to Byron as it appears to have been to society.

He said: 'I know very well that I was for you a *catch*, but now you have caught me, and inspected me in the net, is it not time to throw me back in the water? Is that not how it is done?'

I do not and will never care how things are done. Neither does he, of all men. But I suspect my mother-in-law had begun to spin her webs about him. I know she could do it: for she is a charming woman in many ways, and a clever woman – and cleverness he loves. She has been too subtle to reproach me much, directly. But at Melbourne House I often feel – yes, feel – her attention upon me. At Brocket once I recall standing by the open door of the ice-house and the curious sensation on my skin – like the reverse of a fireside – and that is what breathes upon me from Lady Melbourne's apartments.

I suspect, too, that it was she who roused my poor mother's anxieties. Mama began to speak to me, in her tentative way. About how unhappy I seemed to be making myself. And how when I was a girl I suffered in the same way and they had to bring a doctor in. Well – it made me weep to think of my mother troubled so by my follies – and indeed I would have put an end to them if I could. But it was not in my power – the power was all *his* – and if he had only exerted it to tell me plainly that he did not love me and never would any more, then I would have accepted. With anguish and despair to be sure – perhaps a *final* anguish. No, don't look so alarmed – I speak only of conjectural things, because the truth is he could not tell me this. Because it was not true. The fire still burned, I could tell even when he treated me with the greatest asperity – and *then* indeed I felt the flames lick hottest about us and I have known him call me hell-hag and demon and whore and then I have spat at his face and within the same moment our arms have been about each other and our hands occupied privily—

I beg you excuse me. I wanted only to give an impression of what it was like. Why it *could not* end.

But Mama – she wished me out of an embroilment so agitating, as she feared, to my spirits. And my mother-in-law thinks as always of her ambitions for her family, which I must not imperil by my conduct. Between them I believe they persuaded Byron to go out of town – while I was to be persuaded to go away with Mama and Papa and William to Ireland for a holiday. As if I were ill, and only to be restored to health by fresh air and yellow cream.

I am not ill, I said. Only dying.

'When I am with you,' he said latterly, 'I am bewitched. When I am away from you, I think you a witch.'

I was pleased.

This was in my mind when I made my challenge to him. You may hear it talked of in other terms – in an absurd style, perhaps – no matter – the grand and the absurd are I am convinced like the two points of a ring that does not quite meet. When King Lear cries that his dead daughter will never stir again – and says it five times, never never never never never – is this absurd or grand? or partaking terribly of both? Well, a challenge I intended it – in the purest old sense, as knights in the days of chivalry would stake their honour upon a challenge of combat. This was a challenge of love.

I went to his lodgings in St James's Street. I had on my page's costume and a coachman's coat over, so that I might not be recognized. Alas, the disguise must have become something notorious – for people began to gather when I was hammering at Byron's door, and a servant said he knew me – and in short there was publicity. Which I did not seek – but which, as it happened, answered to my purpose. For there was no shrugging this off – Byron's face said as much when he saw me.

He was dining with his friend Mr Hobhouse – the one who went on his Eastern travels with him. You do not know him? A curious dry long-nosed lawyerlike fellow – quite a foil to Byron's beauty. Astute, though, I am sure – sharp. He does not like *me* – but does not, I think, like any women. When he saw me – the bundle containing my clothes – my fevered state – he fetched the shopman from downstairs to be another witness that nothing discreditable was going on. He was concerned about scandal, of course. I went into the bedroom with Byron, but only so that we could talk privately. And he kept going in and out in his agitation, so they could see everything was decent. There was still a crowd outside the door, you see. Oh, yes, Byron was agitated. I could not keep from weeping as soon as I saw him, and I threw off my coat, and said I was lost unless he saved me. They were trying to part us, I said, and I was to be spirited off to Ireland, and so I had come to him like this. I had come to him, and I would not go: I would not leave that house, unless he went with me.

What did I expect him to say? Well – in truth I do not anticipate the future in that way. That is not my – well, yes, it was forcing a decision on him. But I was in such a wretched state. Imagine a watch or clock-face. Imagine the passage of a minute across it. Now suppose that for you getting to the end of that minute is an unconquerable task, like wading through eternity. Such was my mind.

Besides, Byron did rise to my challenge. The shopman – a brute – was bellowing like a bull to have me thrown out. 'Out with her – into the street with her.' That stick Hobhouse was hovering about muttering, 'Caution, caution.' But when I refused to move Byron gave me a look – it was a sort of admiration – even relief. He loathes uncertainty, you see. And here was a certainty offered. If we were to run off together – why, there would be a clean stroke instead of messy tangles and I knew, I could see in those fearsome eyes of his, that he was tempted. And then he said, holding my hands hard, 'I am yours, Caro, to do with whatever you want. All of me. You know that? But it must be all of me. If I go with you, you must be sure of what you are getting.' And then there was this smile – it was like his own challenge to me.

Sometimes I think he has the devil in him. Quite seriously.

Yes, I was afraid.

Still – I would not and could not leave him – not then – thinking I might never see him more, that my family would have it so, that his friends would see to it. Hobhouse got hold of a dress belonging to a maid. He urged me to change into it and then I could leave unrecognized without a scandal. Still I would not go – and when he became pressing – I know not how it happened but I got hold of Byron's sword which lay on the sofa and I said there would be blood spilt . . .

I meant mine. Of course I meant mine. But it was only his court sword, it would not have cut deep, it would hardly have been sharp.

I know about these things.

Byron got the sword from me at last. He is very strong in the arms. Lame men often are, I think.

Yes, I failed. I think we failed each other. But the *world* was with us – that was the trouble – Hobhouse interfering like some miserable attorney – and that shopman croaking about the reputation of his establishment – and I still believe—

Oh, I left at last. I would not go without Byron – and without a promise that I might see him again. He said, 'Oh, the promise you shall have, Caro,' and Hobhouse fetched a hackney and we got in it. Byron came part of the way with me to Hobhouse's rooms, where they wanted me to change into my own clothes and then go back to Melbourne House. Back to William, to the world. He didn't say much in the coach.

Only – I remember this – 'You have a husband. I don't imagine you would want another.'

No I don't always know what he means nor do I always know what I mean either – do you mean to say you always do?

No, that was not the end of it. He remained in London – he did not fly away from me as everyone was saying he wanted to. So I drew my own conclusions. It is as I have said – we do not know ourselves – and how much more must that apply to Lord Byron, who is so much darker and stranger than other men? Well, I confess I did try to see him, though I had promised my poor mama I would not. You know his publisher – Mr Murray, the Scots gentleman at Albemarle Street? Well, I knew Byron was often there – he would call in after his fencing-exercise at Jackson's – and so I went there one morning, just in hope of seeing him one last time – to ask his forgiveness – because I had heard he hardly went out of doors at night for fear I should come upon him at some dinner or reception and place him in difficulty, for he wanted to prevent any more hurt to my family. Well – there is a little waiting room at Mr Murray's house – you have only to open the door and slip across the hall – Mr Murray talks with his authors in the drawing room – and so I slipped in and waited till I heard Byron come.

Well, I know his footstep, of course.

No – as we are being candid, I can tell you I have never seen the foot bared. Even in – even in intimacy, he keeps it from sight.

I can tell you something else: he does the same with part of his mind.

No, he was not happy at being surprised in that way. Poor Mr Murray, who is a gentlemanlike man, hardly knew what to do. I said it was all my fault.

Everything always is my fault. I am quite happy to accept that. As I accept that I became – distracted – before we came to

Ireland – but you know there is always a reason for everything – and when I wrote him and sent a cutting of my hair, yes my private hair, the sort that is never seen in paintings or statues, which makes quite as much a nonsense of their fidelity to reality as those cherubs or is it cherubim, is that plural or singular, well, those supernatural babies fatter than any baby ever was or should be being lifted aloft by the tiniest wings – such nonsense and yet I am so often reproached for nonsense who would not countenance such an absurdity . . . Well, the hair is an Italian custom between lovers, I have heard of it, and I asked the same of him in return.

No, I did not get it.

It is very difficult to cut. I bled. But blood means love, I think. Heart's blood and blood brothers and blood relations and blood is thicker than water and so on.

Yes, you are right, hate too, your blood running cold and bad blood and what-naught, but there it's another example – like the points of a ring not quite meeting, love and hate, they are much closer to one another than to lukewarmness and liking and milky mild mediocrity which I *loathe*.

Blood, by the by, is indeed thicker than water – instance my poor mama, so perturbed and distressed as she was at my carryings-on and yet never a reproach to me: never a hard word. *That* I got from William's family at last. Oh, yes.

Not from Lady M., not this time. She is, again, far too subtle. You know of her, of course: everyone does. The *grande dame*. I often think she would have made a better Frenchwoman than English. You will be less familiar with her husband: everyone is. Lord Melbourne is not a prepossessing man. He is the colour of his favourite port and just as crusty. Well, my mama came calling at Melbourne House, to persuade me to come away to the country, and then go on to Ireland. It seems they were still afraid of what I might do – that some terrible break was in the offing. I was just coming down the stairs. I saw my mama's face all weary and reproachful and – yes – I grew angry. Even with her. I remembered Naples years ago, when she could not rest for love of a man, and I a mere child comforting her through the nights. And how pleasant it must be to be able to *manage* your affairs of the heart as she has done, neatly, quietly, *properly*...

Disloyal – terribly disloyal – I do not think this now, I only tell you what I thought then – and it was wicked of me. I am wicked. I dread to think what my punishment will be – for everything.

Where was I? Ah, on the stairs. Well, I snapped at poor Mama – saying I would not be shifted about like a lost parcel – that I would go where I chose and it might well be away from all of them – and such things – and then Lord Melbourne appeared. I remember that red face of his coming out of the drawing-room doorway below – seeming to rise on my vision like a horrid gouty sun. 'Oh, well, at least we shall be spared all this commotion – but as a matter of interest, where, madam, will you go?' he cries – I can see his bad teeth mashing away behind his purple lips – and I say, 'I shall go to Byron,' and he snorts like a pig and shouts out, 'Go and be damned. *He won't have you.*'

I have compared myself to a tippler – and just like a tippler I find there are spots of memory that are entirely lost to me – and one of those is what exactly happened next. I am assured I was extremely rude to Lord Melbourne, so much so that Mama hurried away in shock to find Lady M. who can always be relied on to take charge – and I have some vague dreamlike impression of telling Lord Melbourne, quite calmly, that one never knew what men would put up with, as for instance he had stood by that bitch he was married to even while she filled the nursery with other men's children . . . I don't know: it isn't like me, I would never – but I do remember him standing there silently opening and closing his mouth like a fish – there he has been crab and sun and pig and now fish, he makes me quite figurative – and then I was running down the stairs. I mean running: not what ladies do in pretended distress, that hasty tittuping. I went full pelt, out of the house, without so much as a hat, and Lord Melbourne was shouting to the porter, '*Stop her, stop her*,' but she, I, was not to be stopped.

Where was William? Oh, out of the way. Things like this make him tired, he says.

No, I did not go to Byron. No, it was not that I believed what Lord Melbourne had said . . . I'm sorry, where was I? No, I did not go to him because I did not wish to drag him down into these sorry depths. All I wanted was to get away from everything.

I hid in a chemist's shop for a time, knowing they might be looking for me. Then I found a broker to give me money on a ring I was wearing so that I could pay a hackney. 'Drive anywhere,' I said – and off we rattled – I felt so free even as I was so wretched – we got as far as Kensington. There is a surgeon living there – I had heard good things of his kindness – and I presented myself at his door and begged him to give me shelter a while. I told him a little tale of being a seduced creature abandoned by heartless relatives – I have I think quite a turn for fiction. He took me in. The hackney-man I sent back to London with letters of farewell – to my family, to Byron. I raised twenty guineas on another ring and secured a place on the next public coach to Portsmouth. This was resourceful, was it not?

Portsmouth – why, I was going to take the first ship out of the country, of course.

Anywhere.

And yes, to be sure, this did not happen. And do you know who my saviour was – who prevented it – and thereby preserved me for another destiny? Byron.

Mama and Lady Melbourne drove about looking for me, at first. Then they went to Byron's rooms – but he, of course, knew nothing of the matter. He promised to send word if I came there. Then came my letter of farewell by the hackney-man – and Byron somehow persuaded or bribed him to say where I was hiding at Kensington – and so came to fetch me himself. He told the surgeon I was his brother. I shall never forget his look as he shouldered his way into the room where I was hiding . . .

Angry? Oh, certainly. One hardly expected anything else. But there I was in extremity, and there he was – putting out his hand and drawing me back from the brink . . . Well, was this not proof of a regard that for all his denials went beyond – Well, I shall say no more. Only, again, that we do not always know ourselves.

It was he who made me return to London, to my family. He told me of my poor mama's mounting distress – and this could not help but have its effect – but chiefly it was because *he* was ordering me back that I went. And humbled myself to Lord and Lady M., and begged forgiveness of William, and undertook to reform. And agreed to come away to Ireland soon after. So – all would have been well.

I beg your pardon – you are surprised perhaps to see such an abandoned and hardened wretch as me crying. You suspect the crocodile perhaps. I don't blame you. I say all would have been well, but for my poor mama. Her health has always been precarious – and when she was searching for me she spat up some blood – and the next day was found on the floor of her carriage having fallen down in a seizure that deprived her of speech – and that she did not die is thanks to Heaven and none to me, who nearly, I know it, nearly killed her with my behaviour . . .

Yes, she is better, much better now, I thank you.

Byron writes to me here – wonderful gay amusing letters – though I prefer Mama not to know that.

William is very well and hearty. He says the past is like a note writ in pencil, it can always be rubbed out.

Happy? Well, I am – not unhappy, not just now. But what good is that?

Well, here is a thought for you. Now let me see if I can take you over the fences of this one. You'll agree that there are times in your life that are happier than others – yes? And so out of all those there must be one time that is the happiest – yes? – just as among some trees that are taller than others, there must be one that is tallest of all even if only by an inch – yes? Thus there must be one period of time in your whole life that is, taken all in all, the happiest, the truest, the most fulfilled, the *best*. So.

What if that time has already been and gone?

And you know it?

No, no — I'm quite well — I just fancied I heard my grandmother's ghost at last. Saying that in her day they did not think of such things.

Well for them, perhaps. Part of me does long to lace up my feelings in that narrow bodice and tread that old narrow path. But I think it is closed off to us now, whether we like it or not.

Do I think *my* best time has gone? Why — how could I go on living, if so?

LADY MELBOURNE: Lord Byron, how do you do? I am so used to seeing you disappearing upstairs, you must forgive my staring at your *near* and *frontal* approach.

BYRON: Any forgiveness, my dear Lady Melbourne, must be on your part, if you will be good enough to extend it: for I fear that I have been a great disturber of your domestic peace.

LADY MELBOURNE (*with a wave of her hand*): There is peace for now: like the English summer, one is grateful for it without expecting it to last. Besides, you only furnished the pretext. Come, sit by me: I don't bite: contrary to popular mythology, I don't even sting.

BYRON (*sitting down on the sofa beside her*): I have long sought your acquaintance; but in the circumstances . . . I hope you will believe me, and not think it a mere conventional disclaimer, when I insist that it *was* my fault. If you feel Lady Caroline deserves any blame, then I must deserve it doubly. In short — be kind to her.

LADY MELBOURNE: I am never anything else. Indeed she has a true protector in me, did she but know it. I fear the ridiculous creature does *not* see what would happen if it were not for me: but never mind. I am happy to extend forgiveness in any direction, my dear Lord Byron, because of one blessed word you have just pronounced. *Was.*

BYRON: Ah, is that it? I see. I'm glad to have provided such pleasure with a single word – commonly I must cover twenty sheets of foolscap with 'em for that effect. Curious thing is, I once pronounced it the saddest word in the language. (*After a thoughtful pause*): So you are happy that I speak of the affair as a *past* matter?

LADY MELBOURNE: As it must be.

BYRON: Well, so it is.

LADY MELBOURNE: I would be glad to *know* that it is. Are you still writing to her in Ireland?

BYRON (*half smiling*): I see I am in the presence of one from whom it is impossible to hide anything. I am alarmed.

LADY MELBOURNE: Don't be. The fact is, I have lived altogether too long in the world to be deceived. I know all the deceptions—

BYRON: Having practised 'em yourself, eh?

LADY MELBOURNE (*with a reluctant smile*): That may be. Also Caroline is writing to me, and she can never hide anything: so it is a simple deduction. Do you know what you are doing?

BYRON: I think so. Trying to keep her mind at ease – forestall any more grand gestures. I am sure she is capable of taking ship across the Irish Sea by herself, if she gets in a passion again.

LADY MELBOURNE: Perhaps. Oh, I see your reasoning: but the fact is, she must return at some time. And what will she suppose when she does? That she may pick up your love like a piece of sewing half done, and resume it?

BYRON: What a charming, homely image. I had not thought you knowing such things.

LADY MELBOURNE: I have not touched a needle since I was a girl, thank God, nor do I possess a cap, nor do I know any cures involving rhubarb and horehound. I am pleased to say I am the least homely woman in existence. You are evading my question, my dear sir.

BYRON: I always evade every question if I can. But as to *love*, there I can only invoke your rhubarb, and assure you it is not a thing I intend having any truck with, from now on. I have supped full with *those* horrors. In the end love becomes like a deadened nerve that must have the electrical plate clapped to it more and more brutally to rouse a twitch. (*Lounging back, a little uncomfortably, on the sofa.*) I should be very glad, believe me, to be freed from the responsibility of forever *feeling*.

LADY MELBOURNE (*eyeing him narrowly*): Lord Byron, may I speak frankly?

BYRON: I can already see we are going to be on that footing, my dear Lady Melbourne.

LADY MELBOURNE: I hope so. Do you intend marrying?

BYRON (*with a short laugh*): I don't know about *intend*. Is marriage not one of those things that comes to all of us – like death? Or is that another evasive answer?

LADY MELBOURNE: It is a thoroughly sensible answer, as far as it goes.

BYRON: Certainly it has occurred to me that to snatch me out of these scrapes, and to put me safely beyond the reach of imbroglio, the best thing would be a monastery or a marriage. And as I am too much the unbeliever for the first species of imprisonment . . . But all this requires decision. Even before reforming, I must make the decision to reform, and anything of that nature flattens me quite. I have gone back to bed rather than face the decision of what shirt to wear.

LADY MELBOURNE (*smiling*): Then what you need is guidance.

BYRON (*smiling also*): Oh, that is what I have always needed.

And after all Mary missed him: Mr Shelley. Their household myth became flesh in the autumn of 1812, just when Mary made her first visit home after six months in Dundee. Mr Shelley and his young wife were in London, and came to dine at Skinner Street the day after Mary's return.

But Mary was exhausted from a long, retching-rough sea voyage, and blissful bed claimed her for twenty-four hours.

'You were absolutely sleeping like the *dead*,' her stepmother informed her, with a grimace, as if Mary were performing a piece of tasteless mimicry. And meanwhile, downstairs, the Shelleys had been here to dine, and gone away again.

She was interested: not excessively. Scotland had changed her, blowing away fogs of uncertainty, unrolling new experiences with colours in the weave she had never suspected. Afterwards, she tried to remember whether there had been anything in the cramped house at Skinner Street that whispered of prophecy, when she finally came down. There was, she thought, a faint violet scent in the air that was perhaps Mrs Shelley's: several books lay open and haphazard where her father and Mr Shelley had been discussing them: in one there was a slip of scrap paper that had been painstakingly twisted so that it spiralled like a spring. With Jane away at boarding-school, there was no one in the house who would do anything so frivolous. So . . . Yet there was no anticipatory shiver, not yet.

It was Fanny who, in the intervals of pious darning and pen-mending, could not stop talking of their visitors. 'Mrs Shelley is very ladylike. But very natural. Unaffected – yet still ladylike. And very pretty – not that that counts for anything, of course.' She gave Mary a peculiar look. 'And then to see how fond and attentive he is to her – you never saw anything so delightful.'

'And Mr Shelley – I hope he is not ladylike?'

'What curious things you say. He is quite the gentleman – I suppose that is what you mean. But not fine at all – quite careless in his dress, and easy in his manner. I think his hands are especially . . . But of course it's Papa he comes to see, he has read all Papa's writings, and respects him so deeply – I would say reveres him. Though to be sure there were one or two things, political things, that they didn't agree on—'

'Dear Lord – how did Papa bear that?'

'Oh, now you're being satirical.'

But Mary wasn't. She had spoken out of sheer honest surprise. 'Mr Shelley is very tall,' Fanny went on.

'I know,' Mary said, and then at Fanny's look, 'I mean he must be.'

The narrow house above the bookshop was a little less crowded now. Charles Clairmont, her stepbrother, had gone north too, to learn the book trade in Edinburgh. Little William, sole offspring of her father and the Clairmont's unthinkable couplings, was still at home, but he had grown quieter and pleasanter. Sometimes he cried bitterly for no reason, or what his father called no reason. ('Every human action,' he would say, with dusty bewilderment, standing over the sobbing boy, 'must have a cause, direct or indirect. Do you see?') As for Jane, a crowd in herself, she came back from her school changed too. The hoyden had been suppressed altogether. Breasts and hips had done it. She was as conscious of them as someone carrying a loaded tray. She was still Jane in that she was unignorable; but variety was added to irritation, because Jane the aspiring actress was now in continual flux. She altered her voice from sentence to sentence, frowned like an Amazon then simpered like Fanny, covered every spare piece of paper with endless variations of her signature.

They shared a bedroom. When the candle was out Mary was astonished to find Jane slithering in beside her.

'What are you doing?'

'Bundling up. It's what we do at school. We stroke each other's hair and talk and drift off to sleep.' Jane giggled. 'And there's one girl who is *giving* herself to the cook's brother every day behind the wash-house and it makes her so amorous that at night in her sleep she starts pawing you like *this*.'

'Well, get off – you're not at school now.'

Jane sighed and slid away. 'Please yourself.' Back in her own bed she was asleep within minutes, unlike Mary.

Mr Coleridge was in London, and having a rare encounter with success. He had written a play called *Remorse*, and it was put on at Drury Lane. Mary's father took them all to the first night. The story took place in Spain at the time of the Inquisition and palpitated with vengeance and violence, but there were chunks of

227

philosophy too, which marked it as definitely Mr Coleridge's work, and which the actors got through briskly while everyone looked at the gorgeous scenery. In the third act there was a scene of sorcery: incantations moaned and apparitions flickered: Fanny covered her eyes. Mary was absorbed, not so much in the play as in the fact that it had all come from the brain of one man. Creation: there was the true sorcery. The vast house was nearly full, and no one booed or laughed at the solemn parts: this was success indeed. When the curtain came down and the applause roared up Mary's father blinked around in surprise: envy, goblin-like, overtook his face for a moment before he recollected himself and became the benign sage again. Nearby Mary overheard a man say, 'He certainly should feel *remorse* for having written it,' and his companion, in a groaning chuckle, 'He cannot be half as sorry as I feel,' but she darted them a look – which, she found, had a noticeable effect. She was indignant for genius; and was horrified, soon after, to think that those men might have thought she was flirting.

In the theatre Jane was transfixed: coming out, silent and sorrowful. 'I am exiled from paradise,' she said, in one of her new voices. Later, she suddenly turned termagant. She railed at her mother. ' "Jane" – why did you call me that? Why did you degrade me with this damned name – dullest of damned stupid names, damn it, damn it—'

'This language,' clucked the Clairmont, who in matrimonial rows could outswear a coal-heaver.

'Why, why?'

'You know, my dear, it is my own middle name – that is why I—'

'As if I care a fart for that. You have *doomed* me with such a name. Even Mary is better.'

Later, after a quart of mutual tears, Jane sat with her arms tight round her mother's waist and her head on her shoulder, murmuring that she wished no other name in the world. The Clairmont beamed sentiment. 'Natural,' she mouthed to Mary and her father, sitting on the other side of the fireplace with two feet of empty settle between them, yawning as conspicuously as the ocean floor without the ocean.

Still, Godwin was cautiously pleased with the new Mary. 'I see improvement,' he informed her. 'You are stouter in health, I think – but not just that. There was a tendency, you'll be the first to acknowledge, my dear, to wilfulness and stubbornness. It does not now show itself. Yes, I see improvement.' She was silent: he toyed awkwardly with his spectacles. What she could not express, because they were beyond expression, was the deep-burning thrill she still got from such words, and the anxiety that went with it. For though it was bliss to be told by him that she was improving, she knew that the basis of her father's philosophy was *perfectibility*. By striving upwards, man could become perfect. And daughters. But how much further was there to go? Meanwhile Godwin at last fumbled his spectacles into his pocket and went away, discouraged by her silence.

They joined the congratulatory swarm converging on Mr Coleridge's lodgings in Berners Street. Here Mr Coleridge, chubby, sweating, somewhat bruised-looking like an overripe fruit, laughed and nodded and wagged his round head in modesty and talked, talked. Usually he had a circle of listeners. But even when he did not he made an open-handed appealing gesture to his right, inviting agreement from no one. He looked delighted and anguished, as if secretly wishing everyone were gone. The room smelt of books and brandy.

'A musical drama on the fall of man. That is what I contemplate next. What think you?' His owlish lost eyes came to rest on Mary. 'Miss Godwin – grown absurdly fair. Adam and Eve. What think you?'

'I don't think they would allow it.'

'Blasphemy to stage scripture? And yet the medieval guild presented pageant-plays based on Bible stories, and theirs was a true age of faith—'

'But Adam and Eve would wear no clothes,' Mary said, 'and I

don't think the Drury Lane committee would be happy with that, Mr Coleridge.'

'Dismal practicalities. You are right. How old are you now? Fifteen – I can hardly believe it. I saw you as a baby. It seems like yesterday. This is, of course, a commonplace uttered by every grandma from her chimney corner – but the difference is for me it is *true*. I do not know where my life has gone.' He glanced around the room, as if talking of his hat. 'And do you still say your prayers?'

'Not regularly.'

'That means not at all. You are rebelling. Oh, I was the same once. A curse on all your systems and so on.' Coleridge took her hand, considering it as if it were some cunning puzzle. 'You will find in the end, my dear friend, that there is nothing more oppressive than freedom. Shall you always come and see me? When you are grown and so on?'

'Of course, if I can. Why not?'

'Oh . . .' He whispered a laugh. 'I am taking out insurance against the time when nobody does.'

Back at Skinner Street, the Clairmont sighed fatly. 'Dear Coleridge! I am heartily glad for him. He deserves some success at last. The piece is no *Barnwell*, but it will stand. I wonder how much he will make from it?'

'He mentioned a figure of five hundred pounds,' Godwin said absently, peering into a volume of Epictetus.

'Good God.' The row, as Mary thought it would, came to the boil about an hour and a half later. Epictetus went out of the window. Then her stepmother went out of the door. Unluckily she came back.

Less crowded, the house, but no less crowding to the mind. In Scotland, Mary had learnt a mystic lesson from wide silver waters, hills crowned with a cold chaplet of sunlight, spaces and stones. In Dundee she had seen whaling-ships come reeking into the harbour from polar expeditions with their timbers gouged by ice ancient and thick as the bones of gods. The world had not just become bigger – and for Mary it had always seemed intimidatingly, unnecessarily big – it had become charged with new meaning. It was the locus of a million destinies and destinations. She had met people who thought and believed nothing that was thought and believed at Skinner Street. She had made friends who liked her not simply because of her parentage. She had impressed at least one young man to admiration – which, while it was nothing in itself (and neither was he), posed her a startling new question.

Most of all she stood at a new angle to truth. The family and community she had lived with in Scotland were in some ways dour, pious, staid. But they were true to themselves under that iron-bright sky. They did not live a lie. And that was what Mary felt secretly, shamefully, at Skinner Street, where Radical philosophy rubbed alongside unabashed cadging, and the Clairmont bragged of her distinguished connections while emptying the cash-box (which did not take much emptying) on the shop counter.

Which was, by the way, Mary's destiny.

'You may as well familiarize yourself with these things,' the Clairmont said, showing her the day-books and ledgers.

'But I'm going back to Scotland in the spring.'

'Yes – but not for ever.'

And Mr Shelley had gone back to Wales, where he was trying out a sort of rural commune, without calling again. Mary doubted now that she would ever meet him. And sitting behind the bookshop counter, on a high stool made shiny and treacherous by the rubbings of her stepmother's sandbag behind, she imagined herself still here thirty years from now, saying, like Coleridge: I do not know where my life has gone.

Winter 1813: Gossip of the Season, or Town Tattle
Mr Brummell, *otherwise the* **Beau**, *continues to lose such quantities at the* **gaming-tables**, *that we have heard it suggested he may soon be able to exhibit his famous deportment only on a* **Sunday**, *viz., when the* **duns**

*may not take him; and a whisper that he may be falling out of favour with the **Prince Regent** likewise suggests that his reign as the imperator of fashion may be soon at an end . . .*

*We observe that many of our home-grown **Radicals** (or **Francophiles**) are become curiously silent since the late reverses in **Russia** of the supposedly 'invincible' **Bonaparte** (we have never accorded the Corsican adventurer his upstart 'title' of **Napoleon**) and are less inclined to hold forth on the merits of their **retreating** hero. At this rate we do not despair of these drawing-room renegadoes turning patriot at last, and finding a good word to say about Viscount **Wellington** . . .*

*We hear that my lord **Byron** contemplates a return to town, after spending Christmas in the company (we had almost outstepp'd discretion and writ **the arms**) of **Lady Oxford** at her seat at Eywood. The **friendship** betwixt the young poet and the lady, whose undeniable charms are nearer to their **autumnal** than their **vernal** equinox, has been of some months continuance, and seems to have been looked upon with his usual complaisance by **Lord Oxford**; whose given name of **Harley** occasioned that lively jest on the parenthood of Lady Oxford's five children, viz., that they might well be called the **Harleian Miscellany**, on account of having the same number of **fathers**: a libel from which we firmly dissociate ourselves. We do not presume to suggest that this latest intimacy of Lord Byron's has run its course; but we can only draw comparisons from experience, and in this regard, the situation of **Lady Caroline Lamb** is surely instructive. The days when those names were linked are no more – a conclusion to which Lady Caroline herself has lent weight, by an extraordinary **performance** observed at **Brocket Hall**, country seat of the **Melbournes**. We hear that Lady Caroline was sequestered there at the behest of her husband **William Lamb's** family – who are accustomed now publicly to refer to her, with a callousness we cannot but reprove, as the **mad skeleton** – in hopes of an improvement in her unhappy temper. But it came to Lady Caroline's ears that her erstwhile **admirer** Lord Byron had made, in October, a **proposal of marriage** to a young lady – none other than the arithmetical heiress **Miss Milbanke**, niece to Lady Melbourne! We hear that this proposal was not a successful one, though the matter was resolved amicably upon* *both sides; but it appears that the mere proposal struck the mind of Lady Caroline as an outrageous infidelity. Accordingly she mounted at Brocket a* **ceremony***, which in its singularity exceeds even those freaks for which the lady has become notorious. Assembling the letters and gifts she had received from the noble poet, as well as his portrait, she had a stupendous* **bonfire** *laid in the grounds at Brocket, atop which was placed a straw* **effigy** *of her fickle inamorata; and while a set of little maidens from the adjoining village, clad in white dresses made for the occasion, danced in a ring about the outlandish pyre, Lady Caroline had a page read out an* **address in verse** *she had composed for the occasion. We are informed that the style of the composition was not such as to make Lord Byron look to his laurels as a poet, but that for force of sentiment it was scarcely less remarkable than the accompanying* **ritual***, in which his lordship's letters &c. were consigned one by one to the flames, with many expressions of bitterness and execration from Lady Caroline. But lest Lord Byron be heartened by this account, and conclude that her ladyship's interest in him is now at an end, we feel it fair to mention a rumour that the letters were only* **copies** *. . .*

5

Kissing the Mirror

'Now whatever you do,' George said heavily, handing her into the *Elegant* at the Bushel Inn, 'don't worry yourself about me.'

'I won't, George,' Augusta promised.

And, to her own surprise, she found, as the coach swung out of Newmarket, that she was not worrying about him. How would he manage, who would soothe and cosset him when he had his headaches, would he drink too much brandy . . .? One by one the rolling wheels erased them. Leaving her children had been a great wrench: though they had an excellent nurse there was still a feeling at her heart like the socket left by a pulled tooth. But most of all, overwhelmingly, Augusta felt excited.

Opposite her sat a middle-aged clergyman with a long, hard, keen face. Legs crossed, book unopened in his lap, he wagged one well-shod foot and watched the landscape critically. He wore his clerical black as if it were this season's fashion.

'You go all the way to London, ma'am?'

'Oh, yes.' Excitement even overcame her usual reserve. 'I dare say we shall be there before we know it. The coaches go so swift nowadays, they say. It's so long since I travelled anywhere like this, it all seems quite new and thrilling to me.'

The clergyman produced the efficient smile of a man who considers himself good with women. 'You have been a dweller in the country, I take it. Far from the tents of wickedness.'

'Since my marriage, yes. And then there was the bringing up of my babies. So I have been quite out of circulation for some

while. I knew Town pretty well when I was younger – but I dare
say that's all changed too.'

'Family there?'

Oddly enough, she was about to say no, all her close kin were
dead – but what was she thinking? 'Yes,' she said, 'yes, that's who
I'm going to see. My brother – half-brother rather.' And then,
even more untypically, she could not resist it. 'You may know his
name – he is Lord Byron.'

The clergyman smiled thinly. 'Oh, ma'am, now you are
making a game of me.' He opened his book.

'Indeed, sir, I am not . . .' Oh, well. She settled herself to
watch the countryside. East Anglia under a high June sun:
peaceful, sky-domed, awash with light like a Dutch master. A pity
about the jingling troops of soldiers on the roads, the sullen
labour-gang gathered around the overseer's cart, but that was the
times, she thought unhappily, the times . . . Well, *she* knew,
though she was not in the position of those poor wretches. She
knew, at least, what it was to tremble when a tradesman sent in
another bill at Six Mile Bottom: to leave it unopened by her
breakfast-plate while she ate, and then while she saw to the
children, and then while she supervised the kitchen, until at last
she must sit down and with a deep breath open it. (George was
hopeless about such things: they made him ill.) Making ends
meet: she thought she had mastered the tricky operation, but this
year it had become a Herculean task, a desperate tugging together
of unyielding ropes that threatened to pull her apart instead . . .

And so she had written to Byron asking for help.

A huge decision – and hers, though George had a way of
conceding all decisions to her, gracefully like a man opening the
door for you. As the creditors had become more pressing, George
had begun mentioning Byron more, observing how well her
brother must be doing for himself, surely . . . But it was Augusta
who had made the necessary mental leap – for her a strenuous
and painful one. For it meant throwing a new bleak light on her
brother, on that beautiful picture that had always hung in the

quiet withdrawing room of her mind. Also there was the memory of when she had refused to help him. It was all most unpleasant.

Yet his reply, back in the spring, had been genial. He had spoken regretfully of their never seeing each other, ruefully of his various love-affairs, which she had probably followed through the scandal-sheets – and shamefacedly of his own financial embarrassment. It was all to do with the long-dreaded, long-delayed sale of Newstead Abbey, which had run into various difficulties and left him high and dry just when he expected to be flush: but as soon as he *was* in a position . . .

'All very well,' said George gloomily. 'But what about those scribblings of his? They must bring in a pretty penny.'

'He doesn't take money for his poetry. It's the gentlemanly thing.'

'Oh.' George studied his wine. 'God, I feel depressed.'

Then little Augusta fell sick, again, and the doctor at New-market sent a curt note in reply to their summons, recommending a nearby apothecary. It was because of his unpaid fees. George raged. Little Augusta screamed. The apothecary fumbled, wiped his dewdropped nose, breathed gin. And Augusta decided.

At first she wrote a letter. But letters, as the pile of unpaid bills on the same desk testified, were ignorable. She tore the letter up and told George she thought she should go and see Byron in person.

'Well, old girl, I see what you mean. It's been a long time since you saw him, and he is your only close relative after all. A shame if these things are allowed to drop away, I always think. Yes, I er . . . Where shall you stay?'

She had plenty of acquaintance in London; and the family lawyer had extended an open invitation to his house in Bloomsbury Square. Packing, she sighed over her frocks. Her brother moved in the highest circle of fashion: here was his dowd of a sister. But, but: deep down she didn't care, deep down she was elated to be going. (And to be going *away* from George and Six Mile Bottom and family and responsibility? Was it secretly so?

What did that say about her?) She considered these questions, in bed sleepless the night before leaving, and now again in this fast coach aimed at the south horizon; but only as she might have considered a broadsheet thrust into her hand by a hawker. For, after all, it was done.

Those three words: Augusta always finds comfort in them.

The clergyman, softening, finger in his book: 'This heath, ma'am, saw its share of highwaymen in years past. But you needn't fear – those rogues are long gone. The only robbery we need fear now is from turnpike-keepers and ostlers with their ever-open hands.' He snuffled in enjoyment of his own humour.

'Were there ever highwaywomen, I wonder?'

'One hears tales. But, of course, the whole subject is obscured by legend. Dick Turpin was in fact a mere brute of a housebreaker.'

'What a pity. But Claude Duval – surely he was a true gentleman.'

'You are romantic, ma'am: it is charming,' he said, with a correct little bow. 'Your husband does not accompany you to Town?'

'No. Colonel Leigh has so much business on hand at his stables, he cannot quit the country just now.'

'Ah, Colonel Leigh! His name is known to me, of course.' The scandal with the Prince, she thought, but his face gave nothing away. 'Tell me, what does the Colonel think of the war news? Shall Wellington cross the Pyrenees? He may be doing so now, of course. A pity the other powers of Europe have revealed themselves so craven. It has taken Britons to show how to deal with Bonaparte.' He waved a hand in apology for fretting her female mind with such weighty matters.

'My husband was in the Peninsula four years ago – in the retreat to Corunna. There were no rejoicings then. So I should not blame him if he felt a little bitter now that we are all cock-a-hoop for victories: not that he does.'

'Dear, dear. A sad business. Still, I hope these things will not foster the unpatriotic and sceptical spirit one sees growing in certain quarters.' The clergyman looked her over as if quickly scanning a page of dubious theology. 'I supposed you jesting, Mrs Leigh, about your consanguinity with Lord Byron – and yet now I wonder – can it be so?'

'I wonder at it myself, since his fame has grown so great,' Augusta said, in her agreeable way. 'But it is indeed so, sir. Lord Byron and I share a father – the late Captain Jack Byron.' She laughed. 'Do you mind?'

'I could not ask for a more delightful travelling companion,' the clergyman said smoothly, promptly, 'and I raise the matter only in connection with what I was just saying. Lord Byron's pronouncements – forgive me – cannot be heard with quietude by any lover of his country, of law and order, of public morality. His speeches to the Lords, ma'am – such inflammatory demagogical stuff, and on behalf of a set of lawless incendiaries, machine-breakers—'

'I don't pretend to understand these things,' said Augusta the peacemaker, 'but I'm sure my brother has his reasons for all he says and does.'

'No doubt, but are they the right reasons? Here is a man who has the public ear, to a degree seldom known before – and what use does he make of it but to incite mischief and rebellion?'

'My brother is a very singular man,' Augusta said, still calm, smiling. 'But you know, sir, you are hardly likely to convert me against him during the course of this journey.'

He sniffed and reopened his book. 'Of course I would not presume.'

Excitement persisted in her until the evening brought the glow of brick-kilns, signalling the approach to London: then apprehension stirred and prickled. For her companion – chin drooping on chest now, lips pursed as if he dreamed of political arguments – was in a way right: Byron was a public figure, not the untried young man she had known and laughed with in obscure drawing-room corners. What if he had gone beyond her somehow? What if he looked at her (her imagination sketched a yearning beauty on each arm) and looked and said at last, flatly, dismissively, finally, 'Oh,' which she could understand if he did, but what if . . . ? What if . . . ? The words, the thought, pursued her from the coach-inn at Holborn to Bloomsbury Square. Her hosts were used to Augusta's habitual quietness, else they might have wondered what was on her mind. She wrote him a note that evening, and her hand shook.

After the country, night-time London kept her awake: not so much the noises as the spoiling of quiet, like a scribble on a white wall. But she did sleep, and in the morning she found she had undergone a change. She greeted the racket of the streets with pleasure.

It's wonderful, she thought, looking out at the square. A milk-seller with her yoked pails, an ostler leading mews-dulled horses out to exercise, seedy young fellows coming home from an all-night drunk, hurriers, strollers. And, blessedly, she knew none of them.

And they don't know me, she thought, dressing with care. The mirror in her room was superbly clear compared with her own, foxed and fly-blown, at home. She examined the person in it, trying to be dispassionate. Thirty years old, Augusta thought: thirty years gone. Perhaps we should always say that instead of 'old'. How gone are you? I'm thirty years gone. The face in the mirror smiled. I must tell that one to Byron, she thought, they both thought. Interesting: there had been gloom, amusement, anticipation, and yet the face in the mirror had revealed virtually nothing. Quite reassuring. Also the mirror, which might have been pitiless, was not so bad: *she* was not so bad, thirty and a mother three times over, but still . . .

Attractive. Which didn't matter, of course. But it did matter. She had forgotten.

'That's the Byron in you, you know,' her brother said, after commending her looks.

'Now I know why you are happy to see me,' Augusta said. 'When you compliment me, you can be sure of commending yourself also.'

'You have it.' He laughed.

He had called at one, and they were left alone. The sun-filled drawing room with its dance of motes reminded her of their first meeting – how long ago? Time collapsed, fell away.

'It isn't that, though, Gus,' he said, keeping hold of her hand. 'Lord, no, lawks-a-mussy, no!'

All her anxiety fell away too – everything: she could not believe she had ever feared this reunion.

' "Lawks-a-mussy". What a word.'

'Words. Comes from "Lord-have-mercy". Did I tell you I'd turned into a pedant?'

'I'm disappointed. I thought you spent all your time being scandalous.'

'A mere front. Once behind closed doors I get out my hidden teapot and grammar-book – I don slippers – I riot in subjunctives – dreading the moment when I must be called back to claret and love-making, and pretending to like them. Did you ever hear anyone really say "lawks-a-mussy"?'

'There's an old lady in our village who says it all the time. Isn't it a curious thing about old ladies – they always dress and talk the same. Old ladies now are just like the old ladies I knew when I was a child, and yet *then* these new old ladies weren't old ladies at all. So at some point something must happen to you to turn you into one – perhaps overnight – what do you think?'

'To put it to the proof, you would have to sequester a lady of a certain age – imprison her, keep her under glass – under observation at least. You would have to watch in relays. And then – how typical – you just drop off to sleep for a few moments from the sheer boredom of watching a middle-aged matron lie abed and then, *bang*, you wake and it's happened, and you missed it – she's turned, she's turned—'

No, there was no need for fear, there was no strangeness or awkwardness and they were laughing like hyenas again just as if . . . Of course, there were changes. Look at her brother: a man; no longer that unfinished quality, that flicker like a lamp new-lit and burning sulkily. She was proud of him, proud to have his attention concentrated upon her, knowing how many people longed for it. But there was something else, and the deception of the mirror helped her to see it. Byron still shared with her that peculiar quality some called shyness. It was thus: if she had walked into a room, and everyone present had turned their heads and said, 'Go away,' she would have said, 'Yes, certainly,' and done so, without a second thought, sans surprise: because in her heart's core it was what she expected.

'Now, tell me what's fetched you off that damnable heath in Suffolk or wherever it is. Are you—'

'Cambridgeshire.'

'So, are you well? Maritally harmonious? You and George have been busily increasing the population of Cambridgeshire, so I assume—'

'Or is it Suffolk? I am not quite sure.'

'Dear Goose, don't you know where you live?'

'Oh, that's a small matter. George sends his best regards, by the by.'

'No, he doesn't. But I thank *you* for the thought. Is he still out of favour with the Prince?'

'Oh, God, I wish he were not. Byron, I'm so ashamed – but that's why I had to see you. We're so deep in trouble. I was half expecting the bailiffs to be in before I came away. If there were anywhere else to turn—'

'Hush, now you've insulted me. If there were anywhere else to turn, I should hope you'd still turn to *me* – even if we had a millionaire great-uncle half gone in his wits and in the habit of handing out hundred-pound notes. Oh, isn't that a nice picture, by the by? It's what I've always said, Gus. You and I are the only true family each other has, or have – which is it?'

'So much for the grammar-book. But – I do feel dreadful. Coming here to ask you . . .'

'Feel as dreadful as you like, if that's *all* you came for. But confess, ain't you delighted just to set eyes on your shocking scapegrace of a brother, hey, hey?'

'Quite moderately delighted. As a matter of interest, how shocking are you? I'm a married woman and a mother and so beyond corruption, but I do wonder, you know—'

'As a matter of interest. Well, my dear Gus, I'm not shocking at all. I'm merely human, unfortunately.'

'I can see I'm going to have to reproach you for your irreligion again.'

'Oh, I don't say a word against the Almighty – only if we *were* created in his image, it's not a flattering portrait. This may sound hard on the human species, but don't forget I've studied one specimen in detail–' he tapped his breast '–and the conclusions are not hopeful. Look here, I don't know when I can advance you some money, but as soon as I get some, it's yours. Or George's. He won't mind taking it, I suppose?'

'George doesn't concern himself very much with bills and things,' she said blandly. 'So I'm sure there would be no – fuss.'

There were several sorts of ice underfoot here, but by mutual lightness they got across it.

'I don't blame him – it's enough to curdle your brains, all the complications we've had over Newstead. All I can say is that it will be sold, eventually, and as soon as I can raise a thousand on the strength of it – well, will that keep the bailiffs out?'

Every lungful of breath that she had taken in since arriving in London yesterday seemed to gasp out of her. 'Yes,' she said, 'oh, thank you – oh dear—'

'Well, I don't know,' he said chuckling, 'if this is what happens when I say yes, I dread to imagine saying no.' His hand came up and brushed, very gently, the tears from under her eyes.

'I'm so relieved – and glad and sad,' Augusta said. 'Sad that Newstead has to go. I wish I'd seen it.'

'You may yet. You never know what may happen.'

True: rather than a conventional figure, with him those words seemed a declaration of vast possibility.

'Glad and sad,' he said. 'How about bad and mad?'

'I'm not those, I hope. It's funny that they all rhyme, isn't it? All very basic things in life—'

'And *had*.'

'My dear brother, you mustn't be indecent.'

'Why, don't you like it?'

'It's not that, it's just that I've been living in the country for years, and so I probably won't understand it when you are. Oh, Byron, I haven't thanked you for your *Childe Harold* – glad and sad – that's how it makes me feel, and a hundred things besides—'

'Ah, no, stop, I beg you, Gus,' he said, covering his ears, 'this is just what I get from drawing-room harpies and just what I don't want from you.'

'You shall get it anyway. And I want a copy of your new one – what's it called?'

'*The Giaour.* No, I'm not sure that's how you pronounce it. No one is, that's why I titled it so – one sure way of getting it talked about. Come with me to a party tonight.'

'Me? Why?'

'Because you're the one person in London I want to go with. You get my shoulders down.'

'Is that one of these indecencies I don't understand?'

'Go along with you. I'm relaxed – for the first time in *years*, I think. You know, when you're tense and high-strung – without knowing it your shoulders go up round your ears – well, yours don't, perhaps, because you have this most beautiful calm – but mine do and sometimes I cannot get them down – brandy don't achieve it nor a bout at Jackson's nor a sweat nor a purge but here *you* are, and look–' he grasped her hand, and placed it on his shoulder '–down.'

'But I haven't been in society for so long. And won't people stare at me because I'm with you?'

'No – they'll stare at me because I'm with you. Dear Goose, don't you know you'll set every town miss in the shade, like a set of little weeds next a – a gladiolus?'

'No. But if you say so . . .' She found her hand was still on his shoulder, and took it away. 'Oh, Byron,' she suddenly shrieked, 'a gladiolus! What a thing!'

'Any damn flower you like then,' he snarled, laughing. 'Am I a botanist? If you want grubbing in hedgerows you must go to old Turdsworth. Now, he'll make you more sad than glad I warrant. Do you know the old hypocrite has pocketed a sinecure from the government? In return, no doubt, he'll turn out reams of toadying verses saying up with the Tories and down with the people. Thankfully, as before, no one will read 'em. There, I've done now. Yes, the party. Evening affair. Lady Davy's. I'll call for you before ten. You know Sir Humphrey Davy? One of these Royal Institution fellows, electric-chemico-scientifico sorcerers – started out as a humble prentice. Now isn't that piquant enough to tempt you? And we may see Madame de Staël too. The great lioness.' A mock roar. 'But don't be feared of her.'

'I won't,' Augusta said, realizing that her own shoulders were, at long last (how long had it been?) down. 'After all, I have the great lion to protect me.'

Augusta's stay in London: she keeps thinking, this cannot be right.

Why? Because she came to see her brother, and ask for his help, and perhaps to look up a few old acquaintances, and then quietly and gratefully to return to her domestic life in Cambridgeshire (or Suffolk). And now instead of thinking of her children all the time she is temporarily forgetting them; enjoying herself; actually parading about society, accumulating introductions, coming home in the small hours.

And fitting in very well. To be sure, when she was younger she welcomed the King and Queen into her grandmother's drawing room. But this is different: these people are not solid and earthbound, they sparkle across her like shooting stars. Here is Madame de Staël – my absolute opposite, thinks Augusta wonderingly. Big-armed Germaine de Staël, turbaned and toothy, has been all over Europe and made herself famous in every corner of it. In a gallimaufry of languages she says just what she thinks, loudly, which is why Napoleon kicked her out of France. She has lovers. She talks over the top of everyone and gestures with large ink-stained hands. She knows politics and philosophy. She has written vastly and controversially. There is so much of her in every way and in comparison, Augusta thinks, there is nothing to me. And yet, here is Madame de Staël addressing Augusta familiarly at Lady Davy's reception, where the whole company are hovering like eager bees about this great blowsy flower of celebrity.

'This brother of yours–' jab of grubby thumb at grinning Byron who has been teasing her '–he loves to torment. Does he treat you so? Or is it only me because I am up on a height and he knocks me down?'

'He loves to torment,' Augusta says. 'But if you do not respond, Madame, he soon gives it up.'

'Curious. It is a way of controlling or directing the other person's feelings. Make them angry or sad, then you know what they are feeling, you need not fear it as unknown. This is so, Lord Byron, is it not?'

'There, my point exactly, Madame. Impressionable young girls will pick up your works, and become trained to this sort of thing – hardly able to stir for cogitating – forever trying to plumb the depths of the mind. Very dangerous.'

'What journey could be more exciting than to the depths of the mind?'

'Or more terrifying,' Byron says, with a cold smile. 'Thank God we can't do it.'

'What do you think, Mrs Leigh? Has the mind secrets we cannot touch?'

Augusta says, after a moment, 'I don't know – because I can

only think about the question with my mind. Which *is* the question. So it's rather like trying to paint the handle of a brush with the brush.'

'Bravo, Gus,' Byron says delightedly.

'You are indeed a pair,' says Madame de Staël, looking from one to the other and back again, intently, as if there is some fine translucent thread joining them that she can only just make out.

Of course it is Byron everyone wants to meet, and it is his glory she is sharing. But then that seems quite right, because she is a Byron too. Often they will find themselves thinking the same unspoken thought: they both know when to leave a party without either asking: she divines his headaches, he soothsays her moods. So, no feeling of picking up crumbs of regard. If anyone should be at his side through his triumphal progress, it is Augusta.

And yet it cannot be right because she is so—

'Ordinary?' Byron says. 'What the devil put that in your head? It shows you're not, from the fact that you think so. The truly ordinary people are the ones who are always flaunting their personalities at you because they *think* they're extraordinary.'

'Well, I've never done much, I'm afraid,' Augusta says. They are walking in Hyde Park. Already, instinctively, she has the habit of looking at the ground ahead, to make sure there are no awkward places for his lameness – almost as if lame herself. 'No tales to tell.'

'That's because you've got on with life instead of acting it out. You know? Some people have to carry a mirror and watch themselves living to feel they're alive at all.'

'Is that—' She strikes an unexpected shyness. 'Is that the way Lady Caroline Lamb is?'

'Actually I was describing myself,' he says, with what she thinks of as his vinegar smile – a kind of inverted pout. 'As for Caro, what can I tell you? You've probably heard a hundred rumours. We were both to blame. All I can say is that the essence of a firework is that it doesn't last, and that's what Caro wouldn't understand. How's George? Still riding, shooting, racing, all that?'

'Yes,' Augusta says, a little starchy. 'He is very well, and much occupied with his usual pursuits, which he enjoys, so that makes me happy too.'

Byron to her shock seizes her hand and kisses it. 'There – exactly what I hoped you'd say – there's you, Gus, God love you – I do believe you're the only female I know who hasn't set out to change her male from the moment she hooked him. With Caro you must be always jumping through the flaming hoop even when you want to do nothing more tremendous than lie and stare at the wall. Then there was Lady Oxford – you heard about my little sojourn at Eywood? Very comfortable in a leafy, bowery, breakfast-in-bed sort of way. Only she had her plans for me as well. She's always been a politicking woman, you see, and I was to be her agent and lead us to a glorious reform and all the rest of it.'

'Well, I've heard some of your pronouncements, Byron, and really you seem to me the most shocking Radical.'

'Ah, but not the right sort of one. You have to be a party man, and that I can never be. Not unless everyone can form a party of his own. Oh, if we can bury the Tories and all their works I'll gladly take a turn with the shovel, but damn your committees. Besides, I keep thinking of leaving England again.'

'Why? But I know why. You're like a boy with the fidgets. You know, Byron, I think I must be a most peculiar woman. I mean these ladies – like Lady Caroline and so on – they are so free, aren't they?'

'I'm groping for a gallant answer.'

'They are, though. Freedom is what matters to them. Like you, which is why you're never contented. And I don't particularly want to be free at all.'

'Hm. What do you want to be instead? Imprisoned?'

She thinks. 'Warm. Yes, warm – and I do mean physically because I can't bear the winter and I must have a great fire. But just warm, generally.' She shrugs. 'I don't know any better words to describe it. You would, probably.'

'Having the words doesn't always help,' he says, vinegary again. 'Well, Gus, you'll have to come with me, that's all there is to it. When I go abroad again. The Mediterranean – the Levant – you'll feel no cold there. The reliability of the sun there is quite strange to the English mind – almost sinister – you wake up in the morning and there it is. No sniffing and peeping and consulting your corns. When shall we go?'

'Oh, Byron. You're talking as if I were free. Not that it doesn't sound delightful—'

'Freedom is a thing you make,' he says, with sudden vehemence. 'You make it by what you do. That's about the only thing that is left us in this world.'

'Left us by whom? Are you tilting at the Almighty again?'

'Yes, him – His Doubtfulness, call him – but not just that, everything – fathers and mothers and ancestors, blood and bone and damnable dead earth – everything.' He pauses, pale, then laughs metallically as if he has been whispered a bad joke by some hovering sprite.

Gently she says, or suggests: 'You can't set yourself against everything.'

'I don't,' he says, gathering her arm closer to his. 'You are my exception.'

Almack's. Club of clubs. They call it the Seventh Heaven of the Fashionable World. Byron remarks that it must certainly be near heaven, for the air there is so thin he starts yawning as soon as he goes in. And the place does have the dullness of absolute exclusivity. Its hundred-foot ballroom echoes like a bath-house, the refreshments are tepid cordials and insipid claret-cup, the dress codes so inflexible that the dancers plodding their stately polonaises look like penitents in uniform. Entrance to this weekly purgatory is strictly by ticket, procurable only from the half-dozen 'patronesses', society ladies who run the stultifying show. Byron's ripening friendship with Lady Melbourne gives him the password for the Gorgon gang. He wants to take Augusta to

Almack's because it is the grandest thing that you can do for a young woman in Town, and he is proud of her: proud with her. Happy with her, indeed: they need not fear the heaviness of an evening at Almack's because they bring their own pleasure with them, in each other.

A young woman – well, Augusta supposes she is not, at thirty, but she feels it this summer. And a married woman, whereas Almack's is the traditional venue for the coming-out: here you tremble on the precipice of maidenhood, looking at the sleek male sharks circling below. And yet again she feels all new-made, the tired skin of the matron sloughed off, her nerves braced with a sense of commencement. Can this, too, be right?

'Byron, who is that woman staring at you?'

He turns: their heads are so close together, as they perch on one of the Seventh Heaven's incomparably uncomfortable sofas, that she feels his hair brush her cheek.

'I've no idea. She looks as if she's putting a curse on me.'

'Not one of your lovers?'

'God, no. Truth to tell, Gus, I'm finished with all that. I forswear and abjure carnal connection from this day forth.'

'I'm very glad to hear of it. Does this mean you are beginning a thorough reform of all your vices?'

'Reform, no – it's just the surest way of avoiding disappointment. There – I've given her a terrible glare – off she goes like an affronted chicken.'

'To spread your devilish reputation. Why *do* people think you've done dreadful things?'

'Is that a sly way of asking me whether I have?'

'It depends. I mean – if you have done a murder, as some seem to believe, then I'd rather not know.'

He glowers. 'I hid the body in the pianoforte.'

'You haven't got a pianoforte.'

'Curse you, you've foiled me again . . . There are things worse than murder, of course. And I don't mean this woebegone

249

lemonade. Things that fill your average mortal breast with greater abhorrence.'

'Well, I can't imagine what,' Augusta says staunchly.

Byron hesitates. His eyes burn with assessment, he seems to be thinking his way all around her, resolving her in his mind like a complex sum.

'Do you remember I once mentioned to you the things that go on at places like Harrow? Where a lot of boys are all heaped together?'

'I do. And I didn't quite understand. I suppose the bigger boys can be cruel to the littler ones. Bully-ragging George calls it—'

'Oh, there's no end of that. More tyrannizing and brutality goes on in a public school than the foulest slave-market. But you either learn to fight back or go under. No, beyond that there are other things. After a certain age boys grow amorous, and often they grow amorous together.'

'*Do* they?' This is such a novel idea to Augusta that she can only sit for long seconds thinking about it. At last: 'How?'

'My dear Goose, I can't sully your ears, nor the rarefied air of St Almack's, with details like that. Besides, as a married woman you can surely use your imagination.' He sobers abruptly. 'Sometimes it is mere animal appetite that must find release – the prettiest young fellows being cruelly and forcibly used – as happens on shipboard and in prisons.'

(Augusta, about to cry again '*Does* it?', sees his seriousness and refrains.)

'Other times it is – otherwise.'

'And is it not a great crime? I seem to remember once a man standing in the pillory at Covent Garden – I asked my grandmother about it but she wouldn't explain – and the crowd abused him dreadfully—'

'According to the laws of England, where we pride ourselves on such appurtenances of civilization as the pillory, yes, it is. In other countries, among the Turks and Greeks certainly, there are different notions. Different traditions. But, aye, here, law and society between 'em will chew you up and spit you out for the vice of *wrong loving*. You can imagine it must be a powerful temptation indeed if men will risk so much for it.'

'I can believe it.'

Byron gives his nose a tweak and says: 'Could you believe it of me?'

'I could believe the temptation. The – the love. Not the cruelty and force.' So says Augusta, who has been called by unsympathetic connections dreamy, slow, languid, and yet who has made some profound interior adjustments in the last few seconds: the mental equivalent of penetrating an unknown territory and settling there with a few tools and a bag of seeds.

'Dear Gus.' His hand trembles a little as it covers hers. 'You are too good for me.'

'Oh, I don't think I am.'

'Well, I think – I hope I've never been cruel in that way – to anyone. All I see in looking back is various sorts of foolishness.'

'Temptation, you know – I can always understand that. I think it's the most human thing of all. I know that if there is one cake left on the plate, I cannot let it lie, I *must* have it.'

He gives a shout of laughter. 'I don't know that it's quite the same.'

'Isn't it? Well, when it comes to a liking for men, I can quite understand that too. After all, I married one . . . Hush, Byron, you shouldn't laugh so – they'll have us turned out.'

Later, in the carriage: 'Byron, you haven't talked to anyone else about this?'

'There's no one I trust like you.' He shifts uneasily, lowering and extinguishing his eyes. 'There is Lady Caroline – that is, she may have a hint, indirectly.'

'Oh dear.'

'But she must lose interest in me soon. God, I've never loved anyone above ten weeks, even happily: how can she keep it up? Oh, never fear, Gus, I think people in general still incline to the

251

murder theory when it comes to my wicked past. And in truth all I have to reproach myself with – here in England at any rate – are thoroughly pure and ideal attachments. Indeed I just told a lie, because once I did love beyond ten weeks, and it was most purely et cetera, which may tell us something about human nature. It was at Cambridge. How the heart groans when one hears the dreaded words "I remember" – so I shan't burden you with a long tale – suffice to say he was a chorister at Trinity Chapel. Two years younger than me. I heard his voice first, going up like a beautiful thread of smoke: I followed it . . . And then I saw him, and I was transfixed by him, and we were together every day I think until – well, until it ended. His voice had broke, and he had no fortune, and so he was to go into a mercantile house in London. Thus we parted. David and Jonathan. My God, it's so long since I've spoken of this. I kept up with all his news while I was abroad, and I had the satisfaction of knowing he was doing well and thought of me . . . And then I came home and learnt that he was dead of a consumption. Dismal story. Don't know why I'm boring you with it.' He stares out of the carriage window: flickering lights keep editing his expression, now sombre, now uplifted: or is that fluctuation in him, his own quality? 'Do you ever think we're – forgive the Gothic locution – doomed?'

'All of us?'

'No, no,' he says lightly, 'that's for certain. I mean the Byrons specially.'

'I prefer to think we're blessed.'

'Perhaps it's the same thing. Do you really feel blessed, sis? Debts and troubles, and George being – well, George out of favour, and this damned *dubious* Byron name around your neck—'

'Yes, I do. I am the only person I know who literally does count her blessings. Well, look about us. Look at your poor friend from Cambridge – dying so young of consumption. There is so much to be thankful for.'

'Ah, but what if you're not thankful – constitutionally?'

'Why, then, you are very wicked. Byron – you said "here in England" – do you mean there are worse things to tell me about when you were abroad?'

'No, Goose, because I'm not going to tell you 'em. I want to keep at least a portion of your good opinion. But when in Rome, you know – that's all.'

'It's curious, though, isn't it? How countries can be so different in their ways. Of course the Turks are pagans, but the Greeks are Christian, aren't they?'

'All relative. Stand on the shores of the Bosphorus and look up, and you'll see the same sun we see in Piccadilly. Same sun, same moon. Only you stand in a different relation to it. Everything's relative, Gus.'

'Everything's relative . . . Well, I of all people should be able to see that. Because I'm everybody's relative. Oh, that's how it used to seem,' she says, as he laughs. 'Before I was married, when I rotated round my cousins. Round and round I went. But I don't think any of them really truly wanted me there. My God.' Astonished, she looks at the tears falling on her hands. 'How—? I do beg your pardon, I had no idea this was going to happen. I still don't know why it has.'

He leans over and kisses her face. 'It doesn't matter.'

'Wait, I do know why. It's because I'm so happy. Because you are so different from them. You do want me. That's what it is. Happiness. Isn't that a curious thing?'

An evening party at Lady Heathcote's. Do they have a sense, these hostessing ladies in their Mayfair townhouses, of interchangeability, of being mere attendants on the protagonists of a greater drama? Everyone is the hero of their own story, so probably not: but Lady Heathcote stands no chance, Lady Heathcote can only melt into the background when her guests include Byron and Caroline Lamb.

As soon as it becomes known that they are both here, a thrill runs through the reception rooms, already a little feverish from overcrowding in the July heat. Fans fractiously oscillate, ladies dab and dab at their beaded moustaches of perspiration, gentlemen feel they are perishing of their cravats. Byron has found Augusta a quiet seat near an open window where she can feel a heavenly breeze, and she is disinclined to move from it. Thus when something does happen she is not entirely sure what. Signals of commotion reach her; but then an old fat man, breathing cherry brandy, squeezes himself into her nook and begins to tell her about military strategy. When at last she escapes, and makes her way to the supper-room, rumours are flying about.

'Caro Lamb made a scene.'

'It was here.'

'It was upstairs.'

'She threatened to kill herself.'

'My dear, she tried to kill herself. With a knife.'

'Blood everywhere.'

'I heard it was a glass.'

'They took her away.'

'Carried her out.'

'Carried her out actually in a strait-waistcoat. No, I didn't see . . .'

Blood: Augusta finds herself looking at the carpet as if to see a scatter of drops. The mere thought of violence makes her feel faint. Yet the party is going on, and the sound of waltz-music continues from upstairs; and she is rather hungry, and cannot wait about for a gentleman to help her to the food. Afterwards, when the whole town is talking about Lady Caroline Lamb's behaviour at Lady Heathcote's ball, Augusta will be perplexedly aware that her strongest memory is of the excellent cutlets.

'Oh, God,' Byron says later, when she asks him about it, 'it was just one of Caro's scenes. Don't let's talk of it, Gus, it's too yawnmaking and dreary and deadly.' But she sees how perfectly pale he is, as if the blood was all his, drained to the heart's last drop.

He talks of it the next day: though still there is vagueness.

'Oh, it started with the waltzing, I suppose. Caro was going to lead off the dancing and was looking, I may add, entirely happy and tol-lolish and then she catches sight of *me* and all at once she's the serpent of old Nile. "I presume I may waltz *now*," says she – as if I ever stopped her. I said I would be happy to watch her, as she always performed the dance better than anyone. Which I *meant* – but we are so declined into tragicomedy that everything must appear bitter or ironical or what have you. Next she came at me in the supper-room. I was peaceably squiring a lady to the soup-tureen when Caro is suddenly before me – as if she'd risen up out of the floor like a stage devil – and gets hold of my hand and presses something sharp against it. A table-knife I think – it was all over in a trice. "I mean to use this," she whispers. On herself or on me, says I. And then I said very grandly that she could not *wound* my heart more than she already had – beating my breast the while – you see it was all so absurd, there was my poor partner yearning for her mulligatawny and Tom-footman stirring the tea and in front of me this Mayfair Maenad – this Clytemnestra with a butter-knife . . . Well, off she flounces at that, muttering, and I flatter myself that's the end of it for tonight – except, of course, it wasn't. I don't know – perhaps I should have gone after her. But that's just what she wants, because then we are never finished, you see. Anyhow, later she got into a room upstairs where the ladies were pinning up their hair or something, and that's where she made a great to-do of cutting herself. I don't think it was the knife, but I've heard several versions. Some say she smashed a glass and scratched herself with it – others that she struck herself with scissors. There was certainly blood on her gown when she was prevailed upon to leave. The strait-waistcoat I think is a fiction – Lady Heathcote's house is very well appointed, but I don't imagine she keeps a Bedlam wardrobe just in case . . .' He looks quizzically at Augusta: he is nervy, precarious. 'I'm being bright about it because what else can I do? Weep and wail? I can't change her and I can't change myself. Can't she see that?'

'If it's a person you love,' Augusta says slowly, 'then that's all you see. Everything else fades.'

He seems not to understand. But it's her own understanding she is expressing, like a child reading out loud, finding a new world.

Byron's rooms in Bennett Street, St James's. He and Augusta are supping alone. Bachelor-hall, cook-shop fare; and he has sent Fletcher away for completer intimacy. They are even drinking wine from the same glass, for no other reason than that they can: for no other reason than the coming true, as Augusta tells him, of her old girlhood dreams of him, the lost brother with an abbey, innermost of her inner circle.

'No, no,' she says, 'I never did feel alone. Because I always had you in my mind. That's the way it is with me. Even after Grandmother died, I still had her, really, within. I can't make it not sound sentimental.'

'What did I look like – before you knew me?'

Augusta resorts to the glass. 'Like you,' she says presently, imprecisely.

'I was fat. I will be fat again, if I ever let myself go. That's why I eat like this – nibbling like a damn squirrel. The curse of my mother's blood, which of course you haven't got – you with your admirable figure and three children, damn it, how do you contrive it?'

'It must be my exercise. Twice a day I walk half-way across the lawn, and in the evening I mix myself an egg-nog very vigorously. My schoolfriends all wanted to marry you, you know – the you I had imagined. It was either you or Valancourt from *Udolpho*.'

'Equally fictitious personages. Do schoolgirls really talk about marrying?'

'Yes – but it includes a lot of things.'

'Ah.'

'Not what you think. Mostly it was love, embraces, sighs – we looked forward to an unconscionable amount of sighing, as I recall.'

'Now it really does sound like marriage.'

'Oh, and burning kisses. We were all in a state of readiness for those – tried to practise so we would not be found wanting. Some girls did it on their arm, but to me it was never anything but an arm, and most uninspiring, so I tried kissing the mirror. Well, it is a face, after all,' she says at his look, smacking his knee. 'It did give some notion – though of course it was cold and not burning at all. And nothing does truly prepare you, does it?'

'For love? I don't know. I'm not sure that I've ever felt it, in spite of everything. I've sometimes heard my own mind asking, is this it? – have I finally found it? But if it has to ask, then . . .' He refills the glass. 'Mind, it's different for men.'

'Is it?' She drinks, with a floating, insubstantial feeling: great and luminous truths seem to be all about her, if only she could just grasp them.

'Did you ever get your burning kisses?'

Augusta laughs with a throaty sound that surprises her. She is taken up by the way the candlelight reflects on the glass, in a cluster of golden, accurate spikes. 'When George first used to kiss me, before we were married, it would make me so excited that when I was alone I'd have to—' She lifts her face open-mouthed. 'Oh – the things you make me say.'

Smiling, Byron shows his open hands, a gesture of innocence that looks so absurd on him she can only snort. She notices that he has long finished eating. This hunger of hers: she thinks it started when she moved little George to a wet-nurse. She blinks away the image of his face, catlike and scowling, denied the breast he used to knead so unmercifully.

Without her quite knowing it they have moved to the sofa. Cradling the wine-glass she looks around her: gilded pier-glass over the fireplace, portrait miniatures propped on the mantel, a bust of Napoleon with a gold chain hanging round it, books, boxing-gloves, an inlaid dagger, a curious jar.

'What is that – snuff?'

'Attic hemlock from Greece.'

'Dear me. Careful your housekeeper doesn't take a nip from it. The maid's always at George's sherry. Well, that's what George says. I suspect he doesn't know how much he drinks. Of course I shouldn't talk like this.' She looks gravely for a place to put down the wine-glass, but there are so many possibilities.

'Why shouldn't you?'

'Because it's disloyal. And I am loyal.'

'I know. But it's different here, with me. None of that applies.'

'Doesn't it?' She fixes her eyes on his face: she feels that if she can just do that, and not look away, everything will be all right. 'Are the Greeks not a very dishonest sort of people? I don't mean to be rude – only one hears these stories . . .'

'Oh, they lie and cheat about as much as they have to. Which, as they are a conquered people without freedom or hope, is quite a lot. Come abroad with me and see for yourself.'

'I can't go to Greece.'

'Italy, then.'

'I wish I could . . . Are you really going?'

'Yes, it's all fixed. That's to say, I keep thinking of it, and announcing it, and changing my mind every other day.'

That is definitely his arm along the back of the sofa, but she is not quite sure whose hand is on whose knee. There is a sort of indivisible mutuality of sensation. Or perhaps she is just tipsy. Keep your eyes on his: below, a great fall: don't look down.

'And,' he says, 'I have ordered a new portable desk and dressing-case, mahogany you know, lined with velvet, the bottles of silver—'

'Oh, you sybarite. It's funny, when I've had wine I can think of such very good words.' The glass has gone: someone has taken it from her and set it down on the floor. 'What else would you need for these hypothetical travels? Oh, there's another good word.'

'Camp beds. Table. Chairs. Trunks. Canteens.' Each word, like the ticking twitch of a clock-hand, seems to bring his face closer to hers. 'Kettles. Plate. Pistols. Powder flasks. Telescope. Medicine chest. Sword . . .'

Can this be right? And yet it is all relative, after all. Certain contingencies occur, and this is one; and you cannot be prepared for them all, you must just do what seems right at the time, and this feels right, it feels like it never felt before. His knees against hers, hers gently parting, the indistinguishable hands stroking, the two pairs of eyes locked just before the instinctive closing. Augusta consults the indices of her mind, but she finds no black marks. No one in her world cries out with hurt. Adultery – isn't that when you shatter marriage by bringing in some destructive intruder? Whereas this is *Byron* – who has always been there, part of her. She kisses her brother's mouth. A clock strikes. On the floor by the sofa, the candlelight continues its optical experiments on the wine-glass. Presently Augusta's feet sweep upward, but they do not knock it over.

Augusta is staying now with an old friend from her grandmother's circle, Mrs Theresa Villiers, at North Audley Street. Mrs Villiers is descended from Oliver Cromwell, prefers to be called Thérèse, for some reason, and even in this warm summer weather insists on fires in grates and closed windows. This, at least, must be why Augusta has such a restless sleep that night after returning from visiting her brother, and at one point actually jerks up in bed, flapping at the bed-curtains and saying aloud: 'I'm burning up.'

The next morning Augusta goes shopping in Bond Street while her friend pays calls. By arrangement they meet at Green Park.

'Well, my dear,' Mrs Villiers greets her friend, 'did you get what you came for?'

And Augusta, from looking more than usually absent, turns fierce in a moment, as unexpectedly as a lamb snarling. 'What do you mean? What *do* you mean?' And then, herself again, 'Oh – no – I didn't care for the pattern. I have not seen any sprig muslins I fancy for such a long time.'

★ ★ ★

Byron says, with his lips in her hair, 'I'm coming with you.'

'Where?'

'Back to the blasted heath. Sixpenny Buttocks or wherever it is. Well? You are going, aren't you, or thinking of it?'

'How did you know?' she says, though it seems merely natural that he should.

'We'll travel together. We've never done that before. Infallible guide to how you get along, you know. Of course you've got to go back – the children and so forth. George.'

'Yes.' George . . . But here, when she lies with her back against Byron's chest and his arms round her, it's only a name. Step out of this enchanted circle, this pentacle of proximity, and the terrible questions leap up. 'I said I would stay in town for a month or so. George will probably be wanting to go down to Brighton once the July meet at Newmarket ends. So I should be there—'

'And I'll come with you. It'll be a relief not to have to look over my shoulder for Caro Lamb. Did you know she forged my signature to get hold of my portrait from Murray? She's always haunting him but the poor fellow hasn't the heart to send her packing. Let's see, if we travel post—'

'Oh, I had thought of the public coach.'

'Post is pleasanter. Don't fret, I'll arrange it all.' He nuzzles her ear. 'I'll look after you.'

Augusta closes her eyes. Dear God, it is wonderful, just for once, to hear those words.

'And when we get there we can inform George, before he skips off, that I can plug the hole of his debts, at least for a while. He can go down to Brighton with a light heart. So all in all it could hardly be better, could it?'

'Oh, no,' says Augusta, never one for arguing.

At Six Mile Bottom, at first, Augusta believes she cannot stand it and will go mad. Compartments: that is the way she has managed, she realizes. There was what happened in London, and that is one compartment, and there is here with George and the children and the mess and the maid with the boil on her neck and the clouts hanging and the smell of small beer that had burst its keg all over the scullery floor, and this is another compartment entirely and it is wrong, sheer madness, to think they can be brought together. And to look at Byron here – as she finds after the first few anguished side glances – is impossible: he appears *outré*, unbelievable, as if she has brought home an ostrich or a noble savage in bangles and paint.

And then – somehow – it gets better, as things often do with Augusta. She does not so much overcome obstacles as melt through them, like a ghost walking through a wall. George is not at his best – he has been ill with a cold, possibly two, in her absence, and he further informs her that there are scores of things amiss about the house and needing her attention; but Byron, as he can be when he wants, is all unassuming charm. When George starts packing for Brighton, he misses one of his gloves, and Byron goes to great lengths searching for it. He is, George grunts to her, not a bad fellow.

As for the children – there she suffers too, at first. Violently they claw and grasp at her as if she were a tree to be shaken for windfalls. And for a few moments she is terrified of them – these greedy, clutching strangers, making free with her body.

Then she begins to laugh. The children stare, and then they laugh too. The dusty parlour rings with the noise of it. Augusta is giddy with relief: she is not, after all, a monster.

'It's easy to see you're a born mother,' Byron says, watching her. He makes it sound faintly disreputable.

After George has gone, a settling-in. Byron prowls delightedly about the house: he likes the snugness and seclusion. Augusta begins to reconcile his electric presence with the familiarity of shabby upholstery and drain-smells. Though he claims to hate children, they take to their unknown uncle and are soon scrambling all over him.

So, this must surely be right.

And when he steps into her bedroom at night, it is just like London; and she doesn't want to lose that, yet.

Or ever? she asks herself, as she pants, kisses his smooth neck, subsides. But then what does *ever* mean? We can't experience it, we can only experience time. And this time is good. Therefore . . .

She sleeps.

And wakes, to find the bedroom door being inched open, and little Augusta Charlotte's fretful snuffly voice calling for her through the crack. She leaps up, vaulting over dozing naked Byron, reaches the door before her daughter's face can peep in.

'Hush, hush . . . come, I'll get you some water and put you back to bed. Hush . . .'

Byron is sitting up when she returns.

'We must be careful,' she says, handing him his shirt.

'If we went abroad together,' he says, temperately, 'we wouldn't have to.'

'You don't mean they see *nothing* as wrong in the East?' she says, snappishly for her.

He takes her by the shoulders and makes her sit down. 'I mean we wouldn't be known,' he says. 'We'd be free.'

'The children. I can't leave the children. And if they come too . . . then what about George?'

'I don't think it would be quite suitable for him to come too, do you?'

'Byron, be serious.'

'I am being. I think, you know, that I am the one who is taking the whole notion rather more seriously.'

She looks away from him. 'I am thinking of it. But George is my husband — the father of my children — and to just desert him . . .'

'Well, it wouldn't be entirely inexplicable. He's hock deep in debt. He can't leave the country because it wouldn't be the act of a gentleman. But people would understand if his wife took their children to live abroad more cheap and comfortable.'

'Hmm. There's a word for that reasoning, but I'm too sober to think of it.'

He laughs, yawns, tickles her back. 'Specious, probably.'

Next evening the sulky summer breaks into a storm. Thunder commands the heath, with a ripping and spilling of great bundles of sound. Lightning calibrates the horizon. The two little girls give unison screams of ecstatic terror. Repeatedly the groom comes to the door to tell Augusta that George's new mare is playing up.

'She'll kick the stall down soon. That's what I'm afraid of. She'll kick it all to splinters. She will, do this storm keep up.'

'Oh dear. Isn't there anything you can do?'

'Not do this storm keep up. Terrible wicked storm, missus,' he tells her, reproachfully.

'Well, really, I can't change the weather,' Augusta says. Yet she sounds, even to herself, curiously unconvincing.

'What's Uncle doing?' demands Georgiana. She tugs Augusta to the back parlour window. Byron is standing out in the yard in his shirtsleeves, his head thrown back with an exultant look. The first fat drops of rain are sizzling down and blooming on the cobbles.

'Nothing,' Augusta says, then opens the window. 'Byron, what are you doing?'

'Waiting to be struck down,' he shouts, his hair dripping. She has never seen him look so happy.

That night, after supper, they sit with the windows open to the new sweet cooled air.

'How much do you remember of our father?' Byron asks.

'I remember his face. Handsome, gay. Rather wry. He would whistle when he came in. He would pretend to nip off my nose – play little games. Not for long. I think he was always very restless.'

'Ah.' The candle-flames genuflect in the bellying breeze. Byron catches and cups a moth that has been flittering around them. He releases it outside the window, but it heads straight back to the candles. 'No teaching 'em. Now why would nature make them court death like that? Once in Aberdeen my mother was in a black mood – from the gin, or from not having enough money for gin, one or t'other. She sat staring at the fire-screen and grinding her teeth all evening and I – because I knew that the fidgets, as she called it, would set her raging, I sat absolutely still. Did you ever try that when you were a child? I don't think I was afraid of her, though I may have been – it was more an absolute disinclination to face one of her tempers again. I suppose I was pitting myself against her as well, in some sort. But at last I was too cramped, and I had to shift – just a little – in my seat, with the merest of creakings – and immediately her head snaps round and she fixes her button eyes on me and she says, so sharp and distinct: "You little limping brat." ' The moth, wings burned, falls with a click on to the windowsill. 'And now I can't help wondering how long she had been sitting there waiting and longing for me to do something so she could say that.' He flicks the moth out into the splendid night. 'And whether it felt as good as she anticipated. So few things do.'

LADY MELBOURNE: No, sir, I am not going to scold you. Why should I?

BYRON (*sitting down*): Well, I presume you got my letter.

LADY MELBOURNE: Yes, and read it. What then? I may as well say I think you are the greatest fool, but as for scolding, that suggests a moral eminence, and you know I do not pretend to look down from any such thing.

BYRON: Thank God for that. Too much looking upward makes my neck ache. Caro is not about, I hope?

LADY MELBOURNE: I would hardly have summoned you if she were. She is at Brocket.

BYRON: And how does she do?

LADY MELBOURNE: My dear Byron, you are with me now –

you don't have to make this counterfeit of caring how my infernal daughter-in-law does.

BYRON (*smiling, but frowning also*): I would care a great deal more, if she could only be rational. As it is, I wish her no ill.

LADY MELBOURNE: No need, she brings all her ills on herself. She is at present like a barrel of gunpowder, my dear sir, in other words pretty much as always, and now I will be diverted from the point no longer. I must satisfy myself, first, that your letter was not written as some sort of unholy joke?

BYRON: Did it read like one? I wish I'd kept a copy.

LADY MELBOURNE: Tut, that is exactly the kind of indiscretion you must guard against. Above all while Caroline remains – unreconciled. I have destroyed the letter. I cannot destroy what has happened. Nor undo it. Still, you know that must be your object, or as near as possible. You must absolutely put an end to this madness, Byron: you must know that.

BYRON (*sighing*): I suppose. But shouldn't madness *feel* like madness?

LADY MELBOURNE: I have absolutely no idea, I have never suffered anything like madness in my life.

BYRON: No . . . that's why I like confiding in you. How does it feel, though – that sanity?

LADY MELBOURNE: You are altogether too concerned with how things feel, sir: that is your trouble. Now tell me what has happened since you wrote. Or let me guess. You did go back to Newmarket to see her again, in spite of all your assurances that you would not.

BYRON: Oh, I had to. Because the first time I came away with nothing properly settled between us.

LADY MELBOURNE: How so? You said she had decided against going abroad with you – happily for her sense.

BYRON: You don't know my sister – well, in a way you do, since you know me: when she says she has decided nothing, it means very little. She *thought* she ought to say no, but I could tell she was still contemplating it. And why not? Her man's a drone and always will be, and she's got nothing to look forward to but growing poorer on that miserable common where the best conversation you can have is with the horses. So I went back, once her tomfool *mari* was off on the jaunt again, to try and persuade her at last. Yes, and to see her – (*twisting about irritably and biting his thumbnail*) – of course, to see her.

LADY MELBOURNE: Really, you are incorrigible!

BYRON (*with a shrewd look*): If that were literally true – I mean, if I truly were beyond correction – would you still trouble with me?

LADY MELBOURNE: My dear friend, I have not taken you in hand with any notion of morally reforming you. Any woman who would attempt that would be doomed indeed. My concern is to see that you don't waste a promising life by getting into these scrapes, as you call them. And this one is worse than a scrape, Byron: you must know it. Now come: Mrs Leigh said no again, I collect, else you would not be here.

BYRON: Aye, she wouldn't have it. There's her children – and then she's heard about this plague that's going around Italy – and, besides, I think she's still tied to hearth and home and him—

LADY MELBOURNE: As well she might be. Consider, those are not going to go away; whereas what guarantee has she that you will not tire of this – this association?

BYRON (*ferociously*): Never. That is where you are wrong, utterly wrong. My love for Augusta is something – something beyond mere time, beyond the petty and the everyday, beyond and above it . . .

LADY MELBOURNE (*drily*): If only it were. Well, leave that. So, where have you been since you came away from Newmarket?

BYRON: Oh, paying visits. Trying to cure myself. One lady in particular signalled her willingness. No good. I am still so very lost in – in this love.

LADY MELBOURNE: Flirtations and affairs and what-naught are all very well. But they are a palliative, not a cure. You know my prescription.

BYRON: I know it. And it's curious: I should not have supposed you of all people a friend to marriage.

LADY MELBOURNE: I am a friend to marriage in the same sense that I am a friend to castor oil, which I would not recommend for the table but is unrivalled as a purge. Everything to its own uses. I may as well tell you that my niece Annabella has been asking after you again; and I have taken the liberty of giving her an encouraging report.

BYRON: I know – she wrote me herself. Bold in her. She certainly has a very taking argufying way about her – you expect to see *Q.E.D.* writ at the bottom of her letters. Didn't she have some other suitor?

LADY MELBOURNE: Annabella has had many suitors, but none has succeeded.

BYRON: The suitors don't suit – oh, a vile pun, get rid of it. Of course nothing can alter the fact that she turned me down.

LADY MELBOURNE: She would not be the first woman to have second thoughts. I *believe* I detect a certain regret: I can say no more than that.

BYRON (*getting up and moving restlessly about*): So, I must marry or burn, eh?

LADY MELBOURNE: Oh, I don't deal in such dramatic stuff, my friend. I am of this world.

BYRON: Yes . . . and St Paul was a self-serving old turncoat anyhow. Wordsworth on a camel. I must think, think . . . (*Taking out his watch and peering at it.*) And go. Murray is expecting me. My dear Lady M., I wonder you can see in this dim light.

LADY MELBOURNE: Tactful light, sir. You have been writing?

BYRON: Like the devil.

LADY MELBOURNE: Well, that's encouraging, at any rate.

BYRON: Perhaps. I fancy Murray may take against the subject of this poem. (*He lays his hand on the drawn curtains, as if he would yank them open.*) I have drawn on the East again – very well – but the story is of a brother and sister – very ill.

267

LADY MELBOURNE: Byron, you do not suppose you can publish such sentiments?

BYRON: Just for the defiance of the thing – aye, why not? (*He moves away from the curtains, a harsh, absent smile on his face.*) Last season they were raining invitations on me – fighting to have me at their parties – the more tales there were about me the more they loved it. Will they alter now? It's like I once said to Caro – if you want me, you must have all of me.

LADY MELBOURNE: Even if you survived, do you think Mrs Leigh's reputation would?

BYRON: Ah, there's the rub. Of course, if she were to come abroad with me—

LADY MELBOURNE: I do not think she will do that, you know.

BYRON: No. It's a terrible thought – that to protect someone you must stop loving them. (*Abruptly he bows over Lady Melbourne's hand.*) You've had enough of me for now. I will seriously think, my dear Lady M. – most seriously think.

LADY MELBOURNE (*as he leaves*): No, you won't.

(*After a few moments LADY MELBOURNE rises and goes over to the curtains. She pulls them open a little, then crosses to the fireplace and looks at her reflection in the pier-glass above it. Then she puts out her hand and lays it against the glass as if to cover the reflection.*)

Another coach-journey from Newmarket to London, but this time Augusta feels no sense of release or excitement.

Mostly, she feels sick.

'My God.' Byron is writing at the desk when Fletcher shows her in. 'I didn't know you were in Town.' He jumps up and comes towards her with fresh-dipped quill still clutched in his right hand: it makes a trail of bloodlike spattered drops on the rug. 'Damn.' He throws it down, embraces her. 'You're frozen.'

'No, I'm not. I'm pregnant.'

A moment's pause: he looks over her shoulder, frowning as if trying to remember something. 'Sit down, Gus.'

'I don't need to sit down. I've been pregnant before, I'm always very strong right up to the ninth month. Sick, though – prone to sickness. Oh, God, Byron – I couldn't bear it – knowing – not being with you—'

'And now,' he says, steering her in his arms to the fire, 'you will sit down.'

He brings her brandy: she swallows it with difficulty. I could never take to drink, she thinks randomly, and: If you find a vice unattractive, is there any virtue in resisting it? Good question.

'I'm going to stay with Theresa Villiers. But I came here first. I had to see you to tell you. I couldn't do it in a letter somehow.'

'So that's why your letters have been so damned odd. How long?'

'September, I think.'

He hisses a long breath. 'When you say *knowing*—'

'I mean knowing I'm pregnant but not knowing otherwise.'

'Ah. Does George know?'

'Yes. He is half pleased. Half dismayed at another mouth to feed.'

'So it might be either.'

'Yes.' She fixes her eyes away from him, on polished fire-irons in which, for a bewitched moment, she sees herself reflected without expecting or understanding it: as if he has little portraits of her everywhere. She fixes her eyes away, will not look because a traitor part of herself wants to be held by him and not yet, not like this . . . 'Well, what did you suppose? He is my husband: it would look mighty queer if I refused him. Besides . . .' How to explain the complex codes of marriage? How explain, really explain, anything – lacing a shoe, combing your hair, making a fist – if the basic terms are not understood? When George comes to her, it is a small domestic event like winding the clock. Also, yes, it helps solve the conundrum of her guilt, for what after all is he losing? 'Besides . . . it's a different thing altogether.'

Suddenly Byron laughs. 'It certainly is. Lord, it certainly is.'

'Oh.' She is, for her, tindery. 'I'm glad you find it amusing.'

'I don't, though,' he says, still laughing, shaking his head. He seizes the brandy-bottle, pours a glass and swallows it all in one convulsive movement. 'That's it, I don't at all. I love you, Gus, more than anyone, ever, always. I hope you know it.'

'Perhaps I do,' she says, risking a look, 'but, Byron, that doesn't change—'

'I know – that's what I'm saying. Doesn't change a thing, and nothing really can. If the child is mine, then – well, in a way I am not sorry for it. No: why should we be? Conceived in sin and all that – but our beautiful religion instructs us that we are all conceived in sin anyway. If your Jehovah sets the mark of doom on the most spotlessly generated babe that ever screamed at the font, then how can it be worse for ours? If ours. Which we can't know. And still I'm in this unique position for a man confronted with possible paternity. For what I can't offer to do is to acknowledge it, or promise to look after it, or marry you – all of that.'

'I know,' Augusta says: and she does know. Though she wishes she did not have to be dragged into his cosmic feud.

'If we were to come into the open, our lives here would be finished.' He recites it in an ashy voice. 'In another country – far off – we might live differently. But we've talked about that.'

Augusta shakes her head. 'Of course there's nothing to be done, except the one thing. But I do hope—' she can say it only in a whisper, only this once '–I hope it is yours, God forgive me.'

'He will. What else is he for?' Byron kneels awkwardly beside her, his eyes stained with shadows. 'You haven't said it, so I will. The old tales – superstitions – about such a child – and yet you know it is only half blood—'

She puts her fingers on his lips. 'That we'll have to see. Old tales, as you say. I shan't think about that because it's something we can't change anyhow. That's how I look at it.'

He nods soberly. 'And the one thing – the one thing you said there is to be done . . .'

'Yes: we must stop, of course. This proves it.'

'Oh, yes. We must. Yes, I know that.'

She leans into his arms, closes her eyes.

'Now,' she says, her voice muffled, 'we must think how.'

She is not sure who suggests it, but Byron accompanies her back to Newmarket. It is December, and George is in hospitable mood, and Byron is family, so he stays at Six Mile Bottom for Christmas. There Uncle spends much time writing, but he never seems to mind the children barging into his room and clambering all over him: still his pen scratches madly away. Callers come to take wine and seed-cake and exchange the compliments of the season, and Byron comes down amiably blinking to be introduced and stared at; and just occasionally Augusta will see a savage look flash over his eyes, like an indoor cat that spots a bird outside the window. And Augusta thinks – or rather, she doesn't think: for the visitors must see merely a normal family gathering, and indeed leaving aside secret past and unguessable future that is all it is, so why not enjoy it as such? Then one night, undressing and easing her swollen breasts, she is invaded by a memory of her brother kissing them, and after that it is harder not to think.

And yet, still, they are to be together, and in a way that cannot be resisted by thinking or anything else.

Newstead.

'I think it will be my last chance to stay there,' she tells George. 'It looks as if the sale is finally going to go through.'

George is in the stables, looking over his favourite brood-mare.

'She doesn't like this cold, do you, old girl?' he says. He is talking to the horse. 'The old family home. Well, I can understand that. Mind, don't they say it's half a ruin? I hope he'll make you comfortable.'

'I'm sure he will. Thank you, George.'

Beaming at his own magnanimity, George pats the mare's

neck. 'Well, this sale's been long enough in coming. My creditors are getting fidgety. Rot 'em. I've told them they'll get their money. Don't know what more I can do. Oh – how will you travel up there?'

'Byron's coach.'

'Ah. Sprung, I should think, and no draughts.' For a second he looks divided between approval and envy. 'Only I'm thinking of your condition, old girl, and the new young 'un.' This time he is talking to her, not the horse. 'So, have a care.' Suddenly he gives her one of his hearty Georgeish kisses. 'Lud, I never knew such a woman for breeding! Does it run in the family, d'you think?'

'What?'

'Well, when your brother marries – wonder if he'll have a great brood too. High time he did, by the by – twenty-six, ain't he? – tell him from me to look about him. It's the best of all states for a man. Never regretted it for an instant myself. Yes, old girl, you're a beauty, that's what you are.' The horse this time, probably.

Newstead. So few experiences in life are not tinged with disappointment – so even Augusta's optimistic nature admits – that this, her stay at the abbey with Byron in the depths of the coldest winter she can remember, is somehow unreal in its perfection. She thinks of children's stories, fairy feasts that vanish leaving you hungrier than ever, beautiful maidens who are witches disguised: illusions. But they all have something sinister to them, and this does not. This is more like—

'An idyll,' Byron says contentedly, as they stand at the windows of the old refectory gazing out at whiteness.

But for Augusta that word only means something that comes to an end. She prefers an Eden: something we must all have at some point.

At first he is apologetic for Newstead – rambling, half ruined, draughty: in the grandest rooms there are gaping ceilings, boxes of lumber and flower-pots and espaliers and twine and even bales of fodder. The Wicked Lord ran the place down shockingly, and he, he says, has been little better . . . But soon he begins to understand: she does not want Newstead to be like other houses. The moment she saw the old priory west front from the coach, a fabulous fragment standing out against the gander-coloured sky like a titanic engraving of itself, she knew this was her place. And now it is that flavour of vanished glories that she savours in going round it with her brother, cloisters and staircases and galleries creaking with the weight of past Byrons. Even the newer elements have something richly forlorn about them: the young oak planted in the garden by her brother when a boy, the monument to his favourite dog Boatswain. And then the snow: that, too, is entirely right, though he tells her how beautiful the lake can look in summer, dredged with tree-reflections, skimmed by swans. She can believe it, but her Eden needs this snow – great glittering ribbed banks of it, so adamantine and durable it must surely have fallen in nuggets rather than flakes. It seals them off in a self-sufficient world of Gothic crenellations and turrets, fire-places of primeval size primevally blazing, red velvet drapes so heavy it takes two servants to tug them along the rails.

Eden with its innocence: she freely goes back and forth in Byron's bedroom, but she is very pregnant now, and they burn only with the steady glow of companionship. He does no writing: for that, he says, he needs to fret.

'I think I saw a ghost in my dressing room last night, Gus.'

'How wonderful! Of course it would be odd if this place didn't have ghosts. Do tell me it was a monk with a cowl and everything.'

'I'm not sure. Did you ever think ghosts might not be from the past but from the future?'

'I'm thinking now. But then they wouldn't be dead.'

'No, but we would. Just think what they could tell you.' He chuckles. 'And just think if what they told you was "It didn't matter after all." '

One afternoon the baby gives such a decided and accurate kick that she gasps. Byron sits by her and puts his hand to her belly.

'God,' he says, after a while.

'I know.' She folds his hand between her own. 'I know . . . Look, it's snowing again. Our friend the snow.'

While it lasts, they hold the world at bay and decision, that deep dark lake, is frozen over: you can skate on it laughing. But there must, will be a thaw. Every Eden ends in an expulsion.

A letter gets through the drifts, from London: John Murray, Byron's publisher. Byron's new poem *The Corsair* has sold ten thousand copies in a single day.

'This kind of thing is not heard of,' Byron says, looking perplexed, pale, even sick. 'Even Murray says so, and he is a Scot too canny even to scratch an itch. Lawks-a-mussy. Where does a man go from here?'

And what do you do, Augusta thinks, watching drips bead and fall from the castellated eaves above her window, what do you do after your dream comes true? Then it's back to the mess and murk of life: because there isn't anything else.

BYRON: Well – if it turns out to be an ape, then yes, I am to blame. If it's a donkey, it must be Colonel Leigh's.

LADY MELBOURNE: For shame, sir – you amuse me against my conscience.

BYRON: I don't mean to amuse, I assure you. I am in deadly earnest. At least – I don't know.

LADY MELBOURNE: Mrs Leigh will have her confinement in the country, I presume?

BYRON: Yes. Yes, I shan't be there.

LADY MELBOURNE: I'm glad to know it. The more you can be kept from *that* influence the better, I feel.

BYRON: My dear Lady M., you know I have the greatest respect for your wisdom and all that, but really I can't hear you talk of Augusta in that way. It was all my fault.

LADY MELBOURNE: Nothing of this kind is ever *all* one person's fault. I disclaim wisdom, my friend, but I do know women.

BYRON: You make it sound as if you are not one yourself.

LADY MELBOURNE: I was once.

BYRON (*getting up to close the curtains at the window, where a strong spring sun is shining*): I'm afraid you are out of spirits today.

LADY MELBOURNE: Not at all — leave those if you please, Byron, I want the light — not at all, I am heartily glad to have those days over. Their gratifications are much over-prized.

BYRON: I know that myself, but are there any others?

LADY MELBOURNE (*with a faint smile*): I think it is you who are out of sorts, my friend. Come, enough of that subject. Has my niece written you again? Tell me everything she has to say.

Mrs Augusta Leigh's fourth child was born, a healthy girl, at Six Mile Bottom on 15 April 1814. Colonel Leigh, who was not present at the birth, pronounced himself delighted. The child was christened Elizabeth Medora.

'Medora,' George boomed, wetting the baby's head with some cronies, 'after the Duke of Rutland's filly that won the Oaks, you know.'

'Medora,' the vicar mused to his wife. 'Is that not the heroine in Lord Byron's new poem?'

'Medora,' Augusta whispered to the baby at her breast; and thought, daringly, I have survived.

Part Three

What do they know? – that they are miserable.
What need of snakes and fruits to teach us that?

Byron, Cain

Is it a father's throat
Which I will shake, and say, I ask not gold;
I ask not happy years; nor memories
Of tranquil childhood; nor home-sheltered love;
Though all these thou hast torn from me, and more.

Shelley, The Cenci

Heard melodies are sweet, but those unheard
Are sweeter.

Keats, Ode on a Grecian Urn

Part Three

What do they know – that they are miserable,
What need of snakes and fruits to wail us that?

Byron, Cain

Is it a father's groan?
Which I will shake and say I ask not polity
I ask not happy years; nor memories
Of tranquil dip; nor home sheltered love;
Though all these thou hast torn from me, and more.

Shelley, The Cloud

Heard melodies are sweet, but those unheard
Are sweeter.

Keats, Ode on a Grecian Urn

1

Summer of the Sovereigns – Warm

War as a drum. For twenty years the beaters have pounded on the stretched skin of Europe and everyone, even at the furthest edges, has felt the vibration.

And now from France, where the tattoo first sounded in the shade of the guillotine, the roll and rataplan rumbles, rattles, swells to a new stridor and then – at last, unbelievably – stops. The amazing silence rushes in. Peace.

At three in the drizzly afternoon of Sunday, 20 March 1814, Mary Godwin boards the *Wishart* at Dundee harbour to begin the voyage back to London. This is a final parting from her Scottish hosts and friends. Her father has summoned her back home. She is sixteen. The sailor who lifts the slender flame-headed girl on to the yawing deck of the boat is, quite literally, transferring her from her past to her future.

In that future she means to board her own boats – even if she does not yet envisage burning them.

On the same day, at Arcis-sur-Aube a hundred miles from Paris, the Emperor Napoleon flings his dwindling troops against the invading Austrian army of Prince Schwarzenberg, but cannot stop it; while another Austrian column takes Lyons, and the British under Wellington advance on Toulouse.

On 28 March, Mary staggers on her sea-legs up the slimy stairs of a Thameside quay and finds herself once more in the belly of the great city: London, throbbing and pumping and living all

279

around her. She stands and stares, and for a moment it seems she is the only point of stillness in the whole chaotic world. Then she stirs, and looks for a boy to send to Holborn with a message for her father. Come and get me.

On the same day, the Allied armies, Prussians and Russians under Blücher, Austrians under Schwarzenberg, meet up at Meaux, thirty miles from the capital of Napoleon's empire. Now it is all happening very fast.

30 March: at the tall unloved house in Skinner Street, Mary, after sleeping off the exhaustion of the sickening voyage, sees to her unpacking. With great care she lays out and brushes the tartan frock bought for her by her Scottish hosts. The works of Sir Walter Scott have made such things highly desirable: Jane Clairmont moans in admiration, pleads to borrow it, though she is so much more buxom than her stepsister she would never get into it. Mary, suspecting Jane to be quite capable of squeezing secretly into it and bursting the seams, makes sure to lock her trunk. New clothes are not so easily come by at Skinner Street, where, she guesses from her father's evasiveness at her queries, a new financial crisis approaches.

The same day, Paris surrenders to the Allies, while Napoleon races towards it in a light carriage, still hoping to save the lost day.

On 31 March, Napoleon shuts himself up in his deserted palace at Fontainebleau to think. He is not good at defeats. In Paris the great survivor Talleyrand, who all those years ago drank canary wine from a teacup with Mary's famous mother and discussed the Revolution for women, evades an order to leave the city and prepares to welcome the victors: Tsar Alexander of Russia, Prince Frederick William of Prussia, Prince Schwarzenberg of Austria.

On the same day, Mary goes with Jane and Fanny on a walk up to Charterhouse Square, and notices lumps of blackened frozen snow still lying in sheltered places, from the seemingly endless winter.

On 1 April, at Talleyrand's prompting, the French senate invites the younger brother of the guillotined King to come back from exile as Louis XVIII.

On 4 April, Napoleon signs the first provisional instrument of abdication.

On the same day, Mary's stepmother flies into a temper with her father, crying that they will be worse off than ever with what she calls 'two great girls slummocking about the place'. Godwin tries to pacify her with talk of the loan he is negotiating from his young friend Mr Shelley. Mary takes herself off to her bedroom, fireless but blessedly voiceless, and reads *Paradise Lost*. She finds herself warming to the character of the Devil.

On 6 April, the Devil is declared defeated about the streets of London. Napoleon Bonaparte has long been associated with the Prince of Darkness in the English mind, or part of it at least. In some households – like the Godwins' – the news of Napoleon's dethronement is not particularly welcomed because it means the old despot kings are back in charge. Still, peace is good; and Fanny, who is showing odd touches of assertion lately, says: 'Mr Shelley calls Napoleon the worst of all sorts of tyrant, because he held out hopes of liberty only to crush them.' Church bells ring, fireworks coruscate, and the windows of known Radicals are patriotically smashed. (Mrs Godwin prudently decks the bookshop window with celebratory laurel: they cannot afford glaziers' bills.) Even the weather improves: going to bed that night, Mary notices she cannot see her breath.

On 12 April, the last resistance ends as Toulouse falls to Wellington's army. Late that night, at Fontainebleau, Napoleon tries to kill himself with a dose of opium, belladonna and white hellebore. The poison makes him very ill but does not kill him. It will be exile to the island of Elba, after all.

The same day, Mary makes her first visit since her return from Dundee to her mother's grave at St Pancras churchyard. When her stepmother demands to know where she has been all day, Mary pointedly refuses to answer.

On 4 May, the newly created Duke of Wellington enters Paris

for the Allied parade before the newly created French King.

On 5 May, Mary is minding the shop at Skinner Street when a young man comes in and, after glancing absently at some new books on the counter, heads for the door leading to the stairs. Then, with a start, he turns back to Mary.

'I beg your pardon – I was going up to look for Mr Godwin. He does know me. My name is Shelley.'

'I know.' And Mary is astonished. This is the first time she can ever remember speaking in that way – irrepressibly, with no command over what her tongue might say.

'Do you? How?' He looks humorous but serious, as if prepared to drop everything and consider the question as long as she likes.

'Well. You could be no one else.'

'Ah!' He draws the syllable out, seeming to encompass whole worlds of understanding.

Unlike Jane, for whom the term 'devouring stare' might have been invented, Mary is not a frank looker. She glances sidelong or upward through lowered lashes: visually she sketches. Her sketch of Mr Shelley is of a very tall young man, somehow over-tall, so that he stoops a little apologetically: slender and finely made, with tapering fingers, and a long white neck that a woman would be proud to show: dark hair growing thick, drooping, profuse: blue, painfully blue eyes that in their bruised-looking orbits seem to stand forth from the high-cheeked, long-jawed face as if on a carnival vizard.

'Would you,' he asks intently, 'be anyone else if you could?'

'No,' she says. 'But then how could I be? As soon as I became someone else, they would cease to be someone else and become me.'

'Ah, but then—'

A customer comes in, and he breaks off. By the time Mary has finished with the woman, who is grim, awkward, unsatisfiable, he has gone upstairs. But she notices the prints of his fingertips are still just visible on the polished rail running round the counter: watches them fade before her eyes, with a curious sensation like dampness drying off bare skin.

'Mary.'

It is her father, rousing her from a trance of abstraction so deep she almost feels she has been asleep.

'Mary, ask Cooper to set another place for this evening. Mr Shelley will dine with us.'

'Yes, Papa.'

And this is when time changes its nature, and instead of a steady file of dates becomes for Mary a pool: she slips in, surrendering, swallowed up.

Who *is* Shelley?

Digest of Reports on Mr *Shelley* (P.B.)
Prepared for the Secretary of State for Home Affairs, His Lordship the Viscount Sidmouth

Further to your lordship's request for a summation of intelligence gathered since Mr Shelley's subversive activities first coming to the attention of this office (April 1812): – It now appears that Mr Shelley's antecedents are certainly the Shelleys of Field Place, Sussex (baronetcy conferred 1806: first baronet, Sir Bysshe Shelley, Mr Shelley's paternal grandfather) though there would seem to be a condition of lasting estrangement from the family as a result of said activities and others private and matrimonial. Mr Shelley's date of birth, 1792, though has the appearance of almost a youth. Was educated at Eton where he did not distinguish himself otherwise than for eccentricities. Likewise Oxford, from which he was expelled for publishing on the subject of Atheism, a doctrine he has been consistently zealous to propagate. Subsequent quarrel with and dissociation from Mr Shelley senior (of Field Place), followed by elopement with and marriage to (while still a minor) a Miss Harriet Westbrook, daughter of Mr Westbrook, proprietor, Mount Street Coffee-House (NB, not tavern-keeper as previously stated). Has adopted residence in divers parts of the kingdom,

> *in community with Mrs Shelley and other ladies, relations undefined but almost certainly irregular. Seditious activities in Dublin (1812, addresses, publication), Lynmouth, Devon (printing and distributing inflammatory material, 1812), Tremadoc, Wales (ditto). Referral by this Office to the Solicitor for Prosecutions produced advice against taking any present steps but recommended further observation and collation of information in view of Mr Shelley's plain attachment to principles subversive of order, government and religion . . .*

'Thank you – I take no sugar,' Shelley said at the end of dinner, when the Clairmont officiated at the teapot.

'Lord, you will when you taste Mama's tea,' said Jane, who had been noisy throughout, under the mistaken impression that she was sparkling. 'You don't let it draw, Mama, that's your trouble.'

'La! You see how I am treated, Mr Shelley!' sighed the Clairmont, who was coquettish as ever in the presence of a young man; as if it were at least a reasonably frequent occurrence for handsome twenty-two year olds to fall deeply in love with fat stupid old women. La, thought Mary. La. Where did that come from?

'Mr Shelley abstains from sugar on principle,' her father said. 'A laudable one. You know, of course, my dears, where sugar comes from.'

'It is a product of the stem,' said Fanny, at once the dutiful pupil, 'of the sugar-cane plant.'

'A plant cultivated on plantations by slaves,' said Shelley, turning his tranced eyes on Fanny. 'Can you conceive anything more revolting? Human creatures chained, beaten, tortured, so that we may have the trifling pleasure of sweetening our tea.'

'Oh, we have always been friends to the abolition,' the Clairmont said comfortably.

'Yes, but that must wait on our parliament. As soon expect honey from a decaying carcass as expect any good from that heap of idleness and corruption,' Shelley said, smiling gently.

'La, Mr Shelley, you have quite put me off my mutton,' cried Jane.

La. It was catching. How stupid you all are, Mary thought: don't you see he is the last sort of man to be caught by a *la*? They would be tapping him with fans next. She kept her eyes on her plate. She had a terror of meeting his look – a kind of beautiful dismay at its inevitability.

'I should not want to spoil your digestion, Miss Clairmont,' Shelley said, putting up his long hand to push the drooping fringe out of his eyes. It was a gesture Mary had already begun to notice: it was always accompanied by a frown of surprise, as if he forgot he had such a thing as hair until reminded. 'But if I could put you off mutton, you know, I would.'

Shelley ate only vegetables. Even in her father's circles, Mary had never known such a thing: a young man was by definition someone who tucked heartily into brawn and steak. Shelley absently fed himself carrot and greens and bits of crumbled bread. There was nothing hearty about him; but nothing languid either. He was like stretched wire.

'But isn't it natural for people to eat meat?' Jane demanded.

'If it were, surely you would have fangs and claws in order to get it,' Shelley said. 'But to put the hypothesis to the test, the easiest thing would be to take up a live lamb from a meadow, and tear into it with your teeth.'

Jane squealed. 'The things you do say!'

'Well, there is, besides, the wastefulness,' Shelley said, turning to Godwin, who was blandly chewing in – indeed – a sheep-like way. 'Little wonder that meat is the favourite indulgence of the rich. An acre of ground goes to feed a single heifer, whose meat will only grace my lord and lady's table. That same acre might have been sown with wheat, which would make loaves to feed the whole village.'

'But does one really help the slaves by not taking sugar?' put in Fanny, in her slow, anxious way. 'Can it make any difference?'

'Oh, if everyone does it, then the plantations will be ended.'

285

'That's not likely to happen,' Jane said sturdily. 'The head-mistress at my school took so much of it you could stand the spoon up in the cup, and *she* was a tremendous Whig with a portrait of Fox above her escritoire.'

'One can give a lead,' Shelley said, still looking at Godwin.

'This,' Godwin said, then devoted half a minute to chewing – a new, annoyingly great-man habit of his, to begin a speech and then make you wait for it (or had Mary just begun to notice it? Had he always been like this? Was it all a lie? – Yes, the shrine had often been sullied, the godhead had shown a mortal taint, but could it be that the voice from the oracle was not that of a god at all? Not to be thought of. For what did that make her, who was half composed of him?). 'This is a question concerning individual conscience. It is my belief that each man and woman should be guided by it, looking at things as they are, and applying their rational faculties to each question strictly without reference to prejudice or convention. In this way, each will inevitably choose the good. It is also, I think, where my disciple and I–' an almost coquettish smile '–have our differences. You favour political organization and combination, sir, as I do not.'

Mary spoke up. 'Why not?'

Now Shelley was looking at her, but she kept her eyes on her father.

'Because I am a believer in complete liberty. And as soon as ten people concertedly agree on a policy, some liberty is sacrificed, for all ten cannot *wholly* agree. There will be elements in the policy that are not approved by some, but they endorse it for the sake of compromise. Thus the principle of freedom is abandoned. You see?' Her father's smile of complacency suddenly, awfully, fell away: he looked into the distance, lost and sorrowful, like someone contemplating a portrait of himself when he was young. Mary remembered Jane's giggling disclosure: 'Before he wrote to him, Mr Shelley actually thought Papa was *dead*.'

'I have great respect for your principles,' Shelley said earnestly. 'But in times like these, people of like mind must join together and seek practical remedies for our ills.'

'I'm sure you might go into Parliament, indeed, Mr Shelley, to hear your eloquence,' the Clairmont said, meaning nothing much beyond a desire to be talking. 'You should, sir, really you should—'

'Mr Shelley has just given his opinion of our legislators,' Mary snapped at her.

'Oh, I know that, my dear. I do know that. That's not what I'm saying, you see: I'm not saying that.'

Mary faced her. 'What are you saying, then?'

'No, no,' Shelley said peaceably, 'I couldn't, wouldn't, whichever you please. I'm no orator.' It was true that he had an oddly light, unstable tenor voice: sometimes to hear him speak was like listening to someone unmusical trying to sing. 'I hope to change things by my pen.' He bowed to Godwin. 'As you did, sir.'

Godwin wagged his shining head. Mary felt exquisitely torn. It was a kind and delicate compliment: but she wished her father had been honest enough to deny the truth of it.

She jumped: Shelley was addressing her. 'And, Miss Godwin – no one can be better placed than you to appreciate the power of the word. There is not only your father's example, but that of your illustrious mother. I confess meeting you – daughter of such a parent – it's almost as if someone has invited me to take tea with Athene, or shake hands with Sappho.'

For the second time, Mary found herself speaking unthinkingly. She answered him as if they were the only two people in the room, and she risked his eyes.

'I wish I'd known her,' she told him. 'I was only a baby – I have no memory of her at all.'

'Posterity will keep her memory,' he said to her.

'Oh, la, Mama,' Jane burst out loudly after a moment, 'how dreadful if I had lost you so soon as I was born! I think I should always have felt that somehow I had killed you!'

Mary was tolerably confident, from her long habit of self-suppression, that Jane did not see her flinch. (The glowing eyes of

287

the young man across the table, perhaps, but that was different: he was, in all ways, different.)

'But, Mr Shelley, you mentioned a decaying carcass,' piped up Fanny, who as ever was stuck at an earlier stage of the conversation. It was like that when the three girls went on walks: somehow Fanny would get behind, and the shameful thing was that too often you did not even notice her absence. 'And how honey could not come from it – but you must remember your Bible. The riddle of Samson, you know: the bees nesting in the dead lion. "Out of the strong came forth sweetness".'

' "And rebellion is as the sin of witchcraft",' Shelley said promptly. 'That's from a neighbouring book of the same Testament, I think? As I am whole-heartedly committed to rebellion, you may guess what I think of the Bible, Miss Godwin.'

'Oh – I know shocking things have been done in the name of religion,' Fanny said. 'All Papa's history books taught us that. Only—'

'You mistake me. I don't regret what has been made of the creed, but the creed itself. I think the Christian religion detestable: where it is not childish and nonsensical, it is oppressive, and calculated to increase mankind's misery while denying us even the solace of truth. But never mind,' he said brightly, at Fanny's look, 'though I single Christianity out as especially pernicious, I am just as severe on all religions, Miss Godwin – don't take it amiss.'

'To be sure, there is, isn't there, a great deal of hypocrisy about?' cried the Clairmont, blundering past the point as usual. 'But what shall you write, Mr Shelley? If you want to know what sells, you could do worse than consult me – involved in the trade as I am, with my *sposo*, of course.' La and *sposo*: what next, Mary wondered, *et tu, Brute*? 'There is always clamour for German romances – ghostly bridegrooms and horrors. But now Lord Byron's verse-tales are the new taste, the East and all that, and I shouldn't wonder if that's what the booksellers are all wanting.'

'A poet,' Shelley said, diffidently, 'yes, that's the glory I aim at.

If a man would be a world-changer, he must be a poet, or the poet must be in him. But I don't anticipate being any sort of rival to Byron. Walk out into the street and you will easily find someone who has heard of Childe Harold, but you will find no one who has heard of me.'

'Mr Shelley's book is *Queen Mab*,' said Godwin, 'and he is too modest. There is promise. A little raw, but certainly promise.'

'I should like to read it,' Mary said.

'I fancy I have lent my copy,' her father said vaguely. 'Of course it is rather—'

'You shall have another,' said Shelley – to Mary. 'I had it printed myself, and must be my own distributor. It is not the kind of thing to gladden a bookseller's heart, I fear. You write, Miss Godwin?'

'I make attempts, and generally destroy every one,' Mary said.

'Because you feel they are not good enough?'

'Oh, nothing can ever be good enough. And if it's only good enough, then it's not good at all.'

'You speak as if this were your creed.'

'Pooh, Mary's never happy. She always looks on the dark side, even where there ain't one,' said Jane.

Mary was so absorbed in private dialogue with Shelley that the interruption was as startling as if a picture had spoken. Equally surprising was her subsequent discovery that the dialogue was still going on, silently, sometimes without even looks.

'Oh, but the dark side is the most fascinating,' Shelley said, turning vividly to Jane. 'Don't you think? Now, I love horrors. When I was a boy, I used to tell my sisters stories at night – and which do you suppose those little innocents liked best? Stories of princesses and gold coaches? Not they. "Tell us about the Great Snake that lives in the woods and comes slithering out at night," they would say, "and the Great Tortoise that comes out of the pond and tramps all over the lawn—" '

'Oh! Stop it,' shrieked Jane, 'you make me shudder – I think that tortoise is even worse somehow.'

'Do you? Why?'

In all of this, Mary observed, there was nothing of the dreary flirtatiousness of the usual young man, who – even when intelligent – just had to give female company a parade of scampish personality. Shelley was interested in everyone. There was no hierarchy of attention. He gave the same consideration to the boy William's epic account of kite-flying as to her father's philosophical disquisitions.

Such as: 'All fear and horror,' Godwin was saying, 'arises from disproportion, which confounds the sense of reason – as with monstrous size in a creature.'

'Ah, but why is the tortoise worse than the snake?' Shelley said.

Mary spoke: 'Because ordinarily we would not mind a tortoise as we would a snake. The true terror is in the normal gone amiss. A hundred shrieking demons would not appal us so much as a single silent phantom with a face we knew.'

'Dear, dear, how morbid we grow!' her stepmother said, seizing Mary's teacup as if it had been stolen from her.

'All this, of course, is mere superstitious fancy,' Godwin said creakingly. Mary felt various shapes of disapproval pressing against her. Shelley's face (she was no longer avoiding it, was now taxed with the problem of how to stop looking at it) showed that he felt it too, but was sublimely and serenely used to it.

It was Fanny who managed to cast a shadow on him. She asked abruptly, as if rapping the gavel of convention: 'Mr Shelley, how is Mrs Shelley?'

'She is very well, I thank you.' Shelley made the motion of drinking from his empty cup. 'The last I heard.'

'Oh, let me give you some tea, you are quite neglected,' crooned the Clairmont.

'And your dear little daughter?' Fanny pressed.

'Likewise, likewise.' Shelley flung back his hair and stared around him. 'At least, I presume if she were dead Harriet might notify me.' He uttered a jagged laugh. 'Morbid. You are right, Mrs

Godwin.' He continued to look about him, flounderingly, as if he were drowning and none of them were trying to save him.

'People always disapprove what they don't understand,' Mary said to him. And, though it must be mere superstitious fancy, she was sure she could feel the spectral clutch and grasp of hands.

Caroline: in her element. London is *en fête* for the Summer of the Sovereigns – banquets, balls, suppers, operas, fireworks. She is particularly fond of these, perhaps because she is in the habit of setting them off herself, metaphorically. Alas, the festivities include one firework display gone horribly wrong, a pagoda of flame in St James's Park that kills several people.

Byron, of course, draws from that a bitterly ironic satisfaction. The fall of Napoleon has filled him with a savage despondency. He sees the true nature of his hero now, but he cannot approve the victors: it is all sour on the tongue. So she hears, and so he tells her, when he is civil to her, which is sometimes.

Yes: the association is not broken, not quite, not yet. Of course it should be. There have been – not ultimatums – but solemn talks with William.

'You know I am content for us to begin again on our old footing. You know there is no man with less of the Puritan in him than me. I live in the world and I don't expect it to resemble the new Jerusalem. Thank heaven.' A touch of the old William dryness: it still pleases her. She is a poor adulteress: cannot quite complete the revolution, dethrone her love for her husband, weak and discredited though it is. 'So all I ask, Caro, is your promise to try.'

'Oh, William, you have it,' she says, with passionate sincerity: for what people do not understand about Caroline is how hard she does try to control herself. If she really let herself go, there would be earthquakes.

'Then that's all *I* ask.' He smiles. Barely perceptible, that stress on I, but significant. For behind him, he subtly suggests, stand his family: the platoon of hostile Lambs, captained by matriarchal

Lady M., and from them only his tolerance protects her. Oh, she knows it. She knows they, with their big jaws and splendid teeth, would make short work of her, they would have her as a mere snack between their gargantuan meals. A nuncheon, as people are fond of saying nowadays. (Caro, connoisseur of piquant words, delights in this one. Think of me, she says to Byron, in one of their meetings that are not supposed to happen, think of me not as a hearty breakfast, not as a good dinner, but a nuncheon: now doesn't that tempt your appetite? And there it is, she could swear it, beneath the pose of stern rejection the old flicker of amusement, and what may not be blown into life from such an ember?)

But she must be good, she must be – at the very least – respectful of appearances. And so she tries, and yet what is she to do, when she moves in society and so does Byron? Especially this sleepless, mad summer with the Town all cock-a-hoop for the visit of the Allied Sovereigns like a hundred Seasons packed into one. Her element.

Wafted by the blessed winds of peace the conquering monarchs come across the sea, to pay homage to the land that has led the long struggle to lay the ghost of usurpation and restore legitimacy and liberty to the nations of Europe. Well: there is a lot of this sort of language about this summer, and part of Caroline is susceptible to it. Glory and grandeur and heroism – and yet Caroline's other side, the imp and jester, blinks beady eyes at the dubious reality, which she sees at close quarters. She thought no man could be fatter than the Prince Regent until at Devonshire House she is presented to Louis XVIII, the restored King of France – Louis the Gouty, as Byron calls him: a genteelly perspiring grossness spread over two chairs, with a little head somewhere near the top of the cone-shaped bulk. At the opposite extreme, King Frederick William of Prussia, so stiff and bony and soldierly – all joints, she thinks, as if he could be folded up like a piece of his own camp-furniture.

Still, there is General Blücher, magnificently moustachioed and nostrilled and everything a man called General Blücher should be; and Caroline's own favourite, everyone's favourite, the Tsar of Russia. To begin with, there is something irresistible about being a *Tsar* – any grand pumpernickel can be a king – and then he is tall and fair and looks as if he would make a splendid statue and he is surrounded by Cossacks in uniforms that even Caroline's flamboyance could not have devised. And he waltzes: everyone waltzes this summer, and of course Caroline most of all. She even has hopes of taking the floor with none other than Wellington: the great eagle alights in town at last in late June and is soon exhibiting his hooked profile around the salons.

Where, still, she always looks out for that other famous profile. The one that is incised on her heart – and why is it, she wonders, that there is always this triteness about what is most true? For there Byron still is, at the centre of her. Yes, she hates him quite as often as she adores him, but that doesn't dislodge him. In France the statues of Boney are being hacked down from their plinths, but for Caro Lamb the Napoleon of Rhyme, as they call him, still reigns and rules.

And this is the other side of her hectic summer. One day she whisks from Hyde Park Ring to calls to a levée to a dinner to an assembly to bed at four when the midsummer dawn is already breaking: the next day she pursues her private course, her Byron course. Forbidden and difficult, yes, but for the addict even the subterfuges of addiction have their thrill.

Often a Byron day will involve a visit to John Murray, the publisher in his Albemarle Street town-house. The soft-spoken Scot, civil, sober-suited, with the slightly drooping lid of his blinded eye giving him a perpetual look of reservation, and the willowy slip of quick-tongued, copper-curled, blue-blooded oddity – how could they ever have come together? Only through something miraculous, she concludes: only through Byron.

Even more curious, they have embarked on a true friendship. It seems to leave them both a little baffled, as they sit facing each other, sometimes in the glass-domed waiting room, sometimes in the airy drawing room where the changing sunlight runs brilliantly along the bookshelves like a stick drawn along railings.

'I am so fond of this room,' she says, 'I do not know a pleasanter in London. And, yes, I will say it – there is such a sense of *him* in it.'

Murray nods, cautious. 'That may well be. His work has played no small part in our prosperity as a firm. Lady Caroline, I wonder if it is you I have to thank for the basket of hothouse fruit I received yesterday—'

'Yes, I thought you would like it, though if you do not I shall not mind at all, for I sometimes feel that fruit is after all something of an *impostor*, don't you? It is always so shiny and shapely and brightly coloured and then you taste it and so often it is no more than pleasant and in the case of the strawberry, that great imposition, not even that, a mere piece of damp plaster with a *tang* . . . I suppose he has a new piece ready for the press?'

'He has.' Always a pause before a remark from Murray, who seems to inspect it like a banknote. 'I may say it is entitled *Lara*. It is an Eastern tale, though he talks of doing no more in that vein. Of course they have made his fame, but he may wish to turn his genius to other themes.'

'Mr Murray, when you first saw him, did you suppose him marked out for fame?'

'Well: yes.' Lightly he laughs at himself. 'There now, Lady Caroline, you have made me speak romantically, and that is not my wont.'

'You delightful man! And yet you know fame – consider it – is a species of *doom* for those who seek it. Because it is finite. When does fame end? Why, when *everybody* knows you. And in our dear friend Lord B.'s case that is not so very far away. And so when that is achieved, what remains? What but a fall?'

Cradling his knee, Murray studies her thoughtfully: this sheer-muslined exotic who periodically invades his peaceful demesne like a cameleopard crashing into a pony-paddock. And yet he looks forward to it.

'Your prophecy might be true, if fame were all Lord Byron seeks.'

'You think it is not? I ask because I wonder – what it is he does want – what is at the root of it all. Some say he is actively seeking a wife – which you who are so close to him would surely know about.'

'My dear Lady Caroline, I thought you liked my company, not my information: and you know if I had any that I was at liberty to divulge, I would let you have it.'

'My dear Mr Murray, you are so gently firm with me – firmly gentle – whatever it may be – I wish others had been so, and then things might have been – but no more of *that*. I suppose you thought, when I first sought your acquaintance, that I only did so because of Byron.'

Murray scrutinizes this note for a long time. 'I did suppose so, at first: if only because you took no pains to hide it. Now, I think that if my famous author deserted me for another publisher – which heaven forbid – we would still be sitting here having our chats.'

'Oh, yes, sir: I would still come, even if only to remind myself what the word "gentleman" means.'

They sit in silence for a few moments: both oddly moved, though a thousand miles from expressing it.

'Well!' says Caroline briskly. 'Do you know the question that was occupying me as I rode here – for you know my horse is so familiar with the way that I can cogitate all I please in the saddle? The question – I warn you it is deep and theological – can there be any virtue without vice?'

'My first instinct is to say yes – but I fear you are going to correct me.'

'Fear me, Mr Murray? – there was never anyone less to be feared, believe me or not the truth remains – but the question occurs to me because of *you*, who have helped me to see the greatest of all virtues is forgiveness. You have known my sins, and forgiven them.'

'Oh, come—'

'I obtained Byron's portrait from you by imitating his signature, did I not? Was that not thoroughly wicked and larcenous?'

'These are strong expressions. Though I should say to you, Lady Caroline, in a spirit of confidence and cordiality, that what you call imitation the law would call forgery. I don't mean there was ever any question of law in this case. But it would be wise to bear in mind that folly can cross over into crime. I would be glad, for your own sake, to feel that you knew this.'

'Oh,' Caroline says, with a quick bare smile, 'what will be will be, sir, but I thank you – I am a thousand times your debtor for your kindness, both now and formerly because the point is you did forgive me that and – and also my *unannounced* visits. You see – you are a true Christian. And so here is the question: there could not be forgiveness if there were no vices to forgive, therefore is not vice necessary to the world, even a force for good? And how are we to live with such paradoxes?'

'A theological question, as you say, and not one I feel qualified to answer.'

'Oh, fie, sir, you must, you are a good Protestant, and we do not have priests to stand between us and divinity – I tease, of course – only if this thesis were true I wonder might it not be that some people are put upon earth expressly to test the virtues of forgiveness of others? Thus that it is their purpose to be bad?'

'Dear, dear – would these creatures not be redeemable?'

'Oh, no,' Caroline says casually, gathering up her riding-crop, 'they must be damned.'

And back to her element: a reception at Lady Cork's in honour of Blücher, who with unPrussian lack of punctuality stays late at the opera and keeps the guests waiting, bored and a little fractious until Caroline slips out, dons a coachman's greatcoat and hat, and asks the servants to shout hurrah in the hall. When she comes stomping and swaggering in, one deaf, dim-eyed old lady, oblivious to the laughter, curtsies low to the gamine general, then goes home contented to have paid homage to her hero. And then at Burlington House an event that brings together these two strands of Caro's life: a masked ball in honour of Wellington at which Byron himself is present.

To be with Byron *and* in costume: this brings back many memories.

'Does it not?' she says to him, as soon as she can get near him in the crush. 'Don't tell me, Byron, that there is nothing in your mind that is in mine just now?' She lifts her cloak to reveal her slender legs in tight green pantaloons.

'You shouldn't do that,' he says, with a bleak glance. He is in a cowled monk's habit, which makes his pallor quite deathly.

'Why not? I am a married woman, and my husband is present – somewhere – yes, there he is in the Italian dress, see? You of all people have not grown moral, I hope.'

'If I did, would you cease plaguing me, Caro?'

'Oh, it would take more than that,' she says, dancing round him. He is plainly not in spirits, and she is pleased at that: what more cheering sight than an unhappy ex-lover?

'Please instruct me what it *would* take,' he says mordantly, 'so that I may take steps to procure it.'

'Oh, Mr Hobhouse,' she says, slipping her arm through that of Byron's starchy friend, 'I am afraid Lord Byron is in the sullens today. Could it be because all these tiresome kings are out-dazzling his celebrity?'

Hobhouse, dressed in the dashing Albanian costume that Byron has made famous, and looking deeply silly in it, does not know what to say. He would never speak against his idolized friend, but Caroline suspects he is not impervious to the pantaloons either.

'You shouldn't do it,' Byron says again, 'for the sake of your reputation, though I don't suppose you'll listen to me.'

'Why, do you imagine I care what people think of me?'

'You only care what I think of you, which you shouldn't: I can make no difference one way or another.'

'Oh, Byron, what company can you be keeping, to make you so dreary and grandfathery?'

He sends her a smile that in its grimness nearly overbalances her mood. 'Surely such an accomplished spy as you would know that, Caroline?'

She dances away from him: not wanting to hear.

For – yes, in stillness and quiet, beyond the racket of her mind she will admit it – there are other Byron days, days when instead of calling on Murray she goes straight to the source.

Albany: Byron moved here in the spring, into a set of bachelor chambers more permanent than his usual lodgings, and thereby presented Caroline with terrible temptations. Irony is a spur: for Albany House, before being converted into apartments, was once the newlywed home of Lord and Lady Melbourne. To go there, secretly, wrongly, is to cock a double snook at the indomitable in-law – the spiteful spider or withering webster – but beyond that there is the sheer beautiful *accessibility* of Byron's new lair. She can be where he is. Even when he is not.

Oh, at first it was conventional and acceptable enough. She called on him, properly, and he received her – seeming indeed relieved that they could now swim in these lukewarm waters – and she admired the apartment, the high-ceilinged sitting room with the arched windows looking on to the garden, the fire-screen fitted up with a collage of theatre scenes, the Turkish hangings, the macaw that chuckled and damned your eyes in Byron's own accents. Could he tell, when she cooed polite appreciation, that her heart was screaming a thousand times louder that *this was her place*, that to be here was to take him blissfully in at her very pores?

Perhaps not: for after all he is wilfully burying the old magical intuition between them, and it is up to her to tend the sacred flame alone. And that is why, to be in that place, to drink of that draught, she has to resort to other methods.

Not bad in themselves. She waits about the courtyard or the passage until either Fletcher or the strange old witchlike maid to whom Byron is unaccountably attached comes out on some errand, and then she slips in. She does no harm: often she does not even sit down: she stands and breathes, eyes half closed, imagining him, conjuring him. Sometimes she will leave him a note, tucking it perhaps in the flyleaf of a book so that he will come upon it with surprise. Childhood tales of elvish visitation return to her. It makes her smile inside; when she is not weeping. Other times, she must take other measures. There is, she finds, a tradesman's entrance to Albany on the basement level. It is relatively simple to disguise herself in a workman's greatcoat and anonymously penetrate the sanctum through that musty-smelling brick passage. And exciting, somehow.

But, yes, this is the bad Caro: she knows it: the side of her that should be defeated, deposed, sent to Elba.

(William, giving her a curtain lecture: 'Car, you said you would curb these mad fancies to please me.' Yes, she said in true submission, I will try, I will. And then William, eyes glittering, testing the truth of that submission: 'You said you would please me. Please me, my love . . .')

Still she cannot stop it. Albany is her magnetic north. And if transgression is natural to her, as she is beginning to fear it is, then she can only hope and pray that her punishment will not be too severe. (Lately, terrible mystic dreams in which Augustus, dear heavy helpless Augustus, hovers above her bed like a sprite and then, grinning, fades upwards into nothingness.)

After all, she can point to temptations resisted. There is his desk: his papers, letters.

The trouble is, the trouble is (and her eyes still sting whenever she thinks of it), she has lost one of her few moorings. Grandmama Spencer, straight-backed and outspoken to the last, died a couple of months since: Grandmama Spencer who always believed in her and towards the end was beginning – but only beginning – to despair of her. Gone. And now, thinks Caroline – prowling Byron's rooms, circling but not approaching his desk, arching her neck to read the snatch of his dashing sloping script peeping out from a closed notebook – now, there is no one to tell her, even in her mind, when she is doing wrong.

'You have such a bruise on your cheek – what happened?' Mary said.

'Have I, where?' Shelley mapped his face with long fingers.

'Careful, don't touch it.' Careful, she pointed: careful to avoid the jeopardizing contact. 'There.'

'Oh, yes. Ow. Is it very hideous? There's no mirror in my lodgings.'

'How do you manage shaving?'

'I know where my beard grows. I wonder how I – oh, wait, I did have a notion I'd been sleepwalking this morning. Wasn't sure, but the bedroom door was open, and I always close it.'

'Why?'

'For fear,' he said, with a ghostly smile, 'of what may come in.'

She turned and began polishing the glass door of the next bookcase. 'Do you often walk in your sleep?'

'It depends,' he said. He didn't say on what. 'A few times I've woken up in the street. Oh, quite safely. I've always found myself curled up in a doorway or something. And no one has ever bothered me. But then who would notice? We're used to wretches sleeping on the streets, in our Christian polity. Part of an Englishman's traditional liberty, don't you know. Never, sir, never shall I see it imperilled, while there is breath in my et cetera. I don't suppose you have a mirror down here?'

'Not in the shop. I could go up and fetch one but—'

'No. No, I know what you mean.'

They were coming more and more to these moments: unspoken understandings. To go upstairs might flush out the Clairmont, or even her father – for though the girls had never been permitted to interrupt his work, he often left the study for Shelley. But then that was because of the money.

'Aha, here's a thought.' He shrugged off his coat. Underneath he wore – unheard-of – no waistcoat, and his rumpled shirt was open at the throat. It gave him a shipwrecked look. He held the dark coat up above his head, spreading it like a cloak, and peered at his reflection in the bookcase glass. 'Oh, that's a beauty. Like I've been in a proper fist-fight.'

Their reflected eyes met. Her own face, she thought, looked strangely unsymmetrical; also fantastically solemn. But then that was how she felt. Utter joy, she was discovering, was solemn. It did not jingle, it gave out a great profound note like a vast bell.

'I hope you don't get into fist-fights.' She meant it to be jocular, but it came out governessish.

'Not any more. I did at school. When the teasing became unbearable. I would hear something snap in my head.' He lowered the coat and their reflections paled. 'Then I would lash out. I didn't know how to fight. I just – climbed up on my rage and rode it. Rather frightening, really.'

'Why did they tease you?'

'Oh, for being different. The ultimate crime. Now instead of the playground there is society, and instead of my fists I have the pen.' He uttered his high, sudden laugh. 'How self-regarding that sounds. Mary, are you happy here?'

She could not answer. 'You'd better put on your coat.'

'Why? Oh, in case someone comes in. Yes, of course, by the lights of our current social arrangements I'm practically naked.' He slipped on the coat, drooped over to the shop-window where an elderly matron was peering suspiciously in, and pulled a grotesque face at her. 'That was meant to be a Greek tragic mask. Now the Greeks went naked or partially so for much of the time, and their morality was not noticeably harmed by it, quite the reverse, they had the advantage of us in most areas of moral philosophy. Are not clothes, indeed, hypocrisy made visible?' He came back to her, pale, looking abruptly exhausted. 'Now I fear you may think me a mere sensualist – that I am being loathsomely suggestive – it isn't so, Mary, believe me. And yes, I have called you Mary twice, and look, we are still alive. Outraged convention should surely have conjured an earthquake by now.

301

Or at least a whiff of brimstone. Of course I should have asked you first, but I felt I didn't have to, somehow.'

'You didn't.' She looked at the duster in her hand. She was surprised to find how much she hated this trivial object. 'Shelley, can I ask you a question?'

'Anything.' Again with Shelley this perilous sense that he meant it: that even the conventions of speech could not be taken on trust.

'Why did you ask me whether I am happy here?'

'Because it is a matter I care for,' he said slowly. 'Your happiness, or otherwise.'

'And if I were – unhappy?'

'Then I should hope to be able – to try to change that.' All at once he seemed to veer away. 'If I did not think this world could be changed for the better, I would despair. Kill myself, probably.'

'Oh, don't.'

'Ah, there's prejudice creeping in. We still hear the old Mosaic thunder when we mention suicide, and yet it's only an act such as a free human being may make, like going abroad or getting married.'

'But you don't approve of marriage, I think.'

'Quite right. And am married, as you are too gentle to point out. Well, while our social arrangements are as they are, I couldn't secure the young lady's reputation without marriage. In a changed world, she would not be at the mercy of opinion in that way. Nor would any of us be compelled to register our affections like excisable goods, and chain ourselves in official pairs like so many matrimonial carriage-horses.'

'That's why my father and mother married. I dare say she hoped by the time I had grown that things might have altered. But, Shelley, isn't the world simply too strong?' She was swept with despondency – though it left her fundamental joy untouched. Sorrow could not long breathe in this air, with his voice in her ears, and the sight of his nervous hand with its expressive branching vein, and the scent of him, which was curiously warm and sweet like new bread wrapped in linen.

'It is my one great fear that it will be. But we will just have to try.' He took a shilling from his pocket and set it spinning on the counter. 'To change it.'

Guiltily, Mary thought: I believe you are a world-changer, Shelley. *My* world. And I do care for the wider world but not so much, not so much as I care for mine. Change it, Shelley, change my world.

One thing did change: the shop. The place she detested was now, as their rendezvous, almost beautiful. But she shouldn't have been so surprised at the transformation, Mary thought: look how the mere presence of the Clairmonts had turned her home into hell.

He had taken lodgings in nearby Hatton Garden, and came to Skinner Street nearly every day. There was no question of pretexts. He was still in the middle of arranging the loan, or gift, to Godwin, so it was entirely natural for him to be about. Even Mary's formidable brain could not quite follow the complexities of Shelley's finances, but she gathered that he was trying to raise money on his expectations. In the normal run of things, Shelley would have inherited his father's estate in due course. But Shelley did not want it. He did not believe in it: he would rather see it broken up and given away. Then there was the not unconnected fact that his father hated him. All this made money matters difficult: when all he wanted, as he explained to Mary, was to renounce his claim on his inheritance for a modest living now.

'I think he is as much my enemy for that, as for the atheism. Which is revealing in all ways. It is the look of the thing, you see. Respectable son respectably following in footsteps of respectable father. Now if he had been a genuinely pious old donkey, angry at the insult to the religion in which he misguidedly believes, do you think I would have clashed with him so fiercely? But no, you see: it's the look of the thing. He doesn't even give a hang about the Christian religion, deep down: it's a *convenance*, it's a good hat. And the worst thing is, I think he knows that I know this. I've seen through him.' His eyes sparkled: witch's eyes. 'And that's the last thing we can ever forgive someone for.'

Often Godwin invited him to dine. 'Our young friend has not much acquaintance in London, and is I think somewhat at a loose end,' he pronounced, with vague benevolence. True, there was only one friend Shelley introduced at Skinner Street. Thomas Jefferson Hogg: Hogg the aptly named, as Mary thought of him at first. She tried to respect him as Shelley's friend, and as the co-author of the atheist pamphlet that had got them both expelled from Oxford. But she could see only a heavy-set, hard-glaring young man with a lawyer's supercilious sniff and a habit of addressing Shelley by name a lot as if to assert his claim on him. 'Well, Bysshe, it is just as you described it.' 'Bysshe, d'you recall when they had us before the Master and Fellows . . . ?' 'Bysshe, look at the time, we should be going.' Hogging him.

But then she admitted to herself that Hogg could have been as charming as a cavalier and still she would have wished him gone. Because she could not bear to share Shelley – always that name alone, to her, a name she seemed to have heard somewhere before she was born – with anyone.

Not that he was hers to share.

'It will be my daily prayer,' Fanny said before she left, folding her hands prayerfully, 'that Mr Shelley and his wife are soon reconciled.'

'Why, just the other day you were saying you thought she was flighty in her dress,' cried Jane.

'What I said was that I feared there might have been a little tendency that way, and that it might have formed one of the differences between them,' Fanny said painstakingly.

'No man likes to see a dowd,' asserted Jane. She had lately become very stylish, great in ribbons, proficient in poplins. 'Anyhow, it's like Papa has always taught – if two people cease to get along, then it's nonsense for them to stay together.'

'Yes, I suppose,' Fanny said dispiritedly. It was one of those times when you longed for her to say no, to stand up for herself, and when she did not you felt as annoyed as if she had let you down. Poor Fanny. She was going away to Wales for a holiday with friends of the Clairmonts: it was to do her good, she was sickly and fretful lately.

Also she kept talking about Shelley. Mary noticed: she wondered if her stepmother had noticed too. Shelley was as courteous with Fanny as with everyone, while Fanny merely looked as if she longed to do his darning, but you could never tell; and the trouble with Fanny was you never felt inclined to ask – there were just so many fences and hedges to hack your way through before you could get anywhere near a confidence.

But if Fanny is deluded, Mary thought, waiting in the transformed shop to hear his unmistakable step, then what am I?

'Will you,' he demanded, 'walk with me? You and Miss Clairmont?'

'Where to?'

'The Elysian Fields. Or, say, Charterhouse Square. We must make it Elysian with our conversation.'

He smiled, but crookedly: she had already noticed he had days like this, when he looked sensationally ill, blanched and haggard. Then by the evening he could be back to normal. She had thought of Mr Coleridge, and what she now knew to be an addiction to opium, but it surely wasn't that: Shelley did not even drink wine. She suspected that it was somehow part of him. He had his own interior climate, subject to its own storms and spells.

'I would like to, very much,' Mary said, and then came to a stop, and everything seemed to come to a stop, for ever, with him leaning bonelessly on the counter and her half facing away from him dressed in the tartan frock from Dundee and staring fixedly at a pen in her hand that wanted mending.

'But,' he said at last, raking at his hair, 'you're tied to this miserable shop – this wretched servitude—'

'No, it isn't that.'

Well, partly. There might well be complaints from the

Clairmont, not that she cared a fig for those: only that then there might be talk, and questions, and a light might be shone into places she didn't yet know about: didn't know whether they contained only darkness and must, or beautiful secrets.

She burst out: 'Mrs Shelley—'

'Yes?' he said encouragingly, when she could not go on again. 'You want to ask something about Mrs Shelley? Mind, her name is Harriet, so why should we not say it? Because we should not be speaking of her at all?'

'Properly, we should not.' Mary shrugged helplessly. 'I – I know nothing of her.'

'Neither did I,' Shelley said, with a dungeon laugh, 'hence this and thus and hence many things. Harriet is in many ways the most delightful person. Unfortunately they are not the right ways for me, for us, and now we discover this. In a better state of society this would be the occasion only of a rational parting with good wishes upon either side. But then in a better state of society she would not have been so persecuted by a tyrant of a father, so that she had no alternative but to flee from him, *und so weiter*. Here, let me.' He took the pen from her, pulled from his pocket a clasp-knife with an alarming blade.

'Do you always carry that about with you?'

'No, sometimes a pistol. They make me feel safer, somewhat. When we were living in Wales, someone got into the house and attacked me. And the odd thing is I always felt that that was a thing likely to happen. When I look at this world I see the bars of a cage that have been broken through by some huge beast.'

'Are you inside the cage, or out?'

'Ah, that I don't know, none of us does. I only know the feeling of peril on the edge of vision. I read too many Gothic romances in my youth, perhaps.'

'Jane has a great fancy for those.'

'I know – we were talking of them the other day – she has such a ghastly imagination, it was delicious.' Strange, Mary thought, how *physical* this jealousy is: she could almost have sagged to her knees with it. 'You, I think, have too clear a mind for such stuff.'

'I can imagine horrors,' she said baldly, 'all too well.'

'Which is why you don't need the artificial stimulants of the Minerva Press. The imagination – is it not like a limb, how would we get about without it? And yet you know people do.' He handed her the pen: he had not mended it well, though he was blind to it. 'My father wanted to have me locked up in a lunatic asylum. That, at least, when it became clear he could not ship me off to the war to be comfortably killed on a Spanish plain.' Like a dog's, his head sank. 'You can imagine what he thought of my marrying Harriet.'

Shelley had this way of talking about his father as though he was as universally known as Napoleon, or God. And Mary's imagination, which was intense in a debilitating way, like migraine, had pictured nearly all of it: the house in Sussex, Field Place, a place in a field – she saw lush meadows and long shadows and a carriage-sweep leading to a white portico (and there was a part of her, a very small part, that longed for it while the rest of her disapproved of it) and the elegant sisters he was not allowed to see any more and the refined, downtrodden mother and even Shelley's west-facing bedroom where, he had told her, he would stretch his eyelids open with his fingers so as to take in even more of the setting sunlight that flooded the windows. 'Light beyond light – like syrup – like lava.' Yet the father – his likeness eluded her. She tried blending Shelley's high-boned features with the stiff stodge of a paterfamilias, but the result only flickered in and out of life: and sometimes it even showed, momentarily, the face of her own father.

But then how could she envisage a man who hated Shelley? How, she thought fearfully, does that happen? Where does the unfelt poison enter and begin its relentless circuit of the blood?

'But you did marry her,' she said. 'You did marry Harriet—'

'Aye, and there's the offence! "Throwing himself away on an underbred chit" – oh, I can hear it. Now what I should have

307

done, what I was marked out to do, was quietly ascend to my father's estate, and attend the county meetings and sit on the bench and oppress my tenants in the most gentlemanly way possible. And for all this, select the appropriate helpmeet. Look for birth and fortune, though fortune first. View the available female livestock at the assembly ball or social cattle-market. Now marry and produce a prompt heir. After that, if you must, you may amuse yourself with affairs, as long as you are very discreet about them, and keep them in their proper place. This is the world, and thus is all love, sacred and profane, smeared with the dung of the streets.' He seemed about to slam his fist on the counter, but was overtaken with a sudden, transfiguring smile. With Shelley it was as if you were under a cold windy spring sky with cloud shadows racing across the ground – and then, giant gleams. 'I'm sorry. This is not the language of the drawing room.'

'We're not in a drawing room,' Mary said. Faintly smiling in her turn – but not laughing, they did not laugh, and she did not think they ever would. For if they were to have an *ever*, then Shelley would be carrying her to it in his arms across a dizzy chasm by the slenderest of bridges, and there could be no laughter up in that tremendous air.

'Jane and I are going on a walk with Mr Shelley.'

She found her father and the Clairmont together, going over the accounts. Her stepmother's shoe was off and she was rubbing away with obscene gusto at her corn. Her father seemed to take no notice of this at all.

'Mm – ask him to step up and see me when you return, will you?' he said, not looking up. The room smelt of heated stocking. Mary got out.

They walked through scented pockets of tree-shade and shrilling gnat-swarms and Shelley said: 'Everything that is behind me I do not want. Or it does not want me. This is a curious sensation.'

'Yes,' Mary said. Breathing the hot still air was like inhaling warm water. It seemed to leave her brain dizzy and exposed. 'Oh, yes, I know.'

The trouble is this. What Mary is drawing towards, what she is impelled to, is something that does not really suit her. Though she always feels strongly, the mind is her ruler. This mind is accustomed to seeing all round a question. It has the gift of analysis, which is also, perhaps, a curse: while appreciating the beauty of a rose it will also be estimating the length of time before the rose withers. But still she trusts it as a watchmaker trusts the steadiness of his hand.

And her mind cannot approve the dubious shape of the future to which passion is driving her. The shape is shadowy, awkward, chaotic. It is revolution: and that mind has too much logic to believe that revolutions can be accomplished without blood.

Still, it is a mind with a sharp edge, impatient of prevarication: let your yea be yea. Thus, for Mary Godwin the most momentous decision of her life is completely out of character, except for the fact that she makes it.

Harriet Shelley: the wife and mother: young, pretty, fashionably dressed. Mary, with typical thoroughness, tried to comprehend her rival, but could not invest the absent Harriet with much more reality than this.

'I won't speak ill of her,' Shelley said, 'because that suggests blame, and there isn't any blame. Ill influences, perhaps. She bends with every wind, and just now it's her sister, who has convinced her I'm evil. To be shunned and flown from. Perhaps I am, for her, as we do not do each other good any more. I only know that what I felt soon became what I pretended to feel – and that was, after all, not much different – and also that even at the best, it was a shadow. Only a shadow.'

How do you know? she wanted to ask. A shadow compared with what? The reality, the reality of love? These were the coming questions, and she must ask them and then abide by the answers and the consequences. Knowing this produced a kind of cold, livid excitation for which she could only find one comparison.

'How does it feel, do you suppose,' she asked, as they walked, 'when one is about to commit a murder?'

He started, then closed his eyes blissfully and squeezed her arm. 'Thank heaven,' he murmured, 'that I'm not the only one to wonder.'

2

Summer of the Sovereigns: Hot

For the Brawnes, dwellers in the suburbs of history, the great events of the summer of 1814 had no direct significance. And yet they were not untouched.

Uncle John Ricketts, with whom Fanny and her family went to stay for a week, was cautious. He had been a cheesemonger in the City and still had property interests there, and he was shocked at the way some of his old business associates were rushing into speculation. The funds were buoyant because of the new continental markets thrown open by Napoleon's defeat, but it was, he kept saying with a shake of his great grizzled head, early days yet, very early days.

Mrs Brawne, meanwhile, looked discreetly at Fanny's developing figure and thought of the officers of army and navy who would be returning to the assemblies of Highgate and Hampstead. And looking for a fortune, perhaps: but still. One had hopes.

And Fanny was glad the war was over because she deplored all the killing, and because she was bored by the talk of lines and divisions and entrenchments. During their stay with Uncle John they went into Town nearly every day to view the celebrations, and here was life as she felt it ought to be: bright, gay, social.

They saw the Tsar, bowing to a cheering crowd from the balcony of the Pulteney Hotel, and General Blücher riding in Hyde Park and hardly able to get along for clutching well-wishers. Fanny, with her fascination for costume, was entranced by the cuirassiers and Cossacks, the shakos and dolmans, and tried to memorize them for her sketchbooks. She was doing this when the gentleman without eyelashes touched her.

The Brawnes were in Green Park to watch a balloon ascent, with fireworks later. But nothing much was happening yet: there was some problem with the guy-ropes, and the novelty of seeing the great gaudy onion-shaped bag rocking above the treetops was wearing off, and Fanny's eye was beguiled by the glittering uniforms of a group of Russian officers up on Constitution Hill. In the restless press of people she had become a little separated from her family, though she did not realize it until she found herself squeezed up against the gentleman. Who was such by his dress, fashionable pantaloons and hessians, and his speech, which had the dandyish bleat: but Fanny's observant eye took in the soiled and frayed bands at his cuffs. His breath on her face smelt of wine. He had not very much sandy hair, and no eyelashes at all to his red-rimmed eager eyes.

'You like the look of our gallant allies, do you, my dear?' he said in her ear. 'They are a fine set of men, are they not?'

'They are very fine indeed, sir,' she said politely.

'Very fine indeed,' he echoed, smiling harder at her. 'And yet do you want to hear a secret about them? Hm? You look like a girl who enjoys a secret.'

Fanny gazed back into his aching eyes. Knowing she ought to be afraid of him, she found the knowledge destroyed the fear.

'You don't look like a fortune-teller,' she said.

'What's that, my dear?' He squeezed closer, his arm travelling round her.

'I mean, sir, if you can tell so much about me merely by a look. "There's no art to find the mind's construction in the face." Shakespeare, you know.'

'Oh, I know,' he said, though he plainly didn't. His hand was now touching her waist, and giving signs of moving downwards. 'Now the secret I was going to tell you about those Russians – would you believe they drink the oil out of the lamps?'

'I would believe it if someone else told me,' she said, trying to edge away from him.

'Oho.' He was still smiling with his yellow teeth, but not with his lashless eyes: there was something else in them. 'But there's another secret. Do you know where they relieve themselves? Can you think? In fireplaces and cupboards. Even just on the floor – even in company.' Now his hand had moved down to brush her buttocks: Fanny used muscles she did not know she had to squirm sideways. 'Can you imagine that? You know what it means, of course. They get out their weapons there and then – you know what I mean by weapons?'

'Sabres, perhaps. Or muskets.'

'Oh, no, no. I shall have to teach you—'

'Or lances, or flintlocks, or pistols, or grenades–' her voice rose steadily '–or bayonets, or cutlasses, or rapiers, or daggers, or halberds – dear me, it must be one of those, sir? Or do you mean something else entirely?'

Teeth still, but no smile. 'You're a provoking little creature, my dear. Don't you know that's not the way to behave when a gentleman is nice to you?'

'As I am not yet fifteen, I don't expect gentlemen to be nice to me, and if they are it shows they are neither nice nor gentlemen,' she said sweetly. The crowd had parted a little, and she had a view of Uncle John's stiff back. 'But my uncle is there – perhaps we should consult him. Perhaps he will know the name of the weapon that escapes you.'

For the first time, it seemed, the naked eyes blinked. 'I'll bet your uncle has done this,' he hissed, with a last fumble at her.

'With grown ladies he may have done, for all I know. But if he could only do it to young girls in parks, I should think him a sad fellow. But we'll ask him, sir, if you like. Uncle John!'

On Hampstead Heath once she had seen an adder go sliding away into the ferns very much in the same way that the lashless gentleman now disappeared into the crowd.

'Ah, there you are, my dear.' Uncle John mopped his brow.

'Really, this heat is too much. I would suggest we go home, but Margaret is so set upon seeing the balloon go up. But then there is sure to be another ascent tomorrow – and you do look rather flushed, my dear – are you quite well?'

'I'm quite well, Uncle,' Fanny said, slipping her arm through his. 'And we mustn't disappoint Margaret. Look, I think the balloon is ready at last.'

'You're a good girl, Fanny.'

I'm not sure I am, Fanny thought. If I was, I would have been more shocked. I wonder if the Russians do make water in the fireplace? Surely not. It would put the fire out, and I've heard that Russia is a very cold country, so that would make no sense at all.

She smiled. Even if she was not good, perhaps never would be, she felt proud that she had seen her assailant off with nothing more than woman's wit. Rosalind or Viola would have applauded her, she thought.

Uncle John used his elbows, and they squeezed through to where her mother stood with Samuel and Margaret under a fond arm each. The balloon rose and everyone cheered, Fanny as loudly as anyone. She had another success that day, managing to get home and into the privacy of the outhouse before being sick.

Hailstones like dried peas pelted at the window of the bedroom Mary shared with Jane. It was late afternoon – they had gone up to tidy themselves before dinner – but it might have been any time of day from the strange subterranean light: earlier there had been thunder too. Hail, most nonsensical of weathers, Mary thought, it presaged nothing nor cleared the air, and if it moistened the soil it dashed the plants to pieces anyhow. Another proof surely that there was no benevolent deity behind the universe. Like someone exercising a weak limb, Mary kept mentally exercising this thought, which Shelley had demonstrated so clearly, and which had so terrified her at first she could not sleep for thinking of it. Always there had been her father's steady unbelief, but this was different: Shelley made you feel it.

He made her feel many things, not all of them comfortable. In fact, none of them. But feeling, yes, God, yes, more feeling than she thought was possible. It was as if before this she had lived like a tuber, a root, buried in nerveless darkness.

'Damn,' she said softly, as the hail began to turn to fat cold raindrops. The weather had become very important. Good weather meant she could meet Shelley outdoors, freely, intimately.

'Hell and damnation,' said Jane companionably, doing experimental things with her rich black curls in front of the mirror. 'Hell and damnation and the devil take it. Not that one believes in these barbaric superstitions, of course. I wonder what we will swear by when such things are got rid of altogether?'

'We won't need to.'

'Because there'll be perfect happiness and peace, I suppose. Still, I can't imagine not wanting to swear ever. One would have to be a saint. Or Fanny. How does this look?'

'Pretty well. Rather elegant.'

Mary found herself looking – really looking – at her stepsister. Jane had changed, and one saw it without seeing it. Mary still tended to think of her as the competitive little girl craning over her shoulder at lessons and weeping pints of tears. But the person in the room with her was a poised and pretty young woman. Mary grasped at an alarming and exciting conclusion: we were not the prisoners of ourselves, we could leave them behind. And then she wondered: Has that happened to me too? Am I unrecognizable?

'He will come, you know,' Jane said, pins in her mouth. 'He doesn't mind about things like rain. Nor do I, come to that. You won't lose your chaperone. So stop sighing.'

'Am I sighing?'

'Inside you are. Ow, damn! I pricked my tongue. Now there, that's what I mean, there will always be a need for swearing.'

'You're sure you don't mind walking out with us? I haven't thanked you.'

'You never do, but you will one day,' rapped Jane smartly. She

315

had a prompt way of saying these things that made them seem clever, though when you thought about them they didn't make much sense. Her lip curled as the voice of her mother, raised in complaint, penetrated from downstairs. 'Lord, did you hear her rating Papa this morning? People should show decorum when they get old. I don't think I do like this hair after all.' Jane tugged out the tortoiseshell comb and the beads, which came off their string and bounced on the dressing-table. 'Damn again. Mary, what's happening?'

Their eyes met in the mirror.

'Nothing,' Mary said faintly.

Jane, hands inert in her lap, watched the rolling beads. 'You won't leave me, will you?' she said.

'What makes you say that?'

'I wouldn't blame you if you did. If it was me, I would.'

'That doesn't make any sense.'

Jane frowned. 'Not everything has to. You're cleverer than me, but you don't see that.' She suddenly grabbed a bandeau and swept up her hair. 'Shelley agrees. How does this look?'

'You talk about me with Shelley, do you?'

'Well, of course. You're the only thing he wants to talk about.'

The hail had stopped as suddenly as it began. Mary extinguished her flaming cheek against the cool window.

'You haven't answered my question,' Jane said.

'The bandeau looks very well.'

'Not that question.'

Mary headed for the door, stopped: where was there to go? 'I can't answer it.'

'Well, that's the first time ever,' Jane said, with a triumphant grin. But her eyes held longing.

St Pancras churchyard.

Natural that Mary should bring Shelley here, to her own place of communion: the place where her past has its monument, the past she might have had and should have had. Natural, thus, to inaugurate the future here.

And natural for Shelley to wish to come here. He is eager to pay homage at the grave of Mary Wollstonecraft Godwin, whose works he knows and admires, whose name he venerates as the majority of society disdains it. In a way, he knows her as well as Mary does.

And a natural spot for secret liaisons, with its quietness, its shady willows. And natural is their watchword: their belief is that if you truly follow your natural impulses all will be well.

And, besides, anywhere will do. They are at the stage where the world is only a backdrop for their dialogues: where no one is really worth speaking to except each other, the precious thoughts to be hoarded for the next meeting.

At least, Mary is. She believes Shelley is, but she must be sure: cannot live without knowing.

He is talking about ghosts. Jane has a great fancy for such tales; and he, though intellectually he should not accept them, has the same taste. As a boy, he has told Mary, he longed to perform magic, would deedily experiment with powders and retorts like a dwarfish alchemist summoning spirits. Ghosts. If there are such things, they should surely be here among these graves and tombs; but Mary sees none. Only a live one, conjured up by her own mind.

Harriet Shelley: very much alive. The wife, pretty, beribboned, discontented (so Mary's mind constructs the diaphanous image), floating between the gravestones: the ghost who must be exorcized, if Mary is to say what she wants to say. There she is: stare her away. Good, she is fading a little . . .

'Your stepsister would do anything for you, I think,' Shelley says, as Jane takes herself off to stroll by the Fleet River.

'I don't know why,' says Mary, watching the smart figure go away. She feels torn about Jane, who is an ally, a Shelley-enabler, and yet has often been a torment to her.

'Don't you?' He is relaxed, smiling, ready to be teasing and enigmatic.

She is not. 'No. Tell me.'

And being Shelley he does not burble facetiously about women liking to hear their praises. Serious at once, he takes her hand and enumerates.

'Because you are a rare and remarkable being. Intelligent, deep-thinking, truthful, beautiful. And to know you is to admire. Sit down, you look faint. The sun—'

'You are my sun,' she says. And then sits down on the low wall. 'You know that?'

'I would be glad to know it,' he says, his face convulsively working. 'If . . .'

'Ah, if. But, Shelley, on my side there is no if. This is what I must tell you. A woman should never declare herself like this, I know – conventionally speaking – and least of all to a man in your situation.'

'A detestable convention,' he says absently, crouching beside her, eyes fixed on the grass as if botanizing.

'And the situation – the marriage – if I could be sure that only convention holds it intact—'

'If that is all the reassurance you need, then you have it. There's no love between Harriet and me. And I may as well add that I doubt she will be long alone.'

She gazes at the turbulent tendrils of his hair; then up at the gravestones. Yes, fading, going. 'I shouldn't say I'm glad to hear that – it sounds wrong – but it is what I wanted to hear. And even if I hadn't I would still have to say it. If we are to go on meeting in this way, then you should know I love you.'

He starts to tremble. 'Oh, God. It's what I wanted – I didn't quite dare hope for it but . . . You want honesty, Mary? I think so, you wouldn't be Mary otherwise. So yes – I've loved you and wished for your love. But I am not a seducer. That must be clear.'

'I know you're not.' Fading, vanishing: almost gone.

'It is what people will say. If we are to go on – if we go on from this, what we've just said, and make it a beginning and not an end, then it is what people will say.'

'Do you have your watch?'

Frowning, he takes it out.

'Let me see. Very well – this is the time, ten minutes to seven on Sunday the twenty-sixth of June 1814 – this is the moment from which I will never care what people say.' Almost gone.

'Mary . . .'

Gone. 'Yes.' She closes her eyes as his mouth falls towards hers.

'This is a great disappointment. I am greatly disappointed in you. You have greatly disappointed me.'

Thus Mary's father: as if this supreme moment between them were an illustrative lesson in grammar.

They were in his study. Shelley had called earlier, asked to see Godwin alone, then left with a slamming of doors and hasty feet. That had been the first indication. Her father's stony face, on her being summoned here, had been the second. Indeed, she had known all then: a few seconds had been room enough for the vast amazement, shock, realization. Her father disapproved. William Godwin, doyen of the Radicals, widower of Mary Wollstonecraft, disapproved.

'What have you to say?'

Mary thought. 'Nothing really. That is, I have nothing to say that you will like to hear, I'm afraid. Usually that question means explanations and excuses, and I don't think either are called for here.'

Her father sat down heavily at his desk. He shaded his eyes with his hand, as if she were dazzling him – not pleasantly. 'I believe,' he said, 'indeed I am willing to state, that I have never disappointed you, Mary.'

Outside the study door there was the thumping tread of the Clairmont, pacing, impatient for admittance, fuming for her four-penn'orth.

'And at such a time.' Godwin sighed vaguely.

He looked small. Mary thought, with bewilderment: I have shrunk him.

★ ★ ★

Later, the Clairmont had her say: *fortissimo* and *legato* and *agitato*.
Mary had been picking up the rudiments of music from Jane. She
tried, not unsuccessfully, to treat her stepmother's ranting as if it
were a rather poor piece of music. Full of cheap effects and
pointless repetitions. At last the Clairmont turned from her in
frustration.

'The consequences,' she shouted intimately at her husband,
'have you thought of those? She must know the consequences to
her own reputation, and she doesn't seem to care, so that's by the
by. But there are other consequences, don't you see?'

'I do,' Godwin said, 'I know very well and—'

'If this nonsense endangers – I mean, if it jeopardizes . . .' The
Clairmont glanced uneasily at Mary, who realized that she was
trying to find a word that Mary wouldn't understand – as if she
were a child to be protected from the knowledge of a surgeon's
visit! As if she didn't know all the words her stepmother knew,
and more!

'I know what you mean, and I shall make sure and have a talk
with him,' Godwin said. A 'talk': that was always a grave, even
direful word at Skinner Street. 'He may be brought to see that
this – this fantasy need not alter things between us, on a practical
level . . .'

'I am here, you know,' Mary burst out. 'I know everything
you're talking about. And you needn't be afraid. Shelley is still
going to give you that money whatever happens. He won't alter
that. *He* has principles.'

The two faces, her father's long and lined, her stepmother's
fudgy and pudgy, turned in unison towards her: the word 'money'
had done it: for that moment an identical spark was in their eyes.
Look at them, she thought: a couple united not by the best in life
but the worst. Never, never shall I be like that. We.

'Mary,' her father said, tucking his hands under his coat-tails,
'the point of the matter is, he is married.'

'And marriage is an oppressive convention that will ultimately be abolished.' Mary gestured at the portrait of her mother, serenely looking on them. 'Isn't that what she taught?'

'Your mother is dead, my dear,' said the Clairmont, with a ridiculous gentleness, as if she were breaking the news.

'And it's what *you* taught, Papa,' Mary said, 'isn't it?'

'There is the everyday truth of things, and there is the ideal. We must somehow live between them,' her father said. 'I concur with advanced ideas on marriage, as a model for an improved society, but the fact remains that you are a young girl and Shelley is a married man with whom you can form no attachment that does not involve scandal and disgrace, even ostracism—'

There was a lining of kindness to this tawdry stuff, she knew, but she was too unforgiving, too fiercely and consciously young to acknowledge it. 'You shouldn't say things unless you mean them,' she said. 'That is the base of *my* ideas.' They stared at each other across the gulf, hatchling and antediluvian.

'I believe you're set on breaking your father's heart,' the Clairmont said, with the throaty sniff that usually meant she was working herself into crying.

'Hearts don't break that easily,' Mary said.

'If you were my daughter—'

'Oh, please ma'am, things are bad enough without invoking the torments of hell.'

'We must talk,' Godwin said wincing, trying to wave his wife to silence, 'really, we must all have a proper talk.'

'Thank God it's not my Jane,' the Clairmont said, 'that's all – that's all I can say.' Though it was not, far from it.

'Pooh, you call those fireworks?' Jane said. She was sitting at their bedroom window, watching another celebratory display fretting the city skyline to the south. 'You should see the fireworks we have here. The domestic sort but *quite* spectacular.' She chuckled and looked at Mary. Jane was enjoying it all. She was a Clairmont, and throve on chaos. 'What did they say this time?'

Mary shrugged. 'I'm not to see him. They tried to get me to

promise to give him up. I wouldn't, so I am just forbid.'

'Lord, how monstrous they're getting in their dotage!' Jane jumped up and executed a series of nimble dance steps. 'I'll take a letter to him any time you like. They can't imprison *me*.'

'Would you?' Mary's throat thickened. 'Why are you on our side?'

'Why? Because it's my side as well, in a way. I love Mama, but she is an old fool. We can't let old fools rule us. The world belongs to us, after all.' Jane twirled and then folded gracefully at Mary's feet. 'There – *one* movement down. I'll bet poor Shelley is half frantic. What *will* you do? Of course you are not going to give him up, so have you thought how you will go on?'

'No.' For now she could only see the world as a high blank smooth wall, and somehow she must find a foothold and climb.

'Then you should think.'

Strange times.

Outside the summer obtusely blazing away: within doors, Mary restricted to the dusty schoolroom at the top of the house. The princess in the tower, listening out for the footsteps of her go-between, burning for the letters with their angular hard-driven script.

'What does he say?'

'Let me just read it first, Jane, please.'

'Oh! Very well.' An indefatigable go-between, but temperamental. Mary had to be careful. 'I could hardly get along Hatton Garden today – all manner of traffic. Going to St Paul's for the Thanksgiving, I think. They say the Duke of Wellington actually rode in the Prince's carriage with him. I wonder there was room for him to sit. Ha! I shall tell Shelley that joke.'

With the letter, a book: Shelley's poem, *Queen Mab*. Mary read and reread. And wrote, on the flyleaf of the book: it was like a proxy embrace. She poured out her love for him and then, feeling her own words weak and pallid, turned to copying out a love poem she had been reading. 'The whisper'd thought of hearts allied,' she wrote, her hand slightly shaking. The poem was called 'To Thyrza' and was by Byron. Byron who, she thought, would understand.

Strange times, because sometimes the prince still came to the tower. Shelley visited Skinner Street to plead, persuade, argue. And also to talk about other matters: for the negotiations over the gift of money he was making to Godwin still went on. Sometimes at supper her father would even talk about them, neutrally. As if he did not consider this man as the treacherous seducer of his daughter. Or perhaps he could just keep the two things separate. Mary, listening in agony to Shelley's nervous, changeable voice down below, had never understood her father less.

Strange times: Harriet was in London, Shelley wrote, and he was making sure to see her and explain the whole thing to her, unequivocally. This should have been good, Mary thought: but it strengthened her father's hand. A wife present was a more effective weapon than a wife absent. Godwin saw and talked to Harriet. Severe, not gloating, not quite, he presented his version to Mary.

'Mrs Shelley is prepared to view this matter as an unfortunate – let's see – escapade.' Her father snuffled with momentary amusement or amazement at finding himself using such a word: it was as if he had cut a caper on the rug. 'Yes. And in that spirit, she will be glad to have from you an assurance that you did not mean to interfere with her marital happiness, and that if Shelley gave you to understand any such possibility, then you realize now it is regrettable nonsense.'

'There is no marital happiness,' Mary said dully. 'Shelley doesn't love her. He's told her so.'

Later she wondered why she submitted. From that moment in the churchyard, she had never entertained defeat for a second. There could be no turning back. After all, she had given herself to him.

It was the day after her confession: again in the churchyard, in a secluded spot curtained by willows. He half sobbed himself into her. The peculiar intimate pain made her think of pearls and shells. Afterwards she lay folded into his bony chest, in a place that seemed made for her shape, and he looked up through the whiskers of willow at the beaming sky and said: 'This is my birthday.'

Besides, and what was more – much more – she had opened her mind to him, and that she had never done before. Shelley hung on her words, almost literally: his eyes never left her face when she talked, his lips moved faintly as if repeating them to himself in wonder.

'Your brilliance burns me,' he told her. 'Now I see that everyone else has a sort of fire-screen round them. You frighten me.'

'You frighten me, Shelley,' she said. Their heartbeats were drumming together like restless fingers. 'Like a great height. I want to throw myself down it.'

How could there be retreat from this? And yet the princess in the tower relinquished hope and embraced obedience, or made a show of doing so. For the last time Mary obliged her father, and went by arrangement to call on Harriet at her father's well-upholstered house in Chapel Street. Jane accompanied her. 'I don't know how,' she kept saying, 'I don't know how you can do it.' How? Perhaps because she fancied, just for a little while, luxuriating: Mary, who could sleep soundly on a hard bed with a single blanket, needed briefly to wallow in her situation instead of thinking how to solve it.

Curiosity, too: regrettable but natural. To see Harriet Shelley, to see if she resembled the ghost of the churchyard, to see if it made any difference.

Strange times, strange day. Uniquely, Mary stifled her nerves with drink – brandy filched from her stepmother's sewing-case. So she floated over the threshold in a slow trance. The parlour into which a stiff-backed maid showed her seemed to be made of gauze – or was that her legs?

'Chinese wallpaper,' Jane was whispering. 'That's the Prince

Regent's taste. How pretentious they are!' she added enviously.

'I don't know what I'm doing here,' Mary heard herself say, sitting down: the descent seemed to take minutes.

'Should you do that? Shouldn't we wait?'

'Why? What can happen? Will we be shot or stabbed or – or bastinadoed?'

'Curious imagination you have,' said the young woman who had appeared in the doorway.

Mary got up. She wondered if she should extend her hand. But it would take so long . . .

'You're Mrs Shelley.'

'Yes. Mrs Shelley. And that is all that needs saying, I think.' The young woman put her chin up. 'You must be Miss Godwin.'

'I must be, yes,' Mary said sorrowfully. 'Again we have said a lot in a little.'

'Miss Godwin, none of your sophistries, please.' Harriet Shelley walked to the window, where a bluebottle was pounding the panes, and opened it. 'I agreed to see you because I was given to understand you had certain assurances to make me.'

She stood looking out of the window, biting her lip. The breeze stirred her honey-brown hair. Mary gazed in dreadful fascination. Not the churchyard ghost at all: nor any of her subsequent imaginings. No one, she thought, was ever the way you had pictured them: why do we never learn this? Harriet Shelley was a neat, firm-fleshed little figure, braceleted and bandeaued, very much at home. I have never felt that much at home, Mary thought. Pretty oval face: noticeable frown-groove between her brows: it would give me a headache, Mary thought, to keep looking at that every day. Strange day, strange meeting. She could imagine seeing this young lady getting into a carriage from her front door while she and Jane and Fanny went by on one of their walks. A passer-by in her life, not an important figure – indeed, that was just what Harriet looked like: one of those people you look at idly while waiting to be served in a shop, mildly registering them, expecting never to have anything to do with them again.

But this one was important – supposedly: for it still didn't seem real to Mary, any of it.

'I came here because I was made to,' Mary said.

Harriet's chin went up again. 'Well, at least you're honest.' Not sure of herself at all, thought Mary, despite appearances.

'Yes, I am,' she said. 'I can't lie, or I won't. I won't lie about Shelley and me.'

'Oh.' Harriet shut the window with a bang. 'Well. Somehow I doubted . . . Very curious, Miss Godwin, this notion of your being *made* to come. That sort of tyrannizing does not go on in *your* household, surely?'

Mary shrugged. She was beginning to feel a little sick from the brandy: she wished they could have the window open again. 'In truth, I don't know why I am here,' she said.

'Neither do I. Really, in the circumstances, and given what you have just divulged, we can have nothing to say to one another.'

How roundabout she is, Mary thought. Divulged. Is she trying to be clever to impress me? God, I want to run a hundred miles.

'No,' she said, 'I suppose not.' And yet she felt there should be something said – not good, grand, significant, but something: she tried to strain it to her lips, while Harriet's pretty, perplexed eyes measured her.

'You know,' Harriet said at last, 'he's only interested in you because of who you are. Daughter of Godwin and Wollstonecraft. That is very like him.'

Ah, that tone of familiar contempt – just like the proverb. Whatever happens, Mary thought, at least I shall never speak of Shelley in that way.

'I was meant to come here and tell you that I would give him up,' she said. 'And you may not believe this, but I even might have done it, if I had felt that there was anything at risk, anything that might be destroyed by our association. But there isn't, is there? I'll go.' This little speech left her curiously exhausted, as if it were some amphitheatre oration. Blindly she reached for Jane's arm. When she felt the squeeze, she wanted to cry.

Outside Jane said: 'Chinese wallpaper – but hardly a book to be seen, did you notice? And no instrument. No wonder Shelley prefers us.'

'Forty-one Skinner Street,' Mary said. They were back in the schoolroom. 'The only coal-mine in London.'

Jane was putting a new trimming on to an old bonnet. 'Now I don't know what you're talking about. Oh, still dowdy!' She tore the ribbon savagely. 'I wish I knew the French modes.'

'Coal-mines. I remember reading that the air is sometimes very bad in certain places. Poisonous, explosive. A killing air.'

'Oh, surely it's not that bad.'

Isn't it? There were moments when Mary felt that the next breath would be impossible: there was a clutching at her chest and panic in her skull. Shelley, Shelley. Two doors away a silhouette-cutter had a little shop, and on the floor you could see the leavings of his work, the shaving-like outlines from which the profile had been removed; and that was the shape of Shelley in her world, a perfect shape cut out and taken away.

And then, suddenly, he was there.

His last letter had been wild and bitter in its expressions; still, she could not have guessed that he would burst into the house like this. Her father was out, and her stepmother was minding the shop. A torrent of knocks, and then she heard Shelley's voice, choked and fluty, rising up the stairwell of the house.

'Where is she? Where?'

In what seemed an incredibly short time he was flinging open the schoolroom door. Gasping, grim and gaunt, his eyes sunken, he looked like a man hauled up from the depths: his hair, uncombed and sweat-soaked, streamed like water-weed.

'Mary. God, you're there. It felt as if you'd been wiped away – gone.' He hung on to the door-frame, gazing at her with a grin of pain. 'I've tried everything. You've tried. They can't say that . . .'

She walked into his arms.

'Mama's coming,' warned Jane, unnecessarily: the noise was like a carthorse being made to climb the stairs.

'They're determined to keep us apart,' Shelley said, into her hair. 'They won't change. It's hopeless.' It sounded so melodramatic, but then so was the situation: how could one be low-key with this? 'I've told Harriet, I couldn't have been clearer. I love her as a sister, I shall provide for her, but you are my love, my choice. If this is wrong, then I don't know what's right.'

But here came, snorting and blessing herself, the Clairmont.

'Mr Shelley, you should be ashamed. Abusing our hospitality – turning the girl's head with nonsense – and now invading our premises like this . . .'

Invading our premises. Mary very nearly burst out laughing, as she had heard people were prone to do at funerals. The most dreadful moments were seeded with hilarity, it seemed. Nature seeking a balance, perhaps. She thought too much, Jane had told her. Yes—

'The girl is here, ma'am,' she said sharply, 'and her head is not turned. I know quite well what I am about.'

'Your father will never consent, Mary, you may take it from me,' the Clairmont said, and for a moment the hatred showed starkly through, like bone in flesh. 'I know him pretty well – I may say better than anyone.'

'Damn you all then,' Shelley said softly. 'You will finish us. Very well, damn you all, very well—'

Though it was a sultry day, he was shivering: his hands were cold as marble. His eyes were not seeing her as she looked questioningly up at him.

'Shelley, when did you last sleep? Or eat?'

'One good thing about this,' he said brightly, conversationally, shaking his head, 'it returns you to an understanding of what's important. And not so. Love, life and death – these are the essentials.' He dug in his pockets. 'What do you say, Mary? Would they prevent that as well?'

The pistol nearly fell from his shaking hand: Jane squealed. For a second Mary, not usually a fainter, saw the floorboards swim up towards her. She gripped his arm.

'Shelley, please—'

'Oh, never fear – Jane, calm yourself, I won't hurt anyone, I couldn't. I only mean myself. Unless you want to join me, my love? I wouldn't ask it, but I know your courage, and if you did wish to, why – let me see—' He pulled out his handkerchief, threw it aside, came up at last with a little bottle of laudanum. 'That would do it. The quietus. What do you say, ma'am? Is this to be prevented also? Are we to be kept apart even in death?'

'Shelley,' Mary said, low and urgent, putting her fingers on his stubbled chin and turning his face down to her, 'Shelley, my darling, don't talk like this. You're weary – half mad—'

'Ah, but which half? The half that wants to live, or the half that wants to die?' He uttered a cackling laugh, then staggered. Jane screamed again.

'Jane, for God's sake!' Mary snapped.

'My smelling-salts,' the Clairmont cried, as if that would solve everything. 'They are in my reticule – or should be – I didn't see them this morning, now that I think of it, which suggests to me that someone has used them and not put them back, and really I must have things where I can find them. I've told you girls before, it's too bad with all the things I have to do in this house . . .'

Though Mary wasn't listening, a part of her mind did absorb this – her stepmother trying even now to squeeze herself into the centre of attention: it might even have been the thing that tipped the balance, later. For now all she saw was Shelley. And fearful, racked as she was, still she discovered a new joy she thought had only existed in fiction. Again, melodramatic. Being brave for your lover.

'Shelley, I beg you. Put the pistol away, and don't think of it any more. You have my love—'

'But he cannot,' her stepmother said, 'that is the whole point—'

'And because of that love, I want you to go home, and rest yourself, and don't think any more of this.'

'And leave you here in prison,' he said.

'I'm not happy or free, but I'm not in prison, and even if I were, for your sake I wouldn't mind it. But I must have you well – and not like this.'

'Leave the pistol here, Shelley,' moaned Jane, wiping her eyes on a shawl. 'I hate to think of you carrying it about.'

'This is shocking. Shocking.' The Clairmont was hovering and huffing: not saying what was shocking exactly – perhaps the fact that she was being ignored. 'And here is my poor girl frightened out of her wits – she is so easily upset—'

'No, I'm not, Ma, don't talk so.' Jane flicked her shawl at her mother like a whip.

'Corrupted,' wailed the Clairmont, pointlessly holding out fat mourning arms to her daughter. 'Both corrupted.' Absurdity was thickening in the air. Yet Shelley, having pocketed his pistol, still held the bottle of laudanum between finger and thumb, like a delicacy, and still there was a terrible glitter and glow about him.

'Go home, Shelley, and write me,' Mary told him. 'A long letter – a beautiful long letter.'

He nodded. 'Very well,' he said trustfully. He put the laudanum bottle down on the desk. 'I'll leave this here. And go home. And write.'

'She will not receive your letters, sir, as Mr Godwin has told you,' the Clairmont said: then gave a little shriek as Shelley, looking unearthly, whirled round on her. 'Oh! Would you offer me violence, sir?'

'Only if you would take it,' he muttered. He slipped past her to the door: though he left a good foot of clearance, she lurched backwards as if he had pushed her.

'Shelley,' Mary called after him. 'You have my promise.'

At the door he nodded. He seemed suddenly bewildered, as if

woken from one of his sleepwalks. In fact he looked as if he had been struck by the stunning possibility of happiness.

He was gone. Jane snatched up the laudanum bottle and threw it on the fire. Only there was no fire, only a cold grate and unswept ashes; the bottle did not even break. Jane gasped, then began giggling.

Sinking into a chair, the Clairmont said, 'Dear, dear. Now I shall have a bilious attack.' She made it sound like a refreshing cup of tea. Mary watched the woman rubbing lovingly at her breastbone and crooning; and almost felt sorry for her. The Clairmont was so used to cooking up spurious crises: now there was a real one she was curiously unequal to it, like an understudy prepared for anything but going on stage.

'Jane,' Mary said absently, picking up the dropped shawl and folding it, 'you'll give yourself the hiccoughs.'

'No, I won't – oh, rot it, I have. Oh, pat my back, someone. Oh, blast and damn.'

'Such language, child,' her mother said, fanning herself with her hands. 'I can't think where you learnt it. As for you, Mary, I won't say I'm surprised at you – because I'm not, not any more. I will only say one thing.' That, thought Mary, is unlikely. 'Your father – your poor father. After all he has done for you.'

'Yes,' Mary said after a moment, briskly patting Jane's back. 'After all.'

Godwin made no direct comment on this episode. All he said to Mary the next day, on his way to his study and his inviolable routine of work, was: 'I am sad, Mary: sad.' If it was meant to pain her, it succeeded. Even saying tartly to herself, *And you are richer, Papa, richer*, could not quite brace her. But he left her alone. It was Jane who was summoned to the study for the dreaded Talk.

She came with a tremendous stamping up the stairs afterwards, and made the schoolroom door rebound on its hinges.

'Old dry-bones pom-ti-pom long-nose *beast*.'

'I know I have rather a long nose,' Mary said, 'but I didn't

331

think I was quite that bad.' She was only humorous when she was anxious: when she was happy she was solemn.

'I can't carry any more letters for you. It's found out, and I'm forbid. I can't even go out. I've got to stay in like you. I'm imprisoned.' Jane contorted her face in a great suffering sniff, which then altered, as if she had become aware of a beautiful perfume. 'Well. Well, now it really is *our* side.'

The old porter who worked in the shop was amenable to carrying letters between Mary and Shelley – for a small consideration. He needed it, he grumbled to himself: Godwin paid a miserable wage.

Yes – I know you're there. Of course I do. My senses are acute. Supernaturally acute, one might say. But today, as it happens, I do not feel much like talking. Quite a wonder, you may well say. Well, go on, laugh. I am indifferent – perfectly indifferent, today.

Yes, a pleasant little room, is it not? Mr Murray's waiting room – and just up there you will see the drawing room – where *he* is received, the great *he* – but I am not waiting in hopes of seeing him, no, not this time. I don't wish to see him. Believe me or not as you like – but I think you must know at least this of me now and that is I do not *lie*. All my other sins I accept. No, I am waiting for Mr Murray. Just to sit with him a while, if he will be so good, and have a little talk. It soothes my spirits, I find. Dearly as I love my papa I sometimes wish that I had had such a father as Mr Murray – for I think if I went and sat with my papa and said, 'Let us have a talk,' he would look puzzled and say, 'About what?'

And sometimes, yes, I will just sit here and be quiet and think. Very well, and feel *his* influence, to be sure – formerly – no longer.

I know I said I did not want to talk. Here I am talking. Well, there it is. I think a lot of the trouble in the world is caused by our expecting people to be *consistent*. Are you? Always? Look into your heart. I'm sorry, I should not ask that. That is the most terrible thing to ask of anyone.

It is warm, indeed, though I don't find myself incommoded by it. My thinness, you see. Spectacular, isn't it? I do eat. But often it seems to me I can feel the food being burnt up by my body even as I eat it. But there, it is indelicate to talk of digestion. We may heap these obscene mounds of roast and boiled on our plates and gobble them down, but what comes next is not to be mentioned. *He*, by the way, has a great aversion to seeing women eating. Why is that, do you suppose? Well, you know him. Perhaps as well as I – or anyone. I do wonder if anyone does or will – except his wife.

No, no, he is not married. But I know he talks of it. I suspect he discusses it with my mother-in-law, in that witch's lair of hers – coven cavern. There will be a wife, I am certain of that – and perhaps it will be she, at last, who can enter that secret room he keeps locked within him – like a dungeon in one of his own verse-tales. And when that happens – why, I shall be forgotten and less than nothing and now you think I am being silly and self-pitying. Well, you would break in on my reverie. And we are all more or less self-pitying in our private thoughts.

No, I do not care. That is, I do not wish to see him, I do not care to come near him any more. That is not quite the same as ceasing to love – to burn. But I cannot look upon him in the same way now. He is beyond me – horribly.

Well, you warned me. Didn't you? Perhaps it was my good angel then – not that I suspect I have one. Grandmama's ghost, perhaps. Some sensible voice told me, when I slipped into his chambers at Albany and went to his desk, that eavesdroppers never hear any good of themselves. And that if I similarly broke his privacy by looking into his papers, I should regret it.

And so I do. The things I found – they frighten me. And I feel I should not have them, I of all people – it is like carrying an explosive about – or, no, say a young tiger wrapped in your petticoat or your waistcoat.

I remember once raging at him that he could never have loved any woman as he loved me – and he answered, looking thoughtful, 'Not any *woman* – perhaps.' I thought at the time he was just being odd and capricious. Many things are becoming clearer, now.

I never liked to think of myself as a shockable woman – and yet William found me so at first, and tried to teach me the ways of the world, as they are so dishearteningly called – for is that *it*? The world, the whole of it, everything – all like that, shabby, no beauty or truth anywhere? I would shoot myself before I could think so. Well – I am still shockable perhaps. Or simply unprepared, somehow.

I read his letters. Yes, I succumbed to the temptation – but it was so strong. In that sitting room in Albany I was, if you like, re-enacting the fall of our first mother – yes – and now I too am a fallen creature outcast from grace. My own fault. But Eve after all acted only from curiosity and though that was a powerful motive with me I had another – love – my love for Byron, which is a glutton that must take all it can get – even the things that are not good for it.

I came across references – to his time abroad – and to the unspeakable acts that take place in countries such as Greece and Turkey – between men. Yes – of course I knew of such things – and he had alluded to them, when we were intimate – and yet these letters seemed to suggest that he knew them at first hand. Well. He came in and found me there – oh, not with the letters – I had thrust them away – but I must have done it in such a way that he knew I had been at them. Oh, he knew. And he took me up on it, and asked, with the most ferocious smile, whether I was satisfied. 'You see, Caro,' he said, 'I could not put it all in my *Childe Harold* or *Corsair*, what I experienced in the East – there are some matters at which the dear hypocritical English public would blanch' – these were his words not mine I add. 'These matters,' said I, 'are crimes.' 'Oh,' said he, 'but you of all people would not think so.' He drew very close to me as he said it –

examining me. I said I could not believe it of him – that it must have been some madness of the clime. He laughed long. 'You always could make me laugh, Caro,' said he, 'and to think you had no inkling, after what we used to get up to together. But never mind that,' said he, seeing my face – curious, he can still be so kind! – 'never mind that, I will only say, my dear, that if you suppose it a madness of the East, you never saw my page Rushton – did you never hear me commend his beauty, Caro? I'm sure you did – well, he is as English as roast beef and yet, let me assure you, quite a Greek also.'

What did I feel? You are oddly pursuant of what people feel. Most of the time one does not feel, one thinks. Feeling comes after. Oh, I turned from him – I didn't want to hear any more. Because it was not what I wanted to hear about him.

And yet, and yet – I know, that is precisely what he said. He thought that I, who was so scornful of convention, would not condemn him. I could not speak for a time. I saw myself – not as what I wanted to see – and it ached. And then I think I raged a little and said he was only trying to put me off again with these tales – it was a ruse and I would not believe it – and I think then I angered him for with a deadly paleness on him he said, 'Well, Caro, what other letters have you read? Have you read any letters from my sister?' And I was mortified and blushed and shrugged – and said perhaps the odd one but no more – 'Why, why,' says he, 'for this cannot be shame at your intrusion when you have been so thoroughly through my papers – is it because they could not interest you?' And of course he saw that I could not disguise it – the letters from his sister Mrs Leigh were perhaps the least tempting for I supposed them full of news of children and so on – and when I glanced at them I found them peculiarly and cryptically expressed for they say she is a quiet, shy sort of woman with none of his brilliancy and so I could not be bothered to tease them out.

Well. He did it for me. He read out a letter from his sister and explained it to me, there and then. Watching me.

And then he said – devilishly – that he was so glad he could unburden himself of this to someone who was the last person to judge him harshly – Pharisaically – his word – and he actually leant over and kissed me drily upon the lips – saying that if everyone else came to hate him I would surely never change. How bright his eyes were . . . .

I tore myself away. Ran.

Why? You mean, was I shocked and disgusted? Well: it is as I said, I truly believe we do our thinking at the time, and do our feeling later – the reverse of the common supposition. And if I am honest – yes, since then I have felt a revulsion at his sins and yet it is true I loved him and love him still for *being* a sinner. So. I do not really know what I feel.

Only this. Byron told me these things to be rid of me. This is what goes round and round my head – buzzing like a trapped fly at a window-pane – Byron was, is, so determined to be *done* with me that he will go to these lengths. He really does not care for me or my opinion of him. Anything to be rid of me. This – this I do not like.

Well, yes, perhaps stealing into his rooms was going too far – no doubt it would try his patience. I don't deny it.

But it's this: the fact that he hates me enough to tell me the truth about himself.

Think about it, on your way out.

Think about it.

The sea, the sea: *thalassa, thalassa*. Byron had told Augusta about that – Xenophon's ancient Greeks (and she knew they weren't but her mind couldn't help picturing them as *ancient* – white-bearded dodderers in sandals and helmets) coming at the end of a great march across Persia to the shores of the sea and letting out this wonderful shout at the sight of it. In fact, she found this more interesting than the sea itself, which she was not particularly fond of. It was quite pleasant to walk beside – like this, on Byron's arm, with her children scampering along the cliff-path and drawing in the air that was promised to be good for their many ailments – but it went on endlessly and needlessly: she could not look at it for long without wanting to turn away, back to her preferred world of warm, cluttered rooms, solid ground beneath the feet, corners, no vistas.

Which showed how impossible had been that notion of going abroad with Byron. She had, thank heaven, taken up the dropped stitches of reality since then. She was a married woman and a mother, with a husband and home, and she was not to go voyaging. Here – Hastings – was sea enough for her.

And it was all quite respectable. George had migrated north for the shooting: nothing more natural than that his wife and family should decamp to the seaside for a summer spell with her generous bachelor brother, who had rented Hastings House for them all. These things – respectability, appearances – were becoming more important to Augusta, since her resolution.

'I think I would feel better if I knew her,' she said. 'As it is, I only have your word for it. And that, you know, is not to be relied on.'

'Why should you know her? I don't. Oh, yes, I've met her on numerous occasions, and had woundy great talks with her, and now that we have resumed our correspondence there is no end to the screeds we write each other, on every subject under the sun. But as to knowing her – whoever married except wildly, in the dark, desperately hoping for the best? Ain't that a very definition of the dismal institution?'

Byron was in whippy, expansive mood: he loved the sea, clambered up and down the cliffs with the children running after him or clinging round his neck, heedless of his limp. He loved it all – especially, it seemed, the evenings when they all gathered in the drawing room of Hastings House. The family: the mother: the father.

She hustled the thought away.

'There are lots of eligible women,' she said.

'Miss Milbanke is particularly eligible. She is clever and

piquant and thinks I am a great prodigy but does not adore me because she can see there is much amiss with me. Also she will be an heiress, and if the sale of Newstead founders again this may matter – not that I want to take her money and would not but I want any wife I marry to feel secure that one of us at least will be solvent. Also–' he gave the sandy turf a jab with his stick '–she turned me down once before.'

'Is that a recommendation?'

'Oh, do we value the easy conquest? Look at your Georgiana. She loves to run a race with me, but she truly hates it if I let her win – she thrashes me for the insult – and I don't blame her.' He was breezy, too, in discussing marriage, which was their chief subject here at Hastings. Indeed it was partly the motive for the trip. They had agreed, solemnly, that there must be a change.

Or two changes. One was negative, a relinquishing: they must change to each other, she and Byron. This was Augusta's proposal. She could not bear it any longer, the deceit, the secrecy, the stabbings of religious conscience – or, rather, she could see a time coming when she would not be able to bear it any longer.

The other was positive. Byron must find a wife, and then—

'Why me?' he had said, teasing.

'Because it must be one of us, and I already have a husband!'

'Oh, not so you'd notice,' he said.

And then from laughing she slid down a steep slope to tears. He held her. 'I'm sorry,' he kept saying, 'I'm sorry. You're right, Gus – you're always right. I'm sorry.'

So, the matter of a wife. Once it was in train, Augusta felt better. Life, like a tightrope-walker, would regain its balance, and step neatly onward. Byron was mutinous at the decision – she knew – but then he loved her also, and was ready to obey: that was earnest of his love.

And there was a candidate already waiting: Lady Melbourne's niece, the mathematical young lady, the much sought-after Annabella Milbanke. She and Byron had renewed their acquaintance, were eagerly writing to one another: Byron was even invited to visit her at Seaham, her family's place on the far northern coast of Durham. It all made sense, and Augusta could not understand her own reluctance to countenance it.

Unless it was the recalcitrant side of her – the side that she was determined on smothering. The side that inclined still to what she and Byron had had, because it was warm and beautiful and *right* – meaning it had no feeling of wrong about it. Deceptive. Away from him, alone, in thought, in church, she knew it must stop: she measured it against the precisely graded rule of the world and was dismayed. Therefore. Thus. Hence. All expressions of consequence led to the same conclusion: stop it.

And so they would. 'You know,' she had said to him last night, her voice muffled, 'this must be the last time.'

'You know,' she said now, and stopped as a gull swung overhead with a piercing screech that cut her off, like a shrill blast of accusation.

'I do know,' Byron said, caressing her fingers, 'I do know, whatever it is you were going to say. Always do. We never have to work, do we, when we're together? The beauty of it . . . Gus, I won't change, whatever happens.'

'You must change,' she said gently, 'that's what we agreed.'

'Inside, inside,' he said, placing her hand on his chest so the palm ticked to his heartbeat. 'I wouldn't change at all if it were up to me. Well, no more of that. You know Annabella is mightily religious?'

'Yes – though you shouldn't disapprove her for that, Byron – you know my feelings.'

'Oh, I don't disapprove at all. It inclines me the more to her. If we are at odds over something so fundamental, it obviates the possibility of boredom. The prospect of remorseless harmony appals me. Besides – a woman usually sets out to change a man when she marries him, but to have a wife intending your *salvation* is surely to go one better. Thank you.' He bowed gravely as little Augusta Charlotte presented him with a handful of broken daisies. 'You think I don't approach this matter seriously? I do, though. Because it will be the saving not of one but two people. Gus, do you regret anything?'

'I don't know,' she said. And she didn't. Sometimes, quite often, Augusta's mental life seemed to come simply to a stop like this, as an asthmatic will have a fit of breathlessness. Warm, sun-dazzled, tantalized by the stroking of Byron's fingers, she found herself incapable of thought.

'Marriage. Oh, well, our father committed it twice. Our father who art not in heaven, probably. Sorry.'

She pinched him. 'No, you're not. You like to vex. It will come home to you one day, my wicked brother.'

'You mean I must get married *and* go through purgatory? I thought one was at least a down payment on the other.'

She suspended another pinch. 'Byron . . . if you do marry, I want you to be happy. Content, anyway.'

'Oh . . . My belief is that happiness is finite. There's only so much of it in the world, like gold – and a good deal less of it than gold. *Ergo*, you are not like to get more than a scraping of it in your lifetime. And so most people are engaged in a perpetual futility, looking for great nuggets of it that just aren't to be had. I know this–' he smiled sidelong '–because I am the most devoted digger of all. If I find any in the marriage-mine, well and good. I take up my pick and shovel without expectation.'

'You shouldn't think like that,' she said – and meant it earnestly: but as so often with Augusta, it came out mild and conversational. And so she left it.

The trouble was, so much of life seemed a sort of moral military parade-ground, and she was a confirmed scrimshanker. Her mind would never stand to attention. It turned to anything – like the entrancingly perfect print of Augusta Charlotte's bare foot in the sand – rather than serious business, like this of Byron's marriage. It slumped, slouched, and at last snuggled down in the fleecy belief that everything would be all right.

And then there was tonight, and the long passages and thick curtains of Hastings House inviting to privacy's indulgences; and though the drill sergeant screamed that it was not right to do so, Augusta looked forward to it because it was, after all, the last time, or one of the last, or whatever.

Mary said: 'You know what it may mean for your reputation.'

'I know. I really don't care. Reputation is a fig. Do I mean that? A figment perhaps. Or fig-leaf.' Jane was sorting through her trunkful of clothes. 'Besides, I'm not running such a risk as you. You are eloping with a man. I'm going along with the two of you as a companion. It is different.'

'People may not see it so. Other people.' And, for a moment, Mary treacherously wondered whether Shelley would not see it so also. She knew that in the past he had shown a taste for communes: Harriet's sister had been the constant companion of their early marriage. I want him all for myself, she thought; and then reproached herself for a selfishness that Shelley of all people would not have approved. Shelley believed that love, like wealth, should be shared. And Jane had been such a help to them as a go-between; and if Mary was to be sprung from this gaol of family tyranny, then could they leave the other prisoner to languish there alone?

Curiously, she could not remember now where it had come from – the suggestion that Jane should go with them. Somehow it had simply become an agreed feature of the plan. Jane, lively, extroverted, was ready to go at any moment, to walk to Dover if need be.

'People? You mean society? But we don't believe in society. We *scorn* its conventions.'

'I – I have chosen to. Because of my love for Shelley. But I am conscious of the weight of that choice, and I want you to be too—'

'Lord, Mary, anyone would think you're trying to convince yourself instead of me!'

'You're very young—'

Jane spluttered her laughter. 'Hark to Madam Methuselah!'

Then she sobered abruptly and appeared, indeed, young – for a moment, a helpless infant looking desperately about for a familiar adult. 'You do want me to come, don't you?'

'Of course I do.' Mary silently congratulated herself on her prompt answer.

Jane's scalp lifted. 'Well, then. And think what it will do for my French!'

And now the planning is over, and the hot last day ends, with brassy darkening but no real cooling: the humid air just seems to congeal about the house in Skinner Street where Mary and Jane sit, in black silk gowns, blinking at each other by the light of a stub of candle and straining at the small hours' silence.

This should be the time for farewells to fond associations, the patting of a favourite chair, the last long look at familiar rooms. None of this for Mary. She has already taken leave of her mother's portrait. There is nothing here to wrench at her. Only her father.

'Where are you going?' Jane hisses. 'Don't leave me here alone!'

'I shan't be a minute.'

'I'm frightened.'

'What of?'

Jane flounces back in her seat. 'Oh, there always has to be a reason.'

'I shan't be long.'

Just long enough to steal to her father's bedchamber door (his and *hers*, but no thought of that, not tonight) and stand with her fingertips against the panels. Silent tribute of goodbye. Try to collect the scattered feelings. Awareness that this tiptoeing does not feel unnatural: that around her father she has always tiptoed, that to lay the foot flat and freely on the boards is a guilty liberation.

Silent communication. Father, forgive me – no, not that. Anyway it does not require forgiveness. Because – because, Father, I am only choosing to live according to your principles.

–Are you? Are you truly? Or are you punishing me?

–Punishing you for what?

A blast of contralto snoring comes from inside.

–Are your motives not mixed at all, daughter? Consult your understanding. Look closely into yourself.

–No. I'm sick of looking into myself. I want to look into someone else, into their depths, and lose myself there. That's what I want, Father. I thought you'd understand.

–Did you? Really?

Mary takes her hand away from the door, turns on her heel.

–I think I've answered enough questions now. Goodbye.

Just before four, when a sickly light envenoms the sky, the light tap at the door below.

He is here.

The farewell letter stands on the mantelpiece: the thick waxy heat presses on the sleeping inhabitants of the tall house in Skinner Street, like the enchanted sleep of fairy-tale, as the two slight figures slip out and down the street to the post-chaise waiting at the corner.

Jane gasps, half-crying with relief. 'It's just like a book!'

Mary, wrapped in Shelley's arms, thinks: So it is. But please, God, don't let the rest of life be too much like a book. I prefer life to be like life.

'I don't know why I feel so sick.' She stands in the yard of a dirty posting-inn on the Dover road. The morning light makes polychromatic spangles on the puddles of horse-piss and lamp-oil. Mary leans heavily against Shelley. 'I'm so sorry. Need we go so fast . . . ?'

'No. No, of course not, my darling. Only I'm afraid we may be followed—'

'I don't feel sick,' says Jane cheerfully, swallowing a mug of small beer. 'I think I must be a good traveller. I can't wait for the sea.'

★ ★ ★

The sea, the sea. Finally it snarls before them, worrying at Dover beach, at four in the next afternoon.

Jane's spirits have sunk. 'Now that I see the cliffs of Dover that everyone talks about, I don't want to leave them,' she says listlessly, in the inn coffee room.

'You've come this far,' says Mary, taking tea in tiny experimental sips. It seems to be staying down. She has reached an accommodation with the sickness now: surely even the Channel cannot make it worse. 'England isn't everything.'

'Oh, I know that, thank you. I am of Swiss descent, after all. I shall probably be more at home on the Continent than you.'

'Jane,' Mary says, with sudden urgency, 'please, don't be – don't be Janey. There's so much ahead of us yet. You know we have to get along.'

'Oh, but we always do,' Jane says, quite honestly taken aback. 'Don't we? Only–' her lip quivers '–I hope I shan't feel left out.'

'That you never will, I promise,' puts in Shelley, appearing between them. He sinks on to his haunches and places a hand on each of their wrists. Curiously, fatigue and anxiety do not turn him ashy and drawn like Mary and Jane: he actually looks, as it were, more like himself. 'I think we have our boat. It's open and not large. But they are prepared to go now, and if we wait for the packet it might be any time—'

'Yes,' Mary says, rising, 'let us go.'

'Janey. What a word,' Jane says, following with a sigh. 'And what a name.'

Swelling, churning, the sea hurls them this way and that while summer lightning palpitates beyond the restless clouds. Among them, an apricot moon, like the last stable and stationary thing in the stirred universe.

'Keep your eyes on the moon,' Shelley murmurs in Mary's ear, as she clings to him. 'Look – the paleness, the beautiful paleness.

We think of paleness as a *lack* of something, until we remember the moon. Your moon, Mary.'

She smiles weakly, a smile he must be able to feel rather than see, a changing of contour against his cheek. 'You've made me a gift of it?'

'If I could. It is yours – the beauty, the coolness. The feeling of exception. Thank you, by the by. For this. For giving me my life.'

At some point, when stinging waves began to pitch themselves about the boat, Mary must have commended her exhausted soul to her maker, or the deep, and willed herself to sleep in Shelley's arms. Now she wakes with a fumbling disconnection of the senses – is this light? Sound? Pain?

A little of each. She is cramped from lying curled up against Shelley: now he turns her gently about, to where the sky is garrotted by a cord of glowing land, and says, in her ear: 'Look, Mary. The sun rising over France.'

3

Summer of the Sovereigns: Stormy

August the first, and William Lamb, hugely yawning, saunters late into his mother's apartments at Melbourne House, asking for a brandy-and-water.

'You stayed on till the end, my dear?'

'I stayed on as long as I could bear it.' Today the celebrations of the summer have reached some sort of climax, with the Jubilee to mark the centenary of the Hanoverian succession. Only thus, by inserting himself into the general junketings, can the Prince Regent get anyone to cheer for him. 'I would have been home sooner, only there was such a crowd in Piccadilly I could hardly get along. Well, the people seemed to like it. Lots of rockets and maroons, lots of money going up in smoke. The Battle of the Nile on the Serpentine looked very impressive. Or ridiculous, depending on how you're feeling.' He tips back his handsome head in another yawn. There is something unsettling about these yawns of William Lamb's, which are so excessive they seem designed to make a point: how tediously predictable he finds life, how unworldly and naïve you are not to find it so.

But nothing unnerves his mother. 'And how,' she says, watching the drinking of brandy-and-water as if she will have to answer questions on it later, 'is Caroline?'

'Still thrilling to it all. I left her so. It's better than . . .' Leaving it unfinished, he stalks over to a painting representing Potiphar's wife, and regards it airily as if it were an under-secretary unable to explain a shortfall in ministerial accounts. 'I have never understood how this creature is supposed to be seductive. Do you not think that much art is mere flummery, only no one dares say so?'

'She is quieter,' Lady Melbourne says, not meaning Potiphar's wife, 'but that isn't always a good sign. Well, I have hopes. Your cousin Annabella is as difficult as ever to get a plain answer from, but her last letter suggested that Lord Byron is at least corresponding again.'

'Well, well. He certainly doesn't seem to visit you so often lately, Mama.' William Lamb comes away from the painting, his mother's eyes following him like a cat's with a bird. 'If he marries, Caroline will go into fits, no doubt – but, then, she will get over them.'

'Let us hope so,' intones Lady Melbourne, with a sort of diabolic prayerfulness.

'And after that, it's hard to see what more she could do. Yes,' he says to the last mouthful of liquor. 'You know, for all the crowds I had the feeling today that people were a little tired of it all. After all, what now?' He snorts. 'Now that the peace celebrations have gone stale, we shall have to go to war again, just to feel alive.'

'Is that what it takes?' murmurs his mother, contemplating the back of her papery old hand.

Newstead: the last time.

Oh, she doesn't know that, Augusta. After all, the sale of the Abbey is always off and on, and is now in abeyance again, and it may go on this way for years; and as for Byron marrying, that too may be a mirage, ever visible, ever receding.

Yet she knows. And so, with uncharacteristic assertion, has asked Byron after the Hastings holiday whether they may not spend the last of the summer together at Newstead. It is important. Again, she is quite unaccustomed to thinking of anything that is to do with her as important; but this one time the comfortable glass globe of habit, that fits so neatly in the palm, must be tossed away to fall and shatter.

The last time.

Her children pound along the Abbey's ancient passages, slam the groaning doors, shriek their echoes under the cavernous ceilings. Always, she has noticed, children love to make the loudest noise possible: something irreducibly human about this: in the end it explains, perhaps, artists and poets. Yet she has never had this desire at all. She likes the quiet and the dark, and within it a gentle single interchange.

Byron is in comparable mood. He is not writing at all: he lounges, reads, invents for the children games full of the satisfying combination of drama and finickiness, shoots soda-bottles with his pistol. Augusta thinks: He will never be so much himself again. And yet she knows, when they wait for the post, when the latest fat letter like a small tight cushion arrives from Annabella Milbanke, she knows and knows . . .

The kings and generals have bowed their last bow, and gone home – across the Channel, which for years has been a debatable stretch of danger dared by smugglers and bristling frigates, and now is like a well-worn highway where people grumble about the traffic. And the grumbling mood, the jaded temper, is widely perceptible as the fireworks fizzle away. The London parks are trodden brown, the flags are rags, and the surplus soldiers and sailors suddenly loitering and begging on street corners make one uncomfortable. We need a new world.

But for Mary and Shelley and Jane, returning to England after six illicit weeks on the Continent, there is already a new world, vast and alarming and about to claim them. Now, after their approximate honeymoon, they must begin the difficult process of living.

At first there was nothing but charm. Little children speaking French: postilions in boots the size of barrels: fishwives in lappet-caps and men in comical hats who shrugged and grimaced and gesticulated as if mere words communicated nothing at all.

The food was splendidly different, and as Shelley had no interest in food, Mary felt too sick to eat, and Jane would try anything, they were able to give it a scholarly attention.

Then, before they had got properly on their way, a setback. The Clairmont had followed them. A servant came up to the rooms they had taken at Dessein's in Calais and told them, in vivid Calais English, that a fat big lady was after their heads. Mary reluctantly admired. Her stepmother had made the journey without a break, alone: she looked disgustingly well. At the sight of her Jane burst into tears, and there was a long maternal discussion behind closed doors, which must, Mary thought, end in Jane's capitulation. Mary, strolling on the seafront, breathing salt air, tried to assess how she felt about that prospect. Do I want her here with us? Or would I rather defeat her mother, at whatever price? An English papa and mama with two lathe-turned daughters in poke bonnets passed her with stares of undisguised curiosity. Does it show? Does it show that much?

It was Shelley who decided it. When Jane wavered, he took her aside and with a few magical words she was convinced. (What did he say?) The Clairmont stamped up and down the creaking passages of the inn, her mouth set. Coming upon Mary, she glared and slid out the words: 'I blame you. I blame you for all of it.' Then she pounded downstairs to fortify herself with lamb's fry and artichokes before the next packet home. Soon the Channel bore her away again, the boat wallowing low in the water. (Or so Mary imagined. I shall be glad, she thought, to be rid of this malice.)

Then: France.

She had expected a sort of garlicky flamboyant version of Norfolk. Instead it was wild. War and invasion had blasted the landscape and, it seemed, ulcerated the character of the people. Prices for transport and meals shot up as soon as their accents were heard. Men of all ages frankly leered at Jane – seldom at Mary, who found she could quell such things with a look – and getting in and out of carriages afforded opportunities for incredible gropings. 'It is *my* bottom,' Jane wailed at one point, 'and you are not to touch it any more.' After the tourist-primed comfort of Calais, the roadside inns were miserable: sour milk, sourer bread, and the nodular scrunch of rat-droppings underfoot, with occasional glimpses of the rats themselves. Even they looked thin. Burned villages and uncultivated fields made up the view. Postilions shook their heads grimly at the mention of certain roads.

'War, the true curse,' Shelley said, 'the true fall of man. I'm glad we saw this.'

Paris was different: grandly grubby, overwhelming, heaving with beggars, jangling with high-perch carriages containing wealthy hard-eyed men and their diaphanously dressed ladies. For Mary and Shelley's taste there were still too many military trappings, thinly overlaying something that Shelley described as 'horribly Louis XIV' – stiff, formal, trumpety, a tyranny of marble. He struggled to raise money from a banker, who at last parted with sixty pounds. It would have to do. The south was calling them, the Alps, Switzerland: they had read their Rousseau and Wordsworth, and under the jurisdiction of Nature they would be able to breathe and be free.

Not yet. The road south was long, hard and dusty, and haunted by shapes of oppression. To save money they bought a donkey to carry their luggage. It had been so badly treated it could barely walk a mile before staggering: Shelley actually carried it into the next village. When they hired a carriage there was more trouble. At a halt under the furious sun Shelley stripped off to bathe naked in a roadside stream, and their coach-driver declared himself so shocked he drove on without them. (Mary, hating herself, could not overcome her scruples and give in to Shelley's pleas to jump in too. 'I would,' Jane cried, but he wouldn't let her.)

At last the Alps reared into view like distant thunder made visible. This was what they had hoped for: the splendour of sublimity, beauty laced with terror. Mary had dreams of being carried up by an eagle and dropped, to break and bleed, on the pitiless tops of the crags. The littleness and poignancy of the meadows and villages clustered in the valleys struck her with brutal tenderness. In the mountain shadow, Mary clung all the more passionately to Shelley, folding herself into him. They made love often, and often at her instigation: she found it was the one time when you could not think of anything else. They were writing a shared journal, and their bodies interleaved too, formed a carnal palimpsest.

But there would always be Jane in the next room. And often afterwards Mary would wonder if she could hear; and sometimes Shelley would dress and go and talk to her, as if to prevent her feeling left out. Usually it was their favourite talk, the late-night subject of ghosts and horrors. Jane could work herself up to shrieking point over it. Dramatically she would call attention to a strange atmosphere in the room.

'The smell from that awful stable, I think,' Mary said.

'Lord, Mary, I wonder you don't feel it! I declare it goes all through me – like a whisper of death!' Jane seized Shelley's arm. 'You feel it, don't you, I can tell.'

He nodded, his eyes shining.

'I swear, Mary,' Jane said over her shoulder, 'you've got no imagination.'

I can't be all to him, Mary thought at such times. I want to be, but I can't. She tried to accept it, then fear blew a gust through her.

'Shelley,' she said to him at night, when he was on the edge of sleep, 'you must be all to me.'

Smiling he blinked at her. 'That's what I intend.'

But perhaps she meant something else: you must be all *for* me; no one else to have any part of you. Realizing she had a jealous nature, she felt guilty about it, and began planning strategies to hide it as if it were a tendency to secret drinking or opium.

Switzerland and Lake Lucerne: it should have been perfect, but

351

she was learning about perfection. Bruised rainclouds, never quite breaking or dispersing, hung over the crags and pines like their own lowering dissatisfaction. The Swiss were free but burgherish and kept talking about the price of cheese: there were no decent lodgings to be had. Notions of taking up residence here, founding the nucleus of an ideal community, evaporated in the drizzle. Shelley made one of his explosive decisions.

'Home. The winter here – unthinkable. Home it must be. We have thirty pounds left.'

'Is that all? I thought—'

'I've been disguising it,' he said, taking Mary's hands and kissing the palms, 'because of Jane. If she knew how little we had left, I'm afraid she would – you know. Have one of her turns.'

He does not think that of me, Mary thought, with calm pride. Not, of course, that Jane was a rival of any kind: no.

'Will it be enough to get us back to England?' Mary said, at once casting about in her mind for what she could sell. Shelley had already disposed of his watch and chain in Paris.

'If we go by the Rhine boats all the way to the Dutch ports, I believe so,' he said. 'It's how the ordinary folk travel hereabouts – like our carrier-wagons.'

'Well, if it's good enough for them, it's good enough for us,' Mary said stoutly.

Fine words, she thought later, huddled on the windblown deck of a river-boat while German peasants with medieval faces champed sausage, spat, belched, farted, smoked, urinated over-board, and hogged the best places. Clay, she kept thinking, biblically: of clay we are made: who shaped it? Could it not be shaped better? Beyond, she kept her eyes trained on better prospects. The Rhine and its banks seemed shockingly beautiful. Tumbling woods sprouted fabulous castles. Old Europe hung like a horn-note in the mellow air. An old German schoolmaster, one-legged and grotesque but omnilingual, came on board and told them Faustian tales of alchemists and grave-robbers seeking forbidden knowledge in lonely keeps. Jane looked entranced.

Mary felt it. But this was an ending. Holland opened out damply and tamely before them. With their last coins they rode overland to Rotterdam and got a passage on an English boat to Gravesend. They had to wait: out at sea a storm was whipping up to herald their return. The captain set sail at last against all advice. The boat, like a whale, seemed to make the voyage mostly underwater, with occasional plunges upwards into screaming air. Mary thought she would die, though she was not sick: there was nothing to come up, as she was already being sick every morning.

And so English ground again – and no money. Exhausted, they trailed about brown-skied and bad-tempered London, trying to raise funds from various elusive contacts of Shelley's, and a boatman sent by the unpaid captain to make sure they did not default trailed good-humouredly with them.

'Now where next?' he said, as the hackney rumbled off again.

Shelley, blankly staring out of the window, said: 'Chapel Street. By Grosvenor Square.'

'Well, that's an encouraging address, at any rate,' the boatman remarked cheerfully. 'Family, sir?'

'My wife,' Shelley answered, with a pale glance at Mary.

For two hours they waited outside the Westbrook house while Shelley, somehow, talked Harriet into lending them some money. He did it: he was haggard and silent when he climbed back into the hackney, but a purse clinked down on the seat beside him. Did Harriet think this might be the means ultimately of getting rid of Mary? Did she hope that the hackney was to convey her back to her father's house, the escapade over, the erring husband returned to forgiving wife?

It was not going to happen. Please, God, and God forgive me, it was not going to happen.

It is not going to happen, in the first place because Mary's father will not see her.

Absolutely that: she is forbidden to come to Skinner Street – though Jane may, on sufferance, visit there – and he will enter into no communications with her, and worst of all he will not speak to her in the street. This is not hyperbole. A short time after Mary and Shelley have settled into meagre lodgings nearby, they spot Godwin coming towards them along Oxford Street.

His head is down – can it be that he has started to stoop more in these six weeks, and can it be that she is responsible? – and his coat is not brushed, perhaps because it is so threadbare it would fall apart, and he looks as if he carries a great many cares. The intensity of her own reaction surprises Mary: her throat seals, she wants to run to him and help him somehow. Carry something.

Then he looks, and sees. And in his reaction, the opposite of intensity. He subtracts her from the world around him: creates a vacancy where she stands, lips trembling and parted, holding Shelley's tensed arm. Her father walks anonymously past.

Fanny comes to their lodgings. She stands looking about her at the tin candlesticks, the Hogarth prints, the moulting rugs on the crippled sofa, the cane-bottomed chairs, with a sort of defensive fastidiousness. As if, Mary thinks, fighting down a wave of nausea, she could get pregnant here just by sitting down.

Pregnant. 'You knew, of course, about Mrs Shelley?' Fanny says.

'Of course.' Of course. 'Why do you ask?'

'Papa says the habit of answering a question by a question is a very bad one. It shows . . .' But even Fanny's diligence seems to weary of saying what it shows. 'The fact is, you see, that Mrs Shelley is expecting Mr Shelley's child, and so . . . Well, it is what Papa cannot get over.'

'I don't see why,' Mary says, with a smart recovery. 'It doesn't alter the situation. Shelley and Harriet separated a few months ago. They can no longer live happily together. It is unfortunate. But it's like Papa has always taught – the nonsense of people being forced to stay together and make each other miserable in obedience to a mere convention.'

Gingerly, Fanny sits down. 'Yes, but you should hear what

Stepmama says about it.' Fanny's blush makes her look throttled. 'She says – well, in so many words, that they can't have been miserable a few months ago, because he did get her with child.'

'I always knew she was vulgar in her ways,' Mary says, after a moment, 'but I didn't know the vulgarity extended even to her mind.'

'That's my mother you're talking about,' Jane snaps.

'Yes, but it's true.'

'And she seems to think,' Fanny goes on, with fearful looks at both of them, 'that they made you come away with them – like a prisoner.'

'Me?' Jane hoots with laughter. 'Nobody makes me do anything I don't want to do. And what, are you to be the next victim? Shall we steal you away too, Fanny?'

'Don't.' Fanny shrinks as Jane makes a mock-lunge at her. 'It's true I'm not supposed to be here. Strictly I'm forbidden to see you at all. Only I had to—'

'To see the sinful *ménage* for yourself,' says Jane, irrepressible. 'But careful, Fanny – you might be corrupted – indeed I do believe I can see the corruption *creeping* up your skirts—'

'Stop it, Jane. It's not funny,' Fanny says, getting up. 'It's all very well for you – you don't have to feel the horrible atmosphere at home, and hear the quarrels, and see the way there's never any money—'

'No different from before, then,' Jane said. 'And there ought to be money, when Papa's had so much from Shelley. And I'm not Jane any more. I'm changing my name.'

'How?' gasps Fanny, screwing up her eyes as if literally dazzled by her.

'Just by doing it. You can go by any name you choose – Shelley told me, I asked him.' (When? thinks Mary.) 'You just make the name known, and use it, and then it's yours. You see – we can make ourselves in this world. Now there is the true freedom.' Jumping up, Jane moves smoothly into dance steps. 'Claire. That's my new name. If I go on stage it will be much more suitable. And if not – well, "all the world's a stage", anyhow, is it not? Who said that?'

'Shakespeare,' Mary says. '*As You Like It*. Act two, scene seven. Jaques's speech.'

'Pom-ti-pom! Well there you are, it must be right if it's Shakespeare.'

Claire. Claire Clairmont. Biting her lip, Mary has to admit it has a ring to it. She watches her stepsister twirling. How we hate to see those close to us blossoming. Mary knows these bleak truths as Shelley does not. His eyes are fixed on the beautiful tomorrow, the dawn of justice and freedom. Yet if we have perfect freedom, thinks Mary, can we have perfect justice? Thus, what if I were to exercise my freedom to thrust a knitting-needle into my stepmother's neck – which would be, even I can see, an injustice. I think of these things. I still believe, passionately: I believe in Shelley; but I look at what human beings are really like, and I think of these things.

' "Blow, blow, thou winter wind",' Mary says.

Pirouetting, Claire Clairmont shrugs. 'I never know what you're talking about.'

Shelley screws up the letter, such as it is, and tosses it on the fire, such as it is.

'Well, my father refuses ever more adamantly to speak to me, write direct to me, or let me past his gates without the gamekeeper shooting at me,' he says cheerfully, 'and now yours is the same, my darling, and so you see we share everything.' He sees her sad look, draws her head down on his breast. 'I'm sorry. My father is past redemption, but yours – it's different. He will change to us, you'll see.'

'How?'

Shelley considers. 'He will consult his reason.'

'Ah.'

The fire winks out, mockingly. Mary burrows closer to Shelley's chest, closing her eyes. 'Blow, blow, thou winter wind.'

★ ★ ★

More than two years had elapsed since Annabella Milbanke had first set eyes upon Lord Byron at Lady Caroline Lamb's waltzing-party: two years in which their association, though fitful, had been marked by peculiar intensities. There had been regard, there had been warmth, there had been candour: there had been a mutual goodwill very rarely to be found, she believed, between those who have passed the milestone of a declined proposal; and at last there had been, on her part at least, a very positive regret. Annabella was as far as the general run of mortals, from supposing she could ever be wrong – indeed if anything, from a habit of complacency, and a tendency to view her own conduct with unstinting admiration, she was further; yet a critical survey of her past decisions, and her situation, could not but furnish her with a melancholy conclusion.

She had refused Lord Byron's offer of marriage, as conveyed to her by her aunt Lady Melbourne, for principled reasons, which she was so well able to articulate that she wrote them down as an analytical character of the gentleman, and returned this to her aunt with some further notes: the which Lady Melbourne declared herself somewhat perplexed to receive, referring, with a little coarseness, to her niece being up on her high stilts again. Whatever might be the worldly puzzlement emanating from Whitehall, Annabella in the remoteness of Seaham was well able to contemplate unhindered the integrity of her own motives. Of Lord Byron's genius, force of personality, and fascination there could be no doubt: of the sweetness of temper and readiness of understanding of which he was capable, she had had proofs: and even of his attachment, beneath the veil of scorn and contempt, to the highest principles of morality and truth, she believed she could see traces. But she must lower herself in her own opinion, if she were to ignore the evidences of a strong disinclination in her suitor to the domestic virtues, which accorded with a hostility to religion still more to be deplored, and which no revision of judgement could, she believed, ever render acceptable to her conscience, no matter what might be the contrary inclinations of her heart and mind.

Thus she had replied; and Lord Byron had shewn himself the man she believed him, in his temperate and gentlemanly acceptance of her refusal, and his intimation that he would be happy to consider their friendship unimpaired and uninterrupted. – This was gratifying; but while love may have wings, friendship is a more earthbound species of being altogether, and cannot make light of two hundred miles' distance, not to mention the separation of circles between a young lady in the country, and a gentleman about town. – Lord Byron's doings were so much the common talk that there was no possibility of his dropping out of sight altogether; still Annabella had the mortification, as a year and more passed, of finding that she only knew what everyone else knew of this most famous of Englishmen and poets. She sought more personal news, as discreetly as she could, from her aunt Melbourne; but that lady was little inclined to gratify a curiosity for which her scepticism could find no reason beyond the pique of second thoughts. – This Annabella rejected: not angrily, for anger must entail a loss of self-possession, which she could congratulate herself never occurred to her; but with a serene indignation. She had examined her own affections and inclinations so thoroughly that she could confidently acquit herself of any missish yearning for what she might have had. On the other hand, time must produce effects upon the human mind and character, as surely as upon the complexion; and so with Annabella and her feelings towards Byron, which on scrutiny she found to contain more of warmth, and above all more disposition to make allowances, than she had supposed a year ago. What news she did glean of him only reinforced this tendency to wonder if their intimacy had been untimely in its closure: for he had not married nor offered to marry anyone else, and the progress of that admirable soul seemed suspended in mere sensualities. The exception appeared to be the attention he bestowed on his half-sister, Mrs Leigh, and her family; a development which powerfully suggested to Annabella that he was being drawn, almost without his knowing it, towards the comforts and decencies of domestic life.

Annabella was too sincerely attached to her religion to commit the impiety of supposing herself specially intended for some great redemptive work in the world. Still, when Lord Byron resumed their correspondence, with every appearance of regarding their past relation as a stage upon a journey rather than a terminus, she could not help but detect the hand of Providence in so uniting desire and opportunity. From the slough of aimlessness and irreligion, it seemed, he was reaching out a hand; and that he should reach in the direction of Seaham was surely an indication of the inscrutable purposes to which she hoped to awaken his conscience. Whatever might be the common motives of the young woman contemplating matrimony, Annabella was satisfied, as she walked the bracing shore of her native county and read the increasingly ardent letters of her second-time suitor, that hers were of an elevated nature that fortified them against disappointment. For she would be *good* for him.

'Don't know her?' Byron says, by the lake at Newstead. Swallows dipping, sweeping, congregating: autumn making stealthy, benign, gilded alterations in the woods. 'Well, let's see. I have had long talks with her, and even longer letters. I know her likes and dislikes, and the general *way* of her. I know her family, or at least her aunt. All in all, what greater knowledge *can* you have of someone?' He glances at Augusta's face. 'Yes, well. But that's the excitement of courtship, isn't it? The mystery. Finding out what's behind the mask. My God, just think – what if behind the mask there's only another mask, and then another and so on.' His laugh is so loud, unsettling, that a pair of ducks go scattering up from the water with a canvassy clap of wings.

'Stop it, Byron,' Augusta says. 'You're alarming when you're like this.'

'Gus,' he says after a moment, 'is it just Annabella? Or would it be the same with anybody?'

'It would be the same with anybody. And that doesn't mean I don't want you to marry. I want you to so much that . . .' She cannot think of any superlatives: melodrama is not in her line. 'I want you to. We both know why. But I doubt that Annabella Milbanke is the right choice. Leaving my own feelings aside.'

'Ah, yes. Which,' he says lightly, 'you seem well able to do.'

'Don't reproach me, Byron. Please.'

'I don't. How can I reproach you, when you are simply better than me?'

'Lord, don't say that. I'm afraid I'm not a good person at all.'

'And don't you say that, my dear Gus – not ever. And don't let anyone ever say it or even hint it to you.' His lips smile: his eyes are stones. 'I mean it. Kill 'em first.'

'Dear, dear. I'm rather troubled about this murderous future you're setting out for me.' Still, she is warmed. This fierce evidence of love – when she has gently forbidden other evidences – and when their parting is stealing on them, like the surrender of the leaves to beautiful death.

'It is a very well written letter,' she hears herself saying, as she reads it for the second time.

'That doesn't mean anything.' Byron snorts.

'It isn't meant to. Like most compliments.'

'Oh, even mine?'

'Now you're angling for one yourself.'

'Well, if they're all meaningless, it won't cost you anything to give me one.'

'I said most, not all.'

'Did you?'

'I don't know, I've forgotten. Really, Byron, I don't know – do you write all your conversation on your sleeve as you go along? For reference?'

They smile at each other – not quite as if this will be the last time for their laughter and nonsense, but somehow reminiscently, as if it is already half in the past.

'Perhaps it's a trifle out for a letter of proposal. Perhaps I'll put it back in the desk,' Byron says, his face falling.

'And then what?' she says, hating herself.

'God knows.' Blindly, oddly, he limps backwards, right hand extended behind him, until he finds the bell-pull. He rings. 'Oh, I'll send it.' That laugh again, this time echoing flatly around the library. 'What can happen?'

This.

A week later. Byron has been pouncing on every post, but today has offered distractions. First, a wonder: a gardener has found a gold ring in a flower-bed. It is the wedding band of Byron's mother, supposed lost many years ago. His eyes mist as he takes it on his palm.

Second, they have, for a rarity, a dinner-guest: the local apothecary, who has a fine store of gruesome anecdotes. Soon, in unbuttoned mood, Byron is showing him the ring.

'My poor dead mother *yielded* this up today most unexpectedly, sir. And the curious thing is I have a proposal of marriage of my own afloat, and if it don't founder in the matrimonial Biscay, why then I shall get married with this ring.'

And then a servant comes in with a letter. All the way from Seaham.

Byron opens it, turns pale, motions the servant to give the apothecary more wine. Finally he tosses the letter across to Augusta. A glance shows her that Annabella's answer is yes, yes, yes. 'It never rains but it pours,' Byron says, white-lipped. This ought to be very funny. Indeed, later, alone, Augusta howls.

Part Four

'Tis pity though in this sublime world that
Pleasure's a sin and sometimes sin's a pleasure.

Byron, *Don Juan*

That unrest which men miscall delight.

Shelley, *Adonais*

Come then, Sorrow!
Sweetest Sorrow!
Like an own babe I nurse thee on my breast:
I thought to leave thee
And deceive thee,
But now of all the world I love thee best.

Keats, *Endymion*

1

Portrait of a Marriage

It begins with words: an exchange of vows. Nothing is real until we say it.

Augusta, never confident with words, sits long at the bureau in the winter parlour at Six Mile Bottom, looking at the blank sheet of paper as if it were some ill-cooked meal that politeness will force her to eat. The ink has dried on her pen, again.

The letter is, will be, to Annabella Milbanke at Seaham. It is, will be, to introduce herself to her future sister-in-law. Also, at Byron's request, to offer excuses for the fact that he is still in London – that the words have not yet been said.

It was expected, once his proposal was accepted, that he would go directly up to Seaham, be gathered into the bosom of the Milbanke family, and make arrangements with them for the marriage. It is still expected, but it is not happening. Business keeps detaining Byron in Town. It is starting to look awkward.

'You'll never guess,' George said last week, returning from a trip to London, 'who I ran into. Your brother. I congratulated him on the coming event and so on – and then I said–' George gave a reminiscent whinny of laughter '–I said, "When exactly *is* the coming event to be?" Which was rather good funning, I think. You see, some of the fellows are laying bets on whether this marriage is ever going to come off—'

'Oh, George, you didn't tell him that.'

'Lord, no. No, no. As a matter of fact, I commended him for not being in a hurry. After all . . .' George looked hazy. After all, when Byron married, his money would be less available for clearing George's debts. One of the many things they did not say. Augusta is quietly amazed at the number of things it is possible not to say, for years and years if necessary.

'After all,' she said, 'people said unkind things about us when we had to wait to marry.'

'Ow, my tooth's throbbing again.' George has a battery of minor ailments, which he uses as a defence against reproaches. 'Still. It was rather good funning.'

Now her ink has dried again. She puts the pen down. She doesn't know how she feels about it.

Yes, she does. He must marry: they must all settle to proper lives. Once you reconcile yourself to the idea that life should not *be* exciting, then all is well.

A domestic crisis calls her away from the bureau. Augusta Charlotte and little George are quarrelling over the cup-and-ball, though both are too young to do it, as six-year-old Georgiana acidly points out.

'I want, I want,' Augusta Charlotte keeps repeating in a monotone, drily crying. It begins with words, and Augusta Charlotte knows very few for her age, and often she will go into strange rocking silences. Creeping apprehension that there is something wrong with her.

'I want,' Augusta says, 'you all to try and be quiet. I must write a letter.' I should have run away with him, she thinks blindly, yes, I should have. But then . . .

'I want horse,' little George says, having gathered the cup-and-ball to his heaving resentful chest.

'You can't have both,' Augusta says. You can't have both.

At last Byron makes his journey north to meet his new family – stopping on the way at Six Mile Bottom.

'The best inn on the Great North Road,' he says.

'We're not on the Great North Road,' says Augusta; but this is not the time for banter. His face proclaims it. He looks sick.

'Oh, I'm well enough. All these delays have been damnable and pestilential. Lawyers and what have you. God knows what her parents think.' He bends to admire Georgiana's copy-book. 'God knows what I think.'

'Well, Annabella wrote me a very charming letter back the other day,' Augusta says. 'She sounds very impatient to see you, but only in a good way. And she wrote that she considered us almost sisters already, which was kind of her.'

Byron grunts, turning over the leaves of the copy-book with their big looping letters. 'Be careful what you write, little one,' he says. 'People may start to believe it.'

Augusta has a vivid dream that night. In it, Byron announces that he is not going any further. He is not going on up to Seaham: he is staying here, at Six Mile Bottom, for ever. George is quite happy: it is a *fait accompli*. 'I have put my carriage in the coach-house, you see,' Byron keeps saying. 'My carriage is in the coach-house.' Which, in the dream, and with irrefutable dream-logic, clinches it. And life is unlikely heaven until she wakes up, to the sound of Byron's carriage being made ready.

A fortnight later, Byron breaks his homeward journey at the best inn on the Great North Road, where he stormily informs his hostess that the engagement is off.

'What do you mean?' Augusta says, quietly closing the parlour door. It is late, and George has gone to bed with the sniffles, having dosed himself with brandy. Still, she wants discretion. It begins with words. 'You mean she has broken it off?'

'No such luck. I don't know what I mean.' Thunderous, he peers into cupboards. 'Did George drink all the brandy? Oh, never mind. What I want is pen and paper. Ah, this will do.'

'What are you doing?'

'Writing a letter to my beloved Princess of Parallelograms, telling her we shall not be married after all.'

Augusta sits and watches him, his flying pen, his twitching lips. I wish I could write so easily, she thinks. And, surprisingly: the secret of beauty is in the shape of the mouth. Surprising, because such deep pronouncements are not her style. And: oh, Byron, you should not do this to me, indeed you should not.

Byron says, not looking up: 'What's wrong?'

'Why do you suppose anything's wrong?'

'Oh, dear Gus, I'm not a complete fool.' He flings the pen down. 'Though if I had to listen to any more of Sir Ralph Milbanke's interminable shooting stories, or Ma Milbanke's twitterings, I very soon would be. The marvel is that *she* turned out so clever.'

'What is the difficulty, then? Merely your in-laws? You don't have to get along with them, you know. Indeed, it seems quite traditional not to.'

'What about your spouse?' Byron says, throwing himself down on the sofa and gazing up at the ceiling. She watches the expressive movements of his Adam's apple in his white throat as he speaks, like a tiny subsidiary face. 'Are you supposed to get along with your spouse? I don't say wife, because you can't know that. But husband you do.'

'That's not something we should talk about.'

'Now you sound like Annabella,' he said mordantly. 'I'm sorry, Gus. The fact is, she's too good for me. And we don't get along because . . . well, imagine it as a literal sort of getting along, that is walking along together on a journey. But at *every* turning she must know *why* we are going that way, and what does it *mean* that we are going that way . . . Oh, Lord.' His chest bobs in a laugh. 'In truth I feel better now, just talking about it. Just being with you.'

'Well. That is partly a good thing. Partly not, as you well know. But, Byron, you knew she was a very intellectual sort of woman—'

'To be sure – and very interesting she can be. But she didn't take kindly to the wrong sort of interest. When we were finally left alone, I tried to be a little pre-matrimonial with her, and she got into a taking—'

'Byron,' Augusta says, more gently than she feels, 'you shouldn't say these things to me.'

'Shouldn't I?' He sits up, and there is a look of absolute sadness on his face. 'I suppose not. I'm just trying to convey how it was. She was eager, but then it was as if she was frightened of herself. And so she suggested I had better go.'

'Go and what?'

'Oh, make plans for the wedding, of course,' he says, laughing crossly. 'And how am I to do that? When we cannot even be – be *comfortable* with one another.'

'Is that what you think marriage should be?' she says, smiling at last.

'Why, to be sure – I have it all fixed – you comfortably ignore each other's ghastly daylight faces across the breakfast-table, and then you, the husband that is, go and see to the paddock fence where Farmer Mulligrub's sheep got through – and the vicar calls and you invite him to dine next Thursday when you have your wife's tedious spinster cousin coming – she is up in good works and hands out tracts from a little basket – and you may as well get them both over with together – and then before dinner you read the local newspaper and wink at the maid and then over dinner you comfortably ignore each other across the table again . . .' He is prowling about, grimacing, nearly laughing. 'Is this not the thing? Have I not hit it – the hellishness?'

'It doesn't sound so very bad. Byron, you cannot send that letter.'

'Can't I? But I feel so much better for having written it – the choking feeling has gone off – like a hanging man cut down in the nick of time—'

'Well, you have written it, but you need not send it. Think about Annabella. The engagement is made public: there is her reputation as well as her happiness to consider.'

He stops pacing and looks at her, piercingly. 'Why do you care so much, Gus?'

'Tear up the letter, please, Byron.'

After a moment he says, snatching it up, 'For you, I will.'

'Not for me, for her,' Augusta says: but so quietly that the sound of ripping paper covers it up altogether.

It begins with words, and Byron finally sorts out his affairs in London and travels north to Seaham again, to say the words, to marry and be married, just before Christmas 1814.

And stops, on the way, at Six Mile Bottom.

Not a good visit. Snow, ice, Arctic winds that infiltrate the disrepaired house and set the pictures rattling on the walls. George ill with a genuine cold and groaning for horehound and tisane from a cocoon of blankets: children ailing as usual: household fractiously confined, and Byron in a strange glassy state, making gnarled little jokes over Christmas dinner that no one understands. He stays till late on Boxing Day.

'You are certainly making your bride wait,' George remarks, peeling a yellow eye and extending a limp farewell hand from his blankets.

'That's the secret, Colonel,' Byron says. 'That's the secret.'

Augusta, wrapped in a shawl, sees him out to his carriage.

'You'll catch cold, Gus,' he says softly. 'Go inside, my darling.'

'No. Byron, this is dreadful.' She does not mean the weather.

'It has to be.' He holds her and kisses her. Blown flakes of snow interpose themselves between their lips. When he leaves, the snow is in her eyes and she cannot see at all.

It begins with words, and the words are to be said in the cold drawing room of far distant Seaham (special licence from the Archbishop of Canterbury) before the rector of the parish and the Rev. Thomas Noel, the bride's cousin, with the bride's parents in attendance, and the groom's old friend Mr Hobhouse as best man, at eleven o'clock in the morning of Monday 2 January 1815.

All this Augusta knows. And throughout that morning, at Six Mile Bottom, she keeps herself desperately busy, dusting, baking, sewing, anything: anything not to notice the time: anything not to feel the significance. And at last, as if all the while she has a perfectly accurate timepiece in her heart, she puts down her work and walks through to the hall, where there is a long-case clock. She stands before it: to her absolute absence of surprise, she sees that it is eleven o'clock.

'Well,' she says after a beating moment, 'all over now.'

It begins and ends with words.

The honeymoon – or the treaclemoon, as Byron calls it – is spent at Halnaby Hall, another bleak northern pile belonging to the Milbankes. 'I shan't write you,' Byron told Augusta on Christmas night, 'it would be too fantastical.'

But Annabella, the new Lady Byron, does. Long, informative letters. Augusta replies that she feels she knows her already, though this is not true: Lady Byron is as chimerical a figure to her as the Queen of the Fairies. This is because, as Augusta tells herself, she has no imagination. And she is very glad of it: it means she does not have to read between the lines of those painstaking letters, with their assurances that all is well between husband and wife, their stiffly flippant references to her brother's odd little ways. It means she does not have to picture it. Imagination, the torturer.

No, she will have to see this Annabella, Lady Byron, to believe in her. And that is not a thing she intends ever will happen – though she knows, of course, that it will, one day. (Augusta, with her experience, has no difficulty in holding two such contraries in her mind.) Above all, she is firm as she can be in her refusal to join the treaclemooners at Halnaby, as Annabella suggests in her circumlocutory way. If she were in the habit of reading between the lines, Augusta would see there was an appeal for help, but she cannot see it, and even if she did, she is the last person to enlist. God, yes.

She will not go there – but the trouble is, they keep threatening or promising to come here, to Six Mile Bottom.

Partly this is natural. It is the custom to make family visits after a wedding, and she is virtually all the family Byron has. Not natural, though: as Annabella's letters mention more and more her husband's eagerness to introduce her to his sister, Augusta discerns the shadow of a terrible longing. A longing that was meant to have been suppressed and suffocated like an overlaid child. (Dear Lord, where do these images come from? It cannot be her imagination, as she has none.) Well, it must not be. This longing – and it is Byron's, of course, not hers – must not be allowed to revive.

Yet short of saying *I don't want you to* – an almost impossible thing for Augusta's temperament – she cannot see a way of avoiding it. As the snow, which has been a harsh white stare all round them since Christmas, begins to sully and melt, as the ice in the dykes leaves off making its tight-gripping pistol-cracks and slackens to mush, Augusta runs out of excuses and looks to the coming of Byron and his bride like a sort of horrible anti-spring, inexorable as the true one.

Out in the wider world, great things go on that might save her, if only their timing were a little different. The lesser is news, unofficial as yet, from London. Despite her years of country seclusion Augusta, the granddaughter of Lady Holdernesse and acquaintance of royalty, is not forgotten. A court appointment is to be offered to her: Woman of the Bedchamber to Queen Charlotte.

At once she is wafted back to her girlhood, to Grandmother's stately, well-regulated house, to the little grim-jawed Queen and the gabbling King making their incognito visits. The poor King is now a blind and decrepit shell, talking madness in his closed rooms at Windsor; but Augusta is astonished to think that Queen Charlotte, to whose kindness and long memory she owes the appointment, must only be seventy. She is astonished because that past, that world, seems several lifetimes away. It must be because it was before she met Byron.

The appointment brings a stipend of three hundred pounds a

year – enough to stave off at least a few of George's ravening creditors – and the use of an apartment at St James's Palace whenever she is in Town for her duties, which will not be many: attendance on the Queen at state occasions and receptions, most of which are the Prince Regent's business now. All in all it is the first unmixedly good thing to happen to Augusta for a long time – and if only it were formally confirmed, so that she would have to go up to London to be presented. But not, frustratingly, yet.

The greater news is from Europe. Napoleon has escaped from Elba and landed in France, declaring himself Emperor still, rallying troops to his standard, and threatening to tip over again the whole carefully laid banqueting-table of peace. Consternation, disbelief, panic, riot: a rash of bankruptcies as the newly inflated funds collapse again: a rush by many to put their houses in order, plan, pray. But it does not touch either of their households, Byrons or Leighs, closely enough to justify putting off the nuptial visit.

Lack of room might have stopped it, genuinely. But then George, straining from wintertime imprisonment like a dog balked of a walk, seizes on an invitation from a crony to a hunting-party in Yorkshire. One less, old girl: now they can have our bedroom, their maid our dressing-room, and you the spare room. All the difference.

Thank you, George.

The things you dread always come, Augusta thinks, hearing the sound of carriage wheels. But they are never as bad as you think they are going to be.

Well, that has always been her optimistic belief. This will certainly test it. She hesitates, running cold hands down her frock, peering at herself in the little cracked mirror that is all the spare bedroom offers. Is her hair right? Why does it matter? She has found some threads of grey lately: at thirty-two. She takes a savage pleasure in plucking them out.

The carriage has stopped. They must be at the door. Still

Augusta cannot make herself go down. She feels cavernously sick. Wonders, with a lack of interest that horrifies her, whether she is pregnant again.

At last she walks down the stairs, for some reason counting them as she goes. Thirteen, fourteen. Curious how one can go up and down one's stairs every day and never know how many there are.

'Well, sis, you need not have *hurried* yourself so.'

Byron is in the hall. He has a bitter, flaming look. Beside him is a young lady, surprisingly short and slight – why surprising? perhaps because Augusta equates her cleverness with physical presence – in a dove-grey spencer and netted bonnet. A very neat young lady: she makes Augusta think of the ladies in fashion-plate illustrations, who are always doing something very poised and self-possessed like reading or contemplating a vase in profile while wearing perfectly unwrinkled gloves. So much to take in.

'My dear . . .' Augusta half stumbles forward, kisses her brother. 'I'm so glad to welcome you both at last.' Her voice seems quite shrunken. So much to take in. Byron, for example, looks, regrettably, ominously, quite mad. Insane. Turn to the neat young lady. Grab at the small gloved hand. 'I hope you had a good journey . . .'

'Oh, no kiss for your new sister-in-law, eh?' Byron's flush makes his teeth look deadly white, vampiric, ready to bite at you. 'And there I have been telling Bell all about your *warmth*.'

'Oh dear, he is in that humour, I see,' Augusta murmurs, turning to Annabella. A glance of collusion there, sisterhood of suffering? Perhaps not. 'I feel I know you already.' I'm lying. A round, pippin-round face, cherry lips, peach complexion – yet nothing pert there at all, nothing of Nell Gwyn: great dreamy serious eyes, martyr's or inquisitor's perhaps, but certainly demanding of you something grave and unequivocal, calling you to witness. Augusta smiles precariously. 'You'll wish to see your room. Shall I have your bags taken up?'

'I still think it's shabby about the kiss,' Byron says. Embracing his wife, he kisses her apple cheek while fixing his dark-filled eyes on Augusta. 'There. Now we are all friends.'

They should never have come.

It isn't that they quarrel – Byron with Annabella, or Byron with Augusta, or Augusta with Annabella. None of them is on sure enough ground for that. But quarrelling would be pure peace compared with what they have, which is a thousand excruciating variations on uneasiness. Ugly music played by an incompetent player on an out-of-tune violin for hours, days on end.

The first night, Annabella goes to bed early so that brother and sister can talk alone. Augusta smiles and says there is no need: Byron raises his eyebrows at her afterwards.

'What's the matter?'

'You don't have to be so damned polite.'

'Earlier you thought I was not polite enough.'

'Oh, damn it, Gus, can't you see I wanted her to go out of the way? How else can we be together properly?'

'Well. I dare say we have a good deal to catch up on. You must tell me about the honeymoon – and Halnaby – they say it's very pretty country up there—'

'They say nothing of the kind, because you know nobody who has ever been to the dismal sty, thank heaven.' He takes her by the shoulders. 'Now, enough of this small-talk, Gus, for God's sake.'

Sinuously, sideways, she evades his lips. He watches her retreat to the other side of the parlour, where she makes a pretence of trimming the candles.

'If it wasn't wrong then, why is it wrong now?'

'It was always wrong.' His touch seems to have left a fiery imprint; but she is set on revealing nothing. 'But this is even more wrong.'

'Because I'm married?'

She nods. 'Because you're married.'

'And yet, you know, I had never suspected you were a spinster all this time.'

'It's different.'

He laughs, groans. 'How much women can pack into that short sentence. Covers a multitude of sins. Or multiplies a coveting of sins. Augusta, I have been in hell.'

'Byron, you exaggerate.'

Smiling, he relaxes a little, though it is only a faint slackening of an impossibly overwound spring. 'Of course I do. That's what I'm for. Well, what think you of Bonaparte breaking out like this? Do we not live in an age of miracles? Doesn't it show that everything is possible?'

'You know I don't agree with your politics.'

'At least you don't quiz me on 'em. When I say hell, perhaps I mean purgatory. The thing you have to go through in order to be saved. This – you – are my glimpse of heaven. Let me have the glimpse. Then back to the fires and pitchforks.'

Augusta shakes her head. 'Byron – you know we agreed. We must stop *because* of that – the consequences—'

'What, will Bell's thunderous Jehovah – oh, he is indeed, believe me, she would make Cromwell look like a backsliding voluptuary – will he really, you know, consign us to actual hell after we die? For what we have done? A harmless thing that hurts no one?'

'I don't think we can say harmless.'

Byron gulps brandy, then throws back his head to look at her, critically, as if she is a painting with clear signs of fakery. 'The one thing I truly hate – no. The second thing I truly hate is hypocrisy. And you, darling Gus, were the last person I suspected of it.'

'Byron, you're drinking too much brandy.'

'There's no such thing as too much brandy. That–' gesturing up to the ceiling, the bedroom above where Annabella waited, presumably neatly, coverlet turned down, hands crossed on it, no, don't think of it '–is what the world *requires* of us. This–' he seizes

Augusta, hands hot on her waist '—is what our hearts require of us. Well — isn't it?'

Miserably she slides away, averting her face. 'You said — the first thing. The one thing you truly hate. What is it?'

'Oh, myself, of course,' he says, dully, turning away too, taking up the brandy-bottle.

The days are bearable — the slide towards hideousness begins around dinner-time; and the mornings even pleasant. Byron sleeps late, and when he wakes is lamblike, making gentle jests, playing with the children. Augusta and Annabella walk together in the bare, twiggy, brittle garden.

'Your children are very handsome.'

'Thank you. I think so. But, then, a mother's partiality . . . I should think you would like to have children.'

'Why should you think that?'

'Oh . . . well, I suppose every woman does.' But Augusta doesn't suppose that: she knows nothing of other women and does not presume to — they might want to foster walruses for all she knew.

'I see. Yes, it would seem there is a natural inclination. Also, scripturally it is our lot. Also our glory. Thus the pain and suffering is redeemed, made beautiful even. This is rather a wonderful thought, isn't it?'

'Yes,' Augusta says, bewildered. 'Beautiful, wonderful.'

'You sound as if you are not entirely sure. You have had difficult deliveries, perhaps.'

'No, no, no trouble at all . . .' This is not true either: she had a bad time with the last two; but she is trying to flounder back to the point.

'My dear Augusta,' Annabella says in her fruity, fluty way, smiling, 'I am not quite an innocent. I know very well that there was never a birth that cost the mother *no* trouble at *all*.'

'Well — perhaps I overstated—'

'I wonder why. To spare me, so that I shall not be

377

apprehensive? But you need not. I have very little fear of pain. It is kind in you, but really you must promise me not to consider me in need of protection. Small as I am.' A little joke, delivered with an odd mixture of arrogance and timidity.

'Of course I promise.' Augusta feels weary. Often it is like this with Annabella: you find yourself having to labour over some conversational point in which you had no real belief or interest. And yet, Augusta tells herself, she is very amiable: no forward Townish mannerisms. Too good for her, perhaps, she thinks, echoing Byron.

'Augusta, may I ask you something?'

'Anything. You know I want us to be friends – more than friends – sisters.'

'I never had a sister,' Annabella says, frowning up at Byron, who has climbed into the lower branches of the apple-tree with Georgiana, 'so I cannot tell what that must be like. The inevitable limitation of being an only child.'

'I know. I'm one too.' She becomes aware of Annabella's look. 'Well, it always *felt* so. Only half-blood, you know, and we were never together as children . . .' Some untruth here too, but she hasn't the energy to trace it. Annabella saps her. 'I'm sorry – the question.'

'Well, it is this. Why does Byron prefer to spend his evenings with you, after I go to bed?'

Augusta feels as if all the blood has drained out of her: would not be surprised to see it staining the grass at her feet.

'I – I have said to him he should not stay up so – only he is used to it, I'm afraid – in London he would be at balls and card-parties and then come home and write like a madman – and then, you know, as hostess I should keep him company, and we have much to catch up on—'

'You don't understand me,' Annabella says sepulchrally. 'I'm wondering why you are better at managing him than I.' That careful rosebud mouth is colourless, drawn in. 'It is a thing I cannot fail to be aware of.'

There is pain there, and Augusta is always helpless and propitiatory before pain. 'Oh, Annabella, please, you shouldn't think that. Byron is an odd creature – but utterly whole-hearted – for him to marry is a great thing, a greater thing than it might be for most men, and it is on you that his choice has fallen, and he must think so very, very highly of you. Really, don't let his oddities draw you into feeling a jealousy, which—'

'Jealousy?' Annabella stops dead. 'My dear, that can hardly be. You are his sister.'

'I know.' Augusta fumbles for Annabella's arm, for absurdly long moments cannot find it, what is this, has the woman detachable arms . . . ? 'I know. Come. Let's walk on – there's damp there. I know. What I mean is—'

'Perhaps I have been unclear in my meaning,' Annabella says, frowning. 'It is difficult to talk of. I merely meant that I would like to learn – how to put him at his ease.'

Augusta breathes out a long breath. 'Well. Sometimes you can't; but then I think you shouldn't try too hard. He is odd, as I say, and it's best to take his oddity as normality. Often when some mood is on him I'll say, "Oh, you're being *Byron*, are you?" '

'Yes – when I first met him, I observed the women gathering about him, and hoping he would be scornful and satirical with them. And I thought then it wasn't a good thing to feed this element in his nature, which he has cultivated at the expense of the nobler aspect that shines through his writings. The indulgence of such feelings must lead him away from the path towards the good.'

'To be sure,' Augusta says faintly. Actually she had meant you should just laugh him out of it.

Byron has clambered down from the tree and taken Medora from the nurse. Holding the little dark-crowned head under his chin he advances smiling on Augusta and Annabella.

' "How now, you secret, black, and midnight hags," ' he says brightly.

'Yes, Byron, we were discussing you, and whether we should

just push you in the river and have done with you,' Augusta says.

'Excellent. I'll haunt you, mind. Look at this little spiky sweet-briar,' he says, holding Medora up. 'Was there ever such a likeness?'

More blood on the grass.

'To her uncle,' Byron says, as all three stare at the child, staring cryptically into the middle distance, 'to her uncle, I mean. There's the Byron blood for you.' His face falls. 'I shouldn't say that, of course. Because it's doomed.'

'I shall cure you of those morbid thoughts, my dear,' Annabella says, laying her hand on his arm.

'God, I wish you could, Bell.'

Well, thinks Augusta, if not fond, then near enough. For a moment, like a reformed addict sneaking back to the laudanum-bottle, she allows herself her old treat of believing that everything will be all right.

The brooches.

Augusta doesn't share Byron's belief in doom: still, it makes her wonder, the way the brooches arrive when Annabella is there. He ordered them some time ago from a London jeweller: two gold brooches engraved with the letters A and B, and entwined with locks of his and Augusta's hair. The trouble is, they are so beautiful, and to Augusta so meaningful; and *not* to wear them would appear far more peculiar and conspicuous than to wear them.

'I never knew such a brother and sister,' Annabella says, at her most queenly, shaking her head at them.

And Byron, at his most unholy: 'You never spoke a truer word, Bell.'

Guilt: Augusta has never known before what it is to be torn by it in quite this way. It was different from when she felt guilty towards George: that could be dealt with by making compartments in the mind, by considering how far George was from any danger of hurt. But when Byron stays up at night with her, ignoring his wife upstairs, a guilt tears at her that is beyond soothing. (And yet how much more comfortable it is when that doll-like figure has gone soberly trotting upstairs, and they are free of those catechistical questions and shattering silences, that solemn gaze like light through a stained-glass window, that accuracy . . .) Guilt because he should be with Annabella, not her. And then another guilt, because this is − no denying it − what she wants: to be alone with Byron, in candlelight and peace, to relax and talk nonsense, to be her untrammelled self as she can only be with him. It is for her the greatest and most precious part of it − beyond even the passion, which is only a more concentrated form of their lazy love: she can be happy with this. But hence the guilt, because on these long fire-crackling evenings she is getting what she wants. And Byron is not getting what he wants, she knows. Knows even without the way his eyes dwell on her like fingertips.

Madness, yes: unfortunately she *was* his madness.

One night he suddenly embraces her with a moan, and she nearly, so nearly gives in.

'No. No.' She gets out of his arms like an exhausted swimmer struggling on to a bank. 'We mustn't.'

'In my experience that proves that we must.'

'Your wife—'

'Is upstairs.' He sits back and looks up at the ceiling − though seeming to look further, higher, into heaven itself. 'The only thing worse than constantly seeing what you can't have is constantly seeing what you *must* have.' He reaches for the brandy. 'There is nothing like misery to make you epigrammatic. See, there's another.'

'She wants to make you happy.'

'She wants to make a domestic pet of me. You've heard of Pasiphae and the bull? Well, imagine an even more monstrous mating − a curate and a lap-dog. And there you have the *wived* Byron as he will be. Why did you make me tear up that letter?'

'I thought it was the right thing to do.'

'Aha, you said *thought*, not *think* . . . The curious thing is, she does make me happy. That is, she comes as close as anyone could, under the circumstances.'

'Oh, now you're being Byron.'

He chuckles. 'I don't feel as if I shall ever be Byron again.'

The next morning he is more wolf than lamb – a savage, wounded, cunning wolf, at bay.

'So,' he says loudly across the breakfast-table, 'you wouldn't, Gus.'

Augusta manages to make her tea-cup descend, vibrating and splashing, into the saucer.

'No,' she says, after a time of which she has no conception – it might be an hour from the feel of it, yet it can't be as they are still sitting there looking at her . . . 'No, I wouldn't recommend tartar emetic. It is too strong a purge.'

Byron falls to silent laughter, his elbows on the table, his fists on his closed clenched eyes. He could almost be crying.

Later he lies on the sofa and tells them of his visit to the court of Ali Pasha, the Albanian warlord, roaster and impaler of foes, but a genial greybeard with a paunch who invited him to sit at his right hand on a scarlet ottoman while they drank thick black coffee and shared a hookah.

'He liked my *ears*, because they are so small. And he sent me baskets of sweetmeats and sherbet with a thousand compliments . . .'

'It sounds as if the barbarian wished to add you to his harem,' Annabella says sceptically.

Byron, eyes closed, lets out an abrupt laugh. 'Perhaps you're right at that, Bell.'

'You and your pashas,' Augusta says. 'I think you fancy yourself quite a pasha. Lounging there—'

'And I have my harem,' Byron says, opening his eyes with –

impossible yet almost audible – a snap. 'Here. Come, you pampered jades of Asia. I must have a kiss from each of you. Then I shall pronounce on the kisses, and judge.'

Afterwards Augusta remembers that they were all laughing as they did it: but laughter can mean lots of things. He closed his eyes again, and waited half smiling. First Annabella. 'Aha.' Then Augusta. 'Oho.' And then: 'I can tell which is which. Oh, yes.'

'Spring is here. Almost.' In the garden, Augusta contemplates with mild dismay the few crocuses that have not been trampled or uprooted by the children. Some people, she supposes, do not have such rampaging offspring: how do they manage it?

'I greatly love a garden,' Annabella says, drawing her pelisse tight about her, as if to dissociate herself from *this* one.

'I think everything will be better – that is, I think your real married life begins when you have a home of your own.'

'Well, that may be soon. My aunt Melbourne writes that she can secure us a place in London, all being well – at Piccadilly Terrace. A house belonging to the Duchess of Devonshire. Byron says he wants to take it, though it is seven hundred a year – rather dear.'

'My God. Can he afford it?'

'He says – very grandly – that he *will* afford it.'

It is not a bad piece of mimicry, concluded with an impish sideways look. There is fun in her, thinks Augusta. Perhaps we can be friends after all. And perhaps, after all, that will solve things. She doesn't know how, but just the thought is like a warm breeze on her skin.

'Men are strange creatures, are they not?' Annabella goes on.

'All the ones I know certainly are,' Augusta agrees.

'Yes – and their ways – that one never guessed – these appetites of theirs that come and go so quickly,' says Annabella, and now there is a deadly sort of sprightliness about her. 'One supposes it is normal – that what they *like* is then an *abomination* to them.'

'I do know what you mean,' Augusta says cautiously, 'though

perhaps this is just human. For instance – I have a great weakness for sweet cake – and will eat such a great deal of it, and then feel sick at the very sight of it—'

'He does not like to sleep in the same bed with me. By which I mean *sleep*.'

'Oh – oh, I see. Well, that is his way, you know. He must stretch out in bed. I fancy it may be so he can rest his bad foot more comfortably.'

For several seconds she doesn't understand Annabella's stare. Then she understands, and must make her quickest recovery of all. She does not do well.

'What I mean is, if he is anything like my George, which he may well be, for George is my cousin and families are alike, and George is a great one for stretching out and taking up all the room—'

'But Colonel Leigh does not have a lame foot, surely?'

'Prone to ill-health, though – poor George,' Augusta says tensely. 'And men – men are, you are right, they are strange creatures when it comes to these things. And, of course, Byron is strange in *all* ways, that I do know.'

'You seem to know practically everything about him,' pronounces Annabella, looking wonderingly up into her face. 'I think you are the person I must learn from.'

'Lord, no, no,' Augusta cries, 'I'm a very stupid person – quite the stupidest – and to think of anyone learning anything . . .' She falls silent as Annabella touches her arm. She is wearing long sleeves, but there is something about Annabella's small neat hand that always makes you feel as if she is touching your bare skin.

'You shouldn't say that, my dear. You shouldn't hide your light.'

She is so much better than me, thinks Augusta; and for the first time in years has a vivid memory of Grandmother with her cancered swollen face, dying in patient faith, a silent example; and her eyes fill with tears.

And Annabella, seeing them, smiles; as if they are nicer than any children or crocuses.

★ ★ ★

That evening, after dinner, Annabella corrects Georgiana's lesson for her, and begins to talk of education.

Her own: from an early age, prodigious. 'This was in response to my willingness, of course. Not every child, not every girl, will seize on Euclid as I did, or wish to understand the Greek they see in Papa's books. But the strength of curiosity in the very young should not be underestimated, and nor should it be allowed to wither. Let them be overwhelmed, a little out of their depth, rather than undernourished with learning. There is, of course, a great danger with the study of the ancient languages, and that is a tendency to irreligion. So it goes without saying that the firmest foundation in Christian teaching antedates all these. And not mere rote-learning of religious tenets, but the inculcation of a religious approach to *life*. I think there must be high ideals. It is all too easy to recognize, in adult life, when this habit of aspiration has been lacking.'

'The ancients,' Byron says suddenly, 'never mention underwear. Isn't that curious? One would give much to know what Alexander had on underneath, or whether Cleopatra wore drawers.'

Annabella gives him a flat look. 'Aspiration,' she goes on, 'which can be inculcated through the study of history, even of poetry—'

'History, exactly – it *affects* you, what you have on underneath. But it's all a mystery to us, or nearly all. You, my dear, wear drawers, this I know.' A smile at Augusta. 'You, sis, wear drawers also.'

'Hush, Byron,' Augusta says quickly, 'you're talking nonsense.'

'Am I now? Do you deny it? Here's an interesting point—'

'It's indecent to talk like this,' Annabella snaps.

'Nothing's indecent when you're married. That's why they say a marriage *licence*. Anyhow, if it's indecency you want, turn the pages of your ancient Greeks.'

'There are some pages that must be omitted,' says Annabella, calmly.

'Good Gad!' Byron laughs furiously. 'I'm going to have that written up somewhere in brazen letters – the true epitome of our mendacious age.'

'My dear,' says Annabella, 'if you mean to impugn morality—'

'Oh, but I don't.' Byron holds up his hands. 'I have nothing to do with morality. Morality I leave entirely to you, Bell.'

Annabella's jaws work behind tight lips; and then, though Augusta has hardly spoken, Annabella turns on her a look of scalding accusation, as if everything, everything, were her fault.

She is so glad to see them go that the gladness almost overshadows the guilt she feels at feeling glad. Augusta, in knots.

'But you'll be coming to Town soon,' Byron says, while the carriage awaits, Annabella's watching face glumly framed in its window. 'Now your court place is confirmed. Where will you stay? Where else but with us?'

'I don't know if that's a good idea—'

'Dear Gus, all the good ideas ran out precisely three months ago. It's settled.' Going to the carriage he calls out: 'Gus shall stay with us, Bell, hey? When she comes to Town to bend the knee and all.'

'Oh, yes.' Annabella puts her hand out and squeezes Augusta's tightly. 'You must, please.' And now she looks as if Augusta were her last hope in existence.

'You do not seem to have changed at all.'

Little old Queen Charlotte, now defiantly, memorably ugly, raps out the monosyllables like a fusillade. Augusta murmurs her thanks.

'And you still mutter. But no one speaks clear any more. It is so they can tell better the lies. Come closer, I can't see. Well, there is a little change. You are a mother, I think.'

'Yes, Your Majesty. I'm very lucky, I have been blessed with four children.'

The Queen snorts. 'If they are truly all *blessings*, then you are lucky indeed. Still, I suppose they are young yet, to disappoint you.'

'My eldest girl is seven, ma'am. She is here in Town with me – I thought she would like to see the sights.' Also, I confess only to myself, I thought she might help cure the sick atmosphere of that house. Wrong again.

'I regret that your apartment is not ready for you yet. Also, you will find it is not grand. I do not live in the grand style. My court also. Do not look for the grand there. My son's court, now – if it is grand you want, there you will find grand.' The Queen gives 'grand' a more scornful rasp with each repetition. 'Still. You have lived, been living, in the country.'

'Yes, Your Majesty. Not grand at all.'

Queen Charlotte waves that away with a clawed hand, as if to say: too old, too shrewd for banter. 'Where do you stay in Town? With your brother?'

'Yes, ma'am, and his wife.'

'He is married? I never hear anything here.' Another snort. 'Thankfully. There is not much to hear that is good. Especially from the quarter of my son. Mind you, there is *grand* if you want it.' She seems to have forgotten she has just said this. 'And I am a dull old woman. You need not fear your duties will tire you, Mrs Leigh. I seldom require attendance at a ball nowadays. It will be mostly funerals.' She gapes a short, silent laugh. 'I am a mere left-over. But at least my conscience is clear. Who can say the same?' She peers at Augusta. Only short-sightedness. 'And now it seems we must face that monster Bonaparte once again. He should never have been allowed to escape. But then he should never have been allowed to *be*. This is the decline. In morals, in everything. I do not know where it will all end. But my conscience is clear, Mrs Leigh. You will find, as you grow older, this becomes more and more important.' Her cockerel eyes suddenly moisten, but it is only rheum: there is no indulgence here. 'The thing is, above all, to have no possibility of regrets.'

After her audience at St James's, Augusta takes a hackney to

Bond Street. She wants to find a little gift for Georgiana. She doesn't know whether it's her being out of step, or the dangerous uncertainty of the times, but everything seems very dear. Still she lingers, looking in shop windows as if into misty oracle. She is putting off going back to number thirteen – of course it would be – Piccadilly Terrace.

On the Continent, undeclared war as Napoleon gathers his loyal troops about him once again and the Allies, bickering among themselves, muster to meet him: at Piccadilly Terrace, too large, too expensive – too grand, indeed – another undeclared war.

Of course, Augusta thinks, she should never have come. Why, then? Because not only Byron but Annabella asked her to, pressingly. Augusta, no student of geopolitics, views the turmoil across the Channel not wholly with understanding but with a sort of recognition. In the war of Byron's marriage, what is she to be? A buffer state – or an ally to one or other of the powers?

Of course the one thing you cannot be is an ally to both. Wars don't work that way. But it is the one thing she wishes she could be.

There are money troubles, which the echoing house has made worse. Annabella is in the early stages of pregnancy, which Augusta knows can make you emotional. Byron is drinking heavily, which is never a good sign. Also there are quarrels with the in-laws: Annabella's uncle Lord Wentworth is dying, which means Annabella will move closer to inheriting, but there is some family trouble over the matter, which makes Byron violent at the very mention of Annabella's parents. Also they are a very mismatched couple. Also – but no matter how you add it up, the sum of unhappiness is always greater than the parts. Annabella the mathematician must be puzzled indeed.

And Augusta – is she the missing factor in the equation?

Of course, she came because she was asked, but not only because of that. There is still her love for Byron. Like a powerful hound pulling at a lead, it still drags her on. But not to such dangerous places, not now.

'Oh! I do beg your pardon.' A dandified old gent, leaving the shop, bumps into her, though it's her fault: dreaming and wandering. 'I am most terribly sorry.'

'The thing is to have no possibility of regrets,' Augusta informs him amiably.

Not the same love, not the same Byron. Always changeable, now his mood alters with dumbfounding speed. As if he were living ten times as fast as everyone else: as if a flower should bud, bloom, fade and wither all within minutes. If the Byron she loves did not still appear occasionally, she would have gone home days ago. Or would she? Because there is Annabella as well, and Augusta does want to help her, somehow, even while knowing that her presence is the last thing that helps.

'I know you're eating for two, my love, but in the name of God do you have to keep gourmandizing like that?' Byron, yesterday, when Annabella had luncheon brought in.

Augusta tried to take it off. 'Not everyone likes to be forever dieting like you, Byron. Now, are you going to reprove me as well? Because I have a great fancy for one of those cutlets.'

But Annabella, instead of taking heart, joining in, said nothing: she had a way of planting these silences like fizzing charges. She just went on methodically – and even, somehow, martyrishly – eating. And Augusta – she asked God to forgive her for it – found it faintly irritating too.

The evenings have assumed the same pattern as at Six Mile Bottom. Annabella retires early, Byron sits up talking with Augusta. This, alas, is when the Byron she loves is most apt to surface from beneath the fierce saturnine stranger. Alas, because she is always thinking of Annabella upstairs, can often hear her peculiarly dumpy tread from the library above.

Last night Byron said, with an air of perplexed discovery: 'You know, this is what comes of poetry. This is what comes of the dreaming of dreams.'

'What does?'

'*This*. All of it.' With a peculiarly untroubled expression, Byron picked up his empty brandy-glass and hurled it at the ceiling. It smashed, rained down tinkling. The pacing footsteps ceased. 'You see, because of it we think we can make each other happy. More than that, we think we *should*. We accept no limitations. Hence and thus. Now, in our father's time, people knew what was what. No illusions. Marry for money, have tidy affairs, keep the peace, dream no dreams. It was very practical.'

'It sounds horrible.'

'Of course, I don't say pleasant things any more.'

'You do not to poor Annabella lately. Sometimes you are so abusive—'

'And sometimes I am sweet and tender. Oh, Gus, God knows why you came.'

'I was invited to come.'

'And do you do every damn thing you're asked to?'

'Yes, pretty much,' she replied honestly.

Later, feeling she must do something, she went upstairs to see Annabella. She should have prepared more. Annabella, looking very sanctified and early-Christian in a long white night-rail with her hair down around her pallid moonlike face, regarded her in silence.

'I – I've come to say good night. And also to say – well, I think you should go to bed. Not stay up thinking – and I'm sorry, I wanted to say that also, because Byron will stay up so with me, and get to talking, and you must think – you must feel . . .'

Annabella, the graven image, would not help her incoherence. She seemed, merely, to draw conclusions from it.

Now the shopman, with a pointed look, begins putting up the shutters at the window, extinguishing at once Augusta's reflection and her reflections. She has a job to find a hackney, and when she does the driver seems to be in a ferocious, manic, Byronic mood, and takes off at such a speed the carriage feels as if it is plummeting down a steep hill. Or perhaps that is in Augusta: the feeling of rushing downward to waiting disaster.

Very well: but I cannot talk for long. I have many things to think of.

No, not *him* in particular, not this time. Though to be sure he has been much on my mind since I learnt of him marrying William's cousin Annabella after all – after she had turned him down forsooth! – and at first I could not hear her name without agitation. But am better now. The proof of it: yesterday I paid the nuptial visit.

Yes! You would not suppose me equal to it, I dare say. Neither did I. But my mother-in-law came to me and said she was going to pay the requisite call on the Byrons at Piccadilly Terrace and would I come. She added that Byron had specifically urged it. Also that if I did not it would look like a *scene*. Says she with a pruney mouth and her eyes to the sky. So you see even if I do nothing that is interpreted as Caro making a *scene*. Well, no matter, I went, with a great turbulence of feeling that you may be sure but externally calm, yes, unruffled, a lake with swans on it, that was I. Very well, a pale lake.

I don't know what I expected. But not what I found.

Byron shook my hand. His felt like cold, damp plaster. He introduced his wife, saying with a little smile, that of course, he hardly need do so. Well, true: though I cannot say I *know* Annabella – I don't think anyone does. She does not have friends: she has acolytes. Did they look happy? No. And neither did his sister, Mrs Leigh, who was with them – I thought she looked most unhappy of all.

And I remembered those letters.

Unhappy is perhaps not right – it was more painfully expect-ant. Like three actors sent out on to a richly decorated stage with no play-book, no lines, only the knowledge that this perform-ance will make them or ruin them.

I was glad to get away.

Oh, yes, it went through me – the thought – of course it did, like an electrical bolt – that I was *discarded* and *this* was taken up.

Triumph? Not at all. Think about it: where is the cause for triumph in that?

No, I don't know how I feel. It presses about my heart but there are other things there, closer just now. My family. My poor mama and papa were travelling in France when Bonaparte made his sudden *démarche* and have friends among the royalists and so we are all concerned for their safety in the midst of that horrid upheaval – they will I think do very well as long as they travel to the south and away from Paris and the north where all is ready to explode – that is almost literally – and here is my greatest fear, for my brother Frederick. Do you remember him? Probably not – you may have seen him with me as a child – well, since then he has become a most gallant and beloved colonel with the 12th Light Dragoons – fought all through the Peninsula – was the officer who brought the news to Wellington of Bonaparte's abdication – and now he is over there, with the army, waiting for what this reincarnated Boney will try. And I have the greatest anxiety for him, for there must surely be a great clash of arms and I have a superstitious conceit that there is only so much luck that one person can have.

Mine? Oh, I ran through my luck years and years ago. And now I am in arrears. I know I will have to pay, soon enough. But you know me: I shall not go quietly.

It had been Annabella's hope, in extending to Mrs Leigh the hospitality of Piccadilly Terrace, that she might thereby moderate the intemperate behaviour of her husband; who, since making her Lady Byron, had exhibited a temper so volatile that at times she had cause absolutely to fear for his reason. The presence of the sister to whom he was obviously devoted might assist him to that contentment which Annabella, to her infinite regret, seemed unable to foster, though she had made every effort to please, that was consonant with her sense of dignity, of decency, and what was due to herself. As she could not conceive of any alteration in her own conduct or character that could have rendered her a more amiable matrimonial partner, she was obliged from the weary eminence of perfection to view the unsatisfactory scene, and plan how best to improve it. Hence, her acquiescence, and even eagerness, in welcoming Mrs Leigh beneath the conjugal roof – an expedient that did not at all accord with her private opinions on the nature of her sister-in-law's influence.

Annabella had supposed at first that the reforms she sought, in marrying him, to effect in Lord Byron's principles, might be advanced by the promotion of familial affections, and the example of domestic virtue, which Mrs Leigh offered – however imperfectly; for Annabella could not entirely approve what she had seen of the lady's household arrangements, nor that indulgent fondness for her children, which must be laying a regrettable groundwork for their future characters. – Still, she must surely help to turn her brother's mind away from the morbidity and bitterness, which Annabella was afraid even her impressive example was inadequate to conquer. Alas! if Annabella was prone to a fault, as she was soon ruefully to acknowledge, it was a sort of innocence, and a too tardy willingness to believe ill of her fellow-creatures. There had not been lacking indications, during her visit to Mrs Leigh's home in —shire, of the almost incredible moral turpitude that now began to be borne in on Annabella's mind, as lying behind the curious relation between her husband and her sister-in-law. But that very innocence, and her firm adhesion to the principle of her faith, which enjoins us not to be quick to judge, had prevented her interpreting the appalling hints with anything beyond bafflement. – Now, she took up the clew: now, observing that her husband's strange profligacies, violent shifts of mood, and abusive conduct towards herself were not so much ameliorated as sharpened by the presence of Mrs Leigh, Annabella began to pursue the thread, though with a dread of the moral obloquies to which it must lead her, which only the fortitude of her religion enabled her to support.

She was far from a firm belief: yet she was equally distant from a firm disbelief; and in these circumstances, could only signal, as gently as she could, that when Mrs Leigh's turn of duty at court was over, she might be best to quit Piccadilly Terrace as soon as possible, and return to —shire. Mrs Leigh's ready and good-tempered acquiescence returned Annabella again to the state of forgiving allowance that was the bent of her nature. – She reminded herself she was without proofs. But even the shadow of such a suspicion was not to be borne; and it was earnest of the enormities that her imagination had touched upon that Annabella was relieved to say goodbye to a woman who in some regards had been her natural female ally and helper, in the hostile state of discord to which her marriage had descended.

Though Annabella was now in an interesting condition, she could not rely upon her husband's attentiveness. That instability and restlessness, which neither the fervency of her prayers nor the firmness of her example had yet succeeded in curing, had led him to a new pursuit. – He had joined the Committee of Drury-lane Theatre, and was much from home seeing to its affairs. Annabella could not but reprehend the talents that she had hoped to see turned to works of a noble and elevating character being engrossed to the fripperies of the common stage; and she further had reason to believe that he was amusing himself with actresses, dancers, &c., during these absent hours. Yet still she could not think of the moral pollution that must ensue, with the same degree of horror that attended her speculations about Mrs Leigh; for these must be mere wretches abandoned to vice, of whose capacity for regeneration little was to be hoped, and less antici-pated. But when she thought of Mrs Leigh, the one supporting reflection, in the mass of suspicion and loathing that over-whelmed her, was that repentance and redemption might be possible to her too. Providence was inscrutable; and Annabella did not reject the possibility that in choosing her to be the instru-ment of salvation it had intended as its object the sister as well as the brother.

Augusta, in the Newmarket coach with little Georgiana, closes her eyes in bliss as they draw away from London.

'I like Aunt Bella,' Georgiana volunteers. A chatty child with some of her uncle's spark. 'She likes to have big talks. And when she says to tell her everything, she really truly listens . . . It's funny there, though, isn't it?'

And Augusta puts her head in her hands and howls and hoots. Funny. Yes. Only now, only now she is free of it.

Augusta leaves, on 25 June, a London still reeling and fevered from the news, a week ago, of the titanic battle fought and won near Brussels: Waterloo.

Waterloo: some statistics.

The battle involved approximately 72,000 French troops, commanded by Napoleon, with 226 guns, against 67,000 British and Allied troops, commanded by Wellington, with 156 guns, together with the later intervention on the Allied side of the 50,000 Prussian troops commanded by Blücher. There were about 30,000 horses among the armies also. The battlefield was about three miles square. The battle commenced with the firing of French cannon at just before half past eleven in the morning of Sunday 18 June 1815. It was considered over at nine in the evening when Wellington and Blücher greeted each other on the Brussels road. By that time the Prussians had lost 7,000 men: Wellington had lost 15,000: the defeated Napoleon, 25,000. At this time the entire population of Manchester was about 100,000.

Waterloo: a story.

During the battle, at about three in the afternoon, Colonel Frederick Ponsonby, Lady Caroline Lamb's brother, was unhorsed and cut down in a cavalry charge. To a French sabre wound was added the piercing, through his lungs, of a Polish lance. While he lay flattened in the mud beside a ditch he was also trampled by French cavalry and then again later by Prussian cavalry, his body

395

actually bouncing up in the air: a sharpshooter used him as an arm-rest, a battlefield scavenger half stripped and robbed him, and a groaning soldier died slowly and gorily on top of him. After all this he was somehow still alive, as a British infantryman discovered. The infantryman guaranteed the continuance of that life by staying with him all night until the orderlies could come and transport his twisted husk on a blood-drenched stretcher to an overworked and chaotic field hospital the next morning.

Unsurprisingly, the first news that reached his family suggested that Frederick was dead. Luckily, it was corrected, just as his sister Caroline, with her husband William Lamb, reached Ghent. Frederick, Caroline learnt, was seriously wounded and in a military hospital in Brussels. She sincerely thanked God.

Caroline: she is far from the only English visitor to Brussels at this time. They have been thick on the ground even before Waterloo: the gathering of the Allies made the place a social centre, and the night before the battle the Duchess of Richmond held her celebrated ball – soon to be celebrated, indeed, in verse by Byron – from which the young gallants sallied out still in their dancing pumps to prepare for arms. Frederick was one of them: as he tells Caroline, with the splendid irony of the very ill, he came away from the ball complaining that he felt quite knocked up. And now in the aftermath of battle and flush of victory there are more English arriving and renting the best houses in Brussels and creating a miniature social season amid the blood and death.

And yet it is Caroline who gets a name for herself at Brussels: Caroline who becomes an emblem of outrageous frivolity.

Every day for two weeks she sits at her brother's bedside in the military hospital at the Hôtel de Ville. It is not pretty. To get to him she must pass men moaning and dying, shivering, gangrenous: men ruthlessly amputated, lopped and cropped like polled trees. She must inhale suppurating smells, hear the sound of blood-dried bandages ripping away skin. Then there is shattered Frederick, somehow inching back towards life. Characteristically he does his best to be decent, but still he has ague-ish fits, bubbles and spits blood, wets himself in extremity. When he begins to improve he murmurs a wish for an English newspaper, and Caroline goes all over the city to get one, and reads it to him over and over.

The bone-saw that is used to amputate limbs, Caroline notices, is quite small, and its carved wooden handle branches off in a couple of curlicues. The tool-maker who made it gave it this little flourish to look nice. How strange we are, thinks Caroline.

And when she is not nursing Frederick, she takes in the other sights. Commissary carts are still coming in from the battlefield with wounded, and with corpses – those that families have managed to trace and retrieve. Others, many others, must lie where they fell, which means that the trampled rye-fields are a mass of putrefaction. There is burning out there: human fat makes the pyres crackle merrily for days. Making up parties to go in carriages and view the battlefield is the latest fashion. William joins one, and comes back sombre and silent. He washes his hands over and over, then sets about the brandy with determination. 'Don't go,' he tells Caroline. She puts her arms round his neck, but he stares unyieldingly away: he wants to be alone with it.

And of course she goes. The road south out to Waterloo, churned up by endless traffic and then baked hard by the July sun, makes a bone-jarring experience. One of the ladies in Caroline's party complains that she was never more uncomfortable in her life. They get down at the sunken Ohain Road: somewhere about here, as far as Frederick can recall, is where he first fell. A heavy porkish smell in the air: mud, splintered trees, spatterings of gravel, decayed bodies of butchered horses. Embedded in the mud, glints of ordnance, grape-shot, bulging wheel-rims: a powder-flask flat as a saucer. People are picking up souvenirs, but there is less to be found than one might expect – here and there a boot, a stirrup, a blood-soaked epaulette: thieves and scavengers have long combed the battlefield and made off even with the dead horses' harness. There are ragged bits of bone, if you want them. And one lady in buttercup sprig muslin, wilting and bored, poking about with the point of her parasol, lets out a shriek of discovery that brings all eyes upon her. Gasps, a nervous laugh. There on the end of her parasol is a draggled scant-haired skull. The parasol point is protruding through the grinning mouth. Caroline thinks of banquets and pigs' heads served with apples. On the road back she sees a wooden-shoed boy driving a pig. The pig looks fat and lively: they will eat anything, apparently. All this, Caroline thinks, dazed, all this must mean something.

Her mother and father arrive, and take a house near hers in the place Royale. Frederick improves rapidly. Caroline goes to a dressmaker. How would Madame like? Madame would like to live. Live, live. The fatty smoke, death on the wind, begins to disperse. Caroline's new gown is her nudest yet: pale lilac, thinnest muslin, shoulders and back bare. The soldiery parading in the place Royale stare as she skims by. She makes their day. Live, live. The talk is of moving on to Paris, where Wellington holds victorious court. William is morose, but says they may go, if she wants. Of course she wants. Not to want is to surrender. To want is to live.

'Caro Lamb,' people say, disdainfully. 'Her usual flibbertigibbet self. Cares for nothing.'

Augusta, climbing the steps up to 13 Piccadilly Terrace six months after she had promised herself *never* to do this again: with her, again, Georgiana, in sickly health and fretful spirits: greeting her, again, or rather not greeting her but only staring at her, a scarcely recognizable Byron with yawning eyes in a chalk-white face, a face peculiarly emptied of everything but emptiness: coming forward to give her, again, one of her sharp pecking kisses like a tick next to a sum, Annabella – not much changed, in her steady bosomy way, by her heavy pregnancy: Augusta feeling again the simmering awkwardness, tasting again the air that seemed too hatefully tainted to breathe: why, why?

Because Annabella asked her to come for her confinement.

Because of Byron. Duty, affection. Perhaps fate.

'I thought you were another bailiff,' Byron said.

'Augusta has come not to take away,' said Annabella, with sententious fondness, 'but to give.'

Byron snorted, stalking away. 'If only that were true.'

Later, he stepped into her dressing-room and put his arms round her from behind.

'You've put on flesh, Gus.'

'I'm expecting another child.'

'Ah . . .' His breath singed her neck. 'Gus, what are we doing?'

'The traditional thing,' she said, gently disengaging his hands. 'Married sister-in-law coming to help with confinement. Very traditional.'

Moving away, she felt his still presence behind her like an angry fire.

'If we had just done the traditional thing from the beginning,' he said, 'would it have been better?'

Smiling slightly over her shoulder, she said: 'Did we ever have a choice?'

Yes, the house was a nightmare, but then nightmares ended and you woke up.

Byron's debts were such that a bailiff had moved in to make sure he did not try a flit, and to avoid creditors he went out only after dark. Then he would come home blind drunk and desperate. If he did not rage at Annabella he would turn on Augusta, saying he did not need her: the smell of cheap perfume said the rest. Then he would load and prime his pistol, gaze lovingly down the muzzle, set it on the mantelpiece calling it his faithful friend. Or he would burst into hysterical laughter and wild singing of some barbaric chant he had picked up in the East. The servants tiptoed round him, which, as Augusta could have told them, only made him worse. Once, watching him slop yet another brandy into a glass, she said mildly, 'I don't know where you put all that.'

And he smiled beatifically. 'It's all swallowed up, you see, by the void. The craving void inside. Don't you see?'

'I can see that you're very unhappy.'

'Ah, but I'm not, sis. I'm as happy as it's possible for a mortal man to be. And that's the most horrifying thing of all.'

But nightmares ended and you woke up and right to the end Augusta tried to keep hold of her old optimism. Marriages, after all, were strange accommodations, they were three-legged races or jury-rigged ships, they were like the mantelshelf clock at Six Mile Bottom, which kept perfect time as long as it was turned half-way to the wall and propped at a certain angle with a wedge of paper. You only had to look at her and George . . . And even now she saw signs of warmth between Byron and Annabella. He would call her Pip or Pippin: she would call him Duck. She would put up her hand sightlessly when he was behind her chair and he would squeeze it, hovering solicitously over her, sometimes kissing the crown of her head. Indeed, Augusta might even have felt jealous, if she had not sworn an everlasting end to all that. ('Old girl,' George had said lately, admiringly, before turning to sleep, 'I do believe you can hardly get enough of old George.' The admiration was for himself.)

The question, Augusta thought, was power. That was the foundation on which a marriage settled itself. At Six Mile Bottom, she took charge, paid the bills – or found ways of not paying them – raised the children, made the decisions. George rode and hunted and cut a fine figure and swore he would be lost without her. It was all very clear. But here, she thought, the issue was still undecided. Byron stormed and smashed things and seemed always on the verge, when he quarrelled with Annabella, of some final statement, challenge or ultimatum: a matrimonial Waterloo. Yet he was not in charge at all. Annabella presented her rigid suffering solemnity to him and he broke against it, in frustrated spray, like a wave against rock.

If they could only balance out, Augusta thought: balance out the power, and all might be well. The thought was still running in her head like a prayer to a broken idol as dirty-dark December came splashily in and Annabella's time drew near and it became pathetically clear that balance, any balance, was out of the question.

'Of course you should never have married me. Your *first* instinct, my dear Bell, was entirely right. Why did you change your mind at last, by the by? Were there no other sinners to convert?'

'It is not quite right to talk of converting sinners. One may still sin after conversion. It is not sin that separates the Christian from the infidel, but the conviction of it.'

'God in heaven! You know nothing of sins, Bell, nothing. It's all prating. I could show you some *sins*, if you've a fancy for 'em.'

'Byron, please,' Augusta said quickly, 'this is not – this is unpleasant talk for the season.'

'It's not Christmas yet.'

'It is an even more sacred season, Byron,' Annabella said, her neck mottled. 'I am to become a mother.'

'What? You're claiming an immaculate conception? To be sure, you may as well.'

'If you go on this way,' Annabella said, with a roasting glare, 'I swear I shall be brought to bed of a dead child.'

'I can't imagine *you* having any other kind.'

'You see,' Annabella said, 'how he treats me.'

'Yes. And I am sorry for it. But sometimes he seems quite – beyond reason. I think with this immoderate drinking, and trying to clear the debts—'

'Always you make excuses for him,' Annabella said, with a slight, metallic smile.

Augusta hesitated. 'He is my brother. But I hope I do not excuse—'

'Dear Augusta.' Annabella held her hand, rather too tightly: it was as if she were taking her into custody. 'You would make excuses for the devil himself.'

'Why?' Augusta asked Byron, as he threw his watch into the fire and began crushing the fragments with the poker.

'It's mine to dispose of. It's a free action. We don't get many of those.'

'I know you have a great many troubles. But I don't understand,' she said, 'why you must make everyone unhappy.'

'Oh, come – your God does that, and he gets psalms sung at him for it. Besides – misery is like a combustive gas – it *must* expand or else. Anyhow, Gus, we are respectable, Lord we are, and soon we shall have a respectable heir.' He thrust the poker savagely into the fire. 'Funny thing. You know, of course, that I do like to strike a pose. Yet what I hate above all is *pretending*.'

'Did you drink all that bottle of wine?'

'No, I drank that and then half a bottle of brandy.'

'You know it only depresses you more.'

'Does it? I only know it takes more and more to feel anything nowadays. If this is a general rule of life, we are sadly deceived.'

'Oh, Byron . . .' She looked at the white nape of his neck, its delicate flue, the way the dark glossy hair grew irregularly in catchable clumps. She knew this neck: too well. 'Is it because of us?'

He smiled round at her, gently, sadly: the old Byron. 'Oh, my sweet sis, *everything* is because of us.'

Suddenly her mouth felt like a dry wound. 'Byron . . . would it make it better – I mean things here, this house, the unhappiness – would it make it better if I . . .?' She found she could not say it, but she put her hand to the neck of her gown: their old signal.

She heard him swallow convulsively. He looked down at the floor. 'Too late,' he said, as if confiding in the carpet.

Shame swept over her. She got up to go: Byron caught her by the skirts. If Annabella came in now, she thought, how it would look: and yet now it isn't: though in a way it is. It's like he says, everything is because of us. She squinted at him through a lens of unsuspected tears.

'Let go, Byron.'

'This first. Gus, it was my fault. From the beginning and always. You know – if it ever becomes, God forbid, a – a point at issue.' He grimaced at the phrase. 'I must be sure you know that it was all my fault and none of yours.'

She sighed, then nodded. 'You men,' she said. 'Everything always has to come back to you, doesn't it? Even the bad things you must have all to yourself.'

She left him, but not before hearing him laugh the first true, warm, appreciative laugh of her stay.

'My doctor suggests that I should never be left alone with him,' Annabella said, lingering over the layette box, smoothing and refolding. 'This is difficult but not impossible. If my old governess comes to stay, and you remain, and Fletcher and his wife take turns at watching—'

'Oh, surely there's no need for that,' said Augusta, admiring the lace.

'He fears, I think, for my very life, and that of my unborn child.' Annabella's pronouncements were becoming operatic: Augusta, reproving herself, just could not help hearing the two dabs on the harpsichord after this one.

'But this is absurd,' she said, as lightly as she could. 'If he thought that, why has he not sent you away? To Seaham – or, well, to Mivart's Hotel, isn't that where your mother's staying? You could—'

'You don't understand,' Annabella said. 'If my parents were to know . . . Besides, that would seem like deserting him. And that is something I can never – ever – do.' Plink, plink.

'I don't excuse these black moods of his. I think his mind is in a poor state indeed, from various causes . . . But I don't believe it is permanent—'

'He talks of unthinkable crimes. He talks, most alarmingly, of the taint of the Byron blood coming out.'

'Oh, well,' Augusta said soothingly, 'I have the Byron blood in my veins, you know, and there is nothing wrong with me, is there?'

But Annabella was silent. And nobody could produce a silence like Annabella.

By the time Annabella's baby was born, in the middle of a December Sunday with a city sound of church bells trickling through the rheumy air, Augusta felt as exhausted as if she had gone through the labour herself. It was she who had had to manage the quarrels, sweeten the disgruntled servants, welcome the unwelcome visitors, and keep the creditors at bay. An unhappy home generated more energy than a steam-engine.

But at least – surely – with the new baby a new world might be born, a new accommodation. Babies were great promoters of compromise.

'Augusta Ada,' Byron told her, 'after her godmother.'

She was flattered, though *just what we need*, she thought privately, *more As.*

'I was never more proud and pleased – as Punch and peacocks and a dog with two tails and whatever you like,' Byron said, sitting at Annabella's side. 'Proud as Lucifer, aye, that too—'

'Not Lucifer, Duck, if you please,' Annabella said.

And he did look proud and pleased: Augusta never doubted it at the time, and even later, when she began to doubt everything, she could not remember otherwise. Just before the birth he had been at his most erratic, roaming from room to room, swiping the heads off soda-bottles, swearing that once the child was born he would disappear from their lives.

'Why, because I'm a curse, that's why, I know it very well – a curse to you and her and no doubt a curse to the child . . .'

But his baby daughter – a fair, porcelain child whose very cry seemed attenuated and apologetic, as if she scarcely dared assert herself against such overpowering parents – seemed at first to return him to his senses. He left off the brandy, he washed and shaved and put on a clean collar, he made considerate tiptoeings, he cooed. Ah, the unison of the crib. I am a wise old bird, thought Augusta, with astonishment: she had never dreamed of being such a thing.

Then: the cracks.

'Oh, what an instrument of torture I have got in you!' Byron addressed the baby.

Annabella's mouth drew in. 'My dear B, what can you mean?'

'Why, only that we have something new and most wonderfully effective to use against each other in our quarrels, Bell. Isn't that why people have 'em?'

'I don't intend quarrelling,' Annabella said. 'I never do quarrel as far as I'm aware. Nor do I think that is generally a motive for having children. If people end up using them in that way, it is very regrettable; but I cannot conceive that they would begin with such an aim.'

At this moment Augusta felt split, accurately and agonizingly, right down the middle. She sympathized with Annabella, who was hurt: she comprehended Byron, who enjoyed tart sparkling ideas. She wanted to cry out to Byron not to be like this just when they were getting on; she wanted to cry out to Annabella that not everything said by a mercurial man known for sardonic wit needed to be analysed like a mathematical theorem.

Perhaps that would solve it, she thought. Give each of them half of myself. For the sake of peace, she would have done it.

'God,' Byron cried, 'why must you follow me with those damned great eyes so?'

Annabella's great eyes followed him. 'Where are you going?'

'To plant an acorn, and water it with my tears of laughter at our ridiculous situation, and then hang myself from the first branch of the tree.'

'It would snap,' Augusta said. 'If it was a young tree.'

'Oh, Gus.' He went out laughing, or it might have been crying.

'My dear Augusta,' Annabella said, touching her arm, 'you should not encourage him in these fantasies. Not with his mind as it is. It has gone too far.' As well as the persistent look of pitying concern, she had this new voice, a forbearing sickroom voice, only just audible. It forced you to lean towards her like a conspirator. If Byron isn't going mad, Augusta thought, then one of us is. Perhaps we all are. 'Many things are becoming clear that were not so before.'

Later, when Byron came in drunk and wild, Augusta heard him shouting in his bedroom. Shouting at Annabella, perhaps, but there was no sound of any reply. The echo of the high, ruinously expensive Piccadilly rooms made it sound as if Byron was shouting down a well. Augusta wished to go home. Georgiana was chesty in the cindery Town air and kept demanding more attention than her mother could give. The bucolic dullness of Six Mile Bottom was a celestial vision. But there was loyalty to Byron, whether he deserved it or not. Loyalty was grey and insignificant, but you found it at the bottom of your pack when you had used up all the colourful fragile love. But what durable stuff. She would have to stay. Also she had a sense of something about to happen, though she couldn't tell what. Working out the sum of all this ferocity and misery – add perverse passion, take away stability, multiply by resentment, divide by jealousy – was quite beyond her. Unlike Annabella, she had no head for figures.

'Of course we must go,' Byron picked at his mutton. 'I was a fool ever to take this house, and soon they will repay my folly by taking away everything in it.'

'Surely the sale of your library helped,' Augusta said. 'And what about Mr Murray? Surely he would advance you—'

'Murray would undoubtedly do more than such a sensible man should, to get me out of a scape into which I have got myself, and so of course I will not let him. The house must go. Indeed, Bell, I don't know why *you* don't go straight away. Your ma's forever pressing you to go to Kirkby Mallory. Why wait?'

'That does sound pleasant,' Augusta said. She meant the name, Kirkby Mallory: she knew it only as the estate in Leicestershire of Annabella's parents, but the words gave her a delicious picture of knightly ramparts and keeps and, for some reason, heather.

'Do you think so?' Annabella said, in her most deliberate way, turning to Augusta, subjecting her to excessive, unwieldy attention. This must be how it feels to be a piece of embroidery in a hoop, Augusta thought: fixed, stretched, and pierced.

'Unless of course you like living here,' Byron said, abandoning his plate and getting up. 'With all its happy memories.'

Annabella sighed, watching him go. It was a curiously stagy sigh, as if to be overheard by second murderer behind the arras.

'It must be,' she said: aside or soliloquy perhaps. 'It *must* be.'

Either Byron picked up the theatrical tone, or it was the result of his constant attendance at Drury Lane: something made him say, the next night when he, Annabella and Augusta were on the point of parting to go to bed: ' "When shall we three meet again?" '

Augusta was just about to make a trifling joke about there being only *two* witches, but Annabella forestalled her.

'In heaven, I hope,' she intoned, holding up her candle so that her face stood out in masklike relief. She turned and walked consciously, accurately, to the hall door.

Byron said nothing. He was only a novice at that. But in his grimly mocking face Augusta clearly read the message that he would see her in hell first.

Augusta had no idea. Even when Annabella left, early on a wine-cold copper-coloured January morning, and paused in the hall to kiss Georgiana, and said, '*You'll* remember your Aunt Bella, won't you?', even then Augusta did not suspect. The carriage took her away, with her baby a wincing kernel in the midst of a swathe of shawls, and her travelling luggage put up

407

behind; and it was to take her to her parents' house at Kirkby Mallory, while Byron remained behind to see to the winding up of his distressed affairs and the closing of the unloved house. The sight of that baggage had made Augusta wistful, and that day she started, in hope, to sort her own things.

And leave Byron alone, now? She found she couldn't. After the breaking up of his house, he would have to move towards reconciliation with his wife. He was in low water. She could at least paddle along beside him.

So, she had no idea; and then the letter came.

Not the first letter: that was a cosy conventional note from Annabella to her husband, to Duck from Pip, saying she had arrived safely, the baby sent kisses, and conveying love to Augusta, who read it with pleasure. In fact reading it Augusta thought, for perhaps the last time, her characteristic thought: that everything would be all right.

Then, the other letter.

'A separation.'

For a few moments Byron only looked puzzled in an alert, tantalized way, like someone trying to remember a name on the tip of their tongue.

It was never Annabella's intention to reveal the sufferings she had undergone to her parents, even as she fled to the shelter of their roof. She arrived at Kirkby Mallory still undecided on her future course, though firmly convinced that in justice to her child, at the very least, an immediate flight from the matrimonial establishment had been imperative. But at last a mother's solicitude uncovered what fortitude had hid and reason denied. She was compelled to represent to her parents, in the starkest colours of unadorned nature, the monstrous behaviour of her husband, and to confess her own lamentable discoveries, made in the course of researches initiated, as she explained, in pure anxiety for him. She had had secret consultations with eminent doctors, describing to them his symptoms; and on searching, with an excusable breach of privacy, through his personal effects, she had found a quantity of laudanum, and a book by a notorious Frenchman, which in themselves must confirm the worst suspicion. It could not, she insisted, be depravity: it must be madness.

Thus did the generosity of Annabella's spirit incline her to the kindest interpretation, even while the sufferings she had undergone prostrated her. A less charitable observer might have viewed her insistence upon Byron's insanity as the reason for their separation thus: that it ensured her custody of the child (towards whom she exercised such a very restrained tenderness that it was almost indistinguishable from indifference); and above all, that it presented her in the best possible light in these unpromising circumstances. – If a man found her intolerable, then he *must* be mad. If he were in his senses and yet uncaptivated, what must be the reflection on her? However, observers of such an unsympathetic nature having never figured in Annabella's circle, or if they did, being soon banished, the unpleasing thought was not entertained.

Sir Ralph and Lady Milbanke, upon whose good sense Annabella had never, alas, felt herself entirely able to rely, were properly incensed on their daughter's behalf. Her mother proceeded at once to London, to consult with the best lawyers that injured innocence could enlist, or money buy. Annabella, in the meantime, maintained her communications with the scene of battle, by a frequent correspondence with Mrs Leigh, who was able to report to her the progress of Lord Byron's malady, and other domestic details that it might profit her to know. Annabella was forced scrupulously to examine her conscience on this matter of the correspondence, which she represented to her sister-in-law as the mere impulse of continued fondness, when her motives were rather more practical; and when, indeed, she was coming to a clear apprehension, to which her own purity of mind had blinded her, of the degree to which Mrs Leigh was involved in Lord Byron's corruption. But examination found her conscience clear; and it was some comfort for Annabella to find that even after these vicissitudes, the habit of a lifetime was not broken, and that she was no more capable of being wrong than she had ever been.

The letter: Augusta had known it was coming, because Annabella had written to tell her so. Annabella was always writing from Kirkby Mallory, asking for news of Byron, hinting that her departure might be more or less permanent, hinting. And begging Augusta to say nothing of all this to Byron. Augusta managed it, but she wasn't sure how much longer she could bear being torn like this. Undressing at night, she noticed the forming of the vertical line beneath her navel that she always got in early pregnancy, but this time she saw it differently: the visible mark of a person being slowly pulled apart.

The letter: she had known it was coming, and what was going to be in it: in fact she had waited for its arrival, secreted it, and sent it back unopened to Kirkby Mallory with a note saying please, consider, not yet, he may improve, things may change . . . Now Annabella's parents, as Annabella regretfully informed her, were angry with her for interfering, and Sir Ralph was coming to London to deliver the letter by himself. And here it was, in Byron's hand.

'A separation.' He turned the letter over, as if expecting a trick. 'It's from Sir Ralph Milbanke. God. All he ever did was tell dreary stories about county meetings. Sir Ralph.' This simple fact seemed the hardest for Byron to take in. 'And now this.'

'What does he say?'

'He says . . . circumstances have come to his knowledge that convince him it cannot tend to my happiness to continue to live with Lady Byron.' He looked up. 'What does he expect? – we're *married* for God's sake. And he says I should appoint a *professional friend* to discuss terms of separation. What does he mean, a friend who's in a profession, or someone who makes a profession of being a friend?'

It was possible, Augusta thought, to be a little too interested in words.

'Is this her?' Byron said. 'Or is this all the in-laws' work?'

'Oh dear–' she fumbled her coffee-cup on to the tray with a crash '–why ask me?'

But he had fallen to his bemused fingering of the letter again. 'A separation. She said nothing. When she left, she said nothing.'

Suddenly and brightly, as if changing the subject, Augusta said: 'Perhaps it's for the best.'

'How?' He concentrated on her, trustfully. Guide me.

'Well, I think – forgive me – I think you did not love her, or rather you could not get on as lovers, which comes to the same thing.' A depressing thought. 'And neither you nor Bella could rest content with that as – as some couples do. So – to be apart is best.'

'If it were just a matter of being apart . . . A separation, you see. It's different. It's public. With *me*, it's bound to be very public indeed. There must be terms and reasons. The turning over of stones.' His voice had grown dry, spasmodic. 'And the picking up of stones and the casting of them – God, what have we done? That frowsy bitch of a mother of hers, she must be behind it. Well, let it come. I don't care what happens to me. Or her, come to that. There's someone else to consider.'

'Ada.'

'Ada's a baby,' he said dismissively. 'It's you, Goose, you I mean.'

'Oh, what can happen to me?'

He did not answer. He laid the letter carefully down and sat back from it, as if still fearful it might explode. 'When do you want to go home?'

'Go home? And leave you alone, with this?'

'You should. You're best away from me, Augusta – believe me.'

For a moment she thought he was just being Byron. But the use of her full name was unusual: a warning.

'I'll stay,' she said. She risked a contact, reaching out and placing a finger on his lips. She batted the squirming memories

411

away. 'I'll stay. There's an end of it.'

So, her strangest time with Byron: in some ways, the sweetest. It was like that inner circle of the mind into which she would retreat as a girl. Sister and brother, protecting each other against the world. The over-grand house, already half stripped of its furniture, was somehow more homely in the few rooms they used.

Strangest of all, George was there for part of the time. He had come to London to see to some things, as he put it – probably Tattersall's, ratting-matches, and money-lenders – and Byron invited him to consider Piccadilly Terrace his home. George unpacked his bag, but that was about as far as it went. 'Old girl,' he whispered to Augusta, 'there's a devil of an air in this place. Fairly puts me in the dismals. Fellow's like touchpaper. How do you bear it? Mind, I was never in favour of that marriage. Old George may be bluff, but he knows a thing or two.' He spent most of his time with his cronies, and when he was at Piccadilly Terrace developed a nervous habit of poking his head round the door of every room before entering. When at last his credit was exhausted, he told her he was going home. 'And I strongly advise you come with me, old girl. I know he's your brother and all, and you want to stand by him just now, but remember your condition. Strain and all that – you know.'

'I know, George. But I'm quite well and strong. And I think I should stay just until . . .'

Until what? She didn't know. But it was one of George's sterling qualities that he never asked questions like that: she knew best. He sighed and nodded, kissed her and asked Fletcher to wake him early for the journey back to Newmarket. He went whistling. Place gave him the blue devils.

It was certainly quiet. There were few visitors. Byron's friend Hobhouse, whom she had always found irritating, came often and clucked, irritatingly, over what he found. Lady Melbourne made a rare sortie from Whitehall to demand of Byron what had happened and, when she found the situation beyond her control, to grow visibly stiff-backed, remote, polite. She was dissociating herself: the Spider was cutting the threads.

And Byron: he was drinking less, and his moods did not change with such dizzying speed, but still he gave off a crackle, a constant sense of emotional emergency. But there was good reason for that. Annabella was in London now, at Mivart's Hotel, and girding herself for the fight. All attempts at reconciliation had failed, and now the terms of separation must be thrashed out. 'Amicable separation.' Byron snorted. 'What's that? Something like a hostile alliance?' Oh, he was girding too: after the first shock, the numbness and vacancy, he had taken fire, as Augusta had feared he would. He was a passionate man: did Annabella suppose that he wouldn't be so when it came to hatred?

'Of course, she will try to destroy me,' he said quite conversationally, after reading the latest letter from her lawyers. 'And probably will succeed.'

'But that's terrible.' He's being Byron, she told herself: and I'm feeling sick because of the pregnancy.

He shrugged. 'As long as she rests content with that.'

Downfalls: they seem to be in fashion. After Waterloo, of course, the greatest downfall of all – Napoleon sent by the victors to the island of St Helena, a dot in the ocean, and there courteously marooned. No escape this time. We have done with that sort of thing: we have done with Napoleon's sort of thing, and Louis the Gouty has been winched back on the throne of France to the whirring sound of clocks all over Europe being put back thirty years.

A much lesser fall, but revealing in its way, happens at this time also. Beau Brummell flees from the crashing pile of his debts, fetching up at Calais, the perpetual anteroom of the bankrupt Englishman, and facing the prospect of living on nothing a year, and dwindling into a moral example. The champagne boot-blacking has caught up with him. And as he never did anything much but make witty remarks and look exquisite, there is perhaps not much to be lamented in his fall: though his good friend Colonel George Leigh declares it a damnable shame, and thinks uneasily of his own bank account. And the subtraction of that stylized absurdity – of the man who said he never touched the grossness of green vegetables but at last confessed, under pressure, that he once ate a pea – leaves a definite gap, into which deadly seriousness must flow.

A time of exile. Something is ending. The tight little island, triumphant against foreign foes, is growing tighter: a certain sort is not wanted in its midst, as Mr Shelley the spied-upon atheist and republican already knows, as a young medical student named Keats, just about to publish his first poem, will soon know.

Downfalls: they are sweeter, they are more satisfying for the spectator, the greater the height of the fall. Byron's Empire, society, begins to shudder. A corrosive whisper goes round the drawing rooms. Annabella has what is commonly called a large circle of acquaintance, and the propagating zeal of the missionary. What happened? What did he do? What did he do to her? The questions are more important than the answers: questions lead to dethronement, and downfall. It begins and ends with words.

Byron: 'I haven't thanked you. For staying here with me.'

'Yes, you have.' The dining-room windows overlooked Green Park. They had a habit now of setting two chairs here, gazing out, quietly talking. There were few signs of spring: vicious winds got up and thrashed the emaciated trees, the turf was dun. On the other hand, there were few people.

After a contemplative pause he said: 'You know, Gus, you are the only woman I have ever truly loved.'

'Yes.' This was a new place for them, calm, well lit. Was this what was meant by *all passion spent*? 'Yes, I do know. Do you want me to say—'

'No. No need. You're been everything I knew you were, standing by me these past weeks.'

414

An indefinable emotion, proud and sorrowful, shivered through Augusta like the wind through the trees. 'And something else,' she said, striving for lightness. 'I've been something you never thought I could be, I dare say. Clever and wise. Because if I had gone away, after Annabella left, then it would have seemed that I – well, that I had something to hide.' Sightlessly she reached for his hand and held it. 'That isn't why I stayed. Byron, do you really think they are saying these things? – what Mr Hobhouse hinted he'd heard—'

'There's no telling what they'll say with that witch at work. My spousal sorceress. All I can say is she ain't a woman to *spare* – anything or anyone.'

'You're very bitter against her now. I wish it weren't so.'

'I wish *she* were not so. In a way I find her terrifying. Because of her utter self-belief. The most inhuman of attributes . . . You know the time is coming, my darling, when you will have to go. For George's sake, for the children's – I won't say your own, because you're too unselfish to take any notice of that.'

'I know.' Again the wind across the park raged bleakly. Behind her, in the direction of the city, she seemed to feel another tremor, deeper and more menacing. Where the idea came from she couldn't imagine, but she suddenly thought that it must have been like this in Paris during the Revolution: sitting behind closed doors, listening to the rumble and hum of agitation, wondering. 'Soon. Not yet.'

She went – she was summoned – to Mivart's Hotel, to see Annabella. A transformation: Annabella had become someone who summoned, who gave audiences. There was also a military flavour of campaign headquarters: lawyers' clerks with blue bags came and went in the vestibule like aides-de-camp. But in the audience chamber – Annabella's sitting room – the air of sanctity was thickest. Going in, Augusta looked for a ring to kiss . . . But no. At the sight of Annabella's face flippancy went out like a taper.

415

How could that peachy roundness have become so gaunt? And the pallor, which in the heavily curtained dimness shone like moonlight – and the stupendous calm, otherworldly, as of a being centuries old who had seen the sinful generations rise and fall . . .

'Dear Augusta.' Annabella did not speak: she *uttered*. 'You look well.'

Augusta knew it, and was ashamed. Her ample flesh was a sign of her moral inferiority. No matter what I suffered, I would never look like that, she thought humbly.

'How is little Georgy? I often think of her. It's a great sorrow to me that I can no longer see her.'

'Oh, but this is terrible. Annabella, do we – isn't there any way?' Augusta found she was half whispering, as if in church. 'Even a step towards reconciliation—'

'Would be a step towards perdition,' Annabella said patiently. 'My dear, that is partly why I asked you here today. So that there can be no doubt about where we stand. No persuasions, even from those who have my true welfare at heart–' a bare spectral smile '–could alter my resolution, because it is not simply a matter of my *feelings*.' She made those sound fearfully trivial – the concern of mere fleshy creatures, like Augusta. 'It is a matter of my duty to God. I'm sure you understand, Augusta, that upon the point of religious principle, and indeed very salvation, there can be no compromise.'

Part of Augusta wanted to say: Can't there? Compromise was the heart of her belief, in this world and the next. But then she was probably wrong.

'And in the same way, my dear, it is best there be no communication between the two sides – between this establishment, and Piccadilly Terrace – while the matter is dealt with by the law. I regret it, believe me. But there are much greater issues at stake than my regret.' She waved a hand: it was white as bone and enwrapped in a cobwebby mitten. Ghostlike, she rose. Audience at an end.

'But do there have to be two sides?' Augusta said plaintively.

'I'm afraid so. There are always two sides, Augusta. It's best that you remember that.'

The apartment in St James's Palace was in Flag Court, by the tower. You could look down from the sitting-room window and see a little *opera buffo* of sentries, majordomos, clerks and equerries and maids continually enacting in the yard below. This was rather better than looking at the apartment itself, which was creaky and boomy and draughty in authentic Hanoverian style. Augusta was glad of it, though. She had to leave Piccadilly Terrace; all common sense said so, Byron tenderly said so, her own nerves, like a harpsichord strummed by a bad child, said so. But she could take possession of this apartment and so still be in London, still be near him, for a while yet. Until—

'What am I going to do? Anything they say,' he told her, mildly, on the day she moved. 'Oh, I prefer to fight, but one must think of the consequences. She is bringing up such forces – revengeful regiments of 'em – reserves and allied troops – countless artillery pieces – I tell you Waterloo is nothing to what Bella wants to make of this. And, of course, there will be ruin,' he added, even more mildly. 'All I can do, and must do, is limit it.'

Caroline cloaked and veiled, hurrying to an assignation. Just like the old days.

And, importantly, feeling alive. Nightmares lately in which everyone in the world is dead, and has always been so. Hard for her to explain even to herself when she wakes. But part of a growing perception that we are all more or less dead unless we rouse ourselves to knowing we are alive. The sight of Waterloo started it, perhaps, those broad rye-fields sown with flesh and manured with blood. For long ages before we are born, and long ages after we are gone, we do not live: being alive is the exception, a mere fragment: a nap in the long waking day of death.

Caroline, hurrying to her most fateful assignation, at the

townhouse of William's brother George, neutral ground. Breath short and a *pizzicato* of pulse in her thin neck. Just like the old days when she hastened to meet her lover.

Loved no longer. When he dropped her, ground her beneath his heel, for long she was too crushed to respond. But now, the turning, the biting.

Not a word from the servant who admits her to the house, and Caroline does not put back her veil until she is safely in the drawing room. This must be the most secret of her assignations also. The person she is meeting would be damaged if it were known that she had been consulting with Lady Caroline Lamb; and Caroline accepts that. She is pitch, she knows well, and will defile. Never mind. In secrecy and subterranean darkness she can still work and wield, like a sapper digging under the fortifications. Until the crash.

The servant leaves her alone. A sulky fire has just been lit. Caroline stirs it with the poker, kneels by it, wonders idly what it would be like to thrust her hand into the flames. Wonders, with a writhe of terror, whether she should ever have written the letter proposing this meeting, whether this is not the bad Caroline taking control and pushing her down a calamitous slope.

Caroline props her chin on her bony knee, hugs herself, curses under her breath a vile curse learnt from William, and blames the Duke of Wellington.

After Frederick's recovery they moved from Brussels, along with a large swathe of English society, to Paris. Wellington was there and Caroline grew dazzled by him. No Apollonian beauty like Byron but a striking figure none the less with his high hooked nose and desolating pale blue eyes: and about him too the intoxicating air of great deeds and potent destiny. He gave a ball at the avenue Gabriel. Caroline shared a supper-table with him and Sir Walter Scott – who made her think, it was true, of Mr Murray and the book-lined rooms at Albemarle Street and, yes, of Byron – but not for long. This was new, this was other: this was starlight and medals and champagne and it was *alive*, and none of it tasted of that old disappointment and despair.

Until: a couple of overheard remarks.

'I suppose Caro Lamb won't be content until she's stabbed herself for the Duke as well.'

And then: 'I heard Lord Byron is coming to Paris.'

Untrue, as it turned out, but not before it agitated her and, worse, William. Coolly he notified her that watching her throw herself at two famous men simultaneously would be too tiring for him, and that they were to return to England. They had a spectacular fight, which left them with a large bill for broken crockery and glass at their hotel, and a making-up almost as spectacular. Just like the old days indeed. But Paris was spoiled for her. Everything was spoiled for her. Wellington was not Byron: and *Byron* was not Byron, he was a married man, beyond her, gone. Back in London there was nothing for her, nothing but deadness creeping up like sleep.

Until now. With the news of the separation, with the rumours of Lady Byron's wrongs, Caroline is suddenly within his orbit again: and, oh, so alive. She remembers the bonfire at Brocket, Byron's effigy melting and blurring, the letters curling like blackened fists, and her own heart crying, *It's not enough, this isn't enough*.

Air to the fire. A whisk of draught as a door opens behind her. A leap of flame and vengeful joy. Caroline turns.

'Lady Byron. Thank you for seeing me. I do believe what I have to tell you may be of the greatest service to you.'

Caroline, shielded by darkness, whisking home – but now a diversion: raps on the hackney roof, says she has a fancy to go round by Green Park.

There: she raps for the hackney to stop. In an upper window of 13 Piccadilly Terrace, a single light. And, for a moment, Caroline holds out her arms to it. She doesn't know why. But she remembers as a little girl stabbing her favourite doll in the eye with a pen in a fit of vexation, and at once kissing and caressing it in a flood of passionate tears.

419

'. . . The crimes towards you, Lady Byron, of which he is suspected – that is, of which one hears – one cannot help but hear – with loathing and pity and yet – I must confess it – on my part without surprise. For I know him to be guiltier of yet greater crimes. I have seen the written record of them – and had them confirmed, without shame, from his own lips.'

She raps on the hackney roof: what does the man mean, loitering here? Just let her go home, home to William, to poor Augustus, and she will be a good and dutiful creature hereafter . . .

'The unspeakable practices of the East – but not confined to his travels for he *imported* these practices . . .'

Lady Byron – Annabella – closing her eyes and inclining her head. Poor woman, poor, poor woman, thought Caroline: and yet how I used to hate her.

'These are terrible crimes before the law – this I know and expressed my horror – but no words were left to convey my horror at what I *further* learnt from his own confession – a crime before God and, indeed, in that sense no less than a *blasphemy*. I bow, of course, to your religious learning, my dear Lady Byron, but feel sure you will find that word no overstatement when I tell you *who* was involved – when I tell you that I saw with my own eyes letters from this person – from her – in which the frankest and warmest expressions were made to one whom they should never, by all that is moral and sacred, never . . .' She faltered then: her mouth was parched. Annabella poured a glass of canary with her own hands and presented it to her.

Caroline gets out at Whitehall, passes swiftly under the portico of Melbourne House. For a moment she has an acute wish to run into her mother-in-law's apartments and throw herself at Lady Melbourne's feet and tell her what she has done. But the moment dies, and she flits up the stairs.

'I felt I must come and see you – in tribute to your sufferings and the courage with which you bear up – and to offer you this information not, oh, Annabella, not I hope to increase that suffering – but to strengthen your case against him and enable you to have *all* the victory. And yet – though I have seen these letters he may easily destroy them – and he and *she* may simply deny the ghastly truth – so I fear that when it comes to proof—'

'My dear Caroline.' A thrilling funereal voice. 'You said you had heard of his crimes against me. Yet I have made no public profession of those. You see? Knowledge may be disseminated in many ways. And even where the process of the law forbids a public accusation, the duty of the Christian to arraign the sinner allows, nay, encourages us, to make those sins known in whatever way we can.' A faint, reassuring smile: a gleam through Annabella's frost. 'So don't, my dear, trouble yourself about that. You have indeed done me a great service.' She put out her hand, and Caroline didn't know why she hesitated for a second to touch it. 'You could hardly have done more.'

2

Dividing Lines

'Come with me,' Claire pleads. 'Just this once. It will make it easier for me. He's said how much he wants to meet you.'

'Why should he want to meet me?' Mary says.

'The usual reason. He's a great admirer of Papa's. He even tried to get his publisher to give his profits to Papa, only Mr Murray wouldn't do it.'

How eager these geniuses are to give my father money, thinks Mary. And how eager my father is to take it. 'Well, I wish Mr Murray had not been so scrupulous. It might have lifted the burden from Shelley a little. What do you mean, make it easier for you?'

Claire arches her neck, the tip of her tongue poking: just like when she was a child. Not a child now, though: oh, no. 'I mean it will be all the more reason for him to see me. You can imagine how very busy he is just now.'

'I imagine that just now he wouldn't want to be troubled at all, with the whole town up in arms about him. Least of all with visits from young ladies he doesn't know.'

'Oh, he knows me pretty well by now.'

Mary glances suspiciously at her. But Claire has taken up Shelley's new volume of poetry, *Alastor*, and is reading devoutly.

' "I have made my bed In charnels and on coffins" – Lord, Shelley makes me quite faint when he's in this vein. "In lone and silent hours, When night makes a weird sound of its own stillness" – oh, Mary, this is superb and terrible. I must give *him* a copy of this too. He greatly admired *Queen Mab*, indeed he has the most cordial interest in Shelley as a poet and a man – his very words to me – and so you see he will be all the more interested to meet you. Oh, do come. After all, you admire his work, don't you?'

'Very much. But the work and the man are different things . . .' God, how prim I sound. 'Oh, very well. They say he intends going abroad soon. So this may be my last chance to meet Lord Byron.'

There is nothing to show, in the demure figures of the two young ladies crossing Covent Garden amid the cabbage-stalks and sausage-ovens and yawning bosom-baring demireps, that they are notorious women themselves. One especially, the slight flame-haired one, who lives in flagrant sin with the atheist poet Shelley; but there is speculation about the other girl too, the black-eyed rounded one, who shares their illicit household and is commonly supposed to be sharing a good deal more than that. As to how the atheistical rascal achieved this ménage, the general agreement is that he purchased the girls in cash from their father and stepfather, Godwin.

These rumours are not true, but they are not far enough from truth for Mary's comfort. Shelley is still advancing Godwin money – money they can ill afford and for which, true to his austere principles, her father does not express gratitude – even though Godwin is still as inflexibly disapproving of their relationship as any cruel father in a barn melodrama ordering his daughter never to darken his doors again. As for Claire and Shelley – she doesn't know.

Terrible admission. After all, she has given up everything for Shelley: how can she even countenance the possibility that he might be false to her? But that is the wrong language for the Shelley world. And since she ran away with him, any other world has been closed to her.

And she wants it so: if Shelley were a religion, then Mary has

423

been confirmed. When she cannot help wondering, when her jealousy of Claire, who has shared their peripatetic lodgings, on and off, for a year and a half, rises in her like a tide, then she knows very well that she sins against it. But she can't help it.

'What,' she demanded lately, engulfed by the tide, 'do you and Claire find to do precisely, to make you come to bed so late?'

Shelley gave the smallest of sighs. 'I know these strictures come from love, Mary,' he said, in his patient, explaining way, 'but in the end they only rebound back on love and damage it. I love you. That love must be freely given, mustn't it? Not like a rent or a wage or a duty. Now to answer your question, we were talking of ghosts.'

Which in a way she knew: they often did it. Claire would sometimes end up shrieking with manufactured fear, would ask to share Mary's bed or, most annoyingly, would call attention to some disturbance in her room – a pillow or a book moved – which she clearly did herself.

Still, Mary cannot help wondering, and still, even though she knows and admires Shelley's ideas about exclusivity in love. She has reason to know about that, for he is no hypocrite and in the Shelley world there is no sauce that is only for goose or gander. Six months into their marriage (no marriage and yet, sinfully and secretly, she thinks of it as such) Shelley was genially encouraging her to make love to his best friend.

Hogg the aptly named. Hard to imagine now: hard to imagine, above all, that she nearly went along with it. But they were in the first flush of idealism, she supposes. They had sliced through the oppressive knots of convention. So: keep slicing. If you throw the rudder of convention overboard, you must steer with something else – an unexpected discovery, this, for Mary: just drifting doesn't work. You need ideas, of which, fortunately, Shelley has an endless supply. Love, like the wealth of the earth, should not be appropriated but shared out. He greatly loves Mary and he greatly loves his old friend Hogg. *Ergo.*

She did try. It was made easier, perhaps, because she was

pregnant then. She had the first, unanswerable proof of her and Shelley's bond inside her body, and no idea could take that away. Also, because of it she had often to stay at home while Shelley went to town on the usual money-raising tasks, and it was frisking slim-bellied Claire who would, to Mary's bitten-down jealousy, accompany him – and so flirting with Hogg was a sort of getting her own back. Entirely the wrong motive, she knew. Shelley was not thinking of such dark, bitter things when he smilingly left them alone, when he read with approval in their shared journal Mary's valiant attempts to praise Hogg, when he referred to her to his friend as 'our sweet treasure'. He was living his beautiful idea.

And she was failing to come up to it. Oh, there was a certain success. Hogg, sharp-tongued, heavy, bumptious, did grow on her. She managed to ignore the hairs sprouting from his nose in favour of his rather timid, kind eyes: she vanquished him in intellectual disputes and he was respectful instead of seeing his manhood impugned by his defeat. And then, besides, he was doggedly (hoggedly) *there*, while Shelley was elusive. Shelley did have much to do at that time. His grandfather, old Sir Bysshe, died, and left a will about which the whole family were tail-on-end. Shelley went down to Sussex for the reading of the will – and, as he mildly told her, was not allowed under the paternal roof.

'You mean your father wouldn't see you?'

'I mean my father wouldn't let me in the house. No matter, it wasn't too cold, so I sat on the doorstep and read Milton – your Milton, with your name there on the flyleaf, so that cheered me.'

The will made Shelley the heir, after his father's death, of his grandfather's fortune. But there were provisos and conditions, complicated by the fact that Sir Timothy Shelley hated his son so perfectly and wished to throw every obstacle both in his way and, especially, in that of his partner in sin and their illicit offspring. The good side was that money-lenders would now be more generous, knowing they would definitely get their money back one day.

All this meant further visits to lawyers in town, and it was Hogg who kept Mary company, and she was glad of him. But to go further . . . She had nightmares about it, while severely reproaching herself, for after all her mind was committed to the experimental. Was not man's mind launched upon a voyage of adventure, she asked herself when Hogg took her to an institution lecture on electricity. These discoveries had once been stifled by superstitious adherence to old notions, she thought, looking at Hogg's stubby pink hand resting on his knee.

In a way it was superstitious adherence to old notions that solved her dilemma. Hogg was no longer the fiery atheist who had been thrown out of Oxford with Shelley. He was training as a lawyer and inclining to the respectable. He was embracing old prejudices, or having scruples, whichever way you wanted to look at it: scruples that Mary could probably have overcome with effort. But she was quite happy not to make that effort. Hogg drew back: then childbirth intervened, and for a time her baby was everything.

A short time. She was premature: she was named Clara: she looked impossibly tiny when Shelley held her tenderly at his shoulder: she had a little smudge of hair dark like his: she fed well at Mary's breast: after two weeks she died suddenly in the night.

Adventure and discovery. Shelley, she discovered, was not good at comfort. He was too unmanned, wild, lost. Also his ideas did not help him. Mary did not reject them for this reason: indeed she thought, being a pessimist, that it probably made them more likely to be true. But in the deep pit after the baby's death, she found, curiously, it was Hogg who was most effective in pulling her out. Gruffly and awkwardly he said the usual consoling things, tried to lift her spirits, performed solidly the traditional duties towards the bereaved. Meanwhile Claire was Claire.

'I don't understand. It's not as if Claire's to blame for what happened to the baby,' Shelley said, when Mary raged about her stepsister's continued presence. Well, there it was: continued presence, while all that she wanted became absent. And blame: when there was no one to blame for something, whom did you turn on but the person who was usually to blame? And also in this sorrowful aftermath, they needed to be together – just Mary and Shelley, not a commune of souls. She tried to explain these things – but they came out, even she could hear, fretful and complaining. They even, God help her, threw Claire's robustness into stronger relief. Mary crucially lacked what Claire had in abundance: buoyancy. I sink, she thought then and still thinks now, I am a sinker, and I look up at the others bobbing on the bright surface.

Different nightmares then. Her sleeping mind dismissed the Hogg business as the absurdity it was and set to work tormenting her about her baby, who night after night was alive again – a little poorly, but only sleeping – if she had just given the tiny limbs a rub, if she had just been a little more careful – and so on. Just as she began to dread sleep, the dreams began to fade, but not before a sweat-making *pièce de résistance* in which her mother rose up before her, solemnly beautiful as in her portrait, holding the lost baby in cupped sacerdotal hands: gentle inquisitor. Both of us dead, and yet you live? How is this? How, Mary, how?

'You will have, you know, many more,' Hogg had assured her, in his clumsy way, and thrown out his arms as if to express an infinitude of babies. And it is perplexingly true now, now that she and Shelley have another child, three months old and thriving, there is comfort. William. Wilmouse, as they call him. A blessing – though that, too, is not the language of the Shelley world. Nor can she quite acknowledge her feeling of relief to have produced another proof. Because always at the back of her mind there is Harriet. Harriet Shelley the deserted wife, who gave birth to her husband's child not long after Shelley and Mary returned to England from their elopement. Shelley went to see her, pronounced the baby beautiful, promised support: was apparently untroubled. Shelley, limbed like a deer, abstracted nibbler of bread and raisins, is nourished by his ideas, but Mary to her distress finds she cannot quite survive on them. Towards Harriet she feels a gunpowdery mixture of guilt, jealousy, impatience, pity and fear: and the fact that Harriet has two legal children by Shelley only makes the mixture more unstable. Mary loves William for himself, but also for what he does, and she knows this, and feels guilty again.

Nothing to show, though – she has this damnable serenity in her features, sees it reflected in the dingy shop-window where Claire tugs her to peep in and giggle at a display of obscene prints, survivor of Covent Garden's richly dirty past. Nothing to show that she often hates this fizzing stepsister at her companionable side, blames her for the thread of trouble running through the fabric of her new life and wishes her gone. Mary has her ideas too, and one that she cannot get rid of is the idea that feelings should not be mixed.

Drury Lane Theatre: this is where Claire has appointed to see Byron, who is on the theatre committee. Not at his home in Piccadilly Terrace, though Claire has been there: an unhappy place, she says, with a gang of sightseers forever at the front steps slavering for scandal. And the fallen Byron now outdoes the Tower lions or old Bedlam as a sight of London. The scabrous gossip has even reached the peripatetic household of Mary and Shelley, where books litter the frugal dinner-table and Town tattle is generally disdained; but then, as outcasts themselves, they are bound to look favourably on a man who is being crushed by social outrage. But that Claire should bring them together is unexpected. When Claire first let slip that she was writing letters to Lord Byron, Mary took little notice. It was well known that young girls were always bombarding him with letters, longing to play Medora to his Corsair. But Claire kept writing. She was strong-willed and resourceful: she sought his help and advice in beginning a theatrical career, which was different from merely gibbering: and she had a trump card – her background. Invoking the names of Godwin, of Shelley, of Mary herself stirred his interest, and he agreed to see her. This much Claire admits. That he has continued to see her she puts down to her fascination.

'He is a great judge of singing, and he declares that I have the greatest potential as a performer that he ever saw.'

'Did he declare it, or agree it?' Mary, tartly.

And of course Mary wonders. Is it as Claire says, or is Byron merely being good-natured at this stage-struck girl insistently besieging him, or is it something else? Right from the nursery Claire has competed with her. (Distant memory of wicked exasperation, in the garden of the Polygon: Mary turning away and pretending to eat with smacking noises a lump of soil, Claire – Jane as she was – snatching it from her and cramming it into her mouth: her eyes, when she realized. Her eyes.) Mary has Shelley (just, she murmurs, just), she has hooked herself a poet and rebel. If Claire is trying to outdo her by hooking Byron, then – well, then what? It might be a good thing. It might detach her from Shelley. That would be a very good thing. So Mary doesn't know why the mere thought makes her feel uneasy.

Nothing to show, however, when Byron greets them in the Drury Lane green room. He appears very much in command of himself, this pale, negligently dressed, soft-spoken man tossing down a play manuscript and limping forward to shake Mary's hand. Mary notices a pile of books on the table with a wine-bottle, a cap, a handkerchief, and thinks: This is where he hides.

Surprisingly soft-spoken, indeed: not tall compared with Shelley, and a feline gentleness about him, where Mary had expected a sort of human thunderstorm.

'Miss Godwin. You have so many claims on my regard, that to say I am honoured to meet you seems a mere truism.' He follows this with a slight smile, acknowledging the absurd pomposity of it. 'Take a chair, if you can bear with that infernal hammering. The carpenters are turning a prospect of Babylon into the South Parade at Bath.'

'Oh, I love the noise of this place,' cries Claire, walking

showily about to demonstrate her familiarity with it. 'It stirs my blood. Indeed, I do believe it is *in* my blood. I swear my ancestors must have stood in the Roman amphitheatre, you know.'

'Being eaten by lions?' Byron gently suggests.

'Oh! Do I mean the Greek? Anyhow, where they wore masks and were very tragic. Shelley was telling me about it.'

'I trust Mr Shelley is well?' Byron says to Mary. 'I have not the honour of his acquaintance, but I do feel a sort of proxy friendship for him. We have many things in common, not least that our mother country is being distinctly unmaternal towards us.'

'Shelley would agree on that, I'm sure,' Mary says. She and Byron are taking the measure of each other. Oddly, each sees this, neither minds. 'I wish I could give you a better report of him, but he is rather low just now. There is a chancery suit over his grandfather's will, and it has all turned rather bitter.'

'God, is the poor fellow in the hands of the lawyers? Get him out, Miss Godwin, save him before they have his vitals for fiddle-strings.'

'You speak with feeling, my lord.'

'I speak from experience – your only true teacher, and don't he love to use the *rod* to get his lessons home. But you mustn't milord me, please.'

'He doesn't like it,' puts in Claire. Mary inclines her head, thinking that he probably does, sometimes. 'But I was telling you just the other day, you know, about Shelley – how he's at the end of his tether, even thinking of going abroad again – don't you remember?'

Rather proprietorial. Again Mary wonders. But Byron is smooth and bland in reply, revealing nothing.

'The other day? That's the last thing I'm likely to remember. To make life bearable, I'm training myself to forget each day by the time the next dawns. Every morning you wipe the memory clean like a window-pane and gaze into the clear future. I think to found this as a new school of philosophy. After all, love would never stale, because each day there would be that first rapture again.'

'Love would never grow or mature either,' Mary says.

'That would be the choice, or dilemma.' His look is solidly appreciative, as if recognizing someone who drives as hard a bargain as himself.

'Well, you must remember *that*,' Claire says flatly, 'because when I told you, you said you envied him.'

'Going abroad? So I do, but not for long, for I shall go myself as soon as my affairs are settled. Or my hash – which comes to the same thing. So I fear, Miss Clairmont, such influence as I can exert here on your behalf will soon be at an end. You mentioned your ancestry – and to be candid it seems that the best preparation for a life on the stage is to be bred to it. Many of the actors here seem to have been literally born in the wings. Also it is a confounded uncertain profession—'

'Oh, I don't care about that,' Claire says airily. 'I've lived all my life in uncertainty. Our household was the kind where you write epics before breakfast, and the breakfast turns out to be dry bread.'

'Not even toasted?'

'Not when there's no fire. I do not mean it was *low*–' Claire suddenly draws herself smartly up, and without a fichu her high round breasts seem the most unavoidably visible things in the room '–only that there was a true philosophical disregard for frippery.'

'A disregard for frippery can oftentimes be slippery,' Byron remarks, as if to himself. 'Oh, I don't mean to discourage you. I'm no judge, but your singing seems to me the equal of any one hears at Vauxhall. Indeed, the other night you quite sang me out of my senses.'

'I thought you couldn't remember the other night,' Claire says, with a sharp smile; and Mary wonders again.

'You intend a long stay abroad?' she asks him.

'I do not plan a return. I must go for my health, you see: as

431

your consumptive can't breathe Albion's air for the fogs, I can't breathe it for the cant.'

Claire says, with one of her sudden sorties of insight: 'Poor you. But you should have expected it, you see. Because everyone loved you so much, they were bound to hate you just as much in the end.'

'You do have a lot in common with Shelley,' Mary says. 'Though he still hopes for a better England.'

'I'm glad there are some such still about. My only hopes for my country are selfish ones – that it would let me walk down the street without being jeered at; but I can't see 'em being fulfilled, so I shall be off.' Byron turns and nods as the old doorman looks in and coughs discreetly. 'There's a rehearsal coming on, so we had better vacate the room,' he says, rising. Mary wonders if this was deliberately planned. 'Pray give my respects to Mr Shelley—'

'Oh, so soon?' cries Claire, but in a resigned voice, as if used to it.

'Also to your honoured father, if you will.'

'I would if I could,' Mary says, 'but my father does not communicate with me since my going to live with Shelley.' She has a bracing way with the truth, and Byron seems to like it.

'A rum world,' he says. 'When shall we three meet again?'

'It may be sooner than we can guess,' Claire says eagerly. 'If Shelley goes abroad too, as he says he will, then we go with him, and then who knows? – we might all be exiles together.'

'A rum world, and a wide one,' Byron says, shrugging, opening the door. 'Who knows?' He wants to get rid of her, Mary thinks. Now there is something we have in common.

'There ought to be more aunts,' Fanny said to her mother, as they rode in the first carriage back from the churchyard in Deptford to Uncle John Ricketts's house. 'A funeral is a poor affair without a full platoon of aunts all in black, with faces like bulldogs in bonnets. Two aunts is a most discreditable showing.'

'Hush, Fanny, for shame,' Mrs Brawne said. 'Whatever would your poor uncle say?'

'I hope he would agree it is a very poor showing of aunts. Uncle John always liked things done properly.'

Mrs Brawne shook her head. Her weepers wagged becomingly: she was a woman who always looked good in mourning. 'I hardly know what to think of you lately. You were such a good child.'

'Was I? That's disappointing. I must make up for it with a wicked old age.' She groaned and slumped. 'I feel old now. Old with tedium.'

'Sixteen,' her mother said, with a pawky look. 'You have barely begun, my dear: barely begun.'

'Juliet was wedded and bedded by my age.'

'Fanny!' Mrs Brawne covered Margaret's ears.

'And deaded, of course, which rather spoiled things.'

'Talking so, at your poor uncle's funeral.'

What better time? Her bargain with death and its evil still stood: she would grant it no more power than belonged to it. She had done her weeping for kind, stiff-necked, mealy-mouthed old Uncle John when she heard of his death, when it hit her: why turn it on now? It was entirely artificial. But then she often felt like this lately. The world seemed full of transparent frauds that only she could see through. She was forever shouting from the hustings of honesty, though if any honesty were directed at her she ran from it horrified. And she knew it, and laughed at herself for it, wretchedly. She was all to pieces.

At the house the unsatisfactory aunts whispered of the price of ham and swung critical eyes over their raised teacups at Fanny, observing her prettiness and elegance with a certain sourness, as if at the fulfilment of some pessimistic prophecy. Plainly they hoped she was not going to be a flighty one. But I don't know what I am or what I'm going to be, Fanny thought, as angrily as if they had said it. She knew about the prettiness and elegance, seeing no reason to deny them except a simpering false modesty: she knew also their limits – her growth seemed to have stopped at five foot one, and she had an aquiline nose that there was no denying, so she had decided not to, and made a habit of flamboyantly presenting her profile in company. But she meant what she had said about feeling old with tedium. At least, that was how she felt now, because she was doing something she did not want to do, and lately she found that physically unbearable. Her age, she supposed: her mother was always sighing about it. She hated being at an age, envied Samuel and Margaret who could just be themselves and not the living illustration of some hideous folk wisdom.

'Your Uncle John was such a tidy-minded man,' Mrs Brawne said in Fanny's ear, indicating the ribboned will in the porcine hands of the tippling old attorney. 'He said he would never leave his affairs in disorder: nor has he.'

'That wig must be half a century old,' Fanny marvelled. 'And where does he get powder nowadays? Oh, Mama, did you ever wear one when you were young? And did it itch, and did you have one of those little ivory forks to scratch underneath it?'

'My dear child, you make me out to be an absolute relic. When I came out, the fashion was for hair prettily loose or *en papillotes*, though some still did powder. I did not, I never liked it, and then the powder-tax came in . . . Mind, when I was little I did see a cousin of my mother's, who was something at Court she *said*, try to come in our drawing-room door and nearly get knocked flat, for her hair was dressed three feet high and stuck hard with powder and pomade and had, you will hardly believe it, a little model ship on top of it, and she had forgot to duck her head . . .' Mrs Brawne stopped and looked at her daughter reproachfully. 'But we shouldn't be talking of such things, Fanny, and it is very wrong of you to make me do so.'

Someone – the kind of loud, heavy-handed, over-whiskered cousin who always turned up at funerals – was laughing excessively at a remark of the lawyer's. Expectant, probably, Fanny thought. Her mother was too, but not in any greedy way –

Fanny, who could be scathing to her mother's face, would draw a sword over her before anyone else – and besides she had been genuinely fond of Uncle John. So had Fanny, and it was horrible seeing his pipe on that mantelshelf and his backgammon board and penknife, and it was especially horrible when she wanted to be thinking of other things, like Mr Ollard.

'I feel like Romeo,' he had gulped at her the other evening after cards, just before the tea was brought in. Her mind had swarmed with sardonic replies: she felt like a sportsman suddenly presented with a skyful of grouse.

That was what had made her think of Juliet, no doubt. Not her favourite Shakespearean heroine, too moony and precious, and something in Fanny firmly rejected the nobility of brief, doomed love. Surely long, fulfilled love was preferable. Yet another part of her mourned over the knowledge that she would never be a Juliet: never cast such a profound shadow.

Mr Ollard – Francis, he gulped, Francis – was a fair young gentleman she met at carpet-dances and dinners, and flirted with. Only flirting: he did not make her heart pound or leap or any of those athletic things that hearts were supposed to do. Still, she kept thinking of him, because this was more interesting than anything else, somehow. He was tall, narrow, over-eager, twenty, and the son of an Undertaker, Dyer and Mourning-stationer, who had a shop in Highgate full of jet beads and black plumes and mourning card-cases wrapped in black marocain.

'But it must be absolutely deathly! How can you bear it?'

He was sensitive about this, and she knew it, and she could not help but press.

'One becomes accustomed,' he told her earnestly. 'It is not actually so gloomy a business as you might suppose. Black, you know, is very restful on the eye. My father and I never suffer from headaches.'

'Some consolation for being buried alive.'

'Indeed it is not like that—'

'My dear Mr Ollard, why should I care what it is like? It's not as if I shall ever have to live there.'

Tentatively bringing his grin of anguish nearer her, he said: 'Miss Brawne – you are mighty confident on that point.'

'I am. Why would I not be? I can't imagine any reason why I – oh, unless you mean if I were to *marry* you? Good heavens, is that what you are suggesting, Mr Ollard?'

He glanced over his shoulder, appalled: people might hear. 'My dear Miss Brawne, I suggest nothing – I only hint—'

'Why, what's the difference?' Curious: Fanny could not bear to see a horse whipped, shrank from all inflictions of pain – yet she had discovered a new pleasure in this torment. She watched him writhe.

'I do not presume,' he got out, among much lip-licking, 'could not presume – only if I were to presume – I can think of no more adorable creature to – to adorn those premises.'

'Oh. Oh, I see. But I couldn't, you know, because of that,' she said coolly. 'Also the name does not fit nicely in the mouth. Fanny Ollard – there is an awkwardness – it might almost be Yollard, and then there would be all sorts of complications – misdirected letters – confused masters of ceremonies – no, really, it would not do.'

Then, pluckily, he tried to beat her at her own game. He folded his arms with a sniff and said: 'Well, I never would marry you anyway, Miss Brawne – so don't think it.'

'Oh!' She gave him a long, wounded look, then drizzled tears. He had made a good showing, but it was time to finish him. 'Oh dear. I'm sorry – to be such a goose – only one doesn't expect a man to say that to a girl – quite so brutally—'

Gulping, quavering, he made a grab at her hand, catching air. 'Miss Brawne – oh, Miss Brawne, please – of course I *would* marry you—'

'You make it sound conditional!' she cried indignantly. 'You *would*, if I were prettier, and richer, and the only girl in the world, or something like that.'

'No, no . . .'

There was such acute pleasure in playing him like this. The curious thing was the way the pleasure would suddenly go, leaving her on a precipice of perplexity.

'I like you just as you are,' he was saying.

'I don't know why,' she murmured; and he went on to tell her, but she wasn't listening. He was no Romeo, she was no Juliet: that was the way things were: the moon was not available. There was a tiny sigh deep within her, like the scratch of a wainscot mouse in a vast mansion.

The tippling attorney read the will as if he were translating it at sight from Hebrew. But they got there in the end, and Mrs Brawne tearfully blessed her brother John's name. There was a thousand pounds for his sisters, and fifteen hundred in trust for Fanny, Samuel and Margaret until they came of age. The rest of his property was to be sold and divided up among them.

'Not a fortune,' Mrs Brawne said to Fanny, as the funeral carriage bore them back to Kentish Town. 'But a fortune to us, it must be said. I am so thankful. Your Aunt Gould rather put her nose up, as if she thought John had done shabbily by her – but, really, she has a husband in a prosperous line of business, and we – we have stood for years unprotected in the storms of life.'

'That's quite poetical, Mama.'

'It is, isn't it? Why, Fanny, you're crying.'

'For our good fortune.' But it wasn't that, quite. It was just – that was the end of Uncle John. And surely you should leave something more behind you than money.

The will was proved. Mrs Brawne celebrated her new security by being very lofty at church with the rector's wife, who had a frequently mentioned baronet somewhere on her family tree and used to patronize by sending mantles and bonnet-trimmings she had no more use for. ('I shall just wear it once,' Mrs Brawne would fume regretfully, 'because it is, after all, rather pretty.') Then, a spree in town. A new dinner-service selected from Wedgwood's showrooms in York Street after prolonged agonies of indecision. Thence to the Strand, and a painted screen and a set of prints from Ackermann's Repository: into the City, at Fanny's urging, to the Temple of the Muses in Finsbury Square, where the bookshop was like a dream of bookshops, rising into a great rotunda as if St Paul's were transmuted into a library. Finally to Drury Lane, to see the sensational Mr Kean in *Othello*. The great actor was a small man with a growling voice – not what she had expected – but soon she was seduced. He even temporarily overcame her doubts about the play, which she thought turned on a fundamental unreality. Could jealousy be *that* powerful? It was a poor mean emotion. She would run a mile from any man who started grinding his teeth at her in that unconscionable fashion.

'What are all those people doing?' Margaret asked, when they left the theatre: there was a small crowd at the stage-door.

'Waiting to see Mr Kean, I should think,' Mrs Brawne said, bustling her on.

'They've just seen him,' Margaret said, with sturdy logic.

'Lord, how tired I am!' Mrs Brawne yawned and exchanged a look with Fanny. They knew who the crowd was waiting to see. Lord Byron was a frequent visitor to the theatre, and Lord Byron's was the name on everyone's lips just now: the very hackney-drivers were discussing him. But the things being said were not for Margaret's innocent ears. Even Fanny, who liked to think of herself as worldly, was mystified by some of the gossip she overheard.

'What exactly,' she asked her mother that night, 'was this unspeakable thing Lord Byron did?'

'Hush, hush!' Mrs Brawne said in alarm, nearly dropping the print she was holding up against the parlour wall. 'My dear, you must not even allude to it.'

'Literally unspeakable, then. Not figuratively unspeakable, like Princess Caroline's teeth. Dear me. Now I wonder even more.'

'Don't even think of it, my dear. The tone of society, I regret to say, has declined lamentably since I was a girl. The things that are talked of in mixed company. I blame the Prince. Not a good example. One hopes for a reform in manners before too long.' She held the print up above the mantelpiece. 'No, not there. Really I would not trust you, or Margaret when she is grown, to come out in such a society. I would rather quietness – respectability – elegance, yes, but not mere fashion.' She laid the print down. 'I really think this parlour too small for them . . . Fanny, what do you think to our moving back to Hampstead?'

'I think—' And Fanny couldn't go on, because it all came back in the most surprising rush – the ponds and the heath, the broom-tyer, the druggists' shop, the nightingales and the ugly terrible thorn, yes, even that, and her father and the paper boats and the brickfields and the quilted view from the breeze-scented heights. 'I think,' she said, 'I think yes, and you are an angel of a mother, or a mother of angels.'

'Not quite that, I fear,' Mrs Brawne said, with a humorous look. 'We shall start looking at the end of this lease – but come, will you mind leaving your beau behind? The funereal young gentleman?'

'Oh! Lord, it will be a wrench, but I must bear up. And Hampstead, you know, will furnish many more young gentlemen for me to tease and torture.'

'Well, so it will.' Mrs Brawne suddenly kissed her, an uncommon gesture. 'Of course, you mustn't do that too much.'

Byron and Augusta: they make their last public appearance together at an evening party given by Lady Jersey, one of those interchangeable hostesses who were the impresarios of his celebrity and now, fittingly, preside over his fall. At this party, Byron and Augusta are cut.

A short curt word for a short curt act. It sounds, perhaps, insignificant: people at a social gathering turn away and refuse to speak to you. It does not feel insignificant. It is a way of denying that you exist. Even Augusta, who has always been quite comfortable with invisibility, feels the sharpness of the cut, and she knows Byron must feel it more.

'At least,' he says whitely, in the carriage afterwards, 'I shan't be exposing you to any more insults like that.'

'You're really going?'

'I'm really going. The victory is hers. I quit the field.'

'I hate to see you like this. So dark. I'm frightened for you—'

'No, no, hush, don't be. After all, I'm being entirely self-preserving. If I didn't care what happened to me, I would stay. Because she would hound me all the way to the kill, you know. I've no illusions there. D'you know I have lately heard myself compared with Henry VIII, Caligula and Nero? Well, it could be worse. They could be comparing me with Wordsworth.'

At last, the goodbye. Her confinement is approaching, she cannot stay in London any longer, home and increasing family call. Hobhouse, who has been staying at Piccadilly Terrace with Byron, vacates the house for the day so that he and Augusta can say their farewells. But what can one do once the farewell is said? Cry: Augusta does that, and Byron almost chokes himself in trying not to. They keep staring miserably at the trunks piled in the drawing room – not in the hall, in case marauding bailiffs spot them and intuit a flit – and then at their hands.

'I shall write her,' Byron says, with sudden venom, 'and make damn sure she rests content with finishing *me*. Towards you she must be kind – unless she wants my eternal curse on her self-satisfied little head, she will be kind to you.'

'Now I feel better,' Augusta says smiling weakly, 'you're being Byron again.'

He kisses her and holds her: these moments are allowable, being so very finite.

'Where?'

'I thought to look at Waterloo. The abattoir of our national glory. Suits the mood. Then on to Geneva. Hope there won't be too many English there.'

'Who is that very dark young woman waiting outside?'

'What? Oh, not again. She is an odd-headed girl who keeps throwing herself at me. Godwin's stepdaughter.'

'I hope you're not unkind to her.'

'Of course I am. You forget I'm a monster. Oh, I think she wants to go abroad with me, but that would not be a propitious idea for anyone. As far as feelings go, I am really a sort of reanimated corpse walking upright.'

'How horrible.'

'Not much worse than the Prince Regent. Dry your eyes, Gus, you look like the very devil when you cry. I love you.'

'So this is what it feels like,' she says, her voice hollow with wonder, 'when your heart breaks.'

'Yes,' he says, relinquishing at last, at long last, her hand. 'Yes, just about.'

(*Scene, Lady Melbourne's apartments at Melbourne House. A spring morning. LADY MELBOURNE is seated on a sofa: LORD MELBOURNE stands deferentially behind it. Opposite them, two of their grown children, GEORGE and EMILY, thirtyish and fashionably dressed, with the coarsely vigorous look of the Lambs. William Lamb is absent.*)

LADY MELBOURNE: Tut, these tales are always exaggerated when Caroline is the subject.

GEORGE: Caroline *is* exaggerated. She certainly isn't natural. And now if she is to add murder to her tally of eccentricities—

LADY MELBOURNE: That is precisely the sort of talk I wish to have suppressed. I will tell you how it was, and you will oblige me and the family by correcting anyone who says otherwise. She was having one of her absurd games with one of her pages. With firecrackers. These are her latest toy. Lord Melbourne had expressly forbidden their being brought into the house—

LORD MELBOURNE: So I did, by God. Frightened me out of my wits. There are a lot of malcontented Radicals about, you know. Remember France. It starts with shots.

LADY MELBOURNE (*with a long-suffering look*): Yes. Well, this was not a shot, though it was alarming. The page threw a firecracker on to the fire, for some reason—

EMILY: Egged on to it by Caro.

LADY MELBOURNE: That we don't know. It appears that Caroline was shocked too, and angry with him, and on the impulse of the moment threw a cricket-ball that she was holding at him, and it hit his head.

GEORGE (*snorting and pacing about*): Oh, God. Really, Mama, you put the case for the defence very well, but this will not do. The woman is plainly – well, what I have always thought she is.

EMILY (*narrowly*): Why *do* you defend her, Mama?

LADY MELBOURNE: I was not aware that I did or do anything of the kind. My concern is and always has been the reputation of this family, and above all that of William as a public man. My belief has always been that Caroline's conduct should be tolerated and contained within limits, because anything else would lead to greater scandal.

GEORGE: Anything else?

LADY MELBOURNE (*with reluctance*): Anything in the nature of a marital separation. These are so difficult to manage. Publicly they can be calamitous.

EMILY: Lord, yes: only look at Byron.

GEORGE: Did you know he's had a travelling-coach made, patterned exactly after Napoleon's? Was there ever such impudence?

EMILY: Where is this page now?

LADY MELBOURNE: He is being taken care of. His head was cut, and it bled into his eyes, and being frightened he cried out that he was being killed. This frightened Caroline, who came running down saying she had murdered him, and then the rumour got out into the street. It was all a great nuisance. Lord Brougham was calling, and he being eminent in the law took it into his head to speak to Caroline very seriously about the possible consequences of these follies of hers, hoping to do some good. But she being still – excitable, took up a poker and waved it at him saying if she was to be attacked she would defend herself . . . It was all a piece of typical Caroline nonsense.

EMILY: No, it wasn't, Mama. Granted it's not quite as bad as rumour has made it – but it is still bad.

GEORGE: It is too bad.

LORD MELBOURNE: Quite so. I was never so jangled in my life.

GEORGE: It's what I've always said. She's mad. William would never listen, of course, because he was besotted. And because he's too lazy to want a change. But he must listen now. Suppose she had thrown that ball a little harder. What would his loyalty avail him, if Caro was in the Old Bailey dock for murder? Does he think they're likely to give him a ministry then?

LADY MELBOURNE: You need not shout at me, George: my hearing is unimpaired. As to what you've always said, I fail to see the relevance. You are not a doctor—

GEORGE: No, but a doctor is. Oh, you know what I mean. A doctor should look at her.

EMILY: We would need William's consent. We must think how to put it to him. Though if he has any family feeling, he won't think twice. Lord knows I've suffered her embarrassments long enough.

LORD MELBOURNE: Two doctors. That's what you need, or used to – the opinion of two doctors. To have someone committed.

LADY MELBOURNE: Committed. I see. This is what you are proposing.

GEORGE: Come, Mama, it makes absolute sense. A separation is noisy, as you say, and Caro ain't quiet at the best of times. But put her away and she can't raise a fuss. A lunatic asylum has thick walls.

LADY MELBOURNE: A tasteless remark.

EMILY: True though.

LORD MELBOURNE: Not Bedlam. Bedlam is altogether too harsh. Some kind and discreet establishment.

GEORGE (*chuckling*): What, with strait-waistcoats made of silk?

LORD MELBOURNE (*ruminatively*): Perhaps, you know, just the threat is enough. Just to make her change her ways. If she would only promise—

LADY MELBOURNE: One can't trust Caroline's promises, alas. We had better talk it out with William. I don't like this notion, but I can see its utility, certainly.

GEORGE: Ah, and you know, Mama, your head has always ruled your heart.

LADY MELBOURNE (*coldly*): You know nothing of me, George: don't presume.

LORD MELBOURNE (*still ruminatively*): Of course she will have to go. One way or another, she will have to go.

3

Summer of the Monster

They come together like this, by water.

On a brilliant blue lake in early summer, a rowing-boat makes for the pebbly shore below the high white gables of a hotel. In the boat, two men.

On the beach, a man and two women, waiting for the boat to come in.

In the distance, the cold sinews of mountains, and a volatile mob of cloud. And beyond that, everywhere, all over Europe, a sullen blight of rain and storm. Far away in England the hay is ruined and a troubled season looms. But here, today, after weeks of greyness, there is sun on the lake. Sometimes nature is obliging.

One man gets out of the boat with a peculiar strenuous nimbleness, splashes unevenly the last few paces up the beach.

'Byron,' cries Claire to him. 'I saw you from the hotel. So I brought them down to meet you, as you have been such a brute and not come to see me.' She thrusts her hand at him, so he has no choice but to take it. 'Is this not the most delightful and curious thing? Meeting here? Who would have supposed it?'

'No one in their right mind,' Byron says, showing his teeth. 'Miss Godwin, how do you do? And . . .'

'This is Shelley,' Claire says. 'And my sister is known here as Mrs Shelley, to save awkwardness. You know.'

Claire, glowing, her hair a gypsy tumble in the breeze off the lake, is the only one who seems at ease. Shelley, stooping and serious, clasps Byron's hand in a brief, formal, even ceremonious way, as if they are about to Cornish-wrestle.

'Lord Byron,' Shelley says, 'you see a sincere admirer.'

'A rare sight,' Byron mutters. 'I'm glad to know you at last, Mr Shelley.' A stupefying shyness between these two notorieties, which makes Claire roll her black eyes humorously at Mary. Byron gestures back at the boat. 'My companion – Polidori. No sailor. I'd best see to the boat. Will you dine with me later, Mr Shelley?'

'With pleasure.'

'I can't guarantee that.' Byron makes a bow to the ladies – Mary coolly acknowledging him, Claire gaping and yearning – and splashes back to the boat.

Above the Alps, layers of air contend, charged, chilled, superheated, saturated: a meteorological mêlée, a warfare of weather. Sparks will fly.

A month earlier, in London: 'Why Geneva?' Shelley said.

'Oh, every visitor to the Continent must make the pilgrimage to Geneva,' Claire enthused. 'The lake – and the sublime mountains – picturesque and utterly wild—'

'As we have a six-month baby, wildness is not a recommendation,' Mary said.

'Oh, but then Geneva itself is quite the most civilized place – everyone says so – with the most comfortable accommodations. And then there are the associations – Gibbon, you know, and Rousseau – not to mention that the Clairmonts spring from thereabouts.'

Yes, thought Mary, better not to mention that.

'I had thought of Italy,' Shelley said, listlessly watching a web of raindrops interlacing on the lightless window. The grinding lawsuit and the revived enmity with his implacable father had left him haggard: his cheekbones showed like knuckles. 'But anywhere – anywhere appeals. Just as long as we leave.'

'Is not Geneva also where Lord Byron is headed?' Mary asked.

Claire tossed her head, turning away. 'Everyone knows that.' Her neck, Mary saw, was a beautiful bright pink.

Byron left England from Dover on 25 April 1816, disembarking at Ostend and travelling at leisure across the Continent towards Geneva in his huge Napoleon coach, which kept breaking down. Mary, Shelley and Claire left England from Dover on 3 May 1816 and reached Geneva eleven days later. They got there first.

They took cheap top-floor rooms at the Hôtel d'Angleterre at Secheron, outside the town and overlooking the lake, registering as Mr and Mrs Shelley and her sister: one of their compromises.

The first week: 'This is surely heaven,' Mary said. In the heat of the day she read and studied with Shelley in their room: at dusk they sailed on the lake, holding up their faces to the evening breezes, scenting alpine flowers and the juicy new-mown lawns of suburban villas. It was right that heaven should include that comfortably domestic element. It was even poignant, after the soul-shattering passes they had crossed to get here, the blinding white chasms, the huge alien pines that looked more iron than wood. Here humankind gathered, built, tried to make a difference. Mary slept wrapped in Shelley's arms. She thrilled again at the sight of William, full-cheeked and lusty in the keen air, their incredible collaborative being. She even softened towards Claire, who kept talking nervously of Byron's expected arrival, how she would have the pleasure of introducing him to Shelley, how it would all be perfect. Every morning Claire ran down to check the register for Byron's name. The very transparency was endearing, or nearly.

'He's here, he's here.' Claire burst in on Mary and Shelley: a less endearing habit. Shelley was half undressed, though he didn't care. 'You'll never guess – he has put his age in the register as a hundred. I thought I heard a carriage late last night. I wonder why he put a hundred? From weariness probably – or else the weight of his *sins*. I sent him up a note. I told him to reply here to you, it would look better. Have you had any word from him?'

447

'Nothing,' Mary said, forcefully handing Shelley his shirt. 'But he's probably tired from the journey.'

'Also probably rather surprised, my Clarabelle, to find you here waiting for him,' Shelley said genially, wagging a finger. 'Almost as if you planned it.'

'Oh, you hush,' Claire said, slapping at him, 'old skinny-ribs . . .' They fooled and romped, Claire smacking at his bare skin, Shelley at last gripping her arms against her sides and holding her from behind, laughing.

'We should hush, indeed we should,' he said, grinning at Mary over Claire's tousled head, 'our straitlaced Swiss will be shocked at us.'

No reply from Byron, however, all that day. Claire sent up another note after dinner, then went to bed at last with a look of restrained fury.

'It's not just the pleasure of introducing us,' Shelley said to Mary, as they walked in the hotel garden amid a wail of gnats and an itch of crickets. 'Is it? I have a strong suspicion—'

'Yes.' She squeezed his arm. 'I wish we did not have to talk about Claire so much.'

And so, the next morning, Claire spots Byron in the boat on the lake, and the introductions are made, and that evening Shelley and Byron dine together. If they do not get on . . .

But they do get on. 'An exceedingly interesting person,' Shelley tells Mary in bed that night. 'Mad as Ajax. Full of strange prejudices and inconsistencies. Seems to hate a great many things, but really hates himself, I believe. Which has prevented the full expression of his genius. I like him.'

'And Claire?'

'Ah, I thought we weren't to talk of Claire.' He tickles her playfully.

'Did Byron speak of her?'

'Well. It's difficult . . . I hope she doesn't *fix* her heart there.'

I do, Mary thinks, but she cannot say that to Shelley. Neither can she say that she rather likes being called Mrs Shelley. Sweet untruth. That night she dreams of wildly ransacking drawers and closets, until Harriet comes in, bland and genteel in surprise, and politely demands to know what she thinks she is doing? And she wakes just as she is desperately locking her fingers round Harriet's neck.

'It's called breakfast,' Claire tells a bleary Byron.

'Barbarous custom.' Byron bows with hangdog courtliness about the table. 'Mrs Shelley. I suppose I shall get used to it. Do mornings always smell like this? So damned *hearty*.'

'This may account for the intermittent depression of the spirits,' says his companion. Dr John Polidori, brought along as his personal physician: a very young Anglo-Italian, crow-dark, stagily, unnecessarily handsome: thrustful yet ill at ease, with a way of glowering round at everyone as if he suspects them of passing notes under the table.

'You think so? Well, I must write and tell Lady Byron. "It ain't you after all, Bell, it's the digestion." '

'We must try and wipe those miserable memories away,' Claire says brightly.

'Expunge, or sponge, eh? A nice thought. "Not all the perfumes of Arabia", though, et cetera, I fear. What say you, Polidori? – "canst thou not minister to a mind diseased"?'

'I hope to make a study of the pathology of the mind,' Polidori answers cautiously, 'though as a physician I cannot prescribe for . . .' He gives the note-passing look from under his theatrical brows.

'Lord Byron is quoting Shakespeare,' Mary says. 'From *Macbeth*. When Lady Macbeth is tormented with guilt for the murder of the king. It affects her mind and she sleepwalks—'

' "Out, damned spot", of course I know this,' cries Polidori. 'It is a very notable scene for my particular interest, that is somnambulism. My thesis—'

'Brilliant fellow,' Byron says, feeding himself dry toast, 'a prodigy at Edinburgh. Youngest graduate ever.'

'I sleepwalk,' says Shelley. 'What does it mean?'

'Oh, sir, this is a vast subject. The traditional view of distur-
bances in the mind—'

'Ah, but where in the mind? This is what fascinates me,
terrifies me, they come to the same thing,' Shelley pursues. 'Does
this mean that even in a deep dreamless sleep, the mind is in some
degree active – yet without us being aware of it? Thus the mind is
not conscious of the mind? Have we a divided mind, then, or
even two? And if it is disturbance that makes a man get up in his
sleep and walk, then do the emotions persist even in sleep? But
without awareness, this would suggest the emotions are merely a
bodily expression like yawning or needing to make water.'

'These are many questions,' Polidori says. 'But they all seem to
touch on the question of the immortal soul.'

'Aye, there's the rub,' says Byron. 'Suppose we haven't got one?
Suppose yourself a mere mechanism, with the brain as the
clockwork. Now nothing could be more mechanical than sleepwalking – a blind lumbering about, simply because the muscles
have been wound up to go. And sleep, death, these are just the
natural state the mechanism returns to when it runs down.
Meanwhile the earth spins on and the planets revolve and none of
it means a damned thing.'

Shelley stares at him. 'Now I really am terrified.'

The pattern of companionable days: breakfasting, walking, sailing
together. The curious stares of other English visitors, alerted by
gossip, add to their sense of solidarity.

'I swear it feels as if we have all known each other for years!'
cries Claire, picking precisely the wrong image. It is the fact that
they are sealed off from the past that makes them get along.

Byron becomes, to Mary and Shelley, Albé – the name a
fanciful version of his initials. Byron calls Shelley, affectionately,
Shiloh: Mary is Mary. Dr Polidori, who soon begins to reveal
capricious vanities that amuse Byron and irritate Shelley, becomes

to them Dr Pollydolly. Byron never uses Claire's name.

Seated at dinner one day, Byron starts as Claire, at her liveliest, comes up behind and puts her arms round his neck.

'You have the smallest ears I ever saw! I vow I would give anything for them!'

After a moment he bursts out laughing. 'I have heard of poor fellows selling their teeth, and women their hair,' he says, caressing her hands, 'but I don't know the market for ears.'

'Women selling their hair?' cries Shelley in disgust.

'Aye – to wig-makers and such.'

'Here is the aptest emblem of our world.' Shelley throws himself back in his seat as if physically struck. 'Sordid – unjust – destructive of all that is natural and beautiful – and with this ghastliness like a bad joke – can you picture anything more illustrative? A poor woman cuts off her hair and sells it to a profiteer who sells it to a rich fat woman in the guise of a hideous artificial wig.'

'Of course the hair does grow back,' Byron says gently: not mockingly, not quite: there is in his attitude to Shelley something of the respectful indulgence accorded a brilliant child who will soon outstrip you.

'Unlike teeth,' Claire says. 'Ugh, imagine having someone else's teeth in your mouth! Imagine if they started moving of their own accord – talking with the *voice* of their former owner—'

'Why stop at teeth?' grins Byron. 'Only find a surgeon who's a cunning enough artificer, and instead of a glass eye you might have the real human article, transferred from another head – and what would you see with *that* eye, I wonder?'

Watching them, Mary – as ever – is torn. Yes, she thinks, go on, cleave to Byron, and leave Shelley all to me. And yet: Claire is trying too hard, Byron is tolerating her, and Claire has more to lose. Call it pessimism, or a consequential mind.

'I have had a singularly interesting talk with Mr Shelley. He is a man of a metaphysical cast of mind, with many exalted and visionary theories, and a truly radical temper,' says Dr Polidori to Mary, instructively, as if she has never met Shelley in her life. 'We discussed the propositions of Dr Lawrence, the anatomist, that life inheres only in the physical body. Thus our soul, even supposing there is such a thing, does not come from a creator or God. This, I see from reading Mr Shelley's work, is his own position. The curious thing, to me, is that it does not make him unhappy.'

'Shelley's belief, in which I am proud to share, is in humanity.'

'Humanity is a difficult thing to conceive, though, is it not? Rather than Jill and Jack. He has another theory I find hard to conceive, and that is holding women in common.'

'You are mistaken, Dr Polidori,' Mary says, and winces at her own sharpness. 'That is a – a misunderstanding of his beliefs. He, and I, believe that man as a rational creature should not allow love to be tied or impeded by artificial conventions. That is a different matter.'

'Is it?' He narrows the sooty eyes at her.

'Yes. Your tea, Dr Polidori.' Mary, Englishwoman that she is, can make tea do anything. The way she hands him his cup is a firm rebuttal of any flirtatious notions. Dr Polidori accepts it, in both senses.

'I think you would like to learn Italian?' he says. 'If I can be of any service . . .'

Byron, who never seems to notice anything, notices everything. 'Dr Pollydolly has a taking for you, Mary.'

'It's manageable. Claire has more than a taking for you, Albé.'

He shrugs. 'She is a fetching girl, and knows very well what she is about, and here we are among scenes to make the frostiest heart melt, and thereby hangs a tale.'

'This is the art of using a lot of words to say nothing.'

'To be sure – Shiloh has been making me read Wordsworth, and I've picked it up from there. What would you have me say? She comes eight hundred miles to see me – damn it, I feel like an Alp myself, there will be guides clambering up me next – and so what am I to do? I'll not deny being flattered. I slipped out of England in darkness for fear of folk expectorating at me on my way as 'twere – now this is an agreeable contrast, and as such I'm not inclined to over-analyse it. Besides, I didn't suppose you were so *very* protective of her. I can read a look as well as the next man.'

'I would not see her hurt,' says Mary: and the crickets chirp, *Wouldn't you? Wouldn't you really?*

'I admire you, Mary.'

'I hope this is not the same as a taking.'

'I mean truly admire, as in finding you remarkable and impressive.'

'Then that is just as well, because there is a species of talk going about – to do with our party – which I would not see encouraged.'

'Eh? Oh, that we all share and share alike.' He laughs: Mary envies him that. 'How absurd. Mind, it was your father who wrote so memorably that marriage is the worst of all monopolies – hey?'

'I am not married to Shelley. We are – well, the English language does not run to it.'

'Because the English language, beauteous as it is, is enslaved to cant. I admire you even more, by the by. Because I said I admired you meaning your mind and character, and you did not bridle or squeal.'

'I never do either of those things. I may as well say, for the sake of clarity, that I don't want to be your mistress, Albé.'

'What a relief. If only everyone dared to say that it is *not* such a world-shaking matter. And not even, sometimes, that enjoyable. The world would be different. But, please, never tell anyone I said that. Then I really would be ruined.'

The chalet at Montalègre, right on the lake: going in, Mary knows at once. Smells of beeswax and varnish, kindly creakings, broad windows full of water-dazzle. 'Oh, yes.'

'Rather expensive, like everything here,' Shelley muses, poking his head into every cupboard. He always does this on taking any lodging: laughingly, yet without humour, he will tell you it is to check there is no one waiting to pounce on him. 'But cheaper than the hotel. And more private, which is the main thing. I heard a woman call out in the hall this morning: "There's one of Lord Byron's ladies." True, she was wearing spectacles, but still I really must get this hair cut. That,' he adds, with savage serenity, 'or her throat.'

'That path must lead to the Villa Diodati – the place Albé wanted to rent. But they say it's taken.'

'A pity. He does need the privacy. His fame has followed him.'

Shelley eases back a creaking shutter. Light fingers his face like an accusation. Mary senses something, a vacancy needing to be filled.

'Your fame will come,' she says.

He returns her a blank, stricken look, like an actor not recognizing his cue.

'That reminds me,' he says, stirring. 'Polidori was asking Albé, in that pert way of his, whether he had not courted his fame. Albé said it was more the case that fame had courted him, then it had ravished him and abandoned him.' Shelley's smile is awkward. 'He used a stronger word than ravished. We are different in many ways.'

'You like him, though.' She comes and puts her head in her own special spot, on his chest, with the hardness of collar-bone under soft shiftings of shirt and breathing skin.

'Oh, yes. Very much. I can tell that, because I do not feel at ease with him.' He kisses her hair, absently.

Oh, it's you. I thought you might be William coming back.

Yes, we have had a disagreement again. You needn't look like that. It's all very easy for you to judge. It isn't? Well, that is all to the good. Half the problems in the world are caused by people being too quick to judge. What are the other half caused by? I don't know – people being too slow to judge perhaps. How skittish you are today! Or perhaps it's me.

Certainly we've had our excitements lately. Much to do with that book – yes, there is the first volume – pick it up, see – I hope William did not hurt the binding throwing it down so. I have told him before, he does not know his own strength. There: see? *Glenarvon*, A Novel. Yes, to be sure it is anonymous, I would not have sent it to the press otherwise for a thousand pounds – but anonymity, it seems, is the most difficult of author's tricks to pull off, when the matter is sensational, as I confess the matter of this book is . . . Yes, I have turned author. My heart beats with pride to say it though I should not – well, because of the trouble this book is causing. Not that it was *meant* to. Now, I have told you before, I do not lie.

Mr Murray did not publish the book. Though so estimable he is a cautious man I think – and then there is the matter of his most *famous* author or I should say perhaps now *infamous* – who might not take kindly to having such a book come from the same presses as his. Well, there is no disguising it: in *Glenarvon* I have presented, in disguised form, in cloak and domino if you will, my relation with him – with Byron. He is the character called Glenarvon – I the heroine named Calantha – only in some sort, that is I have *altered* things and Calantha dies in the story, which, you know, has not happened to me yet and if it did I should certainly hope to know about it.

She dies of a broken heart, of course: what odd questions you ask.

Well, it's true that William is in the story too – masked – also his family, partly. You must understand that I wanted to *explain*. I have been much traduced. But when one knows all the circumstances . . . Also I do believe I have erred upon the generous side in all my portraits. For who would believe that when I was making a fair copy of my tale I was at that moment being threatened with incarceration in a lunatic asylum?

William's family. All of them – I cannot quite except my

mother-in-law although curiously I felt that if I did have a protector it was Lady M. – she who can hardly find a civil word for me. They called in a doctor – a loathsome creature who kept pressing my hand and asking me nonsensical questions – and I was sent to Brocket with my poor Augustus to wait to hear my *fate* – there were consultations with lawyers – all the time William promised he would not let me be put away nor parted from my son but that was as far, he said, as he could moderate matters, and that we would surely have to separate having so little agreed of late and my conduct appearing in so poor a light once examined. No – not weak – I only think he too quickly *resigns* himself. It is a thing I can never do.

You needn't look like that.

Well, I was summoned back here to Whitehall at last. The house was full of lawyers. I saw William – he looked wretched – bleached and parched – as though they had sucked his blood from him. They were all discussing me in Lady M.'s apartments. Then William came upstairs to me. He had the specimen deeds of separation. 'This,' he said, 'believe me, Caro, is something I never wished to see' – 'Then don't look at it,' cried I, 'there, William, I was always one for the simple solution.' Well, we laughed a little – wept likewise. He said that things might be different if I could moderate my behaviour – things like my pages and the games we have – I said I would make no promises under threat of the madhouse and at that he said, in his true manly way, that he didn't blame me and he would defend me for ever against such a fate, with his strong right arm and his last breath. Then we began kissing.

It is a curious thing – when William and I reach the very lowest point – at the darkest moment of crisis – then it is as if all the old fire flares up again between us and melds us in one passionate flame. Of course, I would not deliberately make it so.

Well, they sent up to find us at last, and there I was seated upon my splendid husband's knee, feeding him little pieces of bread-and-butter – a thing he always liked – and he said to send the lawyers away, he would have no part in any separation on these terms, we would do very well together. Oh, it was wonderful.

Of course, those other Lambs were not best pleased. They may go and boil their heads. With mint sauce.

I do wonder if *he* has read my book. He, B. Oh, to be sure, he is abroad – somewhere – but it is already the talk of the town, and they clamour for another printing, and so it may well fly over the sea – my winged words – and he may see it. Not that I care whether he does or not. He has chosen his path. Let him tread it. And if there be stones—

The path was *not* chosen for him. You do wrong, wrong to suggest it.

I beg your pardon. I thought you said . . . that was why I . . . The mirror? Oh. Well, it was foxed anyhow. I doubt anyone heard it. So, there are two volumes of my *Glenarvon* thrown about. Would you care to throw the third? Well, you know best.

Yes – irony or misfortune or whatever you care to call it, I was seeing my book through the press just as all this was going on – separation – reconciliation – and was a little nervous – but only just before it came out did I really grasp what effect it might have. William did say to me, in his most deliberate way, that he hoped I had nothing up my sleeve . . . Oh dear. No, he knew nothing of my writing, no one did – I wrote secretly, at night, for hours on end. I don't know what it is to be tired, you see. The feeling that in you is tiredness is in me a longing to be tired. It's hard to explain. So, he knew nothing of the book until now – that is, until he found everybody reading it, and looked into it, and saw what it was about, and realized – well, hence this scene.

Yes, I think he was angry: *very* angry. I have had the most furious wild letters from his family, and doubtless he has been talking to them – and all in all it is a great pity.

I am indeed tolerably calm. You see, I fancy they are all – even careful old Lady M. – so absolutely incensed against me now, that they will heap *every* insult on me – sharpen their knives over me so very butcherishly – that William will take my part again. He will stand by me.

Because he must.

On the same day as the publication of *Glenarvon*, Augusta gave birth to her fifth child at Six Mile Bottom. The boy was named Frederick, after some difficulty: George, having already named a son after himself, was rather at a loss. 'Hang me if I know what to call him,' he said. 'Names are a deuced ticklish business. I've never been sure about names.' As George grew older he was finding more things that he was unsure about. Like a failing empire withdrawing troops from province after province, George gave up on large areas of life. The money, now: the money was quite beyond him.

'How much? You lost how much, George?'

'Now, don't fire up, old girl. It's not going to help. You'll only sour your milk. Besides, it's only a little more than what's already owing – ain't it? You know these things. It's all Greek to me.'

The new baby did not feed well: he seemed testy at having been brought into the world at all, like an old man roused from sleep. Augusta Charlotte struck her own thumb flat with a stone, seemingly on purpose, and spent longer hours rocking, crooning, sulking. The local apothecary suggested sea air, pinching his cheek and grimacing as if at his own inadequacy. A bailiff called, mentioned that the house was damnably hard to find, and threatened to arrest George until Augusta managed to pacify him with some trinkets of jewellery. (Byron's brooch winked from the box: no. Never.) In London some old and influential friends of George's began to rally round him, looking out for an undemanding official post with a decent salary. There was Commissioner of Stamps: but that would mean moving to London. Away from Newmarket, from the turf, from hunting and shooting parties. George was wretched.

'I can't see it. What would I do? I do believe I'd go mad.'

'You could still go out to the country sometimes, George – see your friends—'

'Not all the time.'

'Not all the time.' They meant it in different ways. She coaxed her reluctant baby to take the nipple again.

'But what about the house?'

'Well, we would have to sell it.'

'How? I've never been sure about those things.'

'I'll see about it.'

'And where would we live in London? I only know the clubs and what-naught. I wouldn't know where to look.'

'I'll see about it. I dare say I shall be wanted at Court for Princess Mary's wedding. I can see to a lot of things then.'

'You're a marvel, old girl.' George yawned.

In all of this, there was one constant: not a consolation exactly, but a rock standing proud of the gloomy surf. Annabella.

Annabella had no doubts: feared nothing: never changed. She wrote Augusta regular letters, thick as newspapers, thoroughly composed with a beginning, middle and end: you could not help but be abashed by the sheer level of attention you were getting, as if someone were to keep insistently painting you in oils. Her own letters in reply, she feared, were scatter-brained things. But Annabella wanted them. Now that she and Byron were separated, now that Byron had fled, Annabella wanted Augusta. And it was nice, Augusta thought, to feel wanted.

And to know that there was someone with her true interests at heart. Coming dazed and impressed to the end of a tremendous letter, Augusta glowed with thankful humility. This was no ordinary woman who was taking such unsqueamish trouble to pick over the mess of her life. She had always suspected that Annabella was much better than her. Now she knew it. Annabella was taking a cure at Lowestoft, where there was a very serious-minded religious community. Augusta might once have chuckled at that, especially when nudged to it by Byron, but she was changing. It seemed right and fitting that Annabella should find a place there, among the seaside saints. Even the account of Annabella's regimen, in which she ate largely and then took a pilot-boat out to make herself sick, had the true ring of the anchorite's virtue. Lesser beings kept their food down.

And when the letters did not come, Augusta mourned. She only heard from Byron, on his travels, very irregularly. It was Annabella who had now begun to fill the vacancy in Augusta's mental circle. Silence hurt her, as she confessed in one of her own undisciplined scrawls. But in reply Annabella carefully pointed out how difficult it was for her sometimes to forget that the dear sister-in-law she addressed was also . . .

She refrained from spelling it out – just as Augusta, taking her meaning, refrained from naming it to herself in mind. (She always had.) But there was no doubt that Annabella knew.

How? Surely if she had known during the time of her marriage to Byron, she would have confronted Augusta with it. Augusta, too shy to ask, could only conclude that something had been said by someone to betray her. Her mind buzzed like a hive at that, with anger, regret, indignation, shame, thoughts and emotions she could not even recognize. But that was only noise, through which the cool voice of Annabella cut like a pure trumpet-note. This matter between them might be unspoken, but it could not be evaded. In addressing her, Annabella addressed a sinner. There was evil about her.

Augusta, who had never believed in evil, sometimes seemed to feel it diaphanously clinging, like the suspicion of a cobweb in the air.

But the letters resumed. Augusta fell upon them gratefully: Annabella had not abandoned her. Indeed, Annabella seemed to have committed herself to her all the more whole-heartedly. She wrote, in her rather opaque way, of her great hopes for Augusta. She had even got to know Augusta's old London friend, Theresa Villiers, out of sheer mutuality of feeling: Mrs Villiers wrote to Augusta in raptures about her superb and suffering sister-in-law.

A new circle being formed, perhaps: aching with loneliness, Augusta hoped so.

But a circle, of course, implied exclusion.

'When will we see Uncle Byron again?' Georgiana asked her one day.

And experimentally, with Annabella's stern injunctions ringing in her head, Augusta tried it: 'Never.'

The Villa Diodati: it is available after all, and into its capacious four storeys Byron moves himself and his servants and his doctor, Polidori.

The Villa Diodati: handsome if square, whitewashed walls and blue shutters, first-floor balcony on three sides with views down green slopes, clad in fruit-trees and firs like a meeting-place of south and north, across the lake and across vineyards to a dream of rippled mountains.

The Villa Diodati: a comfortable walk from the chalet at Montalègre, and at once Claire is making that walk, and not returning at night. Well, thinks Mary: the inevitable result of importunity and opportunity.

The Villa Diodati: soon open house for the whole Shelley party, where they dine, write, debate, argue, imprint their tense, excited, richly unhappy selves on that scrubbed Swiss woodwork. And where, according to the gossiping English tourists on the other side of the lake, there is a veritable school of prostitution and incest: Laocoon-like tumbles of bare limbs are envisaged.

Shelley to Byron: 'You know, by entertaining me, you are thoroughly spoiling your chances of rehabilitation with the dear hypocritical public.'

Byron, hand on Shelley's shoulder: 'Oh, yes, I know.'

The Villa Diodati: where Mary and Shelley often stay overnight, after late supper and talk, but where she never actually lives – and yet where, quite unexpectedly, she finds herself invited by immortality.

★ ★ ★

461

At Montalègre, she wakes to the sound of William's colicky cry. There is a moon, enough to see his little apologetic face by. She picks him up, kisses, soothes. At six months William has an engagingly precocious look, his chin a pixie point, her own Godwinian sharp nose. He looks as if he could tell you some very interesting worthwhile things. The moonlight wavers: at the open window, a steely sky scrubs itself with frantic rags of cloud: treetops toss. The calm weather is breaking: Europe's foul summer is closing in on Geneva. Mary starts at a moving shadow. The shadow takes form as Shelley, out of bed in his nightgown, standing, swaying, looking down at the empty bedclothes.

He says hoarsely: 'Claire?'

Sleepwalking. He has been free of it for a while.

'No.' Mary steps forward, into a pool of the fitful moonlight. In his poetry, he always links her image with the moon. The silverlit boards feel cold beneath her feet. Cold, cold. 'No, it's me.'

Shelley turns his wildly tousled head in her direction with grinding slowness, open-mouthed, like some creature granted senses for the first time.

'Mary?' He rubs at his eyes, boylike, with the heel of his hand. 'Thank God.' He blinks about, sees William, holds out his arms. 'Let me.'

'Are you awake?'

'Of course.' He gathers the boy into his arms, begins walking up and down crooning to him, his own peculiar nonsense word that always seems to work. 'Yahmani, yahmani.'

'Why did you think I was Claire?'

Shelley shakes his head, finger on lips. 'Yahmani, yahmani.'

Dr Polidori keeps his gallantries in check, but still the black eyes fasten on Mary when they read Italian together. She is reminded, a little, of Claire when she was a young voracious girl called Jane who could not stop staring at her new stepsister as if there were nothing in creation like her.

'What is the Italian for "brother"?' she asks him.

'*Fratello.* Or for little brother, *fratellino.*'

'Then that is what I am very happy to find in you, Dr Polidori. *Fratellino.*'

The dramatic eyebrows pucker. 'Yet I am surely older than you.'

Mary, not quite nineteen, thinks: Nobody is older than me.

But Polidori accepts, if he must, being her *fratellino*, all the more as there is a grating between him and the other members of the party. Claire, now sharing Byron's bed if nothing else, is inclined to be lofty with the young physician whose role as a companion conflicts with hers. Shelley is plunged into gloom by Polidori's loud and insistent reading out of his own bad plays. Byron is divided. One day Mary climbs the steep path to the Villa Diodati to find Byron and Polidori breakfasting on the wrought-iron balcony above the colonnade.

'Come, my good doctor, don't you see a lady there in need of a gentlemanly arm?' Byron cries.

'Yes.' Polidori rises scattering crumbs. 'Wait, please, Mrs Shelley – I will come down to you—'

'Wait, wait? – where's your chivalry? Jump over,' Byron chaffs him, 'it can't be more than eight feet.'

So Polidori jumps over the balcony, landing in a heap on the muddy path with a yelp of pain.

He has sprained his ankle. Byron, all contrition, is the one who carries Polidori into the house, puts cushions to his head, stands over him gnawing his lip and white-faced. Mary wonders if he is thinking: *I have lamed him: made him like me.*

But Dr Polidori laid up on the sofa is an even more demanding companion. And meanwhile the stormy weather curtails Byron and Shelley's daily sailing and throws them all together, indoors, and on their own resources.

Shadows like the flapping of great wings, as the night wind off the lake, sown with sporadic rain, pounds open the windows of the long drawing room, bellies the curtains, flattens the candle-flames.

'Oh, I would have been a chemist, if I had not been what I am,' Shelley says, after talking of the retorts and crucibles and galvanic troughs with which he filled his college rooms. 'Everything else is *about* life, but that is life itself. Unlocking its secrets – how far might we not go, if we were not encumbered with the false shrinkings of piety? What about flying? Why do we restrict the balloon – wonderful invention, my hair stands up to think of it? – we limit it to going over Vauxhall Gardens on some wretched royal jubilee, when we could be exploring the interior of Africa – even the moon, if it could be linked to some power, electrical perhaps – why not?' He stalks to the windows, pulls the snapping curtains aside, points to the palpitations of lightning above the heads of the Jura. 'Think how much power there is there—'

'But how to control what nature disposes?' Polidori puts in. 'How to harness it, draw it down?'

'How? Surely the same question must have been in the minds of the first men, when they gazed at fire – a forest fire, a volcano – something beyond them, they thought, beyond their power.' Shelley darts over to the hearth and kneels, his face witchlike in the glow. 'Yet here it is. We have it. We think nothing of it. It is entirely in our power. Hence the beautiful myth of Prometheus, the god who gave fire to mankind. But the true Prometheus must have been a man, a thinking and daring man, who first understood how fire could be caught, tamed, made—'

'Or woman,' says Claire, 'for it's always women who make up the fires nowadays, you know. In fact I never knew a man who could lay a good fire.'

'Your galvanic balloons,' Byron says, roaming away from Claire, 'they would make mighty puissant engines of war.'

'*If* they were put to that use,' Shelley says.

'Which they surely would be. If we have no compunction about butchering fifty thousand men on Waterloo field just to put a discredited crown back on a fat man's head, what wouldn't we do with more power?'

'That is, if our moral development does not keep pace with the growth of our knowledge. But that it can do, if all the impediments to it, all the lumber of superstition and bigotry, are swept away.'

'I'll gladly join you in the sweeping,' Byron says, sitting down again. 'I'm less confident of the inevitability of human happiness. We will always be at the mercy of the gale—' Byron steadies a picture that has been almost shaken off the wall by the shrilling draughts '—even of our own flesh.'

Shelley, fire-gazing, shakes his head. 'Not once we have gained control over it. If the secrets of life itself are yielding to our science, then surely that day will come. Dr Darwin is reputed to have seen life spontaneously generated in a piece of vermicelli kept in solution—'

'That is a doubtful case,' Polidori says, 'and I think you may be assured that I know about such things, my dear sir. But certainly the bare principle of life seems to have been restored to dead tissue by the application of electrical force, on many well-attested occasions.'

'When we have dethroned God,' Byron says, 'I wonder, will we be any less alone?'

From the mountains, thunder growls a few sultry bars to itself, and Claire squeals. 'Now hark – hark at what such talk does. My flesh is actually creeping . . .' She turns to grab Byron's arm, but he has risen from the settle and sidled away again: he and Shelley are like early dancers at a country assembly, Mary thinks, prowling the echoing room like that. Balked of an arm, Claire seizes the cushion and, after looking about her, throws it at Mary – who to Claire's disappointment neatly catches it.

'You're very quiet, Madam Mope,' Claire says. Mistress of the unanswerable statement.

'You missed,' Mary says, tossing the cushion back. 'But I don't think it was me you wanted to hit anyway.'

★ ★ ★

That night in the guest bedroom of the Villa Diodati Mary and Shelley make such furious loud love that once she has to place her fingers hard over his mouth to quieten him; and at the last he hauls her, with his odd wiry strength, so that she is on top of him, and gazes almost submissively up at her plunging and looming over him, with the still air so humid that she sees actual drops of sweat fall in beads from her drooping hair on to his forehead. A whipcrack of thunder shivers the window-panes: the lake begins to hiss with savage rain.

'God, God,' Shelley groans presently. 'That's what I need.'

'No, you don't,' Mary says, her lips against his shoulder: damp, pale, tender-cool.

'At times like this I do.' He sits up, cradling his face. 'It's not true that we are always alone, is it?'

She can't find an answer. Thunder delivers an oracular comment. She puts a trembling hand through her hair, and it prickles and crackles under her fingers. Somewhere someone is up, probably Byron the incorrigible night-owl, and a little candle- or lamplight trickles into the room. By it she can see every one of Shelley's vertebrae. Anatomy of Shelley. This, she thinks before she can stop herself, will be him when he is dead, just this.

'It's not true,' she says, in between two bell-like beats of her heart.

Fantasmagoriana.

'Oh, does that mean they are gory?' cries Claire, peering over Mary's shoulder at the rare book of tales Byron has procured.

'Yes.' Easier: otherwise she ends up seeming a pedant.

'From the German,' Byron says. 'And you know what a ghoulish goblinish set the Teutons are. Takes their mind off their devilish food. As this damnable summer continues no summer, I thought we might give up and call it winter. Stir the fire come nightfall, close the drapes, and gather about to hear ghost stories and curdle our blood, or bloods.'

'Oh, Shelley will love it! Is he still in the garden? I must tell him – he will fairly shriek.' Claire runs off.

'You know these things make her terribly excitable,' Mary says to Byron: thinking, Not just her.

'Oh, everything does,' he says, taking up the book. 'I have just peeped into it – there is a delicious one here about a severed head coming to life. Another about a grey apparition that walks by a lake talking gibberish. Oh, pooh, thinks I, it's only Wordsworth.'

'Shelley has not converted you?'

Byron scowls. 'I see *something* in him. If only he did not see so much in himself. Why should I care what he feels when he beholds a daisy? This beside the fact that he's a turncoat and Tory toad-eater. Speaking of which, do you know Coleridge?'

'Oh, Mr Coleridge, yes, I've . . .' She flushes faintly, feeling schoolgirlish. 'I've known him since I was quite small. I hid under the sofa once to hear him recite *The Ancient Mariner.*'

'Of course, he was in your father's circle then, wasn't he? Before he went cringing back to Church and King. I saw him just before I left England. He wrote and asked if he could call. It was a novelty then for anyone to want to see me, bar a bailiff or an exorcist, and I'd always thought a deal more of him than old Wordsworth, so I said yes. He brought some new poetry. I thought the spring had dried up altogether, but this – this was magnificent stuff, it *was* the mariner, held you with its glittering eye, made you sadder and wiser, wilder, I don't know what. And needed a publisher, if you please, which is why he approached me. Such the prevailing taste. The prophet is not without honour except, and so forth – never fear, I shan't quote the Bible at you any more. Scots upbringing. Murray I hope will publish him at my urging. Thus I do some good in the world.' He scowls again.

'And you? Has the spring dried up too?'

He shrugs. 'I'm adding a third canto to *Childe Harold.* It wants copying. Shelley tells me of your fair hand. If ever you have leisure, I'd be glad. And you can tell me what you think – not too candidly.'

'You are dissatisfied?'

'That sentence describes me so entirely – enduringly–' he kisses her hand '–that I should have it engraved somewhere – not above the door here because they'd charge me for it – not on my breast for it would hurt – but somewhere. More locally, appositely, yes. Dissatisfied. I have a whole wild-beast show in my heart, and my verses are little fat lap-dogs.' He chuckles suddenly. 'Gory. Lord. What's her mother like?'

'Mrs Godwin is my stepmother,' Mary says, stiffening.

He chuckles again. 'That's no answer, though it is.'

'Why do you ask?'

'Oh, because all women grow to resemble their mothers, supposedly. Not that that much matters in this case. These new poems of Coleridge's are quite in the German ghostly style, by the by. There's one that has quite stuck in my mind. I must give it out to Shiloh some night, see if it shivers him. Is Dr Pollydolly leaving you in peace?'

'We understand each other.'

'He complained this morning that we all talk about him behind his back. Of course, once a person says that, you do . . . God, look at that rain – coming down like a plague of Egypt – you'll not get back to Montalègre tonight.'

'You're being Biblical again. Do you have a God, Albé?'

'I want none of your Gods or immortalities. We are punished enough here on earth without imagining some celestial preceptor to add to it.'

'But why are we punished?'

With a smile of the greatest gentleness, he says: 'Everyone must answer that for themselves.'

Firelit frieze of faces: Byron with his rake's pallor and full lips, Claire round-cheeked and suspensefully blinking, Polidori a frown and Mr Punch nostrils, Shelley all shadowy concavities of jaw and cheek. Mary, reading out a ghost story, is inside her face and cannot see it, though she suspects it is the least revealing of all.

468

Afterwards, a silence, broken by a sudden hissing tumble of wood in the fireplace. Everyone jumps. Nervous laughter, stretchings.

'The Germanic spirit,' says Polidori. 'I have often wondered if it is a consequence of the Teutons being untouched by classical culture. They are still, in a sense, dwellers in the forest.'

'The forest dwells in us,' says Shelley, as if to himself.

'Read the one about the fatal kiss again,' urges Claire, 'the father's curse—'

'The thrill doesn't survive repetition,' says Byron. 'We need fresh terrors. What do you think? Do you have to be a German to conceive these things? I don't believe so. My old nurse was a good Calvinist Scot, and her mind was stuffed with horrors. If I stayed awake after nine the devil would come and take my eyes and mash 'em like boiled eggs. Religion is such a comfort, isn't it? Let's try it. Each of us to write a ghost story. Something to outdo those untouched Teutons. Something to freeze the blood.'

'Oh, Lord, I'm sure I shall think of a thousand things,' cries Claire, 'the only trouble will be what to put down first.'

'Well, what say you?' Byron cocks an eye at Mary like a winking ember. 'Mrs Shelley, do you accept the challenge?'

'I'll try,' Mary says, after a moment; but already Claire is talking over her.

Under the dripping balcony, Shelley sits with his long legs folded up in a position that to anyone but him and a marionette would be excruciating: propped on his knees, his open notebook, covered in his chaotic script interspersed with typical drawings – disembodied eyes, winged figures. One attenuated hand grips his own head, as if to hold it in place.

'Whenever I try for the ghastly,' he says, 'my father keeps popping up . . . Have you thought of anything?'

Mary, jigging William on her knee, shakes her head. The baby seems to have made the connection between her and the

469

delicious motion, and grins his delight into her face: wonderful goddess.

'Polidori has begun his. You can't yield the palm to *him*. You have fifty times his wit. And sense, and taste, and everything.' Shelley scribbles a violent zigzag, tearing the paper. When he dislikes someone, he cannot moderate it. They become an affront to him.

William turns his drunken head to gaze at his father. Mary contemplates the miraculous contour of his cheek.

'I just can't think of anything,' she says.

Going in to dinner that evening, Byron asks her: 'Have you thought of a story yet?'

'No. Have you?'

'I have something in train. Slow and sticky. I find prose prosy now. I want rhyme. Without it I'm like an old carthorse let out of the shafts. Perhaps you're thinking too hard.'

'I don't think I'm thinking at all.'

'Good. That's when the best ideas come.'

'Where from, do you suppose?'

Byron shrugs, then goes to the hearth and lifts up a corner of the rug with a poker. Beetles scuttle, frantically seeking darkness.

'There,' he says.

Past midnight, and they are still talking by firelight in the long drawing room: behind their circle of chairs, a great bulk of darkness, an angry spatter of rain, a burglar wind trying the shutters.

'I doubt I can give you it as Coleridge recited it to me,' Byron is saying. 'He has a voice like soft bronze. But this is the part that haunted me. Christabel's father has given the shelter of his roof to this enchanting creature Geraldine, but she isn't all she seems. She undresses in Christabel's chamber. Now we see it.

"Beneath the lamp the lady bowed,
And slowly rolled her eyes around;
Then drawing in her breath aloud
Like one that shuddered, she unbound
The cincture from beneath her breast;
Her silken robe, and inner vest
Dropt to her feet, and in full view,
Behold! her bosom and half her side—
Hideous, deformed, and pale of hue—
O shield her! shield sweet Christabel!" '

Byron's voice lingers like bright smoke in the air. Mary turns from him to Shelley, to say something in admiration. Shelley, open-mouthed, is staring at her in horror.

'Shelley?'

'Give me a light,' he mutters, staggering upward to his feet and lunging at the candle on the mantelshelf. 'Light—' Now he is screaming. 'For God's sake, light . . .' He covers his face with his sleeve, howling, blind, running from the room.

Mary is on her feet, but Dr Polidori stops her with an officious hand. 'Our friend has had a fit of the nerves, I think. Too much agitation. Allow me to see to him.'

'Poor Shiloh,' Byron says shakily, watching Polidori go. 'I didn't mean to succeed that well. Has he been sleeping lately?'

'About as much as usual,' Mary says.

'Less, I'd say.' From Claire.

Something in Mary snaps. 'What do you know about it?'

'We've all been trapped indoors too long, I think,' Byron says – peaceably, yet with a dark twinkle of amusement.

'I thank God that *I've* got strong nerves,' Claire says, with satisfaction, plumping herself into the vacated seat next to Byron, and searching for his hand. But she does not find it.

Polidori tells Mary: 'He is sleeping. I have given him ether. A curiously excitable constitution. He uses no stimulants?'

471

'No, no.' Mary can't imagine it: Shelley gets drunk on existence. 'Why did he – he seemed to fear me.'

Polidori's eyes devour her: or, at least, courteously nibble. 'Again, the excitability. Too great a power of association. He said that the witch-tale made him think of a story he had heard once, about a woman who had eyes where – pardon me – where the nipples should be. On the breasts,' he adds superfluously.

'How horrible.' Mary pulls herself together. The dressing room is lit only by a single candle, and her flush must be undetectable: surely. 'Of course a physiological impossibility. Thank you, Dr Polidori, for taking care of him.'

'This was no more than any physician would do. I was glad, however, to be on hand. While he recovered, he talked, and I flatter myself I have a sympathetic ear. Mr Shelley is, I believe, much exercised by the question of his wife. I believe the name,' he goes on relentlessly, 'is Harriet.'

'Yes – you are correct, Harriet Shelley, Mrs Shelley, I have met her, in London,' says Mary, gustily.

'I think it is a great sorrow to him that they could not agree.'

'It is always a pity,' Mary says, wrigglingly uncomfortable: his gaze on her is like wet clothes clinging. 'Whenever this happens – but you well know, sir, Mr Shelley's views and mine, about the relation between men and women. If love has ended, then it is a nonsense for them to remain shackled together.'

'Certainly a courageous philosophy. Severely rational. It impresses me. But must it not rest upon a mutual cooling of affection? Suppose that for one party love has *not* ended?'

'I don't see what this has to do with Mr Shelley's health. May I see him now?'

'Oh, Polidori is a great deal of a fool, and a little of an honest man,' Shelley says the next day, and bounds down to the lakeside in the rain. 'Come on – run with me.'

'Shelley – wait. Are you quite recovered?'

'Better than that.' He turns and catches her in his arms, kissing her wet face. 'I am not only restored, I am improved. The good doctor did not let blood, but I feel as if I have been relieved of some. Bad blood. Come on.'

Laughing he tugs her in his hectic wake. Rain and wind snatch her gasping breath: otherwise the lake might have heard her scream, the scream of ultimate bafflement. How can you love someone so much, and not understand them at all?

The nightmare.

Dreams only live in sleep. Haul them up into the waking air, and they flap, flex, and glassily die. But still: they can be used, sometimes. Sometimes, they are food.

Mary – she has never told anyone this – has often had abnormally vivid dreams of reading. She has never told anyone because it seems such a homely occupation for the dream-world, where traditionally one rides naked or flies from steeples; but these dreams delight and frustrate her. The pages she sleep-reads are spellbinding narratives in which she is partially inserted: she half spectates, half participates. And in the morning she cannot recall a word of them. The nightmare has something in common with this. It takes place in front of her eyes, but she does not merely look on: she is involved in some way that she cannot grasp. There is a room like a chemist's. The figure at work among the apparatus is tall, slender, fungus-pale, with a scholar's high shoulders: like Shelley? But she cannot see the face. The scholarly figure knows she is there: she has made some sort of assent that binds her here, compromises her: it troubles her. Trouble fastens itself to the great shape visible among the rods and membranes, becomes tongue-swelling dread and panic because the shape is dead flesh becoming alive. This is the wrong way, her dream-mind says and repeats, but such momentum now, the momentum of life unstoppable and undeniable as the quickening in the womb. This is the wrong way, and she flees, and soon she is half looking, half being again in a dark bedchamber, away from that stirred and questing shape. In the curtained bed, the thin figure, scholar, creator, author of this outrageous woe, stretched out in uneasy rest: alone? No: she is in the bed too, her dream-hand knows the feel of the tumbled black hair, and she too stares abjectly up as the bed-curtains are slowly parted and the great living shape, wrong, wrong, looms and fills the space and unglues at their two selves a yellow, new-seeing eye.

Byron, the next morning: 'Have you thought of a story?'
    Tentatively she says, 'Yes, I think I have.'
    He nods, quite unsurprised.

Places we cannot go – for even Mary hardly knows how she gets there: not the physical place, the rickety writing-table at Montalègre with Shelley's Virgil propping one corner and a cockchafer whirring in the window-casement: but the place she inhabits, in thinking suspense, as she dips her pen: a place lit by strange brain-stars, blown about by cross-winds of memory. One of these gusts brings her something from the time of her elopement with Shelley – the Rhine-journey home – a place-name, heard, seen, Gothically inscribed on a sign or handbill? No matter: take hold of it. *Frankenstein*. Keep that. Other winds whirl: she turns her mind about.
    Now we must leave her.

The weather relents, just a little. Shelley and Byron depart on a sailing-trip together round the lake: they will be gone a week. 'You men,' Claire says, as if that means something, indeed as if it means everything, as if she has long ago plumbed them all to their uttermost depths. After they have gone she stands at the highest window above the dock at Montalègre and watches the cream petal of their sail float away. She sings softly to herself. Mary has never before heard her sing *softly*, even to herself.
    Later she suspects she hears the sound of crying from Claire's room, but she is disinclined to follow it up and carries on writing. I would like Claire much better if I did not have to live

with her, she thinks abruptly; but is disinclined even to follow the thought up. She turns a fresh sheet of paper. Her story is expanding around her, taking up all the room.

The storm is like a hammer and they are the anvil. Mary sits up in bed, watching the wildness at the window, until there is such a bright lightning-stroke she feels as if her eyeballs have been scribbled on with a cold metallic pen. She goes to check on William: sleeping untroubled. Their new Swiss nursemaid, cool-headed handsome Elise, is to Mary's surprise trembling and muttering prayers at each smack of thunder: you'd think her used to it.

Then, as Mary gets back into bed, the thunder makes a noise beyond noise, taking over the world for half a stunning minute, and at the end of it she sees nightgowned Claire stiff and beseeching in the doorway.

'Mary – I can't bear it—'

Mary nods. 'Come – come then.'

Claire makes an anguished tittuping dart across the floor-boards, as if dodging the lightning-bolts, and jumps into bed with Mary.

She lies there shivering in Mary's arms, which she has somehow got Mary to put round her. Lightning reveals them to each other in moments of fabulous detail. There is a film of perspiration on Claire's forehead. Mary puts up a hand and smooths away the torrid curls.

'You're so pretty,' Claire says timidly.

'No. You are.'

'Me?' Claire's eyes widen. 'I always thought – I always thought that *you* thought–' she giggles uncertainly '–that I was a fright.'

'You know what thought did.'

'No, what?'

'I forget. Some wise old saw about thinking being bad for you.'

'Well, it is. I hope they're safe out there.'

'They've probably gone ashore on the south side by now. To

475

explore the Rousseau country. Shelley's been reading *La Nouvelle Heloïse.*'

'I think Rousseau's a beast in many ways, don't you? Those coquettish heroines, only there to please men. I have no wish to be a mere *object* of passion.'

'Better to be a subject of passion,' Mary murmurs.

'You're so slim too,' Claire says, burrowing closer as the shutters rattle again.

'So are you.'

'I'm not,' Claire says quietly. 'Feel here.'

'That's just . . .' What? Claire never overeats. Mary, hand on Claire's belly, counts several blinks before she can speak. 'Did you miss your courses?'

'Ages ago.' Claire stiffens into a gnawing silence. A savage gash of thunder splits the sky overhead. Rain begins, spectral archers firing over the lake. 'The other morning – at Diodati – I was sick before I could stop it. Soiled the bedsheet. Mary – don't say anything to anyone. Please.'

'Very well.' Mary takes her hand away, finds it grabbed by Claire's, hot and clammy. 'But you know – sooner or later—'

'Then later.' Claire's jaw works. 'I know it's just an affair. I know he doesn't love me.' A slow tear ploughs down her cheek. She squeezes Mary's hand, then releases it and shifts a little away. Thunder booms bombastically, flagging. Claire adds: 'I mean Byron, of course.'

'Disgusting.' Anonymous British tourist at the Hôtel d'Angleterre, training a telescope (the canny hotelkeeper is hiring them out for just this purpose) on the Villa Diodati across the lake. He can just make out the clean bed-linen airing on the balcony.

'What is it?' Anonymous wife tugs his sleeve.

'Women's petticoats. Several of them.'

'Where are the women?'

'Ah.' He shakes his head. 'Within, no doubt. Going naked.

Disgusting. It's true what they say about that set. A league of incest, and worse.'

'What could be worse?'

'Ah, you never know.' He raises the telescope again.

'May I see?'

'In a moment, my love, in a moment.'

'You've turned shy,' Shelley says to Mary quizzically in their bedchamber, on the first night of his return.

'No.' She pushes the weather-stained coat off his shoulders, pushes him on to the bed, straddles his lap, kissing him. 'Is this shy?'

'At the dock, then. You only pecked me on the cheek. Are you angry with me?'

'Is this angry?' Presently, holding his head on her breast, she says, 'Because of Claire. Because of the kiss she would not get from Albé.'

'Aha.' He kisses her fingers. 'Kind in you. Especially—'

'Especially when I can't bear her for much of the time. But then I can't bear myself for much of the time . . . Did you and Albé talk of her?'

'Not much,' he says: unhappy admission. 'It's not that he doesn't care for her—'

'It's just that he doesn't care for her very much. Shelley, she's pregnant.'

'Yes.' He nods. 'Well, so one gathers.'

They have talked of it, Mary thinks. You men. Still, she feels a sting at being the last to know.

'He is a curious fellow,' Shelley says lying back, gleaming and pale. 'At one point we got caught in a squall near the rocks. The waves came over the boat, we were awash, and then we found the rudder had cracked, and so – so I thought this was death. And I sat down to wait for it in whatever spirit I could manage – only I could see Byron measuring the distance to shore with his eyes, quite unperturbed. Of course this is a man who swam the

Hellespont. No doubt he could have swum to safety with ease, and was probably calculating how he might pull me along with him. The odd thing is that I almost dreaded this more than drowning.'

'Why?'

He shrugs, smiles, face turned a little away from her. 'If I could say why, it wouldn't be odd . . . We must talk about what we are going to do. About Claire.'

'Yes,' she says: and her heart sinks so deeply at that word 'we' she can hardly believe it is not audible, like a bucket in a well.

Another trip: this time up to Chamonix: this time Shelley, Mary and Claire. Byron stays at the Villa Diodati, wishing to be alone.

'But he won't be alone,' Claire protests, 'with Dr Polidori there.'

'We shall see the *mer de glace*,' Shelley promises her, 'and that drives out every other thought, they say.'

They do. Mary feels as if she needs another mind, just as one needs two hands. How else to contain the ever-growing story she brings in her portmanteau, and the trouble with Claire, which is caught up like spillikins with her and Shelley and Wilmouse and Byron and her stepmother and her father, *and* this?

This is the world of ice, remote peaks, primeval rocks: nakedness, brute bulk, sick-turning perspectives: sublimity. They have all made free with that word before, but for all their talkative definitions Mary realizes she has simply thought of it as another type of beauty. Wrong. She is too dwarfed and diminished by it for that. The ripples in the glacier are the size of villages, yet the dumbfounded mind still perceives them as ripples: it is all it can do. Here there are new colours, or conceptions of colours: the glaring whiteness of ice and snow is like some unsuspected sensory impression, like heat or hunger. If the crags above the vapour are grey, then she has only ever had a dim comprehension of what grey is. This is the colour mixed, she thinks, by the first painter in the first days. The religious tone of the thought catches her by surprise. Living with Shelley, one thinks of God like the slave trade or the Tory Home Secretary. She keeps the erring wonder to herself.

Fortunate: as Shelley, though dazzled and stricken and for a long time wordless as Mary, comes to a different conclusion. Here he has found his confirmation: there is no God.

'That desolation,' he mutters, as they warm themselves around the great open fire in the hotel-lodge at Montavert. 'There's your symbol. Not cross or crescent. The way the ice breaks those great pine-trees. No stopping it. That hostility. Yet it isn't – that's just it, we have to give it our human word, because even that makes it better, to imagine enmity, to say the world hates us when it really doesn't. It's just everlastingly indifferent. No feeling. And meanwhile the ice creeps forward. Inch by inch.'

'I feel as if it's creeping over me,' says Claire, tired and unhappy, and almost unrecognizable because of it.

'So it is,' says Shelley excitedly. Ideas can make him heartless. 'Over you and me and all we love. Those rocks – think of the limitless ages they've seen. And that will go on, and on. Eventually, some say, the whole earth will be lifeless and desolate and even the sun will go out.'

Claire stares at him as if he had pronounced an obscenity. 'Why should the sun go out?'

Shelley smiles: still unconsciously cruel. 'Is there any such thing as a candle that lasts for ever?'

'It's horrible. Stop it.'

'Oh, I can't stop the process, no one can.' Suddenly he takes in Claire's haunted expression and becomes at once the Shelley Mary fell in love with, beautifully, and alas. With the tenderest impulsiveness he puts his arm round Claire's shoulders. 'That's why we must all keep together, all of us. We are all we have.'

In the hotel register, Shelley writes in Greek under the heading 'Occupation', the three words 'Democrat, Philanthropist, Atheist.'

And under the heading 'Destination', in French: 'Hell.' Mary has seldom seen him so cheerful.

Return to Geneva, Mary carrying seeds of Alpine plants in her bag, landscapes of ice in her mind, her story still kicking at her like a child in the womb. Shelley has read it so far, heaps praises, urges her on. He is full of ideas himself: they scribble companionably. Everything should be perfect.

Everything should be perfect, but there is Claire: if Mary were the sampler-stitching kind, she would embroider those words and frame them.

'Why didn't Albé want me there?' she asks Shelley, after he and Claire return from a conference at the Villa Diodati. Claire has gone silently upstairs. 'It can't be that he fears to offend my maiden modesty.'

Shelley's look is constrained: he doesn't like that kind of joking. 'There were matters to be discussed,' he says vaguely, getting down on the hearthrug with William. 'To do with Claire's condition. And you as her stepsister – almost sister really—'

'Not really. Does Albé doubt the child is his?'

'God, no.' A little too prompt, Mary thinks: but she will let it pass. 'No, no, the discussion was about how the child is to be brought up. Claire – I'm glad to say Claire didn't adopt an unrealistic position, at last. Byron has made it plain from the beginning that he wants no permanent liaison – with anyone.'

And least of all with Claire, Mary thinks. And how did Claire manage to accept such terms, and carry on? Was it really out of rivalry for me? In which case, all this, all this trouble and pain I see coming, is my fault. There's a comfortable thought for you.

'Byron will acknowledge the child, and see to its upbringing,' Shelley goes on, doing conjurer's passes with a shilling piece in front of William's absorbed eyes. 'The suggestion is that the child spend the first seven years with one parent, probably here on the Continent. It will not be placed in the care of any stranger. The birth is to be in England. All this took some thrashing out.' Mary, noticing the shadows under his eyes, can imagine: Shelley the well-wisher ground between the egotistical wheels of Byron and Claire.

'The birth in England,' Mary says. 'Where and how?'

For a moment Shelley does not answer. He puts the shilling into William's curious hand. 'See how he turns it over to examine it. Seeing both sides. Oh, yes, you'll do well, Wilmouse. English money – odd, it makes me quite homesick. Mary, she must stay with us. Where else? I doubt your father would welcome her. And besides, she is one of us – part of us – isn't she?'

'Is she?' Mary must have said it out loud, but he doesn't seem to have heard.

'I told Byron that I would gladly take the responsibility of looking after her and the child, through her confinement, and until things are settled between them. Claire is happy with that.'

'Oh, I'm sure she is.'

He regards her sadly from the rug, with eyes identical to William's. Two innocents: she the cawing crow on her perch of bitterness.

'There are letters from home,' he says. 'I'll show you. Not good. The lawyers passing on the latest delights from my father. He'll block every penny due to me unless I return to England. I'll have to go back, if only to fight him. Also from Skinner Street. Your father still demands more money. I must confess he – he is not what I thought him.'

'Which of us is?' Mary says. 'Well, then, home it must be. I don't mind that.'

'And Claire with us?'

'If I really minded that,' she says finally, 'then that would make me a monster. Wouldn't it?'

'It's all a great pity, but she knew what to expect,' Byron tells Mary. 'In London she stalked me to my lair, and there I told her precisely what I felt and didn't feel. Did I not have a care for her reputation? I did, but it was nugatory. Her reputation was already quite sunk by her association with you and Shelley, and she very plainly said she didn't give a damn anyhow. Now we have the inevitable result, and must see to the practicalities as best we can.'

'You're actually quite old-fashioned, aren't you, Albé?'

He looks braced by her, as by a gust of fresh air. 'I'm glad we understand each other. When do you go? I shall miss you.'

'No, you won't.'

A letter comes from Skinner Street, from Fanny. Mary and Claire, reading over it, come to one of their rare moments of unanimity.

'Poor Fanny,' Claire says.

'Yes. Poor Fanny. It sounds grim.'

Pious, dull, dependable, Fanny is weathering the emotional storms of Skinner Street, where debts multiply in Godwin's impractical hands, and the Clairmont, temper souring with every wrinkle, lashes out in all directions, but usually Fanny's. It is typical of Fanny – even exasperatingly so – that she gives an account of all this without feeling in the least sorry for herself. She seems to expect no better in life. All she asks is for news of the exciting Lord Byron, a little vicarious thrill, no more; and to be remembered.

'I just wish she had more spirit,' Claire says.

'I don't suppose she ever will now. We should take her a gift. Something special.'

At a jeweller's in Geneva, city of locked gates and scrubbed sills, goldsmiths and instrument-makers, they hover over bracelets and lockets.

'But what could she *put* in a locket?' Claire remarks, her hand absently cupping her belly. 'Whose picture – whose hair? You see the difficulty. Tsk. Poor Fanny.' Now the words are like a curse of impatience.

'That watch is pretty. Practical too. I think she would like that.'

'So she can look at it and see just how *very* slow the time goes when you're an old maid.'

'We'll take the watch.'

Claire gives a gold locket a lingering look. Well, Mary thinks, he won't give you his picture or hair either.

The gates of Geneva swing open for the morning coach to Dijon. On board, Mary, Shelley and Claire, with Elise and Wilmouse: in the sky, the sun that will one day go out like a candle, now shining brilliantly and sending valedictory glints from the summits of the Jura: in Shelley's portmanteau, entrusted to him by Byron for delivery to eagerly waiting Mr Murray in Albemarle Street, the new cantos of *Childe Harold*: in Mary's, her yet unfinished story. In the coach besides, a freight of memories, passions, fears, enough to make it lurch and sway without the unevenness of the cobbles.

'Goodbye, my darling,' Claire whispers, her face pressed against the window-glass: then sinks back with wet eyes closed. 'Thank God I have you.' With her eyes shut it is impossible to tell who she means – Mary, Shelley, or both. Though Mary has her own ideas.

Everything is not going to be all right.

It was difficult to tell at what point, during her summer stay in London, Augusta began to believe this new, hard, salt-dry creed. But the transition was certainly made, oh, yes: and it was as irreversible as the loss of virginity.

Probably it was the money at last. And not the talk of money, dispiriting as that was: the endless fruitless negotiations over the prospect of an official post for George, and how the debts were to be met out of it if it came, and how the house at Six Mile Bottom was to be sold, and what it would leave them. What it came down to – perhaps, she thought, it always did – was cash. After paying the dressmaker's bill for the court gown she had to wear for Princess Mary's wedding, Augusta found she had very little. When she had paid for her letters, a hackney, and a dinner, she had none at all. And George's banker, she found, would not honour the draft he had given her. She sat in her apartment at St James's, sniffing dust, staring into the empty grate, and thinking: I live in a palace and I have not a penny. For a delirious few minutes she pictured seeking an audience with the Queen and asking her for the loan of ten shillings.

Theresa Villiers pressed the sovereigns into Augusta's hand, folding Augusta's fingers over the coins. A dramatic gesture: her old friend was full of these lately, much more Thérèse than Theresa.

'I can't thank you enough.'

'No, no.' Theresa shook her head, returning to her seat in a peculiar stiff-backed floating way. It reminded Augusta of something. 'These are small matters in the great scale of things.'

'Not when you realize you can't re-use the same tea-leaves any more.'

Theresa did not smile. She seemed to have got out of the habit. 'Have you heard from Lady Byron lately?'

'Oh, yes. She is kind enough to write very frequently.' The last letter had been so long Augusta had had to put it down and refresh herself with the pale thrice-brewed tea before carrying on reading. The matter was exacting too. Annabella was taking her very seriously in hand.

'And – *him*?'

'My brother?' Augusta said, trying to ignore the sepulchral emphasis, wondering again who it reminded her of. 'I had a letter a few – a little while ago.' She couldn't remember how long it was, though she could feel the hurt.

'And you still communicate with him?'

'As far as I am able,' Augusta said uneasily. 'Why?'

'Oh, my dear, I am just a little surprised. I don't allude to these reports of his behaviour abroad. A ménage with two women, one of them dressed as a man, they say. I pay no heed to such things. But you know I have had the pleasure of Lady Byron's acquaintance, indeed friendship–' Ah, thought Augusta, that's who you remind me of '–and I have been impressed, deeply impressed, by her sufferings. And by the way she has risen above them – pursuing the spirit of true Christian redemption.'

Augusta said sincerely, 'Oh, yes, she is a very good woman.'

'I'm glad you see it, Augusta. From the talks Lady Byron and I have had – I did begin to fear you might be lost to such impressions. From your association with *him*.'

Again the tomby boom. Awkwardly, Augusta said, 'I have always tried not to take sides. I have the greatest sympathy for Annabella, but still Byron is my brother. Now that it is over—'

'But, my dear Augusta, it isn't over. You know he is the talk of the town again since this book of Lady Caroline Lamb's—'

'A very silly spiteful woman,' Augusta said stoutly, 'and not at all a good writer. I do think rather poorly of Byron for ever confiding in her but, then, we all do foolish things in love.'

Theresa gave her a pitying look.

'Well, *I* do, at any rate,' Augusta said, with a limp laugh.

'It is far from over,' Theresa said, mournfully shaking her head. 'My dear, don't you see? You have admitted to me that you still write to him. This is as much to say you are *unchanged* towards him.' Theresa's cheeks grew pink. 'In spite of what is *known*.'

'I'm not sure what is known,' Augusta said, her tongue curiously dry and thick in her mouth. 'I'm aware that all sorts of rumours have been flying around ever since the separation. But now that Caroline Lamb is being such a noisy bore again, one wonders how many of them come from her.'

'But has Lady Byron not suggested to you the worse possibility? My dear friend, don't you think that it was Byron himself who . . .' Theresa closed her eyes for a moment: pure Annabella '. . . who *betrayed* you?'

'I don't know what you mean,' Augusta said. How small her voice sounded. She would have been fiercer, but there was the money: besides, would her old friend say such a thing if there were no truth in it? She didn't know what to think. She didn't want to think. She closed her own eyes in sudden weariness, and when she opened them found that Theresa had stolen close to her, with a look of profounder pity.

'I know, my dear, I know,' she said, patting Augusta's hand. 'It is terrible to think of. But look on it as a necessary stage.'

Annabella was coming to London. Augusta wanted to see her. She put off a return to Six Mile Bottom, though her turn of duty at Court was over and George was begging for her return. She couldn't say why seeing Annabella was so important to her. Perhaps it was something to do with certainty. She had so little of it: Annabella had so much.

And then there was what Theresa had hinted. Though Augusta put it away, in the place in her mind where she penned recalcitrant thoughts, it kept breaking out. The only solution was the truth, and for that she trusted Annabella. Annabella *was* truth, Augusta thought. That was what made her so fascinating, and so difficult.

Annabella was just as eager to see Augusta. There was much that they needed to say to one another, she wrote, that could not be properly said in a letter. She would call upon her sister-in-law at her chambers in St James's Palace. The announcement sent Augusta into a flurry of tidying and cleaning and riffling her wardrobe. She changed in front of the mirror a dozen times. It was almost as if she were expecting a lover.

Then, just before Annabella's arrival, two letters. Pieces of paper, Augusta thought: how they can affect our lives. What would it be like if paper had never been invented? Better, perhaps. One was from a money-lender, full of veiled unpleasantness. The other was from George, reporting that he was off north to a shooting-party, as she did not choose to return home to her family. Augusta Charlotte had had another fit: the apothecary had raised the question of confining her in an asylum. George could not cope. And the kitchen-maid had given notice. Really, old girl: expect better of you.

Augusta wept. She had never known such a crying-fit. It was like falling into water rather than weeping it. How long, how loud, she couldn't tell. But her face was plainly ravaged by it when Annabella arrived.

'My dear Augusta.' Annabella seemed to choose the words after reviewing a number of alternatives. She looked irreproachably slender, clear-skinned, ringleted, neat in unadorned white lawn: you could imagine she had been just unwrapped from a box full of tissue-paper. 'If I have chosen an unhappy time to call, I can very easily go away again.' She sat down.

'No, no.' Augusta scrubbed at her face. 'Don't go. I'm so very glad to see you – I've been feeling so dreadful. I beg your pardon – this is not what you wish to hear—'

'Oh, my dear, but it is,' said Annabella, in her most thrilling organ-like tone; and Augusta was lost. She sank down opposite her, with a final heart-fetching sob.

'It's just – oh, so many things – and I've always tried to keep cheerful but now I can't – all I can think is, I must have been a very wicked person for all this to happen.'

Annabella reached out and took Augusta's hand between her own. Her great clear dollish eyes fixed Augusta's: her breath had a strange sickly sweetness.

'My dear Augusta, I'm afraid that is the truth.'

Augusta looked down at her sandwiched hand. She couldn't speak: or rather she didn't want to, she was content to abdicate the responsibility of speech. Let Annabella do it: she was much better at it: she was much better all round.

'But now that you see it,' Annabella went on, 'there is hope. Do you understand me, Augusta? I have tried in my letters to convey to you just how much I know and how I came to know it. I realize these are unhappy things for you to contemplate. For they involve not only the recognition of your own sin – and it is, believe me, my dear, a grave and imperilling sin, one that I *must* as a Christian try to save you from – but the sins of another. One whom we do not name. One who has I fear not only corrupted you, but has made a public boast of it.'

'No,' Augusta said. She tried to withdraw her hand, but

Annabella kept her tight, fond hold. 'No, he would not.'

Annabella sighed. 'This is what I feared. That you are still – to some degree – in his power. For your own peace, my dear, you must learn to see him differently. How else do you suppose your secret was noised abroad?'

'I don't know,' Augusta murmured. 'Oh, Bella, you know I don't like to think ill of *anyone*—'

'I know it,' Annabella said, with a smile of sombre humour, 'oh, I know it. I'm afraid that is what made it easier for him to corrupt you. Was it not so? My dear, I can't think – I can't bear to think that it was you who was the corrupter.'

'No . . . I don't think so.'

'The proverb says that confession is good for the soul. And you will find it so, my dear, believe me. If you are suffering now, it is because of that guilty burden – and I can't bear to see you suffering so, Augusta, really I can't, especially when it may be in my power to help you. You can yet be saved, my dear. But there must be a change. Do you dare it? Will you dare it with me, Augusta?'

'I don't know – yes – oh, Bella, you must help me.'

Annabella cast her eyes up thankfully. 'I have so wanted to hear you say that. I thank God for this opportunity. I shall help you, my dear, I shall make it the aim of my existence.'

'Oh, you needn't do that,' Augusta said, with a weak laugh: then saw at once that was wrong. She corrected her face.

'No effort is too great for such a task. I won't say it's a matter of life or death, my dear, because of course you know–' now it was Annabella's turn to laugh, a kind of otherworldly gasp '–you know it goes beyond that, my dear, to the salvation of your eternal *soul*.'

Augusta shivered. For a moment poor noble Grandmother was before her again, her cancered face, her spotless spirit.

'If I have been wrong – so very wrong,' she faltered, 'then I am truly sorry for it. Really, Bella, I never meant to hurt anyone . . .'

Annabella was patiently shaking her head. 'My dear. I see we must go into this thoroughly. Your principles have become rather mixed up. We must always repent the sin itself, not its consequences – the offence against God, not the offence against others. Do you see? And a sinful thought is just as bad as a sinful deed. Just because that – that association is broken does not mean that you are out of danger. You must scrutinize your heart, when you hear his name, when you recall his face, when you read – above all when you read his communications.'

'He does not communicate much,' Augusta said sadly.

'Ah! But he still does – and, oh, my dear, how revealing that you *regret* his neglect.'

'Well, of course I do.' Augusta was finding Annabella's stare uncomfortable: she looked vaguely away and said, 'Tea – how remiss of me, I haven't offered you any tea—'

'Damn the tea,' Annabella burst out, crushing Augusta's hand: then, exhaling that pearlike sweetness, 'but do not damn yourself, my dear Augusta. Consider what must be done. Are you not taking refuge in a pretence? The pretence of a natural, sisterly affection, and no more than that. When in truth—'

'I can't just abandon *all* feelings for my brother,' Augusta said, pulling her hand from Annabella's grasp. It almost seemed to tear the skin. 'Surely that would be just as unnatural as – it would be unnatural.'

Annabella sat back with a sigh, then rose, decisively. 'I was wrong,' she said, on her way to the door. 'Forgive me. I had thought you ready for these things.'

'Bella, wait. I *am* ready – I mean, I want to know what I should do for the best.'

Annabella presented her high-shouldered back for a few moments: then turned. 'Do you, Augusta? Do you really want to know? Because there can be no half measures. And, my dear, I know you have a *tendency* to those: yes?' She allowed a small smile. 'The tendency has led you into great difficulty.'

'I'm afraid it has,' Augusta said wretchedly.

'Well, no more. I will help you to a better way, my dear.

Harder, it may seem, but, oh, so much better.' Annabella came back and seated herself. 'I believe I will have that tea in a moment.'

'I'll go and see to—'

'In a moment, I said, my dear. You see, Augusta, you are still evading: what *shall* I do with you? Well. You say he does not communicate often.'

'No – though I have written and written to him. But, then, I dare say, with him travelling about—'

'My poor love.' Annabella imprisoned her hand again. 'How you give yourself away. There is one way to be free of that pain, Augusta. You know it. I set before you your only chance. You must sever yourself from him entirely, and for ever.'

For a minute Augusta withdrew her attention from Annabella and listened to the noises beyond: the clock above the courtyard gate chiming the quarter-hour, the chocking sound of a horse being led out to exercise, somewhere a mild coo of pigeons. Somehow these seemed to her the last pleasant sounds she would ever hear.

'How am I to do it?' she said at last.

'You must maintain the strictest vigilance on your heart, my dear. If you allow yourself even one kind thought about him, you are betraying yourself. You are betraying me. You are betraying your God.'

In Augusta's mind, Grandmother turned her terrible swollen face on the pillow. Kind pale dying eyes quizzed her. How would this troublesome granddaughter of hers get along without her guidance? Would she be good?

Augusta nodded. 'I shall try,' she whispered.

'Very well,' Annabella said. 'Now when you write to him – as, of course, you must in order not to arouse his suspicions – it must only be on the commonest topics, and in the most neutral tone possible. And everything he writes to you, you had better show me.'

'Everything?'

'If I am to protect you, Augusta, then nothing must be hidden. You know nothing is hidden from God. Even if you suppress your feelings, God sees them. It is for that reason that suppression is not enough. You must kill them. You must kill your feelings for Byron.'

His name, Augusta thought in a dazed way, his name: I leap at it, and I mustn't, this must be the last time.

'One feeling only you may retain, and that is forgiveness,' Annabella went on. 'That, of course, is your duty.'

'Is that what you feel for him, Bella?'

'Oh, my dear, my feelings are not at issue.' Annabella now gathered both Augusta's hands – hot, plump, restless hands – into her own delicate cool ones, and did not let them go. 'You must think of me as your guardian angel.'

4

Fault Lines

Bath: it was, Mary thought, the most unShelleyan place imaginable, with its slightly outmoded gentility, its tea-table gossip, its tribe of half-pay officers and clergymen and twittering spinsters living on three per cents. The lodgings he found for them were right next to the Pump Room itself – the nexus of fashionable vacuity. ('They talk about bonnets,' she told Shelley in bewilderment, after trying out the morning Pump Room parade: never again.) But it was, of course, a healthful spot, and discreet in that it was a long way from London and the Godwins, and no one knew them here. Discretion: because of Claire, visibly and grumpily pregnant. It's because of Claire that I'm here, Mary thought, drifting in the parasol promenade of dullness along Milsom Street, then groaned inwardly: even her own enmity bored her.

At first Claire went out a good deal: she was loud in her determination not to let pregnancy inhibit her. Then she came back crying. 'I have been stared at by six old tabbies today,' she wailed, flopping heavily down in the fireside chair. 'Two in Sydney Gardens, two in the circulating-library, one in the colonnade and one in the damned bloody double-damned Abbey Churchyard.'

'That's what old tabbies are for,' said Mary.

She meant to soothe: she failed.

'You have no feeling – none at all,' Claire cried, glaring hate through her tears.

'Mary feels for you just as I do,' Shelley intervened. 'What she means is that these stares are inevitable with society still stuck in superstitious ignorance. We are pioneers, Claire, leading the way into new territory, and I'm afraid that means the going is rough. You can bear it, though: I know you can.'

Claire was soothed. Mary's feelings: admiration: thankfulness that the wailing was over: envy at her own incapacity: jealousy at Shelley's rapport with Claire: irritation that he *could* always manage her, instead of being unable to, which would make their cohabitation intolerable, which would mean Claire would have to go: and guilt for most of these feelings. Not bad for a Tuesday afternoon. Thank God for her work. Mary sat down at the desk to the sound of portcullises and drawbridges.

The curious thing was, she understood Claire entirely. Even when she found Claire going through Shelley's letters, and turned furiously on her, she understood. Claire still hoped for a letter from Byron, though she would not get one: failing that, she would ransack Byron's letters to Shelley for references to herself, even if they were not pleasant, or, worse, if there were none at all. Mary understood because she would have done the same. Understanding did not prevent the vicious quarrel, which ended with Claire smashing a glass paperweight and running in tears to Shelley. Not bad for a Thursday morning.

Shelley said to Mary, after several hesitations: 'I wish you could be kinder to her.'

'I am as kind as it is in my nature to be. And that is, actually, quite kind: I believe I am capable of being rather a decent person all round, if I were only given a chance. If I could only live somewhere, not grand, quiet and near water, and with *you* and you only—'

'Mary, I've told you, we'll find somewhere after the winter, somewhere along the Thames.'

'We. The mysterious plural.'

'I've made the decision to shelter Claire as long as she needs us. Would you really have me go back on that? I can't believe it.

493

That's not you. All I ask is that you remember her difficult situation.'

'I'm hardly likely to forget it. Oh, why did she have to go after Byron so? And why did he have to tire of her so? Mind, *that* I understand. I'm horrible today, Shelley: I know it.'

'You're a little cross,' he said mildly.

'Oh, well, if you want domestic harmony you should have picked Fanny instead of me.'

'That rather sounds as if I inspected the Godwin ladies and then made my choice.' His voice was light: his face stony.

'I told you I was horrible. She worshipped you, you know.'

Shelley looked startled. 'Did she?'

Fanny, poor Fanny as one automatically called her, was much in her mind lately. Several letters from her had come from Skinner Street, more pained and gloomy than ever. She said she could not see the point in anything. This seemed to Mary quite a reasonable response to living with the Clairmont. And though Fanny's tone of uncomplaining complaint still annoyed her, she could not help thinking – now and then – of how less difficult life might have been if Fanny had been the confidante and conspirator of their elopement instead of Claire.

But, of course, Fanny would never have done it: she was too conventional, too cowed by home. Which shows how alike Claire and I really are, Mary thought: bleak conclusion. She pulled up the drawbridge again.

Metaphorical drawbridge: and metaphors can only do so much. The news could not be kept out, nor the letter, the letter from Fanny with its strange disjointed phrases about reaching her last destination.

'Shelley, look.' Mary passed the letter across. 'It's marked from Bristol. What on earth would Fanny be doing in Bristol?'

'Fanny? I don't believe it,' Claire said. 'She was always frightened even to go to Baggnige Wells on a Sunday walk. Think of that!' She laughed with satisfaction.

'She talks of never moving from this spot.' Mary watched Shelley's face. 'Do you think—'

Shelley was on his feet: the breakfast-things went flying. 'Oh, God.' He gripped his hair: he was white. 'God, I must go and find her.'

'She doesn't say where she is—'

'I'll search. That is not the letter of someone in their right mind. Where do the Bristol coaches leave? Is it the White Hart?'

'Oh, Shelley, it's cold,' Claire cried. 'Don't take cold – you'll need your hat.' Shelley never wore a hat. Just like her mother, Mary thought: anything to be talking. And: God, I know what's going to happen.

Shelley came back from Bristol, exhausted, at two in the morning. 'No news. I've asked everywhere I can think of. Nothing. But Bristol's such a big place.' Standing, hollow-eyed, he swigged cold tea. 'I wish I liked beer.'

'Perhaps she's going across to Ireland,' Claire said. 'Mary, didn't your mother have connections there? I'll bet that's it. Yes, that's it. Oh, I felt a kick – I swear that was a kick. Shelley, come and feel – just here.'

He did so, wearily. 'I can't feel anything. I'll have a doze – go back tomorrow at first light.'

'Not there – you felt the wrong place.' With compressed lips Claire watched him collapse on the sofa. She snorted. 'All this for Fanny!'

The news: three days later. Shelley had extended his search to Swansea, and came back from there in a rainstorm, tenderly cradling a local newspaper inside his coat.

Detailed report of mysterious suicide at the Mackworth Arms Inn, Swansea. Mary read it with Claire reading over her shoulder. At some point Claire's quick breath went away.

An unknown young woman, travelling alone and giving no name, had taken a room at the inn, secured the door, and

495

proceeded to swallow a fatal dose of laudanum. At her side she had left a note, with the signature erased, saying it was her intention to put an end to a life that had begun unfortunately, and had been only a cause of pain to those who had tried to promote her welfare. The young woman carried nothing that might serve to identify her, but her stays were embroidered with the initials M.W., and she wore a gold watch of Swiss make.

Claire had retreated to the fire, sat staring into it, holding her belly grimly as if to protect it from something, something that had got into the house.

'M.W.?' she said.

'Our mother's initials,' Mary said. Our mother. Fanny, my only true sister — well, half-sister: still closer than anyone except her father, closer than Claire: dead. Now we must see how we feel: now we must climb a new mountain.

'Lord. Those stays lasted well,' Claire remarked.

Wonder of wonders: Mary's father, for the first time since she had eloped with Shelley, wrote her a letter.

A letter brimming with caution. Godwin urged Mary, and through her Shelley and Claire, not to go to Swansea to claim Fanny's body or arrange a funeral. Unidentified, she would be quietly given a parish burial: if they involved themselves, then all the scandal of suicide would attach to them. And there had been, Godwin hinted, quite enough scandal.

'It makes a cold sort of sense,' Shelley said. He had been in sombre but gentle mood since the news: often he came across the drawbridge and worked at *Frankenstein* with her, reading, suggesting, polishing. Such near-perfection, while Claire lamented her swollen feet.

Near-perfection: Shelley's poetry was at last attracting attention. Leigh Hunt, the editor of the Radical *Examiner*, had devoted an issue of the periodical to Young Poets. There he was: Mr Reynolds, Mr Keats, Mr Shelley. And there was an appreciative letter from Hunt too, only a little spoiled by its incidental request for money.

'Oh, he shall have it,' Shelley said cheerfully. 'It's different with Hunt. He's always getting up funds for liberal causes. The relief of prisoners – he's been one himself. They threw him in gaol for libelling the Prince Regent in his paper. One wonders how it's possible to libel the Prince: what bad thing can you say about him that isn't the plain truth? I shall call on him next time I go down to London. He's living at Hampstead. Hunt, not the Prince. Oh, and he wants to print my "Hymn to Intellectual Beauty", only he has lost the manuscript.' He burst out laughing. 'Doesn't this sound like an admirer of mine?'

It was the last time they laughed together, before the next news.

Shelley went down to London in December. He was looking for a house to rent along the Thames Valley. While there he called on Leigh Hunt at Hampstead, dined, stayed, was introduced to Hunt's numerous family and his friend Keats, was delighted at finding himself among kindred souls. He came back to Bath in soaring spirits. The next morning, there was the letter.

Mary was still in bed: they had stayed up late making love and talking. She opened her eyes to find Shelley, up and dressed, wandering about the bedroom with the letter in his hand.

His face.

'Shelley . . . ?'

'From my publisher. I asked him a while ago to look out for Harriet. Because I hadn't heard anything of her lately.' He sat down on the bed: the letter shook in his hand like a fan. 'This is why.'

Another newspaper cutting, this one from *The Times*. Another report of a young woman's suicide, this one by drowning. When life turns strange like this, Mary thought, when it exhibits these striking symmetries, we do not like it: it is too much like art.

Harriet Shelley had been found dead in the Serpentine. She

was pregnant. She had moved out of her parents' home, leaving the children there, and taken lodgings alone. That was all that was known.

'The inquest jury were merciful,' Shelley said. 'They didn't deliver a suicide verdict, so she could be buried decently. Not that that matters to her, of course, as she is dead. Dead, dead.' He seemed to be trying the word out on himself, like a chemist with experimental doses.

'Oh, Shelley.' Mary, after an inexplicable hesitation, put her arms round him.

'I didn't love her any more, but she was the mother of my children, and I still wished her well,' he said tonelessly. 'I would gladly have seen her more, helped her more, but that family of hers wouldn't have it. I always hoped – my one great hope was that she would find a real, true love of her own, such as we have. Well. It seems she found – something.' His voice ran out.

'She must have been – well, not in her right mind,' Mary said against his shoulder: then she stopped too. All words were inadequate. Also she had to take serious charge of herself, because what she must not do, above all, was allow her imagination to work. It was difficult, because she had been cultivating her imagination so intensely through the writing of *Frankenstein*, but from now on she must curb it, she must not let herself picture Harriet (*neat soft brown hair*) and the round belly and the dark winter's night and the fall and plunge (*skirts fluttering floating*) into dark water. She must not. Because – well, because she must continue to live. (*At Harriet's expense.*)

Shelley took the coach to London again the next morning. Mary went with him to the inn-yard. Christmas was only a week away – though they did not celebrate it – and the basket of the carriage was heaped with unplucked fowls. A goose's dead eye inspected her as she reached up to kiss Shelley's cold face. She could almost feel the conflicts going on inside him, like a shaken soda-bottle.

'Mary. The children – it may be odd at first. Difficult. But they will love you—'

'Hush, yes. I'm prepared for whatever – whatever comes.'

He was going to seek custody of his children by Harriet. He was confident: Mary less so. She was sure Harriet's family would contest it, and Shelley's was not a name that any court would look kindly on. What would make the greatest difference to his chances, of course, would be if he regularized his relations with Mary. In other words, marry her. This was all more or less known, more or less unspoken between them. Mary with her deliberate self-discipline managed to suppress any visions of this new future as she did of Harriet's death. Only now and then did she fail: now and then Harriet's ghost would not be contained. She would see it – as now in the frosted inn-yard – from the utmost corner of her eye, an admonitory flicker, a mere grazing of vision. Reminding her. So, now you not only have my husband, you will have my children as well. Satisfied?

'What's wrong?' Shelley said.

'Cold,' Mary said shivering. 'Just cold. You ought to be wearing a waistcoat.'

'I'm not cold,' he said: and said it, curiously, with a sort of defiance.

'Greedy, that's what you are,' Claire scolded William, scrubbing viciously at his jammy mouth. William never protested at these things: it was as if he thought, like everyone else, Well, that's Claire. 'There'll not be so much jam for you presently. When Shelley brings the *other* children here, you'll be the smallest. And you'll be helped last at the table. And I dare say you won't like *that*.' She sat down heavily and wept into her hands. Of course, it was her own place she was afraid for, Mary thought: would Shelley look about him and think he just had too many dependants? She needn't fear that: it was the last thing you needed to fear from Shelley. Alas.

★ ★ ★

Mary, who had never thought to marry at all, ended up having two marriages.

There was the real one, which took place at the church of St Mildred's, Bread Street, in the City of London, on 30 December 1816. And there was the ideal one that she entertained in a secret place of the mind.

The real one came about because Shelley wrote her from London that a marriage would strengthen his custody case, and that therefore reason dictated that they compromise their principles on the needless absurdity of the institution for the sake of expediency. In the secret place of her imagination, Shelley proposed to her ardently in a grove, because he loved her, and marriage would show it to the world.

For the real one she wore her usual day-frock and bonnet: in the secret place, there were white satin and lace veils. And in the secret place, her father was there to give her away full of dignified pride, a pride that he had always had in her no matter what she did: whereas in the real one he was there – oh, yes, *now* he was reconciled, now came the invitations to dine at Skinner Street, now that things were proper – but he was a faintly embarrassing figure, smirking, perspiring head shining, mentioning to everyone near him that his son-in-law was the son of a baronet and heir to a substantial property. (Feet of clay: how about shins, knees, legs of clay? How far did it go up?) And, of course, in the secret place her father was solitary in his dignity: whereas the real wedding was blighted by the presence of her stepmother, who contrived to cough loudly throughout the service, so as to be noticed.

And the ideal wedding was to a Shelley who had never been married. The real one was attended by that corner-of-the-eye ghost, flitting out of the church porch, hovering in the vestry as Mary took up the pen and neatly inscribed her new, forbidden name: *Mary Shelley*.

The secret place would remain secret. It was a place of such banal conventionality – she admitted it – that it would have disappointed and dismayed her new husband if he had known of it. So, though Mary was happy, very happy, to be marrying Shelley, the whole thing had a familiar tint or taint. Like the floating bubbles in the surface film of the eye, it was so ever-present you ceased to notice it. Guilt, guilt.

Two weeks later, in Bath, Claire gave birth to a daughter. She named her Alba. During the labour she gripped Mary's hand, said that if she died she was heartily sorry for all their quarrels, and then yelled a long, complicated and comprehensive curse on the person, name and lineage of Byron. After the birth, a change. Claire was passionately maternal.

'How alarming.' she said. 'How frightening to love something so very much.' She offered Mary an unguarded look. 'I'm not a bad person, am I? Only, you know, society will say it.'

'Society's opinion is founded on barbaric prejudices—'

Claire shook her head impatiently. 'I know all that. But I just want to hear it, just once.'

'You're not a bad person.'

'Thank you.' Claire smiled down into the baby's gnomish face. 'I'll pretend you said that as if you meant it.'

Mr Leigh Hunt. You must have him in his setting, for it is an essential part of him, he is a great lover and collector of things, a bower bird adorning his nest. Hampstead then, specifically that part of it called the Vale of Health, a hollow in the hills amid copses and holly-bushes and, oddly, washing – lines and lines of it: there is a tribe of washerwomen living in shacks on the Heath who use these well-aired slopes for drying. Not inappropriate for Hunt, who adores domesticity.

'Talk to me of the beauty of the Alps, and I will gladly listen and sympathize. Talk to me of the beauty of the *fireside*, and my heart throbs with yours.'

Cottage of white stucco, with a neat white fence and neat garden-plot. Inside, benign chaos. Children scream and tumble, half undressed: Hunt loves children, has already suggested that Claire's baby might be brought up among his brood, the more the merrier. Heaps of books, music-sheets, manuscripts, busts, potted plants: walls crowded with prints and engravings: careful when you sit down, remove the unstrung guitar, the cat, the set of proofs. Here is big-bosomed genial Mrs Hunt with an infant under one arm and the other up to the elbow in wet clay – she is a sculptress. Here is Hunt himself, tall, drooping, charming in silk dressing-gown that points up the slight exoticism of his looks – there is some Creole ancestry in this glowing dark man with the sort of glossy curling hair that can only be called locks. A playful mouth, a playful manner.

'Mrs Shelley, I require you to cut the bread-and-butter again. I make no apologies for exacting this labour from a guest. It is because you do it so neatly and beautifully. The effect is aesthetic. It is a gastronomic sonnet – a comestible sonata. I must have more of it.'

Playful but serious. A poet himself, he is an encourager of poets, friend and host to artists of all kinds, and a determined Radical voice when most such voices are silenced. The times are inimical to liberal ideas. Repressive laws, repressive acts flourish in the post-Waterloo air. Under Hunt's hospitable roof, kindred spirits can meet and breathe easier. They are always dropping in, staying to dine, debate, argue, to sleep on the rug-strewn sofas.

'The times are so very bad,' Hunt says, cracking nuts and eating them with a boy's noisy relish, 'that the only position open to the thinking man is optimism. As they cannot possibly get worse, they must get better – so I for one look to the future with the greatest cheerfulness.' He bends his delicately attentive blinking look on Mary. 'You, my dear Marina –' his pet name for her – Hunt is a great bestower of pet names, even on his set of Shakespeare and his walking-stick '–are not an optimist, I think. I intuit a belief that whatever *can* go wrong will go wrong.'

'I hope I am not so superstitious as that,' Mary answers, a little uncomfortably.

Hunt presses her hand. There is a feminine gentleness about him, a willingness to leave large areas unresolved, that she has never known in a man, not even Shelley.

'Of course there is your husband's chancery suit, which must give you cause for – well, a foreboding feeling. He has told me all about it. Ah, the law! It has been rather a brute to me in the past, when I mustered the courage to square up to it. Which was not easy for a congenital faint-heart.'

'You went to prison for your beliefs. I see no cowardice in that – quite the reverse.'

'You are very good. Ignore that smashing noise from the kitchen, by the by – my ear is attuned to such things, and tells me it is a tea-plate – a mere tea-plate, of which we have an ample sufficiency – at least, we have some. I know we have *some*. Now there is a child been sick – I know that sound also – poor lamb. I think this an opportune moment, my dear Marina, to talk in the garden. I believe it is dry enough. No, I am indeed a faint-heart, you know, and that is why I had to *brave* something. Can you understand this?'

'Courage is the overcoming of fear, not the absence of fear.'

Hunt squeezes her arm. 'Shelley was right about you. And in just the same way, I write so very much because I am at root a profoundly lazy being. Ditto, I am cheerful, because if we are not, we – well, where are we?'

'Hell,' Mary says.

'*I* was right about you. You know, I feel inclined to put in a blow for Shelley in the *Examiner* – were it not that association with *me* would hardly help his case. But one longs to point out that there seems to be one rule for the subject and another for the Prince. That irreproachable model of the domestic virtues was not kept apart from his child. These are sorrowful matters. There is a happier one – is that not Shelley I see thither, with my Thornton? The boy adores him. He takes him on much longer rambles than my poor spavined Londoner's legs can manage. Yet Shelley looks as if a wind would blow him away!'

'He does – but it wouldn't.'

'Ah, there is a great strength in him.'

'Partly. Also he would convince the wind that it was in the wrong.'

They are staying with the Hunts while the house Shelley has rented in Marlow is made ready, and the stuccoed cottage with its crowded *bonhomie* makes a great impression on Mary. She realizes it is the first true home she has known since her girlhood in Dundee. She longs to re-create it when they get to Marlow, even down to the brood of free-spirited children. If Shelley does not get custody of Harriet's children – for Harriet's family are mounting a powerful case against him – then there will be their own: even before the missed menses, Mary has a presentiment that she is pregnant again. And, of course, there will be little Alba – and Claire.

Hunt's domestic tolerance has even made Mary resolve to rub along better with Claire. A relatively easy resolution when she is a hundred miles away; and even then, with the cosiness of fireside parlour games going on around her, a cold mad voice inside Mary irrepressibly speaks. *She deliberately went and got pregnant by Byron in sheer competition with you – and also to make sure that no other man would have her afterwards, which would mean having to stay with Shelley, right at Shelley's side for ever, and of course he won't see it . . .*

'I can see Mrs Shelley is thinking of an acrostic to beat us all,' Hunt says, twinkling at her: and she wonders how much he does see.

Endless callers: Hogg the aptly named is one. And fortunately, transparently, Hogg is determined to see nothing but Mrs Shelley, respectably married lady, wife of his old university friend, certainly not a person that he ever attempted or contemplated going to bed with. He tends also to put up his hoglike nose at Mrs Hunt's uncovered bosom and, lawyerlike, to talk people doggedly down. No, that is a past Mary wants nothing to do with. Not yet twenty, already Mary sees her past as huge tracts of time: she has crossed continents to arrive at today.

Callers: Hunt promises her: 'John Keats. You have not met him? You shall, the very next time he makes the tramp out from London. How shall I describe my excellent young friend? I must use similitudes. Picture me a botanist, eagerly collecting my specimens in the flowery meads of literature. My greatest discoveries I carry home trembling and exulting. Now Shelley is a fabulous orchid found perfuming some exotic spot. Keats is a hardy alpine lodged in barren rocks. An unpropitious history. Orphaned young – his father kept an inn, I believe – and consigned to guardians, and acting pretty much as guardian himself to his young siblings – and set at last to the medical trade, of which I candidly confess I have the greatest horror. He has told me a few tales of it – of operations and dressings and what-naught – but I hush him. I told you I was a coward. And I am thankful that, though he is now qualified to practise as an apothecary – can one say to apothecarize? – he is *not* going to pursue the dismal profession. He chooses poetry instead. For this I hope to take a *little* credit.'

'You encouraged him to that most insecure of vocations.'

'My dear Marina, of course I did. Because he has genius, and genius must follow its destiny. I would have done the same for Shelley, but he stands in no need of it. He knows what he wants. Your husband is, you know, magnificent.'

Hunt, short-sighted, has this way of peering closely into your face, as if to be sure it is you he is talking to; and then, when he sees that it is, looking delighted. Certainly he does it with Mary. She wonders if he does it with everyone: though it doesn't matter. She likes him anyway. There have been few enough flatterers in her life.

Callers: Mr John Keats.

Of course this is not his home, but still to see Keats, unlike lounging, piano-tinkling, slipper-toeing Hunt, you must dispense with setting, because he is so very separate from it. This young man is compact and self-contained. He has, Mary thinks, a *just* quality – that is, he seems always to have just come in, or to have just thought of something, or to be just on the edge of decision. When she first meets him, he has just woken up from an overnight sleep on the Hunts' sofa. This arrangement might have been more uncomfortable if he were taller but, as Mary sees when he rises to shake her hand, he is not much over five feet. Younger than Shelley, too, though the hand he gives her is rough, knuckly, full of tamped strength. An exceptionally beautiful face, slender-nosed, rich-lipped, with wide high cheekbones, challenging eyes in slightly bruised-looking orbits. Wiry body in navy coat with silver buttons, loose neckerchief, cream trousers of the sort popularized – how strange to think of it – by Byron. Abundant chestnut hair, springing rather than curling. The infinite differences between people, between men: between Shelley's mandarin abstraction when he pushes back his hair and the way Keats puts up that stocky hand and thrusts his hair away, businesslike, ready for anything.

'Mr Hunt has told me a lot about you,' Mary says.

In return, a merely expectant look, as if she has left a sentence half finished.

'You live in London, Mr Keats?'

'Cheapside. But I think to move out here – Highgate or Hampstead, away from the press of the city.' He looks about, hurriedly clears a seat for her. Mrs Hunt has been cutting silhouettes here, and he gathers up the spiralling black waste, like so many funereal apple-peelings, and earnestly regards her with them in his arms. 'You and Mr Shelley likewise, I think.'

'We shall be moving to Marlow soon. Buckinghamshire. A pretty spot. But close enough to town. Perhaps you could put those on the fire.'

'To be sure.' He does so, smiling with a little inward constraint. He is unused to women, Mary thinks: or, rather, he cannot stop thinking of them as women.

'I like the peace of the country. Mr Hunt will help you to find a lodging hereabouts, I should think. He mentioned your brothers?'

'I have two very dear brothers with whom I live at present. I don't know whether we shall carry on this arrangement. I gather, from all manner of indications, that a poet should live alone.' Not a blush but a kind of high, angry, conscious colour when he talks of being a poet, as if prepared for fisticuffs over the word.

'Alone, but not lonely, one hopes.'

'I've never understood how people can be so afraid of loneliness,' he says, decidedly. He speaks, Mary thinks wryly, as if he has fifty years of experience behind him.

Later, when the room has already filled up with callers, Shelley comes in, his nose in a volume of Spenser, and Hunt makes the introduction. Shelley's long sinuous arm comes out to shake hands as he bends from his benign abstracted height: his precise fluting voice contrasts with Keats's faintly chesty townsman's tones: and Mary is struck by the intuition that they will get on only so far. They have many things in common, but they are the wrong things, and so the awkward differences protrude, tripping like tree-roots.

And, she supposes, they are rivals. When Hunt spoke of fame a little while since, she saw the kindling in Keats's intense eyes. It does not seem likely – in the privacy of her mind she is candid – that either of them will find fame of the Byron sort. Still they court the same goddess: and Mary knows what rivalry feels like. Claire is coming down to join them soon: there was a fulsome letter this morning confirming it. Shelley: 'I've missed her.' Oh, Mary knows what it feels like. Tastes like, at the tingling back of the throat.

Abruptly she has to run out of the stifling room. Pregnancy sickness, of course. As she goes, she notices Keats's gaze on her; and she seems to carry with her to the earth-closet, like clinging streamers, a whole tangle of his observant emotions – sympathy, speculation, wonder. Also thankfulness: he is domestically untrammelled, no nausea fits or accouchement plans will affront his muse.

Mrs Hunt follows her. Her experienced fingers, colourful with paint, strokes Mary's hair back from her forehead as she retches.

'There we are, dear. Thought I'd better follow. I just knew. Men never notice anything, do they?'

Shelley and Keats walk together on the Heath, later. Mary observes their return from the window of the attic bedroom she and Shelley share with a nursing queen tortoiseshell and her litter of kittens, a tailor's dummy, the maid's wardrobe, and two tea-chests full of books. She thinks of the strange, unfathomable paths that have brought them together, brought her and Shelley together, her and Claire, all of them and Byron. She has a long moment's terror, failing to see any pattern, cornered by the monstrous conclusion that there is none, anywhere. When Shelley comes up she seizes him desperately.

'Hullo, hullo, my love, what would you have, kisses, more?'

'Kisses. You.' Why she loves Shelley: he is never disturbed by emotional demonstrations of any sort. 'Did you have a good talk with Mr Keats?'

'We went over a fair stretch of ground. Spenser and so on. Our tastes differ. I gave him some advice, which I gather he means to disregard. Don't publish when you're young: wait.'

She looks up in surprise. 'But you have.'

'Oh, I would never advise anyone to do what I have done.'

He says it casually. And only later does she feel that this is an admission: like a stone dropped into a deep, deep well, it echoes long after.

Callers: there is the painter with the bald bespectacled bulldog face, who comes to dine and stays to argue when Shelley's atheism breaks out. The painter is a Christian: he pities Shelley: Shelley energetically rejects his pity.

'You speak of my inability to believe,' Shelley says. 'This is not the case – it sounds like a sad lack, as if I hanker after grace and all that detestable nonsense. I do not believe in Christianity because it is untrue, because it is an imposture foisted upon the people and made the pretext for the most dismal series of oppressions of the body and the spirit in the history of mankind—'

'You speak of the spirit.' The painter's spectacles are steamed and there is gravy on his chin. Yet he does not look absurd somehow: not to Mary. 'You acknowledge the existence of the spirit – yet whence do you suppose this spirit comes if not from the hand of the Creator?'

'The human spirit cannot know where it comes from, only that it is. That it must look to and worship a creator is itself the mischievous creation of the worst side of the human spirit, the side that is fostered by the delight in power and the love of tyranny, the side that makes kings and priests.'

'And, of course, there is a better side,' puts in Hunt peaceably, 'the side that promotes kindness and mercy and fellow-feeling – call it by what name you will, Christian, pagan, it is the true human spirit and we all, I think—'

'This bad side,' splutters the painter, 'how do you suppose, Mr Shelley, it is conquered? Is that in humanity's power too? By what mysterious agency does humanity *recognize* its own bad side? A curious self-regulating mechanism, this humanity, like a clock that winds itself. Do you not propose that old impossibility of lifting oneself up by one's own bootstraps, sir?'

'We have been taught to regard these things as impossibilities, by those same kings and priests. Who first of all would have prevented their subjects even from reading the Bible of your religion in their own language – an indication of how they will always seek to withhold and prevent truth—'

'Ho, then, you propose that when a man or a woman feels the beautiful consolation of the Christian faith touching their innermost *soul*, sir, they are merely the dupe of a worldly conspiracy?'

'Consolation. You have hit upon the most revealing word. Consolation for what? Suffering. We must be consoled for life, because life is made intolerable, life is filled with suffering, and the suffering comes from the injustices and inequalities that are inflicted upon us, and which might be remedied, which *must* be remedied by a new social organization—'

'You are going to put an end to suffering?' the painter cries, nearly launching out of his seat. 'Will a parliamentary act put an end to the stillborn child, the consumptive – the cancer in the breast?'

'The progress of science surely will put an end to such things,' Shelley says coolly, 'if it is allowed, and not hindered by blockheaded superstition.'

'And the *mind*?' the painter says, scarlet, struggling. 'Do you not comprehend that the mind may suffer – suffer torments as great – greater than those of the body? Have you never heard of suicides? Never thought of the wretchedness that must have driven them? And you propose to *cure* this by the application of a political poultice? As well as denying them – depriving them of the consolation of eternity, when their lives were so unhappy—'

Shelley's knife falls with a clatter on to his plate. Mary intercepts an anxious glance from Hunt. Everyone seems to contemplate the sudden silence without daring to touch it. And there – out of the corner of Mary's eye – yes, there she flits again . . .

Then Shelley nibbles a piece of bread and says, in his most languorous way, 'I understood your beautiful religion condemned such people to hell.'

'That is not my belief,' the painter grunts.

'I did not think it could be. Because you are plainly a man of warm and generous sentiments,' Shelley says, with a little bow.

'Ah!' Hunt beams. Flit, flicker.

Keats, seated next to Mary, has been silently watchful throughout this. She turns to him. 'Do you believe in ghosts, Mr Keats?'

He seems to make some momentary adjustment before

answering: it reminds her of herself on the Continent, when she prepared to talk to someone in French. 'I believe that people see and hear them. Feel them.'

'But that isn't the same as their actual existence.'

'Isn't it?' He looks truly puzzled. 'What more could there be?'

A hard exultation, the next day, in Shelley's eyes: a letter. 'I have more evidence,' he says, 'that Harriet was actually unfaithful to me before we separated. So, one sees.' He does not say what one sees. Consolation, thinks Mary, watching him play witchy horror-games with Hunt's squealing, half-thrilled, half-uneasy children: we all find it where we can.

Albion House, Marlow. Mary tries to suppress her satisfaction at its roominess, its elegance. Sash windows indeed, she reproaches herself: what a thing to think of: yet she cannot resist opening and closing them. A library. A walled garden with a cedar. Oh, yes: here I shall finish *Frankenstein*, she thinks, setting out the manuscript on her desk: here my Wilmouse will grow and thrive, she thinks, showing him the chalk slide made by Shelley down a mound in the garden: here my new baby will be born safely, please God – and don't tell Shelley I prayed that.

And here comes the not unexpected news: Shelley has lost his chancery suit. He is not to have custody of his children by Harriet, who will remain with her family. Shelley rages against the Lord Chancellor, then takes off on one of his long, punishing walks by the river. And here too is Claire, with little delicate enchanting Alba. Claire still stubbornly disbelieving when her long effusive letters to Byron in Italy go unanswered: Claire disappointed, embittered perhaps. Still, there is no need for her to say it.

'Well, my sweetling,' she addresses Alba, 'you are not to see your Uncle Shelley's other children after all. He is, you know, very upset. But I don't think Mary is – I think she's quite relieved, because they might make him think of Harriet, and we have got *rid* of Harriet.'

Is it design or chance that she says this just as Shelley appears, worn and dusty, in the doorway?

A Bridge of Sighs

Augusta: it had been her lifelong habit never to throw anything away in case it came in useful. (Correct that: her habit since marrying George.) And now, look: after all that, there was so little. So little to show. Luckily the house, in a decent, dreary, shadowy street off Montagu Square, was let furnished. Still, now that they were installed, the effect was forlorn. Don't make a mess, the nursemaid instructed the children: but Augusta thought, Yes, let them, at least it will cover the vacancy.

Six Mile Bottom was nearly – not quite – sold. It had been a long, wearisome business, complicated by George's being unable, at first, to prove he had any title to the house in the first place. It had been the Prince Regent's gift, and that channel of communication, of course, had long closed. There were still some formalities to be dragged through – for Augusta: George could not manage these things. George had not accompanied her in the move to the rented house in town: it would only depress his spirits. He had gone to stay with a hunting friend until things were settled. Augusta had supervised the move herself, brought five fractious and ailing children in the public coach to London, and then, within weeks, been delivered of her sixth.

Emily: tiny, frail, plaintive, an absolutely unpeaceable baby: product of lean times. She developed thrush in the mouth, which made breast-feeding a torment. When Augusta, after long convalescence, made her curtsy at court the little old Queen, herself dropsical and half paralysed, gasped aloud. 'Mrs Leigh, you are a shade.'

Was she? Augusta took up the question on a blustery March day, the first day that the weather and her physical recovery had allowed her to go out on a proper walk. She came back to the usual rowdy dinner of bread-pellets, protests and sulks – no two of her children liked the same things to eat – but, unusually, she decided to have wine with her dinner. And afterwards, when the children had been consigned to bed with the same noisy chaos, she elected to have more wine. And took it up to her bed-chamber: why not? The parlour was cheerless, the fire smoked, and besides she was mistress of the house.

Unusual for Augusta altogether, this mood of assertion. She knew it was probably wrong: she could hear the murmur of conscience, as Annabella had taught her to do. Annabella's guidance, her unquenchable vigilance and unwearied advice, had indeed made a new Augusta. This – this weakening – was an extraordinary lapse. But the walk had brought the blood to her cheeks, and so had the wine, and it was so long since she had felt any blood in her at all – any glow. She wanted to be good (she *must*, as Annabella had taught her) but she did not want to be a shade, not just yet. She refilled her glass and sat down to look at herself in the dressing-table mirror. On the dressing-table, her hairbrushes (she was shedding more lately, she was sure), tooth-powder (she had lost a tooth after Emily's birth), bottles of scent carefully eked out (the attar of roses almost gone), books. She had done a lot of reading during her confinement. On the top of the pile, two new novels sent her from Albemarle Street by Mr Murray, called *Northanger Abbey* and *Persuasion*: below, covered, hidden – but there – Byron's verse-drama *Manfred*.

She was not sure how it had got there. Surely she had put it away. Annabella regarded it with absolute horror, and Annabella was her moral yardstick. And *Manfred* had shaken Augusta too when she first read it. Manfred the sorcerer, dwelling a solitary outcast in the Alps, racked by guilt for a secret and unforgivable sin at last revealed as love – love for his sister . . . Augusta, having extracted and opened the volume somehow, unconsciously, snapped it shut. No letter from him lately. She drained her glass and confronted her reflection.

'Is that all we are, then? Women – are we just there as inspiration? Muse? Subject for a poem? Object, really.' She said it out loud, quite without meaning to, and the effect was as if she posed the question to the woman in the mirror. The woman had a strong, sensual, fleshy face: a wicked face, Annabella would say, and she would be quite right.

'You don't understand,' the woman in the mirror said. 'It wasn't like that. Our love – all of it – it was different. It was perfection.'

Augusta was shocked. She lowered her gaze from her own eyes.

'A fine piece of perfection,' she murmured. 'When poor Annabella suffered so. Although I know – that isn't the main thing, that's what she's taught me. It's the offence against God that matters.' She looked up.

'I don't believe in God,' the woman in the mirror said, picking up her glass and refilling it.

Augusta recoiled, almost dropped the glass. 'This is terrible . . .' she moaned.

'I don't believe in *Annabella*'s God.'

Augusta stared at that glowing imperious face. Its lines shifted a little and she recognized it: Byron. Byron in her.

'You know why he doesn't write,' said the mirror-face sharply. 'Because your own letters are such *nothings*. Because Annabella must read everything first. Because he cannot understand you. Because he supposes it is over.'

Augusta closed her eyes, took a sip of wine. 'He is inside me. I must never let him out. I must never – even this I must never do again. It is over.' She set down the glass, opened her wet eyes and, turning away from the mirror, went over to her bed and knelt to pray to God – to Annabella's God, the only one there was now – for forgiveness of her sins.

★ ★ ★

It had been Lady Byron's unhappy, exacting, but necessary task to bring Mrs Leigh to a true appreciation of the dangers she incurred by her infamous conduct; and she could now comfort herself with the evidence of some degree of success. The unconscious and unashamed tone with which Mrs Leigh had been accustomed to refer to the matter of her brother, and which had revealed beyond doubt the deplorable extent of her corruption, was no more. Mrs Leigh, after indefatigable efforts by Lady Byron to awaken her to the wickedness of her behaviour, was now properly subdued by the painful awareness of repentance. – Lady Byron's satisfaction at beholding the change she had wrought in Mrs Leigh was compounded by the knowledge that it had been nearly all her own work: for though she had for a time enlisted the help of Mrs Leigh's intimate friend Mrs Theresa Villiers, in convincing Mrs Leigh of her grievous culpability, there were signs now that Mrs Villiers regretted the part she had played, from some trifling notions of disloyalty. Lady Byron could only mark this infirmity with a wry smile, and pass it over with a sigh. Her own mind was too firm, her convictions too secure, to countenance such backsliding. She knew that a careful vigilance must be maintained over Mrs Leigh, to ensure that she never again entertained a warm thought towards her notorious brother, and to make certain that her eternal soul was no further imperilled; which could only be guaranteed, given the lady's propensity to moral feebleness, by an everlasting estrangement from him. A careful attention must be paid, too, to Mrs Leigh's children, who were fond of their Aunt Bella, and happily susceptible to her influence. – It was up to Lady Byron to make sure, by precept and advice, that they never looked except with abhorrence on their uncle's existence.

This was a lesson she had already begun inculcating in the infant mind of her own child, little Ada: whom she was teaching, with admirable thoroughness, to detest her father. An unsympathetic observer might have remarked that an equal diligence was not employed in the matter of maternal love, and suggested that the looks of deep respect that the little girl was accustomed to give her formidable mother were indistinguishable from stares of terror. The same observer might have objected that Lady Byron's campaign of reform upon Mrs Leigh was in some sort a species of revenge, which, the proper object – her lord – being unattainable, must be turned perforce upon Mrs Leigh, with all the pitiless persistence of a disappointed and resentful nature.

But such observers were not to be found in Lady Byron's circle, which was of a devout character, the incremental object of devotion being Lady Byron herself. Any doubts about the impeccability of her own conduct and situation, were fully answered by the confidence of her supporters, and the content-ment of her mind; which at this juncture found matter for the profound reflection to which it was prone, in news of a solemn kind. – Her aunt, Lady Melbourne, was mortally ill. That same worldly and indestructible Lady Melbourne, who had first brought her and Byron together, was dying slowly and painfully. What must be the struggles of such a burdened conscience, such a stained soul, in preparing to meet its Maker? If they could not finally be imagined, then it was not for want of trying on Lady Byron's part: but here her historian is unequal to following her. Let other pens dwell on guilt and misery.

(*Lady Melbourne's bedroom at Melbourne House.* LADY MELBOURNE *is in the bed, dozing: she is obviously in the last extremity of illness. The bedclothes are tented over her swollen leg. Beside the bed, cupping-glasses and an array of medicines.* LORD MELBOURNE *sits close by, looking lost.* WILLIAM, GEORGE *and* EMILY LAMB *are seated at a little distance. Through the drawn window-curtains, a shaft of spring morning sunlight.*)

GEORGE: She surely can't take any more laudanum. It would kill her.

EMILY: That would rather defeat the object.

(GEORGE *chuckles.* LORD MELBOURNE *darts him a furious glance.*)

GEORGE: Sorry. Sorry, Papa. Only, you know, it's so ghastly. One ends up laughing for sheer ghastliness.

EMILY: Has she asked for anyone today?

LORD MELBOURNE: Eh? What do you mean? You mean a divine?

EMILY: Lord, hardly. I don't imagine Mama would want to talk religion even now.

WILLIAM (*his head in his hands*): She doesn't need to. She is a good woman – the best of women.

LORD MELBOURNE: She did ask for someone. Yes. She asked for Caroline.

GEORGE: Good God, what does she want the mad skeleton for?

WILLIAM (*glaring*): Kindly do not refer to my wife in that way.

EMILY: Why? She *referred* to all of us in that wretched book of hers. I don't know why you trouble to defend her.

WILLIAM (*muffled*): Someone must.

GEORGE: Where is she, anyway? Haunting that publisher fellow again? She positively smells of the shop lately.

EMILY: It must have been the opium talking. (*Getting up and examining the medicines.*) Rygrathee Oil. Do these doctors really know what they are about? Is it the flying gout, or what? Those convulsions. And she looks so dreadful.

LADY MELBOURNE (*startling her*): I am dying, not deaf.

EMILY: Oh, Mama, are you better?

LADY MELBOURNE (*turning her head about with great difficulty*): You were not listening. Well, you never did. Listen now. While I can speak.

LORD MELBOURNE (*clutching her hand*): My dear, my dear.

LADY MELBOURNE: That I never was. Still, we grew used to one another. Emily, remember what I told you. Keep your husband contented, and make love to Lord Palmerston: he is the man. George, control your temper and get into Parliament. William – where are you, William?

WILLIAM (*in tears*): Here, Mama.

LADY MELBOURNE: This weakness . . . You know what I want for you. Office. High office. You must work for it. It's only this indolence of yours that holds you back.

GEORGE (*spitefully*): Not *only* that.

(*LADY MELBOURNE groans and writhes, shaking her head.*)

WILLIAM: Mama, what is it? Shall I call down for the doctor? I think he's still downstairs . . .

LADY MELBOURNE: Fool. Fools.

LORD MELBOURNE: Oh, my dear, my poor dear . . .

GEORGE (*covering his nose and mouth with his handkerchief*): Dear God. Ugh.

(*There is a sound of frantic footsteps on the stairs. CAROLINE rushes in, flushed and agitated.*)

CAROLINE: Has she called for me? How is she? Is she— No! (*She screams and runs to the bed.*) Lady Melbourne – oh, my dear Lady Melbourne, speak to me! No, no!

LADY MELBOURNE: . . .

(*Caroline falls sobbing down by the bed. EMILY and GEORGE exchange a glance over her head.*)

Compromises: they seep upward like damp. The early spring of 1818 sees Mary and Shelley standing by the church font at St Giles-in-the-Fields, London, baptizing their children.

William, and the new baby Clara, born in the golden September days by the river at Marlow: Clara, pretty and fragile as an autumn leaf. And baptized with them – of course – Claire's little Byronic sprig Alba, now named, at Byron's written request, Allegra. She and Wilmouse are inseparable. Give him a handful of raisins or sugared almonds, and he immediately thrusts half of them, or more, at Allegra. Mary watches with mingled pride and annoyance. Even in the next generation, this sharing, she thinks.

'Compromises,' says Leigh Hunt, when they dine with him, 'are, I feel, of two kinds. Those made in a *slinking* spirit –' his honeyed voice conjures up some wonderfully slithering, yet utterly harmless creature '– and those made with the noblest of motives. You, as I understand it, wish to ensure your legal title to your little ones, in view of the absolute malice the law has shown you in the past. What could be nobler, or more comprehensible? If I thought my children were threatened, I would do anything to protect them. I would even turn Tory. Perhaps.' He goes laughing to the piano. 'Miss Clairmont, will you sing?'

Keats is there: earlier he and Hunt and Shelley had a competition to write a sonnet on the Nile in fifteen minutes. Hunt came off best. Now Keats sits down by Mary in his curled, leg-nursing way.

'So you are going to Italy.'

'As soon as our affairs can be wound up. Mr Shelley has been in indifferent health, and is advised to try a southern climate.' She offers a sudden smile, which must look horribly inappropriate; but she is trying to disguise some very mixed feelings. Regret at the end of a dream, the house by the river, the domestic hearth and sash windows: Albion House is left behind. Another flight, in essence: the baptisms are all very well, but Shelley still fears the vindictive law snatching Wilmouse and Clara from them: abroad they will definitely be safe. Knowledge, too, that she has urged Italy as their destination because Byron is there, and will take charge of Allegra and even, possibly, Claire. Meanwhile her father still hounds Shelley for money – which is, she well knows, another reason for Shelley to want to get away. Yet she worries: how will her father manage without them?

'You will be leaving the scene of your success,' Keats says.

Frankenstein: it is published, read, talked about. Men say it must be by Shelley. The Tory reviews fulminate against its impiety. And her father – her father, to whom she dedicated the book, is proud of her. He tells her so. And by the by, about the money . . .

'Not something that can ever be said about me,' Shelley puts in. 'Success. You'll have seen how they tossed and gored my *Revolt of Islam*. Is your long poem finished, Keats? I wish you joy of it. If you cannot please the public or the critics, you may as well be hanged. Or come out to Italy with us. We'll sit upon the ground and tell sad stories of the death of kings.'

'I could not go so far even if I would,' says Keats. 'My brother Tom is ill.'

'Bring him,' Shelley says vaguely. 'The sick – the disappointed – we'll carve out a little community in the Tuscan hills – with a sort of Dantean inscription over the gate. "None that smile may enter here." You know, it's the way they hate not just your poem, but *you* that is so perturbing. I half expect to be pelted in the street for having written it.' He wanders away. More than half, Mary thinks.

On their last night in England, the Hunts come over to their temporary lodgings in Great Russell Street for a farewell dinner. Shelley, tired from packing, falls asleep on the sofa. Amorously entwined, breathing wine, not seeming terribly sad, the Hunts tiptoe out blowing kisses. Claire takes herself off to bed, her head full of Byron. Mary begins clearing up. And then a timid knock: her father.

'My dear. I could not entertain another departure without a parental valediction.' Sometimes it is difficult to believe, until you are reminded, that he really talks like this. She goes to embrace him, but he is already turning to look at Shelley on the sofa. 'Exhausted, I should think. Perhaps this is not the time to raise the matter of our financial arrangements.'

'Oh, Father,' Mary says sorrowfully.

'Mrs Godwin sends her good wishes, by the by.'

'No, she doesn't.'

'Compromises,' Godwin says. 'By their nature, they involve some sacrifice or abandonment of principle. Yet as a philosopher one cannot condemn them outright. My reconciliation with your husband seems to me one of the necessary compromises without which the world cannot function.' He rubs his sharp chin. It ought to look scholarly: Mary cannot help seeing the acquisitive gesture of the miser. To erase the unpleasant image, she seizes him and hugs him.

'Bless you, my dear. Be sure and write me with your address the moment you are settled. There. Are you sure we shouldn't wake him?'

The house. It stands in an ample garden, shaded by mulberry and plum trees, at the end of a lane overlooking Hampstead Heath. It is quite new, white-stuccoed, red-roofed, with arched recesses over the tall windows and wrought ironwork before: an approachable house. In fact it is discreetly divided into two, with separate entrances. In one half live the Dilke family: Mr Dilke, whose sturdy, stocky, sober figure can be observed trudging down the lane from the coach-stop at South End Green after his work in town, built the house in concert with his bachelor friend Mr Brown, who at the moment lives in the other half. Sometimes one or other of them will let their half for a season. Hampstead, with its assembly-rooms, eating-houses and balmy heights, is growing in popularity, and there is always a demand for good rented accommodation. (An upstart culture of villas and clerks, sneers the conservative press.)

The house: it is inanimate, of course, but like all houses it has its atmosphere, its past, its special feeling.

The house waits.

Fanny Brawne – Miss Frances Brawne of Elm Cottage, Red Lion Hill, Hampstead: eighteen years old. Going on twenty-eight, sighs Mrs Brawne. She has a lively daughter, much admired for her quickness and wit: just occasionally she wonders what it would be like to have a nice mousy girl, who enters a room rather than crackling into it like a train of fire.

'Fanny, really you should not have laughed at that gentleman quite so much last night.'

'Which one, Mama? I can see I'm going to have to keep a little tally – like a dance-card with a pencil on a string. Was it the one who declared, against all the evidence of his senses, that I was a Dappled Fawn?'

'It was the singing gentleman.'

'Well, now, Mama, I must reprove you, and be to you a most unnatural serpent's thankless tooth child thing, because I did not laugh at the gentleman *per se*. As you well know, effect depends upon the *tout ensemble*.' Fanny regards herself in her mother's mirror. 'Lord, what a hook-nosed fright! I shall quite push Mr Kean off the stage, for I am born to be Shylock. The *tout ensemble*, anyhow. And when the gentleman adds a small Welsh wig to a large fat head, and then sings a song in which we are required to believe he is a shepherd called Strephon gadding through the glades, then I protest that it is more than flesh and blood can bear.' She swoops, kisses her mother's lace-capped head – Mrs Brawne after due consideration has taken to caps, badge of the matron, hopes resigned to the next generation – and is gone.

So many faces. Hampstead has plenty of society. Not only the balls and concerts, but private entertaining: the place is rich in hosts and hostesses offering everything from banquets to impromptu carpet-dances with tea. So many faces to be recognized, quizzed, marvelled at: Fanny feels she could never tire of human physiognomy, its strangeness: chins that look like noses, eyebrows that meet in the middle, teeth yellow and big as a sheep's: grotesquerie, beauty. The French *émigrés* from Church Row, with their buttery skins and withdrawn eyes. Rosy, doll-featured Mrs Dilke, their best friend in the village. Mr Brown who lives in the other half of Wentworth Place, with his bald pate and long, sensual face. Mr Keats, the young poet who lives at Well Walk with his brother. And at any time a new one may appear. This, this is what it is to be young: this sense of limitless possibility.

Mr Keats.

Yes, thinks Fanny, when Mrs Dilke introduces them at a supper-party, I have seen that face before, glimpsed it somewhere. I remember that eagerness.

'He is quite unconventional,' Mrs Dilke told her, 'careless in his dress, and singular in his manner.'

All true. But you did not tell me he was like this, thinks Fanny: giving me this feeling of beautiful trouble.

Afterwards, she cannot remember what they said to one another.

A second time, at the Dilkes': the drawing room crowded, several big-chested thigh-slapping officers from the barracks at St John's Wood, seeking to dazzle in their regimentals. With Fanny, failing.

'If I pull on that braid, do you come all undone like an unpicked scarf?'

'Ho, ho.' He actually says that: as if he has learnt to laugh from a book. 'You may try it, Miss Brawne, if you like.'

'No. Only if I could knit you back together differently. One might make a decent greengrocer or draper out of you, perhaps.'

'Pooh, do you really think you would like me better as a draper?'

'It wouldn't be difficult to like you better, as I don't like you at all.'

Wounded officer falling, his comrade steps boldly into the breach.

'*I* have a friend who wears a scarf made out of the locks of hair of all the women he's had.'

'How amazing!' says Fanny. 'That you have a friend, I mean.'

Sometimes it's like an orchestra. They gather around her, and she directs them, a *forte* here, a *diminuendo* there. But there is someone who is somehow resistant to her conducting, and plays his own tune.

'Will you oblige me by leaning a little closer, Mr Keats? I wish to make Mr Swain jealous.'

Keats, emerging from his shade of watchful quietness, frowns. 'I see no Mr Swain.'

'That's because you don't have my eyes. Everyone for me has two names, Mr Keats. The real one and the appropriate one. The real one is arbitrary and nonsensical. Would you say that I am characterized by *brawn*?'

'I might if you vexed me enough.'

'That is not gallant, and you know what I mean. Now when you assign a title to a poem, you don't choose any old arbitrary words, do you? You choose a title that suits. So I call that gentleman with the thin legs and weak hair Mr Swain, because he is so exactly *like* a swain, or how I have always fancied a swain in poetry. Or, rather, not fancied it.'

'A sad fate for a fine old word. You would rather have a lover than a swain, then?'

'Mr Keats!'

'I speak of words. With words. If I lean towards you, Miss Brawne, I shall do it because I want to, not to save you from Mr Swain.'

'That would be an unpardonable liberty, and I only allow the pardonable ones. Besides, Mr Masterful has gone in to cards, and if I do any leaning in, I want him to see it and be jealous.'

He sits back, studying her. Those wide cheekbones: she has an acute image of a sculptor lightly pressing both thumbs into damp clay, creating him: stepping back from the beautiful intensity.

'My name for you,' he declares, 'shall be Minx.'

'Why, I ought to be insulted.'

'You ought to be, indeed, on a daily basis: it might do you good.'

'And now I have yours. Mr Sobersides. You had better climb up on that chair, Mr Sobersides, if you mean to give us a sermon.'

His eyes glitter – and she sees: he thinks she means a mocking reference to his height. She may be a minx, but she is not that sort of minx. Besides, his form is perfect. She hurries on from this uncharacteristic thought. 'Speaking of sermons, did you hear that monstrous dull sermon the vicar maundered through on Sunday? I had to keep sticking myself with a hat-pin to keep awake. Once it made me shriek out because I had stuck it too hard but I turned it into a groan of devotion.'

'All sermons are monstrous.'

'Oh, Mr Keats. I hear you move with Mr Leigh Hunt's set, but are you absolutely an infidel?'

He shrugs. 'I have lived in the world, Miss Brawne.' He has a tense, waiting look: it is as if he expects her suddenly to throw a ball or an apple and he must catch it or pay some tremendous forfeit.

' "I had rather have a fool to make me merry, than experience to make me sad." Shakespeare, you know.'

'I do know,' he says, smiling. 'And for the love of Shakespeare I will forgive much.'

'Lord, I haven't done much to forgive yet. You ought to see what I can really do.'

'I may forgo that pleasure,' he says, attempting a drawl, yawning. But he cannot take his eyes off her. She knows that, because she cannot take her eyes off him.

Mrs Dilke, calling at Elm Cottage, talks of Keats to Fanny's mother.

'He would be very glad to come to dine, I'm sure, my dear. As for what he does, he is as you have seen him.'

'Oh, he is quite the little poet, to be sure,' Mrs Brawne says – making Fanny see her through a burning mist. She has always regarded her mother as quite a sensible creature: whence comes this drivelling idiocy? What can there possibly be about Keats to make him a 'little poet'? 'But he cannot make his way on that.'

'What about Lord Byron?' Fanny says. 'His works sell in their thousands.'

'He was a lord before he was a poet,' says Mrs Dilke, who is from Yorkshire stock and has a downright way that is sometimes just a little irritating. 'No, Mr Keats qualified as an apothecary – or a surgeon, I can't recall which – but he won't take it up. He is all for poetry.'

'And no family to dissuade him, I suppose,' Mrs Brawne says mournfully.

'He has family, but they are all younger than him. A brother emigrated to America, and another very sickly whom he looks after, and a sister much younger who is with guardians.' Fanny stops, becoming aware of her mother's surprised look. 'We were talking of it. You know how inquisitive I am.'

'I know how quickly bored you are, my dear,' her mother says, 'so he must be very interesting.'

He is: his talk. Fanny loves talk. Some of what she likes to call her bee-awks (her brother Samuel's innocent mispronunciation of *beaux*) are tongue-tied around her: she ties them up with her tongue, perhaps. Keats can meet her.

'Do you not dance, Mr Keats?'

'I do not.'

'Spoken in a tone of decided objection. But what can *be* the objection to this harmless amusement?'

'A very simple one. I can't remember dance-steps. The last time I attempted a quadrille, there was utter confusion, which one lady traced to me with the words, "Oh, *you're* the one who's spoiling everything." '

'How very cruel of her.'

He bows ironically. 'A tribute indeed, from the expert.'

'Why, you know nothing of me.'

'Oh, I have observed you. Plaguing and teasing.'

'If the men didn't like it, they wouldn't come back for more. After all, you are here, aren't you?'

'Do you class me with your bee-awks?'

'No, because you plainly don't care for me at all.'

'Well, you plainly don't understand me – or, rather, I can't say that – because you could never do anything *plainly*.'

'You mean I am so very devious?' she says – breezily, because she is hurt.

'No, I mean nothing *plain* can come from someone so beautiful.'

'Oh – oh, ravens and carpets, and blue cockerel honeycomb—'

'What the devil—'

'I can't think of anything to say, but I must fill up the silence.'

'Must you?'

'Yes – oh, needles and cups, bamboo water paper, Mr Keats, does this mean I can number you among my bee-awks after all?'

He licks his lips, and then again. 'I – I think you are very beautiful and fascinating, and I think you know it. And I do not wish to be a parlour Lothario, holding your fan or picking up your glove. I am not sure I wish to be subject to any feelings at all.'

'Now I don't know what to think.'

'An excellent state to be in. That's when the best ideas come.'

'You are an odd quiddical creature. I know that's not a word, I just made it up.' Deliberately she removes her glove and drops it on the floor. 'An experiment.'

After a moment Keats stoops to pick it up. As he raises his eyes to hers the symbolism of the moment seems to flash between them in all its complexity, absurdity, and pain. And Fanny feels a single rasp of fear, too late, that this was never planned, this was never part of her story, that a ghost or murderer has entered the comedy in the second act and nothing, truly, can ever be the same again.

Keats comes to dine. Mrs Brawne warms to him and he to her: they both possess warmth to begin with. But her pretty faded eyes keep recurring to his open shirt-collar; and after dinner one of those braided officers comes in, and hearing the conversation turn on Leigh Hunt, announces that the fellow should be horsewhipped for insolence to the Royal Household.

'Well, he was put in gaol,' Keats says, with a pugnacious look, 'which was enough, for speaking the mere truth.'

'They say his set are pagans too,' the officer plunges on, pink-cheeked. 'Setting up pagan statues and altars – absolute atheists.'

'They can't be both,' says Fanny, reasonably. 'If you're a pagan you believe in some sort of gods, but they're the kind who have goats' legs and misbehave themselves.'

'Atheists, how very horrible,' cries Mrs Brawne, with a shudder, as if at cockroaches in the kitchen.

'Oh, I have met Mr Shelley the atheist, more than a few times, and there is no harm in him,' says Keats.

'The one who ran off with Godwin's daughters!' says Fanny, excited.

'Good God.' Now the officer is crimson. 'He is beyond anything. He lives in an irregular ménage.'

'Well, I saw nothing of that,' Keats says. 'Mind, he is the sort of man who might well end up in the wrong bed out of sheer absent-mindedness.'

'Oh, I say, sir. Company, you know – mixed company.' The officer wags his head at Keats.

Fanny can certainly detect the patronage, and Keats, she suspects, is as sensitive as a prodded snail. 'Yes, Mr Keats,' she says energetically, 'you must recall, it is all right to talk of ménages, but not of beds. The French makes it decent, apparently.'

'Oh, my dear Miss Brawne,' puffs the officer, chesty, 'you are making fun of me.'

'Lord, you have noticed it at last.'

'It would not do for me,' Keats gently says as if to himself, while the officer gapes. 'I could never share.'

Sometimes he is awkward. Sometimes the mere act of coming into a room seems to overset him, so that he looks ready to back out of it again; and then there will be baleful silences, graceless stubbornness, suspicious looks, especially at women. At such times Fanny is tempted to run rings around him, or would be if he were anyone else.

Then he will be different, glowing and animated, his talk whisking and rippling like the tail of a kite, garlanded with fantasy, nonsense, puns. Above all talking of poetry lifts him up – almost literally: his stature seems to grow, his tight, stocky shoulders to broaden. And when he talks poetry, it is not as someone boring on about their favourite subject – Fanny knows plenty of those: he becomes it. Mrs Brawne asks him one day what made him turn to poetry.

'There is nowhere else to turn,' he says, smiling raptly, inwardly, almost as if he were alone. 'It's a question of – being alive. Would you say, my dear Mrs Brawne, that a fish swims in water?'

'I suppose I would if asked,' says Mrs Brawne timidly, 'though I never am, really.'

'But would you say it swims in water in the same way a man swims in water?'

'No,' Mrs Brawne answers, after long thought, 'but pray, Mr Keats, don't ask me what the difference is.'

'Poetry is the difference. It's like water to the fish.'

Margaret, Fanny's little sister, walks assertively in with her bonnet on back to front. 'What's Mr Keats saying?'

'He's saying he's a fish,' says Mrs Brawne seriously. And then they laugh. But Fanny understands.

She understands, even when he is difficult and withdrawn. Her intuition follows him like a spotlight. One morning, walking on the Heath with Margaret, she sees Keats trudging along slowly up ahead, and she knows at once the question she must and does not want to ask.

'Mr Keats. How does your brother do?'

He has walked heedlessly through the old sand-diggings at the top of the hill, and his shoes are caked. He looks down at them in puzzlement as he says: 'Not well. I thank you, Miss Brawne – I wish I could give a better report.'

'What is his illness?'

Keats stares away into the distance. 'There is consumption in our family. Our mother died of it. Tom has brought up a deal of blood again, and . . . You know I was educated for a doctor myself. I walked the wards at Guy's. I fear there is no mistaking the signs.'

'Our father too,' Fanny says simply. And, quite spontaneously, reaches out and takes his hand. Not a masculine shake, not a lover's caress, but something other, something entirely and uniquely appropriate to this moment, this spot among the ferns, these ten entwined fingers.

'Thank you,' he says, and, very direct: 'I shall have to go on by myself now.'

'Of course.'

Again perfect understanding. And yet, the swift clouded thought passing over her: I wish he were nothing to do with death.

'They say poor Mr Keats's brother isn't long for this world,' Mrs Dilke tells Mrs Brawne over tea.

They give an identical, meaningless sigh that irritates Fanny. She hopes she won't be so mechanically *appropriate* when she gets old.

'Those rooms in Well Walk will be too large for him on his own,' Mrs Brawne says. 'Still, one never knows. It might be the thing that makes him look to his future.'

'Oh, but he does. He is going to write an epic poem that will be the making of him – Dilke is convinced of it, and you know he is no tender judge. The reviews have been so very severe on him, and he has been so much attacked that a lesser man would give it up, but not Mr Keats.'

'A lesser man – or perhaps a sensible man?' Mrs Brawne says tentatively. 'I'm sure he does have promise, but so do many odd young men who like to scribble. And as he is, with no money or family or prospects – well, it is a painful lack, ma'am. I am not entirely unacquainted with that pain. And it seems a pity he has turned his back on what is at least a steady profession. Still,' she concludes briskly, unaware of Fanny's look, 'really it is none of our business.'

It is Mr Charles Brown, Keats's friend and the Dilkes' bachelor neighbour – prematurely bald, heavy-lidded, genial, and occasionally when wine emboldens him to be found among the bee-awks – who tells them that Tom Keats, nursed by his brother to the end, has died.

'Nineteen years old,' he says sombrely. 'No more than that. No more than nineteen.' Then looks pensive, as if wondering whether a little more, twenty or twenty-one, would have been any better.

Fanny walks, alone, shaking off Margaret's pleas to go with her, down to the ponds, and finds the old thorn. The years have made it if anything more gnarled, unearthly, and hideous.

'Now,' she says aloud, 'leave him be.'

Tom Keats, no more than nineteen, dies in Hampstead and is buried among aldermen and corn-chandlers at St Stephen's, Moorgate, an old City church near the inn once kept by his father. At just the same time Queen Charlotte, after seventy-four indomitable years, lies in state at Kew having passed indomitably away in her armchair with the Prince Regent holding her hand.

Among the official mourners in the great slow cortège of carriages making their way to Windsor for the funeral the next evening is Augusta, with only George's valet as her attendant. She welcomes her solitude. There are many thoughts, also much genuine grief. Not for Augusta her brother's fierce contempt for the royal family: they have done too much for her personally including, now, giving her and George and the children a permanent home in a modest set of apartments in St James's Palace. Now at least, whatever happens, there will be a roof over their heads. The counting of blessings as well, then, as the thoughts. Memories flare alongside the torches that light the way up the hill to the Castle. The poor old King – in there somewhere still, blind and lost and unknowing – in the days before his decline, commending Augusta's beauty, congratulating poor good Grandmother, gabbling about Handel. As the carriage strains up to St George's Chapel, Augusta finds herself weeping, in a way entirely new to her: without groaning or shaking, without resistance, even without sound: the tears smoothly traverse her face like raindrops on glass. Tears mingling gratitude and apology, remembering how they had tried with her so hard. Grandmother and the King and Queen and her foster-family in Derbyshire, everyone – and how badly she has failed them. She enters the torchlit chapel knowing her presence here is an affront, a wrong note in the music, a stain on the cerements: evil, in a word. And the only hope is, that she knows it. What is that devotional phrase used by Annabella? *Convinced of sin*: that's it, that's exactly it. Augusta is convinced.

And though her children await her and need her, though there are the usual scores of domestic matters that will claim her, Augusta finds during the service that she likes it here. She almost wants to stay among the lofty shadows, and gently moving banners, the smell of dust and desuetude: not go back out to the living world just yet, and poison it.

It happened again at Christmas: always Fanny's favourite season.

Falling in love, the never expected thing. But Fanny genuinely hadn't expected it. Since the Brawnes had moved to Hampstead, stepping into its busy genteel social life like a warm bath, Fanny had spent most of her time enjoying herself, literally. It was as if there were a beautiful dress in her wardrobe that at long last fitted her – and suited her. Fanny revelled in being who she was and where she was. She loved dancing, music, cards, dining, flirtation. She could not have borne mere triviality, but there was plenty of ballast in the Hampstead circle, artists and scholars and parlour politicians: the mixture, in fact, was just to her taste. She had found, to her own surprise, that she was not shy: that she could manage a certain style on their limited income: above all, that she could keep a roomful of young men dangling on her every word. With the odd exception, they were no more distinctive to her mind than backgammon-men. This was how she liked it: the unseriousness.

And now Christmas, and John Keats running all through it like a thread in shot silk, like a tune in the head, like the weather. He was coming to dinner on Christmas Day.

'John.' Sitting alone, looking out at the bright wintry heath, Fanny tried it out. 'John.' Again, unexpectedly, she relished that plainness. The backgammon-men were Georges and Philips – as far as she knew. She had never thought much about it, because she simply hadn't expected to look for this. The unexpected thing.

Deep down she had been a little afraid of it. Might it not have a dark otherworldly shape, like the thorn?

'So you have moved in with Mr Brown at Wentworth Place, Mr Keats. Margaret, don't kick Mr Keats under the table. Nor me, thank you,' Mrs Brawne said over dinner. 'It's a charming house, is it not? We rented the half ourselves when we first came to Hampstead. Elm Cottage is pretty, but I do not find it so airy. I have said to the Dilkes that if ever they shift to town, as they talk of doing, I should like to have the first refusal.'

'That would make us neighbours, Mr Keats,' Fanny said. 'I'm not sure how you would care for that. I might always be wandering through and disturbing your concentration.'

'Precisely what Mrs Dilke's cat does. But only the mother cat. The kitten never comes near me, but the mother cat is quite drawn to me. Can you think why?' Keats addressed Margaret: he often seemed more at ease with children than adults. 'I've asked her. I've felt her pulse, and examined the lines on her paw, and given her milk and studied the leavings like tea-leaves, but I can't fathom it.'

Fanny sent him a look. 'Is this as much to say, I am a mere puss?'

'Oh, I'm fond of cats.'

He wore no mourning for his brother. She understood why. But in deference to the occasion he wore his cravat high and stiff. After dinner, when he was at the piano with her helping to sort her music-sheets, she said: 'You look as if you're being slowly strangled.'

'I feel it.'

'Then loosen it, do.'

'Would your mama mind?'

'Of course not . . . You do not ask whether *I* mind.'

He scrutinized her. 'I don't care for that sort of teasing generally. But with you I could listen to it all day.' He seemed almost to offer it as a scientific observation.

'Shall I do it all day, then? Mind you, if you like it, then I am simply being obliging, which is dreadful. I could not bear to lay my head down at night knowing I had been obliging all day. It would seem like a day wasted.'

'I put this on to oblige you. And to oblige you I shall loosen it.'

'You make me sound quite a tyrant to you.'

'You could easily be so. If you chose.' He chuckled, his head down. 'There is so much in words, isn't there? Turn them another way – they catch a different light. You have chatted and tiffed with a dozen men in just this way, I should think. And I'm flattered, because I know I'm not like them to look at.' She opened her mouth to say something – he really thought, did he, that he ranked below the six-foot swaggerers with their vacant displays of teeth? – but he went hoarsely and swiftly on: 'But the curious thing is, though the words are the same the meaning is quite otherwise, and if you were to call yourself my tyrant and I your vassal or slave it would not be drawing-room blather, it would be true. It would be real.' He placed the music in her hands. To her utter fascination she found she could clearly see the bold beating of his heart through his shirt-front. 'Are you going to play now?'

Later, the village carol-singers came to the door. In the cold spent afternoon, the sky the colour of ashes, it was natural for Fanny to slip her arm through Keats's as they stood at the door and listened to 'Virgin Unspotted' and 'Remember O Thou Man' sung with shy off-key sincerity. When Margaret insistently shoved herself under his other arm he only smiled.

'You mustn't mind my daughter, Mr Keats,' Mrs Brawne said

afterwards, when the singers came into the hall for slices of yule-cake and beer.

'Oh, I don't mind her at all, Mrs Brawne.'

So it happened at Christmas, amid that dark radiance, lustre of evergreens and blood-drop berries, smell of roast goose and chestnuts and punch-spice: even though it was never meant to happen. After Mrs Brawne called for the candles they had games of spillikins and charades, and then Keats and Fanny read out parts from Shakespeare, and then Keats made up for Margaret a long, complex fairy-tale with enough goblins and cloaks of invisibility to satisfy even her exacting taste.

Then they were left alone. Mrs Brawne saw Margaret to bed, and Samuel, a discreet youth, absented himself.

Fanny said: 'Mr Keats, I wonder if you would like to have this.' Again she wondered how it had happened. She had bought several of the fashionable Tassie gems from the shop in Leicester Square on her last trip to town, but what had made her choose this one with a picture of a Greek lyre, and what had made her put it carefully away and then make sure it was in her pocket today . . . ? Well, however it was, the same thing had happened to him. He drew out a book – Leigh Hunt's *Literary Pocket Book*: he had inscribed her name in it.

They sat holding their gifts, nervously looking at each other.

'Is this,' she said at last, 'what they call an understanding?'

'Yes,' he said, and reached over and kissed her. More roughness of beard than she expected from that fair skin. Sweet breath. Strongly pressing communicative lips, reminding her somehow of the way a cat thrust its urgent purring head against you. Their open eyes reflected astonishment at each other as he drew back. 'If it is an understanding – then it must be on the understanding that you understand—'

'Oh, Lord, stop.'

'That you understand my position,' he persisted. 'What I can offer you. Or rather what I can't yet. I have no money nor expectations, only my pen. I have not made my mark—'

'Yes, you have,' she said, and greatly daring, took hold of his hand and pressed it flat against her breast above her heart. 'Here.'

'I should also tell you,' he said, after a long moment, his tongue thickly stumbling, 'that I never meant to fall in love. Didn't want to. Don't want to—'

'There, we understand each other again. I'm going to give your hand back now, because I can hear Mama coming.'

'And my heart?'

'No, no, you can't have that back. I'm keeping that, Mr Keats.'

It was unexpected in its coming – and unexpected in the way it worked. She had supposed, insofar as she had ever thought about it, that love crowded everything else out: which probably accounted for the dreadful dullness of lovers, who had no other thoughts in their head. But Fanny had her love for Keats and lots of other things as well – even more perhaps. Dancing with other men, teasing and flirting with them, was no less amusing than before, and more piquant. In this augmented life even a slice of bread tasted better. It was as if, up till now, she had played on a piano with only the white keys.

He was going with Brown on a month's visit to Chichester.

'You'll miss me a little, I hope?' she said.

'You should hope for more than that.'

'A little will do.'

'This is where we differ. For me, a little will not do.'

'What, sir, would you have me be miserable because you're not here? And they talk of women's vanity.'

At school Fanny had had a friend whose skin was so flaringly sensitive you could write your name on it with a finger. Sometimes she felt that the skin of Keats's emotions was like that: and the temptation to inscribe and inflame was irresistible.

Her mother watched them wrangling together, smiled. It was the sort of smile that meant a polite reservation of judgement, not happiness.

'My dear,' she said at last, 'if I did not know better, I should

537

almost suspect you of an attachment to Mr Keats.'

'Dear Mama, you have plainly thought about that sentence so long and so carefully that I feel I should give it an equal attention. So let me sit down and think about it.'

'No, my dear, really, it is only a remark. I was talking to Mrs Dilke about him – and she agrees that he is a very odd young man in many ways—'

'Thank heaven for it!' Fanny said sharply. 'It's not as if there's an insufficiency of *bores* in this world.'

'But you know,' Mrs Brawne said, with a timid look, 'it is not just what a person is, but what he does.'

'Surely they are the same.'

'They are decidedly not,' Mrs Brawne said, undecidedly. She did not quite know how to be comfortable with Fanny any more: as if her daughter were a roaring fire and she lacked a screen. 'My dear – all I ask is that while you are not of age, you have a care to be guided by prudence and discretion. Do not betray your whole future for the sake of the present. It is very hard, I know, when you're young, to remember that there is such a thing as the rest of your life.'

'What a dismal phrase,' Fanny said, making a face. 'The rest of your life – like remnants, leavings, left-overs.' Then she laughed and kissed her mother. She even had a relish for these disagreements nowadays, like vivid passages in a play. This must be what Keats meant about poetry: everything in the universe enhanced.

'Now you thought about me all the time you were away, I hope?'

'Indeed I didn't, because I managed to do a deal of writing.'

'For shame, Mr Keats, your lady fair is supposed to be your inspiration.'

'I didn't say she wasn't.'

'You're out of sorts, I think.'

'Oh, a trifle. I have this sore throat that won't go away. And then a worse malady has been afflicting me. Jealousy. The news that Murray sold four thousand copies of Lord Byron's last canto has got down into my vitals and gnaws there.'

'I liked Byron when I was younger. My taste is altered now. Well, I'm relieved, or should I say disappointed? I thought you meant you were jealous about me.'

'Oh, I am.'

'Good.' She laughed. Keats did not, quite.

Part Five

Not in vain,
Even for its own sake, do we purchase pain.

Byron, *Epistle to Augusta*

If I have erred, there was no joy in error,
But pain and insult and unrest and terror.

Shelley, *Julian and Maddalo*

I had a dove and the sweet dove died;
And I have thought it died of grieving.
O, what could it grieve for? Its feet were tied,
With a silken thread of my own hand's weaving.

Keats, *Song* ('I had a dove')

Part Five

1

Falling, Again

No one is watching the woman on her way towards death.

She is seen, unconsciously witnessed. A pale, slight, grave-faced woman of not much more than twenty, in a sober grey walking-dress of English make, strolling down to the quays of the Porto Mediceo.

Shockingly pale, deathly pale perhaps? But this is Leghorn or Livorno: an Englishwoman is far from a rare sight in this port where English merchants have long traded and where English sailors feel almost as at home as in Portsmouth. And the hour is the sharp dusk of the Mediterranean: above the red roofs and the spiked web of rigging in the harbour the sky flames, but down in the narrow streets with their grated windows and shuttered cellars and blind alleys there is already a purple dusk like the bloom on grapes. It is easy for the young woman to slip like a ghost (which she is not, though she has seen them) down to a quiet spot on a half-rotten quay, like a crazy crutch staggering into the glowing sea, away from a clutch of fishing-boats where a few fishermen are mending nets, gossiping, whistling. A gull scavenging for fish struts affrontedly out of her way. She notices the amazing sleekness of its head, like something carved, surely, not feathered. And standing at the end of the quay, looking down into the water, she wonders if that will be the last thing she ever notices.

Stop her.

Perhaps, Shelley had said, perhaps after all they had better keep little Allegra with them, rather than send her to Byron's care.

'But that's why we brought her to Italy,' Mary challenged him. 'This is what has been long agreed by everyone.'

Wincing, Shelley nodded. But, but . . . 'Claire is so attached to the little one. It's all very well if she can count on continuing to see her at certain times, and knowing she is well cared for. But Byron writes so very vaguely on this matter, I cannot be sure—'

'He is quite certain that he wishes to have the charge of Allegra,' Mary said. 'It's Claire he doesn't want to see, or have anything to do with.'

And God forgive me, she thought, I understand him perfectly.

'Then there are these stories about Byron,' Shelley said uncomfortably. 'The way he is living in Venice.'

'There are stories about us, and always have been,' she snapped back. 'It doesn't mean they're true, does it?'

Since their Lake Geneva summer, Byron had made his home in Venice, and Venice had made much of him. Wherever he went, he was famous or infamous, but he had never been quite so talked about. The *grand signor Inglese* in riotous, scandalous, voluptuous residence at the Palazzo Mocenigo on the Grand Canal: even in stately and cultured Milan, where the Shelley party first stayed on arriving in Italy, he was a byword. Perhaps, Shelley had suggested, this was not after all a place to send little Allegra. And Claire vacillated.

'I can hardly bear to part with her. I could weep tears of blood at the thought of it. But I do want her to know her father. And as he is going to own her – and considering who he is – and now he has sold Newstead at last and is clear of debt and well set up – well, surely it will be a great thing for her, will it not?'

Yes, good. But then Shelley mused that Allegra might be brought up with them, as their own child, and be none the worse . . .

Oh, much the worse, for Mary. And it was not that she didn't care for Allegra, a rosy little charmer with her mother's quickness:

not at all. But Allegra brought up by them would mean a household united for ever, Wilmouse and Clara and Allegra, Shelley and Mary and Claire, and who belonged to whom would become imprecise, blurred, irrelevant . . . So her fears whispered, invoking bad memories of Hogg the aptly named with his ghastly wooing, conjuring images of herself and Claire and Shelley actually joined together like the paper-chain men that Shelley loved to cut out to amuse the children. Oh, much the worse.

And it was Mary who broke the impasse. Let Elise go along with the child to Venice. Elise, their Swiss nurse: capable, handsome: Elise, her rounded hips seeming always to be swaying, taking up the room, even when she sat down: who seemed always to have just been looking at you, even when her eyes were far off. Yes, good. ('I shall miss Elise,' Shelley said. Yes, good.)

So little nameless Allegra with her little trunk packed was sent off by the lumbering unsprung coach to Venice with Elise to become Allegra Byron. Claire, after a passionate weeping-fit, emerged on to one of her bleak plateaux of honesty. 'I suppose,' she said to Mary, 'it was what I wanted, when I first sought him out. It can be rather terrible, you know, to get what you want.'

(Thus, the steps leading to this place, the jetty above the sea, shards of water-light nudging the rotted timbers below and across the lilac bay the declining sun a disc dabbled with gore.)

And then all was well, of course all was well. Elise sent regular reports from Venice: Allegra at Byron's house was being treated like a little princess, dressed in short trousers trimmed with lace, cooed over by contessas. The Shelleys – and Claire – settled in a villa at Bagna di Lucca, a spa town in the hills. They rode. They went down to the casino to peep at Princess Pauline Bonaparte, Napoleon's sister, who was taking the waters, and to watch the English visitors dance stiff-jointed quadrilles while cicadas shrilled in the chestnut woods beyond the open windows. Clara, who had just started walking, followed Wilmouse round the laurel-shaded garden of the villa, a fat-legged, determined attendant, and they were both as brown as eggs.

Shelley worked. His brain was dry and he was refreshing it with translation: the *Symposium* of Plato. Mary, making a fair copy, looked up in shock.

'He, yes, I mean he,' said Shelley: he had been watching. 'This is usually suppressed in accounts of ancient Greek manners. I was startled at first. But I have thought my way round it. Though they were in advance of us in so many ways, their treatment of women was still arrested at a barbaric stage. Women were so cabined and confined and uneducated that there could hardly be any loving companionship between them and men. Hence the sexual love between men.' He went to the window and eased back a shutter: a giant blazing light immediately took possession of the cool study. His slender silhouetted back to her, he went on: 'But really this is looking at it in the wrong way. Because the love is the thing. The rest is machinery. Oh, yes,' he added, as if a voice had challenged him, 'the love is the thing.'

Then came the letters from Elise in Venice.

'I don't understand,' Mary said to Shelley, while Claire, crooning and cursing, noisily packed a bag in the bedroom next door. 'What does she mean to do? What *is* there to do?'

'I suppose she wants to see for herself where Byron has placed Allegra. Also part of Elise's letter is rather difficult to read, and that in itself troubles her. Mary.' He put his hands on her shoulders. 'She has a mother's natural anxieties.'

Funny how men understood those better than women, Mary thought, before she could stop herself. 'If they're in the care of the British Consul, they must be in perfectly good case. Probably the Consul's house is a much more suitable place than Albé's house.'

Shelley shrugged, and began hunting through his trunk. 'She wants to see for herself.'

'What are you doing?'

'Well, I must go with her,' he said reasonably. 'Yes, Paolo might go along, but you wouldn't want her to make a two-hundred-mile journey across Italy with just a manservant. I'm sure.

Besides –' he thrust his hopelessly crumpled shirts into a valise, true Shelleyan packing '– it may be a question of negotiation. And with Byron––'

'He hates me,' Claire said, appearing in the doorway. She was pale and again unhappiness had made her searingly honest. 'Or at least he's so indifferent to me that it amounts to hate.'

'If he were indifferent,' Shelley began, 'then––'

'Words aren't everything, Shelley,' Claire snapped. 'He hates me because I happened just at the time when his wife had left him, and he was being cut in society, and everyone had turned against him. I remind him of that. I know it very well, I know what reaction I can expect if I turn up at his door. So if you will help me, Shelley, I shall be very glad. If you don't mind, Mary?'

And so, what was there to say?

Shelley and Claire left for Venice in a one-horse cabriolet. Mary tried to work. Shelley had urged her to try writing a play: her father's letters, in between abusing Shelley and asking for money, suggested she write historical biography. Everyone knew what was best. Mary's mind was more expert in the worst. She had not seen that flitting ghost from the corner of her eye lately: but alone in bed she had a piercing nightmare (or dream – with Mary it was the same) in which Shelley announced that he was not coming back to her. He was in Venice, and so was she somehow: she stood beside a canal, and Shelley was in a gondola going gently by her, and he waved and said that as rational beings they understood when the time had come to part, did they not? And beside him in the gondola, wearing a carnival vizard – was it a woman? Was it Claire? Was it Byron? The gondola glided away, leaving her standing, looking down at the rippling water . . .

(As now she stands, gritty boards under her shoes, looking down at the thirsty Mediterranean as the sun struggles gloriously and drowns in the horizon.)

She woke from the nightmare to brilliant light and heat like an orchestral *tutti*. Giving up the attempt to work, she played in the garden with Wilmouse and Clara. At some point, sitting on the grass, she drifted into reverie, and came out of it to find Wilmouse holding a grizzling Clara with difficulty in his arms.

'She's not very well,' he confided. 'I'm hugging her better.'

The Italian doctor from the town smiled and diagnosed a mild infantile fever. 'But she will not eat,' Mary told him, in the careful Italian she had learnt from Dr Pollydolly, and he replied, 'Good, that is the best thing, to starve the stomach.' Discussing it in Italian made it all seem formal, operatic, unreal. The still smiling doctor rode off in the blazing afternoon, disappearing into the sunlight as if it had absorbed him.

Clara was still gripy and feverish when the letter came from Shelley at Venice.

It was like this. He and Claire had gone straight to the Consul's house, and found a warm welcome: the Consul and his wife were excellent people, and they had seen Allegra and found her very contented there. Then Shelley had gone on alone to the Palazzo Mocenigo to call on Byron and discuss the matter with him. Knowing how Byron felt about Claire descending on him, he had had to play it carefully. So he had told Byron that the whole Shelley party had travelled to nearby Padua and, being so close and Claire naturally anxious about her child, he had taken it upon himself to call and enquire. It was subtly done. Byron was delighted to see him: they talked and talked, in his gondola, on the sandy stretch of the Lido where Byron took his daily ride. Byron seemed to want to revive the old stimulating days of Diodati, and soon proposed that the Shelleys and the children and Claire should move into his summer villa at Este outside Venice. Claire could easily see Allegra there, as much as she liked, but there would be no unwanted intimacies to embarrass anyone.

A perfect plan but for one thing. It was based on a fib. Mary and the children were not at nearby Padua at all: they were two hundred miles away at Bagna di Lucca. But all would be well if she packed up the house and came at once. Shelley gave her directions – start at four in the morning, go by post-chaise to Lucca, then hire a *vetturino* to Florence, post from Florence to

Este – sent fifty pounds for her expenses, and signed off with kisses.

It was August. The journey took five days across the stony roads of Italy baking in kiln-like heat. Mary's twenty-first birthday passed unmarked. Clara yelled when Mary lifted the leather shades of the coach-windows, yelled when she lowered them. Her little bowels ran constantly. Wilmouse, uncomplaining, covered his nose with orange-peel. Teeth, just teeth, said Paolo, handsome, thick-necked, always a little too ready with an answer. Often in the hills they had to get out while the horses toiled up the slope. Customs officials stuck their hands in for tips, beggars for alms. Mary's ankles were fettered with scarlet flea-bites.

This was the journey that Claire could not be expected to make alone. Yes, she thought it, over and over. She even thought it until she had exhausted the anger and resentment it produced, and began to make excuses on the other side. What did she love Shelley for? His reckless spontaneity – like this. His helplessly generous nature – like this. His treatment of her as a reasonable human being and not a trembling little rose – and so on. If she loved him for these things, could she hate him for them? Could she?

As for Claire, she was the occasion of it all, of course, but then she always was. When it rained, Mary would not have been surprised to look up and see a cloud in the shape of Claire.

She reached Este, at last, to find a paradisal scene. The villa Byron had lent them was an airy fantasy overlooking the plain of Lombardy: here Shelley and Claire were already settled with a radiant Allegra, and Shelley had a study in the summer-house. He showed her it proudly. She felt like the serpent.

'Clara has been so ill all the way. Is there a doctor hereabouts? I really think she is no better.'

'Poor little Ca. I've had a wretched stomach and so has Claire. Food I think. There is a *medico* in the town, I'll send for him. I have the Prometheus myth in my head. A verse drama – what do you think?'

She thought Clara was dangerously ill. So, her black eyes

549

round with alarm, did Claire. So at last did Shelley. The local doctor was an idiot. Teeth, teeth. Paolo nodded sagely. Shelley had heard great things of Byron's own physician in Venice. Venice it must be. Another start before dawn, another dragging journey, this time by horse-drawn barge along the Brenta canal. Elegant villas set about with trellised vines and arbours came slowly, slowly, into view, faded. Clara, yellow and wasted, convulsed feebly on Mary's lap. The sun rose and mounted its harsh guard. Finally the lagoon of Venice glittered ahead of them: slowly, slowly they were piloted across. Then, at the customs house, panic.

'I've forgotten my passport.' Shelley turned his white, blank face to her. 'It's in the summer-house.'

'They must let us through.' Surprise at her own measured voice: inside there was skirling and shrieking.

The guard on duty was a very young man, nervously fingering an embryonic moustache. Shelley gave him a torrent of violent beseeching Italian: cowed, he waved them through to the gondola-stage. Mary had caught only the words '*My baby is dying.*'

Shelley put her ashore at an inn, then took off again in search of the physician. She walked up and down the hallway of the inn, noticing things: the damp smell, the way the canal-water continually reflected on the ceiling, the little earthenware charcoal-pot carried by the page of a lace-mantillaed crone to warm her skeletal hands in the cold night, the bare brown legs of the inn-servants who passed and repassed and at length began to gather round her, offering advice in an incomprehensible dialect, crossing themselves when they looked into Clara's contorted face.

Steps that bring Mary here, to the stirring waiting sea, to the brink of an end. Here is one step: that Venetian inn hallway, and Shelley coming back at last breathless and desperate, and meeting Mary's eyes as she turned to him. She was still holding Clara in her arms, but Clara's struggles had finished a few minutes since.

They buried her on the salt beach beyond the lagoon.

'Shall I prate to you of Providence?' Byron said afterwards. 'Or hold my tongue?'

'Prate to me of something,' Mary said.

So he talked to her of Venice, his new fiefdom. The little life was gone: let us not speak of it: instead, here was the abundant, overripe, cheese-mite life of the city on the water. Byron – who had undergone his own sea-change, who was somewhat Venetian in his splendid seediness, his face heavy, his hair too long at the back for the receding brow – showed them around. With difficulty Mary observed her duty to be impressed. Gondolas reminded her of floating coffins. The Doge's palace was awash like a great privy. In the gloomy interior of St Mark's feral dogs loomed at you with gaping, dripping mouths. The steps up to the Rialto were slippery with heaped refuse. There was much beauty, but you could not unpick it from the ugliness.

Something about this appealed to Byron.

'Now there's a healthful sight,' he said one morning, when the Grand Canal ahead was almost blocked by rafts and barges heaped with fruit. 'Fresher than Covent Garden.' Buyers were darting nimbly from boat to boat. In front of their eyes a noblewoman had her servant-boy slice open a water-melon with a knife and then, throwing back her veil, thrust her painted face into its moist flesh, champing. Byron laughed. 'This is not so much breakfast as supper. They've been up all night, gaming or whoring, and now they'll go home to bed. Ah, *dolce far niente*.'

He knew this, of course, from experience. While shepherding the Shelleys he was conforming himself to the decencies, but it was plain how he usually lived here, in the city known as the brothel of Europe. Palazzo Mocenigo had obviously been hastily prepared for Mary's visit – no half-dressed mistresses dangling about – but there was no disguising its raffish flavour. Byron's apartments were up an echoing marble staircase on the *piano nobile*: huge painted ceilings, Chinese wallpaper, gilt chairs, moulting Turkey rugs, smell of lamp-oil and verbena and mould. Above, the servants' floor: he had lost count of how many he had and let them live pretty much as they liked: thence came sounds of singing, quarrelling, frank fornication. Below, a cavernous floor given over to Byron's abandoned carriages and his animals – dogs, cats, parrots, monkeys, crows, a fox. The subterranean stink and noise seemed in some obscure way to please him, or say something to him. This, this is what is underneath it all, perhaps.

'How do you work here?' she asked him, listlessly: it seemed an impossibility, but then so did everything now.

'With great ease and facility,' he said smiling. And he had: there was a new verse-tale, *Mazeppa*. He asked Mary if she would take it, run her critical eye over it and produce a fair copy: of course it would be a lot of work.

Yes, work, please. Byron understood that: he was an acute judge of unhappiness. And did he understand, did he see the yawning gap between her and Shelley, the gap that could not be filled by any tender murmurs of consolation and mutual sorrow? Did he understand how she could hardly bear to look at Claire? – Claire who was the only reason they had ever come here – even though back at the villa in Este Claire was all kindness, all sad strokings of her arm, all solicitous urgings of Allegra to come away and not bother Aunt Mary. (Pretty sparky Allegra who was alive and well and Clara was dead.) Perhaps he did, but understanding could only do so much, and Mary felt herself unwanted, with her dry, stony, level grief that in this volatile world could only look like coldness. She stayed immured at Este, copying out Byron's poem in her neat, clear hand. Shelley spent much time with Byron, at Mocenigo, riding on the Lido, talking. All the talk that he and Mary could not have, that Mary could not trust herself with (you gave me Clara and then you killed her, you have given me my life and yet you destroy it) he seemed to pour out to Byron.

'Half the ladies of Venice are in love with him,' Mary said at last, with a deadly sort of levity, 'and now you as well.'

Shelley was silent for an age before he answered. 'I'm trying to understand him,' he said slowly. 'He is intimate with these troops of women, none of whom he cares for. He doesn't mind how he procures them. And then there are these youths – I don't know what to call them. And yet he knows how disgusting this all is. He's not blind to it – quite the opposite. It's as if he's trying to prove something about life.'

'Life does that for us,' Mary said. They looked emptily at each other: the look led nowhere.

Venice, under any circumstances, was not for them. South, south: there the warmth would thaw. Heal. So, via Rome, where she gazed uncomprehending at grass-grown ruins and insolent vaunting domes, laboriously down through waste and bandit-haunted country – troubled though by nothing worse than ravening mosquitoes – to Naples, where sky, bay, Vesuvius, all seemed to tally with something in her mind at last. This was a landscape of dreams – good dreams.

For a couple of months it remained so. Their lodgings were in the Riviera di Chiaia, grandly overlooking the Royal Gardens and with a wide view of the bay: just to use the eye was to be occupied for a whole day. Wilmouse was thriving: their old nurse Elise, whom he adored, had elected to come back to them. Claire was tolerable. And Shelley – well, he wasn't there, not the whole of him. Dutifully he went sightseeing, noted his impressions, wrote. But he was more a phantom than a husband. Sometimes, pouring coffee or opening the window for air, Mary found she had quite forgotten his corporeal existence, thinking of him more as a memory or an image. In bed she turned away from him. She could not imagine doing otherwise. This was how they lived. It was a way.

Life, like some odd hobby, went on elsewhere. Once or twice she came across Elise and Paolo kissing in the kitchen. Mary was coming to mistrust ever-shrugging, ever-innocent, eyebrow-wrinkling Paolo, or to mistrust him more. But when she mentioned to Elise that she did not think an attachment to him a good idea, she got only a sniff and a pout. Well, let them get on with it.

Then Paolo, still blandly shrugging, was caught with his coat-pockets full of purloined money. Elise wept when Mary told her Paolo must go. Elise was growing thick around the middle. Ah. The old story.

'He must marry you,' Mary said.

Elise stared at her — angrily, it seemed — through her subsiding storm of tears.

'He cannot.'

'To be sure he can. He has no prior attachment, has he? And though I think him a great rascal, you seem mighty romantic together. And even Paolo cannot leave you to face the world alone in that condition.'

Elise stared again, then shut her mouth with an absolutely audible snap. 'As you say. Yes. I would like to be married.'

So they lost both Paolo and Elise. Mary, watching them go off to be married at the British Embassy, tried to hush an inconsolable Wilmouse, making him impossible promises. Shelley always strongly disapproved that as a way of pacifying children. But Shelley had absented himself. The whole business of Elise seemed to have deeply upset him.

He came home late that night. He had been wandering down by the shore: she could tell from the grains of sand that dropped on to the pillow beside her, the briny smell. For a moment it made her heart open: only a moment.

He put his hand on her shoulder. 'Mary.'

She did not actually shrug him off: she gathered herself, stiffened, sent out silence: it was enough.

He sat up. The blackness was tinged with red from the smoke-glow of Vesuvius. 'Where are you, Mary?' he asked.

'Here.'

She felt rather than saw him shake his head. 'No, you're not.' He lay suddenly back as if struck. 'I've got to fetch you back.'

Silence fell. The vast inches between their bodies teemed with misunderstanding. Mary feigned sleep. She was extremely good at this. Growing up with Claire, you had to. She lay thinking, wondering how Elise was getting along. At some point, before falling asleep at last, she mentally remarked how big Elise's belly had been, considering she and Paolo had only met a couple of months ago.

There were terrace gardens below the villas of Chiaia di Riviera, and it was here that she saw Shelley with the shawled baby in his arms. She was at the window: he waved up at her.

She went down. It was February: here, soft and mild. Nurse-maids were airing children in the gardens, and as she came up to Shelley, who was cooing his old refrain, *Yahmani, yahmani*, to the baby, Mary assumed it must be one such that he had asked to hold. Again her heart nearly opened. Then: 'Look,' he said, showing the little dark head. 'Isn't she beautiful?'

'Yes.' Mary glanced around. 'Where—'

'Beautiful,' he went on. 'Her name is Elena Adelaide. Elena Adelaide Shelley.'

Mary, reaching out a yearning hand, froze. 'This is a poor joke.'

'No, no, no. I have been to the town hall and recorded her as our child. It's easily done. Look at her, Mary.'

'No.' It was at Shelley she looked, his dramatic boy's eyes, his cheeks stinging with anxious hope. His dark hair, put aside with that absent hand. She turned and blindly stumbled away from him.

He came after her, running, the baby mewing protest at the motion. 'Mary – I want to make it up to you—'

She spun round to him. 'You're mad.'

'Oh, I know that,' he said dismissively, as if she had mentioned the weather.

'Whose is that child?'

'She is ours. She can be ours—'

'Who does that child belong to, Shelley?'

'Now, come, you know that no human being can be the mere possession of another—'

She hit him in the face. It was not a slap. The baby mirrored his open-mouthed look.

'You've chosen the wrong moment to lecture me,' she hissed at him. Rare, this temper, but fierce and exquisite.

'A child belongs with those who love it most,' he said, his tone still gentle, unaltered. His lip seeped blood. 'Surely. The baby is Elise's. I've been to see her. Paolo – Paolo won't acknowledge it or support it, because it can't be his. He is an unreasonable brute. Look at her – what can that matter?'

'If not Paolo's, whose?'

Shelley kissed the top of the little head, leaving a dab of blood. 'Who can say?' There was a kind of unanswerable finality in his tone. Shelley did not hit: but he had his own flintiness. Weeks and months passed in swift review through Mary's brain: her turned shoulder, Shelley wandering disconsolate. Who can say? 'If Paolo won't provide for her, then I have engaged to do so.'

'You mean pay for her maintenance? Or something else?' Mary took a step back: the child was reaching out a hand.

'If we adopted her,' Shelley said perseveringly, 'then think – think of the joy of seeing her grow, of—'

'I don't want to see her grow. I don't want her. I want Clara. I want Clara back.' Entirely without warning Mary was crying, wailing, helpless – babylike indeed: she could feel her mouth grow square as she sobbed. Even in the midst of this terrible abandon, her mind worked like a faithful secretary, noting that this was the first time she had said it since Venice, the first time it had come out. 'I want her. It hurts.'

'I know,' Shelley said. 'I know. I'm sorry. I just thought – well, it was wrong. I wanted to stop it. The hurt.' He looked as if he would have embraced her, but the baby was in the way.

They left Naples at the end of February, aiming to spend the spring in Rome. Shelley had sought out foster-parents for Elena: Mary did not ask for details. They travelled slowly by way of Gaeta, where olive and orange groves tumbled down to a spangled bay and they seemed the only people in the world. They stayed at a clifftop inn, built it was said on the site of Cicero's villa. She seemed to hear a melancholy boom of ancient memories in the buffeting sea that night: the world was wide and old, and mortality was lonely. She turned to Shelley and caressed him: they made love, subsided into a silence that enshrined a new covenant.

Why now? Why ever? Who can say? A voice deep inside Mary said: *At least it was not Claire he turned to.* But it was faint. Mary was growing adept at walling these voices up behind thicker and stouter courses of stone.

In Rome, a return to life. The world, which had been a dismal fresco of flatness, took on three dimensions again as the light of interest brightened. Interest: it seemed so long since Mary had felt it, and now it was rampant in her. Presentation to the doddering Pope, whose translucent skin reminded her of that of a new-shorn lamb. Carved signs outside the windowless shops – a Turk's head with a pipe for a tobacconist, a cardinal's hat for a tailor. A pockmarked prostitute breezily making her bargain with her mark directly underneath the towering marble of the Arch of Titus. A gang of chained prisoners digging up weeds in St Peter's Square, heads down, while their guards, heads down, leant on their muskets and diced for coppers. Returning life, too, in her companions. Shelley had the wrapped, indrawn look that indicated inspiration. He took pens and paper each day to the spectacular ruins of the Baths of Caracalla and wrote madly and perilously, perched on ruined steps and shattered columns. Claire still fretted over Allegra and peppered Byron with hopeless letters, but she was becoming confident in Italian and was applying herself seriously to her music and – Mary noticed it with a sort of abstract admiration – was now really a thoroughly cosmopolitan young woman. (Alas, moaned Mary, behind the bricks: for what man now could suit her? Only someone like Byron. Or Shelley.) And Wilmouse, too, chattered in macaronic Italian and scrambled about the grass-grown Coliseum, a little blond barbarian, while Mary sketched and then laid down her pencil and allowed herself, daringly, just to sit and be content: just to be.

And she was expecting another baby. When she told Shelley, he sat in silent concentration, his spatulate fingers spread out on her belly.

'You won't feel anything for ages yet,' she said amused.

'Oh, I know. I'm doing magic. Putting a spell on him. Her. A spell of . . .' *Protection*, she thought, '. . . of deepest magic.' He laughed, though with a sort of longing. He had often said he dreamt of being a medieval alchemist. She could just see him, wild-haired, zodiac-robed, among cobwebbed tomes and bubbling retorts.

Unexpectedly, so many miles from home, she met someone straight from the Skinner Street days, a spirited Irishwoman who had been part of the Godwin circle and now lived in Rome, quite independent, making her living as a painter. The next thing they knew, they were sitting for their portraits.

Shelley was happy to have a picture of Wilmouse, but he hesitated at first about having his own portrait made: he saw it, with his odd touch of puritanism, as vanity.

'Oh, pooh, you've never had your likeness taken yet, and it's high time,' Claire told him. 'After all, Byron has been painted a score of times. And they say he watches the progress of every picture, to make sure it flatters him, and that they make his nose straight instead of turning up at the end – which it does, have you noticed? Allegra has it.'

Shelley laughed. 'How absurd. Well, as you wish.' Claire could often breeze him into things. The laughter was genuine. He really did not care what he looked like, and could not imagine anyone else doing so.

'You're living in the Corso?' The painter was surprised.

'Rather fashionable, I know,' Shelley said deprecatingly. 'But central, convenient.'

'Oh, it's not that. It's just that with a little child – you know the summer is malaria season in Rome. And it's always worst in that part of the city. The air, you know. That's why I live up here. Never had a touch of fever.'

Up here was the Via Sistina, directly above the Spanish Steps. They wasted no time. There were rooms available in the next-door house. Mary silently congratulated herself once they moved in. You could feel the air was sweeter here. And it was more congenial: a lot of artists lived in the district, flower-sellers sang their wares outside the windows, you could stroll without bumping into platoons of English nursemaids. Perhaps someone was watching over them, after all.

The day before Wilmouse fell ill, Mary had been cutting his hair. On impulse she kept some of the bright yellow tendrils in her purse. They outlasted him. They were still bright ten days later when Wilmouse, William Shelley, three and a half years old, died without a sound on his bed, where malarial fever had put him through unimaginable torments before a kindly coma supervened.

They buried him in the Protestant cemetery. Mary thought, in as much as she thought anything: Make a little room there. Put me in. I am the walking dead. Walking, just: she broke down on their return to the Via Sistina, and Shelley had to carry her up the steps to their lodgings.

Steps. The last step, then, to this place, where Mary stands with her feet protruding over the edge of the jetty, and demands an answer from her courage.

They came straight here to Leghorn from Rome – intolerable Rome that had gobbled Wilmouse into its titan maw. The villa they rented was outside the town, secluded amid vineyards and toast-coloured cornfields with the sea on the other hand: a retreat. Shelley made it doubly so. At the very top of the house was a glassed-in room, like an overgrown skylight, and this he made his study. 'My tower,' he called it. He ascended early each morning and plunged into work. That was his answer, to beat out flat the hard lump of grief. But alone. It was apt that no one but he could bear the ferocious heat of that glass room.

Meanwhile it was Claire who fussed over Mary, clumsily trying to nudge her towards an acceptance of life. She even postponed a trip to see Allegra rather than leave her. But even in Claire's ministrations there was an unspoken assumption, or presumption: we will do this, we will get you better, and then we can recommence life. Mary, who could still hardly bring herself to speak to Claire, was quite unable to tell her the bleak truth that there was no getting her better, that she did not seek to be better, that life was not going to begin again.

And from her father, a sternly philosophical letter, reproving her for indulging in selfishness and ill humour. 'Do not,' he scolded her, 'put the miserable delusion on yourself to think there is something fine, and beautiful, and delicate, in giving yourself up, and agreeing to be nothing.' Meanwhile, he was in debt for rent arrears, so if that immoral man she had married should care to keep his promises and send some more money . . . Shelley was wild. Don't open any more letters from him, he stormed. He was finished with Godwin.

Not a choice for Mary: her father was family, care, grief, things you were never finished with. Unless you made one simple decision.

Oh, she had thought of it in the abstract: the answer to the question of despair, like a mathematical equation. But it was her father's letter that had made the thing a concrete possibility in her mind: the last step to this watery place. Equations. Wrong again, Mary, he was telling her: not good enough. Her mother's unfortunate spirit in her, perhaps. She knew all about her mother's suicide attempt, from the typically unsparing memoir of her written by her father. Well, follow the steps. Mary had in effect killed her mother, by being born. Then, through her own choices, through Shelley and Claire, she had killed her own two children. Now there was another, new in the womb. Was it not ordained, inevitable, that she should kill this one too? Yes, let them go together. Now she understood why that corner-of-the-eye ghost followed her everywhere. Harriet Shelley, who had drowned herself and her unborn child. Her exemplar. Her victim. Her guide.

Full circle. Oh, yes. That was why Mary could never embrace Shelley's whole-hearted atheism: because she saw that the world turned on grim cogs of atonement and retribution. I was the one who drove Harriet to death, just as surely as if I had stood behind her on the bank of the Serpentine and pushed. Now the cogs turn. And isn't that her old familiar ghost there, rising out of the dark sequined sea like a mermaid, waving and calling – inviting? Shelley once said he would give all science's discoveries just to know that somewhere there was such a thing as a mermaid. Water, water everywhere. Her legs trembled. She was weeping and afraid. A hand touched her arm, grasped it.

'Signora. Signora.'

She turned. It was a beggar. Old, toothless, face like seamed leather and bright with an immemorial habit of speculation. His grip was so strong. His other hand, open, dirt-grained, came out towards her.

'Something, something for the poor. A little something . . .'

Mary stared. Was this meant to happen? Presumably, as it had happened. She glanced back out to sea. She could not see the beckoning mermaid. The beggar retained his clawlike grip, peering up into her face. He did not care if she killed herself, it was not that, he wanted money. Now, what was she to take from this? Could you be saved by irony?

She spoke, and her voice felt as strange and rusty as if she had not used it for a year. 'I have nothing to give.'

'There must be something.' The beggar put his head wheedlingly on one side. 'Signora, there must be something.'

She had no money on her, none at all. You didn't need it where she was going. Suddenly she laughed, and that felt as strange as if it were the first time in a decade. The laugh got mixed up with tears. The beggar waited, watchful, dodging about her.

'There must be something. Signora . . .'

On the breast of her dress there was a simple brooch-pin with a pearl head. She drew it out and handed it to him. He studied it, shrugged, pocketed it. He sidled away, just to the other end of the quay, keeping his eye on her, perhaps she would produce more pieces of jewellery . . .

There must be something.

It was quite dark when she got back to the villa. Claire was waiting at the door with a storm-lantern. 'Where have you been? I've been half sick—'

'On a long walk. Where's Shelley?'

'Still working. Lord, I've been so afraid for you—'

'Why?'

Claire held up the lamp with a frown. 'Always there has to be a reason. Come in, I saved some soup for you.

Mary sat down. She looked at the soup in front of her, then picked up a spoon. Yes, this is what we do. Steps.

'I do know how you're feeling,' Claire said, standing over her.

'Do you?' Mary sipped, swallowed. 'How?'

'Through imagining it. Imagining what it would be like to lose Allegra.'

'Oh, God, don't have imagination, Claire. Whatever you do, don't have that.'

Steps. Mary lives, or acts as if she is alive. The days succeed each other, instead of collapsing inward like a house of cards. There is a sort of comfort in mere sequence.

News from England brings Shelley raging and incandescent out of his glass tower. The tyranny that masquerades as government has shown its true colours. A peaceful crowd, men, women and children, gathered to hear a reforming orator in St Peter's Fields, Manchester, has been dispersed by a cavalry charge. Eleven people were killed by the swords of their own countrymen and hundreds injured. The government has congratulated the magistrates and soldiers on their prompt action. Already, in bitter reference to the victory of Waterloo, the event is being called the massacre of Peterloo.

'Now here,' says Shelley, preparing to write on it, looking ecstatic with anger, 'is a real tragedy.'

On the move again, to Florence, where the best medical attendance is to be found. As Mary's belly grows, so does her anxiety. The fact that in her own mind she does not deserve this child makes her all the more protective of it. Shelley urges her to visit the galleries with him, to view paintings and statues, to read widely, to take in the vastness of the world. She tries: but must confess, at last, that she prefers to lie on the horsehair sofa in their rooms in the creaking oil-smelling *pensione*, and wait.

Gently Shelley suggests: 'It's a great deal to place on one little life.'

'What?'

He hesitates. 'All your happiness.'

After a moment's thought, she kisses him. They glance at each other in the dry aftermath of lips. Often their kisses are like this now: not lacking warmth, but with a certain dubiety, as if they both expect something to happen that doesn't.

'I don't expect happiness,' she informs him.

No omens good or bad, no foretellings or conclusions: Mary will have none of that: one step at a time. That this labour is her easiest, two hours from first pains to easy delivery, means nothing and should be taken as meaning nothing. The cogs still turn, and nothing can be taken on trust.

'A fine boy. A very fine boy. You must be very pleased, Mrs Shelley.' There are several English couples staying at the *pensione*, and they come upstairs to tiptoe in and offer sedate congratulations. She is quite glad of this – not too glad, that would not do, that would invite reprisals from fate – rather than the more fulsome Italian response to a birth, blessings and cheek-pinchings. She must be careful, they must all be careful. The boy is, indeed, a very fine boy, a beautiful boy (careful), but take nothing on trust. Bank up the fire, for the winters here are cold: none of that lemon cordial, for it spoils her milk.

Percy Florence Shelley. He grows quickly, thrives and fattens, reveals his grandfather Godwin's nose – and what is Godwin but a survivor? – still, caution, caution. Snow ornaments the domes and campaniles of Florence. Bitter winds funnel down into the city: at night the shutters groan and snap and sometimes Mary wakes in terror, flinging herself upright.

'It's all right,' Shelley says sleepily, reaching for her. 'I'm here.'

She evades his arm. She knows he's there: that is not the consolation she seeks. She goes to the cradle, and reassures herself of her son's sleeping warmth. From behind she hears something that may be snow caressing the window, or else a sigh.

2

Passive Resistance

You have not heard from me yet. Never fear, I shall not try your patience. I abominate a bore above all things. I simply want to tell you how it was, before – well, never mind.

Miss Brawne, yes. You may call me Fanny. And what am I to call you? Very well. Now at least we are on a sort of terms, if we should end up hating each other.

Well, because I am going to tell the truth, and in my experience there is no more reliable way of causing trouble between people.

Does that mean I prefer a comfortable lie? Oh, you don't know me very well, do you?

His poetry is so very beautiful – in the overwhelming undeniable way that a woman is beautiful – that one can forget his essential toughness. He got into a fight with the butcher, who was mistreating a kitten, and he won. I could imagine it, for all that he is not tall: that coppery head of his thrust low, fists windmilling. He said he was always doing it when he was a boy. He looked sheepish: he isn't proud of it. I suspect he feels this shows something about him – some mark of lowly origins. I catch that too when he talks of Mr Shelley the atheist, with whom he was on friendly terms rather than being his friend.

'Shelley is going to reform the world,' he said once, 'and as such he has no time to notice such things as coats and shoes, as long as they are expensive and of the very best.'

And speaking of atheism – well, there you may see this toughness too – toughness of the mind. He will have no truck with the Christian religion, and as I have a solid faith, which I hope I don't prate about, we have had our tiffs over it. But with Mr Keats it isn't the sort of puppyish sneering at religion that one hears goes on in Leigh Hunt's circle. He said to me once that he could no longer believe from the day he saw what a woman looked like with a cancer in her breast, when he was a student at Guy's.

Fine talk for a courting, you may say. Well: it's true I have sometimes teased him for his seriousness. Yes, and then the more serious he becomes the more one must tease.

'Your face goes the most perfect pearly pink when you're angry,' I said to him.

'I'm sorry,' said he, 'if my complexion displeases you.'

But it didn't, doesn't. This is the thing: I like him all the more for it. Teasing can mean love – and he who has such a fine intelligence can surely understand that. I hope.

Well, yes, there is more to teasing, I admit. It is an exercise of power. But consider – compared with men we women do not have physical power in our bodies, nor power in society or the world – we make no orations and sail no ships and gloriously flatten no cities. But over the card-table or the dance-floor we may hold sway. It may not be nice, but it is true. There, what did I tell you about truth?

I think also his life has demanded a good deal of toughness from him. First losing his parents when he was so young, and having to be, as it were, the head of the family almost from a boy. A guardian who was not at all sympathetic to his nature, and still seems to obstruct him at every turn – and then training to be a doctor, and mopping up after the most ghastly operations, and all the while his head full of poetry but his conscience telling him he must not give in to it. Then one brother going off to America and the other, poor fellow, dying of a consumption – well, I have no taste for the pathetic so I will stop, but you can see it has been one loss after another, and he has truly been through the fire.

No, I don't say these things to him. He would hate to see himself as an object of pity. That's his toughness too, you see. And why should one pity him, in truth? He is a wonderful young man, and a genius. This is not partiality. Ladies often declare their favourite gentlemen are geniuses on the strength of a few verses, certainly, but it is different with Mr Keats. As proof of this, I would only say that my taste generally runs to wit and humour, and Mr Keats's poetry is not of that kind – it is not 'my' kind at all, if you like. And yet I know that it is, as we used to say at school, beyond anything great.

Frightening: yes. Sometimes, I admit, I am a little frightened at what has happened. I look back over my life and think: How was I ever destined for this? One does not expect to meet a genius at a Hampstead carpet-dance. That sounds rather funny. Meet, and love, I should say.

Yes, I love Mr Keats. Consumedly. Yes, privately I call him otherwise, I call him by his first name, but really you must leave us some privacy. If there were no privacy, how would we ever have scandal?

Talking of fire – well, I was, a minute ago, really you must pay attention – he said to me, not long since, that the thought of me was like a fire. He was drawn to it, even as he feared that it would burn him up.

Yes, I was mightily pleased. Oh, I would much rather be the fire. Think of the other elements: earth is rather too plain and sluggish, and I hope I have too much sense to be forever floating about in the air, and water has something too cool about it for my temper, which is, I know, a little too much on the lively side. He says beautiful things, often. He says hurtful things too, sometimes, when one or other of us is in what I think of as a fiddle-strings mood – all twanging and tense. And when he is jealous. Oh, he is dreadfully jealous. Sometimes I can hardly believe how much. It seems so absurd.

Well, his toughness: because he has needed it so much, I fear it may have run out somewhat, when it comes to his work. You know his poems have been most shamefully abused by the reviews, *Blackwood's* and the *Quarterly* and such, and they have the power to make or break a man in Mr Keats's profession. Of course they attack him for who he is quite as much as his writing. He is associated with Leigh Hunt and the Radicals; and then they have got hold of his background, and his being trained for an apothecary, and so they say he is ill-bred and a Cockney and much more in that style. Really it is contemptible. And he tries to shake it off, but I know he cannot. It has wounded him in some very acute precise place.

After Mr Keats returned from Chichester, we moved next door to him and thus began the happiest time of my life thus far . . . I'm sorry, I had promised not to bore, and there I was rambling away, so I thought I had better press on at once. Telling you how it was.

Yes, Wentworth Place, that delightful double house: the Dilkes moved out of their half to take up residence in London where their son was at school, and so we moved in. Now, before you say a word, it was Mama's decision. We had stayed there before, and found it the pleasantest of lodgings, and we knew the Dilkes would not have left any unsavoury surprises in cupboards and so on (oh, you would be surprised), and Elm Cottage was draughty, and so we went. And yes, there on the other side of the party wall, there to be bumped into at any time in the shared garden, were Mr Brown and his good friend Mr Keats.

How can I explain it? Dear Mama was actually very fond of Mr Keats – a different thing from approving him as a suitable match, to be sure – but her face always lit up when she saw him. (So does anyone's, if they have sense, and a heart.) Besides that, Mama is very far from being a fool – though of course I would never tell her so. It is no kindness to flatter parents, because they will end up spoiled. She saw that there was an attachment between Mr Keats and me, and so instead of tearing us apart, which is always the one thing guaranteed to strengthen it, she decided to test it by throwing us together. So there must be an issue one way or another. Yes, no fool, Mama.

So: the happiest time. Nothing is more provoking than hearing of another person's happiness, I do realize, so I will be brief. I will mention only – oh, when Mama would say to me, not looking up from her sewing: 'Perhaps Mr Keats would like to come to tea,' and I would kiss her and run next door through the garden, and his face when he saw me, and how I would be an unconscionable time asking him that simple question. Or when we walked together on the Heath up towards Spaniards' Inn, and he told me how he had met Mr Coleridge one day taking his stroll on the Heath and how Mr Coleridge never stopped talking the whole time, his voice fading in and fading away like the rumble of a coach coming towards you and then going into the distance, and how he had been proud to shake Mr Coleridge's hand on account of the poetry he used to write but it was a puffy, flabby sort of hand and Mr Coleridge's talk of a similar kind – something about mermaids and whether he believed in them. And Mr Keats lifting me over a puddle and saying he would like to do this for ever – so I turned round and he lifted me back over it and so we went on for some time, laughing like mad people. And once after dinner Mr Keats trying to explain to me his ideal of beauty in poetry and then saying, 'Oh, hang it, here it is,' and he put his hands on my shoulders and turned me to the mirror on the wall.

Here it is. Oh dear.

Oh, and seeing him take a chair out to the garden, under the plum-tree, and watching his bent head there under the shade, writing, and somewhere in the leaves I could hear a nightingale.

Well, enough of that. You want some good, strong, interesting unhappiness. Very well. Mr Keats went away. Ah, your expression of relief.

This was not an ending. He went to spend the summer on the Isle of Wight, and I did not know when he would come back. But we wrote, oh, how we wrote. Why did he go? To think, to

569

work. Yes, here is a tasty little morsel of unhappiness for you: he could not work when I was so close by. His mind was not free. Regrettable consequence of falling in love with a poet, you see. Now if I had only fallen for one of those red-coated chuckle-heads from the barracks at St John's Wood, they would have been quite content to think of nothing but me all the time, having nothing else worthwhile in their noggins anyhow. But with an artist you may find you are a distraction – even a threat. Mr Keats would sometimes talk of my capturing him and imprisoning him. Now I know that those are conventional figures, old as the hills. Even the chuckleheads would sometimes say they were my slave and so on. But Mr Keats was not using the words lightly.

I tried to take them lightly, of course. Because taking things lightly is my habit – my creed, if you like.

And I mentioned that he was jealous. Well, again it is rather like with the teasing: show me the woman who claims she does not like making her lover a little jealous, and I will show you a shocking liar. Sometimes I didn't mean it. I met Mr Keats's friend, the young artist Mr Severn, and remarked what a handsome man he was. A mere statement of fact – also he reminded me of Mr Keats a little. But Mr Keats took it much amiss, and I had to reassure him. But then there were other times when I did dance and chat and flirt a little, and not mind it coming to Mr Keats's ears, because – well, he once said he had put pepper on his tongue the better to enjoy the coolness of wine: and so surely love is given a relish by not being too safe and comfortable.

This is rationalizing after the fact, to be sure. If you want the absolute truth, there were times, during his absence on the Isle of Wight, when I became quite taken up with enjoying myself at a card-party or a dance, and being admired (oh, you do *not* like being admired? – let me shake your hand – for you are the first and last person ever who did not), and talking nonsense, that I quite forgot about him.

Not for long. Always before bed his face and voice would float about me, and I would reread his letters, and long to see him again. But sometimes, yes, I did not think about him. And if for you this is incompatible with true love then you will probably not wish to hear any more from my lips. Very well, if so – though I would suggest that you have perhaps read more about love in books than actually experienced it.

Well, you should say something nasty to me back, then.

Was that it? No, it will do very well, thank you. Now we are even.

The trouble was, Mr Keats was always thinking of *me*, even when he did not want to, even when it was a torment to him. And this I could not help. Situated as he was, he grew bitter sometimes. He set great store by independence – an absolute independence of soul, no less – and now that was gone. Love is a strange business, and it seems to me that all those who have written about it in verse and story have only scratched the surface. No one sings songs, for instance, about the burden of being loved: but it can be a heavy one.

Sometimes he was very depressed. The obscurity of his literary reputation, his money troubles, the niggling ill-health that was a great fret to a man of his energy – and, to be sure, his prospects of marriage, or lack of same, all would heap up on his heart, and the result would be a dreadful darkness of spirit. Once I was reading one of his letters, and I found that my little sister Margaret (why do I say little? Ten years old, twenty in impudence, thirty in worldliness) had crept up and was reading over my shoulder.

'Ugh!' cries she. 'Wishing he could die by taking poison from your lips! I hope I never get a love letter like *that.*'

'The likelihood of your ever getting any kind of love letter is exceedingly remote,' said I, chasing her out of the room. She was so charming when she was a baby.

Of course I did not like it when he fell into this morbid temper, still less when I was the occasion of it. I think it possible to be loved too passionately – or, at least, too *extremely*. Ugh, said Margaret, and once she was gone I did not know whether to laugh or cry. Some girls might like such notions – poison on the lips and so on – but they would be great readers of trumpery Gothic novels full of ghosts and dungeons, and I have always preferred a sprightly comedy.

Also I did not like it when he talked of death. Not at all.

And so it was that when I felt the burden of his love oppress me, when I felt his love as an *infliction* (is that a word? – never mind, press on, you can look it up later), then I would often rush off to dress, and seek out a dance or a party. Even if it were only a pianoforte hop, as Mr Keats used to call them (he couldn't dance, you see, and he would sit by the wall glaring so balefully as if we were all fools), so long as there was plenty of company and talk and, yes, frivolity. I would talk nonsense and crack jokes right, left and centre (no, I didn't say they were *good* jokes) and watch the men jostling. Did you ever see one of those jugglers at a fair, who spins plates on upright sticks, a dozen of them all twirling at once, and he darts from one to the other and keeps them all going? Well, it was like that. Just keep everything spinning up in the air, never let anything fall to earth, and all would be well . . .

And then all at once I would realize how much those chuckleheads bored me, and I would dream of Mr Keats and that aching look of his, and his arms round me. Oh dear.

He talked much of my beauty. I reproved him for this. First, because I haven't got much (oh, nonsense – take a good look at this nose – you'll need to walk all round it), and second, because I felt it was not right for him to brood in that way. 'I don't much care to be brooded on,' I said once to him, 'as if I were a clutch of eggs.'

And he looked at me in delighted surprise and laughed. In fact that was often the way when we were together. But when we were apart, this melancholy would come on him, and he would paint me in its sable hues. There, you see, I can be flowery too. Never fear, I shan't do any more of it.

If there is one thing more tedious than someone telling you of their happiness, it is someone telling you of their woes, so I shall simply mention that when Mr Keats came back from the Isle of Wight I was in somewhat of a smarting state. He had written so strongly of the way he was trying to drive the thought of me out of his head – indeed, to *wean* himself from me, those were his disconcerting words – that I hardly knew what to think. And when he said it would be better if he did not come back to Wentworth Place, I could only reply that he must do as he pleased. So there, pooh to you, and so on. How childish lovers can seem – perhaps that is why love is so alarming, it reduces us to children again, little and vulnerable and powerless in a great world we do not understand. Now I philosophize. What next, think you – breaking into song? Well, to be brief, and serious, I was absolutely hurting when he came back, and even mutinously thinking that love should not be like this.

But regretting our attachment? Oh, no: never. And now I am being serious. Never.

He had taken a lodging in town. He was going to write dreary stuff for periodicals and be thoroughly sensible and not live in Hampstead where we would have continual sight of each other. He came to Wentworth Place to tell me so.

And as soon as he set eyes on me, and I set eyes on him, that was the end of that.

At the risk of indecency, I must ask you if you have ever held someone so close that you can hardly tell whose heartbeat is whose?

He said to me: 'I cannot breathe without you.'

He asked me to accept a garnet ring. You may imagine how I felt. Actually I hate it when people say that – 'Dear reader, you may imagine my transports of ecstasy &c.' – it always seems that they cannot be bothered to find the words. But in truth they are difficult to find. I felt as if I were looking into the heart of a wonderfully, terribly bright light. I felt as if some room with which I was comfortably familiar had suddenly revealed the presence of an unsuspected door, leading who knew whither.

Poor Mama. She noticed the ring, of course. I believe she made three full circuits of the parlour, cleared her throat till it was sore, and plumped up the cushions so many times they presented quite a pummelled appearance, before she could mention it.

'So, my dear,' she said, 'I take it you are to be congratulated upon being engaged.'

She said it so dolefully that I had to laugh. Though the laugh stung a little.

Well, there was nothing else to call it, though it was an unconventional sort of engagement still. 'I can hold you to nothing,' Mr Keats had said, 'because I have nothing to offer you.' And that, of course, what was what troubled Mama.

'I do wish you joy of it,' she said at last, holding my hand, and looking sorrowfully at the ring. 'I like Mr Keats extremely: there is something about him.' Her eyes had their old pretty look: then she shook her head. 'But I would lie if I said it is all I hope for you, Fanny.'

I kissed her, and said not to mind it. Later I heard her saying to Mrs Dilke that she hoped the match would not come off. This all felt very curious. I had never pictured myself as one of those rebellious girls, defying their parents for a romantic attachment. You can never tell, can you? Said Miss Brawne with dazzling originality.

So, for good or ill, we were together again. Only a wall dividing us – and that can be hard at times: I will say no more. Christmas approached: my favourite season, as you know, and all the more so now, because it is when Mr Keats and I came to our understanding. Well, now we were closer than ever, but it was not such a happy season all told. First, he was still suffering from the sore throat and general poorliness that had afflicted him since the end of the summer. Often he could not accept invitations. I could, and did. And where once I had rather enjoyed making him jealous, in the spirit of lovers' games, now I did not, yet could not help it. If I even showed some animation in conversation with a man at a party, he would reproach me bitterly for it.

'You are quite irrational,' I remember crying once. 'The gentleman you refer to is fifty if a day, and has large clumps of hair growing out of his ears. I do believe you would prefer to have me shut away like some harem-woman out of Lord Byron's verse-tales.'

'Do you really believe that?' he said, in a sort of interested way.

'Yes. No. Not literally . . . Oh, but you know,' said I, 'you are so very possessive of me.'

'Oh, God, yes,' he said earnestly. And then his smile broke out. You often find – that is, I often find that I have been unconsciously waiting for that smile, like waiting for the sun to come out. 'Possessive of. Possessed by. Everything. It's terrible, isn't it?'

'No,' I said.

And then there was the other trouble. His brother. Now, they are a close family, and I think Mr Keats suffered all the more from watching his poor brother Tom die of a consumption because his other brother – George – was far away in America. An emigrant, you see. (Of course you did not suppose he was a Red Indian.) Well, after Christmas George Keats came over from America, and stayed at Hampstead. Which ought to have been a good thing. Reunion of fond brothers and so on.

It was not. I don't know the whole of it, but I do know that George Keats had lost nearly all his money on colonial ventures that did not pay, and so he had come home to get some more. Who from? – who else but his brother. Directly or indirectly – for I know Mr Keats had been giving his brother money he could ill afford – and now here was his brother wanting to set in order, as he put it, their whole estate. The money left in trust from Mr Keats and his brothers was tied up in rather a complicated manner. Dear old Uncle John Ricketts would have understood it, but I didn't, and neither I think did Mr Keats. I am convinced their guardian, who had the charge of it, was not scrupulously honest. I am even more convinced that George Keats came back to England to drain off all he could of that money, with no thought of fairness to his brother.

No doubt in his own mind he excused himself that his need was greater. He had a wife and child. But he did not stop to consider that Mr Keats might soon want these things. And if Mr Keats has a fault, it is generosity. So, more trouble.

You will have gathered that George Keats was not a favourite of mine. He was much with us at Hampstead over the new year, and told tales of Ohios and Mississippis (I don't see why that name has to be *quite* so long) and generally carried himself off well. He was a buttoned-up, bustling sort of man in a frock coat, rather bald for his age, and also, I thought, rather pompous. He seemed to look with pitying disapproval at his poetical brother – as if he longed to brush him up and turn him into a pert, prosperous clerk.

I believe the disesteem was mutual. He was polite to me, but I am sure he was thinking: *flighty*. You know, the term applied to women who show signs of enjoying life. You may be thinking the same, of course.

So I was not sorry, at the end of January, to see him go. He took the coach for Liverpool and a sea-crossing back to America, his pockets full of misgotten money. I do not think Mr Keats was sorry at the parting either – and yet he was his brother, and Mr Keats's affections were always so very warm, and so I think there was a touch of guilt to make him more miserable.

I said to him: 'Patty –' our cook-maid '– made two puddings yesterday. One came out light and golden and altogether admirable, the other would have broke a paving-stone. Yet they were made by the same hands and with pretty much the same ingredients. Curious the difference.' I could not abuse his brother to him, you see, but I could say it like this. Perhaps, though, I simply associate George with what happened after, in the bitter beginning of the year.

There had been a hard frost all January, and Mr Keats, troubled with his cough, seldom stirred abroad. Then February seemed to bring a little thaw, and he went to Town upon some business – to do with his depleted finances, I fear – and came back to Hampstead by the latest coach. Though the days were milder, nights were still severe; and he travelled home, as I later discovered, on the outside of the coach, and without his greatcoat. Mr Brown told me later that when his friend came in, he supposed drunkenness for a minute, for Mr Keats could barely walk straight. He was weak and feverish, and with a great oppression on his chest. Mr Brown sent for a surgeon, who bled him and settled him to rest. I knew about the surgeon next day, because I was friends with his wife, and I called on her, and so I heard. But I did not hear the whole of it until the next afternoon, when Mr Keats told me. Mr Brown had wanted to keep me in ignorance, for fear that I would agitate him.

Mr Keats called, sat a while admiring Margaret's drawings, and being curiously quiet. I spoke of my anxiety for him hearing he had been ill; and at that he stood up and said: 'Walk in the garden with me, will you?'

This I thought strange, for it was still dreary weather for outdoors: still, I put my arm through his and went. The ground was very hard, I remember, so hard that one could not imagine plants ever flourishing in it any more than on a surface of marble. There was a cold white stare of light from the winter sky. I wonder now if he took me out there so that I should see, properly, his face: the pallor of it, the way the bones stood out. I saw. It was wretched to see; and I kept thinking of him in the summer, sitting here at work with one hand resting on the top of his head, and the nightingale singing.

He said: 'My darling Fanny, you know that I was trained for a doctor.'

'Oh, don't do it,' cried I at once, for he had talked lately of going off to be a ship's surgeon if his writing still failed. 'You will have to saw off limbs in a smell of smoke and rum, and when you come back you will talk in such an odd salty language I shan't be able to understand you.'

He just smiled faintly, looking at me. I think it was then that I became alarmed. I pressed his arm. 'Let's go in, Mr Keats. You have a fever—'

'In the blood,' he said, stock still. 'If I have a fever, it is in the blood.'

'That is very lovely, if you mean by it your love for me,' said I, 'but let's go in—'

'Perhaps I do mean that,' he said, with the oddest, most melancholy smile. And then he took hold of my hands and told me. 'When I got indoors the other night, I was dreadfully chilled, hectic-feeling. But, curiously, I felt rather better. Brown made me go straight to bed nonetheless. He came up after me with a glass of brandy. Getting in bed I coughed, and brought up blood. Brown had a candle, and I took it and inspected the blood. My training, you see. It was arterial blood – one can tell by the colour. There is a sort of frothy brightness . . . I know what it means, Fanny. It means that, like poor Tom, I shall not . . .' he seemed to hesitate for ages, though it can only have been seconds, for there is only one word, only one '. . . I shall not live.'

Now what did I think? Many things. I thought of my father, growing weaker, unable to lift Samuel off the ground. I thought – I am afraid I had one overwhelming thought. Thus: *I wish this had not happened to me.*

And then I undid the thought. Because whatever happens to us is meant to happen, and we must see it through.

'There is no telling how the disease may progress,' he went on. 'Some bear up. Some sink. But I had to tell you – at once. So that you may decide what you want to do. In these circumstances, you may wish to be released from an engagement – which I would quite understand – and you only have to say the word—'

I kissed his mouth quiet.

'I do not,' said I, 'wish to be released from the engagement, Mr Keats. Now or ever.'

And after a time we went back into the house together.

I didn't weep then or after. Why? Because if I were to weep now, what could I do later? There would be a time that would need all my tears. No, no weeping now. But perhaps that makes me a sharp, uncaring miss.

There, I have done. You have suppressed your yawns very well.

Shall we meet again, you say? That I don't know.

I don't know.

For no very clear reason, Mary finds herself thinking of her unknown, unseen father-in-law.

Sir Timothy Shelley, Bart., of Field Place, Sussex. She keeps picturing him – neat grey wings of hair, stubborn jaw, squirish riding-coat – and his house too, the place in the field, and farm-buildings and summer-houses and lanes full of cow-parsley and beaver-hatted and bonneted neighbours coming up the drive in gigs to call and talk over corn prices and the assize ball.

Why this? She long ago ceased to trouble her head about Sir Timothy, who would never be reconciled to them. He is a father, and fathers are by nature tyrants. Perhaps it is the fact that he never stirs, that he is always to be imagined *there*, in the bountiful and rooted homestead on the English downs. In other words, home. Perhaps – and this is not a nice thought – she is secretly willing him to die at last, so that Shelley will inherit, so there will be a home. Not so much for herself but for her infant son. Percy Florence, the precious, so-far, touch wood and please God, survivor.

Home. It is only a word. But then a deep, thrilling note drawn from a cello is only a sound.

It is not as if they are houseless, like the pullulating beggars of every Italian town, like the beggar who accosted her on the quay and whose face she sometimes brings significantly to mind like a playing-card turned up by a fortune-teller. They have a decent lodging: Pisa now. They have moved on again, to a city that strikes Mary as dull and provincial. When that tediously leaning tower went up, Pisa was an important place: now it is half empty, grass grows in the streets, seedy noblemen with oiled whiskers and dirty linen parade pointlessly in their lumbering carriages.

But their lodging is cramped – this in a town where half the peeling houses stand vacant – and Mary and Claire grate relentlessly on each other.

'Do you know,' Claire says brightly, one morning, 'you and I have fought every day now for three whole weeks?'

'I thought it was longer,' Mary says.

Of course Claire is missing Allegra, and Byron's recent behaviour has made matters worse. He has a new and, it seems, enduring mistress, a young married Italian woman named Teresa Guccioli. There is here a tradition of licensed adultery: the lover becomes the woman's *cavalier servante*, hovering by her in the opera-box with her folded shawl over his arm, while the husband winks at it and even, possibly, feels relieved that she has something to keep her busy. Byron the rule-breaker has gone further. A separation looms. He and Teresa are much together at Ravenna, her family home, and Allegra is much with them. Claire burns and seethes.

'What if she learns to call that garlicking strumpet *Mama*?'

'Knowing Byron's constancy, she will soon have to unlearn it,' Mary says, with tart consolation. She has her own reasons for coolness towards Byron just now. Obliging mutual acquaintances have passed on some remarks made by Byron about their ménage, and his reluctance to send a child to a household where they live on green fruit and indiscriminately share beds. Shelley, unperturbed, has written him a courteous and dignified letter of rebuttal – this the Shelley she fell in love with, and still loves, though the love struggles in a mesh of blighting circumstance – and there will be no lasting estrangement. But it is a sign that their private lives, even in exile, are public. Another sign rises with a sickly glow from the south, from Naples.

A letter from the foster-parents of Elena Adelaide, the baby girl Shelley had helplessly, hopelessly offered her in the gardens, sends Shelley off on one of his sudden exhausting walks. He returns with his clothes white with dust, his face burnt and unearthly.

'My little Neapolitan,' he says. 'She has died of a fever.'

What to say? The first, cruel, unforgivable thought that leaps to mind: Good, good, why should she have life when our little ones were robbed of it? Or: I'm sorry, sorry for the death of a child I still don't understand, still don't know the father of, you or someone else, still don't know how I'm supposed to feel about it except for this nagging guilt that I am not sufficiently virtuous and idealistic to love her as you wanted?

Life with Shelley: a series of these absolutely unprecedented situations. You need to learn a whole new vocabulary of emotion. Mary loves learning: but sometimes she grows tired.

She says nothing. Shelley sighs, and goes in search of Claire.

There is no more talk of the little Neapolitan – or there would not be, if it were not for Paolo, their ex-servant. Plainly Paolo has drawn his own conclusions about the baby's paternity, and has talked to any of the English community who will listen. Laboriously written, curiously polite and, as it were, smiling letters have arrived requesting sums of money, if he is not to tell all he knows about the Shelley household. Shelley consults a lawyer, quietly fumes. The lawyer is reassuring: once detected, he says, the blackmailer is easily crushed. But of course the words have already been said, and words, as Mary knows, have infinite power. They may have affected Byron: they certainly affect her.

'These grubby trivialities,' Shelley says, taking up an English newspaper sent by Leigh Hunt, 'when there is so much at stake in the world.' Politically he is at his most inflammable just now. He has taken to wearing a ring inscribed with the words *Il buon tempo verra*: the good times are coming. Risings in Spain and southern Italy have roused his hopes while news from England has damped them. After the massacre of Peterloo he wrote urging the people to resist passively without resorting to their oppressors' violence. But the arrest and trial of the Cato Street conspirators, a clandestine group of Radicals who planned to assassinate the cabinet, seems to show that counsels of desperation have won the day – and lost it. 'Now every reformer appears a murderer,'

Shelley says. 'It could hardly have gone better if the government had planned it themselves.'

'I would not be surprised if they did,' Mary says absently. 'Shelley, what do you think of the babe? Does he not look a little colicky?'

'My love, he looks no different from this morning.'

'That's not what I asked you,' she says, to his retreating back.

He thinks she fusses too much over Percy Florence's health – she knows that. There is, perhaps, a superstitious side of him that fears too much care will actually invite the dreaded stroke of fate. Preferring the alternative, Mary frets and cossets. And in bed she is not receptive. She does not want, is unequal to, another pregnancy, another cycle of sickness and anxious hope, another frail hostage to epidemics. Shelley is not a man to persist, or upbraid: still, she wonders if he feels, as he silently turns on the pillow, that he is being punished. She wonders, indeed, if she is punishing him without knowing it: for their losses, for Elena, for the ever more draining presence of Claire under their marital roof.

Lots of wondering and thinking: not much talking. The circle of friends they have made in Pisa perhaps observe this, and one has a practical suggestion. A distinguished physician of Florence seeks an English governess for his children. Would this not suit Claire, with her talent for languages, her rapport with children?

Suit her? No: Claire sticks out her lip at the thought of leaving them, or rather leaving Shelley. But she reluctantly accepts that she will have to forge some sort of independent life of her own. Either that, thinks Mary, or we will murder one another some fine day in a dispute over a hairbrush. She can just see it happening. The Florentine doctor must be her saviour. *Il buon tempo verra*.

'Hunt gives a sad account of poor Keats,' Shelley says one night, before blowing out the candle. 'He is consumptive. Had a fearful haemorrhage of the lungs. Brought on, I'd wager, by all that abuse the reviewers heaped on him. There are faults aplenty in his writing, but it's not those they talk of. The whole thing is sheer party animus and malice. They have ridden over him like the soldiers at Peterloo.' With a sharp, disgusted breath he conjures the darkness. 'I shall write him and invite him here. If he is in a consumption the doctors will surely advise a warm climate, and there's no better air than Pisa. He can stay with us. There'll be room enough with Claire gone.'

Ah, blessed words. The prospect is so enticing Mary could almost turn and embrace him. Almost.

Every night Fanny sent Keats a little love-note to be placed under his pillow.

She did wonder sometimes, as she penned them, whether there had ever been a love like this. They were living next door to each other, they were engaged but not publicly, they had no discernible future and yet no real present either. It sounded dreadful, but she found it could be beautiful.

'You always find something different to write,' he said admiringly.

'Praise indeed. I am half ashamed to pick up a pen when it's *you* who'll read it.'

'Me? I'm no exemplar, my darling girl. I'm an impudent Cockney who should go back to the apothecary's shop, remember?' Keats smiled jaggedly. Though he was out of bed now, the sour touch of self-pity showed how ill he was still.

'Your day will come. I was never more sure of anything.'

'After I'm dead perhaps. The curious thing is, in certain moods I know, as I know the sun in the sky, that I am a poet. It almost doesn't matter that no one else agrees, because the conviction is so strong and woody and everlasting. All though me like the sound of a clarinet. There's fine fevered nonsense for you. I love you, Fanny.'

'I'm pleasantly aware of that, sir.' She looked away, shyly.

'Funny. I resented you. Your effect on me. I thought you took me away from poetry – being poetry yourself. You were destructive. Lord –' he rubbed frenetically at his blanched vein-tender forehead '– this life, we have to learn things in it so quickly, too quickly. Not long ago I was afraid of love. Thought it would chain me. Drain me. Now that love is all I want. It's this double-damned sickness that's chaining and draining. Shall I stop talking now?'

'I love you, John.'

His feverish eyes seemed to grip her like fire-tongs. 'Oh, I shall hold you to that.'

'How is Mr Keats today, my dear?' Mrs Brawne asked.

'He is much improved, Mama. The heart palpitations have quite gone off. He is even preparing to walk into Town, to see to the publishing of his new volume.' Fanny stole up behind her mother and trapped her in her arms. 'Are you very disappointed, Mama?'

'Fanny, what can you mean? I am a silly sort of woman, no doubt, but I think I can say I have never been considered an absolute monster. And only a monster could be disappointed by Mr Keats getting better, surely, unless I have mistaken your meaning, my dear, for you are terribly quick—'

'You know what I mean, Mama. This troublesome *mésalliance* continues.'

Mrs Brawne took hold of her daughter's hand and sadly examined it. 'You still wish to marry Mr Keats, of course.'

'I don't wish to, dear Mama, I mean to.'

'Yes, to be sure,' Mrs Brawne said vaguely. 'I was talking to Mr Brown, by the by, and he will surely be going away for the summer. Mr Keats cannot keep the house on his own – so he will have to move elsewhere.'

'And thus will not be next door. Do you really think proximity is all that keeps us together?'

Her mother sighed. 'I wish your father were here.'

'Why?' Fanny stiffened. 'Because he might talk me out of it? But why would he? He was seen as quite a bad match for you,

Mama, wasn't he, and yet I'm sure you don't wish you had married somebody else?' She paused: there was a horrible power in knowing you could hurt someone so effectively. 'Unless you do. Perhaps you had rather have married some rich strapping fellow instead of a poorly failure like Papa. Is that it? Is that the lesson you wish to impress on me?'

'Fanny', her mother said in a tone of melancholy discovery, 'you're cruel.'

Fanny walked out of the room. 'Life is,' she told herself, on the way to Keats, 'life is.'

Keats's new lodging was at Kentish Town. Not far if he was in health, when he was a vigorous walker: but in this condition, he was a world away from her. There was no question of her visiting him alone – even mortality could not alter the conventions – and Mrs Brawne, without actually refusing, always seemed to find ways of being unable to go with her. Fanny wondered, a little scornfully, whether this was her mother's feeble attempt at punishment. It was a new experience to feel scorn for her mother: new also her impatience with the conventions, for before this she had always found that she fitted in comfortably with society. She recalled the exciting surprise of her first glass of wine: this was not unlike it – her first tingling of rebellion.

He managed to visit at last on a violently hot day in early summer. The Heath looked seared and above the ponds the quivering air seethed with gnats: in the garden at Wentworth Place blackbirds scuttled under shady shrubs as if flight were an intolerable effort.

'This heat doesn't help you, I'm sure,' Fanny said – apologetically, as if she were responsible for it: his silence as they walked unnerved her.

'It rather feels as if what's in my chest has got out and taken possession of the air – as if the world is a mere reflection of what's going on inside me. Sounds like Wordsworth – you know – the

585

way the hills exist just to tell him things about himself.' He spoke in a brittle unhappy burst of energy, then returned to silence.

'Well!' Fanny said finally, brightly. 'I'm gratified to find that you have missed me so very much, you are absolutely struck dumb by the joy of our reunion.'

He stopped, but did not look at her. 'Have you missed me?' he said.

'Oh, I've spared you the occasional thought, amid the delicious whirl of my—'

'You see,' he said, and the words seemed to be shaken out of him, like spasms, like coughs, 'you see, Fanny, I can't help it but I think, I can't stop thinking that that is literally true.'

'You mean about me and the delicious whirl? Which sounds like a pastry-cook's confection by the by, possibly with almonds and cream. John. What is it?' She regarded him in perplexity, the sun like a live coal on the nape of her neck, her eyes dizzy with spikes of tremendous light.

'I hear things. From our mutual acquaintances.'

'Now, you of all people should know, if they are *our* acquaintances, then the word *mutual* is redundant, because it already means that . . . What do you hear?'

'Lies, probably. The trouble is I hear them before the rational mind can rouse itself and say they're lies. I hear about you, going to parties, and flirting, and enjoying yourself.'

'Enjoying myself. God forbid.'

'Yes. In the unlikely event that there is such an old monstrosity, God forbid. This is what I am just now, my darling. A tyrant and wicked. Instance: I don't want you to be happy, if it means you are happy without me. Is that, perhaps, a perfect definition of love? Anyway, I lie awake and imagine and imagine, and it is all morbid nonsense, and I can't stop it. Well, there we are. At least I've broken the silence.'

'John, this is your illness talking—'

'I know, eloquent, isn't it? You must tell me if this is too much. What I feel for you. It certainly isn't fair, I think. For example, I want you to be prepared to die on the rack for me as I am for you.'

'But, John, nobody is likely to strap either of us on to a rack. We are living in the nineteenth century in an eminently civilized country . . .' But she stopped, because somewhere inside she did understand. 'I didn't think – when I wrote you about that party at Mrs Rodd's—'

'Ah, yes, that one cost me a good hour of jealous foot-stamping rage. Actually foot-stamping.' He laughed huskily. 'I can only assure you that I do know what a pathetic spectacle this presents. You could not possibly despise me any more than I despise myself. Yes – I'm out of sorts, my darling, and I'll tell you why – pausing only to observe that I was always inclined to believe that it is women who never say what's the matter with them until they have first punished you with bad temper, and here am I doing the same thing – the reason is, what the doctors tell me. About my condition. It is made worse by excitement. It is made worse by emotion. In order to live, I must not feel. There are two things that make me feel most intensely. They are poetry and you, though I shouldn't really call them two things because I can't separate them any more, but anyhow they are the most important things and—' His voice ran dry and stony, his eyes bleakly fixed away. She pressed him to sit on the garden-seat with her. The wooden slats were as hot as a grate beneath her thighs. 'And they are bad for me. Love is bad for me. You are bad for me. I cannot get over the obscenity of this, the unfairness. It challenges all my ideas. I have no conventional faith and I don't see the Almighty in a waterfall like Wordsworth and I can't believe like Shelley that if we change politics everything will be perfect, but I do love life and think the world is frequently beautiful, beautiful beyond expression and reason, and so that in itself must mean something vast, and now comes this, which is such unthinkable unfairness – pure unfairness, a colourless unadulterated extract of unfairness, and I can't think why or how life can contain such unfairness, something so flagrant must mean something too but I can't see what . . .'

He hung his head, speechless at last. His hand came groping blindly for hers. She was only thinking what to say for a few moments, but she traversed whole landscapes of feeling during that time.

'Everything you say is true. Yet I wouldn't change anything, John. No – I wouldn't – simply because we are together here now, and that's all. It's all I care for and all that matters. It's a question of – well, a bright golden sovereign, or a lot of grubby halfpennies. And that sound, by the way, was the door, which means Mama has taken Margaret out to the baker's shop, and so we may go in and be private. Yes, come along. Now – sit there – there on the sofa. Now let me undo this. Oh – no, indeed, I don't know what I am doing, darling John. But I do know what I am doing.'

3

A Ring and a Circle

In June Fanny's brother Samuel went to try out a junior position in the City, and had his long curling hair cut so severely she could hardly look at him without thinking of shorn sheep. In the same month her sister Margaret was discovered to be padding her bodice with rolled-up stockings, because two of her contemporaries at school had begun to grow a bosom and she, as she confessed with despair, had not. Patty the cook-maid had a quarrel with Mrs Brawne, packed her bags, and returned in tears having got no further than Holly Bush Hill. Fanny bought a new morning-gown and made a muslin flounce for an evening one. And Keats, going home by coach from visiting his little sister, suddenly found his mouth filled up with blood.

These things had to be accommodated together, in the same life, in the same mind and heart. Nobody thought Fanny a heroine for doing it, least of all herself. But she did wonder how much more she could bear, when she heard that he had had another haemorrhage, alone and helpless in his Kentish Town lodgings.

More doctors. They counselled him against living alone: Leigh Hunt took him in. It was kind, though the rampaging of Hunt's numerous children, Keats wrote her, tended to counteract the kindness. All the doctors were agreed on one thing: another English winter would kill him. 'I must go south with the swallows.'

She was no heroine, but life was asking her some fiendish

questions and somehow she was managing to answer. Above all she was having to deal with love, love fierce as combustion, potent as poison, in a way that twenty uneventful years in genteel quietness could not have prepared her for. Keats's feeling for her shone in her sky like a baleful and perpetual moon. Sickness magnified his possessiveness, his jealousy.

There was no one she could talk to about it. Friends of her own age now seemed to inhabit a different world. She watched them like a mermaid on a rock gazing at land: marvelled at their simple cares, their trifling quarrels, their direct desires. Sometimes she envied them. She envied them when, after she had spent a rare evening at the Dilkes', Keats got to hear of it and sent her an agonized and agonizing note reproaching her for not caring.

It was then that she found she did have someone to talk to, quite unexpectedly.

'My dear,' Mrs Brawne said mildly after dinner, 'you never ate a bite. Do you have a bad report of Mr Keats, perhaps?'

'It's more a matter of his bad report of *me*,' she burst out. And then she found herself talking on, and her mother was actually listening, without comment, with no fastidious drawing back from confidences. 'Is it fair to be so harsh on me because I enjoyed myself at a party, as he calls it? Hardly a party – indeed that fruit-punch Mrs Dilke serves makes it more of a penitence – and it's not as if I put vine-leaves in my hair and danced a tarantella on the table. Oh, but I know how he suffers thinking of me, and how wretched his position is, and his illness makes it worse. *I* make it worse. Oh, Mama –' she had a helpless sensation like coming to a last stair and finding only emptiness '–I do believe, in a way, he is dying of me.'

Mrs Brawne seemed to think about this for a long time, her hand to her cheek, as if she were sitting for her portrait and had forgotten she was doing it.

'It all depends,' she said at last, enigmatically. 'My dear Fanny, I do not like to think of you being made unhappy by any man – a

thing I have hesitated to say for fear of getting my head bitten off.'
She smiled timidly.

'Have I been doing that a lot lately? I'm sorry. I hardly know what I'm doing.'

'Only a little. And it's quite natural and understandable. The thing is, being in love doesn't necessarily make people nicer. Oh, my dear, the whole thing is natural and understandable – even Mr Keats being so unreasonable. I don't approve it, but I can see why it is. He sits alone and broods about what you may be doing and wears out what strength he has in brooding. I remember when your father was ill – the way his mind seemed absolutely to throb like a wound . . .' Mrs Brawne gathered herself abruptly, as if pulling up at a turning she did not intend taking. 'Also I like Mr Keats, perhaps better than any man who . . . But as your mother who loves you, my dear, I still cannot think this attachment a good thing. You talk of what you are doing to him – but my concern is what he is doing to you.'

'He is not doing anything to me, Mama, except loving me dreadfully and being unable to bear it—' She stopped with a small smile. 'And there goes your head again.'

'I was going to say,' Mrs Brawne resumed, 'what he is doing to you under these circumstances. I know he is not a cruel man, any more than you are a cruel girl, despite the head-biting. But circumstances have made a sad hard bed for you both.' Mrs Brawne grew flurried, realizing her metaphor sounded indecent. 'I wish there were something one could do.'

'Well, you could accompany me to see him, Mama.'

'Yes, to be sure – but beyond that, I mean.'

In July Samuel's hair had grown out in hedgehog spikes, and he tried flattening it with bear's grease, to even more fearsome effect. Margaret gave up her bodice-stuffing, but began yearning for a lap-dog. Patty had a wart on her cheek removed by a mountebank at West End Fair with the result that her face swelled up for a week. Fanny set herself to learning some German verbs. And

Keats's new volume, *Lamia, Isabella, The Eve of St Agnes and Other Poems*, was published, and this time the reviews – some of them – began to acknowledge – awkwardly – that the man they had vilified was perhaps a genius after all.

Yes, after you have half killed him, thought Fanny bitterly. It was a melodramatic thought, no doubt, but she was learning that even melodrama could contain a truth. And irony, which she had thought of as a literary device, infected the very air she breathed now. Keats was getting a reputation just when he was too ill to appreciate it or build on it: his country was taking notice of him just when he would have to leave it.

Before the fogs and chills of autumn: that was when he would have to sail for Italy, the place all the doctors agreed would most benefit him. Shelley had written to him from Pisa, urging him to come and stay the winter there and be looked after by him and Mrs Shelley. A kind offer, though Keats was also half inclined to Rome, insofar as he was inclined at all. He did not want to go, even though going meant living: because, as he wrote her from Hunt's house, going away from Fanny meant not living. Ironies again. There was a greater one preparing for her.

On a warm musky August evening, just when night began to press its hazy screens against the windows of the parlour at Wentworth Place, and the lighting of the first candles sent mouselike shadows running for the corners of the room, there was a knock at the front door.

'I'm sorry, ma'am,' Patty said grumpily, putting her swollen face round the parlour door, 'only there's a visitor.'

'It's I who – who should apologize for calling at this late hour.'

Keats almost fell into the room. The combination of breathlessness and formality made him seem as if he were drunk and trying desperately not to show it. At first sight his eyebrows and eyelashes looked as if they had been absurdly emphasized with charcoal. Then you realized that was because his face was sensationally white.

To her own disgust, Fanny could do nothing but gasp and stare where she sat. It was her mother who rose, literally, to the occasion. She got up and took Keats's arm like an absolute hostess. 'My dear Mr Keats, not at all – I'm sure such old friends need not stand on ceremony, and besides, quite a welcome surprise to see you in Hampstead.' She steered him to a chair. 'I would say that you must be feeling better to make the journey, though I am rather afraid, if you don't mind me saying so, that your strength is a little overtaxed. Patty shall bring you tea – but what say you to a drink of water first?'

'You are very good.' Keats fumbled out his handkerchief, mopped his face with it, coughed into it. These were very private rituals, Fanny could tell, and only some tremendous sacrifice of pride allowed them to be seen. She could tell too, as his eyes met hers above the skin-white handkerchief, that something new and final and terrible was here – like some strange, vast room which she had not knowingly entered, but which was now all around her, containing her in its alien splendour. 'I set down my bags in the hall – I mention it in case anyone should trip over them. The fact is, I have left my friend Hunt's house, and intend coming back to Hampstead. Until such time as - as—'

'As you make your journey abroad,' Mrs Brawne supplied, nodding helpfully, 'to restore your health. Very understandable. Not easy to find a lodging in Hampstead at this season, mind, though perhaps you . . .' Looking at Keats, Mrs Brawne's brightness faded a moment: she turned and shooed Patty. 'Some water, Patty, if you wouldn't mind.'

'I went to ask at Well Walk. Where I lived with Tom. No reply there. So I thought – as I was so close by . . .' He jabbed the handkerchief back into his pocket, struggled through his cold sweat for urbanity. 'Fanny, I'm glad to see you, so very glad, and yet I fear I have quite *diminished* you with surprise at my sudden appearance.' The weak flash of his old word-loving tricksiness, like a modest Christmas gift from a friend fallen on hard times, moved her at the root of her heart.

'My dear Mr Keats, you have a high opinion of your powers

indeed,' she said, in a sort of parody of her social self, 'supposing you could affect me in any way quite so drastic as diminishment.'

'Diminution,' he said, gazing at her.

'Bless you. Oh, John, why have you left Mr Hunt's house?'

'A disagreement – just a disagreement.' Keats gulped the water thrust at him by a resentful Patty, who did not enjoy anyone being more ill than her. 'My fault, I think. Of course it is a very crowded household at the best of times.' It was to do with me, thought Fanny, interested to find how clairvoyant she had become.

'I don't think you will find any room at Well Walk, Mr Keats,' Mrs Brawne said, calmly sitting down, calmly taking up her needlework, and then calmly adding: 'Of course we have a room to spare here, if you would wish to stay with us. I do not,' she added with decision, looking up and around as if at an assembly of accusers, 'I do not see any reason why you should not stay here with us, Mr Keats, until you sail.'

And there were reasons, there were reasons aplenty why a young man should not come to live under the same roof as his fiancée, and for a mother to make the offer was even more irregular. Mrs Brawne did it. As fathers should never be heroes to sons, so with mothers and daughters, and Fanny was saved from adoring her mother as a heroine for this by one truthful consideration: her mother was being generous, her mother was being unconventional in the breadth of her sympathy, but her mother was also thinking: why not? It can't matter: it can't matter now, now that he looks like that.

He was not ill, now. He was an ill person. His whole being was defined by what was happening to his body. It was brave of Mrs Brawne to take him in on that understanding too: the consumptive was a demanding presence, and this one was doubly demanding because of the love.

The love no one spoke of in the modest confines of that house, where Margaret went into his bedroom every afternoon for a chat and to recite her French lesson, where Samuel would lounge in too at evening and tell rakish stories in his boyish-gruff voice, and where Fanny sat by his bed to read to him, to talk, and sometimes merely to subsist in a brimming silence shaken only by the rattle of pots in the kitchen or the rap of the butcher's boy at the back door.

Normality: it was only when you became aware of it that you realized there was nothing normal about it at all. Fanny found herself awake to a peculiar essence about everything: panels of sunlight on the bookcase, the tingling drone of a wasp, the woody flesh of a bitten apple. Unchanged, the house yet throbbed with his presence. The floorboards creaked differently for bearing him, the tick of the parlour clock commented that Keats is here, Keats is here. And meanwhile that love went on. Not awkwardly: very sweetly. He was an invalid and this was a love with special considerations and yet no, it did not totter forward on walking sticks, not in her heart – and not in his, that she could see from the incandescence about him, the passion revealed through his wasting frame like a nervous hand in a worn glove. Yet they both knew that this was a time in suspension, that while they sat together through long mild mornings quietly exploring each other's presence in word and look, something was happening, their story no longer in normal type but bold, italicized, bracketed: momentous.

Leigh Hunt came to visit. He brought a basket of cherries. 'I wish I could say from my own garden. But the tree in my own garden is obstinately unfruitful. I have clambered into the lower branches in hopes of finding at least a few shy sweets hiding in the leaves, but the effort is – you'll forgive me a vile pun? – fruitless. All the more frustrating in that the tree in next door's garden, its twin in every respect, positively groans with cherries. So, I hopped over the fence and committed a little larceny – or a just redistribution of wealth, if you will. Also it has long been my intent to test out, in a spirit of scientific enquiry, all the old adages that have been handed down to us. I have already proved to my satisfaction that a stitch in time saves nine, and the theorem that good wine needs no bush I have had convincingly demonstrated, so now let us sit and test the proposition that stolen fruit tastes sweeter.'

Liking ease and grace, Fanny liked Hunt without quite trusting him. That blithe and mollifying manner – was there nothing it was unequal to? It soon smoothly took over after the first start of shock at Keats's gauntness and pallor. Delicately removing cherry-stones, one boneless crossed leg swinging, Hunt talked brightly of Keats's forthcoming voyage abroad as if it were a pleasure-trip on the Thames, and praised his new volume in playfully extravagant terms. 'And I am delighted to find that I am no longer a voice that crieth in the wilderness,' Hunt said. 'Now there is a whole choir of us, even if the wilderness is still a mite stony and locusty. Oh, I know sales are slow, but even Byron did not sell at first. You are becoming known, my friend.'

'A pity,' Keats said, with a shadowed look, as if from the folds of an actual cowl, 'that it has come so late.'

'Late, not at all,' Hunt breezed. 'You are but five-and-twenty. To adapt your own phrase, you are a young palmer in love's eye –' he twinkled at Fanny '– and in fame's eye too.'

Keats only bowed his head and shrugged. Fanny, as so often now, knew what he was thinking: knew that he had nearly said not *so late* but *too late*.

Later, after Hunt had gone, she brought him candles and fresh water, and found him going over his manuscripts with a distant, puzzled expression, as if they were someone else's. 'It's all unfinished,' he said, without glancing up.

'I remember you once saying to me,' she said, sitting down by him, 'that if the day came when you looked over your work and found it perfect, you would know you were no poet.'

'Did I say that?'

'Perhaps not, but it is a very good thing to say, and so I make you a present of it – graft it on to your past somewhere, it will soon take, and you will think it quite your own.'

Smiling, he put the papers aside: then repeated softly, 'It's all unfinished.'

She paused in a moment's understanding. 'Perhaps it always is. For everyone. John, you know you shouldn't tax your strength with work—'

'No, no. All my strength is for one thing now. If Italy should – if Italy does restore me – then perhaps I can begin again. The trouble is, how am I to get there?'

'Now, I have not told you this before, and you must not be too overcome by it, but on the sea they have these excellent contrivances called boats, and if you get in one, rather like getting in a bath in reverse, then you'll soon find . . .'

He was smiling willingly: her fun now was like sunlight to a plant – or an invalid. But the core of seriousness never left him. 'A boat it shall be. But how I am to survive the boat . . . Italy is the place to work on my health, but to get there I must risk my health on a sea-voyage. Like soldiers having to march uphill to a battery. And, of course, I don't want to leave. The thought of leaving here—'

'And leaving Patty's unsliceable beef and sliceable gravy, to be sure, and the draught in the privy and Margaret's hideously tuneless singing, yes, it must be an unbearable thought—'

'But I see you.' He caught her hand. 'All the time. The one thing I yearned for, and thought I wouldn't be able to bear even if it came – it's here, and it's beautiful, and I must leave it. What—' He flinched and stared about the room as if at some physical assailant. 'What does it mean? How can this be made *right*?'

She felt his smothered raging through his pulse for a few seconds, like a bee trapped in a glass.

Then he suddenly said, with a gasp like a man coming up from a dive: 'Yet I wouldn't change anything, that's the maddest part. Not a thing. I saw Hunt's wife doing a drawing exercise once. She had placed a basket of flowers in the corner of the room, and she proceeded to draw it by drawing everything there except the basket of flowers. And there it was, this perfect silhouette . . . So with this. It contains the shape of you.'

Their fingers brushed, and then they were embracing desperately, looking away: only thus, as if catching themselves unawares, could they express the killing love.

Seeing him all the time: yes, she had that dream made flesh now, with no partings, no unsatisfactory meetings and misunderstandings and apologies. All that was cleared away. There was only the horrible beauty of this time, its golden venom. Strolling alone one morning down Well Walk, she heard a sharp rustle in the trees above and then, to her everlasting astonishment, a squirrel fell like a stone through the leaves and landed at her feet. A dead squirrel: whatever had killed it, it bore no mark: perhaps it had simply died of whatever squirrels died of, and there it lay on its back, the creamy fur of its underside rippling a little in the breeze, its ceremonious red tail spread out like a fluffed fan. One never saw a squirrel this closely: never had the chance to appreciate its intense beauty. Death and its chances. She gazed. Then she hurried on with spangling sight.

Her mother said, sorting threads: 'Mr Keats was talking this morning of your engagement, my dear.'

'Yes?'

'Yes. Discussing the matter with me, you know, in view of his having to go abroad for a time. Apparently he has offered to release you—'

'And I have refused.'

'As he told me. He wanted to know what I thought. I said that I wished you both to be happy, of course. And that in these difficult circumstances, certain conventional expectations might be set aside. There, I'm nearly out of the silk twist again.' Mrs Brawne looked up at her daughter, and it was as if their eyes were meeting across a chasm. 'Well. I consider it might be best, in view of your devoted attachment, that you marry at once when he comes back from Italy, and live here with me.'

They were all artists now, choosing their words with infinite care and delicacy. She had said *when*, Fanny noted as she embraced her mother, not *if*.

Preparations.

They were agonizing, but really they were not extensive. Keats had only carved out a very little space in the world. There was a trunkful of clothes to be packed, a boxful of books to be distributed among his friends, a handful of letters to be written or, as it turned out, dictated: Fanny wrote them sitting by his bed. From his mind to her hand to the page: it made them one. They were so very much one that the parting seemed an impossibility even as it stole towards them.

'Now that I have you I must lose you. And yet I couldn't have had you otherwise. There's a conundrum to while away the shipboard hours,' he said.

His companion was to be his friend Mr Severn, the artist. Fanny was glad of that, because Mr Severn was young and energetic and might, she thought vaguely, somehow lend a little of his abundant life. That Mr Severn also seemed faintly mistrustful of her was something she could bear: she was growing used to it, having detected it in Mr Charles Brown and Leigh Hunt and others – this unspoken suspicion that she was bad for him.

Of course I am, she thought. Don't any of you understand him?

Preparations: she sewed a new lining for his travelling-cap, they cut and exchanged locks of hair, he gave her the miniature portrait Severn had painted of him, they looked together at maps, tracing the journey to Rome where an English physician was ready to take on his case, and agreeing that it would be very easy. And she gave him a white cornelian to hold in his hand.

'Is it a charm?'

'It's whatever you want it to be.'

He clasped it. Keats's hand was dry, tough, and knuckly, twenty years older than his face.

'In other words, it's me,' she added.

Preparations: they had to end, be complete at last. September brought to the Heath the prompt mists and chills that must send him away. His passage to Italy was booked on a brig called the *Maria Crowther*, sailing from Tower Dock. The morning of his departure was the thirteenth. Fanny watched the damp apple-tints of dawn with eyes smarting and sensitized from lack of sleep. In his room she found him dressed and standing, somehow braced-looking, like a sentinel.

She walked into his arms.

'Now,' she said scoldingly, 'when you come back—'

'Oh, don't.'

'When you come back,' she insisted, 'I shall want a good husband, and if you're not sure what makes one of those, I have plenty of good strong advice for you—'

'Oh, don't.' His mouth was in her hair and his voice had failed: she felt the words on his lips, a silent shape.

Hunt had come over to accompany Keats to London. He was downstairs, charming Patty. Everyone had a painfully spruce and expectant look: Margaret, trying not to cry, kept giggling. Mrs Brawne gave Keats her hand. 'You know you will always have a home here, Mr Keats.'

From nowhere he produced a bright smile. It was like hearing a long-forgotten tune. 'I know,' he said. 'In a way, I think I shall always be here.'

Mrs Brawne squeezed his hand, then seemed to feel the inadequacy of the gesture: yet nothing else was proper: at last she backed away like a confused schoolgirl. At any other time, Fanny thought, at any other time it would have been funny: but there was never going to be any other time.

Her mother, her brother and sister waved them off from the top of the steps at Wentworth Place. Hunt, carrying Keats's luggage, walked on a little ahead, whistling faintly. Fanny and Keats walked together, but they had nothing to say, because they had everything to say.

They waited at the coach-stop on the corner of Pond Street. The sun was up and its light came through the trees like blades. Hunt walked up and down, still making a toneless whistle. Fanny and Keats stared at each other, then at the north road, intently, as if the coming of the coach were some awesome comet-like possibility. He coughed into his handkerchief, bundled it away.

'Do you have a clean one?' she said.

'In my pocket. And more in the top of my luggage.'

'Good.' Good, oh, in that case everything is all right. This is why we invent gods and heroes: we humans are too thin and trivial to be equal to such moments, we are smaller than our own emotions. And here is the coach.

A stray pup was yapping at the wheels. Hunt shooed it away before handing up the luggage, but it came back, nipping at his heels. The coachman laughed a rich laugh full of carelessness. Keats climbed up. Fanny held his hand. They said something, probably goodbye: the words made absolutely no mark on her consciousness, might as well have been Hebrew. Keats settled back into the coach with the angry stony look that she knew meant, in him, the utmost grief. Hunt sat opposite him and waved an expressive hand as the coach shuddered away. Fanny blew a kiss. How nonsensical, she thought numbly. We do not blow a kiss at all, we just make a gesture with hand and mouth. Understanding is all. At the end we are left with symbols. A kiss, a ring, a stone. She walked home alone. Her mother exerted herself hugely in tact. Fanny withdrew to her room, opened her bureau, and wrote in her pocket-book the words 'Mr Keats left Hampstead,' as if that were all – and it was – to say.

What do other people do?

An unusual question, this, for Mary. What other people do, how they live, has long been a matter of indifference to her and

Shelley, on stern and fixed principle, and indeed it is the principle she learnt from her father's lips, little as he has practised it. Live freely according to the light of your own mind and conscience, not that of convention or tradition, and let others do likewise.

But what if you do that, and it still doesn't work? What if there is still dissatisfaction? What if there is a life like hers and Shelley's – taut, problematic, edged with unspoken unanswerable questions? Does it perhaps show that you are on the wrong road altogether?

Lately she has been rereading Tom Paine, friend of her mother, trumpet of the American Revolution, and she keeps thinking of those ringing words in the Declaration of Independence: *life, liberty, and the pursuit of happiness.*

She asks: 'Shelley, do you believe in them?'

Shelley is always prepared for such a question. 'Absolutely. As the rights of every man and woman, absolutely.'

'But how can you pursue happiness? That assumes that you know what it is, and it's just there like a deer or a hare and you pursue it. Shouldn't you pursue something else – something worthwhile – and then, it may be, the happiness will come as a consequence?'

'Oh, Mary,' he says, with a look of sad surprise. 'I think this world has soured you.'

And she wants to question the surprise, and the word 'world', but doesn't, and they paddle on together in their tepid pool of misunderstanding.

So, what do other people do, how do they manage? – a question that would have been difficult to answer before, simply because she and Shelley lived in such isolation. But here in Pisa, where they are now comfortably settled on the Lung'Arno amid decaying riverside *palazzi* like toothless grandees, they have for the first time more or less continual company. Cheap roomy Pisa is a favourite gathering-place for travellers, and soon the Shelleys are part of a circle.

Look around the circle: see how they do it. This splendid exile, exotically moustached yet sensibly bespectacled, is the Greek Prince Mavrocordato, man of the hour. Across the Adriatic the Greeks are rising up against their Turkish oppressors, and a new sun is rising there for the liberal spirits of Mary's generation, just as her mother's looked to Revolutionary France. Courtly, cultured, Mavrocordato is too serious for flirtation: it is a friendship of equals that develops between him and Mary, she teaching him English and he teaching her Greek from a shared medium of schoolroom French. From him she learns enthusiasm for the cause of Greek freedom, of which he is one of the leaders: she becomes expert in massacres and military supplies. Shelley, of course, admires him too, but not without a curious constraint, which he can only express by saying with a shrug: 'The Prince doesn't like me.' Perhaps there is some form of envy. Mavrocordato is, after all, a leader of men, whose words are actually heeded, who will really make a difference. Unless there is a more straightforward jealousy of the Prince's attentions to his wife – yet no, surely not from the man who nudged Mary to get into bed with his friend Hogg, who deplores possessiveness in human relations. If so, he has no need, simply because Mavrocordato has his myopic eyes fixed on greater things. How to live? Have a mission, have a cause. One answer.

From the weighty presence of the Prince, turn to a very different member of the circle. Emilia.

It was Claire – of course it would be – who on a vacation visit to them first began the acquaintance with this pretty little piece of Pisan poison. Emilia is nineteen, the daughter of the Governor, well educated, darkly beautiful as a sleek young black cat, and a prisoner. That is, she is being kept at the school attached to the convent of St Anna while her parents angle for an eligible husband, and spends long, dreary hours soulfully floating about in a couple of Gothic rooms overlooking a kitchen garden while waited on by half-wit servants. And Mary, at first, feels quite as sorry for her and interested in her as Claire and Shelley, and visits her frequently in the gloomy rooms where the caged birds and the painted Madonna stand like twin emblems of her forlorn condition. Emilia writes them elegant little notes full of sighs and tears, *sospiri* and *lagrime*, swears by her favourite saints eternal friendship with her *cara* Clara and her *caro caro* Percy and, sometimes, her *cara* Maria – though she has a little fear that her *cara* Maria is not so fond of her as the others, can it be?, though her *caro* Percy says that it is only her way, that *cara* Maria only appears a little cold and stiff and reserved . . .

While Mary has Emilia's manipulative measure long before the requests for money begin, it is different for Shelley. She knows it and – almost – understands it. Shelley, lover of Gothic romances, enemy of patriarchal tyrants, champion of the oppressed especially when young, beautiful, and female – well, what more could there be in Emilia's case? The high-walled convent – barbaric superstition: the negotiations for a husband – heartless convention: even the parental despotism has an appropriate twist, for the father is married to a young and jealous stepmother. In other words, Emilia is another Harriet to be chivalrously rescued. Or another Mary.

How often, Emilia sighs, she wishes she were her *cara* Maria's sister – even her twin sister – would that not be wonderful? Her *caro* Percy agrees, he is transported by the idea . . . No, thank you, thinks Mary: I have had enough of sharing with sisters. Listening to Shelley rhapsodize on the virtues of his latest cloistered heroine, she wonders how long it will be before the illusion turns to disillusion. And then she is horrified at herself: not for what she thinks of Emilia, but for what she must think of Shelley, if she can view him in so detached, so satirical and, yes, say it, so *cold* a light.

Yet she has not ceased to love him, God, no. It is as if the love has become hopelessly tangled and knotted, like some skein of yarn recovered from a drawer. There it is, but how to use it, how to save it? What do people do? Emilia: make people feel sorry for you. Another answer.

Now step forward the two members of the Pisan circle who

should furnish the most promising example – because they are the only people Mary has ever met who faintly resemble Shelley and herself. The Williamses, Edward and Jane, are English but exotic, wanderers upon the earth, young and liberal and a little scandalous. Edward is a sturdy, fresh-faced idealist who went to India and a lieutenancy in the East India Company via the navy. He wooed and won the delicious Jane, unhappily married and separated from another officer: they snapped their fingers at the world, eloped, and had children while touring Europe. Where they differ from the Shelleys is in their closer proximity to ordinariness. Edward wants to write a play, and sketches a little and not very well, and Jane is adept at arranging flowers and trimming headdresses, but they are not artists and never will be and, above all, they lack that difficult yearning. Edward is an outdoors man, happiest while riding or walking or sailing: Jane, excessively beautiful, languid, lily-like, is superbly at home in the drawing room, blossoms in the polite inexcitations of the fireside, does not so much talk as converse. They fit into the world far more neatly than Mary and Shelley could ever do.

What is it, then, that the Williamses do? That's just it: instead of doing, they are content to be: Edward glowing from a tramp into the pine-scented hills, Jane disposing her long sex-charged limbs on a sofa. Another answer, then: don't do anything.

Interesting, but no good for Mary, with her lean, restless spirit. But the Pisan circle is to receive a new member who will perhaps understand this best, and to whose coming she looks forward with an anxious sort of pleasure: Byron.

He comes to Pisa from Ravenna, where Shelley has visited him in his eccentric *palazzo* full of free-roaming peacocks, monkeys, crows, cranes and goats, and where he has fruitlessly involved himself, along with his mistress's family, in the secret societies for Italian liberation. It is Shelley who has persuaded him to join their circle, and added to it the notion that they should form a kind of literary government in exile along with Leigh Hunt, who is making plans to come out from England to renew his health and escape his debts. Together they will found and write a radical journal to counterblast the Tory rags at home: kindred spirits on the Lung'Arno. Shelley is excited, Byron agreeable. It is left to Mary to find him a house to rent for the mistress and the menagerie.

Not, though, for Allegra. Byron has sent his little daughter, in the Italian style, to a secluded convent to be educated. Claire has been a volcano since hearing this news, and it is the question of Claire that makes Albé's arrival in Pisa problematic. Claire has spent all her vacation time with them – and would spend more if Shelley had his way – and one medium-sized provincial city is not enough to contain a Claire and a Byron together, any more than gunpowder can be kept in a paper flask.

'You needn't fear what will happen if I see my beloved brute,' Claire says. 'I would not do anything rash, for Allegra's sake – though what further punishment he could inflict than walling her up in some beastly convent I can't conceive.'

'It does not suit our ideas, perhaps,' Mary says temperately, 'but it is the Italian custom for young girls.'

Ignoring her completely, Claire asserts: 'It's that macaroni-gobbling trollop of a contessa he's with. She's behind it. She'll have no rivals for his affections, which is sheer nonsense as anyone with a particle of sense knows that Lord Byron, the poetic beast, is constitutionally incapable of maintaining *any* affections beyond a fortnight. Oh, I don't care about her. I wanted to see my Allegra.' She sobs drily, then crams a ratafia biscuit in her mouth. 'If she ends up like poor Emilia, I'll put a knife in his heart.'

'If she ends up like Emilia, she'll do very well,' Mary snorts.

'You're jealous of Emilia.'

'Oh, Lord, if I thought that was anything . . .' Mary cannot be bothered even to finish the sentence.

'I won't see him, I know,' Claire says, with ferocious gloom, ripping the lace from her balled handkerchief. 'He'll do anything to avoid me. I suppose, after all, this is my punishment. I was determined to have him: I wrecked my life for the chance of him. It seems hard, though. One action, one turn of a card, and all your days are shaped for ever. Don't you think?'

'It seems hard,' Mary agrees.

Claire, often an accurate prophet, is right. All her friends urge her to return to her respectable post in Florence rather than dabble in the sullied waters of Byron again, and when Shelley also, sadly, urges it, she listens. On the road outside Pisa the public coach taking Claire away passes Byron's Napoleonic juggernaut, coming into the city with its train of horses and servants.

'Yes, I saw her,' Byron tells Mary later. 'We exchanged a mutual glance of proper loathing. Now how are *you*?'

'I am as you see me, Albé.'

'Still a damned fencing clever sort of woman, eh? I like the house you found me, only it's too big: I must have company every night, lots of it. It looks as if I shall find it here, thank God. I have been too entirely Italian for too long, my talk has become operatic, I need some good puddingy English ballast to weigh me down. You must all come and see me. I go mad when I'm alone.'

'But you are not alone. You have Signora Guccioli.'

'Oh, Teresa is one of the most magnificent beings in creation, and probably my one true last attachment, as far as it goes. But you can still be alone with a lover. My God, you can.' Byron's hair, always tending to the widow's peak, has receded further, and he is expunging the flesh from his sensual face with one of his punishing diets: his look is naked and unposed, as if he has just risen from sleep. 'How goes it with you and Shiloh? I ask out of mere idle curiosity – and also he has been raving to me about some chit of a schoolgirl who resembles an ideal vision or something.'

'Oh, Shelley's Italian Platonics – they are pretty much done with, now the girl is married after all, and quite happily,' she says, with a shrug and a thin laugh, and then realizes how closely

Byron is watching her: more closely than anyone has for a long time.

'A pity,' he says, quite gently. 'I had thought you two, you know, true and enduring and all that.'

'Nothing endures but disappointment.'

'Is that a line of mine? It sounds as if it should be.'

'Now stop it. You know your *Don Juan* is the finest thing—'

'Aye, is it? But it's still only a poem. I don't know, I begin to sicken of words, and hunger for deeds. Is this like a man sickening of fornication, and hungering for marriage? I devoutly hope not. You've met Mavrocordato, of course. There's a thing to do. Greece, where we come from – everything that makes us worthwhile, at any rate – Greece, calling for our aid. Not words but deeds. Terribly romantic I know. Ignore me, I shall probably forget it over the next bowl of punch. Shiloh's a good man, by the by: one of the few genuinely good men I've ever met.'

'How can you tell? she asks, with interest.

'Unlikeness to self. Why, do you doubt it?

'I don't have to answer all your questions, Albé.'

He gives her a look at once respectful and critical. 'You never answer any of them,' he says.

So, Byron joins the circle, and soon vitalizes it, giving extravagant dinners and parties at his house just across the mustard-coloured musty-stinking river from the Shelleys'. Often he goes with Shelley on shooting expeditions – only to shoot at marks, for Shelley will not kill on principle, and Byron will not do it since he shot a bird and wounded it and then, seeing its throbbing dying beauty, spent hours of anguish trying to keep it alive. Other times they go into a huddle with Edward Williams over plans for a boat, for they both delighted in sailing on Lake Geneva back in the days of Dr Pollydolly, and Williams knows about such things, and the sailing along this coast is incomparable. And sometimes after these mornings Mary finds Shelley a little testy and melancholic – perhaps because Byron is still Byron, the man whose life is forever vaunted in capital letters, and he is still that obscure atheist whom nobody reads.

There is one subject sure to bring out this difference between them.

'Aye, aye, it's a great pity about young Keats, I don't deny,' says Byron. 'He had promise, no doubt, and the Tory reviews were being quite like themselves in stamping on it. But a man must rise above these things, and not let himself be snuffed out like a candle by a cold draught of criticism.'

They are on a walk through the orchards outside the city, and Shelley says nothing for a moment, narrowing his eyes at the mellow November sun though the trees, a lattice of bright honey. He forbears from pointing out – Mary reads it – that Byron has grown so sensitive to the stares that his notoriety produces in the streets that he has himself driven in a closed carriage to the city gates in order to take this exercise.

'He was of a susceptible temperament, I know,' Shelley says at last. 'But it does not excuse the robber that his victim was carrying a fat purse. Injustice is injustice. What was done to Keats was a crime, no more nor less.'

'My dear Shelley, you are too good for this grubby world. But you know, if a man's scribblings don't tickle the public, there's nothing to be done. Murray continually gripes at my *Don Juan* because the ladies don't buy it like they bought my corsairs and such trash.'

Again a silence: and Mary thinks, as Shelley must be thinking, that at least Byron has known what it is to be admired: unlike Keats, and unlike Shelley. Curious how you can still divine your lover's thoughts, even across gulfs of estrangement. The mind outlasts the heart. She glances back, impatiently, at the walls and red roofs of the city steeped in yeasty light. They have been out long enough now, she needs to get back to little Percy Florence, he frets without her.

'Well, I still wish he had come to Pisa, instead of Rome,' Shelley says. 'Of course it can have made little difference in the end. But I wish I might have seen him one last time.'

★   ★   ★

Yes: I know I said we might perhaps meet again. But I wish it might not have been under such circumstances as these.

Indeed, I am not sure I wish it at all. Pardon me.

Yes, the Heath is common ground, and there is nothing to prevent your going this way also. Certainly not the sense of intrusion, which you so obviously lack.

Yes, I dare say you have seen me walking here a lot. It is what I do lately. No doubt it is much remarked upon. And my thinness and paleness likewise, well, there we are. The mourning dress accentuates those, of course.

I do it – I walk and walk like this – because I cannot bear society just now. Only solitude is tolerable. Miss Brawne, the girl who adored parties. I think my sociability was often a grief to him. Well, well.

Oh, and I have been over to the pond to look at that ancient thorn and, do you know what? – it is just a very old and ugly tree. It does not do or say or mean anything. This is the last appalling truth about death: it isn't anything. Just a subtraction from what is.

And I walk, I walk because I have always found walking a stimulus to thought. Above all, to the imagination. I remember him telling me that ideas would often come to him like a powder-train when he made the walk from London to Hampstead. The imagination – it was as important to Mr Keats as sight, as the use of the limbs. And I keep trying and trying to imagine it – to picture it – what happened after he left here.

And I can't. Not to my satisfaction.

I mentioned this to Mama or, rather, she prised it out of me. She was shocked and said I shouldn't think of it, that it would make me ill.

But it is making me ill.

You understand? Well, I'm obliged to you for that – though really, no, I don't see how you can help me. But very well. I'll tell you what I know.

Most of it I learnt afterwards from Mr Severn. Mr Keats wrote
as best he could – not to me, we knew that would be unbearable
for him – but to Mr Brown, until he was no longer able – but of
course one suspects that much is being held back: that one is
being spared. Suffice it to say that their voyage to Italy was as
wretched as I feared – fretted with storms that must have been a
severe trial to one as sick as he, though Mr Severn says he kept his
spirits up wonderfully – and ending with their being unable to
disembark at Naples for ten days because of the quarantine – ten
more days cooped in a foul-smelling cabin under a hot sun, for a
man in his condition . . . Well, they were let ashore at last, and
travelled by *vettura* up to Rome, along an atrocious road,
victualling at the most beggarly inns. It almost sounds as if one is
being punished for illness, does it not? In Rome Dr Clark, who
had agreed to treat him, had found them lodgings at the piazza di
Spagnia. Apparently this is in the foreigners' quarter of Rome,
and a very delightful spot: fine views across the city, and in the
square a Bernini fountain. I wish he could have delighted in it.

Oh, for a very short time it appeared there was some
improvement. The climate seemed to suit. Under the doctor's
supervision he took some exercise, and even rode a little, and Mr
Severn rented a piano and amused him with music – he was
utterly devoted in his attention to his friend and I am not
surprised, because that is what Mr Keats brought out in people,
when they were worth anything – and they had meals brought in
from a *trattoria* nearby and ate together in their sitting room, and
Mr Keats read and dozed and listened to the playing of the
fountain and the cries of the flower-sellers. You see: I have tried,
I have striven with my imagination and I worked up a picture of
sorts – not an unpleasant one. Incomplete, of course.

And then it darkens.

It happened at Christmas. The strangest and saddest Christmas
he had ever known, Mr Severn said. Mr Keats took a very
decided turn for the worse. He brought up blood by the cupful.
He grew weak and despairing and Mr Severn hid the laudanum

and the razors for fear of what he might do. He talked of this 'posthumous life' of his. You see that telling gift never left him. Soon he was confined to his bed. The sufferings he underwent made him, at first, what he had never been – angry and irritable – he tipped over the coffee that Mr Severn brought him, he turned to sulk at the wall. But that did not last: he would not have been Mr Keats if it had. He grew milder as he grew weaker. For hours together he held in his hand the white cornelian I had given him. I believe he spoke of me, and our broken life together, in terms of the most anguished regret, though again I think Mr Severn spares me.

And then – of course – Mr Keats died.

I knew he was going to. The reports that came to Mr Brown and my mama – well, it was plain. Still, when Mr Brown came to tell me the news, it was all I could do to remain firm. Not to run, wail, tear.

Why remain firm? A good question. Perhaps because I feel there is more respect in that than in abandon. Also you know I am in a ticklish position. I am not his widow, though I consider myself so: even our engagement was not public. The world does not recognize our tie. It is all inside – burning.

He died on the evening of the twenty-third of February. He felt the tide rising in him, and he was covered in cold sweat, and he asked Mr Severn to lift him up in his arms. He told his friend not to be frightened, and thanked God it had come. Mr Severn could hear the phlegm boiling in his chest as he sank away. And there, there was the quiet end of him.

I wish he had not gone. The southern air did not save him. He might have stayed here, among all those who loved him, and died so – I don't know. I don't know if it would have been any better. Don't ask me.

The day after he died, the authorities insisted all the furniture and linen from his lodgings be burned and the woodwork scoured, because of his being consumptive. It is as if the world tried to rub out all trace of him as soon as he was gone.

He was buried in the Protestant cemetery at Rome. Mr Severn says it is a beautiful place and fit for a poet. Dr Clark had daisies planted on the grave-turf. That I can picture – that he would have wanted – but Mr Severn says also that it is near something called the Pyramid of Cestius, some ancient monument, and that I cannot conjure for the life of me. Pyramids – what had my John to do with pyramids? Why did he have to go so far away from me, to a strange place where I can't follow even in my mind – I have tried and tried but I can't bring it to life in my mind – and that is twice a death.

Very well. Tell me, show me, help me.

I want to see – yes, the piazza di Spagnia, that's the place. The church above the square – not like our English churches I should think. Twin towers, yes, open bell-towers – and what are those tall trees like palms? – oh, and I have pictured it rather grey yet those tall houses are a wonderful warm russet colour. Tiled roofs, yes, that I pictured, and the painted shutters and the little balconies – oh, now which one is number twenty-six, which one is his? Very well, I'll be patient. It is all much more splendid than I thought – that fountain in the shape of a boat forever sinking, and especially those steps, those fabulous terraced steps, sweeping down like a marble waterfall. He must have marvelled – I hope he was well enough, for a time, to have marvelled.

And this, this must have delighted him – this curious parade. They are artists' models, you say? And this is where they ply for hire – actually dressed in their costumes, saints and madonnas and brigands. Oh, I know this must have delighted him. You see, he always believed that we are most free when we learn to be someone else – that the self can be a prison. When he watched a bird pecking about on the gravel, he would enter into the bird and peck about with it. This is what it meant to him to be a poet. Yet he was so cruelly imprisoned in his flesh at the end . . . I beg your pardon. Yes, I would like to see inside number twenty-six.

Second floor. The stairs must have been a trial. Surprisingly cool, though, shaded. I can smell violets – those flower-sellers outside. Let me stand and look a minute. This – this is where he died. And yet it is not deathly, that is where I had imagined it quite wrong. Plain and fresh. Limewashed walls and a red-tiled floor – that I never guessed. Small – there are just these two rooms? – yet I prefer that, somehow I pictured him dying in some hideous great salon full of decaying tapestries.

And this was his bedroom. The windows on the square – he would have liked that – when we nursed him at Wentworth Place we always flung the drapes and windows wide, let the world in to him. Oh, I never expected that – the embossed ceiling – are they daisies or roses? No matter. I like to think he had them to look at as he lay here. They are Keatsian, somehow.

Yes, it is better, a little. It can never be good, of course.

I would like to see the grave, yes – that is, I don't know if I will be equal to the sight itself. But if you can just give me a picture of the place – and that damnable pyramid. No, I am not crying. That's rain. Well, dew, then. The form of precipitation is immaterial. Come, let me see.

The Protestant cemetery. Well, how curious for us to see ourselves thrust out beyond the civilized limits, like suicides or Jews. Once again I find my notions were rather narrowly English – one imagines graveyards as flat – a flat plot of grassy ground about a grizzled church with headstones breaking out like orderly mushrooms from the neat turf. But here – I see slopes bearing a tumble of upright trees – they must be cypresses, yes, and there is myrtle and flowering oleander – how densely green it all is, and scented, and crowded with those tombs and slabs and urns and bits of ruins, and all lightly scored with the chirruping of some sort of insects that I do not much wish to see. Indeed this is not deathly either: in its quiet way it teems. And now I see the pyramid I don't mind it. It is just another monument. It isn't vast. It fits in. It is all reconciled here, life and death and past and present: those silver-grey headstones seem to grow out of this rich earth in just the same way as those silver-grey tree-trunks.

I grow profound. I'm sorry, it's because I grow nervous –

indeed I must ask if the lamp-wick of our imagination, wonderful as it is, may not be turned down now. I am thankful for all of this. I have seen something, absorbed something. But I cannot look at the grave. I have heard about it, about the sculpture of the broken lyre, about the words he wanted on the headstone. But I cannot look at it.

Well, can you?

What do other people do?

Another answer: invent or reinvent yourself.

This is the answer Mary garners from the final, flamboyant addition to the Pisan circle – Edward James Trelawny.

Trelawny: even his name is like a sword-thrust – if only with a cardboard sword.

He arrives as an old friend of Edward Williams, who in his sturdy, stuffy way has been telling everyone about him – Trelawny, sterling fellow, Cornishman, coming to Pisa, can't wait to introduce – but is soon friends with them all. Trelawny is a man of appetite, greedy for people as for drink, food, experience, admiration, love, but above all hungry to know Byron and Shelley. For him scandal is an inducement. In fact, he has made himself in their image.

'Dear God,' Byron confides to Mary in an urgent whisper, after long post-prandial talk with the Cornishman, 'this man terrifies me. I am *responsible* for him. He sleeps with a copy of my *Corsair* under his pillow. He *is* the corsair, in his own imagination. The heroes of those damnable verse-tales of mine are his inspiration. I have written this man's Bible. Is this not magnificent – absurd – above all horrifying?'

'Not flattering?'

'It ought to be, no doubt. But he's in for such a disappointment once he comes to know me. Oh, I don't know – imagine if you actually met your Victor Frankenstein, for example.'

'How do you know I haven't?' Mary says, but her voice is as ever quiet, and Byron is already moving away.

Big as a colt, shaggy-haired, with a white, aggressive smile framed by glossy moustachioes, Trelawny squires Mary about the social season of Pisa like some courtly Cossack. He plies her with tales of his adventurous past (seafaring, shipwrecks, duels, piracy), about half of which she believes. She is happy with this: she has come to the conclusion that a certain amount of lying, like the priming of a pump, is necessary to keep life going. Absolute honesty would bring everything to a shattering halt.

Though he is a Byronic hero made flesh, Trelawny is equally fascinated by Shelley. 'I have never before met a man who seems to me so supernatural. Next to him I feel gross – I feel as if I have twice the human portion of flesh. He is this rare spirit, in every sense of the word. And yet a lionheart too – did he not steal you away, Mrs Shelley, from an oppressive dungeon of a domicile, and your sister too—'

'Claire elected to come abroad with us,' Mary says sharply, 'that is all.'

'Did she? One can hardly blame her.' Trelawny never notices bad temper. 'What woman of spirit would refuse such an adventure? I don't understand bide-at-homes. They only live half a life.'

'That half, however, may be of very good quality.' *Oh, Mary, the world has soured you.*

'I like the way you think. A Scot would call it pawky.' Trelawny lifts her hand and places on it a soft whiskery kiss. He does this frequently, almost as punctuation to his conversation. 'Did I ever tell you about the cabin-boy on the *Dauntless*? Can't have been above eleven – took a dose of chain-shot in the groin. Nearly cut in two. But he'd always wanted to go to sea, and be in a sea-fight, and the glory of dying so was a joy to him, and so he kept singing and making jests even as his life bled away. When he saw the first mate weeping he damned his eyes, yes, he did, and told him he had not an ounce of regret.'

'How horrible. How dreadful. Just when I think I've heard the worst of the world, you come up with something fresh.'

Trelawny laughs hugely. 'Oh, I spare you, Mrs Shelley: I could freeze even your blood if I wished, with some of the things I've seen.'

'*Even* my blood?' Sharp again.

'Why, the authoress of *Frankenstein*, I should think, is not easily scarified.'

'Oh! I see.' You did not mean, thank heaven you did not mean, that I am already frozen, cold, heartless. 'Scarified, by the by, Tre, does not mean scared.'

'It does when I use it. I hear Shelley took a skiff on the river when it was in flood. Mighty courageous again, or foolhardy – which would you say?'

'As he does not swim, I would say foolhardy in the extreme. But I am a little prejudiced against sailing, because right from a girl the sea has always hated me and whipped itself up into a storm as soon as I get on it.'

'Ah, you can make friends with a storm, once you know your business. When I first ran away to sea, we went though the worst storm to hit Biscay in fifty years. Waves above the mastheads. I found myself laughing like a hyena, I can't say why. But Shelley, now, he would understand, I think. My lord perhaps not: he is rather more worldly than I thought him. Shelley was reciting some of *Childe Harold* the other day over billiards. "What nonsense is that you're spouting?" says Lord Byron. I was a mite shocked.'

'You want people to live up to their works.'

'But of course,' he says, with a biting smile. 'You know, ma'am, Shelley is a damned lucky fellow. I hope he knows it.'

'Oh, Tre, I ought to tell you we don't go in for gallantry.'

'I do,' he cries, and as if in illustration aims a perfect killing swipe with the ivory tip of his cane at a wasp that has been hovering round her hair. In fascination, ear tingling, Mary watches the insect spiral to earth.

Dancing is something she has not done for a long time – Shelley, stork-limbed and abstracted, would soon destroy any dance-set – and part of her still disapproves its essential triviality as she waltzes in Trelawny's bearish arms at the masked ball of the Pisan *veglioni*. Another part of her studies this situation with an almost detached interest. The great question, what if your life had gone differently? Other choices, other paths. Many of the dominoed gossiping fan-waving ladies here, for example, do this all the time: having been suitably impressed by a suitable pair of bearish arms they have suitably married them, and now they flicker like insubstantial butterflies between dance and tea-table and card-table. And are, presumably, satisfied.

'Aye, I've had to eat rats before now, when the victuals ran out and the sea was like damnable glass. They are really not so very bad. Your heathen Chinese, now, will readily eat dog, and the one and only time I was driven to that it was utterly horrible. A good fat bilge-rat, infinitely preferable. Not dissimilar to kid.' The quadrille ending, Trelawny bows and tickles her hand with his moustaches. His mask makes him look even more absurdly dashing, also strongly sensual. Yes, one might have taken another path, thinks Mary, and found much there to please: and Tre is a splendid sort of man, and dressing and flowers in the hair and ices and promenades are quite enjoyable: and already I am very slightly bored.

'You never, I notice, stay till the end of the evening,' Trelawny says, handing Mary her shawl, and flashing an incidental smile at a lady dressed as a much *décolletée* Queen Elizabeth. 'It's because of your little boy, isn't it? You can't be long away from him.' Like many self-absorbed people (and immediately there, Claire comes to Mary's mind) Trelawny can be acutely penetrating. Not caring much aids the seeing.

'He is very dear to me.'

'And comes first, eh? Natural, natural.' Trelawny is already heading for the royal presence.

Is that the truth about her? Probably. Percy Florence seems robust now, but then so did Wilmouse at two: you can never tell. Her mind is like a permanently flexed muscle about him, never relaxing. Her son is her sun, the fixed centre around which she moves. And there can be, must be, only one sun in the emotional cosmos. This is the belief that above all separates her from Shelley now, Shelley who would fill his sky with suns, with Mary, with Claire, with Emilia – with Jane Williams.

'He is a damned lucky fellow, I say again,' Trelawny says again, at an evening party in the Palazzo di Chiesa. 'I hope he knows it.' He is at Mary's side, and both are looking in the direction of Jane Williams, who is seated in one of her usual dreamy pictorial attitudes, this time with a guitar on her knee. The guitar, beautifully inlaid, expensive, is a gift from Shelley, who sits crouchingly close by her in devout sun-worshipping guise. Well, easy to understand, in an abstract way, the fascination: such undeniable beauty, such shady eyelashes and tumbled ringlets, and above all that quality of domestic siren, spreading her enchantments amid the teacups. A dry mermaid: a Percy Circe. Even the sound of the guitar, blandest of instruments, suits – charmingly uninteresting like the things Jane says.

And yes, Mary supposes this is jealousy. But of a very peculiar kind. Instead of snarling, it tamely wears the muzzle and hangs its head. It is weary. Something to do, perhaps, with the fact that she has discovered she is pregnant again, and can summon up no good feelings about it at all. There is only foreboding. The unmistakable tightening across the belly is like the delivery of some extravagant purchase she will not be able to pay for.

The thing that is wrong with me is that I do not *thrive*, she thinks, as Byron with his little dim-witted cat-clawed mistress and vinous parties and opiate of cynicism thrives, as Claire always thrives, even resentful as she is at her temporary exclusion and just lately in manic mood, peppering Mary with wild letters about her concern for Allegra in the convent and even proposing that they descend on the place and kidnap her. Mary, picturing a carriage bucketing out of the convent gates with Shelley whipping the horses while Claire bats away the clinging nuns with her parasol, hardly knows whether to laugh or cry. She tries to pacify, promises they will talk about Allegra when they all move to the coast for the summer. For this is the plan for the colony, as they now call themselves – Shelleys and Williamses and, when they finally get here from England, the Leigh Hunts – as soon as suitable houses can be found around the Bay of Spezia. Shelley and Edward Williams are completely sea-haunted now, with Trelawny's buccaneering encouragement. Shelley is having a sea-going vessel built, a schooner, and Byron – of course – is having one built too, a bigger one. Boys with paper-boats competing on the pond, Mary thinks. Oh, Mary, soured.

Claire arrives in Pisa as the circle begins to break up for the summer. There has been the usual hugger-mugger in making sure she and Byron are kept apart, but it should be easier when they make their move, because Byron has elected to go further down the coast to Leghorn for the summer.

'So, it will be just like the old days!' Claire says boisterously, kissing Mary, laughing because she knows Mary does not like it.

'Perhaps, but let us hope for a better eventuality.'

'Pom–ti–pom!'

Odd how comfortable this is, like the feel of an ugly but serviceable dress.

'And how is my brute, not that I care – does the little Pope-worshipper still need to shave her sideburns, and has she stuck a stiletto in his back yet, which she surely will one dark night, not that I care about that either?'

'Wouldn't you do the same?' Mary enquires.

'Only in daylight, and from the *front*.'

Claire it is who accompanies the Williamses to the coast on a house-hunting expedition, buoyed by flattering remarks from Shelley. 'Not much,' he says fondly, 'that you don't know about fitting up neat quarters.'

'There's not much I don't know about anything,' crows Claire, as they set off. 'I am indeed a woman of the world!' Jane Williams already looks exhausted, or more exhausted than usual.

Soon after their return, Mary is taking a mental inventory of her potted plants, wondering which she can transport safely, and wondering, in fact, at their profusion: she having never before settled anywhere long enough to cultivate anything beyond a cut flower in a vase. Roots, roots. Tweaking and watering, she suddenly becomes aware that Shelley has silently entered the room and is watching her.

'Hail to thee, blithe spirit,' she says.

'There's a letter from Byron.'

'A letter? That diet really must have weakened him, if he can't walk over from the Lanfranchi.'

Shelley, after a moment, laughs uproariously as if she has said something superbly witty; and now she knows something is very wrong.

'It's Allegra,' he says at last, and now she sees the tears standing in his eyes. 'Byron has just had the news. She caught a fever in the convent at Bagnicavallo, and she has died.' Turning to go, he adds almost conversationally: 'Claire will go stark mad.'

How they manage it, or try to: all agree, Shelley, Trelawny, the Williamses, that Claire must not be told yet, not while she and Byron are living in the same town, because she will assuredly go wild against him, and the joke about the stiletto may become real. Get her away: get to the sea at once. They pack up hastily: no time for sentimental goodbyes to the Pisan house that has almost been a home; the potted plants are thrown on the dung-heap. Shelley, a whirlwind, arranges for their luggage to go by water, thrusts Mary and Claire and little Percy into the first coach for the coast with Trelawny as their escort and instructions to take whatever summer house is available.

'I'll follow. I won't be long. I have only a few matters to see to.'

'Lord, Shelley, you're like a man possessed,' Claire says. 'Is somebody out to get you?'

'No one new,' he says, with a bleached smile.

'Shall you be making your farewells to the brute? Withhold my love, if you do.'

'Yes,' he says, tonelessly, 'yes, I shall.'

And so they take her, chattering all the way, to the coast, and there at Lerici, overlooking the Bay of Spezia, they find there is only one house to rent – only one, as if it has been waiting for them. No choice. Full of doubts, wearied by the negotiations, preyed on by Claire's cheerfulness, Mary at last signs the lease on the Villa Magni.

Houses enclose, structure, and define our lives. At the Villa Magni, in a kind of still trance of repulsion, Mary reviews the other houses in her life. The pepper-pot house in Skinner Street, loud with inharmonious voices. The guilty dream of a house at Marlow, with its sash windows and seductive burgher comfort. The creaking woodwork of the chalet at Montalègre and the sonorous draughts of the Villa Diodati above the stormy lake. All of them, even the worst, she found a way of fitting herself into, as a cat will find a spot of sunlight. But there is no fitting into the Villa Magni, a house that hates her.

It used to be a boathouse, and still it is as near to a ship at sea as a house can be, poised right above the violent inky bay with its lower floor open to the lash of waves and sand. Above is the terrace and the only habitable floor. Mary, Shelley, Claire, Percy Florence, the servants, and also the Williamses are packed into it, as there is no other house for them. Their bedrooms surround a central hall that has to do service as a dining room, not that there is often much to dine on, as they are remote even from such supplies as can be got from Lerici, a starveling hamlet of fishing-cottages across the bay. Below the house a little jetty and a strip of beach form the only link with the outer world: behind it, to landward, steep hills loom, choked with dark impenetrable woods. This is it, says the Villa Magni: there is only this house, and the sea, as there is only life and death.

From the first moment, agonized though he is over Claire, Shelley loves that sea.

'Everything else stays still,' he says, 'but this. Turn your back on it for five minutes, and you find it's changed.' True: the bay can go from black tempest to blinding serenity in what seems an eyewink. And that is partly, perhaps, why it afflicts Mary with loathing, this sea that will not leave you alone, that is like a person who never stops talking. It truly makes her seasick.

And the house too is what they bring to it: that news, carefully carried like a corked and sealed poison. A few days after they settle in, Claire goes for one of her indomitable walks on the turbulent beach, and Shelley and Mary gather in the Williamses' bedroom to discuss how best to uncork the bottle.

'A woman's touch,' Edward Williams keeps saying, in his solemn stomachy way. 'I'm sure a woman's touch is needed,' though it is only Jane he looks at when he says it.

'I feel it should be me,' Shelley says, his head in his hands. 'I am responsible.'

'Responsible, my dear Shelley, how so?' Edward puffs. 'It was not you who consigned the child to a fever-ridden convent. If anyone—'

'I mean,' Shelley says gently, very firmly, 'responsible for Claire. She has no one else.' And still no one looks at Mary.

'Byron will not write her, I suppose,' Williams says.

'It would be disastrous if he did,' Shelley says. 'If Claire were to learn that way—'

'If Claire were to learn what?'

She is there, in the doorway. There is a smudge of sand on her cheek and her rich black hair has come down and she has never, Mary thinks emptily, looked so beautiful.

Shelley jumps to his feet. 'Claire—'

'What? Learn what?' Her eyes flick from one to the other of them. 'Something about Byron? What should I learn about that brute that I don't already know?' Then she swallows convulsively as if someone has thrust something hard and bitter in her mouth. 'Is it Allegra?'

Shelley takes a step towards her. 'Yes.'

'Is she dead?'

'Yes, Claire. I'm sorry, she is,' says Shelley, taking her hand; and at that moment Mary understands what Trelawny meant about Shelley's courage.

'No, no, no.'

'I know. I know. I know.'

Claire has done very well so far, has impressed everyone with her strength. But now the night has come. The wind batters at the salt-cracked shutters of the Villa Magni as the knowledge of her loss batters at her mind. Mary holds her. Percy Florence sits at their feet banging his toy drum and then expectantly looking up as if for applause.

'My little one—'

'I know. I know.'

'You *don't* know.' Claire tears herself away, swatting and gasping.

'But I do,' Mary says with hurt, hurt that she recognizes like a distant landmark. 'After all, I—'

'You still have *him*,' Claire says, so vehemently that Percy freezes, drumstick suspended, before her pointing, shuddering finger. 'And I've got nothing.' Her arm drops: she liquefies into boneless grief. 'Nothing.'

And now, if ever, is the time for Mary to say: That's not true, you have me, your sister: you have me, you have Shelley, you have us. And even now she cannot say it. Her own silence falls on her like a curse.

When Claire at last sobs herself to sleep, Mary covers her with a shawl and then goes to the window. Lerici shows its usual senseless weather. The wind has dropped, and the sea simmers under humid air. Crazy stalks of lightning spring up on the far lip of the bay. Down on the beach the local people, strange, staring, barefoot creatures who seem more like castaways who have adapted to their bleak strand than a native community, are dancing by torchlight and singing in some dialect Mary cannot understand, singing songs that have no apparent key or form or rhythm. Everything now seems made for bafflement, and the thought occurs to Mary that perhaps this is what the world is really like; and what is happening is merely a fall of scales from the eyes.

'Shelley, help me.'

Claire fingers the lock of Allegra's hair, sent by Byron along with her miniature at Shelley's request. It is Shelley also who has gently passed on to her the details of the funeral arrangements, the little lead-lined coffin that is to be shipped home to be buried at Harrow.

'I will in any way I can. Is it the matter of the burial? I leave it to you, but I truly advise that it's best to accede to his plans, because you will only bring yourself more grief.'

'Not that. I can't – oh, let that go as he likes. It can't matter now she's dead. It's Allegra alive I want.'

'That I understand,' Shelley says conscientiously. 'I would like to offer you some hope. The rejection of religious illusions that we have always adhered to makes it difficult, in conventional terms at least—'

'No,' Claire says, stamping her foot, 'not that. I mean when she *was* alive. You saw more of her than me – you went to see her that last time, when you visited him –' she seems physically unable now to pronounce Byron's name '–in Ravenna, and you must – you must remember things about her. More than you told me. Please.' She seizes Shelley's hands in her own. 'Help me, Shelley.'

He nods slowly. 'Very well. To begin with, her hair was a little lighter than you would think from that lock. And she was wearing a little gold dress that brought out the colour in it . . .'

So it goes on. How much he actually remembers, how much he embroiders or invents, Mary is not sure; but certainly he sets himself to the task as diligently as if he were working on a long poem, and he succeeds at it. From Shelley, day by gruelling day, Claire gets a consolation that Mary cannot supply. She clings and cleaves to him in her grief: Edward and Jane sigh in admiration of

625

the sterling part he plays. And Mary is left clutching a dismal handful of possible reactions, like a batch of addled eggs. For she and Shelley are further apart than ever now, and his puzzlement one morning at seeing her run to be sick in the basin, before he mutters, 'Oh, yes, of course,' speaks volumes, and she knows that she must end up behaving badly. It is only a matter of time.

It comes.

Claire returns to Florence for a while, but Shelley presses her early return. She is best off here, here is where she belongs, though he fears for her health with all this travelling in the heat . . .

'She's as strong as an ox,' snaps Mary, from the well of worry and sickness and irritability and the unaccustomed pain, surely too early, down in her womb that wakes her every morning. 'As you well know, travelling never has hurt her in the slightest.' (She stands in the hall of the Venetian inn with the water-light rippling on the ceiling and in her arms her baby Clara still, still.)

A momentary frown, and then Shelley visibly gathers himself. He has to remember to do it, you see. Has to remember it's Mary, make allowances. 'I'm sorry, my love. It must seem we think about nothing but Claire just now. Only think what she has been through – and if she seems to be bearing up well, remember she does have that bouncing way about her, and deep down she may still be crying out—'

'Just now,' Mary spits, 'it's not just now. Always, it's always been Claire. I pity her about Allegra, I truly pity her, and yet I just can't help thinking here it is again – Claire again, stepping between us. Whenever you and I have suffered or struggled, there she is in the middle of it. Don't you see?'

He is staring at her with what looks like honest bewilderment. 'But don't you see,' he says, 'that very often it's been Claire who's kept us going?'

'Oh!' Almost absent-mindedly, she picks up her teacup and throws it at the wall. 'Oh, so you mean I haven't been enough for you?'

Truthful to the last: 'Not always,' says her husband.

'Not always,' she echoes him dully. She looks about for another teacup, but most of them were broken in the move to this place, to damnable Lerici, the howling place that hates her, the place where the truth comes out.

'Well,' says Shelley, freshening, as if ready for a good meaty discussion, 'I don't think one person ever can be.'

'Go to hell with your thinking.'

He flinches. Nothing to throw, yet that got him right between the eyes. 'Yes,' he says, shrugging, turning, 'I probably will.'

Houses define us, define too our relationships, and the Villa Magni is an expression in stone and crumbling plaster of the estrangement between Mary and Shelley. For he is in love with this place of her mutual hate, thrills to the precipitous loneliness, the wildness, the lack. And his love is confirmed when on a tempestuous May morning a sleek new craft beats into the bay, an eagle among the dowdy starlings of fishing-smacks: Edward and Shelley's boat, the *Don Juan*.

'She doesn't sail,' Shelley says dreamily, after he and Williams take the boat round the bay for the first time, 'she flies.'

She. Mary remembers – surely several lifetimes ago – standing on the deck of the ship that was to take her to Dundee, and her father, benignly pedantic, remarking on the feminine appellation always given to boats, and the why and wherefore. She suffers a moment of acute longing for him. Or, at least, a longing for him to exist: her true father, not the hypocrite and bankrupt despatching begging heartless letters.

Shelley is out in the boat every day as spring becomes in June sudden, fierce summer. A stifling waxy heat lies across the bay: the iron-gold sun hangs in the sky like an instrument of torture. Mary sits or lies in the airless shade of the terrace, sweat-drenched, listening to the servants quarrelling, sometimes looking out to the bay for the elongated triangles of white, the *Don Juan*'s sails, heading in for the beach. Sometimes: not with any particular expectation. She lives here, Shelley lives out there. Sometimes their lives intersect, that's all.

'It makes me wish the earth really was flat,' Shelley says one evening (to Jane). 'Because then you could sail right to the edge of it.'

'And then what?' puts in Mary. But Shelley only shakes his head and smiles. (Jane too.)

But now here is Trelawny, neckcloth piratically streaming, teeth incandescent in his sunburnt face, and surely Trelawny will be the one to revive her spirits. Trelawny is dining at their dismal board (little stinking fish that are simply all bones, like needles of fir-trees, black bread, palate-glueing figs) because he is taking Byron's new boat, the *Bolivar*, down to its owner at Leghorn, and he puts in at Lerici to see his old friends. And, unwittingly, to rouse Shelley's envy, for the *Bolivar* is almost as grand as a man-of-war. Boys on the pond, thinks Mary.

'Mrs Shelley – you are blooming,' Trelawny says, with his usual ticklish salute.

'No, I'm not.'

'Ah, that suggests you don't feel it. But your mirror will tell you otherwise.'

The gallantries are a little perfunctory, as if Trelawny cannot bring himself to believe in them.

Later she does look in her mirror. She never has bloomed in pregnancy, and the pale, baleful image tells her nothing out of the ordinary. But it is, Trelawny said, what you feel, and Mary feels wrong, somehow, deeply wrong: on the ominous edge of something, like the hated house on the edge of the clawing shore.

Her miscarriage begins in the night with a sensation as if a shepherd's crook is teasing out her insides. It continues with such sluicings of blood, such sickening vanishment and liquefaction, that while she can still think Mary thinks: Now we will find out if there is such a thing as a soul, because my body is just going away, so quickly, all of it, like a pat of butter on a griddle.

The nearest doctor is miles and hours away – but why think

about such things as doctors, why be so conventional? – soured, Mary, soured – but at Lerici there is an ice-house, and Shelley sends for the ice and when she begins to slip from the blood-slimy grasp of consciousness, and the brandy and vinegar proffered by a mewing, shivering Claire do not work, he heaps the ice on her and round her, briskly, forcefully.

'Live, live,' he hisses. And when she droops again he piles blocks of ice into the hip-bath, his own hands purpling and numbed, and lifts her bodily into it. 'Live, live.' She is not sure how long it has gone on: hours probably: the window is bright with morning, and Shelley's voice is like a bark now. 'Live, live.' He makes it sound like a violent threat: more like die, die. Drifting in and out of delirious dreams as she is, she cannot be sure what she says, but she has a feeling she asks him at one point: 'Do you really want me to?' And, oh, that she has to ask: Oh, God, let her die for that.

But Shelley does not let her die, nor, perhaps, the Almighty. Mary returns to life through a long corridor of pain and grief – grief of a feeble, unsurprised sort. She realizes she never expected to keep this baby. The fates have already been lenient in allowing her to keep Percy Florence: she is in arrears with the punishment. And besides, there is the malice of the house.

She bathes tentatively in the sea, supported by Shelley. It does her good: he is right again. 'Dr Shelley,' she says, with a weak smile, as they walk back up the beach.

'A patient patient,' he says, patting her hand.

And, yes, this is good, doctor and patient is better at least than the bitterness of division. But it is not how she wants them to be, not for long: she wants the love back. But she does not know how to conjure it. She does not know how to do magic.

Back to life down the long corridor, and at the end of it a new beam of light: Leigh Hunt and his family have finally arrived in Italy. Predictably penniless, they have landed at Genoa and will go on to join Byron at Leghorn. Thinking of Leigh Hunt with his shiftless warmth and his chaotic brood, Mary feels an almost unearthly joy. Perhaps it is because she knows the urbane Hunt would politely regret the dampness of the Villa Magni and find that mad chanting of the torchlit villagers no more than an absurd curiosity. He is reason, and they need reason here.

Instead, there are nightmares. Mary is troubled with them every night of her convalescence, but she cannot remember them, she only struggles awake trailing vague threads of dread and oppression. Different for Shelley.

She has just stirred from a doze when she finds Shelley standing at the foot of the bed, screaming. The screams, shrill as a woman's yet with a man's chest behind them, go through and through her.

'Shelley, remember – Shelley, remember—' The words are the formula they use for rousing him from his sleepwalking episodes. But they don't work now, or he can't hear them for his own screams, and Mary in terror stumbles out of bed and gets past him and across the windy hall and hammers at the Williamses' door. Her legs are still unsteady from the miscarriage and shock does the rest: she hits the floor as Jane snatches the door open.

It is Edward Williams who manages to wake him. His throat is a little sore from the screaming, but otherwise he seems well, calm, lucid. Lighting a candle, staring fixedly into it, he tells them what happened.

'I saw visions. They were not fleeting or hazy: they were full of the most meticulous detail, like Dutch paintings. You were all in them—'

'Dreams, you mean, of course, my dear Shelley,' says Edward.

Shelley hesitates, shrugs. 'If you will. First I saw you and Jane – you were all covered in blood, and the bones were sticking through your skin, and you came staggering in to me and cried, "Get up, get up, Shelley, the sea's flooding the house, it's all coming down . . ." And so I ran to get Mary – but I was already there. I could see myself standing over the bed and throttling her – my hands on her throat – and so I must have screamed.' He scratches his head as over some abstruse puzzle, then catches

Mary's eye. 'Don't look like that, my love. I'm always having these visions of myself lately. I met myself strolling on the terrace. He asked me, or I asked myself, "So, how long do you mean to be content?" ' From looking sprightly he turns abruptly ashen and exhausted. 'Sorry. I wish these things would only disturb me and not you. I'd better get some sleep – proper sleep.' He blinks speculatively around like a tired child ready to curl up anywhere. 'We're going to meet Hunt tomorrow.'

No, not tomorrow, not after this: Mary is so desperately insistent that Shelley, usually inflexible about changing plans, gives in. Still, it is only a postponement. He is eager to welcome Hunt to Italian soil and even more eager to give the refitted *Don Juan* a run on the open sea. With her speed, she can reach Leghorn, fifty miles down the coast, in half a day. So he keeps assuring Mary, still nervous and fretful: it won't be long.

'I don't want you to go.'

She has just come back from her dip in the sea, with cold, sugary sand still clinging to her toes, and her voice has something of the same needling quality: she can hear it.

'You fear you'll relapse without Dr Shelley?' he says lightly. 'I doubt it. You've come on so well. And I shan't be away long.'

'It doesn't matter how long. You're still leaving me alone in this – this place.' Superstitiously she refrains from calling the Villa Magni an insulting name: not when it can hear her. Head down, she towels her stinging feet.

'You won't be alone. You'll be with Claire and Jane.'

'That *is* alone.'

The old wryness: it makes him smile, if a little reluctantly. And what she should have said, of course, was *I am alone without you*. But it only passes through her mind, and then, like a dusty book consigned to a shelf, it joins the vast sad library of things left unsaid.

'Well, she's rigged and provisioned,' he says, 'and we can't delay any more. Hunt's expecting us. With a fair wind tomorrow noon we should be at Leghorn before dark.'

'Promise me one thing, then,' she bursts out. 'Promise me you'll look for another house for us. Anywhere – up the coast, Leghorn – as long as it's not here. I don't want to live here any more.'

Now he looks weary, and faintly affronted. 'Why?'

'Because – because I have a bad feeling about it.' She slumps back in surrender. There. She has come up with the lamest, feeblest piece of stupidity, and she is exhausted and defeated.

'I see.'

She opens her eyes to see Shelley nodding, thoughtful, grave; and she realizes that she has said something prodigiously right, that this, far more than the most urgent matter of practicality, is something he takes very seriously.

'I see,' he says. 'Yes, in that case, we should move. Yes, my love, I promise: we'll find somewhere different.'

So, the next morning, and a blaze of heat quivering over the bay like some titanic gong-stroke that never dies away. So, Mary watching from the terrace as Shelley and Williams walk down the beach, Williams buttoned-up and stocky, Shelley a long, nervous streak in reefer jacket and white nankeen trousers. So, a wave. So, presently, under the molten height of noon, the elegant white triangles arrowing out of the bay.

Four days later, a letter from Shelley arrives at the Villa Magni, a bustling sort of letter full of news about Leigh Hunt, how he flung his arms round Shelley on seeing him, how Hunt's wife is ill from the voyage, how Byron, with swiftly diminishing patience, is putting up Hunt and his large family on the ground floor of his house in Pisa, and how Shelley is cheerfully trying to keep the peace between them all and make plans for the launch of their periodical which Byron wants to call the *Liberal*. . . . No mention of finding another house.

'Well, after all, he can't do everything,' says Claire, while Jane nods in decorative agreement.

Gusts and squalls shake the house night after night. Both

Shelley and Williams have promised a prompt return. Every morning Mary looks out for the racing sails of the *Don Juan*, but sees only the feluccas of the local fishermen. Jane begins asking, plaintively, 'Where *are* they?', as if Mary could answer her. Mary's legs are still weak from her illness, and when she walks about the house she finds herself hanging on to the furniture just as if she were on board ship herself. Then she dreams she is, and wakes in the night to a thunderstorm like a colossal cannonade trained on the house. Percy Florence wails in fear. She hugs and hushes him, watching the lightning paste the walls with ice-blue. In the morning, the sky is clear, the bay troubled only by small spiteful cross-winds, but there is a humid tang in the air that is the opposite of freshness.

And still no white sails.

'This cannot be right,' Mary says over breakfast, and meets Jane's frightened deer eyes.

Percy Florence, still unsettled, grizzles and clings. Claire insists on hunting through Shelley's papers for a coastal map that Mary knows is not there. 'If there is one, they will have it with them. Anyhow, it can tell us nothing. It's fifty miles, and they made the outward trip in seven hours. We know that.'

'Still,' Claire says, 'still,' and carries on, getting everything in disorder, getting dust over her clothes, getting at last thoroughly bad-tempered. Still, it is activity: understandable. Outside, the wind begins to screech again. Jane keeps tuning and retuning her guitar, until Mary feels those little squeaking keys are tightening not the strings but her own humming nerves.

'I'm going to Leghorn,' Jane suddenly announces.

'How?'

'Someone from the village will take me. I'll pay someone to row me down there.'

'They won't,' Mary says. 'Not in this weather. They've more sense.' And after a moment she realizes what a terrible sentence that is.

The next day is Friday, when the mailboat from Lerici brings the week's post. And it will bring, surely, a letter from Shelley explaining that he is staying on in Pisa or at Leghorn for some entirely comprehensible or even Shelleyan reason. Instead, there is a letter addressed to Shelley from Leigh Hunt. Mary scrabbles it open, and finds Hunt hoping that his dear friend arrived home in one piece, as such a shocking storm blew up just after his departure . . .

'This cannot be right,' Mary says again. She finds she is sitting down, with absolutely no memory of having done so.

'Well?' Jane says. 'Where *are* they?'

Mary passes her the letter. 'Monday,' she says. 'They sailed from Leghorn on Monday.'

Claire, who has been gazing out to sea, abruptly turns and closes her eyes as at an obscenity.

Emergency, the midwife of harmony. Swiftly they agree: Claire will stay at the Villa Magni to wait for news here, Mary and Jane will go straight away to Byron's house at Pisa.

The journey, by boat and then jolting, flea-teeming *vettura* inland from Lerici, is exhausting, and it is midnight when they arrive at the shut gates of Pisa; but Mary does not really feel tired, in as much as she suspects that she is probably asleep anyway. What she thinks has perhaps happened, is this: she is actually sixteen, and she is sitting behind the deal counter of the bookshop downstairs at Skinner Street, chin in hand, while her stepmother stomps above and her father pores in his study, and Claire is still a hoydenish schoolgirl called Jane, and Lord Byron is only a distant famous name, and she has never yet met Mr Shelley, and everything that has happened since then is merely her long, long dream as she dozes through the dreary brown London afternoon. And presently, surely, she will wake up.

Because that would make more sense than this, she thinks, as she tugs at the sepulchral bell in the dark courtyard of the Palazzo Lanfranchi: much more.

And only in a dream, surely, could she have such presence of mind, when she is greeted with astonishment by Byron's mistress Teresa Guccioli, to make her desperate enquiry in neat Italian: '*Sapete alcuna di* Shelley?', and to note that Claire's strictures on plump pretty Teresa are very unfair, particularly in regard to her hairiness, though she does have a marked way of looking at all women, even those who cannot possibly be rivals, just as a well-fed house cat will still gaze at birds.

But no, they know nothing of Shelley – unless her Byron has heard . . . Byron appears, dressing-gowned, unshaven, blinking, troubled.

'No. He sailed from Leghorn on Monday afternoon. I thought he must be back at Lerici long since. Trelawny was going to take the *Bolivar* alongside him, but there was some trouble with Customs and he had to stay in port.'

'Did they sail into a storm?'

Byron hesitates just an instant. 'Trelawny says it was turning unsettled when they left. A squall. God, you look like a ghost.'

'I am one,' Mary says, turning to Jane. 'We must go on to Leghorn.'

'Wait – stay here with us,' Byron says, 'at least tonight. The Hunts are in possession of the ground floor, heaven help us. I swear there's one more brat every morning. Stay up here as our guests, sleep, then in the morning—'

'I can't, Albé,' Mary says, pressing his hand, feeling the dart of Teresa's black eyes. 'Can you get us fresh horses?'

A few hours later they clatter into Leghorn. Night and sea-mist are being peeled away by a steely dawn. They put up at a waterfront inn and Mary, seeing the huddle of warehouses and quays, remembers an earlier part of this incredible dream when she stood on one of those timber docks and tried to deliver herself to the sea and could not. Did she promise the sea a life then? And has the sea now claimed its debt? Surely not, surely not even in dreams . . .

'I saw them go.' Trelawny, summoned to the inn, takes hold of a hand each from Mary and Jane: for a crazy moment they seem about to play ring-a-roses. 'This I can tell you. I watched them go through my glass. They had hoisted full sail and I saw them out of the harbour brisk as you like. After that I went down to my cabin to sleep.'

'And did you sleep?' Mary asks. Jane stares at her for such a ridiculous question. Only it is not so.

Trelawny drops his eyes, shakes his shaggy head. 'It turned a little too rough for sleep,' he says.

'Tre, they have not been heard of since Monday,' Mary says, her hand going numb in the grip of his great paw, a surprisingly realistic sensation for a dream. 'Please tell us truly what you think this means.'

'It means we must search the whole coast,' he says, too heartily. 'That is, I will. I shall set in train every enquiry – everything possible. You should go back to Lerici and wait there, in case – well, you should go back. I'll escort you. Have you fresh horses?'

Jane says: 'You mean there is hope?'

'There's always hope,' he answers promptly. Mary studies his face. The trouble is, that dashing beard always was a good disguise for lying.

And, of course, it would be here, at last, that the news comes: here at the hated and hating house, the Villa Magni, where for an unthinkable week they have waited, Mary and Jane and Claire: waited like, Claire says, the three witches.

'Why the three witches?' Mary asks.

'Oh, there always has to be a reason,' Claire says, bursting into tears.

The sea is up again. Foam spatters underneath the terrace. When Trelawny arrives, that evening, his boat-cloak is dripping and his long hair plastered like seaweed. Water, water everywhere.

'Mrs Shelley. I told you, I think, what a wonderful man I thought your husband – I hope I did, because it impresses on me more and more, how vastly honoured I was to know him—'

'Oh. Oh.'

'There is an inexhaustible joy and recompense in knowing and admiring such a man. Even when we can know him no more in the flesh. I'm sure you will agree with me.'

'Oh.'

'The bodies have been found. Washed up on a beach near Viareggio. I have seen – there is no doubt. Besides other things, your husband had in his pocket a copy of Keats's poems, and this survived, better than – well, there can be no doubt. I still say I am proud, so proud, to have been his friend and even to be the one chosen by fortune to bring you this news . . .' Trelawny's hand grips her elbow. 'You should sit down . . .'

But she is not fainting, not Mary: only fathomlessly amazed and terrified to find that this, which should be the moment when you wake up sweating, is not, and that the dream is no dream, and that the worst nightmares are the ones you live.

4

Landings

These people coming out into the lamplit Strand are theatre-goers, and that smart new unpretentious building is the Lyceum – a theatre, yes, but not one of the patent theatres like Drury Lane and Covent Garden, which are the only ones licensed for legitimate drama. It's sometimes called the English Opera House, and anything it puts on has to be seasoned with music, because that's how the unpatented theatres get round the official proscription. As you can see, that doesn't worry the public, who have come in numbers to see – well, we'll ask. Pardon me, sir.

Three pieces, an afterpiece, and a jig. Indeed, a full programme. But the piece you particularly came to see? *Presumption, or the Fate of Frankenstein.* Ah, yes, founded upon the notorious novel. You have read it, sir? And a good thing too, else you would not have recognized it – I see. I gather there have been certain liberties taken with the original. Certainly, it must be odd to see Frankenstein singing an *arioso*. But there were felicities, you say – the first appearance of the monster bursting in at the top of the stage stairs. Yes, that must be impressive. The actual moment of creation is not shown? Yes, I see your point. That might be interpreted, in certain circles, as blasphemous. No, I can tell you are not of that opinion—

Oh, you are, madam? Well, please, tell us what you thought of the production. I see. Yes, one hears that there have been protests against the staging of this story, with its daring theme. Very well, 'blasphemous', is your word. May I ask why you came to see it, if such is your belief? To see just how bad it was. Ah, yes, of course. But it has held that stage for a month now, has it not? Oh, more shame to us for it: I see.

And you, sir, might we ask – yes, sorry, very sorry to intrude, but we were just canvassing opinion on the merits of *Presumption* . . . You also think it vastly inferior to the book. And you speak with some authority . . . ? Indeed, there is something strikingly familiar about your face. Are you not Mr William Godwin? Then if we are not very much mistaken, that young lady at your side—

Mrs Shelley. This is amazing. And might we ask what you thought—

More amusing than amazing, I see. Still, to find your work actually on the stage, in whatever form, must be quite a revelation – you have not long returned to England, I think, after . . .

Yes. Yes, of course, many apologies. Thank you. Good evening.

Well. You'd never guess, would you?

It was one of the new steamboats that brought Mary, the widow, back to these shores, from Calais to Thameside: safer than sails, not so beautiful: perhaps that means something, for the future.

Having lost Skinner Street through indigence, her father now has a new house and shop not to pay the rent on, situated in the smoky Strand near St Clement Danes. Here Mary spends the first few weeks of her return to England, having nowhere else. No, unfair: Godwin, cornered by age, is a gentle, tamed creature to what he was, and is even proud of her, while the Clairmont is only a muted version of herself, gaspy and piggy-eyed, as if slowly disappearing into her own fat. Still, not for long: still, only temporary, as Mary supposes everything must be in this new bereft life. The trip to the Lyceum is one of her rare ventures into a city at first unrecognizable in its flashy rebuilding. Mostly she stays indoors, looking after Percy Florence, thinking, remembering. The parlour fireplace before which she sits is surrounded by blue Dutch tiles, each tile bearing its own little separate picture.

The eye goes in jolts from one to the other. And, likewise, the sharp tiles of memory.

One: Trelawny, escorting them back to Pisa, his big male smell filling the carriage, their three widowed faces pale and damp as putty in the swinging lamplight. (Three widows? Well, what else can one call Claire?) Trelawny has done everything: seen to the packing and sending on of their luggage by water, the closing up of the Villa Magni. Yes, now it has happened, the longed-for leaving of the hated house, but no good now. Nothing now can be good: ever.

'We must have a proper funeral,' Mary says. Jane groans. They think her cold when her voice is so level and decisive. As if despair can be warm. 'I want him to be laid to rest near our Wilmouse – our little son. In the Protestant cemetery at Rome. Where poor Keats ended too. Can it – how can it be done?'

'I'll find a way,' Trelawny says.

Quarantine laws in Tuscany require that the bodies be buried with quicklime on the beach where they were discovered. Shelley, her Shelley, hastily shovelled over like some piece of stinking flotsam – no.

'I'll find a way,' Trelawny repeats.

Another: Mary in her old bedroom at Pisa, looking out at the yellow Arno, knowing what is happening on a bleak stretch of beach along the coast. She could not go, but Trelawny has told her what he means to do, and she can imagine it, if she dares – and why not? Isn't this the imagination that conceived *Frankenstein*? Why shrink, then, from the thought of the decayed flesh exhumed from the sand, placed upon the iron pyre Trelawny has brought from Leghorn, and burnt there under the open sky?

Another, later: Trelawny faithfully giving her an account of the cremation. Byron and Hunt were there. Hunt wept: Byron, after a time, stripped and swam a while out to sea, as if to challenge the destroying element. When the flames grew high, they all tossed frankincense and salt and wine on the pyre. Trelawny spoke, committing his friend to the winds and air. A properly pagan ceremony. At last, the collection of the ashes in a lead-lined oak box, to be taken to Rome. Trelawny pulled out what he believed to be the heart, which had survived blackened but intact. Hunt begged it from him as a memento. They came away in Byron's carriage, with the last wisps of smoke disappearing above the blue sea.

'Now he is one with the earth,' Trelawny says: and scrutinizes Mary, as if doubting that she believes it.

Another: sitting opposite Leigh Hunt in a coach – though she cannot remember where they might have been – and Hunt saying: 'My dear, if you were like this with Shelley, I profoundly pity him, and am almost tempted to say he is better off where he is.'

'He may well be. At least now he has no supposed friends to sponge off him.'

'Ah, yes, money, of course, yes, let's get our priorities right. You are really quite conventional-minded, aren't you? How ever did poor Shelley bear it?'

The quarrel has blown up over, of all things, Shelley's heart. Mary wants it: Hunt refuses, at first, to relinquish it. Below that, of course, enormous roots go down and down. Shelley's heart, that shrivelled cake of leather, is many things: his memory, his reputation, his identity, his love. As soon as a man is dead, the truth of him goes off into the air like disappearing smoke.

'You don't let many people see this side of you, do you?' Mary says.

'Only people I don't care about.'

'Or who are of no material use to you.'

'I do wish you could rise above the grubbily material just for a moment. Can't, can you?'

'I'm sure your wife feels the same. This latest birth has quite exhausted her. Have you no notion of restraint, or don't you care?'

'It's so revealing, that you don't think the woman can feel any active desire. What a splendid quarrel we're having. Shall we stop it soon? Only I'm getting to the stage where I invent things to feel instead of feeling them. Rather like Byron all the time.' He smiles impishly and with tremendous malice.

'We would never have spoken like this when Shelley was alive.'

Hunt yawns. 'Finally we agree.'

This is a strange one: the parting with Claire. She is going to Vienna, where her brother Charles Clairmont is settled, and where she hopes to find a governess's post. There is nothing for her in Italy and nothing, above all, to keep her with Mary now that Shelley is gone. They both know it: neither can say it. In the end they kiss, embrace, and then stand uncertainly in the inn-yard, waiting for someone to say something.

It is Claire as last, with advice.

'You should go home,' she says.

'Should I? Not you?'

'Oh, I've been turned into a wanderer now: I should only fidget back there. But you . . . Besides, you have your little boy. He needs something.'

'What?'

Claire shrugs. 'What none of us has ever had.'

Mary digests this. 'Is it true Trelawny wants you to marry him?'

Claire gasps. 'What do you know about that?'

'You've been very thick with him. I'm not entirely insensible.'

'Pom-ti-pom. I'm saying nothing to that. Except this – I shan't ever marry.'

And the odd thing is, for once Mary believes her.

Genoa: here Mary is uncomfortably sharing lodgings with the Hunts, subsidized by Byron, and here on this crowded tile is a picture of the three adults and seven children squeezed into a smoky parlour, the only room in the building with a proper fireplace. Six of the children are Hunt children, which as Leigh Hunt has a theoretical objection to discipline makes them equivalent to twelve. The other is three-year-old Percy Florence, whom Mary is trying to teach his letters from a box sent by her father from London. A sweet, biddable boy, huddling close to Mary in exclusive adoration and shrinking from the savageries of the Huntlets. Home, thinks Mary. Home. But how to live? Byron has pointed the way, engaging her services to fair-copy his *Don Juan*, prompting her to write essays for the *Liberal*: her old ally, the pen. But will she be able to do it? She feels adrift in her own self-doubt, and wonders whether to write a little note to Byron at his house nearby in Albaro, asking him to call. But she hesitates because she feels Hunt's berrylike speculative eyes on her. He has already hinted that she relies too much on Byron, that their long tête-à-têtes must create a dubious impression, that she is a nuisance and a drag on him.

Curiously even here she and Hunt still understand each other. Hunt drops these hints because he knows that the same applies even more to him: he and his litter are entirely living off Byron's generosity. And there is, she reflects, only room for one leech on a vein.

Another curiosity: since Shelley's death, nobody seems as nice as before, including herself.

'Yes,' Byron says, prowling up and down her fireless upstairs sitting room and blowing on his fingers, 'you should go home. That is, you should stop dithering about the matter, and stay or go.'

'Ah, this is that sort of harshness which is supposed to be good for the bereaved.'

'No, it's just ordinary harshness. Now, come, how are you going to stay? If I were going to stay in Italy, I would try and help you – not that that would be easy with Hunt thrusting himself between us. He's decided I'm going to support him and his tribe for ever now. It ain't so, Lord, it ain't. And truly, could you bear to be with them anyhow? *Ergo*, my dear Mary, it's heigh-ho for the white cliffs, the grey rain, and the black puddings. Home, and make your peace with your papa, and while you're about it, as I've suggested, do what Sir Tim asks, and secure your boy's future.'

It is Byron who has appealed on her behalf to Shelley's father. Probably letters from someone with Byron's reputation are not likely to mollify stubborn old Sir Timothy Shelley of Field Place: probably he has them placed, by gloved hands, on the manor bonfire. In any event, her father-in-law will do nothing for the woman he still sees as one more of his son's delinquencies, like poetry and atheism. He does have one offer to make. He will undertake the bringing up of little Percy Florence, on condition that she permanently surrenders him and all rights over him. So that is the end of that: though Byron cannot quite understand her refusal.

'I'd sooner die,' she says. 'Secure his future? With strangers, without his mother?'

'Oh, well, you know I never quite understand the fuss about parents. Mine were no manner of good to *me*.'

'Yes, but not everything comes down to you, Albé. A thing still exists, even though you haven't experienced it.'

'No, it doesn't,' he says cheerfully. 'Your Shiloh was the best, most unselfish human being I ever met – not that that's saying so very much – but I'm afraid he was entirely on the wrong scent, and the world will always think so. I'm your man of the future, Mary. Imagine a great horde of me, all advancing towards the horizon with looking-glasses in their hands, saying, "But what about *me*?" There's the world for you. Yes, I've been drinking brandy, an indulgence I got quite under control for a while, by the by, after my marriage turned me into a toper. This is an isolated incident. It's because of the things I've got to say.'

'To me? Oh, damn, there, I'm doing it.'

'To you, to Teresa. Not that it's anything new. What I've got to do is convince everyone I mean it. Have you heard from Mavrocordato of late?'

'No. I thought he must have a lot to do, with things going on in Greece.'

'Things are going on in Greece, indeed, perhaps more than we can imagine. And that's why I cling to this notion of going there. Yes, to observe for the London Committee, that would be very well and I'd be glad to do that, but I want to *do*, you see. Can you understand that?'

'I suppose I can. But Shelley always believed that to write, to think, is also to do.'

'Perhaps it is if you can think like Shelley. I've written too much. My hair's going, my wits probably likewise. It's time I did something. I've had Greece in my mind since I first went abroad. Now they are fighting. Blood is spilling. I'm not welcome here any more, since I got tangled up with Teresa's family in this fearfully amateur rebellion. But the Greeks will have me more than willingly, and their rebellion is real. I've got the *Bolivar*, I've got money, I've got my name. I am actually very serious about this.'

'I see. Does Teresa know – I mean, does she know how serious?'

'I've always said that Teresa would be my last attachment. We have endured pretty well, and are now at that charming stage where we forget for long hours that each other exists. Yes, practically married, if you like. It will be a slow estrangement or a quick parting, I think: she may take her pick. She will do very well: she is made of india-rubber, and there I don't exaggerate.' He grimaces at himself, at that reflexive flippancy. 'No. There's only one woman who truly loves me, and she is far away – as far as it is possible to be.'

'And by that you don't mean Lady Byron, of course.'

'The old witch. Oddly enough, when I heard she'd been ill I felt sorry for her. Unless I was really feeling sorry for little

Legitimacy – Ada – knowing how her blessed mother would take it out on her. You see, nothing is ever Bella's fault, and of course nothing can be the Almighty's fault, and so whose fault must it be when things go wrong? Why, whoever's close by her. You probably know why I played the dog in the manger about poor Allegra. Because of little Legitimacy. Because I already have one child being thoroughly taught to hate me, and I didn't want another, and so I dug my heels in and kept her away. Yes, you'll have gathered, nothing is ever my fault either. This is the last time I'm ever going to refer to Allegra, by the by.'

'Did you ever talk to Shelley about that?'

'Good God, no.'

'What did you two used to talk about, I wonder?'

'Men don't talk to each other. They merely strike a series of conversational poses.'

'You're doing it again. That's you, not men.'

'I shall miss you, Mary.'

'Will you? Hunt says you're sick of me.'

'Of course he does, and I hope you tell him I'm sick of him. Which is the truth, as it happens. But it's an impossible situation, all of you depending on me. You hate it, I know, which makes you fractious. Hunt loves it, which makes him jealous. That's why you've got to go home, as you know. And make your own way – which I still think would be easier for you if you truckled to Sir Tim, who surely can't be far off the coffin, but you're not going to, so I'll hold my tongue.'

'No, I'm not going to. He was our enemy when Shelley was alive, and now – well, in a way things are no different. I married Shelley – for ever. It doesn't stop. It's just that I must carry his name to the future on my own. And I shall. People will read him and understand him at last. He didn't have the chance to build his own monument, so I shall build it for him. No one else can do it.'

'It will be a lot of work – and if you're intent on supporting yourself too—'

'I will do it. But, oh, Albé, I feel old.'

'Well.' He thinks about that. 'The important thing is to go on feeling something. Mary, a favour. Will you be with Teresa when I leave? It will help.'

'You mean my glacial and even heartless calm will set her an example.'

'You're always ahead of me. She may bear up: she may see me going to Greece as just striking another pose. Striking a pose, or making a stand: who can say?'

So: the lemon-scented garden of Byron's villa overlooking the harbour of Genoa, and out there in the low glitter of evening the brig *Hercules*, bound for Greece, already laden with Byron's supplies, writing-desk, medicine chests, uniforms, horses, dogs; and making towards it, a small boat. In the boat, among others, Trelawny – for how could the incredible Trelawny refuse to join such an adventure? – and sitting in the bows, unmistakable in a blue nankeen jacket and open collar, white-skinned and still, Byron.

In the garden, Mary stands beside Teresa Guccioli in a silence lined with the song of cicadas, wondering what to say or do. In Teresa's face, puffed with weeping, the utter bleakness of knowledge: knowledge that it has all been no good, the tears, the ringlet-twirling, the foot-stamping: for the first time, her will has not been enough.

'We should wave,' says Mary suddenly.

'He cannot see us so far.'

'Perhaps. Still, we should wave.'

So they do. Something in Mary, perhaps her mother's astringent spirit, comments on this: for is this not women, immemorially, standing on shores and waving while the men go off heroically to define themselves?

'Now,' Teresa says, 'we are both widows.'

Mary, crossing potholed France by *diligence*, with her baggage and Percy Florence, an uncomplaining little boy who seems to have taken a good look at the world and decided that resistance is futile. At a tumbledown inn outside Paris a high-booted postilion hands her from the coach and lifts down Percy Florence and then peers with perplexity at the empty inside.

'*Votre mari?*'

'No,' she answers him. 'It's just me and my son.'

So, London, and her father, and one more tile: a very simple picture, but painful to look at. It is a newspaper cutting, preserved by her father, from the *Courier*, reporting her husband's death.

'Shelley, the writer of some infidel poetry has been drowned: *now* he knows whether there is a God or no.'

Tempting, just to sit in that tiled nook, drowsing, like the old woman she feels, stroking her son's curly head: withdrawing. But too tempting, too much like sinking. She rouses herself, and walks. She calls on such acquaintances as will receive her – not many: the English social neck seems to have stiffened during her absence. She goes to the theatre and with hardly any definable emotion beyond disbelief watches the play they have made (without permission or payment – none needed) out of her book. She walks, out of the loud, staring city, into the countryside of the northern heights, beyond her mother's grave, noticing the differences after her sojourn under Mediterranean skies: the curious afternoonish quality to the light even in the morning, the scrubby restlessness of cloud and wind, the clotted strength of the green and brown tones in the oil-paint landscape. She walks to Highgate, and calls on her old friend Mr Coleridge.

Fifty now, jowled and pursy, Coleridge lives a retired life in the house of the benevolent surgeon who controls the opium and makes sure he changes his linen. Here in a dim, wainscoted parlour he smiles her a vague welcome and talks, talks, as if he has never stopped talking all the time she has been away.

'. . . I condole with you, my dear, for there are losses which

seem to the sorrowing spirit beyond the reach of philosophy –
this I can attest from my own late case, not strictly comparable,
but cognate, at least cognate, and that is my son, who lives,
heaven be thanked, but is estranged from his father, it would
seem permanently. Oh, such griefs, how can philosophy be equal
to them? and yet you know something quickens in that very
womb of despair, for to conceive of the possibility of comfort,
even while bewailing its absence, is to vouchsafe the possibility of
its existence – it lies behind the veil, so much lies behind the veil,
no wonder we wish in bitterness of spirit to *deny* the veil, to rend
and tear it. It would seem there is something fatal to young
genius, for there was that young man Keats, you knew him I
think – I met him one day on the hill-path and we conversed,
and afterwards I shook his hand and I was never more appalled,
for "There is death," I said to my companion, "there is death in
that hand." Or is this retrospective clairvoyancy – is it all such
indeed? – I fancy not, and suspect that all the area of experience
placed under the opprobrious heading of *superstition* would
reward the serious researcher – the superstitious may indeed be
said to occupy themselves – perhaps excessively, but perhaps not,
who is qualified to pronounce? – in examining the veil, in
peering at its tears and inconsistencies, glimpsing perhaps even
incidentally and without comprehension what lies beyond? And
cognate too with this is, surely, the act of imagination, in which
the mind makes what it will of nature – the given world is a given
merely, that is, it is the clay which the mind moulds and shapes
according to its own will. Here the visionary and the poet stand
upon the same ground, above all I would say when *young* – for I
observe the more we have seen, the less we have to say. So it is,
alas, with me – where once my mind was a magus conjuring
nature into a thousand chimeric shapes, now it is a mere
house-steward, pottering in flapping slippers, the drudge of the
dullest work that nature can devise to mock our waning, forced
to think of bills and tradesmen's circulars. And yet I wonder is this
very disappointment not in itself a spur to new reflection? The

fact that we have nothing left to say may mean that the things necessary to be said are beyond our current grasp – and thus that when, as too often happens, I write the title-page of a new work and then cannot write any more, what is being demonstrated is that I inhabit limits and boundaries of thought, I stand upon impenetrable and wonderful frontiers – hence, in what appears stasis there is in fact progression, just as the inertia of a solid body is in fact an *action*, that is because the inertia by definition *persists*, and so merely being is a kind of doing . . .'

Coleridge ceases: his large grey boy's eyes stare. Mary has broken down in silent, hot, bleeding, paralysing tears: at last. Nothing she can do, no knowing how long these tears will last, perhaps a few moments or the rest of her life: nothing to do but surrender.

Coleridge blinks, shuffles awkwardly forward and pats her hand.

'I know, my dear,' he says. 'I know. There is a great secret, and it is this: that human life is intolerable.' The round eyes glitter. 'Now you have found it out, you mustn't tell.'

When the news came from Greece, Augusta was counting her blessings.

This was a regular habit of hers, a kind of moral exercising. Sometimes it required concentration and effort – as today, when the children were more than usually demanding and George more than usually absent – but concentration and effort, as Annabella had taught her, were among the qualities she sorely lacked. That was at least partly why she was a wicked person, she now saw. She did not try.

So, she set herself to it, and there were her children at the top of the tally, troublesome though they could be, all seven of them, though poor Augusta Charlotte more than the others because her mind was not right, and Medora more than the others because – well, she was thoroughly healthy, but there seemed something different, something almost too brilliant and delightful about her.

Odd, because she was after all from the same parents: of course: impossible, even wicked to think otherwise. (Another lesson Annabella had taught her: even her thoughts were like ill-trained vines, and needed smartly tying up.)

And after the children, George: yes, he had his faults, as who had not, but there were cruel husbands who shouted at the children and smashed furniture and abused their wives and even beat them, and George, thank heaven, was not like that. So, a blessing. And then there were these apartments in St James's Palace, a blessing indeed when their finances were more squeezed than ever by school fees. But at least there were no bailiffs at the door and they had not had to run off bankrupt to France like George's old friend Beau Brummell.

And then there was Annabella. Not that Augusta saw her nowadays, but there was always correspondence, and she could keep her guardian angel in view by that means. This was one blessing she never forgot to count: having someone who cared so much for the well-being, not of her body, but of her soul: cared so much that she was prepared to be stern and exacting with her: cruel, as Annabella had explained, to be kind. Oh, yes, she was very lucky.

Perhaps the mirror was not a place to look for blessings when you had passed your fortieth birthday. Still, even there she managed to find them. She had her hair and teeth, she told herself.

And lately, tentatively, as it were secretly, she had tried adding a new blessing to the index of benediction.

Byron.

Secretly, because as Annabella took such pains to show her, her association with Byron was a matter only for shame and penitence, and even in thinking of him there was peril. But that, Augusta dared to think now, was the old Byron: the Byron who was cut by society, driven into an exile of shadowy dissipations and proliferating scandal. Now there was a new Byron, who had gone to fight for a noble cause, devoting his energy and his fortune to it. Since he had arrived in Greece – setting up his headquarters at Missolonghi, raising and paying for a troop, working to reconcile the quarrelling Greek factions – his name had begun to appear in the newspapers again, and without the usual garnish of prurient innuendo: even with respect. Again secretly, Augusta had made cuttings, putting them away quickly in her writing-desk as if hiding them from herself. And yet why? – wasn't this Byron a man, a brother, to be proud of? A blessing?

But she still wasn't sure. As Annabella had taught her, the devil could find the most persuasive arguments. She dare not quite add him to the list. So things stood when the news came.

An ordinary Friday in May: George had been at Tattersall's, and then at the Cocoa Tree, and it was nearly dark when he came in. So nearly that he grunted his surprise at seeing her sitting there with no candles.

'Asleep, old girl?'

'No.'

'Oh. Thought you must be, sitting here in the dark. Got the megrims? I say, was that Hobhouse I saw down in the yard? What was he after?'

'George, Byron is dead.'

Fumbling with tinder and flint, George froze. Then he got the candle alight and came over to her. Several expressions flickered over his face: one, regrettably, was avarice, because there was sure to be a legacy. And weariness, because he was going to have to comfort the bereaved, and that would be rather a fag. But there was sympathy: yes. George did well. Deep down she knew he was a fool and a wastrel, but still there must have been something that kept her by him, and this was when it came out: he did sympathize. He did listen. He did his best.

'He's dead. My brother is dead.'

'Oh, old girl. Surely not.'

'It is certain.' She wept quietly. 'Mr Hobhouse brought me a letter – from Fletcher, Byron's servant. He was with him when he died.'

'Oh, old girl. Don't upset yourself. Terrible thing. What was he, six-and-thirty? Shocking thing. Johnny Turk did for him, did he?'

'Well . . . it was sickness. This place – this place where he was quartered – Missolonghi—'

'Funny old name.'

'It is very unhealthy, Fletcher says – low-lying, like a swamp, all damp and pestilential—'

'Ah. Breeds fever. Knew a place like that in the Peninsula.'

'Fever . . . Yes. I cannot think of a fever carrying my brother away and yet it did. Fletcher gives the most heart-rending account of his last days – I have read and read it and it is so very terrible—'

'Don't read it any more, old girl.'

'But I can't help it, George, because this – this is the last of him, do you see? The last of him, ever.'

'I see. Terrible thing.'

'It started when he went riding in the rain, and he came back to the camp soaked to the skin, and he was seized with shivering all that night. The next day began his fever – pains in the joints – still he tried to keep active but he grew rapidly more ill – while all about this wretched bleak place there was the most terrible rain and wind day after day. The doctors who attended him wanted to bleed him but he would not have it. I know he always hated a bleeding. He called them butchers and told them to get away—'

'Good for him. Don't like 'em myself.'

'But still he grew worse, he became delirious and could not support himself to stool, and at last he consented to the bleeding and they took a pound of blood from him. Fletcher says it was all most miserable confusion – the doctors disagreeing and the servants not understanding each other's language and the Greeks crowding about the house for news of him – and in his lucid moments he knew, he knew what was happening, he knew it was death—'

'Old girl, old girl.'

'There were more doctors fetched, and they kept bleeding and purging and blistering him, and then at last he couldn't get up from his bed any more. Fletcher says he kept talking in his delirium, trying to tell him something – and that he mentioned me – his dear sister he said. That's the part that makes me cry, George, I don't know why, and perhaps it's very selfish—'

'Not at all, old girl. Never mind it,' said George, looking very slightly bored.

'I'm glad though – I don't mean glad – but I'm relieved, really that his suffering did not go on long after that. Fletcher says he grew quiet at last, and then he seemed to sleep though the final day, and then there was a great thunderstorm in the evening, and in the midst of it he opened his eyes and closed them. And then he was gone.'

'Shocking thing. Never more shocked in my life. Still, as you say, a release. Well, old girl, we must have mourning – do the thing properly. Will they bring him home for a funeral, do you suppose? Happy to be chief mourner – do it properly. I say, is there any of that cold gammon left?'

After a long, still moment, Augusta stirred. 'Yes, George. Of course, you must be hungry. I'll get you some.'

She rose, went blind and sure into the unlit pantry. Gammon, Cheshire cheese, some capers. Her hands were quite steady now. At the centre of her was a huge invasive grief, dislodging and displacing: it was almost as if she were impaled on it. Bread, butter, soda-water. And yet somehow she was surviving it. Somehow the springs of life still flowed – even perhaps a little more strongly. Knife, napkin. In the extremity of sorrow, Augusta found herself equipped with understanding: in that darkness she saw. Yes, it was a blessing, the greatest of all her blessings: though he was gone, she had had Byron, and the pride of it rushed in like air to lungs. He loved me and I loved him, she reminded herself: this I can say: this can never change. She had not dared think it – feel it – for years, and now it was as if she were regaining the use of a paralysed limb. She considered Annabella for a few moments, then did not think of her any more. In her greatest loss Augusta discovered a victory.

Yes, it's me, Caroline – who else would it be? Where have you been? Oh, it doesn't matter. Nothing matters.

You've heard, of course.

I have so many regrets.

I have been drinking brandy. I quite often drink brandy. But I do not drink it as often or as much as they say I do. As often or as much, is that grammatical? I ought to know, I am a woman of letters you know – just ask Mr Murray – I have written more stories since *Glenarvon*, to be sure they have not fared so well but then, you know, they are not concerned with *him* and so – you know—

I was very good. In case they say I wasn't. They – I mean the Lambs, William's family, those wolflike Lambs who so want to sink their teeth into me, not that there is much meat to be had there – I look dreadful, don't I? A faded scarecrow. You needn't lie. Oh, they're worse since poor Lady M. died. She was better than all of them, in a strange way. Only old Lord M. rubs along with me pretty well. We curse at each other, and we both nurse our headaches companionably after the brandy, and all in all . . . Well, that will not last, for the others want rid of me, the wolves, and I don't doubt they will succeed at last. But they can't say I wasn't good, when I heard the news.

'Caroline,' William said, 'behave properly, I know this will shock you – Byron is dead.' And though I reeled from the shock and grieved mightily I did, I did indeed behave properly. I thought of him dying in that outlandish spot so tragically and I thought of how he might have lived and been happy and I thought of the things I had done in my bitterness of heart and my brain fairly throbbed and seethed with it yet, and I am very proud of this, I kept a fair command of myself. Also you know I had been ill lately with a fever of my own – a bilious fever the doctor called it – laid me rather low for a time and so I was not strong. Curious dreams I had when I was feverish. About him – Byron. He was bending over the bed and staring at me and I thought it was a premonition of death. Of my death. No, I had not dreamt of him for years.

Very strange, is it not?, and when I say I wonder if there is not some curse upon me you will smirk no doubt – yes, you will – the Lambs would, I can see them now – only consider this. After I had acquitted myself so well, here was I at Brocket recuperating, and at last I went out one day in the carriage, my first airing since my sickness, and the countryside was all green and smiling – though there was a thundercloud in the sky like a great dark plume – and William was riding ahead to make sure the road was fair. And at the turnpike he came upon a funeral procession passing by. Whose was it, asked he – oh, my God, it was Byron's.

For you may know they brought him home to be buried at his family vault in Nottinghamshire – and the cortège went slowly up from London and so it passed by our very gates at Brocket. And I did not know this for they had kept it from me as best they could, sick as I was, to spare me the agitation and perhaps wishing to see it – do you understand what I mean now by a curse? 'That was Byron's hearse,' William told me finally – he had to, of course. To learn like that, so suddenly and unexpectedly, that his mortal remains were *there* – just *there* . . .

Oh, no one will hear. That's the advantage of roomy old Brocket – you can *scream* all you like. And everyone should have a *screaming* place, don't you think?

Well, it set me back – I fell very ill again – my mind was much troubled – now came on those distresses they had feared in me – and indeed I do not feel that I have been quite well since then.

I wish I had not said things about him. I wish I had not tried those revenges. My excuse was love but is it not odd that the passion makes us inflict cruelties and treacheries that we would never consider in indifference? Thus, are people not kinder to each other when they are indifferent, and would the world not go along better without strong feelings in it? And yet how bleak, how terrifying! What do you think, what do you think is the answer?

Yes. Probably I should not think of such things. The brandy helps, a little. But still.

I have so many regrets.

Standing at the front parlour-window of her lodgings in Kentish Town, Mary watched the funeral cortège pass by. Pages, mutes, a black horse bearing the baronial coronet on a cushion, and then the hearse. This was the reduced cortège that would continue to Nottinghamshire: earlier, when it set out from Westminster, there were forty-seven carriages following the procession, and the streets swarmed with people. It was like, as her landlady remarked, a regular hanging-day.

Mary watched with a dull sense of unreality. The world was a broken mirror, fractured into impossibilities. Albé, with his capricious vitality, dead – how could that be? And Albé, her loved, flawed, often exasperating friend, transformed into this national hero whose body had lain in state for two days while crowds fought for tickets to see it – how had that happened? And Albé following her own Shelley to the grave so soon, when she had counted on him to be a landmark in her featureless aching world – how was this possible?

And most perplexing of all – how was it that she was left alive when they were all gone?

Percy Florence was tugging at her to be picked up and shown the spectacle. With a deep sigh Mary lifted him and placed him on her hip. He was still a slight child, not heavy. The groan was for another burden: the burden of survival.

Epilogue

Womanhoods

Caroline: yes, though these rooms in Conduit Street above a tailor's are so very unlikely as a setting for her – with their cracked window-panes, dirty cushions, bamboo wash-stand, copper coal-scuttle – that is she, standing before a flyblown looking-glass in the darkened bedroom, swaying, crooning to herself. A waltz, perhaps: it's hard to tell. The wine-bottle on the dressing-table is empty.

The Lambs have finally got their way, of course: or, William has finally tired of her: or, she has finally wrecked her marriage. Whatever the interpretation, the result is the same. There has been a legal separation, and William's family lost no time in having her turned out of Melbourne House, and this is the place she has ended up in. Rent, four hundred and fifty pounds a year, and she has a maid, and rides in hackneys, and so we are not talking about destitution. But loneliness, hopelessness, pointlessness, perhaps. She misses her son Augustus, though his infirmities have grown more obvious as he nears manhood: Emily Lamb has been heard to remark that he resembles Frankenstein's monster. She still corresponds with Mr Murray, who is always kind to her. She is looked upon as mad, sad, and tedious to know. She reads, thinks, remembers.

Now she stops her swaying, as if a sudden thought strikes her, and darts with the old vivacity to a card-table that is heaped high with books. They scatter and tumble as she pulls one out and riffles impatiently through its pages until she finds, with a little mew of satisfaction, the page she wants. Read over her bony shoulder: then we must leave her.

> *O snatch'd away in beauty's bloom!*
> *On thee shall press no ponderous tomb;*
> *But on thy turf shall roses rear*
> *Their leaves, the earliest of the year,*
> *And the wild cypress wave in tender gloom:*
> *And oft by yon blue gushing stream*
> *Shall Sorrow lean her drooping head*
> *And feed deep thought with many a dream,*
> *And lingering pause and lightly tread;*
> *Fond wretch! as if her step disturb'd the dead!*

> *Away! we know that tears are vain,*
> *That Death nor heeds nor hears distress:*
> *Will this unteach us to complain?*
> *Or make one mourner weep the less?*
> *And thou, who tell'st me to forget,*
> *Thy looks are wan, thine eyes are wet.*

Augusta: the poem is one of her favourites by her brother, and here she is reading it likewise, in her old creaky crowded apartments at St James's Palace. A grandmother now, which means, unfortunately, she has even more dependants to support, for her eldest daughter has not made a prosperous marriage. Most of her time, indeed, is occupied with her problematic family; but still she cherishes her brother's works, letters, and mementoes, and maintains a vigilant watch over his memory. It was because of this that she agreed, soon after his death, to the destruction of the memoirs he had left, and which she feared – Byron being Byron – would sully his reputation. Thus they were fed to the modest flames of Mr Murray's fireplace at Albemarle Street, and Augusta was satisfied; though – Byron being Byron again – she has never doubted that his life will be made the pretext for irresponsible and sensational fictions.

And that is partly why, as the biographies and reminiscences have begun over the last few years to appear, she has fallen out with Annabella at last. Annabella has been a little too eager, in Augusta's eyes, to rewrite Byron's history as well as his will. It is a pity, because Augusta does not like to be at odds with anyone; and it is the more awkward as Medora speaks so fondly of her Aunt Bella, and vice versa. Well, that need not be spoiled; and surely even Annabella would not stoop to turning Augusta's own daughter against her: surely.

Augusta turns the page, thinking, or hoping, or trusting – what else is there? – that everything will be all right.

Fanny: it is eight years since Keats died, and there she sits at her writing-desk in Hampstead, again in black, pondering a letter that has shaken her world. It has happened, again, at Christmas.

No evergreens here, though, no bowls of punch: this is a house of mourning. A month ago her mother took an unshaded candle out to the garden, and a gust of wind caught it, and her gown went up in a flourish of busy flame, and after a couple of days came the slow and unpeaceful death that it was hard to imagine Mrs Brawne deserved. As Samuel died last year – a consumptive – Fanny feels very much alone. Margaret is young, a beauty, a social butterfly: what Fanny was. This is Fanny's place, at home, quiet, walking in shadow, looking backward.

And now comes this letter to disturb her grey peace. Fanny stares at her own hand – thin, knuckled like an old woman's, she thinks – and at Keats's ring, but what she sees are images of leaf-mould, of roots and slumbering seeds, being probed and turned.

The letter is from Keats's old friend Mr Charles Brown, currently travelling in Florence, but still doughtily faithful to Keats's memory. In fact that is his point in writing to her. He wants to bolster Keats's reputation. Leigh Hunt has published some reminiscences, which make him seem like a mere pitiful invalid. That, Brown says, is not the Keats they knew. He wants to do justice to his friend by writing his biography: also printing such of his poems as have not been collected.

And this will include, naturally, poems addressed to her, which is why he seeks her permission. His proposal will mean her being somewhat brought out of that privacy and obscurity which have been her chosen refuge; but he is sure that when she considers what a change may be wrought in the wronged reputation of her lover, it will seem a small sacrifice . . .

Yes: oh, yes, she understands. And she would do anything to help Keats earn the acclaim he was denied in life: yes, oh, yes. And it is not at all like her to be afraid – yet somehow she shivers at the digging of those roots, that light breaking in.

It is, perhaps, because while Keats had no fame, she could keep his memory all to herself. The world could not have him: she nurtured his ghost alone, here in Wentworth Place where the rooms still echoed to his voice. She has hunched over her grief for Keats like a miser's hoard, and now she quakes at the thought of giving any of it away.

'I wish,' she says aloud, 'that he had not been a poet and a genius, and that we had lived together as man and wife with no doom, and no brilliance, utterly unheard of till the end of our long, contented days.' She says it aloud because she wants to confess it, just once, and because she knows she is not going to write it to Mr Brown: she is going to say yes, and unlock the hoard, and face the ultimate fear of returning to life.

And she will let the world have the poems, like this one that she takes from the desk, copied out in her own hand, and long imprinted on her mind.

Bright star! would I were steadfast as thou art -
Not in lone splendour hung aloft the night
And watching, with eternal lids apart,
Like nature's patient, sleepless Eremite,

> *The moving waters at their priestlike task*
> *Of pure ablution round earth's human shores,*
> *Or gazing on the new soft-fallen mask*
> *Of snow upon the mountains and the moors -*
> *No - yet still steadfast, still unchangeable,*
> *Pillowed upon my fair love's ripening breast*
> *To feel for ever its soft swell and fall,*
> *Awake for ever in a sweet unrest,*
> *Still, still to hear her tender-taken breath,*
> *And so live ever - or else swoon to death.*

Mary: she has done it. She has recently celebrated - or quietly marked - her fortieth birthday, and while counting blessings is not at all her style, she has taken stock of her satisfactions. Percy Florence Shelley has just gone up to Trinity College, Cambridge; and she got him there, paying for his education through years of Grub Street toil. He is a pleasant, plump young man who shows no signs of doing anything out of the ordinary, ever. When indestructible old Sir Timothy finally goes to his reward, Percy Florence will come into his estate, and it is hard to imagine anyone more suitable.

Godwin has died, peacefully, full of years, supported at the last by, of all things, a government pension. Which left the Clairmont, old and confused, with no one to turn to but Mary. And Mary did it: she did not give way to old animosities, she successfully petitioned the Prime Minister, Lord Melbourne - formerly William Lamb - for a pension for the widow: she even heard the Clairmont thank her, not too grudgingly.

And closest to her heart, she has seen Shelley's reputation rise, and now a publisher wishes to put out for the first time a complete edition of his poetry - something old Sir Timothy has always blocked: but now be damned to him, there is no resisting the demand, and Mary is to edit and annotate the whole work.

So, to that end, she spends days and nights among his chaotic and voluminous papers. It is a strange, surprisingly physical experience. The whole of their life together is there: tissuey layers of memory. There is the dry salt smell of the Mediterranean on some of the papers, and on others Alpine rain has smeared the ink: over all there are Shelley's peculiar sketches and curlicues, and one fingerprint so perfect and fresh-looking you could almost think his living hand had just made it. She laughs, sometimes: sometimes weeps. And then wipes her eyes, and continues with her work.

Music, when soft voices die,
Vibrates in the memory -
Odours, when sweet violets sicken,
Live within the sense they quicken.

Rose leaves, when the rose is dead,
Are heaped for the beloved's bed;
And so thy thoughts, when thou art gone,
Love itself shall slumber on.

JUDE MORGAN

The King's Touch

'A fresh, fascinating and illuminating insight into the life of the Merry Monarch. Jude Morgan writes with style and understanding' Reay Tannahill

This beautifully crafted novel brings to vibrant life an era famous for its dramatic events – the Plague, the Great Fire of London, the Dutch Wars – and notorious for its sexual licence and scandal. It was an era in which the King of England became a byword for sensual indulgence – enjoying passionate affairs with women and nurturing an addiction to witty company, horse-racing, and high living – while maintaining a strong hold on his throne amidst intrigue and violence.

Yet Charles II remains, as he was to his contemporaries, an enigmatic figure. In *The King's Touch*, the story of this remarkable man and his turbulent times is told from a unique and enlightening perspective – that of the first-born son he loved above all others, but who would never become his heir . . .

'Conjuring up in extensive detail the politics, fears and licentious behaviour of the Restoration court . . . Morgan is careful to challenge the preconceptions of his historical characters' *The Times*

0 7472 6758 8

review

If you have enjoyed **Passion**, you may enjoy the following titles
also available from your bookshop or *direct from the publisher*.

FREE P&P AND UK DELIVERY
(Overseas and Ireland £3.50 per book)

The King's Touch	Jude Morgan	£7.99
The Mysteries of Glass	Sue Gee	£7.99
The Many Lives and Secret Sorrows of Josephine B	Sandra Gulland	£7.99
The Linnet Bird	Linda Holeman	£6.99
Small Island	Andrea Levy	£7.99
The Distance Between Us	Maggie O'Farrell	£7.99
The Lamplighter	Anthony O'Neill	£7.99
Scheherazade	Anthony O'Neill	£6.99
The Passion of Artemisia	Susan Vreeland	£7.99
Girl in Hyacinth Blue	Susan Vreeland	£7.99

TO ORDER SIMPLY CALL THIS NUMBER

01235 400 414

or visit our website: www.madaboutbooks.com

Prices and availability subject to change without notice.